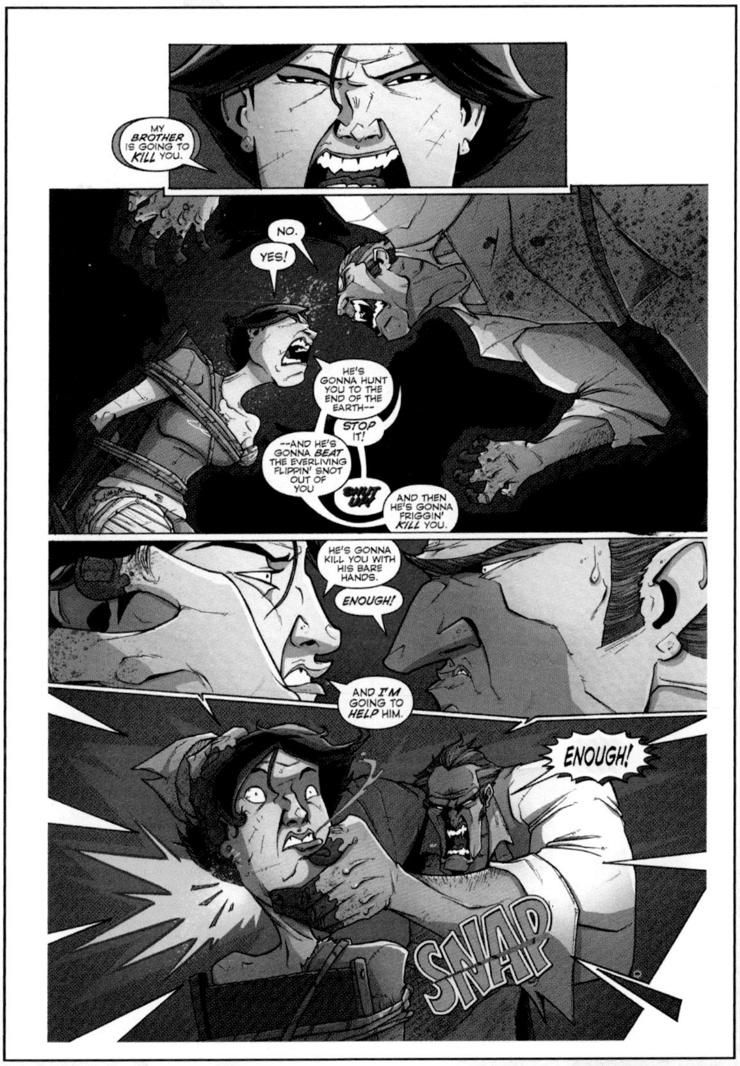
MY BROTHER IS GOING TO KILL YOU.
NO.
YES!
HE'S GONNA HUNT YOU TO THE END OF THE EARTH--
STOP IT!
--AND HE'S GONNA BEAT THE EVERLIVING FLIPPIN' SNOT OUT OF YOU
SHUT UP
AND THEN HE'S GONNA FRIGGIN' KILL YOU.
HE'S GONNA KILL YOU WITH HIS BARE HANDS.
ENOUGH!
AND I'M GOING TO HELP HIM.
ENOUGH!
SNAP

image comics **presents**

The Omnivore Edition
Vol. IV

written & lettered by
John Layman

drawn & coloured by
Rob Guillory

created by John Layman & Rob Guillory
design by Guillory & Layman

IMAGE COMICS, INC.
Robert Kirkman – Chief Operating Officer
Erik Larsen – Chief Financial Officer
Todd McFarlane – President
Marc Silvestri – Chief Executive Officer
Jim Valentino – Vice-President

Eric Stephenson – Publisher
Ron Richards – Director of Business Development
Jennifer de Guzman – Director of Trade Book Sales
Kat Salazar – Director of PR & Marketing
Jeremy Sullivan – Director of Digital Sales
Emilio Bautista – Sales Assistant
Branwyn Bigglestone – Senior Accounts Manager
Emily Miller – Accounts Manager
Jessica Ambriz – Administrative Assistant
Tyler Shainline – Events Coordinator
David Brothers – Content Manager
Jonathan Chan – Production Manager
Drew Gill – Art Director
Meredith Wallace – Print Manager
Monica Garcia – Senior Production Artist
Jenna Savage – Production Artist
Addison Duke – Production Artist
Tricia Ramos – Production Assistant
IMAGECOMICS.COM

Dedications:

JOHN: This one is for the homies.

ROB: For Amelia. And to anyone who has ever launched a revenge blood quest.

Thanks:

Taylor Wells, for the coloring assists.
Tom B. Long, for the logo.
Comicbookfonts.com, for the fonts.

And More Thanks:

Rich Amtower, Jeff Branget, David Brothers, Ryan Browne, Dan Burgos, Charlie Chu, Robert Kirkman, Jeff Krelitz, Adam Levine, Maricio Malacay, Mike Norton, Allen Passalaqua, Kathryn & Israel Skelton, Skybound, Fiona Staples, Sweet Joshie Williamson, Brian K. Vaughan and Maki Yamane.

Plus the Image gang of Drew, Jonathan, Emily, Branwyn, Ron, Jennifer, Tyler, Meredith and Eric.

And for Kim Peterson, Carter Layman, April Hanks Guillory and Aiden Guillory.

Chew #35 SDCC cover inspired by Quentin Tarantino.

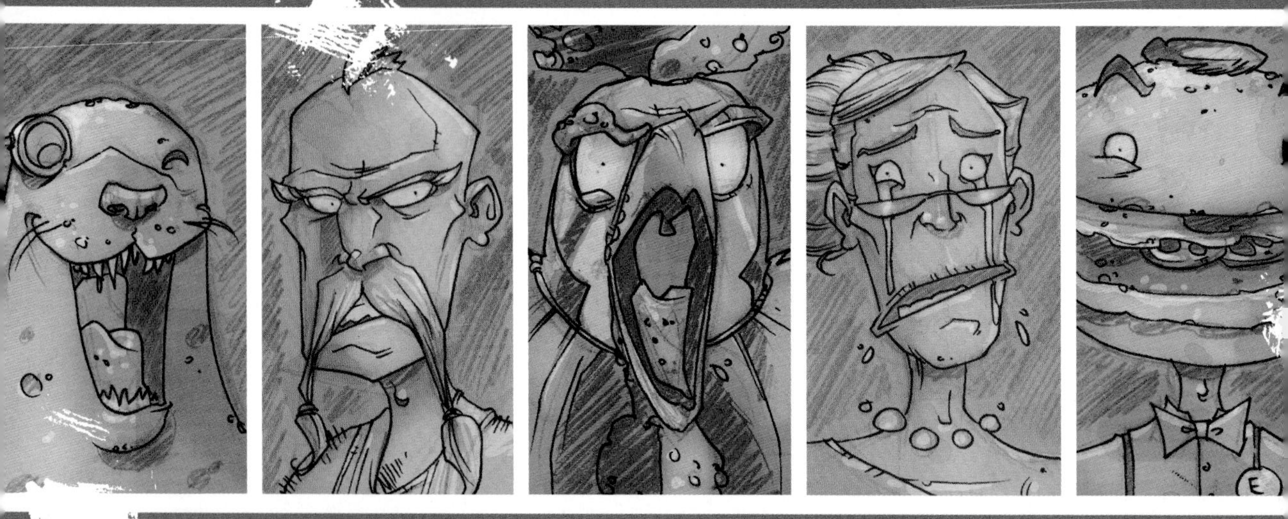
E

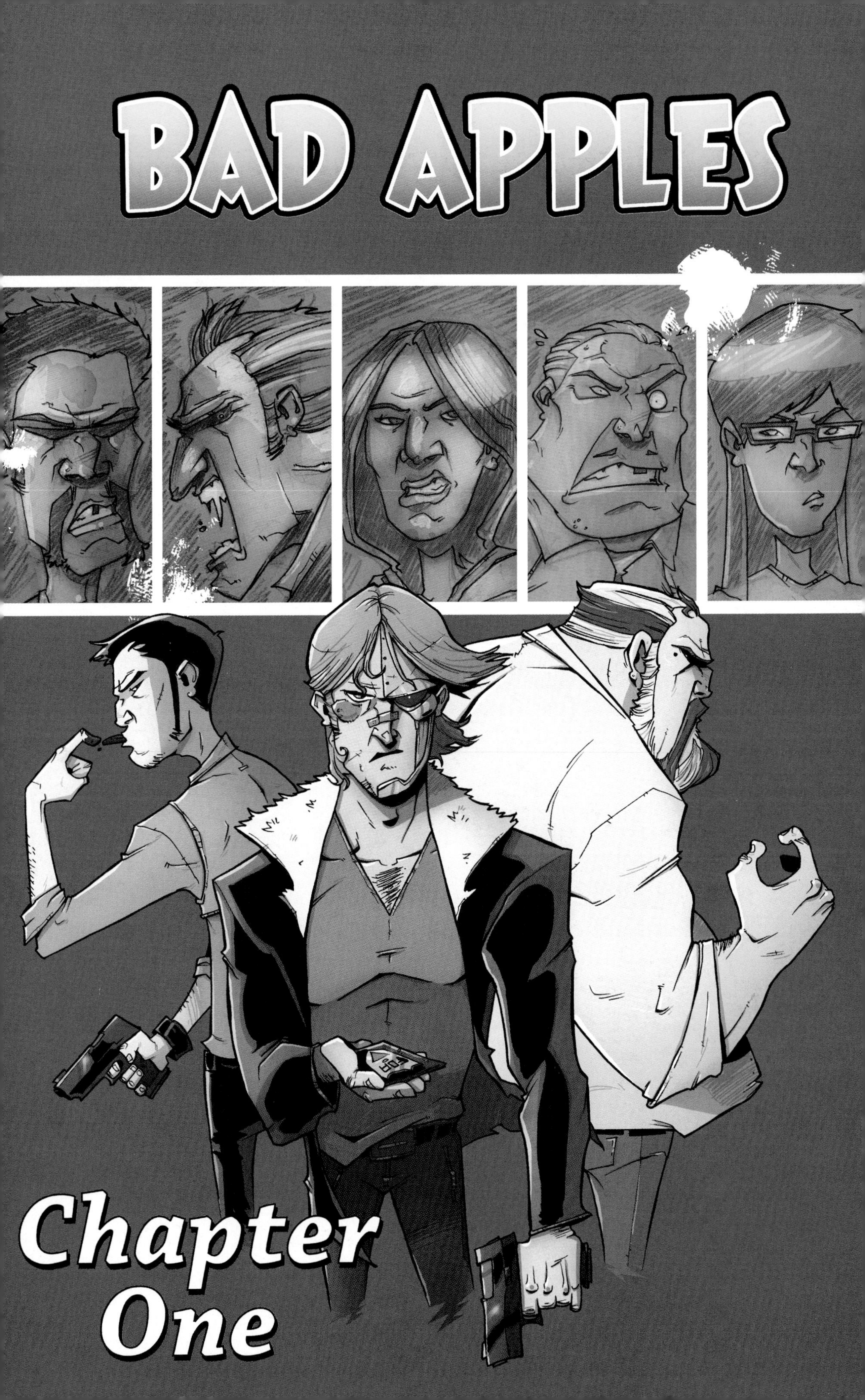
BAD APPLES
Chapter One

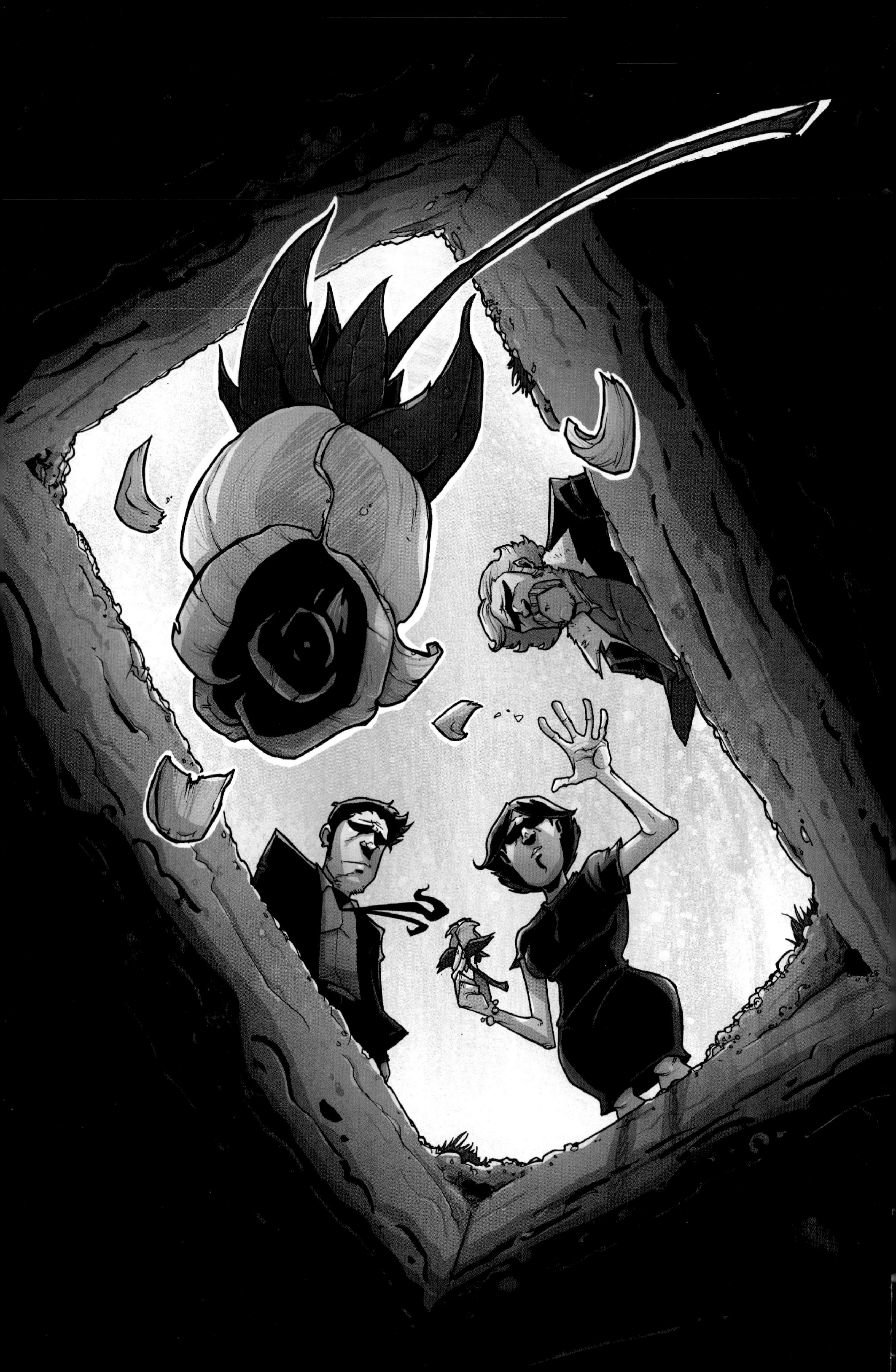
ROB!

Issue #31 cover

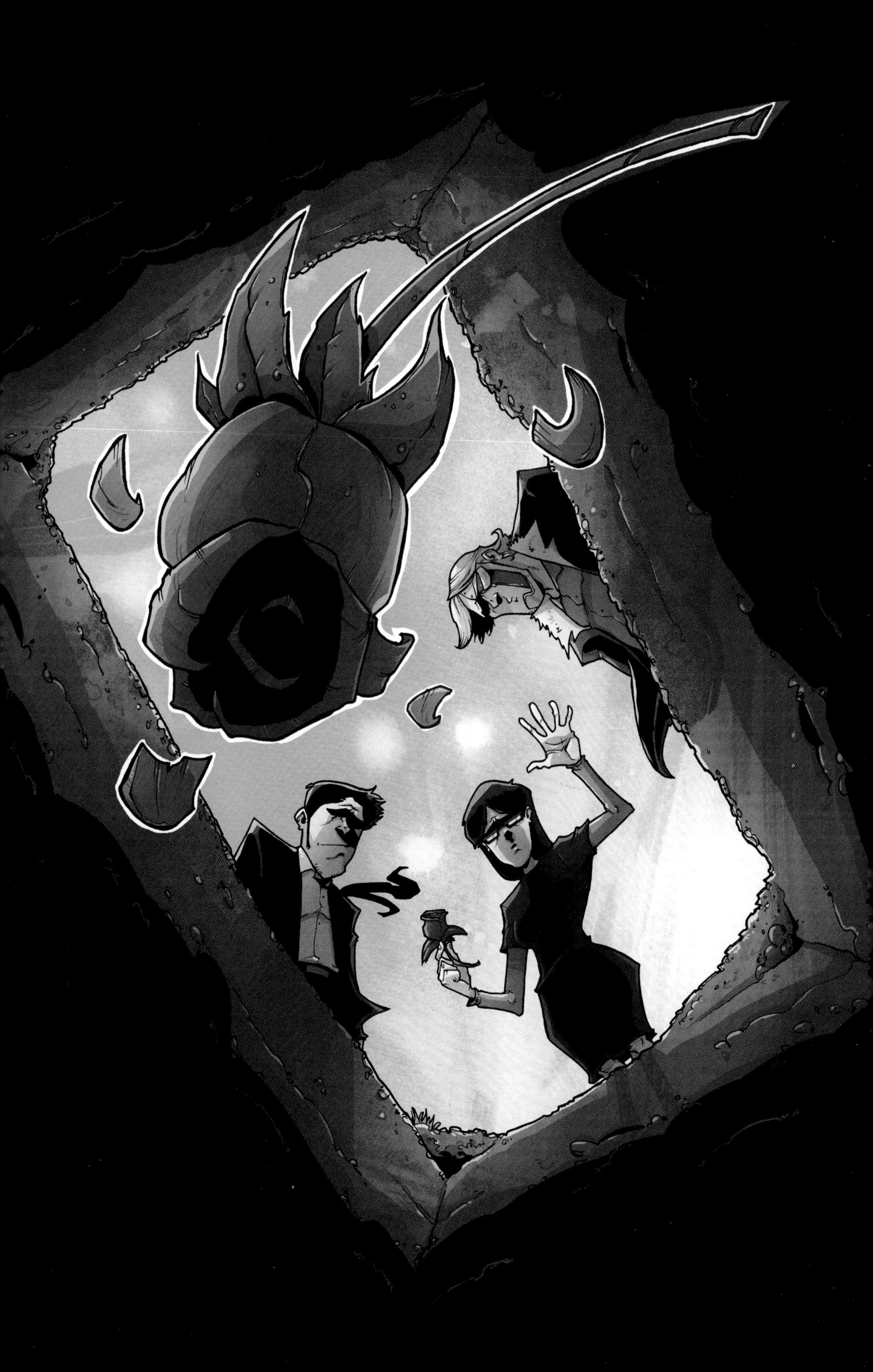

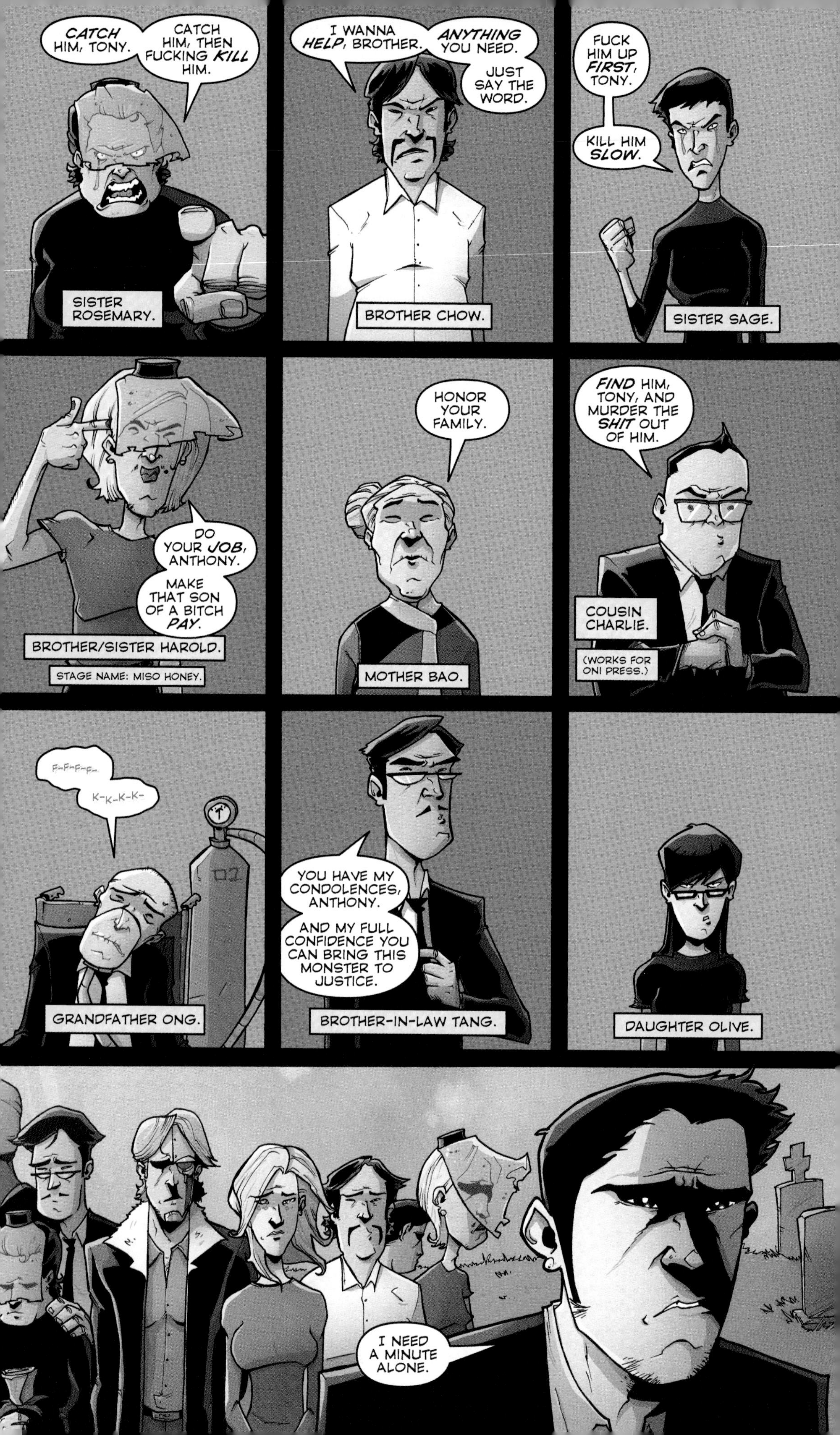
CATCH HIM, TONY.
CATCH HIM, THEN FUCKING KILL HIM.
SISTER ROSEMARY.
I WANNA HELP, BROTHER.
ANYTHING YOU NEED.
JUST SAY THE WORD.
BROTHER CHOW.
FUCK HIM UP FIRST, TONY.
KILL HIM SLOW.
SISTER SAGE.
DO YOUR JOB, ANTHONY.
MAKE THAT SON OF A BITCH PAY.
BROTHER/SISTER HAROLD.
STAGE NAME: MISO HONEY.
HONOR YOUR FAMILY.
MOTHER BAO.
FIND HIM, TONY, AND MURDER THE SHIT OUT OF HIM.
COUSIN CHARLIE.
(WORKS FOR ONI PRESS.)
F-F-F-F-
K-K-K-K-
GRANDFATHER ONG.
YOU HAVE MY CONDOLENCES, ANTHONY.
AND MY FULL CONFIDENCE YOU CAN BRING THIS MONSTER TO JUSTICE.
BROTHER-IN-LAW TANG.
DAUGHTER OLIVE.
I NEED A MINUTE ALONE.

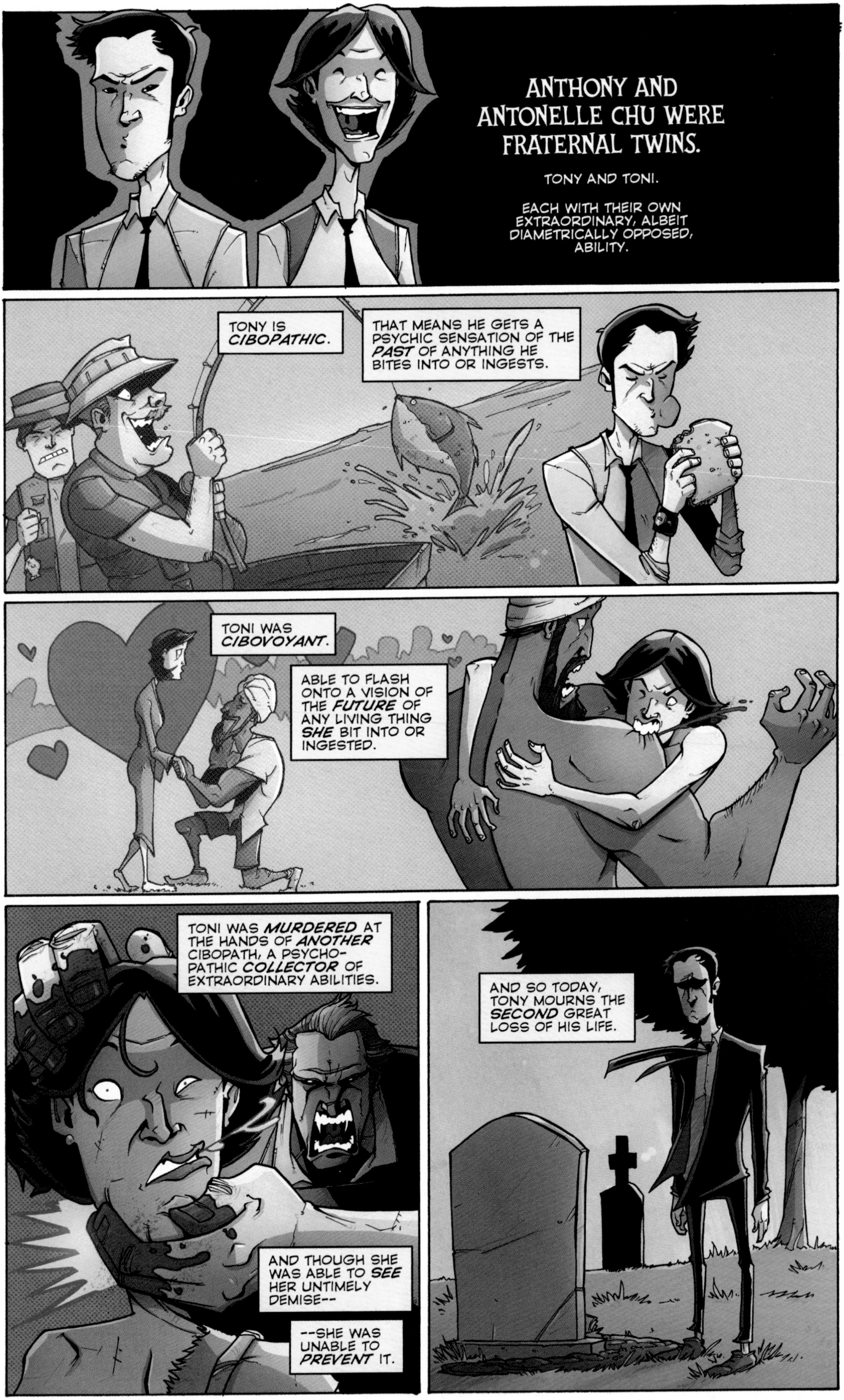
ANTHONY AND ANTONELLE CHU WERE FRATERNAL TWINS.
TONY AND TONI.
EACH WITH THEIR OWN EXTRAORDINARY, ALBEIT DIAMETRICALLY OPPOSED, ABILITY.
TONY IS CIBOPATHIC.
THAT MEANS HE GETS A PSYCHIC SENSATION OF THE PAST OF ANYTHING HE BITES INTO OR INGESTS.
TONI WAS CIBOVOYANT.
ABLE TO FLASH ONTO A VISION OF THE FUTURE OF ANY LIVING THING SHE BIT INTO OR INGESTED.
TONI WAS MURDERED AT THE HANDS OF ANOTHER CIBOPATH, A PSYCHOPATHIC COLLECTOR OF EXTRAORDINARY ABILITIES.
AND THOUGH SHE WAS ABLE TO SEE HER UNTIMELY DEMISE--
--SHE WAS UNABLE TO PREVENT IT.
AND SO TODAY, TONY MOURNS THE SECOND GREAT LOSS OF HIS LIFE.

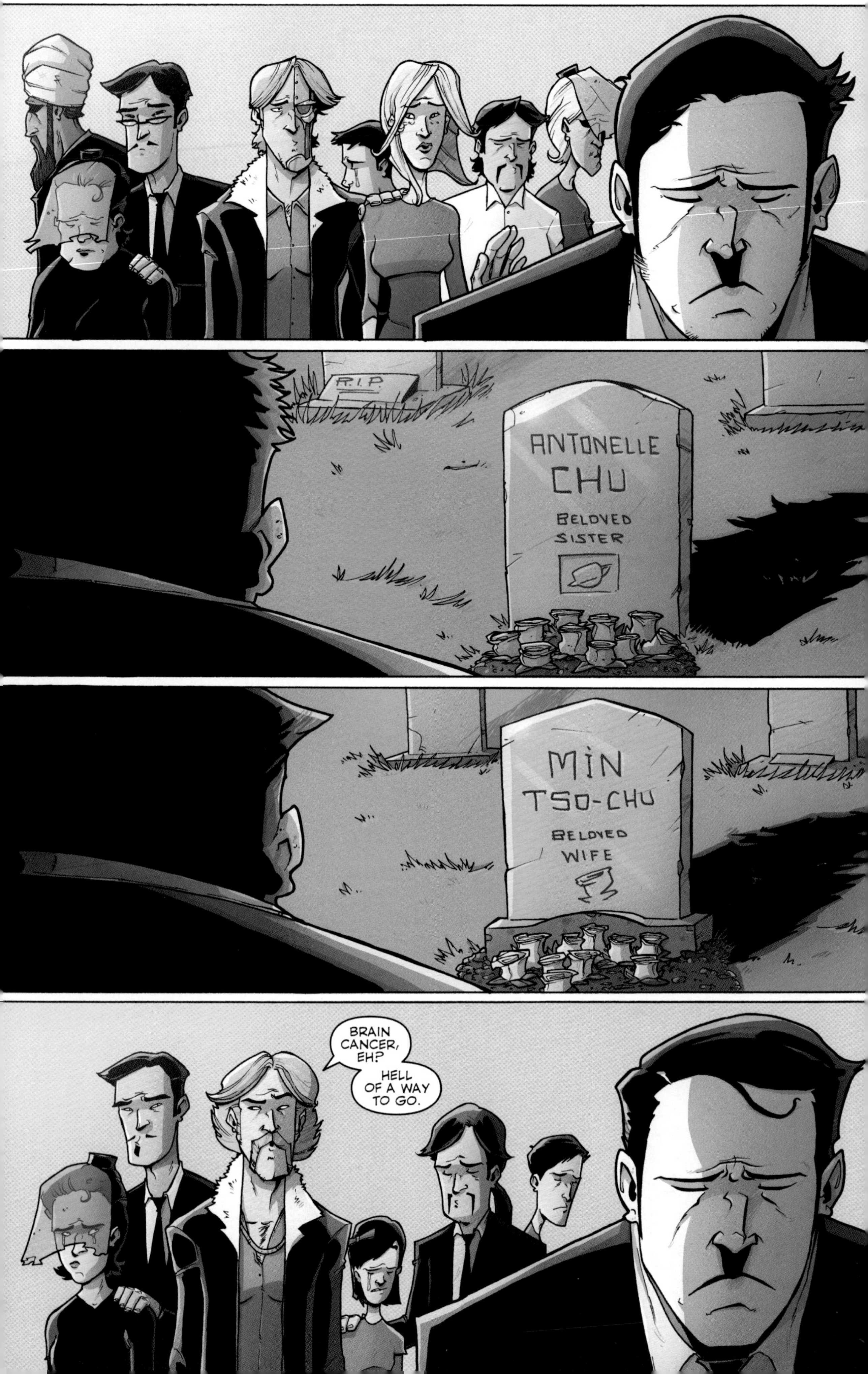
R.I.P.
ANTONELLE CHU
BELOVED SISTER
MIN TSO-CHU
BELOVED WIFE
BRAIN CANCER, EH?
HELL OF A WAY TO GO.

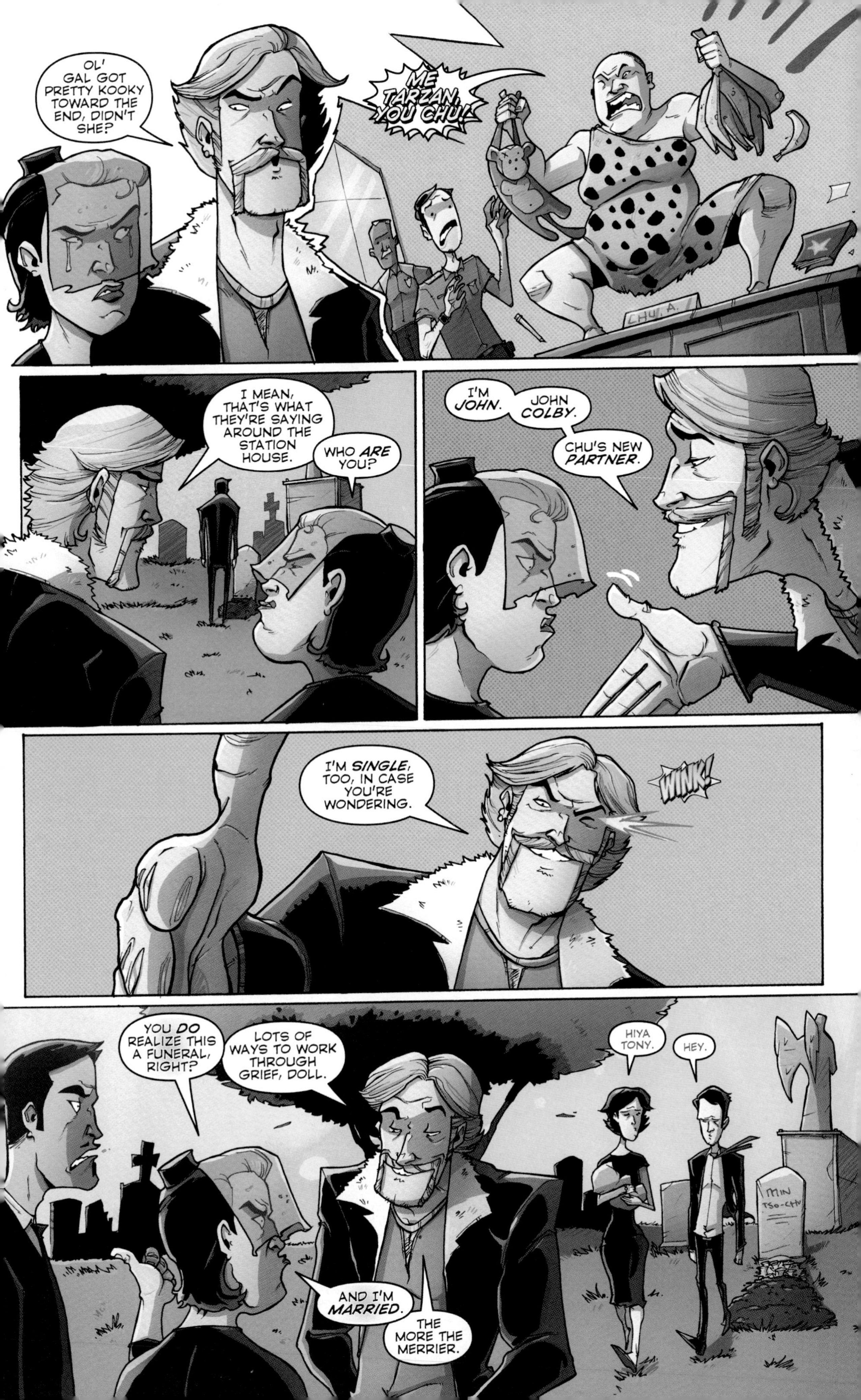

OL' GAL GOT PRETTY KOOKY TOWARD THE END, DIDN'T SHE?
ME TARZAN, YOU CHU!
CHU A.
I MEAN, THAT'S WHAT THEY'RE SAYING AROUND THE STATION HOUSE.
WHO ARE YOU?
I'M JOHN.
JOHN COLBY.
CHU'S NEW PARTNER.
I'M SINGLE, TOO, IN CASE YOU'RE WONDERING.
WINK!
YOU DO REALIZE THIS A FUNERAL, RIGHT?
LOTS OF WAYS TO WORK THROUGH GRIEF, DOLL.
HIYA TONY.
HEY.
AND I'M MARRIED.
THE MORE THE MERRIER.

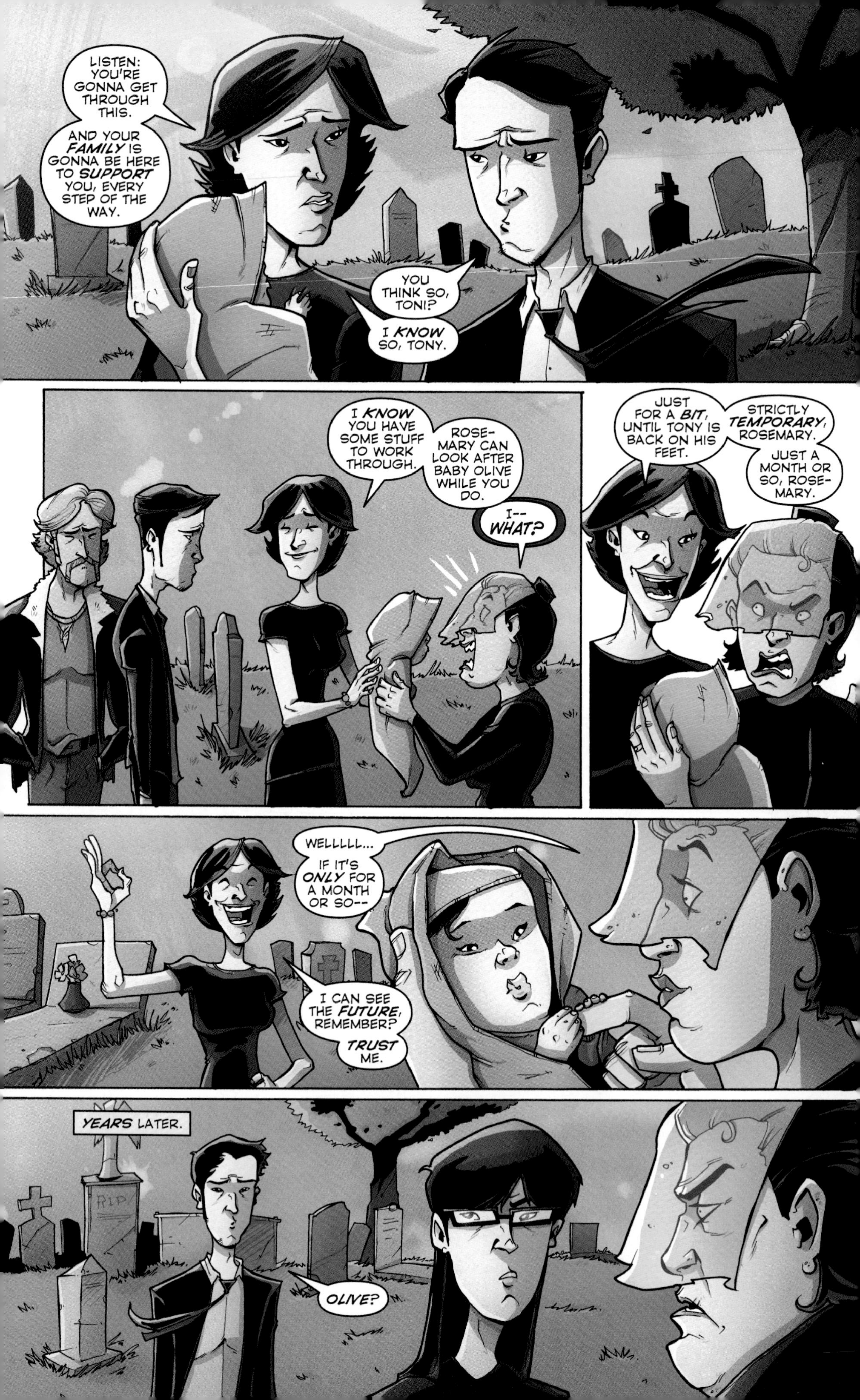
LISTEN: YOU'RE GONNA GET THROUGH THIS.
AND YOUR *FAMILY* IS GONNA BE HERE TO *SUPPORT* YOU, EVERY STEP OF THE WAY.
YOU THINK SO, TONI?
I *KNOW* SO, TONY.
I *KNOW* YOU HAVE SOME STUFF TO WORK THROUGH.
ROSE-MARY CAN LOOK AFTER BABY OLIVE WHILE YOU DO.
I-- *WHAT?*
JUST FOR A *BIT*, UNTIL TONY IS BACK ON HIS FEET.
STRICTLY *TEMPORARY*, ROSEMARY.
JUST A MONTH OR SO, ROSE-MARY.
WELLLLLL...
IF IT'S *ONLY* FOR A MONTH OR SO--
I CAN SEE THE *FUTURE*, REMEMBER?
TRUST ME.
YEARS LATER.
RIP
OLIVE?

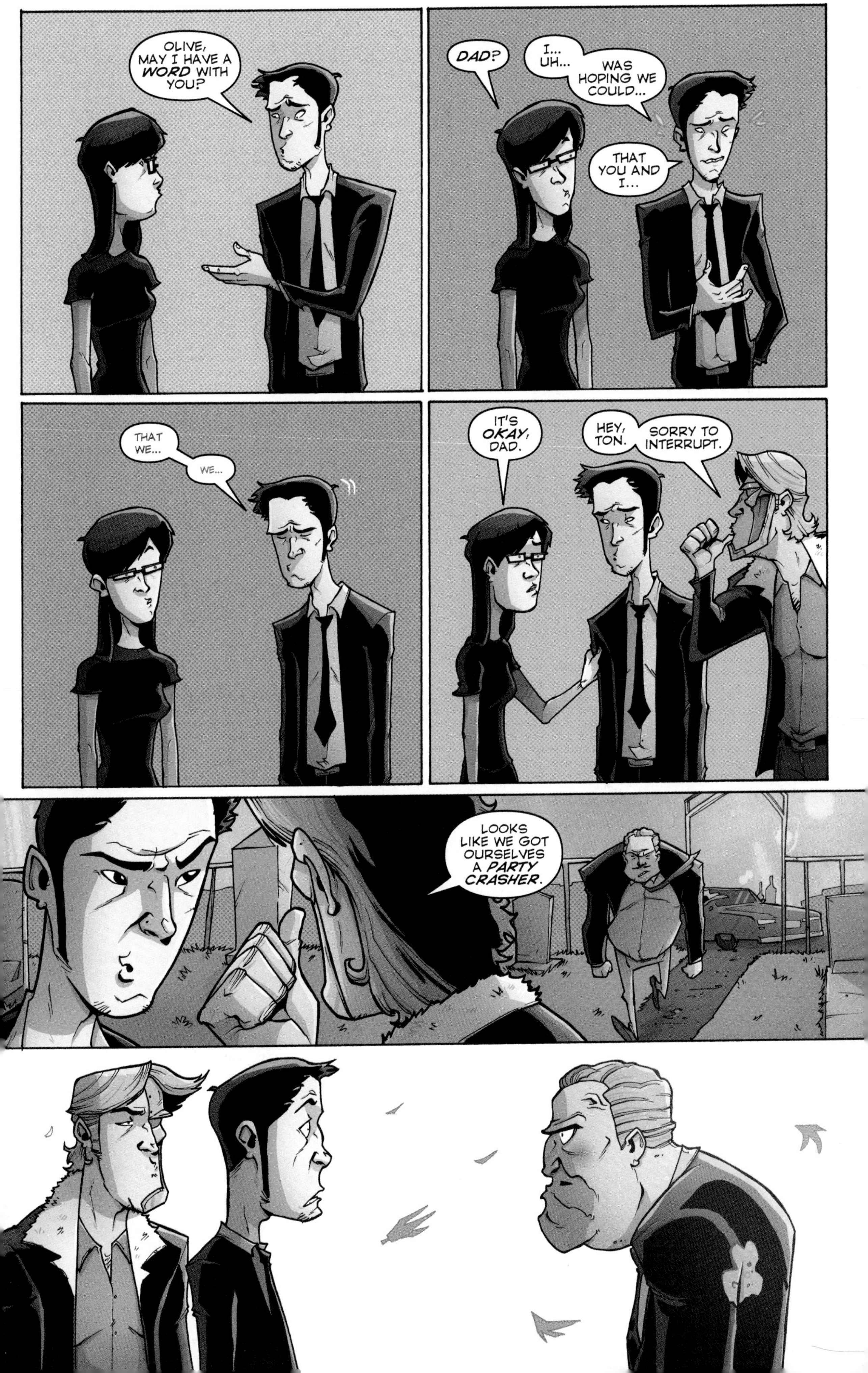
OLIVE, MAY I HAVE A WORD WITH YOU?
DAD?
I... UH...
WAS HOPING WE COULD...
THAT YOU AND I...
THAT WE...
WE...
IT'S OKAY, DAD.
HEY, TON.
SORRY TO INTERRUPT.
LOOKS LIKE WE GOT OURSELVES A PARTY CRASHER.

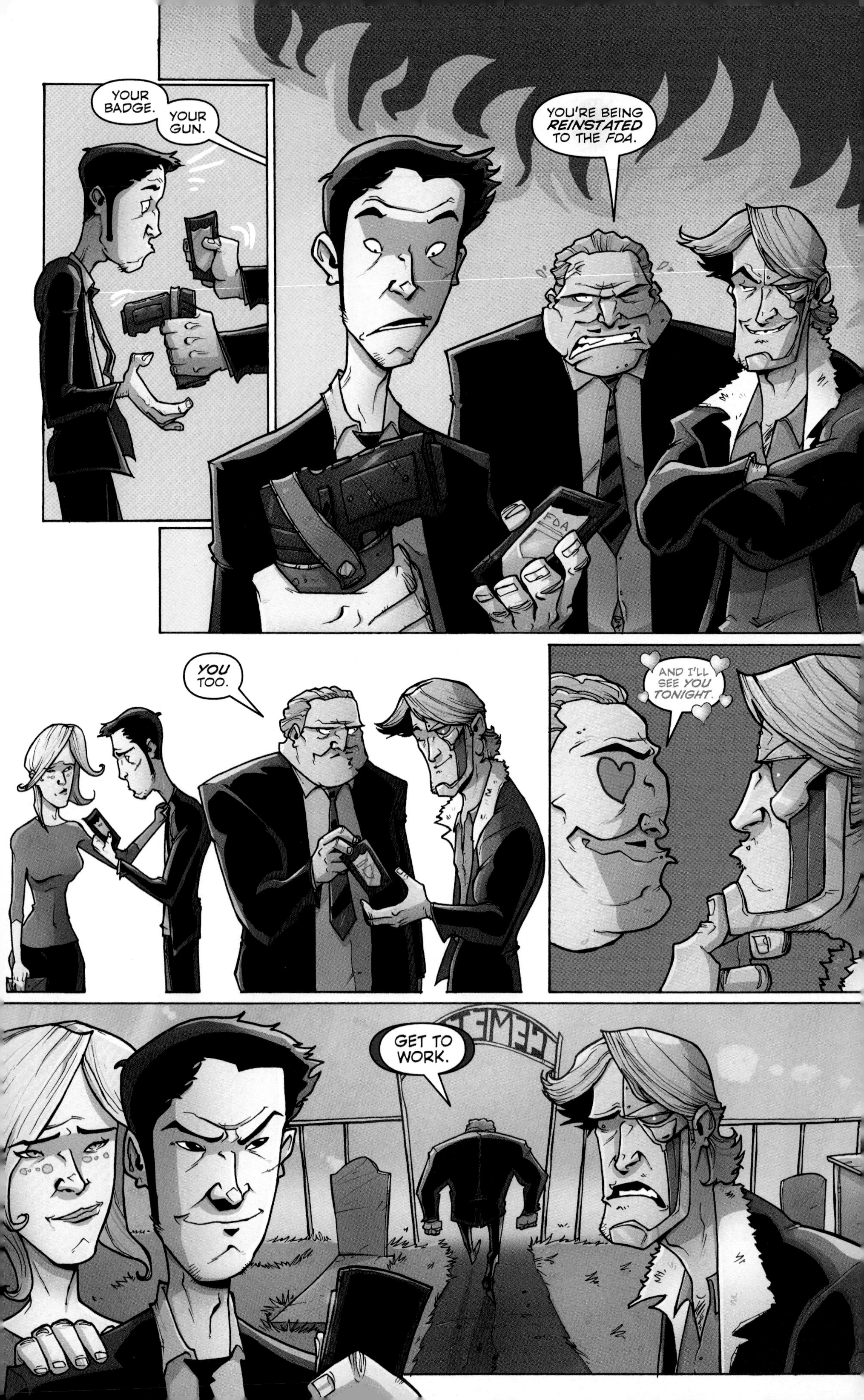
YOUR BADGE.
YOUR GUN.
YOU'RE BEING REINSTATED TO THE FDA.
FDA
YOU TOO.
AND I'LL SEE YOU TONIGHT.
GET TO WORK.

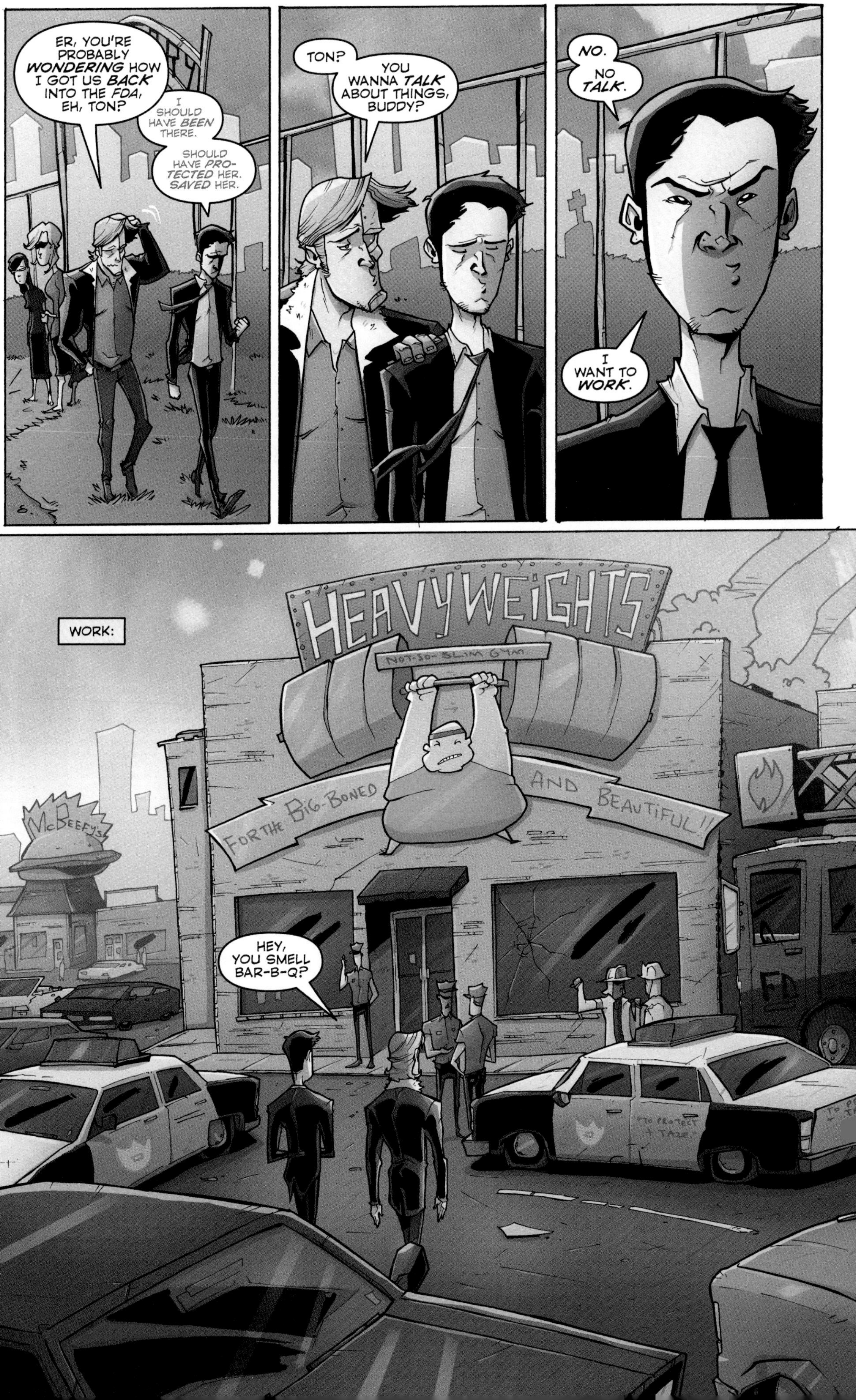
ER, YOU'RE PROBABLY WONDERING HOW I GOT US BACK INTO THE FDA, EH, TON?
I SHOULD HAVE BEEN THERE.
SHOULD HAVE PRO-TECTED HER. SAVED HER.
TON?
YOU WANNA TALK ABOUT THINGS, BUDDY?
NO.
NO TALK.
I WANT TO WORK.
WORK:
HEAVYWEIGHTS
NOT-SO-SLIM GYM.
FOR THE BIG-BONED AND BEAUTIFUL!!
McBeefy's
HEY, YOU SMELL BAR-B-Q?
TO PROTECT + TAZE
FD

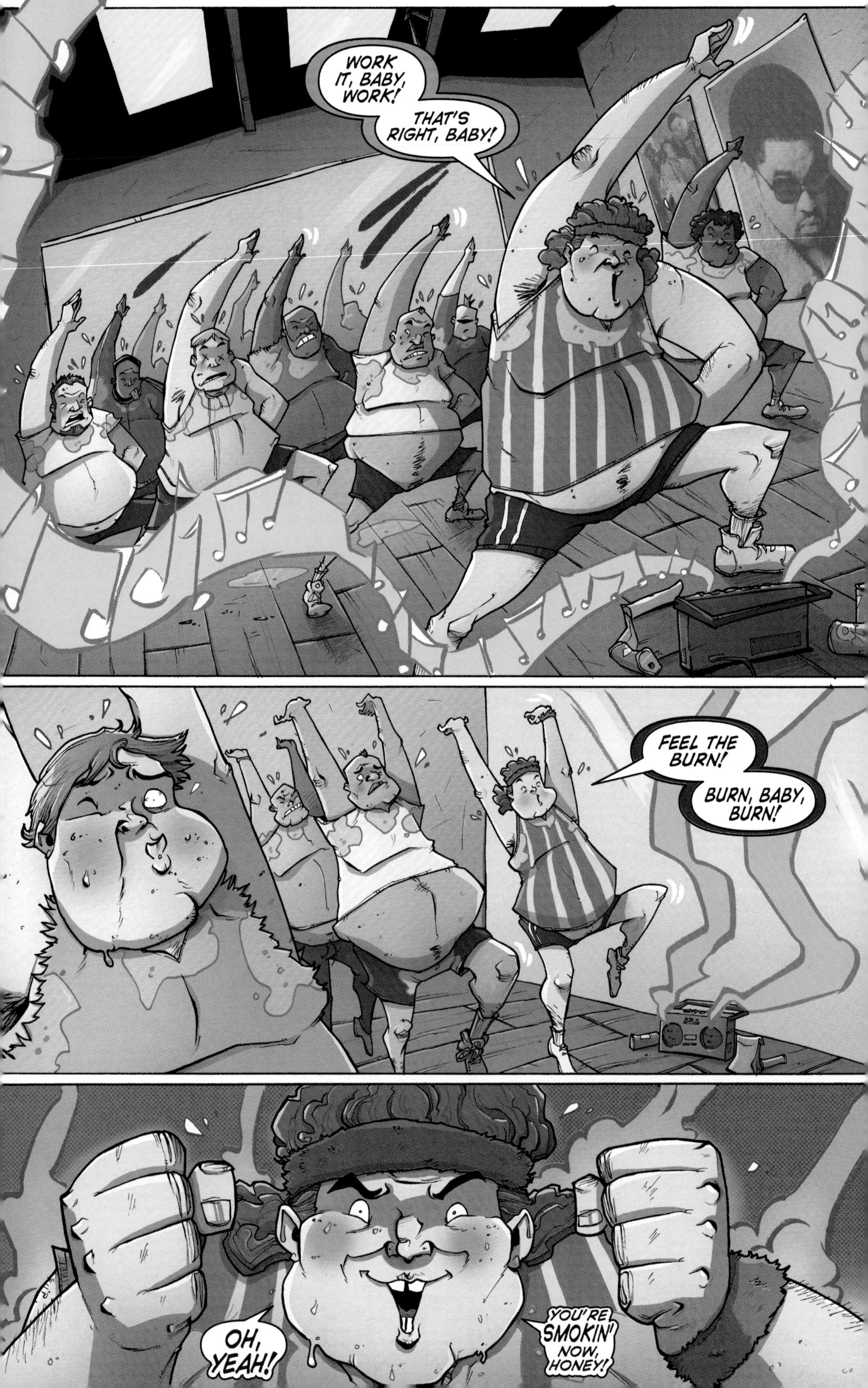
WORK IT, BABY, WORK!
THAT'S RIGHT, BABY!
FEEL THE BURN!
BURN, BABY, BURN!
OH, YEAH!
YOU'RE SMOKIN' NOW, HONEY!

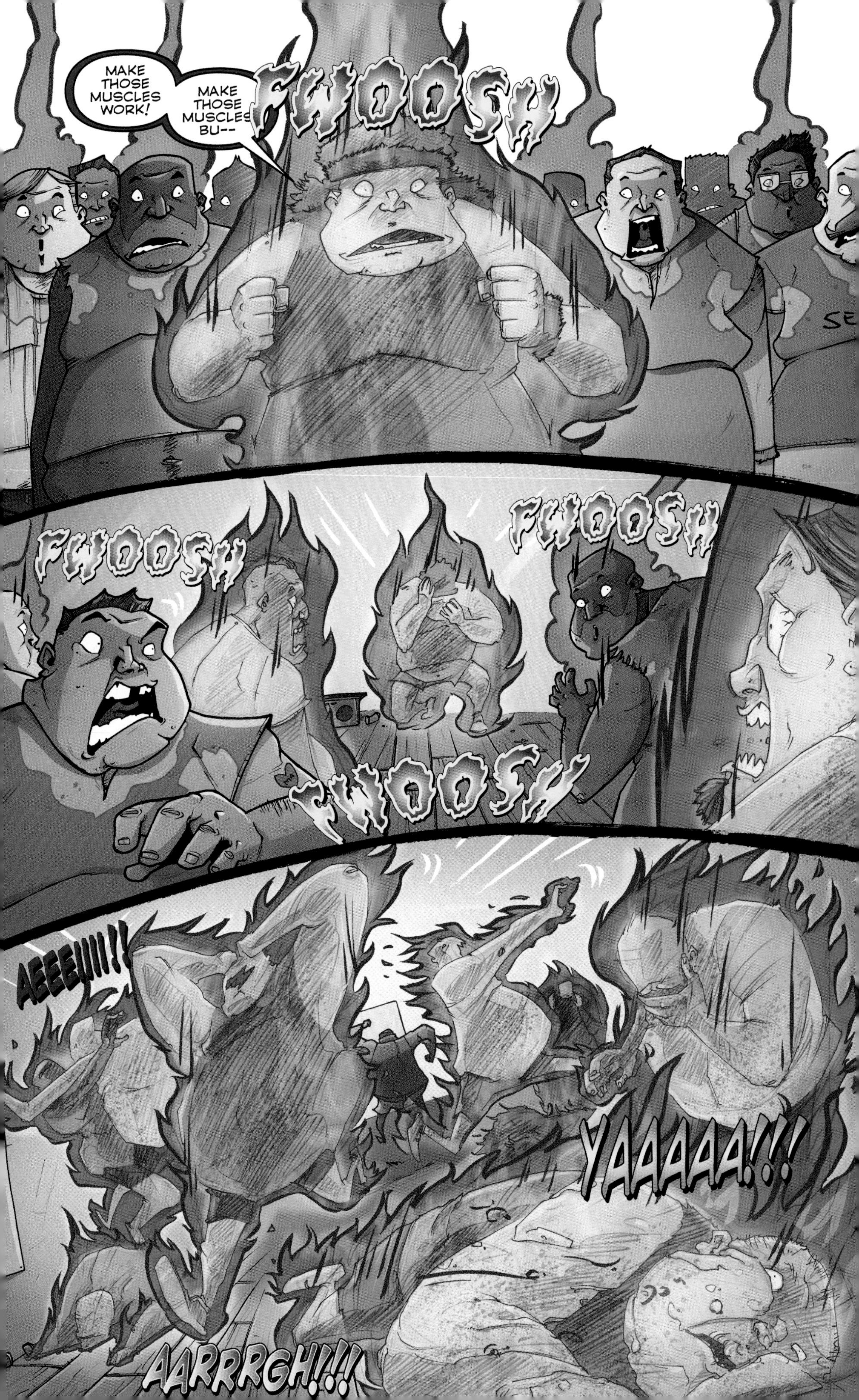
MAKE THOSE MUSCLES WORK!
MAKE THOSE MUSCLES BU--
FWOOSH
FWOOSH
FWOOSH
FWOOSH
AEEEIIIII!!
YAAAAA!!!
AARRRGH!!!

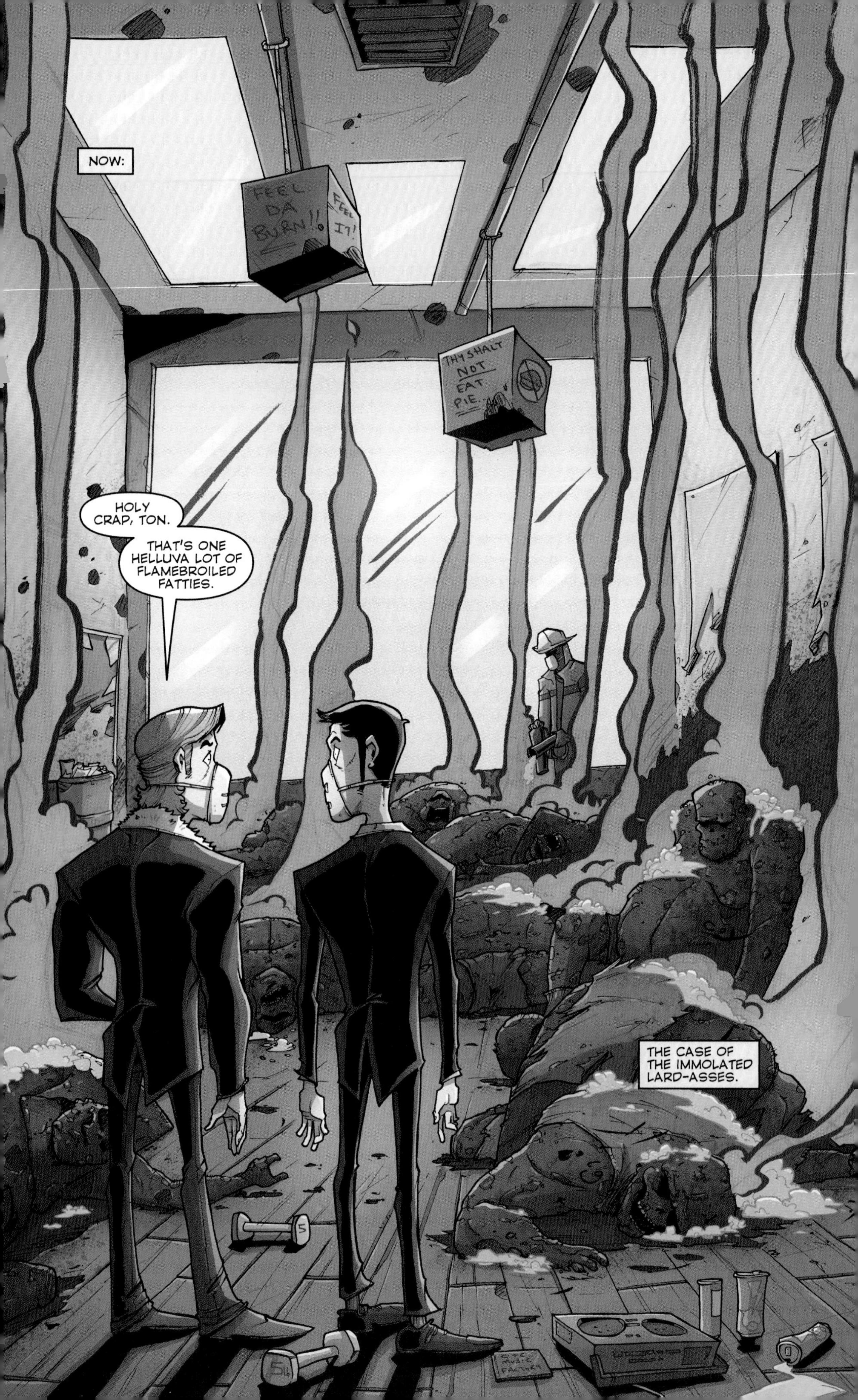
NOW:
FEEL DA BURN!!
FEEL IT!
THY SHALT NOT EAT PIE.
HOLY CRAP, TON.
THAT'S ONE HELLUVA LOT OF FLAMEBROILED FATTIES.
THE CASE OF THE IMMOLATED LARD-ASSES.

THE SCORCHED SUMO.

PILEDRIVE DA BUM!!

TONY, I GOT CAESAR ON THE LINE.

WE BETTER GET A MOVE ON.

TURNS OUT THIS IS *NOT* AN ISOLATED INCIDENT.

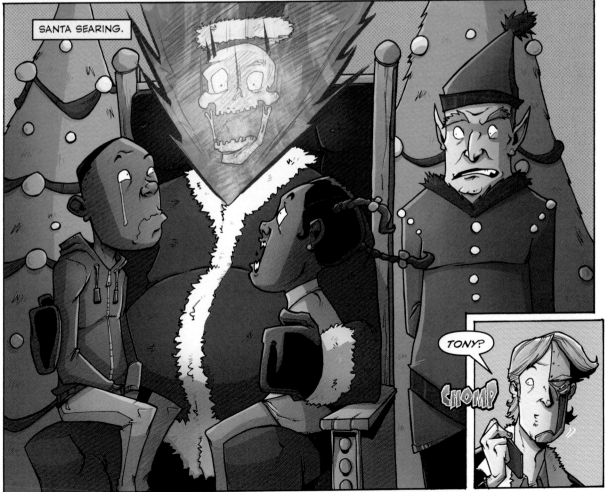

SANTA SEARING.

TONY?

CHOMP

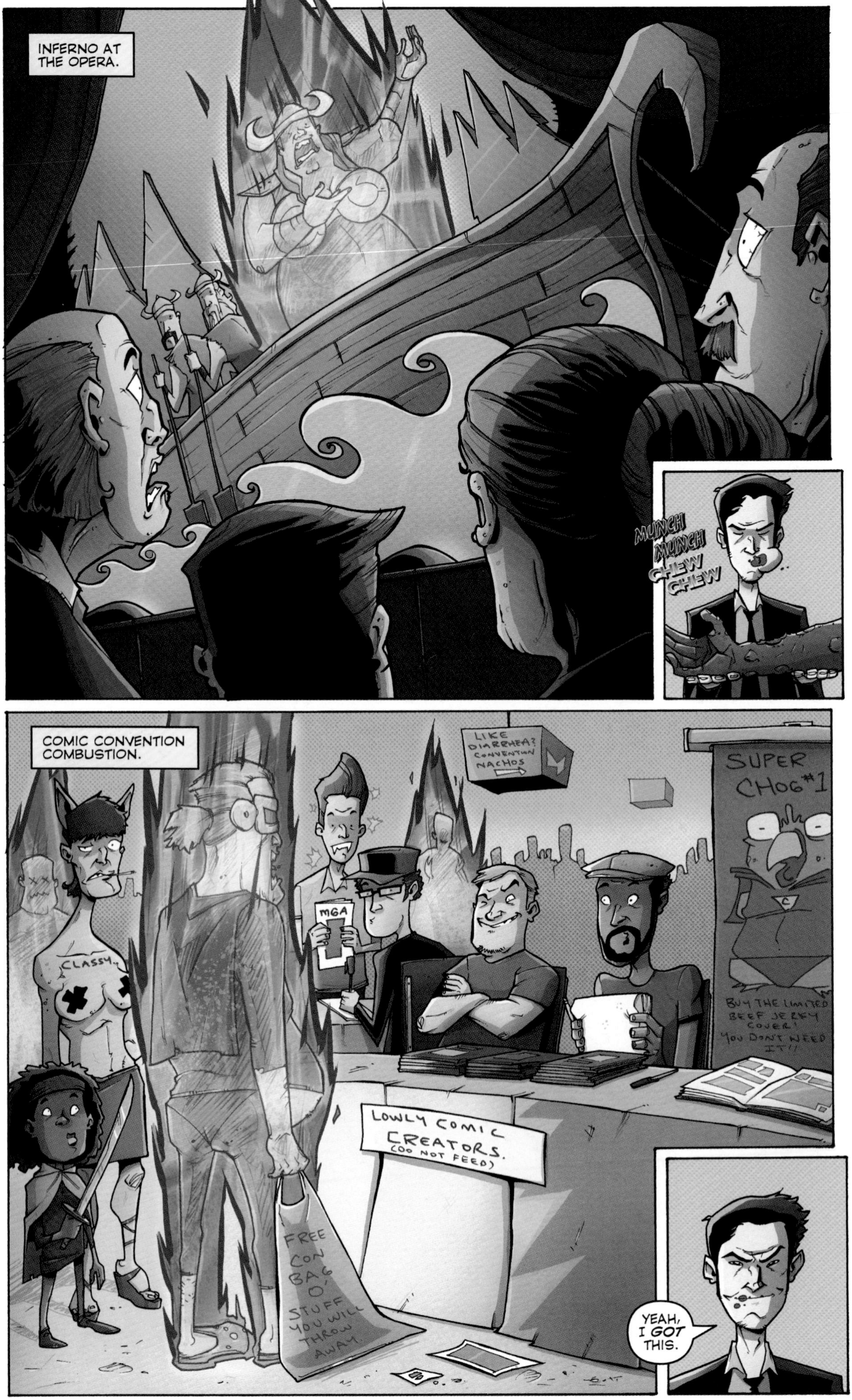
INFERNO AT THE OPERA.
MUNCH MUNCH CHEW CHEW
COMIC CONVENTION COMBUSTION.
LIKE DIARRHEA? CONVENTION NACHOS
SUPER CHOG #1
BUY THE LIMITED BEEF JERKY COVER! YOU DON'T NEED IT!!
CLASSY...
MGA
LOWLY COMIC CREATORS. (DO NOT FEED)
FREE CON BAG O' STUFF YOU WILL THROW AWAY.
YEAH, I GOT THIS.

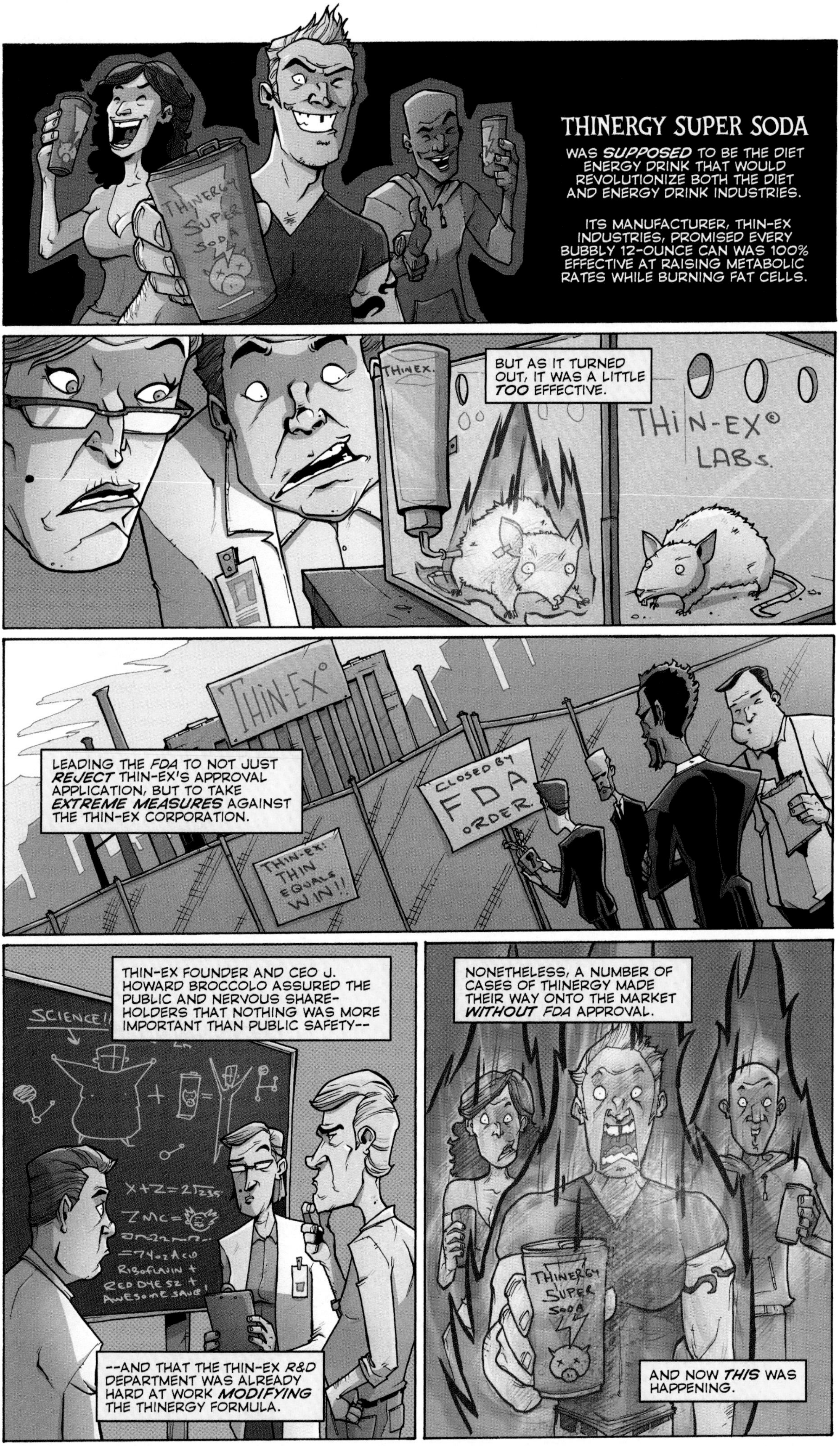
THINERGY SUPER SODA
WAS SUPPOSED TO BE THE DIET ENERGY DRINK THAT WOULD REVOLUTIONIZE BOTH THE DIET AND ENERGY DRINK INDUSTRIES.
ITS MANUFACTURER, THIN-EX INDUSTRIES, PROMISED EVERY BUBBLY 12-OUNCE CAN WAS 100% EFFECTIVE AT RAISING METABOLIC RATES WHILE BURNING FAT CELLS.
THINERGY SUPER SODA
BUT AS IT TURNED OUT, IT WAS A LITTLE TOO EFFECTIVE.
THIN-EX.
THIN-EX© LABS.
THIN-EX©
LEADING THE FDA TO NOT JUST REJECT THIN-EX'S APPROVAL APPLICATION, BUT TO TAKE EXTREME MEASURES AGAINST THE THIN-EX CORPORATION.
CLOSED BY FDA ORDER
THIN-EX: THIN EQUALS WIN!!
THIN-EX FOUNDER AND CEO J. HOWARD BROCCOLO ASSURED THE PUBLIC AND NERVOUS SHAREHOLDERS THAT NOTHING WAS MORE IMPORTANT THAN PUBLIC SAFETY--
SCIENCE!!
RIBOFLAVIN +
RED DYE 52 +
AWESOME SAUCE!
--AND THAT THE THIN-EX R&D DEPARTMENT WAS ALREADY HARD AT WORK MODIFYING THE THINERGY FORMULA.
NONETHELESS, A NUMBER OF CASES OF THINERGY MADE THEIR WAY ONTO THE MARKET WITHOUT FDA APPROVAL.
THINERGY SUPER SODA
AND NOW THIS WAS HAPPENING.

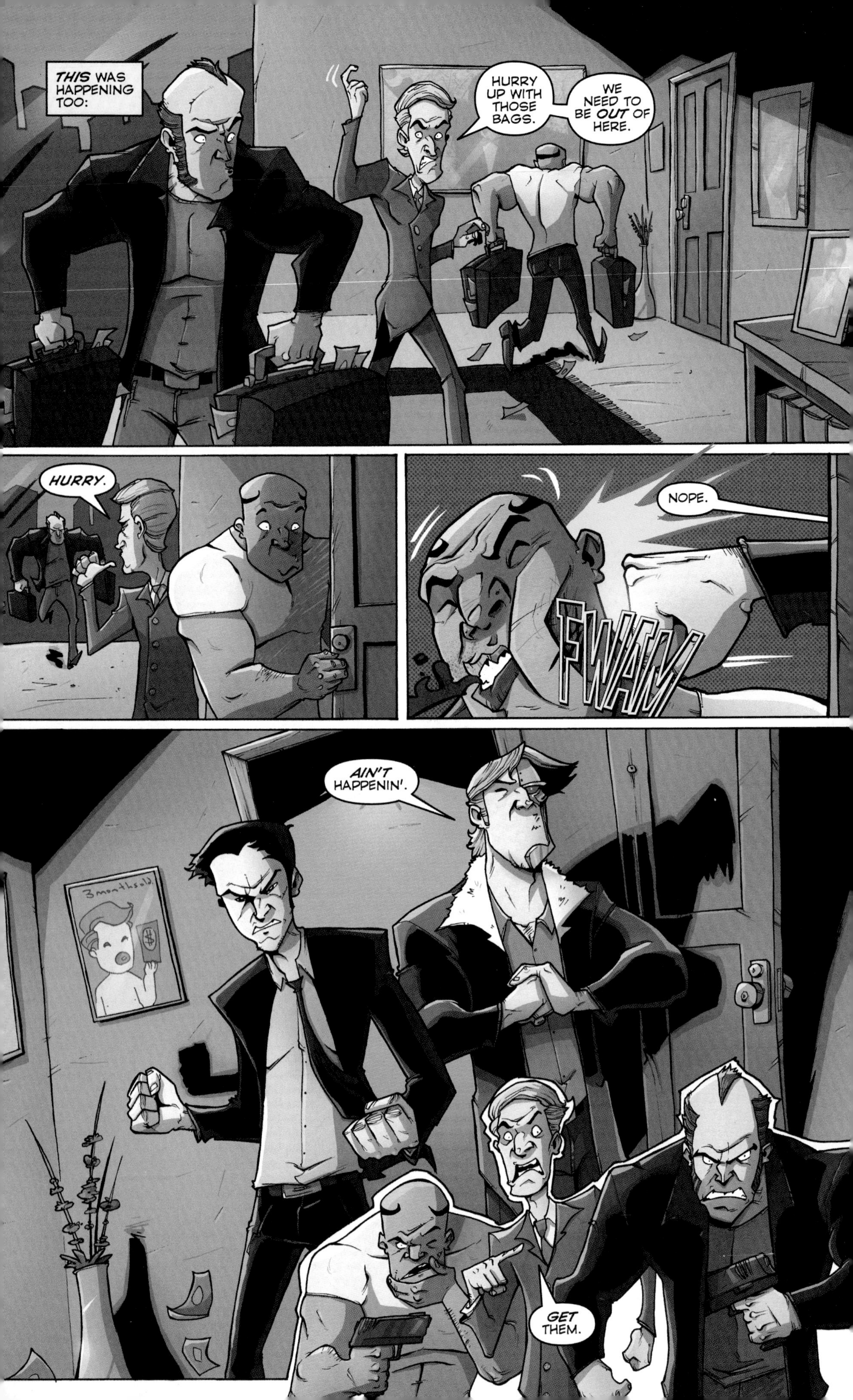
THIS WAS HAPPENING TOO:
HURRY UP WITH THOSE BAGS.
WE NEED TO BE OUT OF HERE.
HURRY.
NOPE.
FWAM
AIN'T HAPPENIN'.
3monthsold
GET THEM.

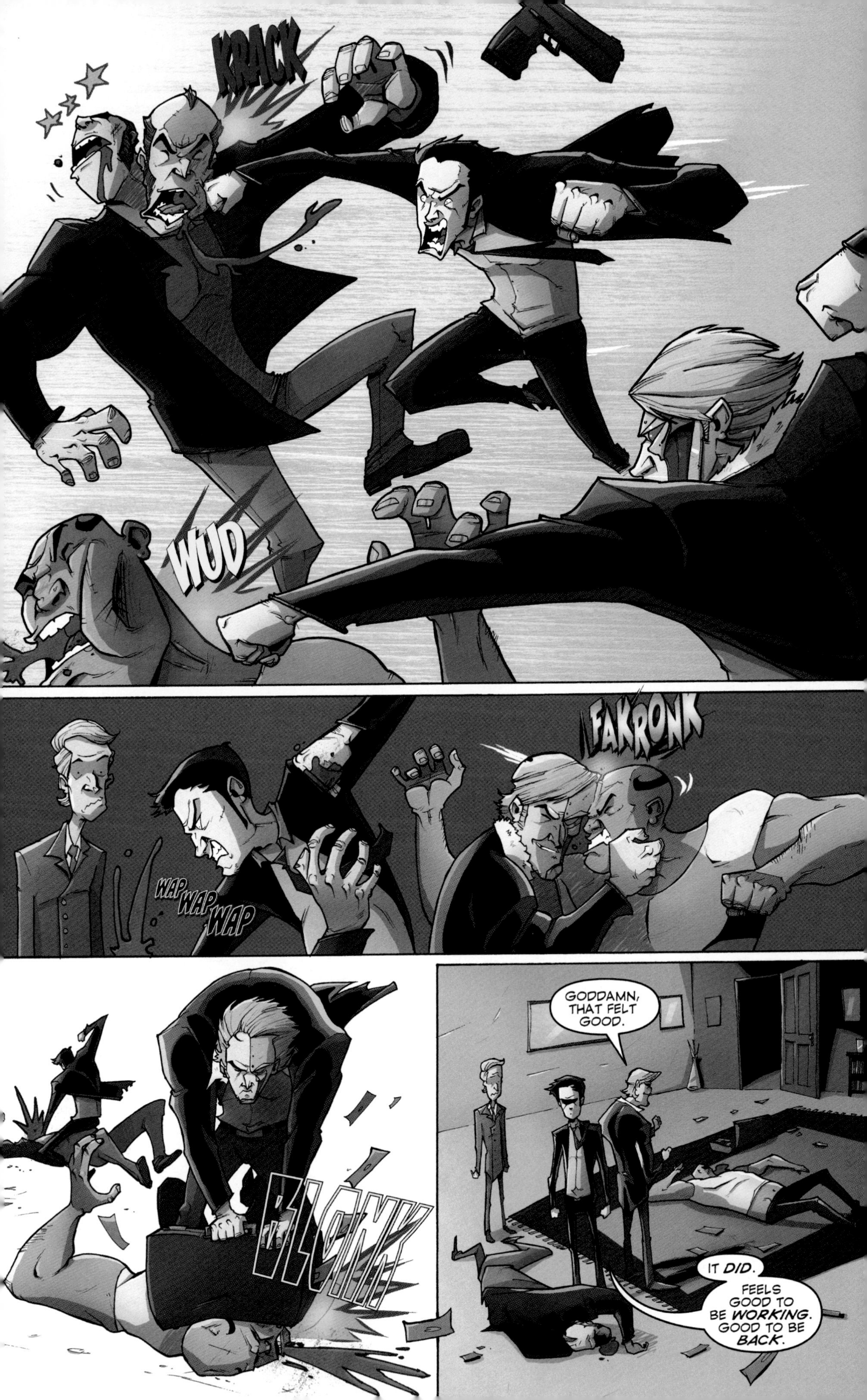
KRACK
WUD
FAKRONK
WAP WAP WAP
BLONK
GODDAMN, THAT FELT GOOD.
IT *DID*.
FEELS GOOD TO BE *WORKING*. GOOD TO BE *BACK*.

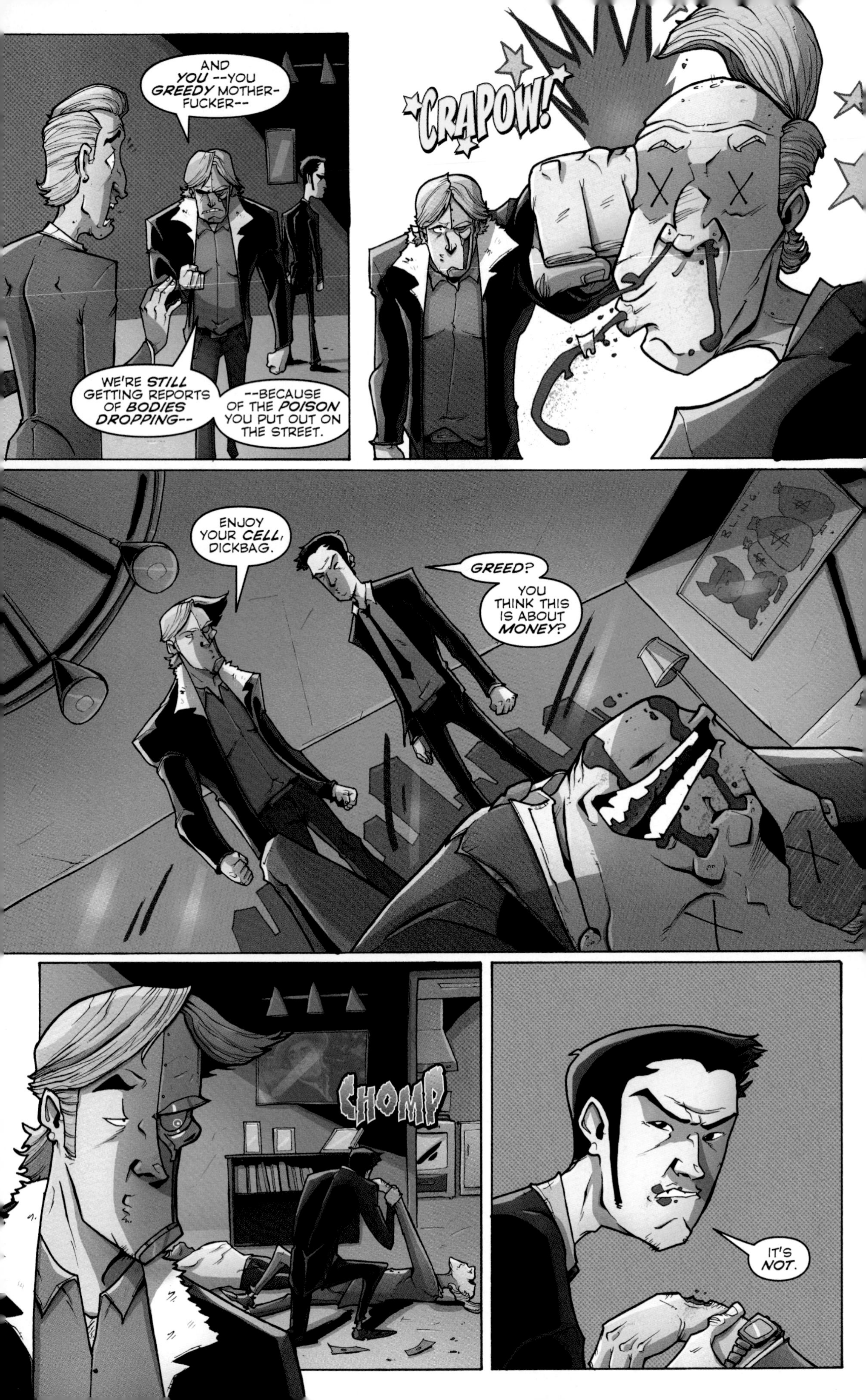
AND *YOU* --YOU *GREEDY* MOTHER-FUCKER--
WE'RE *STILL* GETTING REPORTS OF *BODIES DROPPING*--
--BECAUSE OF THE *POISON* YOU PUT OUT ON THE STREET.
CRAPOW!
ENJOY YOUR *CELL*, DICKBAG.
GREED?
YOU THINK THIS IS ABOUT *MONEY*?
BLING
CHOMP
IT'S *NOT*.

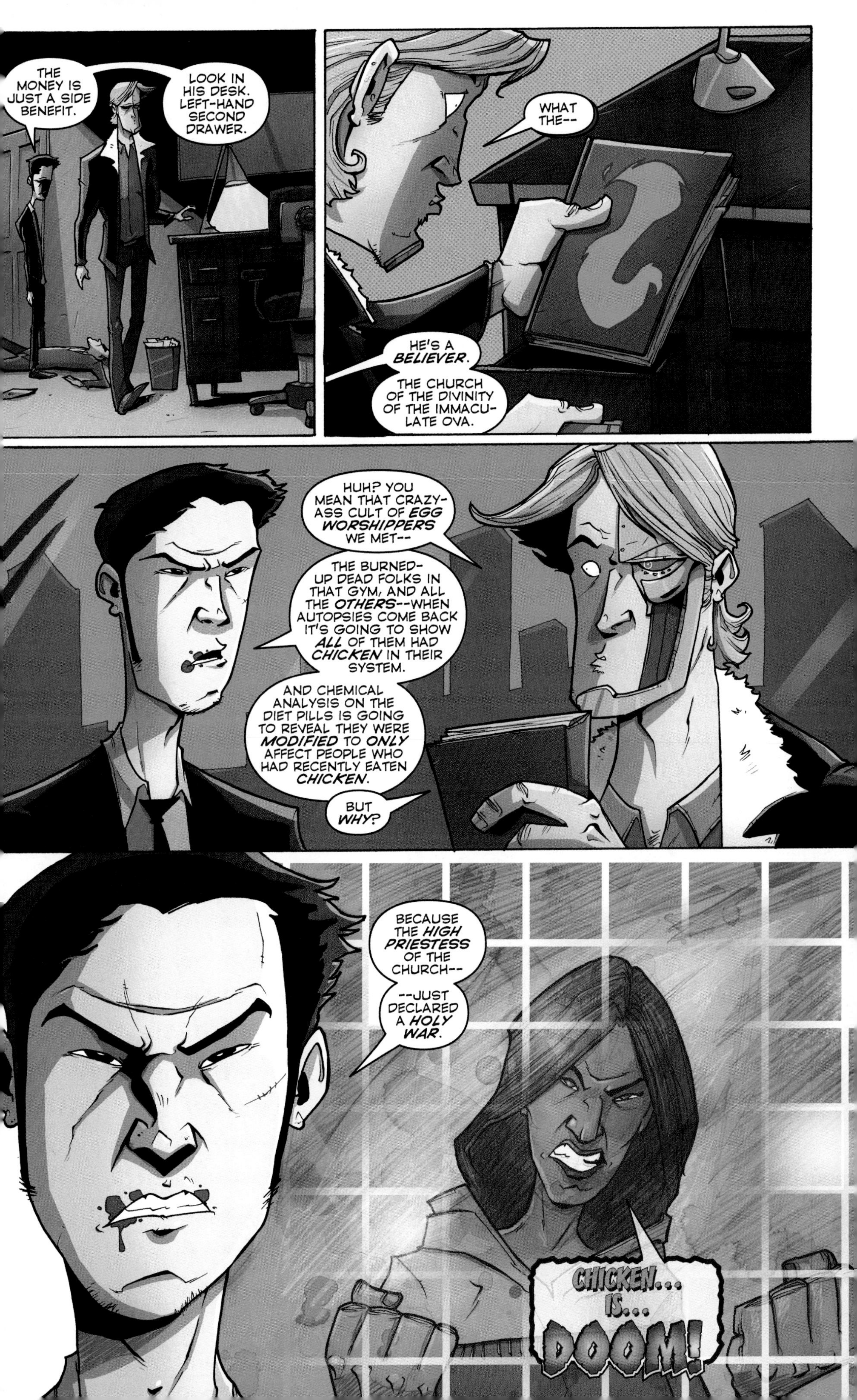
THE MONEY IS JUST A SIDE BENEFIT.
LOOK IN HIS DESK. LEFT-HAND SECOND DRAWER.
WHAT THE--
HE'S A BELIEVER.
THE CHURCH OF THE DIVINITY OF THE IMMACULATE OVA.
HUH? YOU MEAN THAT CRAZY-ASS CULT OF EGG WORSHIPPERS WE MET--
THE BURNED-UP DEAD FOLKS IN THAT GYM, AND ALL THE OTHERS--WHEN AUTOPSIES COME BACK IT'S GOING TO SHOW ALL OF THEM HAD CHICKEN IN THEIR SYSTEM.
AND CHEMICAL ANALYSIS ON THE DIET PILLS IS GOING TO REVEAL THEY WERE MODIFIED TO ONLY AFFECT PEOPLE WHO HAD RECENTLY EATEN CHICKEN.
BUT WHY?
BECAUSE THE HIGH PRIESTESS OF THE CHURCH--
--JUST DECLARED A HOLY WAR.
CHICKEN... IS... DOOM!

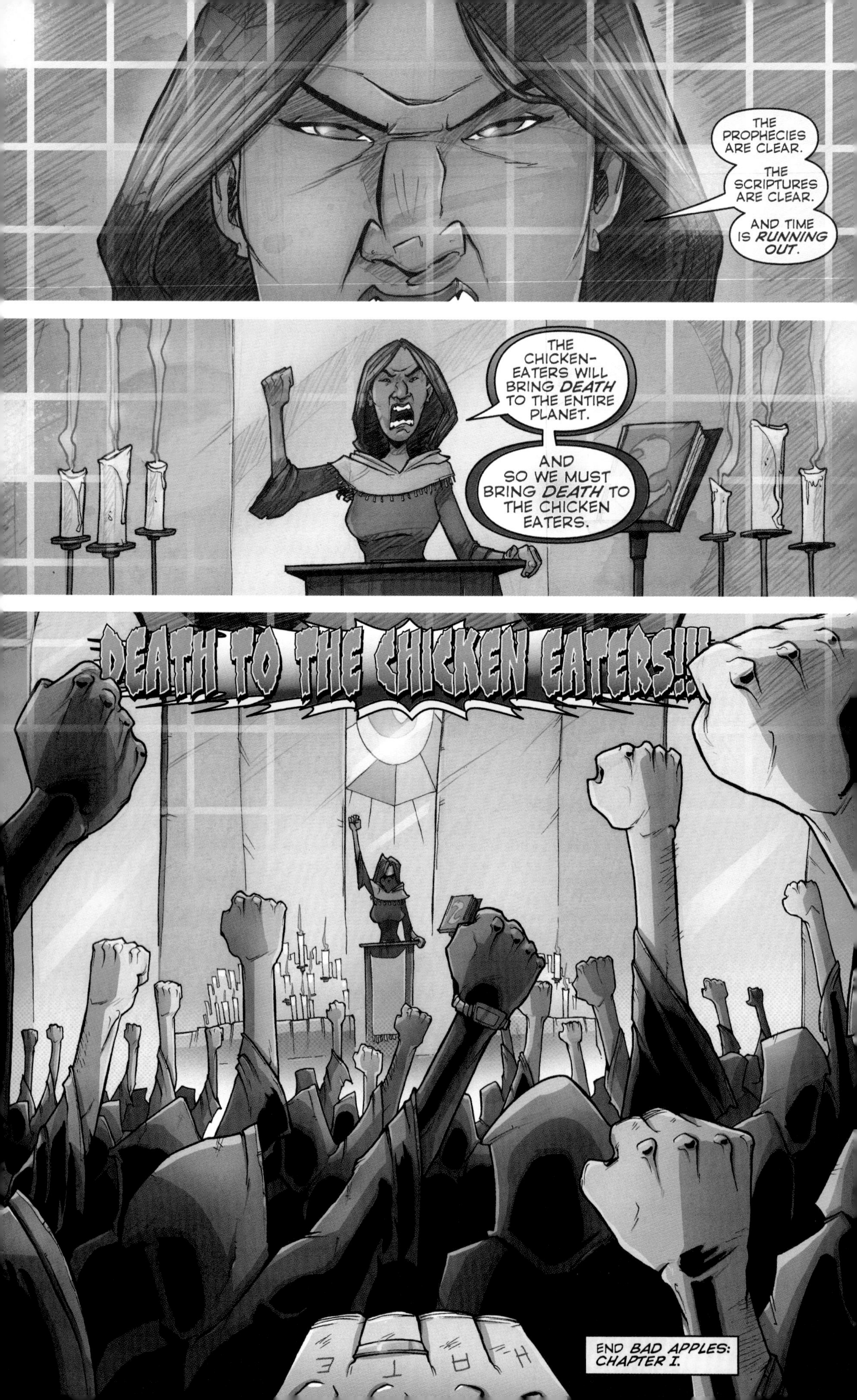
THE PROPHECIES ARE CLEAR.
THE SCRIPTURES ARE CLEAR.
AND TIME IS *RUNNING OUT*.
THE CHICKEN-EATERS WILL BRING *DEATH* TO THE ENTIRE PLANET.
AND SO WE MUST BRING *DEATH* TO THE CHICKEN EATERS.
DEATH TO THE CHICKEN EATERS!!!
H-A-T-E
END *BAD APPLES: CHAPTER I.*

Chapter Two

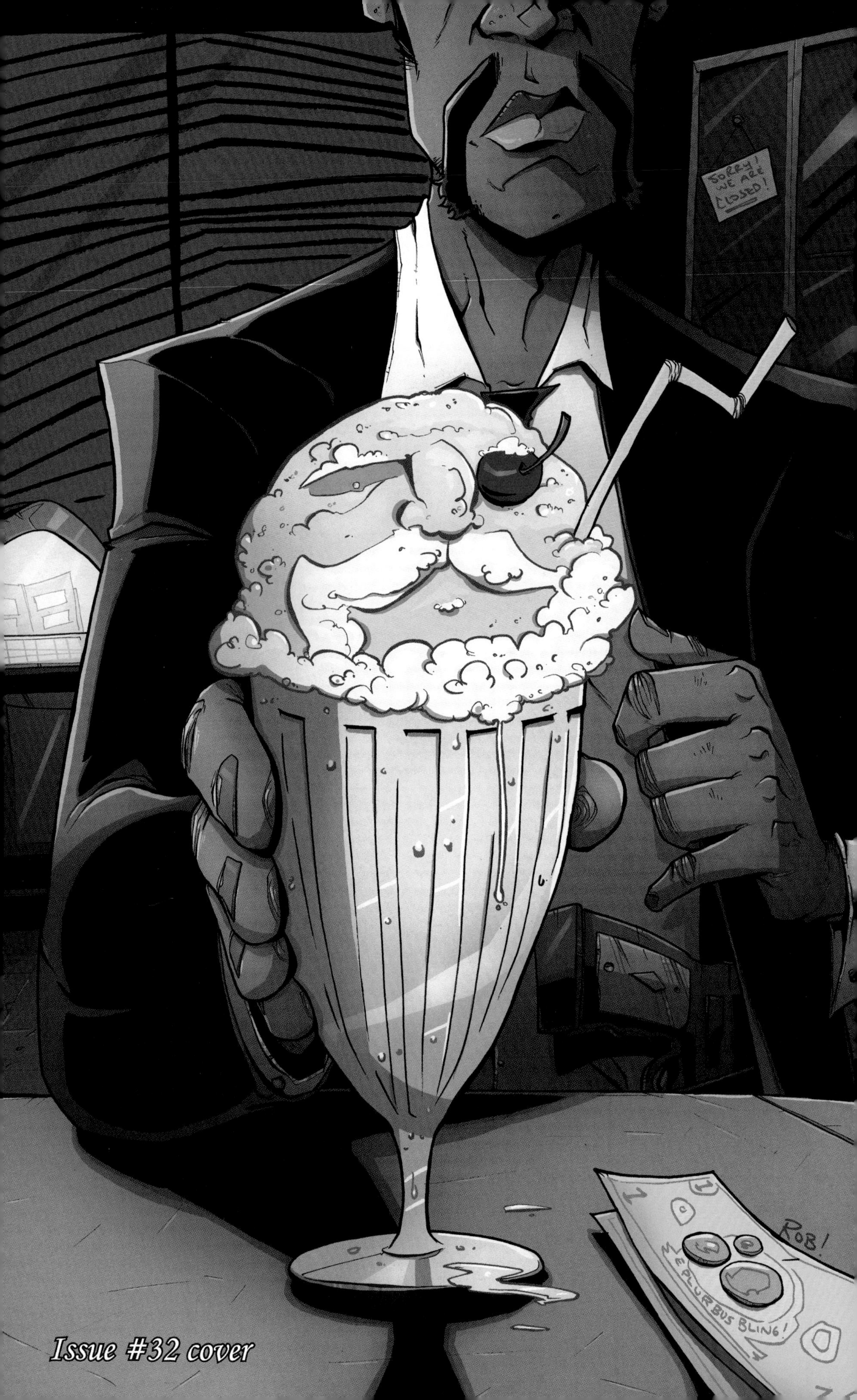
SORRY! WE ARE CLOSED!
E PLURBUS BLING!
ROB!

Issue #32 cover

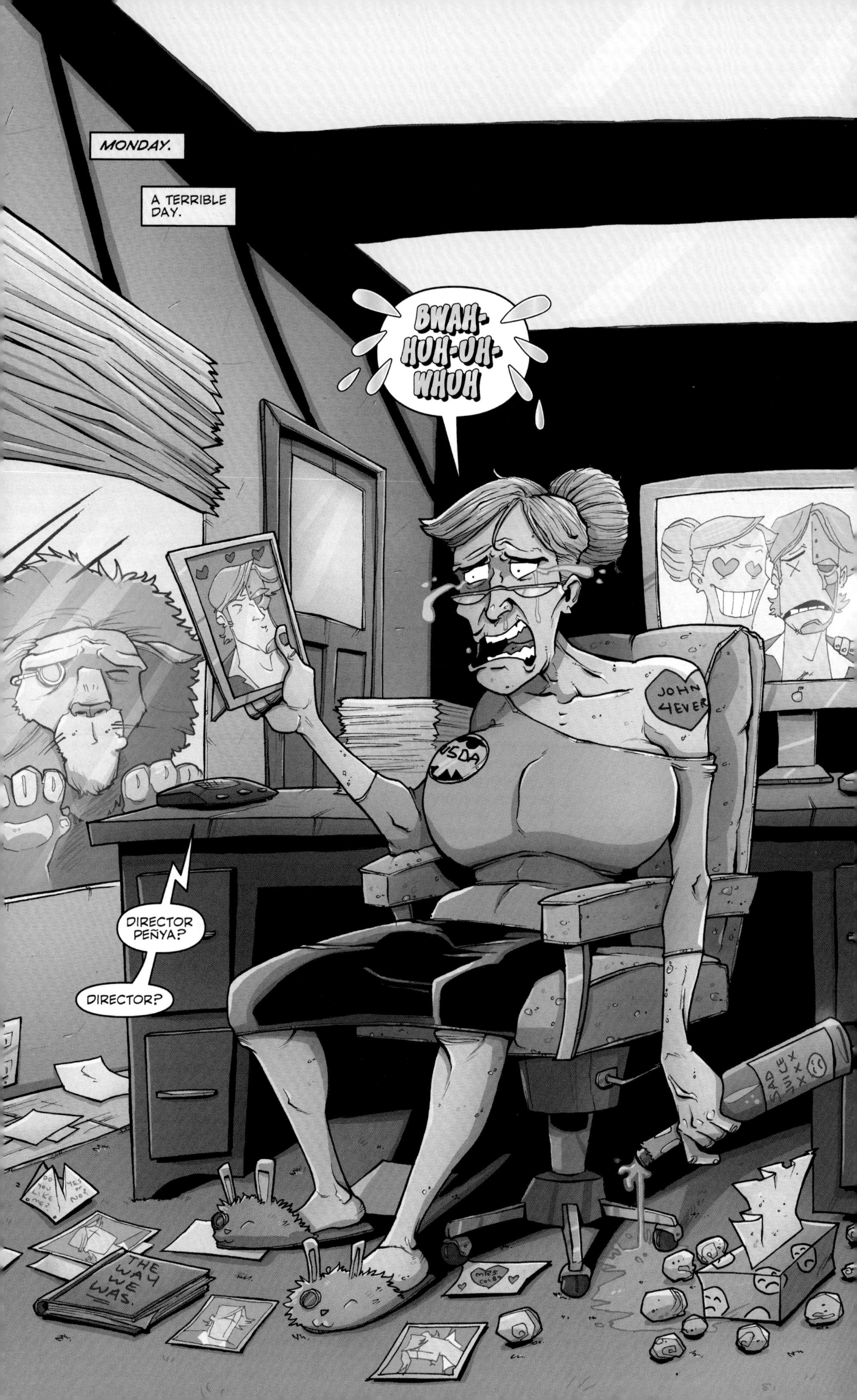
MONDAY.
A TERRIBLE DAY.
BWAH-HUH-UH-WHUH
JOHN 4EVER
USDA
DIRECTOR PEÑYA?
DIRECTOR?
SAD JUICE XXX
THE WAY WE WAS.

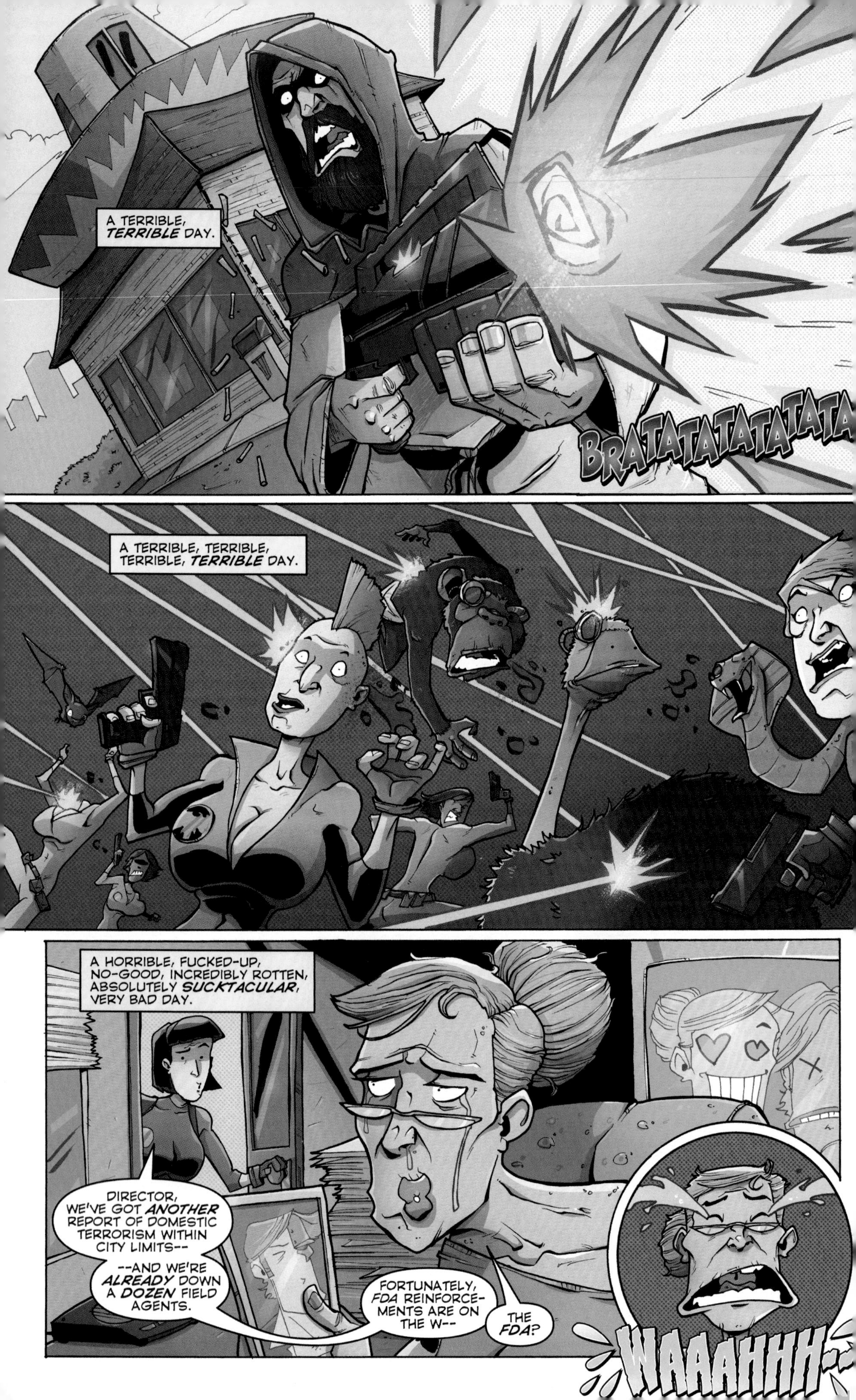

A TERRIBLE, TERRIBLE DAY.
BRATATATATATATA
A TERRIBLE, TERRIBLE, TERRIBLE, TERRIBLE DAY.
A HORRIBLE, FUCKED-UP, NO-GOOD, INCREDIBLY ROTTEN, ABSOLUTELY SUCKTACULAR, VERY BAD DAY.
DIRECTOR, WE'VE GOT ANOTHER REPORT OF DOMESTIC TERRORISM WITHIN CITY LIMITS--
--AND WE'RE ALREADY DOWN A DOZEN FIELD AGENTS.
FORTUNATELY, FDA REINFORCEMENTS ARE ON THE W--
THE FDA?
WAAAHHH--

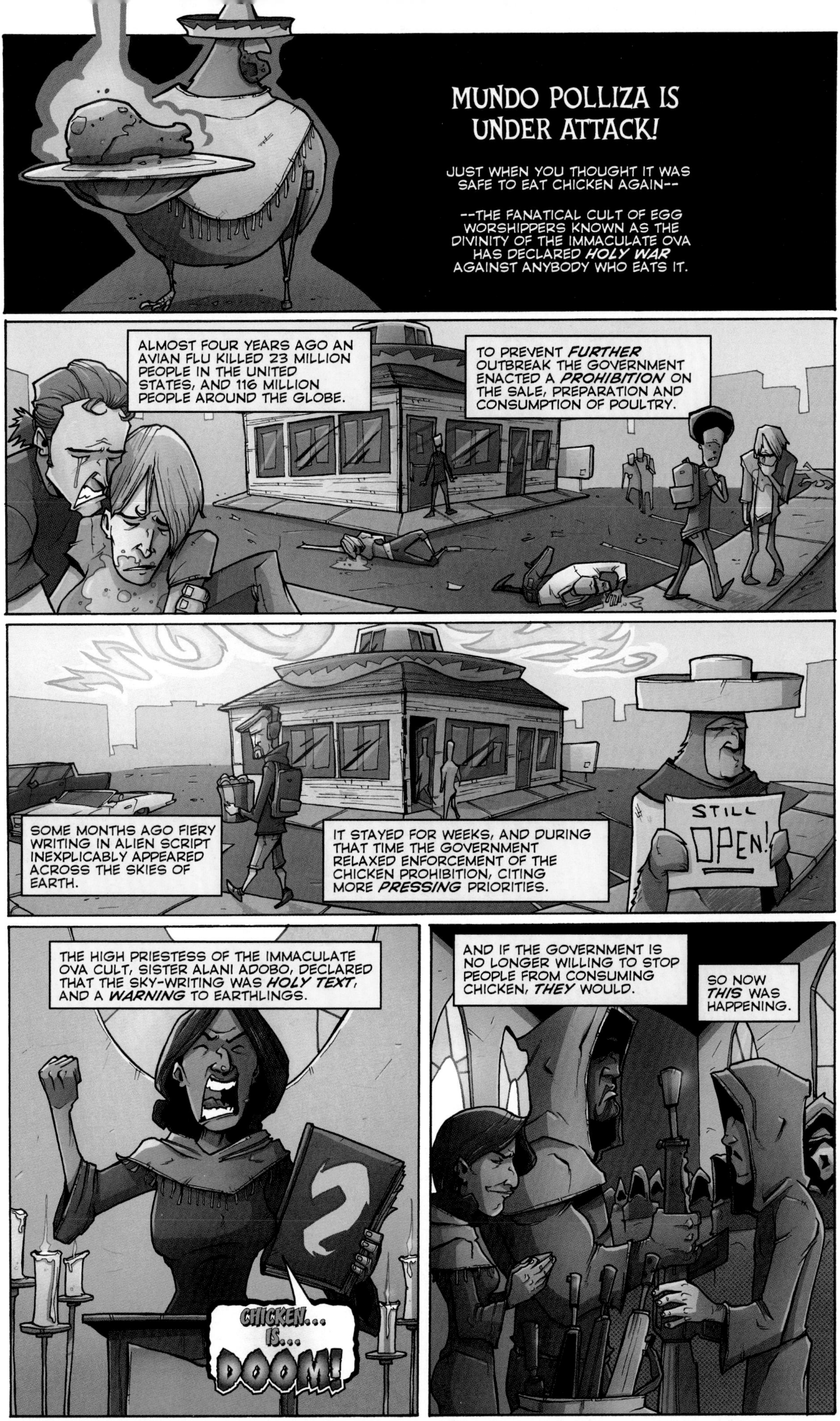
MUNDO POLLIZA IS UNDER ATTACK!
JUST WHEN YOU THOUGHT IT WAS SAFE TO EAT CHICKEN AGAIN--
--THE FANATICAL CULT OF EGG WORSHIPPERS KNOWN AS THE DIVINITY OF THE IMMACULATE OVA HAS DECLARED HOLY WAR AGAINST ANYBODY WHO EATS IT.
ALMOST FOUR YEARS AGO AN AVIAN FLU KILLED 23 MILLION PEOPLE IN THE UNITED STATES, AND 116 MILLION PEOPLE AROUND THE GLOBE.
TO PREVENT FURTHER OUTBREAK THE GOVERNMENT ENACTED A PROHIBITION ON THE SALE, PREPARATION AND CONSUMPTION OF POULTRY.
SOME MONTHS AGO FIERY WRITING IN ALIEN SCRIPT INEXPLICABLY APPEARED ACROSS THE SKIES OF EARTH.
IT STAYED FOR WEEKS, AND DURING THAT TIME THE GOVERNMENT RELAXED ENFORCEMENT OF THE CHICKEN PROHIBITION, CITING MORE PRESSING PRIORITIES.
STILL OPEN!
THE HIGH PRIESTESS OF THE IMMACULATE OVA CULT, SISTER ALANI ADOBO, DECLARED THAT THE SKY-WRITING WAS HOLY TEXT, AND A WARNING TO EARTHLINGS.
CHICKEN... IS... DOOM!
AND IF THE GOVERNMENT IS NO LONGER WILLING TO STOP PEOPLE FROM CONSUMING CHICKEN, THEY WOULD.
SO NOW THIS WAS HAPPENING.

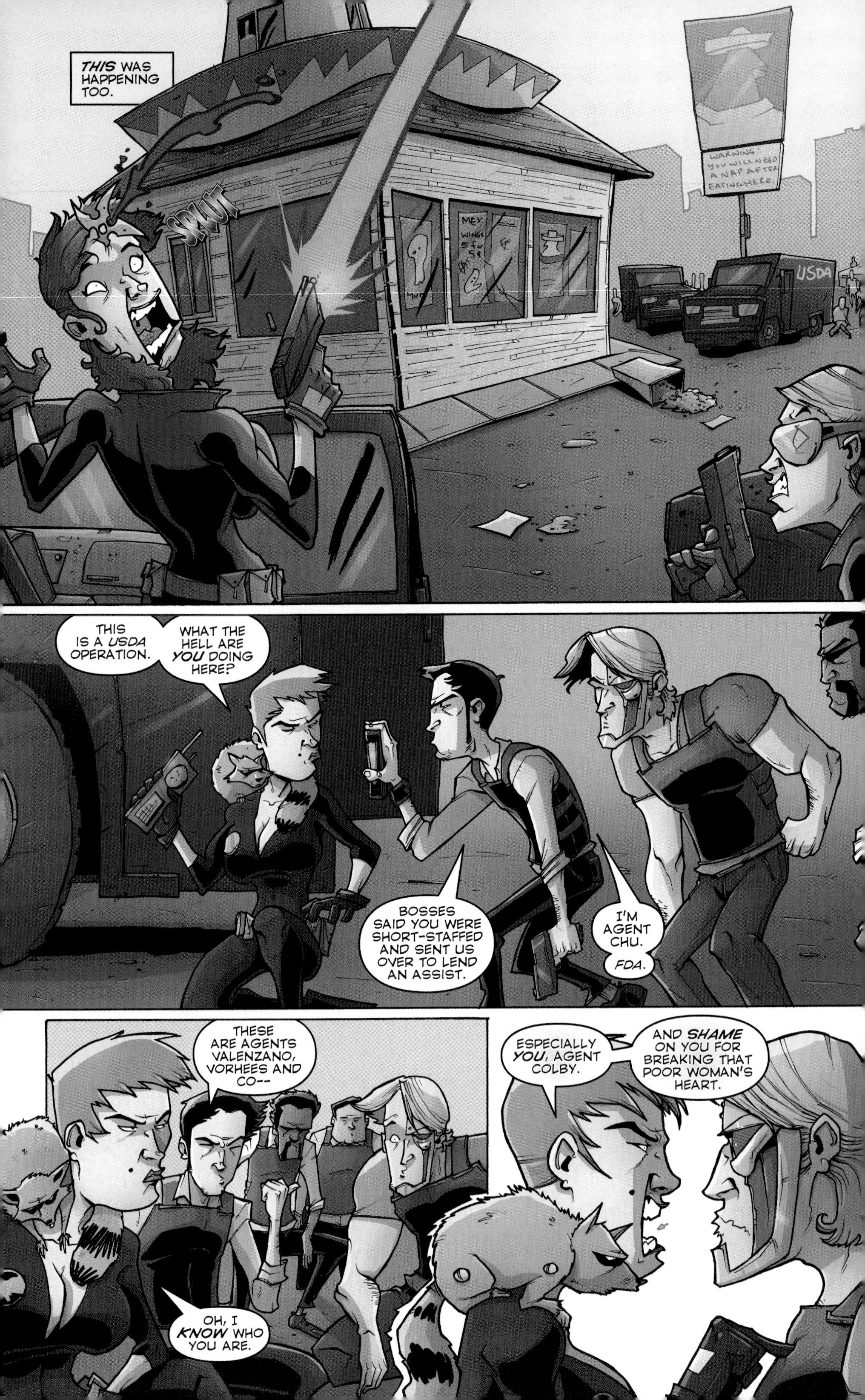
THIS WAS HAPPENING TOO.
SPLUT
MEX WINGS 5 for 5¢
WARNING: YOU WILL NEED A NAP AFTER EATING HERE.
USDA
THIS IS A USDA OPERATION.
WHAT THE HELL ARE YOU DOING HERE?
BOSSES SAID YOU WERE SHORT-STAFFED AND SENT US OVER TO LEND AN ASSIST.
I'M AGENT CHU.
FDA.
THESE ARE AGENTS VALENZANO, VORHEES AND CO--
OH, I KNOW WHO YOU ARE.
ESPECIALLY YOU, AGENT COLBY.
AND SHAME ON YOU FOR BREAKING THAT POOR WOMAN'S HEART.

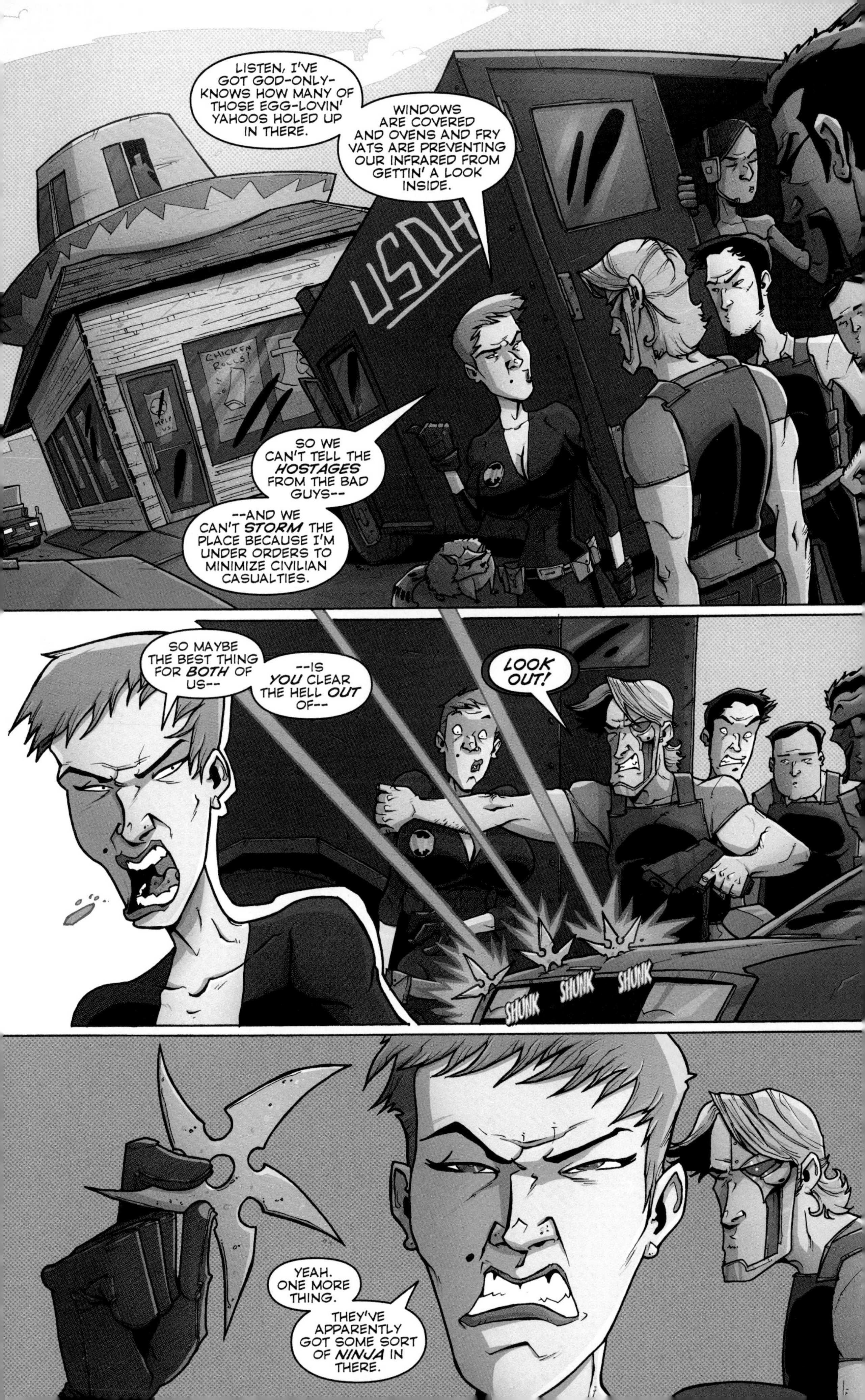
LISTEN, I'VE GOT GOD-ONLY-KNOWS HOW MANY OF THOSE EGG-LOVIN' YAHOOS HOLED UP IN THERE.
WINDOWS ARE COVERED AND OVENS AND FRY VATS ARE PREVENTING OUR INFRARED FROM GETTIN' A LOOK INSIDE.
USDH
CHICKEN ROLLS!
HELP US.
SO WE CAN'T TELL THE *HOSTAGES* FROM THE BAD GUYS--
--AND WE CAN'T *STORM* THE PLACE BECAUSE I'M UNDER ORDERS TO MINIMIZE CIVILIAN CASUALTIES.
SO MAYBE THE BEST THING FOR *BOTH* OF US--
--IS *YOU* CLEAR THE HELL *OUT* OF--
LOOK OUT!
SHUNK
SHUNK
SHUNK
YEAH. ONE MORE THING.
THEY'VE APPARENTLY GOT SOME SORT OF *NINJA* IN THERE.

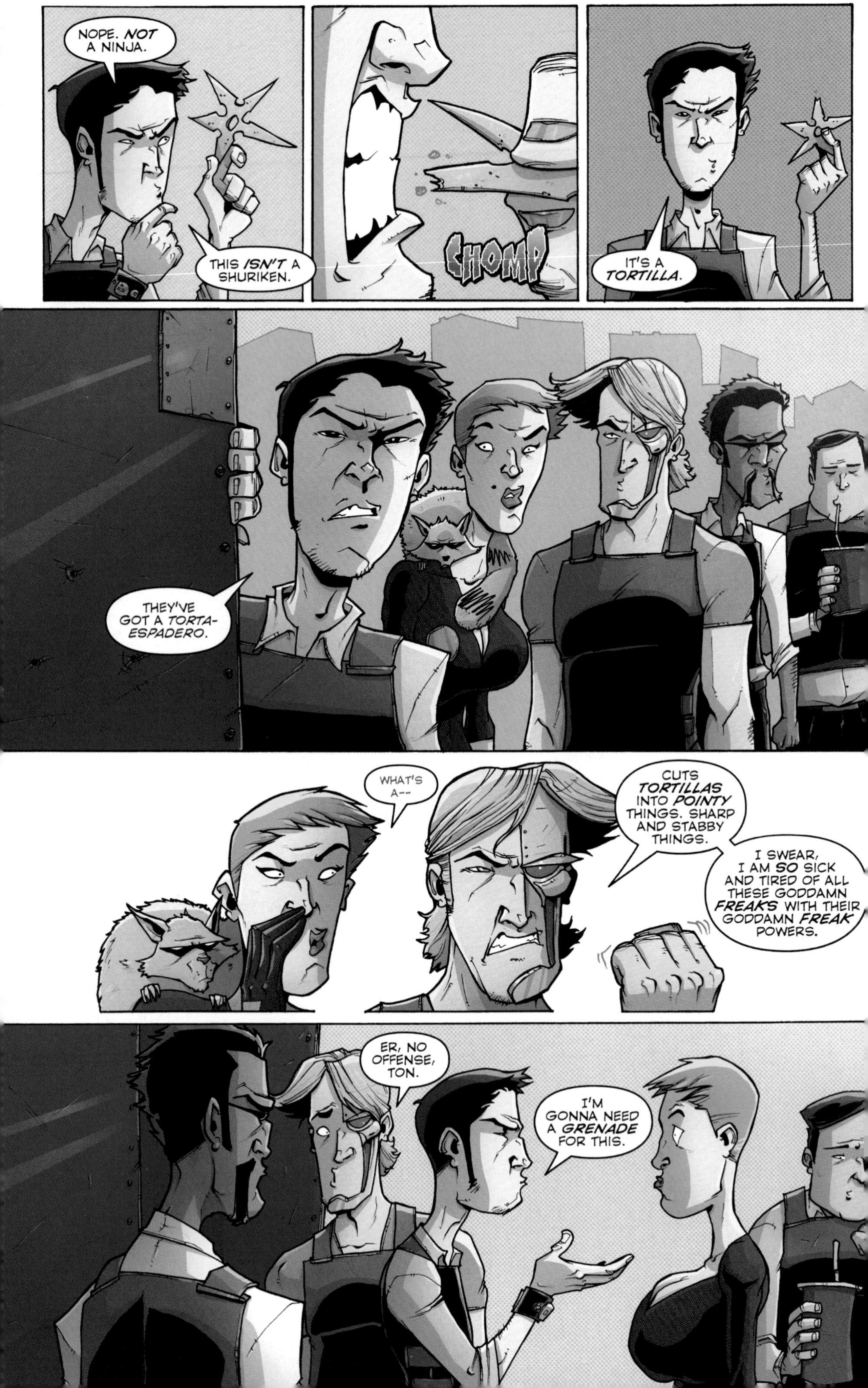
NOPE. NOT A NINJA.
THIS ISN'T A SHURIKEN.
CHOMP
IT'S A TORTILLA.
THEY'VE GOT A TORTA-ESPADERO.
WHAT'S A--
CUTS TORTILLAS INTO POINTY THINGS. SHARP AND STABBY THINGS.
I SWEAR, I AM SO SICK AND TIRED OF ALL THESE GODDAMN FREAKS WITH THEIR GODDAMN FREAK POWERS.
ER, NO OFFENSE, TON.
I'M GONNA NEED A GRENADE FOR THIS.

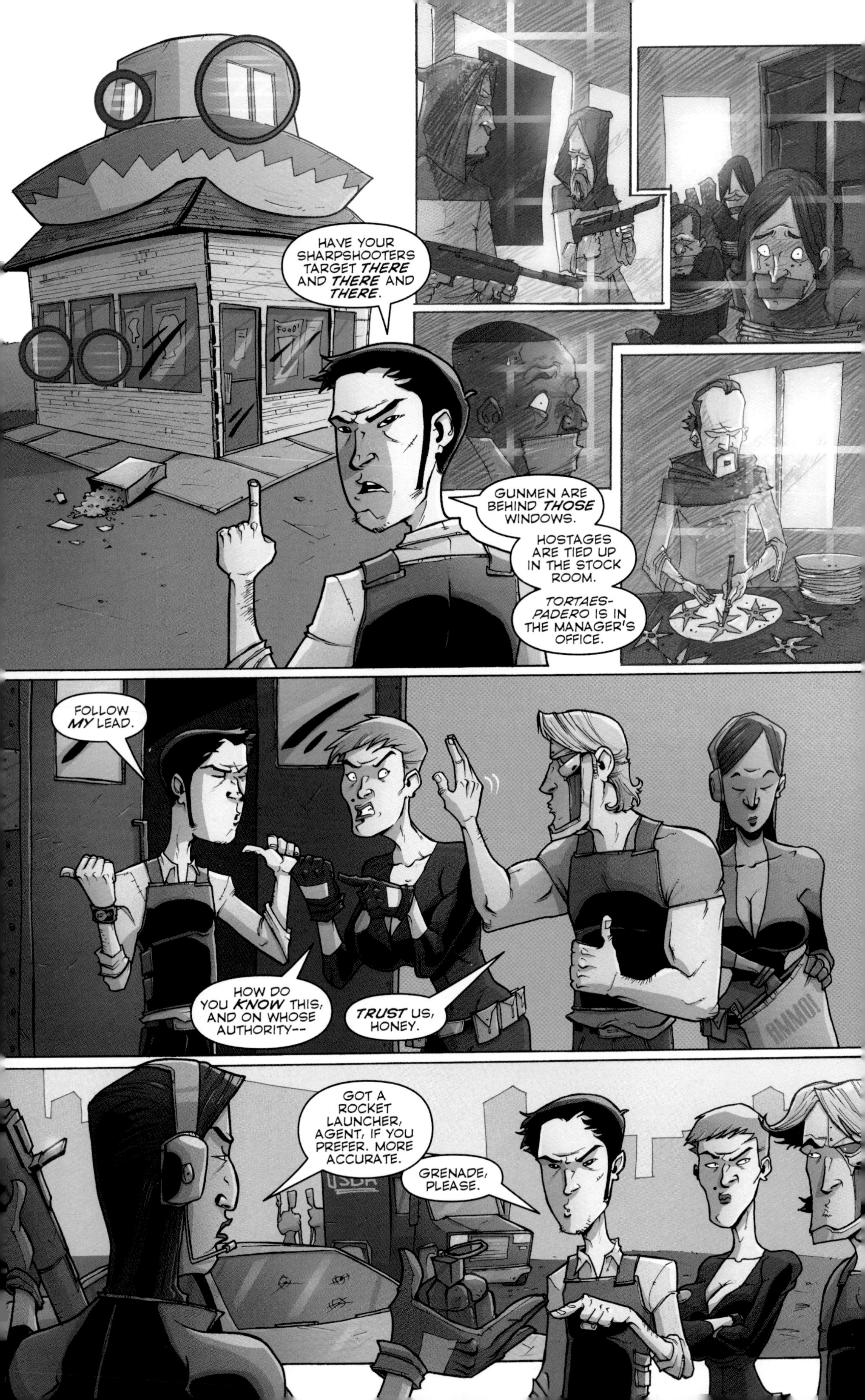
HAVE YOUR SHARPSHOOTERS TARGET *THERE* AND *THERE* AND *THERE*.
GUNMEN ARE BEHIND *THOSE* WINDOWS.
HOSTAGES ARE TIED UP IN THE STOCK ROOM.
TORTAES-PADERO IS IN THE MANAGER'S OFFICE.
FOLLOW *MY* LEAD.
HOW DO YOU *KNOW* THIS, AND ON WHOSE AUTHORITY--
TRUST US, HONEY.
AMMO!
GOT A ROCKET LAUNCHER, AGENT, IF YOU PREFER. MORE ACCURATE.
GRENADE, PLEASE.

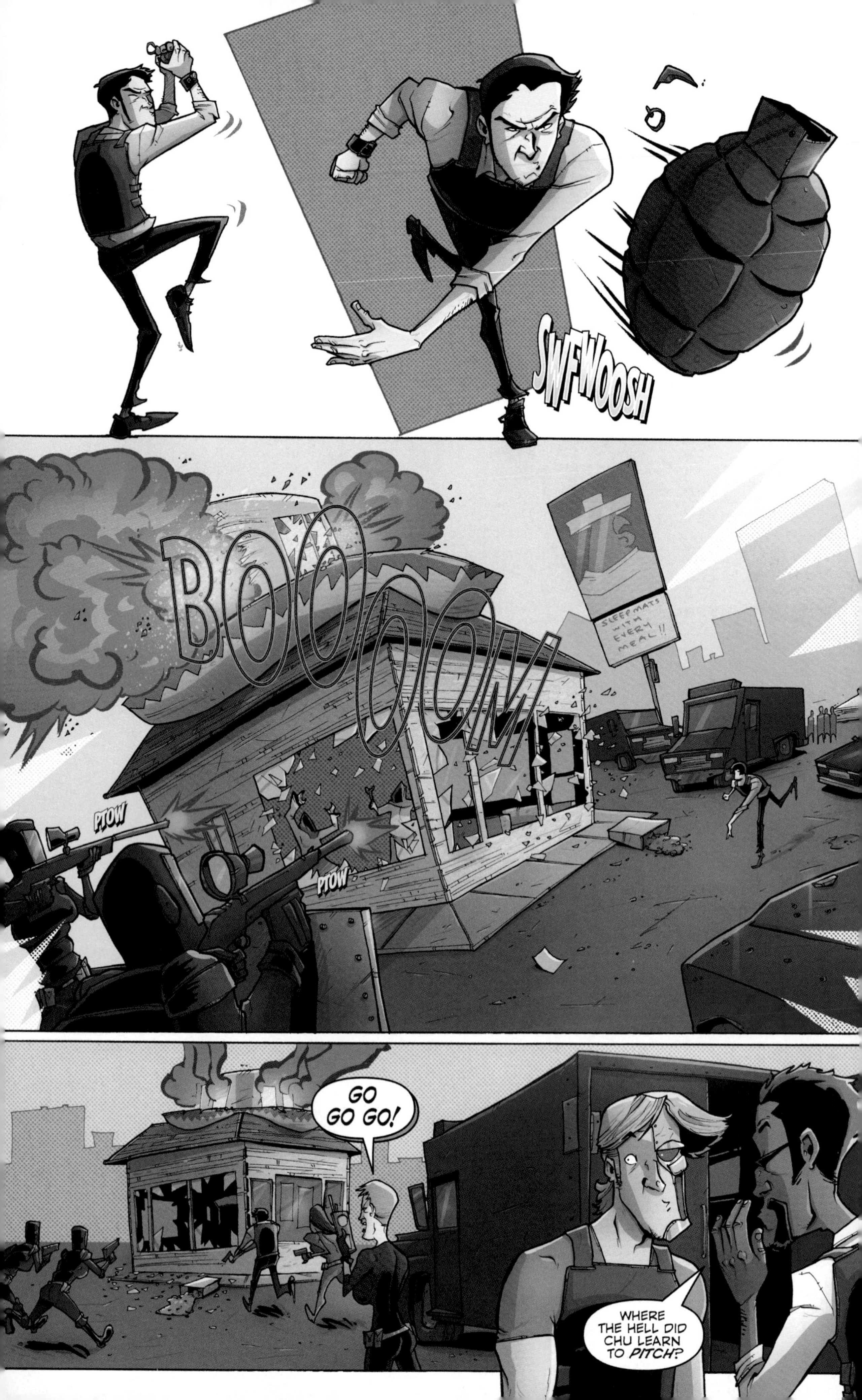
SWFWOOSH
BOOOOOM
SLEEP MATS WITH EVERY MEAL!!
PTOW
PTOW
GO GO GO!
WHERE THE HELL DID CHU LEARN TO *PITCH*?

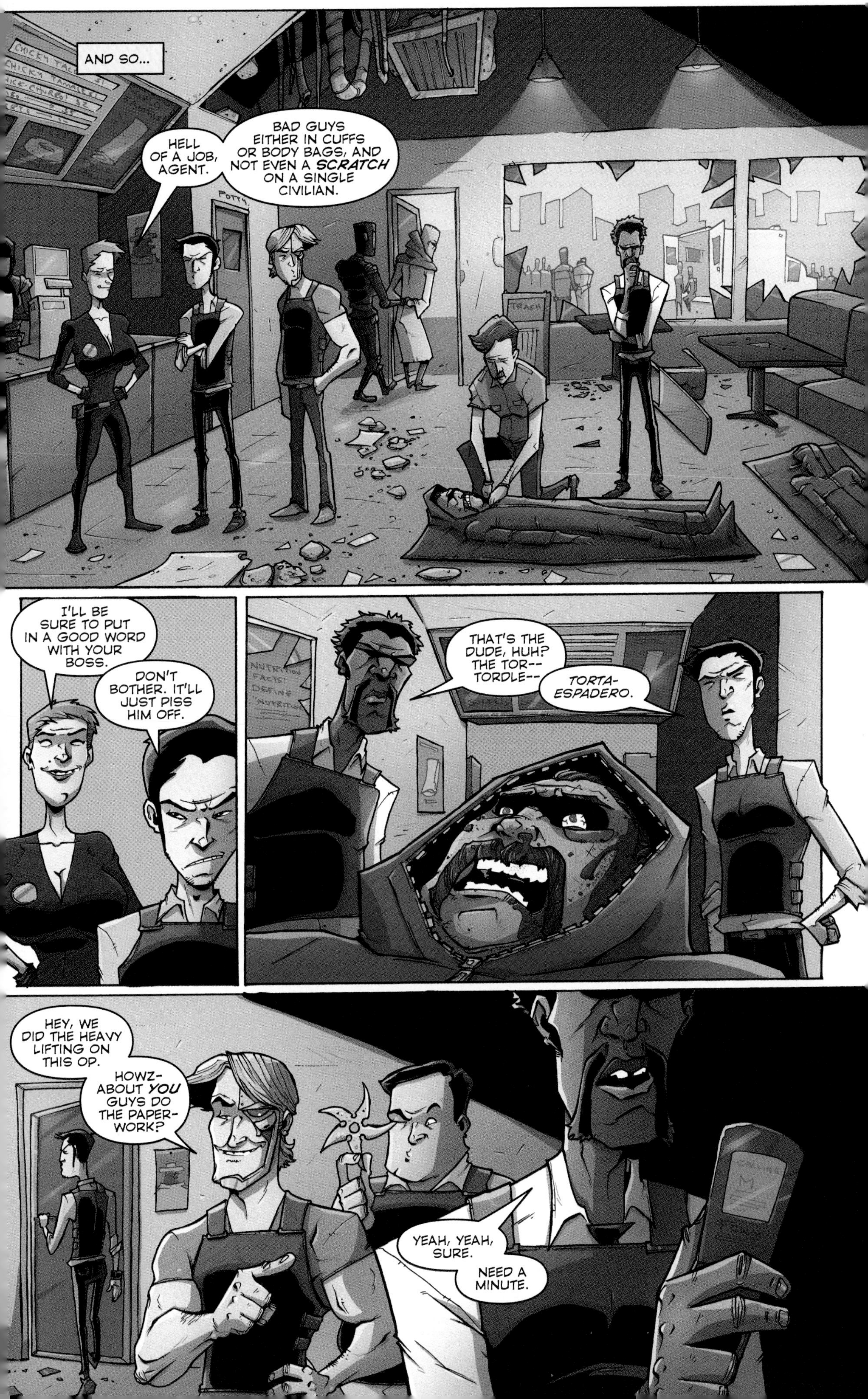
AND SO...
HELL OF A JOB, AGENT.
BAD GUYS EITHER IN CUFFS OR BODY BAGS, AND NOT EVEN A SCRATCH ON A SINGLE CIVILIAN.
POTTY
TRASH
I'LL BE SURE TO PUT IN A GOOD WORD WITH YOUR BOSS.
DON'T BOTHER. IT'LL JUST PISS HIM OFF.
THAT'S THE DUDE, HUH? THE TOR-TORDLE--
TORTA-ESPADERO.
HEY, WE DID THE HEAVY LIFTING ON THIS OP.
HOWZ-ABOUT YOU GUYS DO THE PAPER-WORK?
YEAH, YEAH, SURE.
NEED A MINUTE.

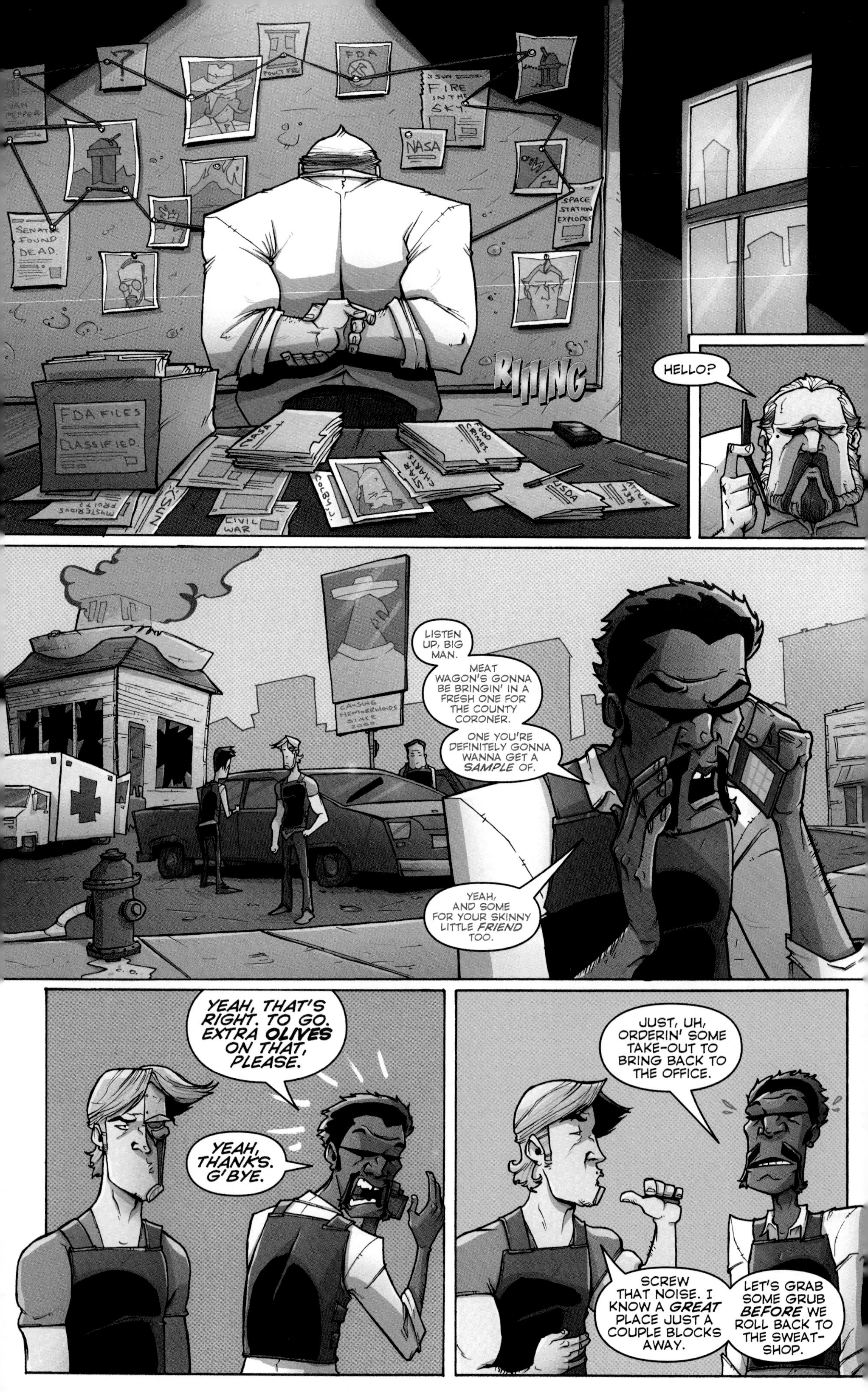

SENATOR FOUND DEAD.
FDA
FIRE IN THE SKY
NASA
SPACE STATION EXPLODES
FDA FILES
CLASSIFIED.
RIIING
HELLO?
LISTEN UP, BIG MAN.
MEAT WAGON'S GONNA BE BRINGIN' IN A FRESH ONE FOR THE COUNTY CORONER.
ONE YOU'RE DEFINITELY GONNA WANNA GET A *SAMPLE* OF.
YEAH, AND SOME FOR YOUR SKINNY LITTLE *FRIEND* TOO.
*YEAH, THAT'S RIGHT. TO GO. EXTRA **OLIVES** ON THAT, PLEASE.*
YEAH, THANKS. G'BYE.
JUST, UH, ORDERIN' SOME TAKE-OUT TO BRING BACK TO THE OFFICE.
SCREW THAT NOISE. I KNOW A *GREAT* PLACE JUST A COUPLE BLOCKS AWAY.
LET'S GRAB SOME GRUB *BEFORE* WE ROLL BACK TO THE SWEAT-SHOP.

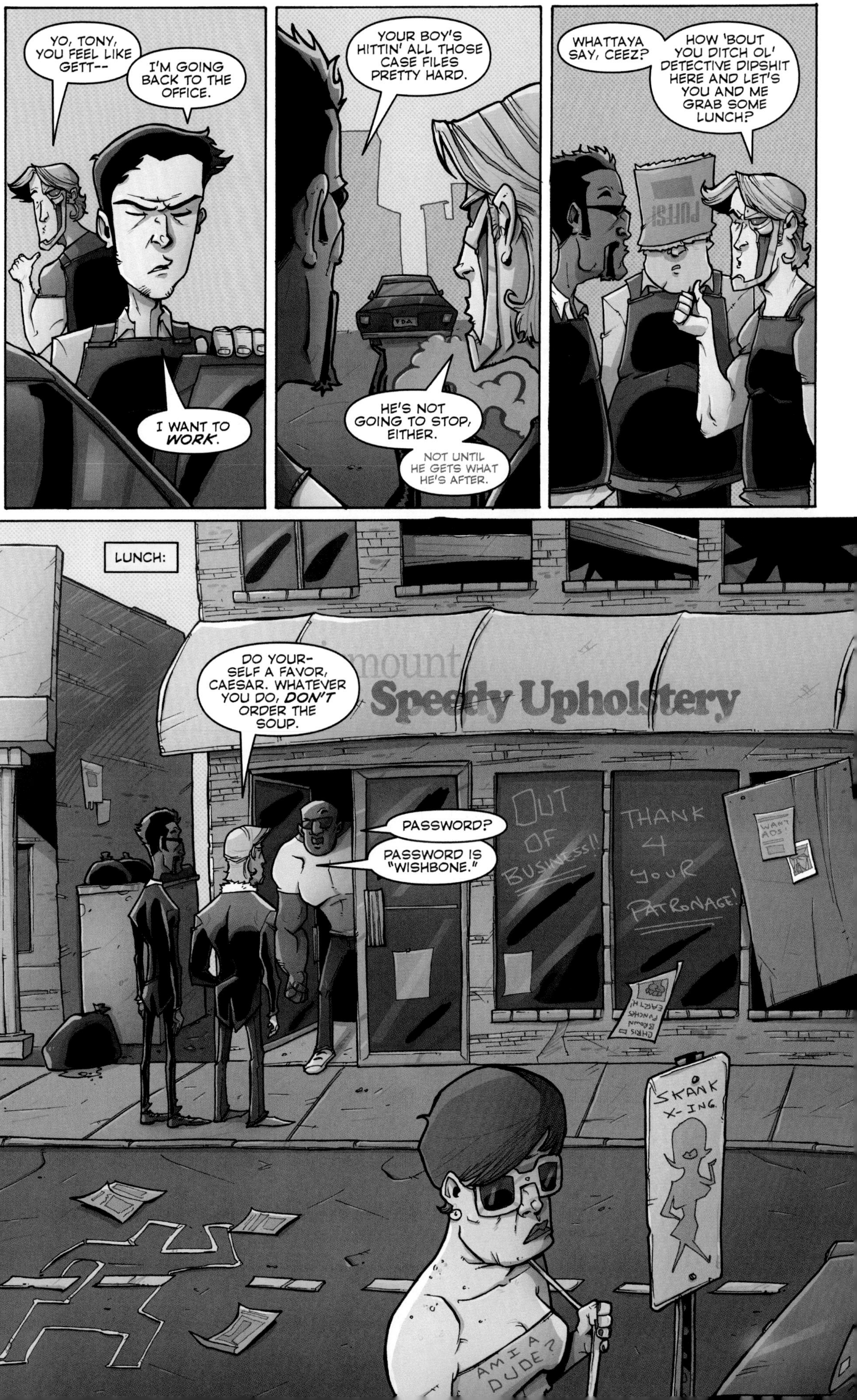
YO, TONY, YOU FEEL LIKE GETT--
I'M GOING BACK TO THE OFFICE.
I WANT TO *WORK*.
YOUR BOY'S HITTIN' ALL THOSE CASE FILES PRETTY HARD.
HE'S NOT GOING TO STOP, EITHER.
NOT UNTIL HE GETS WHAT HE'S AFTER.
WHATTAYA SAY, CEEZ?
HOW 'BOUT YOU DITCH OL' DETECTIVE DIPSHIT HERE AND LET'S YOU AND ME GRAB SOME LUNCH?
LUNCH:
Speedy Upholstery
DO YOURSELF A FAVOR, CAESAR. WHATEVER YOU DO, ***DON'T*** ORDER THE SOUP.
PASSWORD?
PASSWORD IS "WISHBONE."
OUT OF BUSINESS!!
THANK 4 YOUR PATRONAGE!
SKANK X-ING
AM I A DUDE?

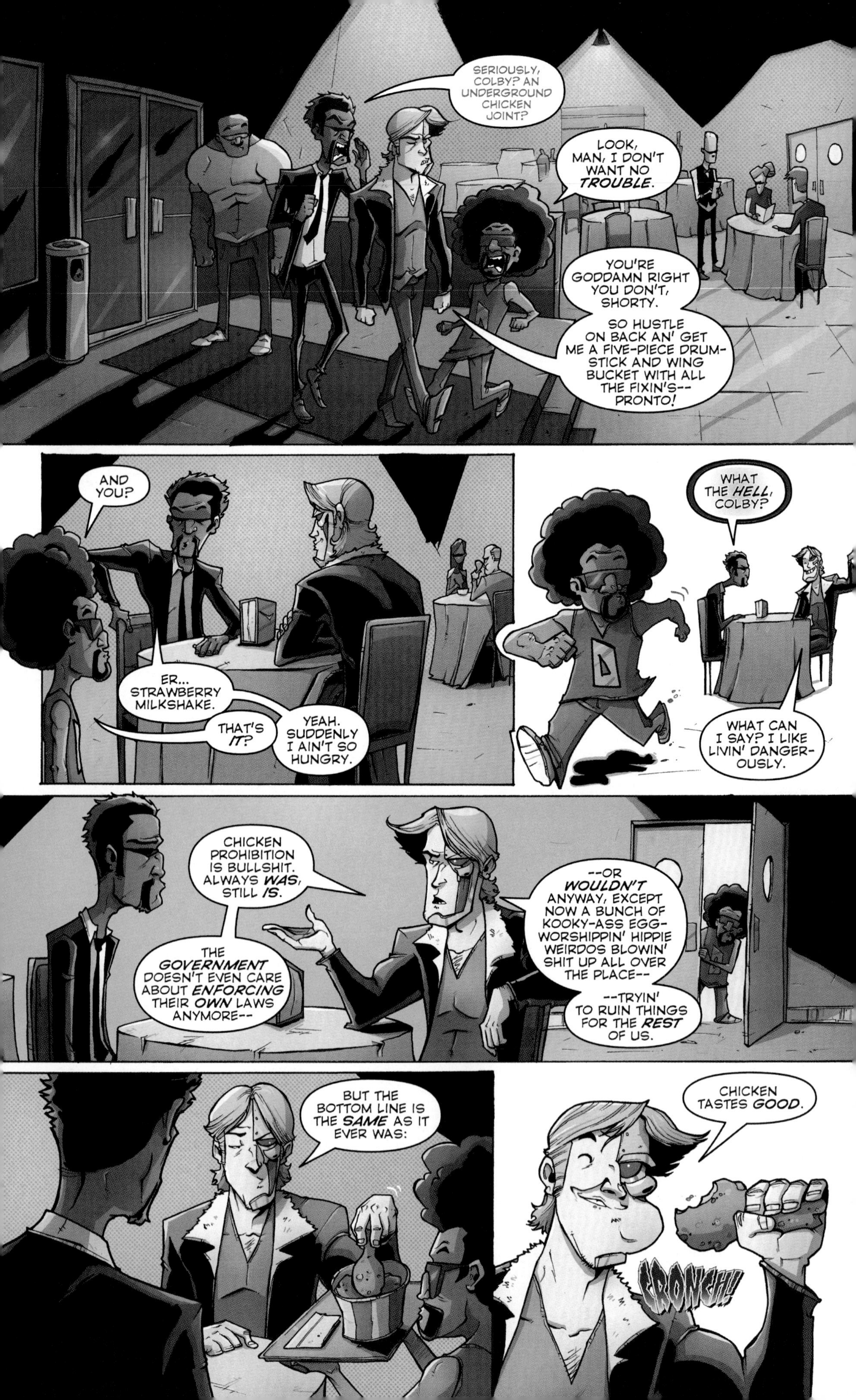
SERIOUSLY, COLBY? AN UNDERGROUND CHICKEN JOINT?
LOOK, MAN, I DON'T WANT NO TROUBLE.
YOU'RE GODDAMN RIGHT YOU DON'T, SHORTY.
SO HUSTLE ON BACK AN' GET ME A FIVE-PIECE DRUM-STICK AND WING BUCKET WITH ALL THE FIXIN'S--PRONTO!
AND YOU?
ER... STRAWBERRY MILKSHAKE.
THAT'S IT?
YEAH. SUDDENLY I AIN'T SO HUNGRY.
WHAT THE HELL, COLBY?
WHAT CAN I SAY? I LIKE LIVIN' DANGER-OUSLY.
CHICKEN PROHIBITION IS BULLSHIT. ALWAYS WAS, STILL IS.
THE GOVERNMENT DOESN'T EVEN CARE ABOUT ENFORCING THEIR OWN LAWS ANYMORE--
--OR WOULDN'T ANYWAY, EXCEPT NOW A BUNCH OF KOOKY-ASS EGG-WORSHIPPIN' HIPPIE WEIRDOS BLOWIN' SHIT UP ALL OVER THE PLACE--
--TRYIN' TO RUIN THINGS FOR THE REST OF US.
BUT THE BOTTOM LINE IS THE SAME AS IT EVER WAS:
CHICKEN TASTES GOOD.
CRONCH!!

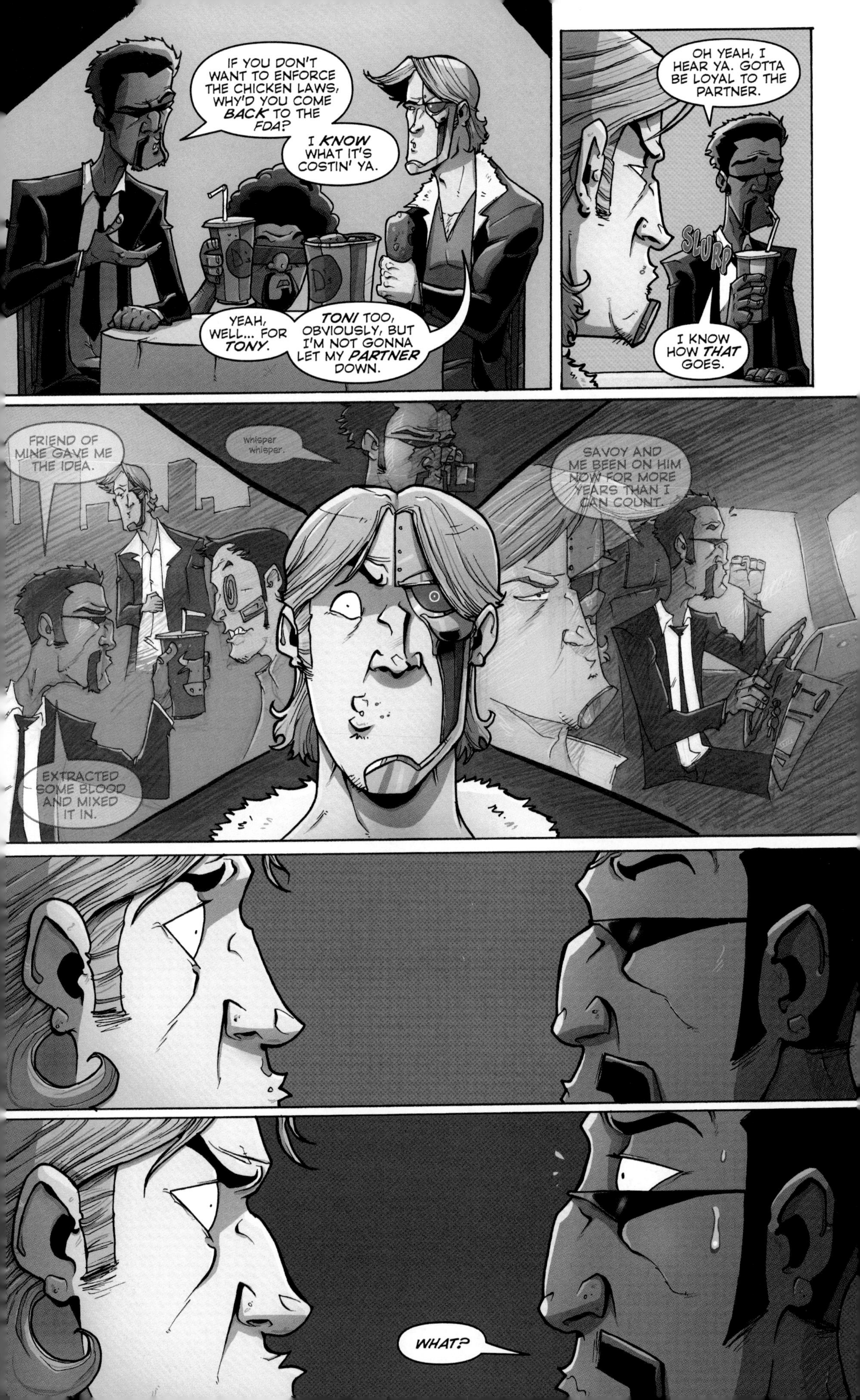

IF YOU DON'T WANT TO ENFORCE THE CHICKEN LAWS, WHY'D YOU COME BACK TO THE FDA?
I KNOW WHAT IT'S COSTIN' YA.
YEAH, WELL... FOR TONY.
TONI TOO, OBVIOUSLY, BUT I'M NOT GONNA LET MY PARTNER DOWN.
OH YEAH, I HEAR YA. GOTTA BE LOYAL TO THE PARTNER.
SLURP
I KNOW HOW THAT GOES.
FRIEND OF MINE GAVE ME THE IDEA.
whisper whisper.
SAVOY AND ME BEEN ON HIM NOW FOR MORE YEARS THAN I CAN COUNT.
EXTRACTED SOME BLOOD AND MIXED IT IN.
WHAT?

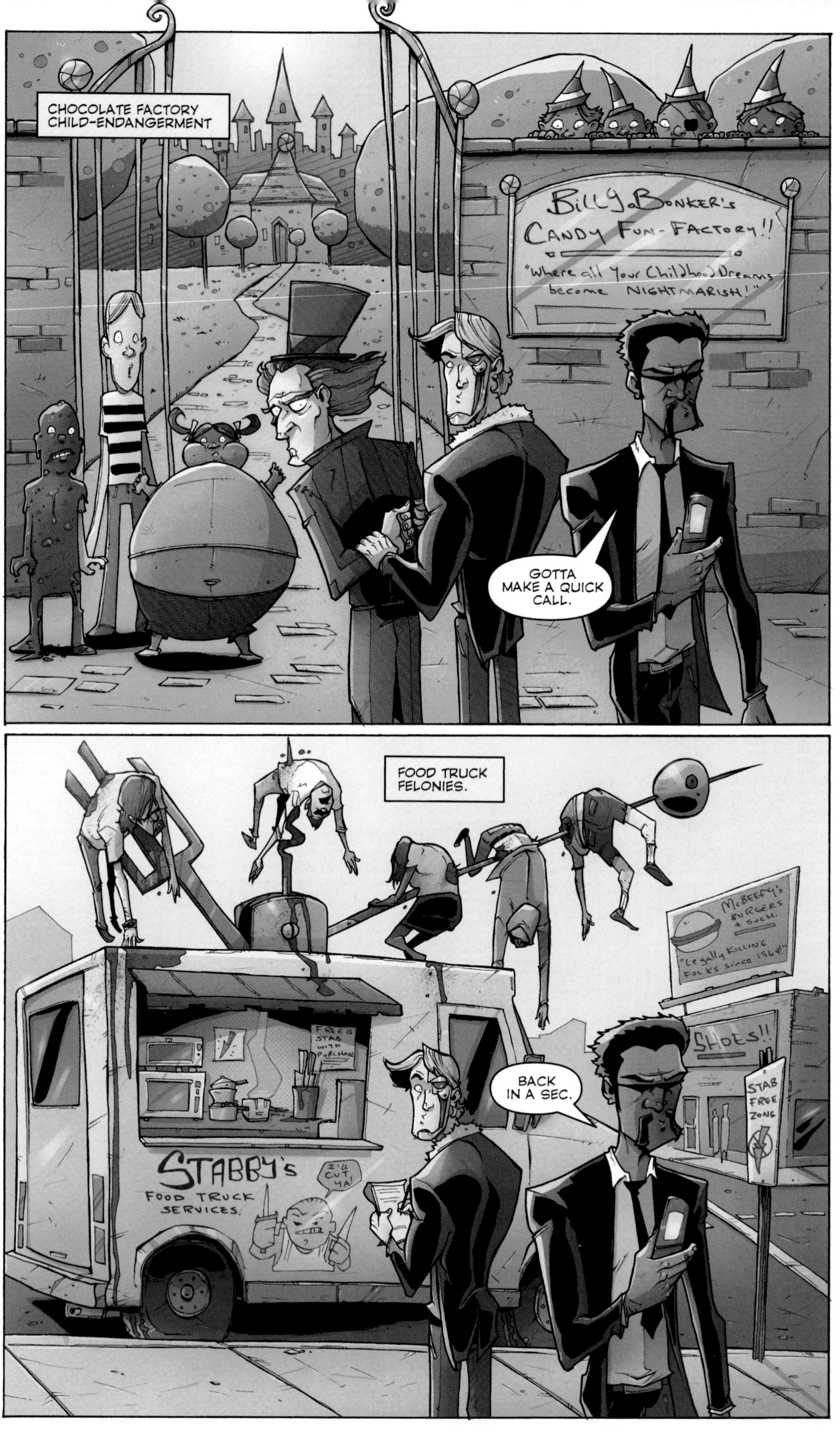
CHOCOLATE FACTORY CHILD-ENDANGERMENT
Billy a Bonker's
Candy Fun-Factory!!
"Where all Your Childhood Dreams become NIGHTMARISH!"
GOTTA MAKE A QUICK CALL.
FOOD TRUCK FELONIES.
McBeefy's Burgers & Such.
"Legally Killing Folks since 1964!"
FREE STAB WITH PURCHASE
STABBY's FOOD TRUCK SERVICES.
I'LL CUT YA!
SHOES!!
STAB FREE ZONE
BACK IN A SEC.

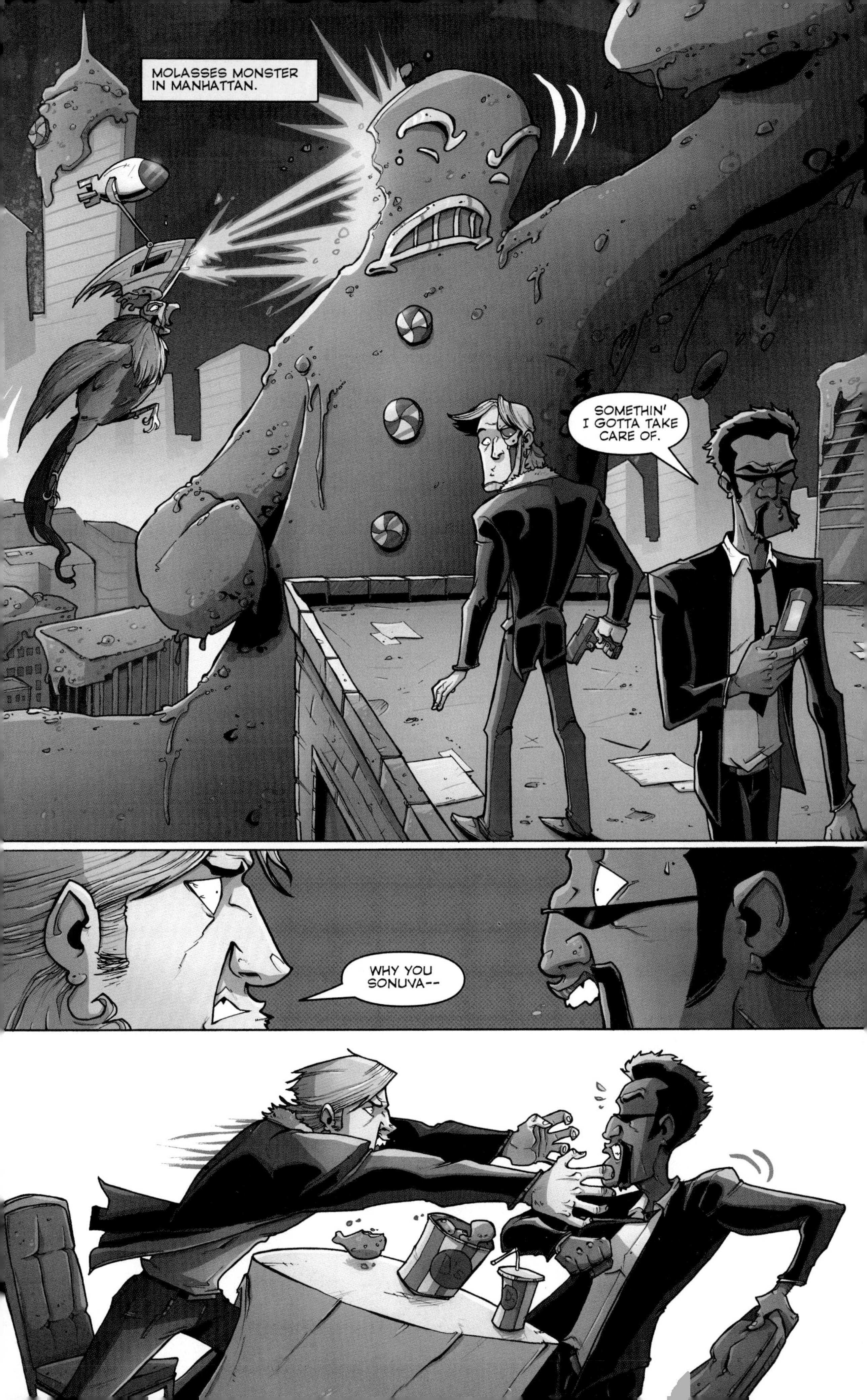
MOLASSES MONSTER IN MANHATTAN.
SOMETHIN' I GOTTA TAKE CARE OF.
WHY YOU SONUVA--

KaWHAMM

YOU'RE *STILL* WORKING WITH HIM.

SAVOY.

WHAM

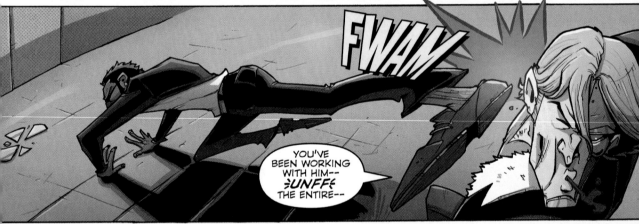

FWAM

YOU'VE BEEN WORKING WITH HIM-- ≥UNFF≥ THE ENTIRE--

CRACK

SWAM

THE ENTIRE TIME!

SKPOW

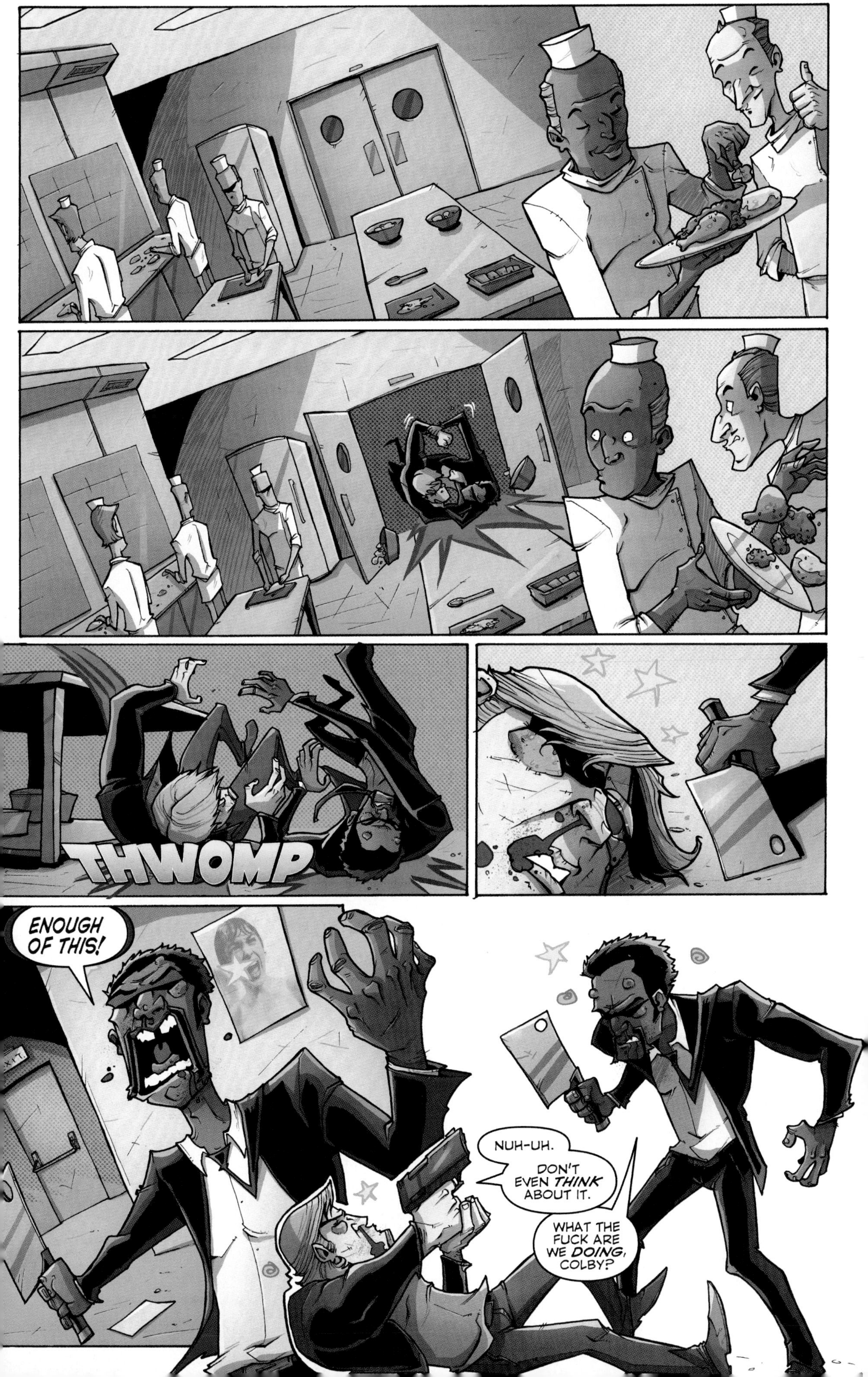
THWOMP
ENOUGH OF THIS!
NUH-UH.
DON'T EVEN *THINK* ABOUT IT.
WHAT THE FUCK ARE WE *DOING*, COLBY?

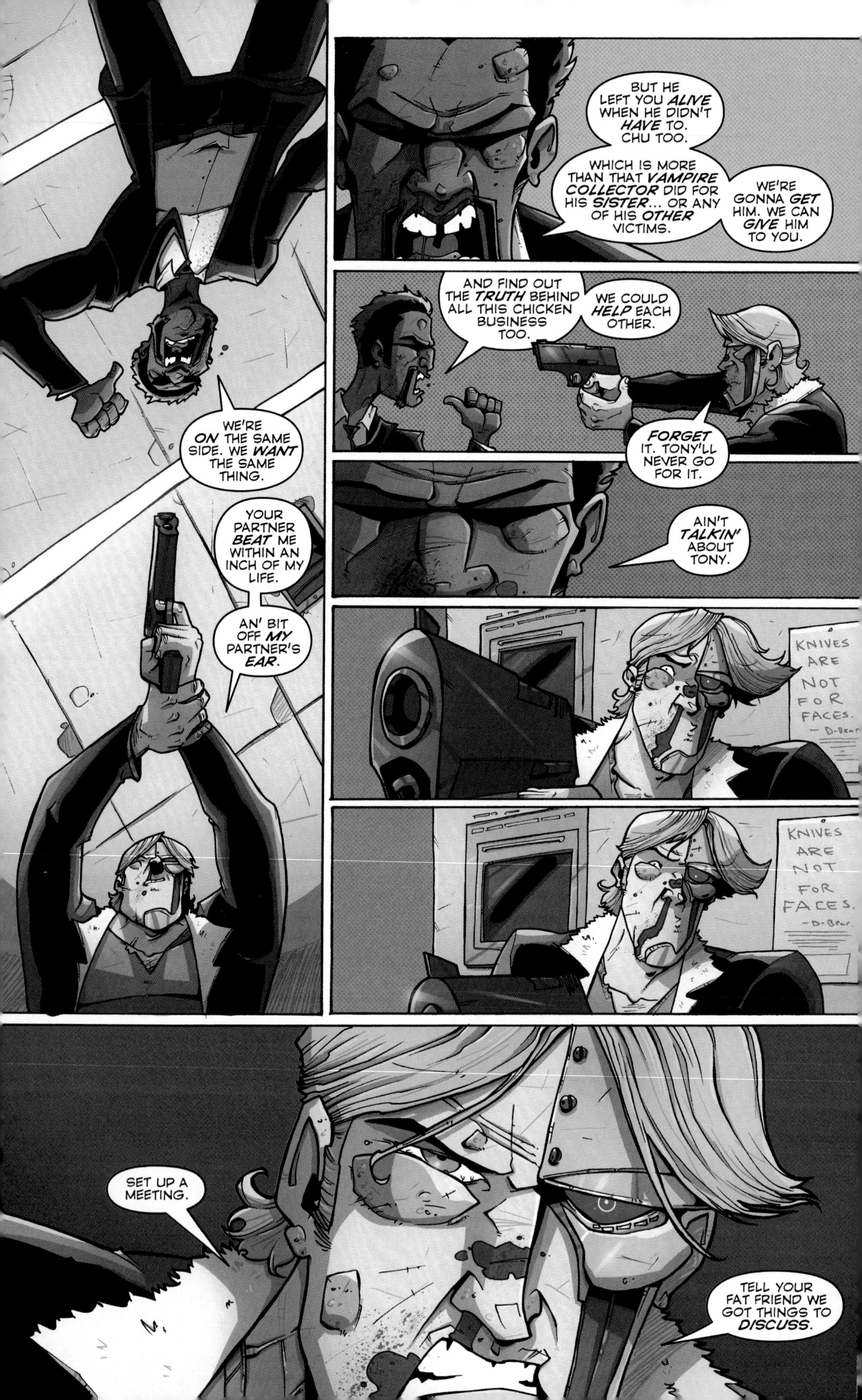
WE'RE ON THE SAME SIDE. WE WANT THE SAME THING.
YOUR PARTNER BEAT ME WITHIN AN INCH OF MY LIFE.
AN' BIT OFF MY PARTNER'S EAR.
BUT HE LEFT YOU ALIVE WHEN HE DIDN'T HAVE TO. CHU TOO.
WHICH IS MORE THAN THAT VAMPIRE COLLECTOR DID FOR HIS SISTER... OR ANY OF HIS OTHER VICTIMS.
WE'RE GONNA GET HIM. WE CAN GIVE HIM TO YOU.
AND FIND OUT THE TRUTH BEHIND ALL THIS CHICKEN BUSINESS TOO.
WE COULD HELP EACH OTHER.
FORGET IT. TONY'LL NEVER GO FOR IT.
AIN'T TALKIN' ABOUT TONY.
KNIVES ARE NOT FOR FACES. —D-Bear
KNIVES ARE NOT FOR FACES. —D-Bear
SET UP A MEETING.
TELL YOUR FAT FRIEND WE GOT THINGS TO DISCUSS.

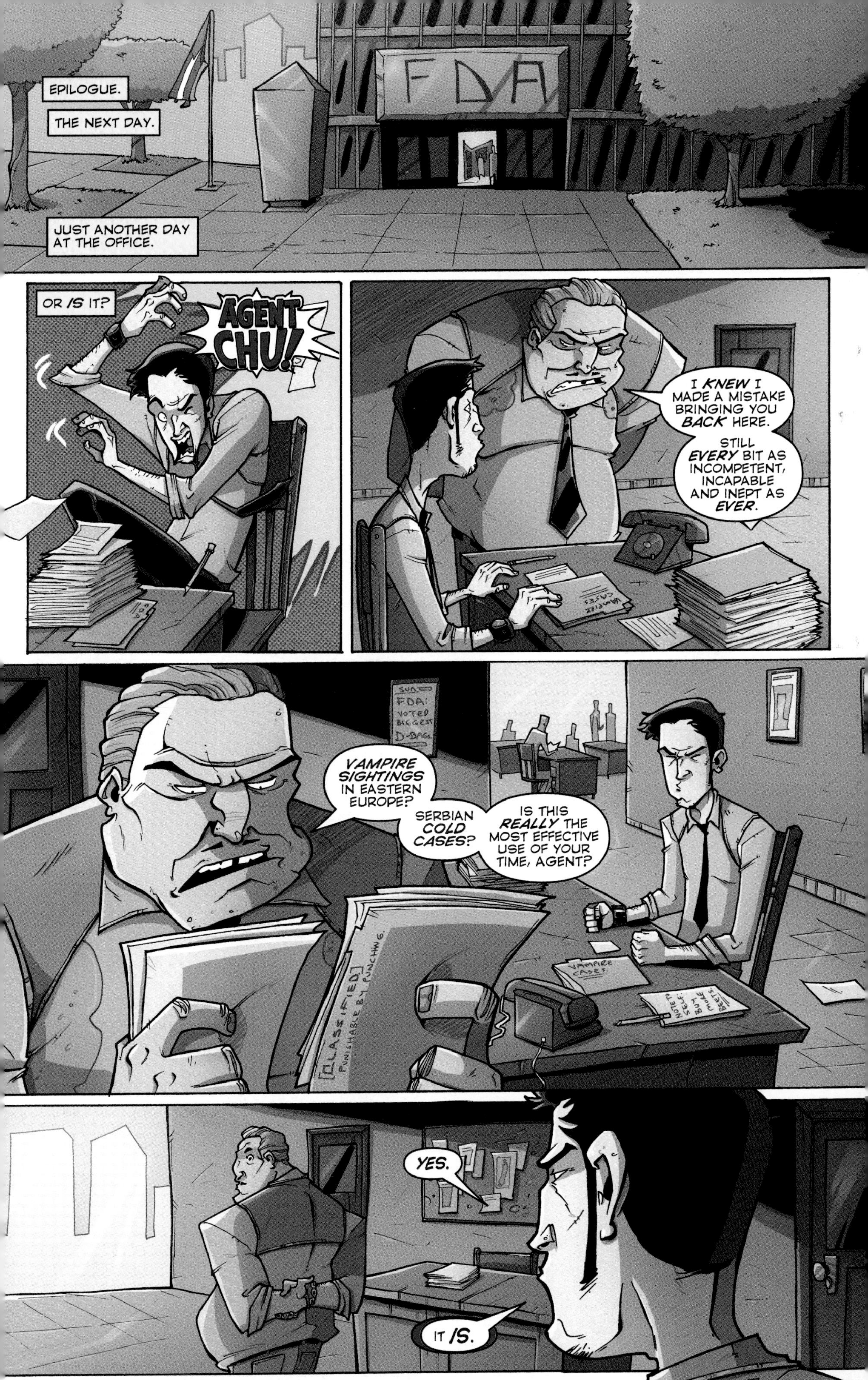
EPILOGUE.
THE NEXT DAY.
FDA
JUST ANOTHER DAY AT THE OFFICE.
OR IS IT?
AGENT CHU!
I KNEW I MADE A MISTAKE BRINGING YOU BACK HERE.
STILL EVERY BIT AS INCOMPETENT, INCAPABLE AND INEPT AS EVER.
VAMPIRE CASES
SUN FDA: VOTED BIGGEST D-BAG
VAMPIRE SIGHTINGS IN EASTERN EUROPE?
SERBIAN COLD CASES?
IS THIS REALLY THE MOST EFFECTIVE USE OF YOUR TIME, AGENT?
CLASSIFIED PUNISHABLE BY PUNCHING.
VAMPIRE CASES.
NOTE TO SELF: BUY MORE BEETS.
YES.
IT IS.

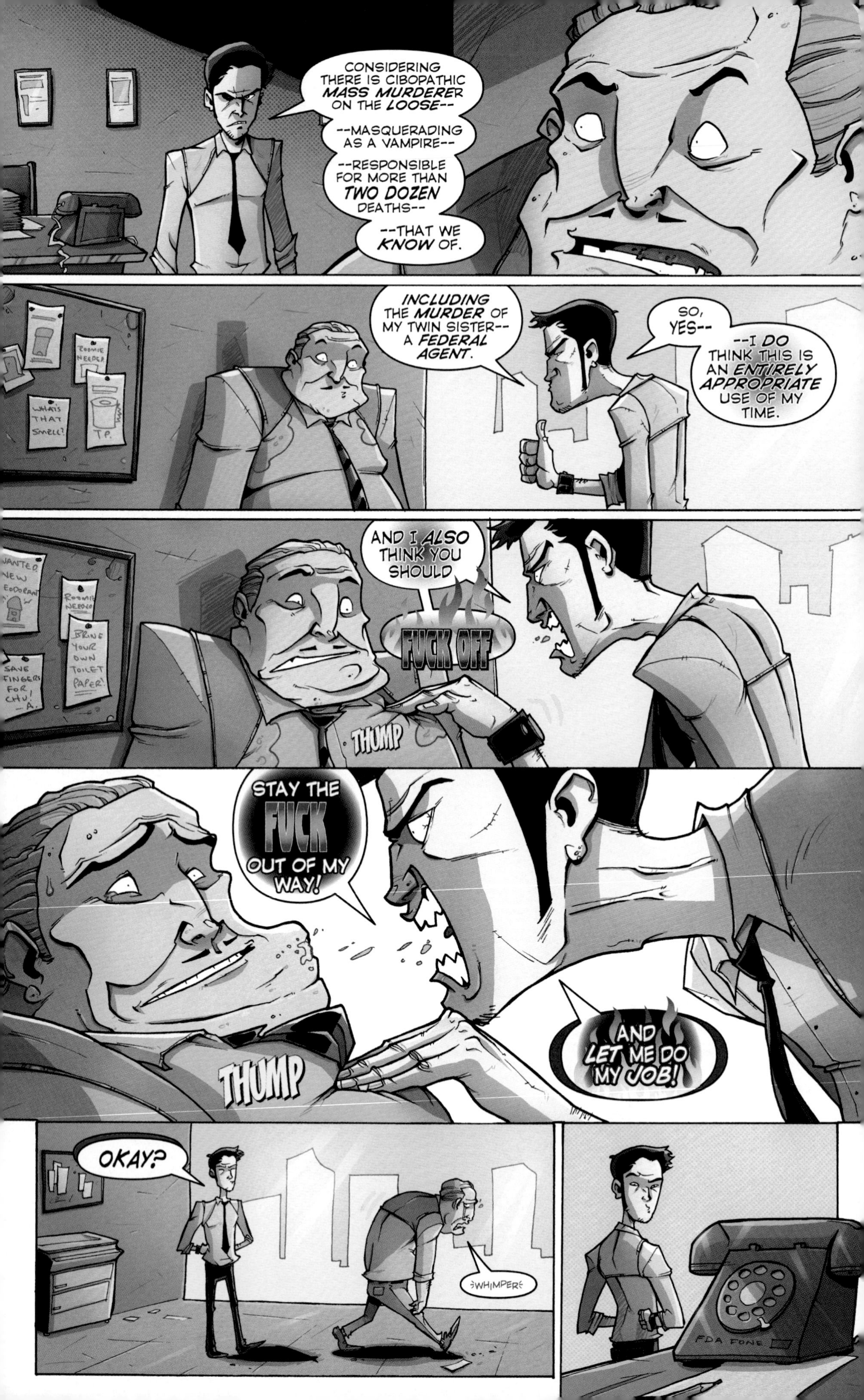
CONSIDERING THERE IS CIBOPATHIC MASS MURDERER ON THE LOOSE--
--MASQUERADING AS A VAMPIRE--
--RESPONSIBLE FOR MORE THAN TWO DOZEN DEATHS--
--THAT WE KNOW OF.
ROOMIE NEEDED
WHAT'S THAT SMELL?
T.P.
INCLUDING THE MURDER OF MY TWIN SISTER-- A FEDERAL AGENT.
SO, YES--
--I DO THINK THIS IS AN ENTIRELY APPROPRIATE USE OF MY TIME.
WANTED NEW DEODORANT
ROOMIE NEEDED
BRING YOUR OWN TOILET PAPER!
SAVE FINGERS FOR CHU! -A.
AND I ALSO THINK YOU SHOULD
FUCK OFF
THUMP
STAY THE FUCK OUT OF MY WAY!
THUMP
AND LET ME DO MY JOB!
OKAY?
WHIMPER
FDA FONE

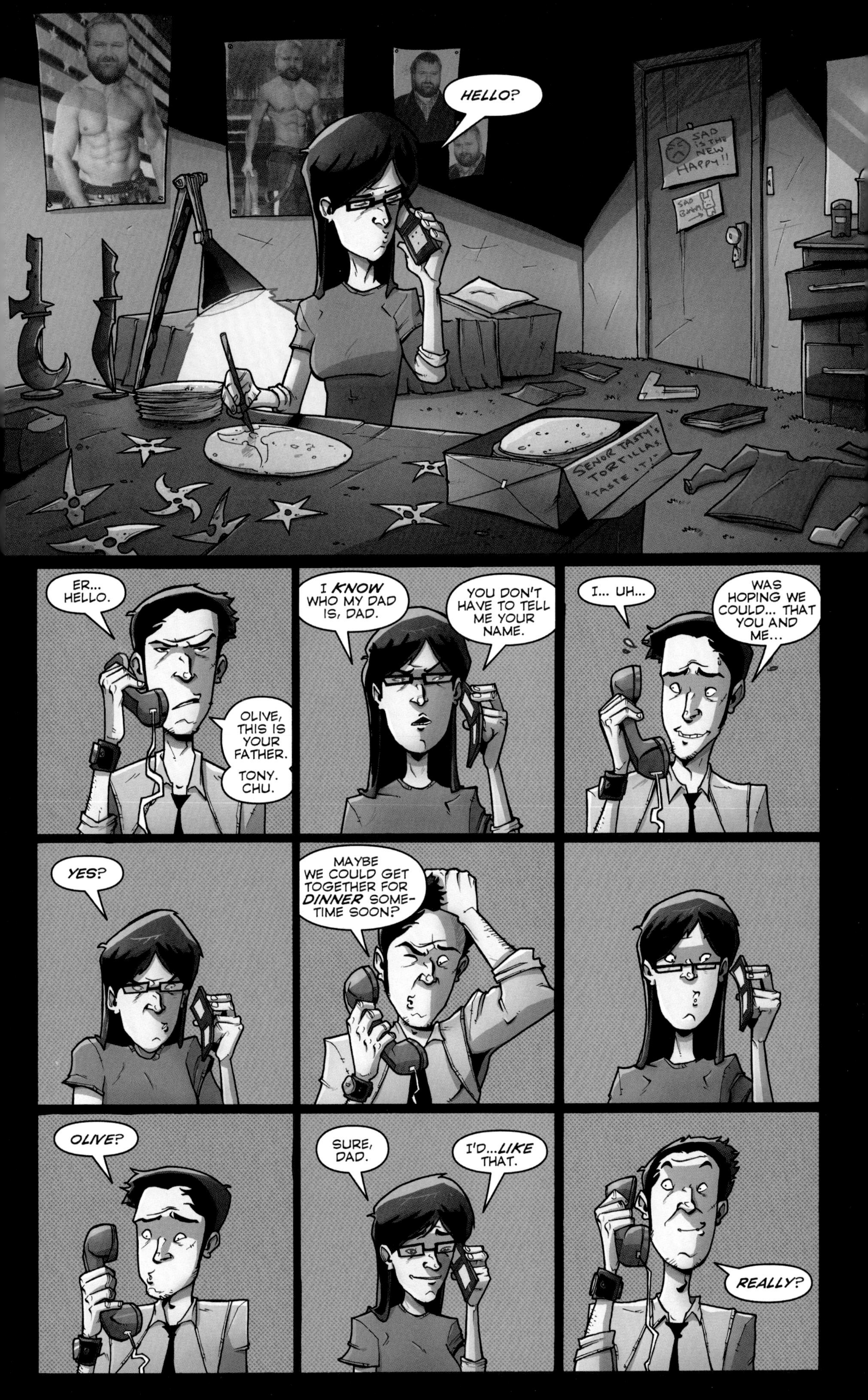
HELLO?
SAD IS THE NEW HAPPY!!
SENOR TASTY'S TORTILLAS "TASTE IT!"
ER... HELLO.
OLIVE, THIS IS YOUR FATHER.
TONY. CHU.
I KNOW WHO MY DAD IS, DAD.
YOU DON'T HAVE TO TELL ME YOUR NAME.
I... UH...
WAS HOPING WE COULD... THAT YOU AND ME...
YES?
MAYBE WE COULD GET TOGETHER FOR DINNER SOMETIME SOON?
OLIVE?
SURE, DAD.
I'D...LIKE THAT.
REALLY?

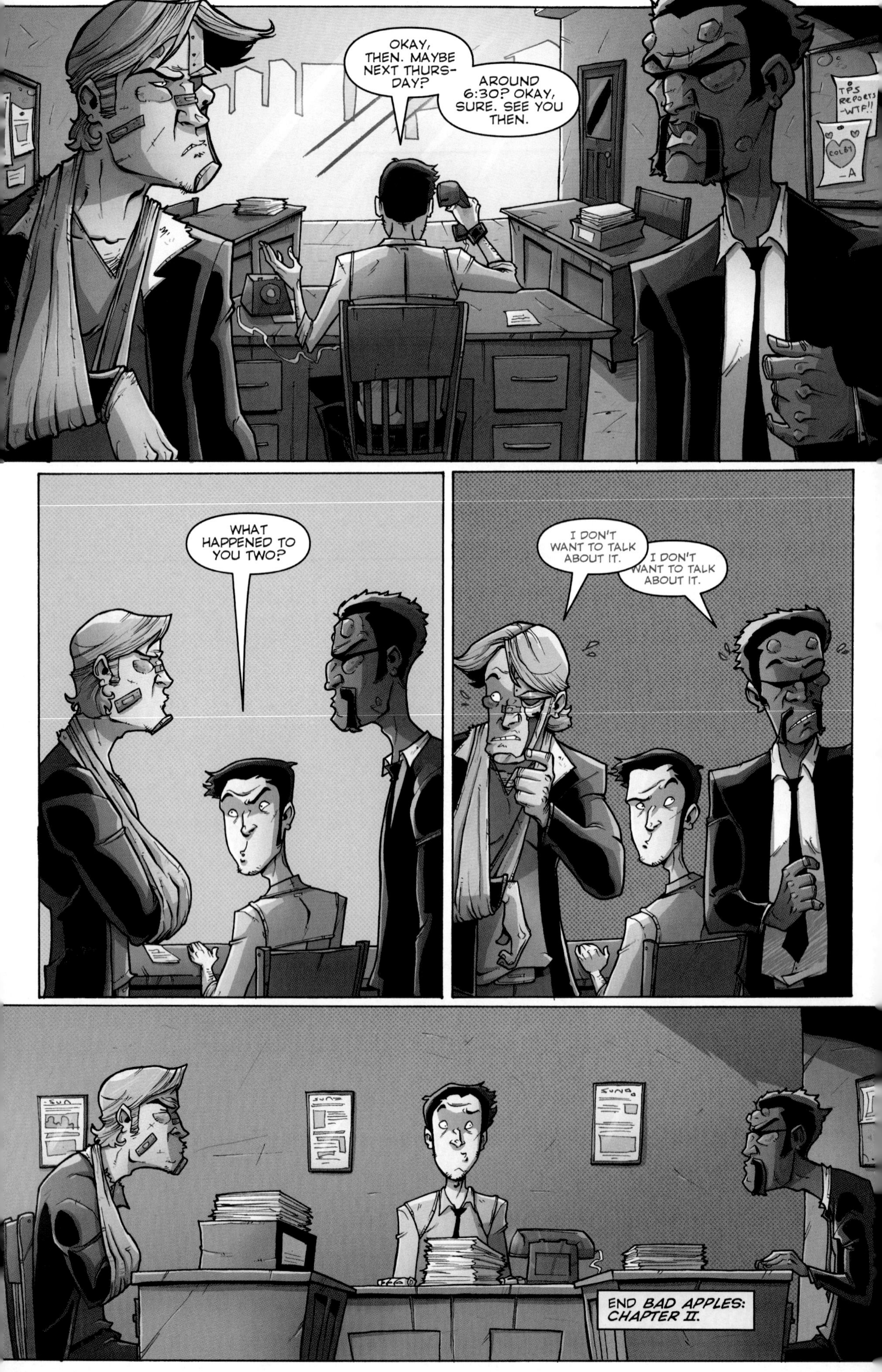
OKAY, THEN. MAYBE NEXT THURS-DAY?
AROUND 6:30? OKAY, SURE. SEE YOU THEN.
TPS REPORTS -WTF!!
COLBY -A
WHAT HAPPENED TO YOU TWO?
I DON'T WANT TO TALK ABOUT IT.
I DON'T WANT TO TALK ABOUT IT.
END BAD APPLES: CHAPTER II.

Chapter Three

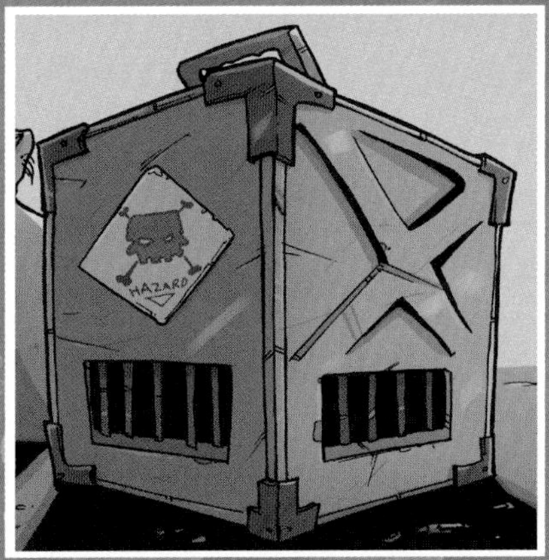
HAZARD

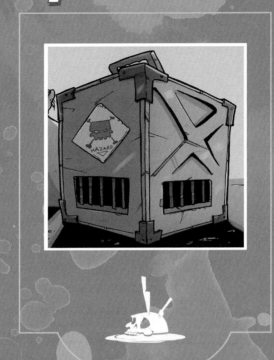

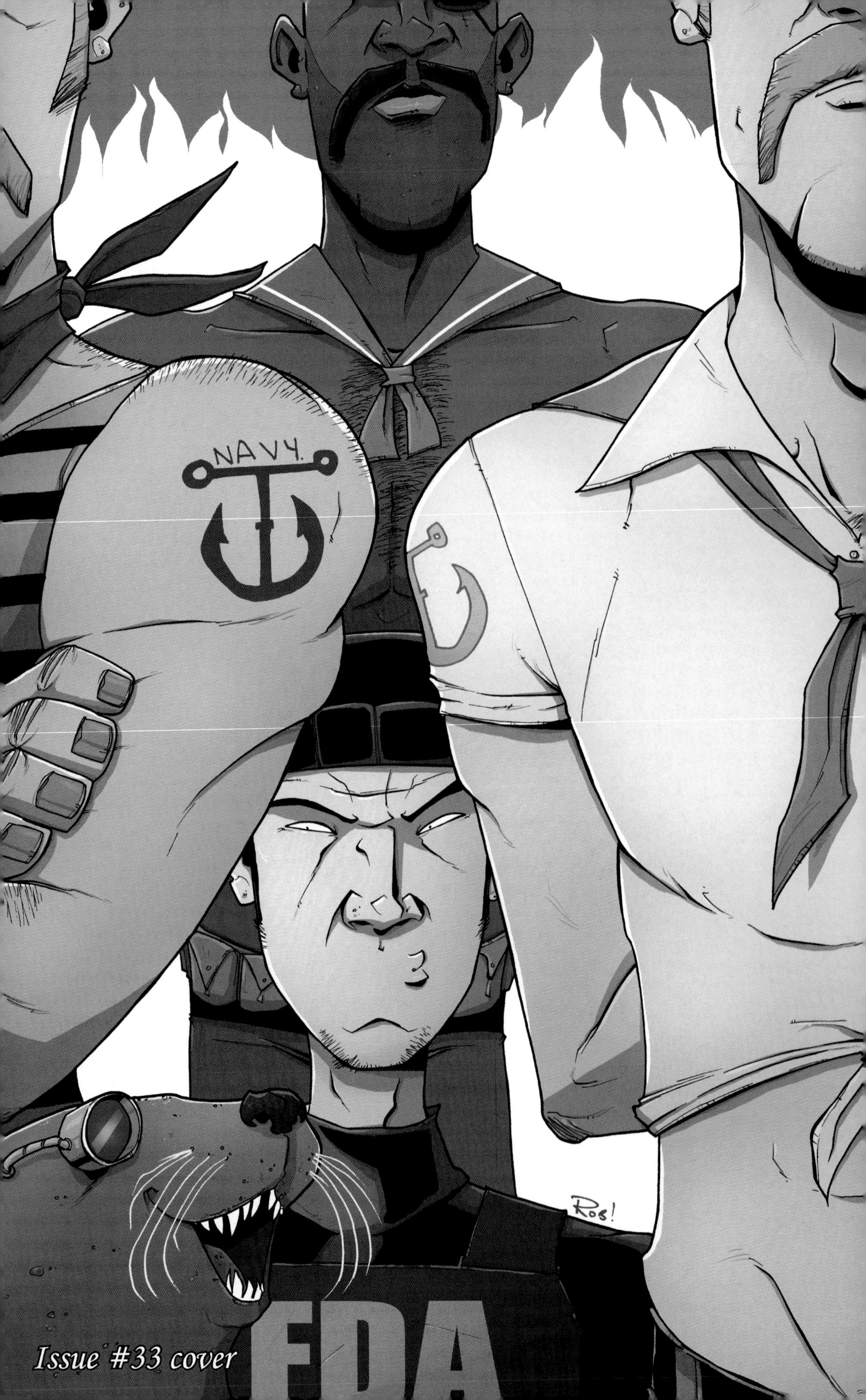
NAVY.
Ros!
FDA
Issue #33 cover

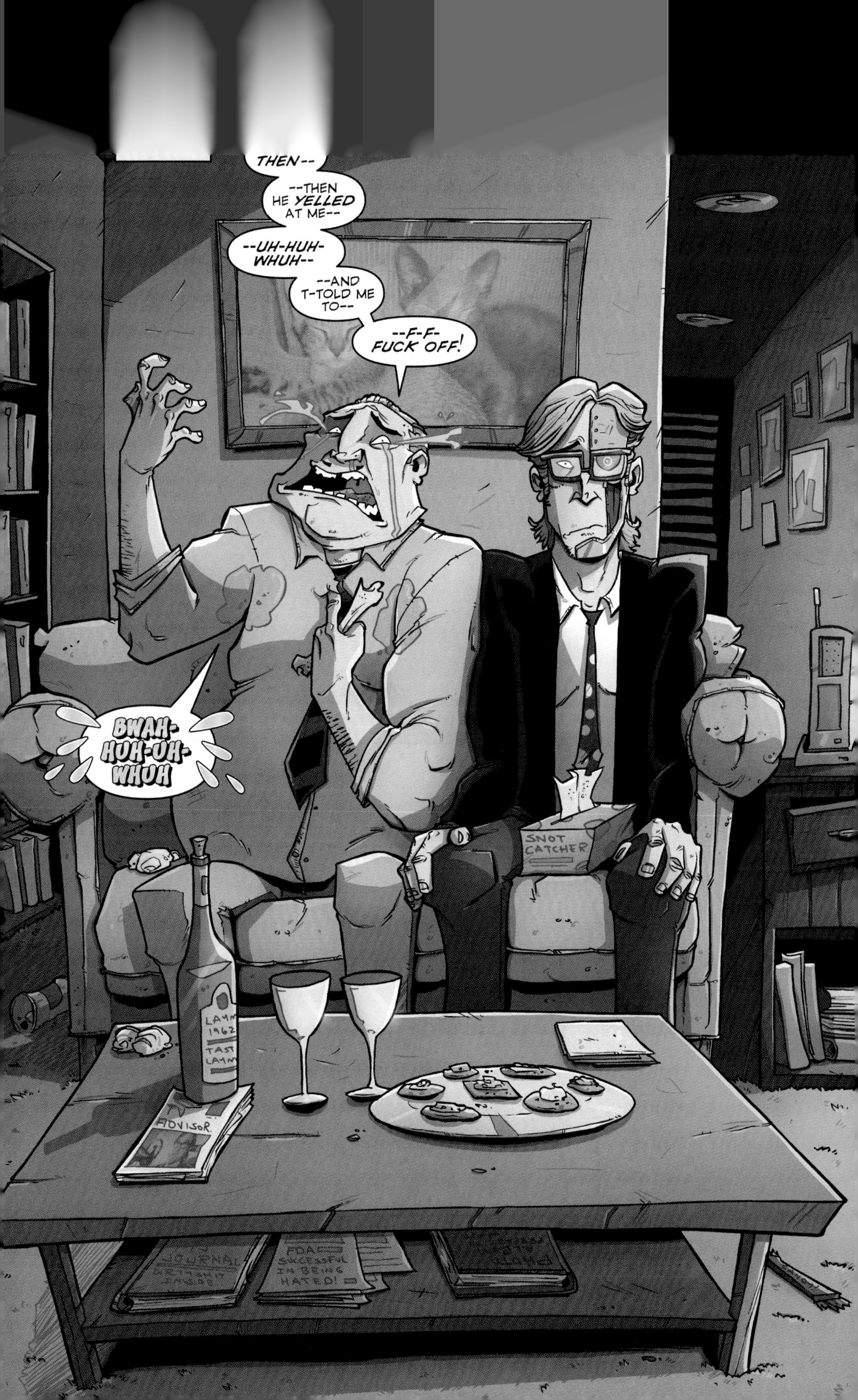
THEN--
--THEN HE YELLED AT ME--
--UH-HUH-WHUH--
--AND T-TOLD ME TO--
--F-F-FUCK OFF!
BWAH-HUH-UH-WHUH
SNOT CATCHER
TV ADVISOR

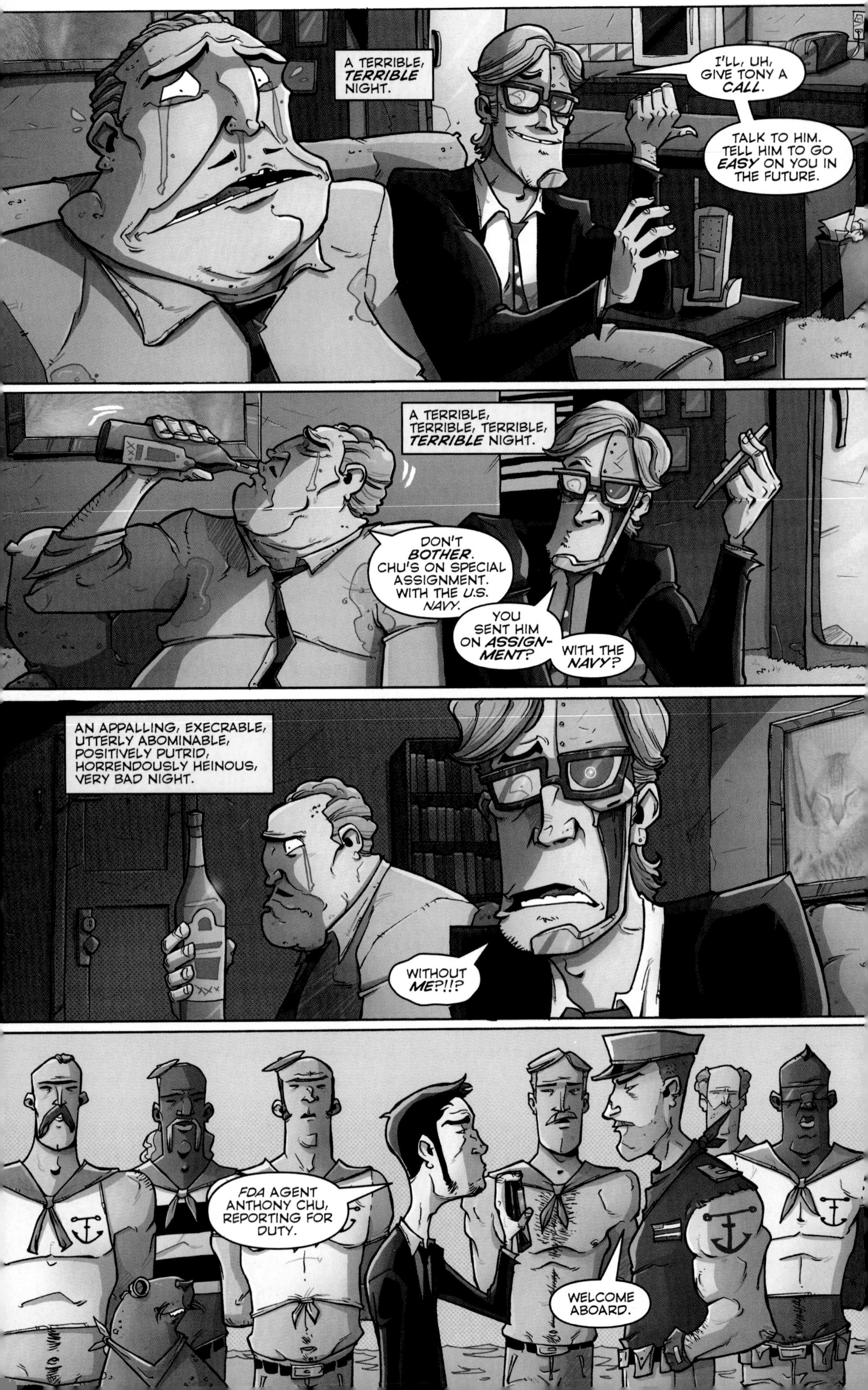

A TERRIBLE, *TERRIBLE* NIGHT.
I'LL, UH, GIVE TONY A *CALL*.
TALK TO HIM. TELL HIM TO GO *EASY* ON YOU IN THE FUTURE.
A TERRIBLE, TERRIBLE, TERRIBLE, *TERRIBLE* NIGHT.
DON'T *BOTHER*. CHU'S ON SPECIAL ASSIGNMENT. WITH THE *U.S. NAVY*.
YOU SENT HIM ON *ASSIGNMENT*?
WITH THE *NAVY*?
AN APPALLING, EXECRABLE, UTTERLY ABOMINABLE, POSITIVELY PUTRID, HORRENDOUSLY HEINOUS, VERY BAD NIGHT.
WITHOUT *ME*?!!?
FDA AGENT ANTHONY CHU, REPORTING FOR DUTY.
WELCOME ABOARD.

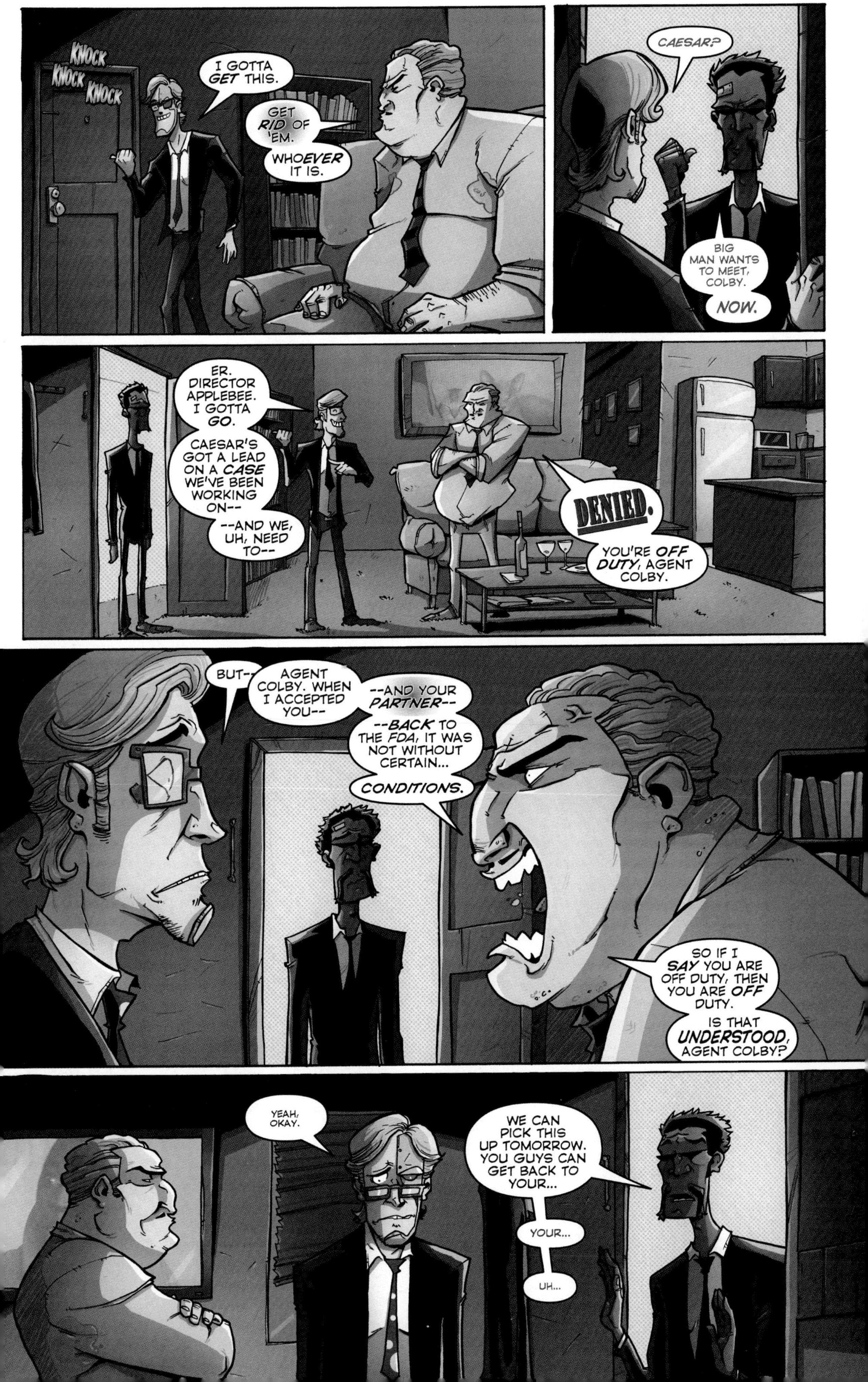
KNOCK KNOCK KNOCK
I GOTTA GET THIS.
GET RID OF 'EM.
WHOEVER IT IS.
CAESAR?
BIG MAN WANTS TO MEET, COLBY.
NOW.
ER. DIRECTOR APPLEBEE. I GOTTA GO.
CAESAR'S GOT A LEAD ON A CASE WE'VE BEEN WORKING ON--
--AND WE, UH, NEED TO--
DENIED.
YOU'RE OFF DUTY, AGENT COLBY.
BUT--
AGENT COLBY. WHEN I ACCEPTED YOU--
--AND YOUR PARTNER--
--BACK TO THE FDA, IT WAS NOT WITHOUT CERTAIN...
CONDITIONS.
SO IF I SAY YOU ARE OFF DUTY, THEN YOU ARE OFF DUTY.
IS THAT UNDERSTOOD, AGENT COLBY?
YEAH, OKAY.
WE CAN PICK THIS UP TOMORROW. YOU GUYS CAN GET BACK TO YOUR...
YOUR...
UH...

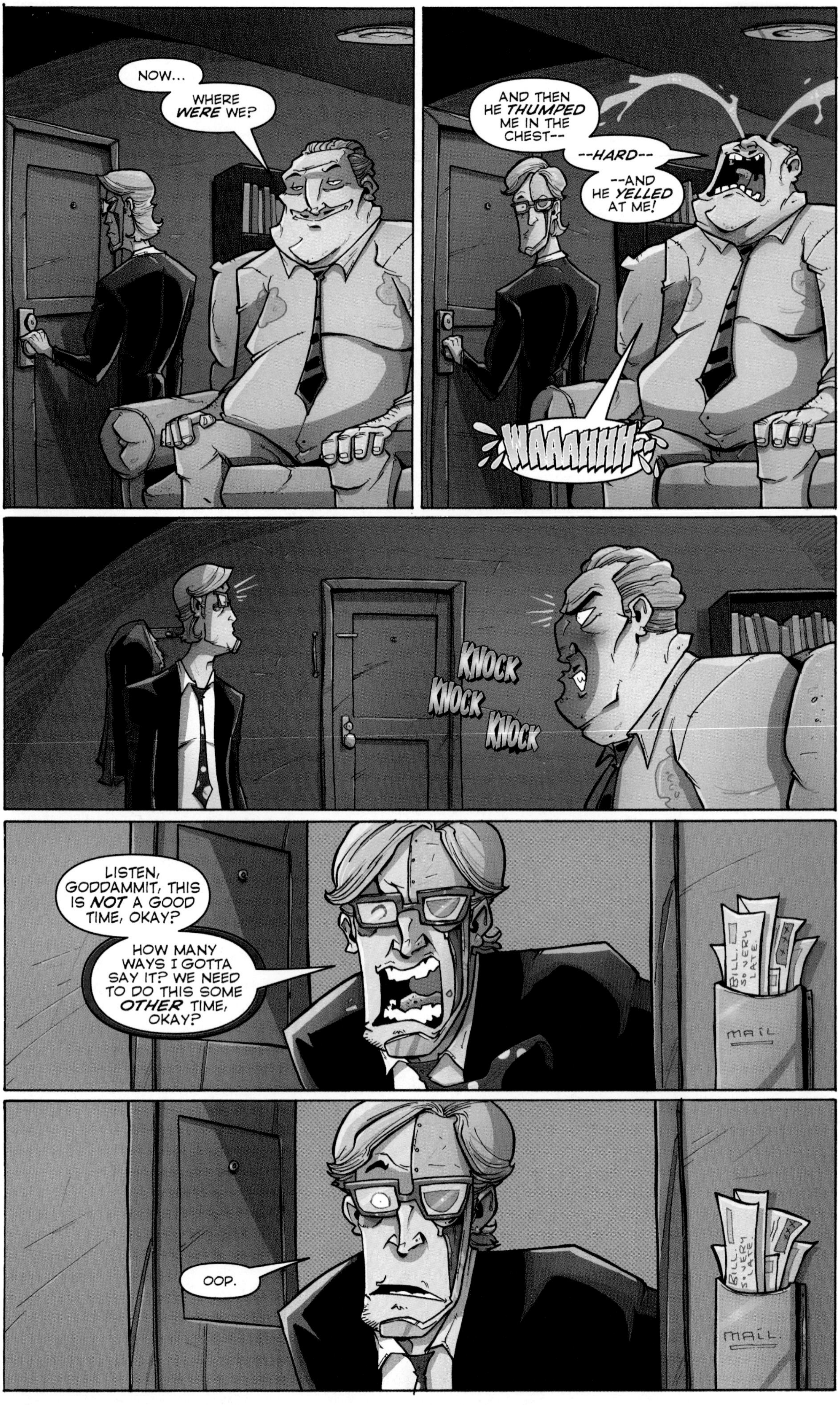
NOW...
WHERE *WERE* WE?
AND THEN HE *THUMPED* ME IN THE CHEST--
--*HARD*--
--AND HE *YELLED* AT ME!
WAAAHHH
KNOCK
KNOCK
KNOCK
LISTEN, GODDAMMIT, THIS IS *NOT* A GOOD TIME, OKAY?
HOW MANY WAYS I GOTTA SAY IT? WE NEED TO DO THIS SOME *OTHER* TIME, OKAY?
MAIL
OOP.
MAIL

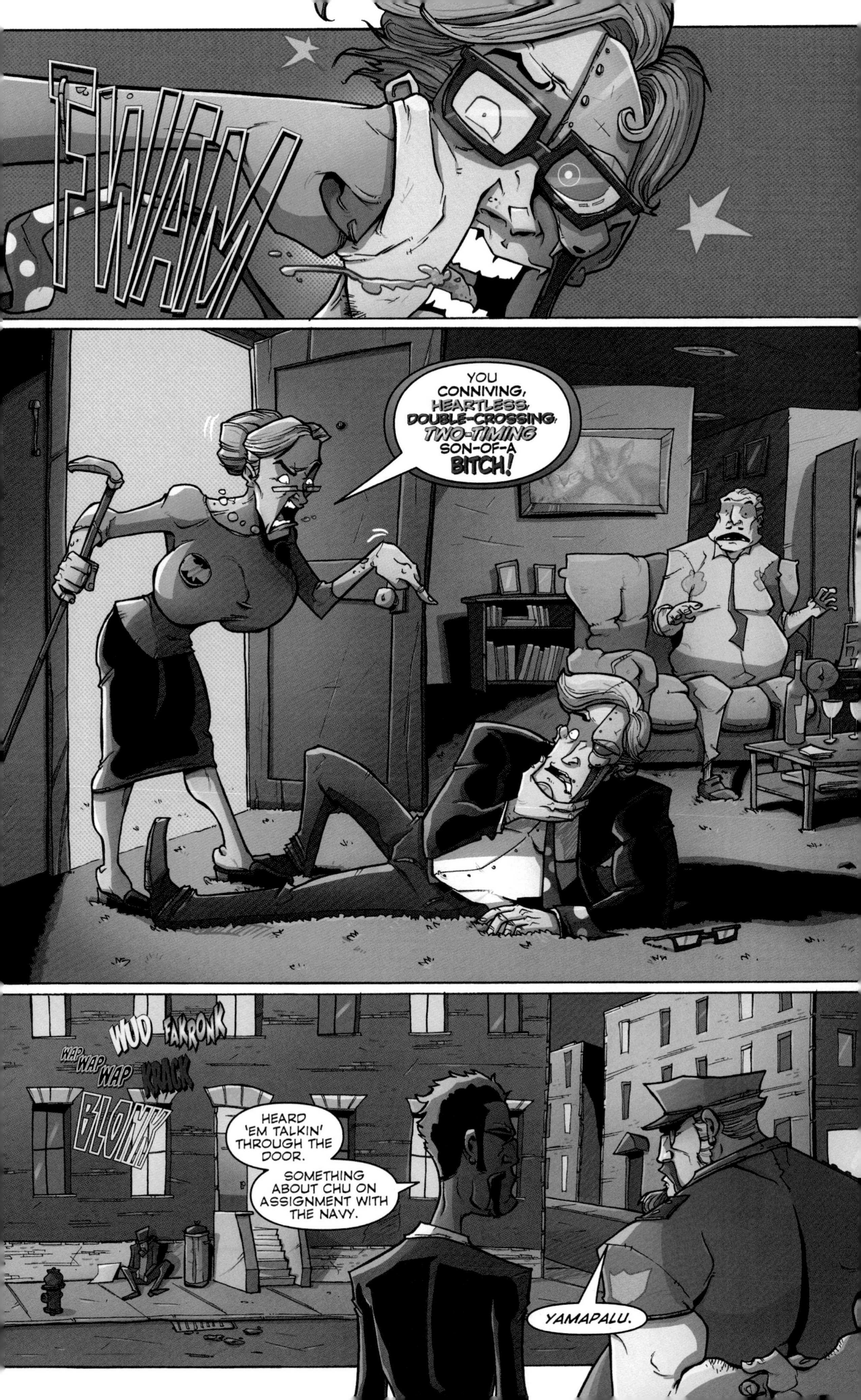
FWAM
YOU CONNIVING, HEARTLESS, DOUBLE-CROSSING, TWO-TIMING SON-OF-A BITCH!
WUD
FAKRONK
WAP WAP WAP
KRACK
HEARD 'EM TALKIN' THROUGH THE DOOR.
SOMETHING ABOUT CHU ON ASSIGNMENT WITH THE NAVY.
YAMAPALU.

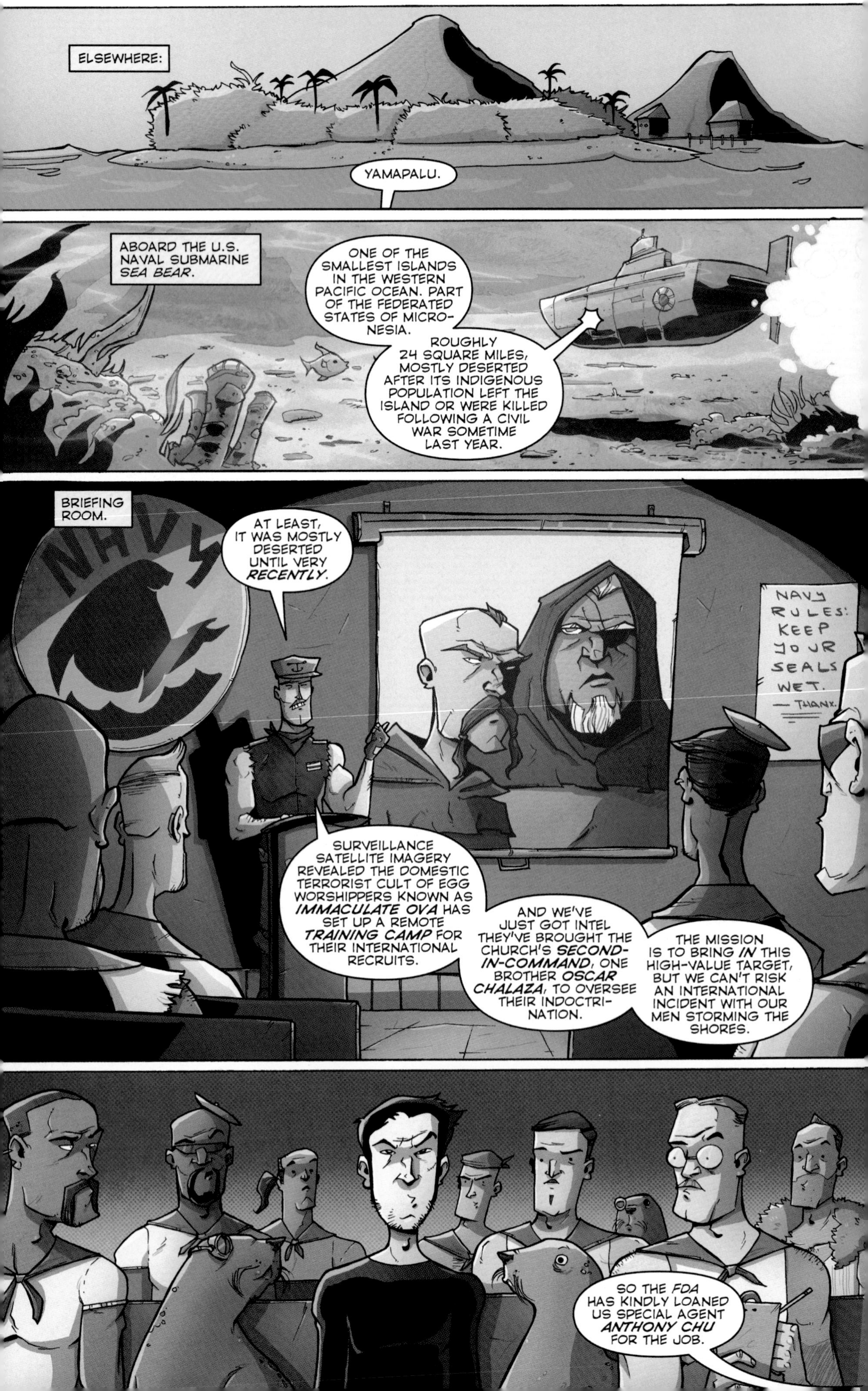
ELSEWHERE:
YAMAPALU.
ABOARD THE U.S. NAVAL SUBMARINE *SEA BEAR*.
ONE OF THE SMALLEST ISLANDS IN THE WESTERN PACIFIC OCEAN. PART OF THE FEDERATED STATES OF MICRO-NESIA.
ROUGHLY 24 SQUARE MILES, MOSTLY DESERTED AFTER ITS INDIGENOUS POPULATION LEFT THE ISLAND OR WERE KILLED FOLLOWING A CIVIL WAR SOMETIME LAST YEAR.
BRIEFING ROOM.
AT LEAST, IT WAS MOSTLY DESERTED UNTIL VERY *RECENTLY*.
NAVY RULES: KEEP YOUR SEALS WET. — THANX.
SURVEILLANCE SATELLITE IMAGERY REVEALED THE DOMESTIC TERRORIST CULT OF EGG WORSHIPPERS KNOWN AS ***IMMACULATE OVA*** HAS SET UP A REMOTE ***TRAINING CAMP*** FOR THEIR INTERNATIONAL RECRUITS.
AND WE'VE JUST GOT INTEL THEY'VE BROUGHT THE CHURCH'S ***SECOND-IN-COMMAND***, ONE BROTHER ***OSCAR CHALAZA***, TO OVERSEE THEIR INDOCTRI-NATION.
THE MISSION IS TO BRING ***IN*** THIS HIGH-VALUE TARGET, BUT WE CAN'T RISK AN INTERNATIONAL INCIDENT WITH OUR MEN STORMING THE SHORES.
SO THE *FDA* HAS KINDLY LOANED US SPECIAL AGENT ***ANTHONY CHU*** FOR THE JOB.

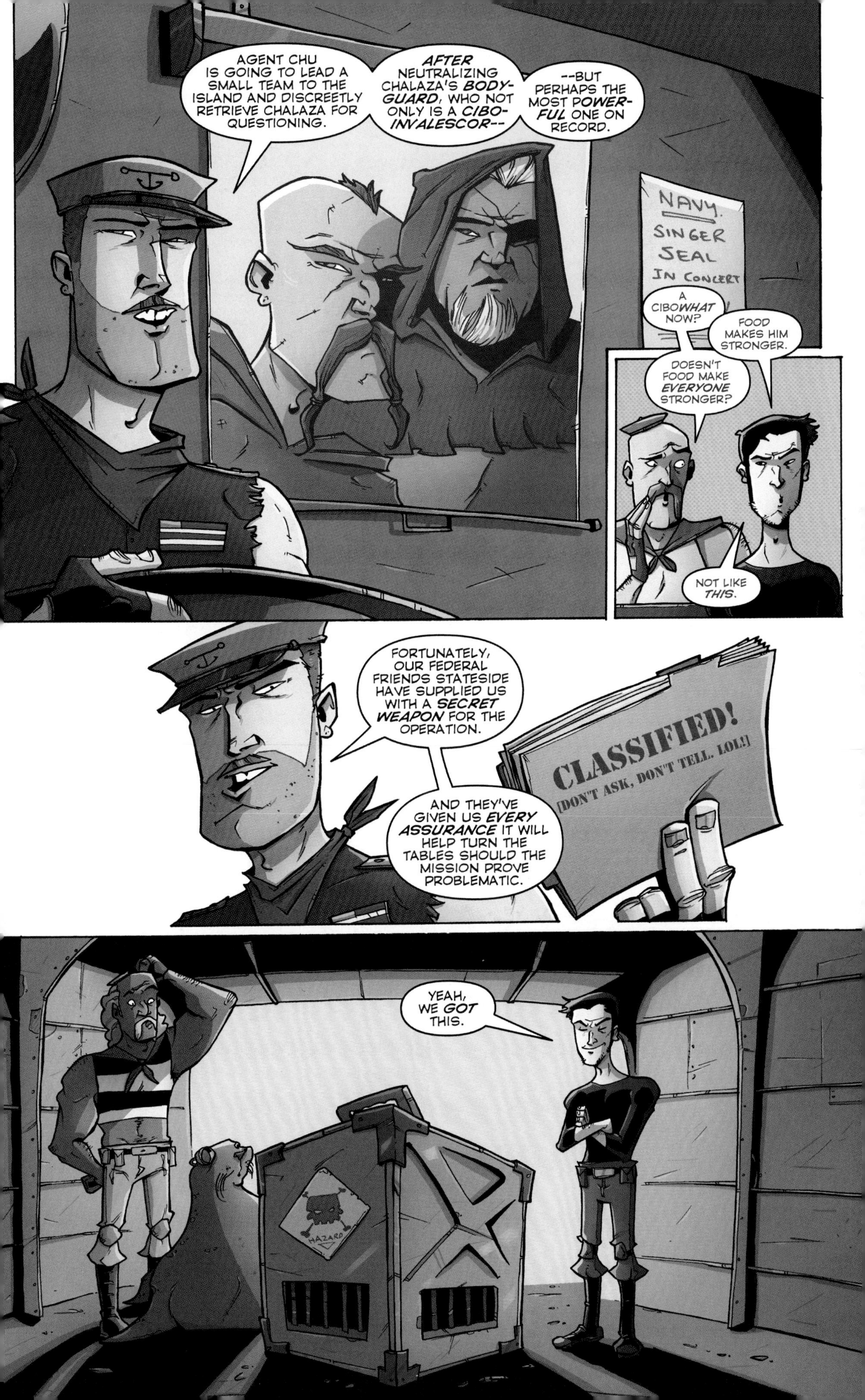
AGENT CHU IS GOING TO LEAD A SMALL TEAM TO THE ISLAND AND DISCREETLY RETRIEVE CHALAZA FOR QUESTIONING.
AFTER NEUTRALIZING CHALAZA'S BODY-GUARD, WHO NOT ONLY IS A CIBO-INVALESCOR--
--BUT PERHAPS THE MOST POWER-FUL ONE ON RECORD.
NAVY. SINGER SEAL IN CONCERT
A CIBOWHAT NOW?
FOOD MAKES HIM STRONGER.
DOESN'T FOOD MAKE EVERYONE STRONGER?
NOT LIKE THIS.
FORTUNATELY, OUR FEDERAL FRIENDS STATESIDE HAVE SUPPLIED US WITH A SECRET WEAPON FOR THE OPERATION.
AND THEY'VE GIVEN US EVERY ASSURANCE IT WILL HELP TURN THE TABLES SHOULD THE MISSION PROVE PROBLEMATIC.
CLASSIFIED!
[DON'T ASK, DON'T TELL. LOL!]
YEAH, WE GOT THIS.
HAZARD

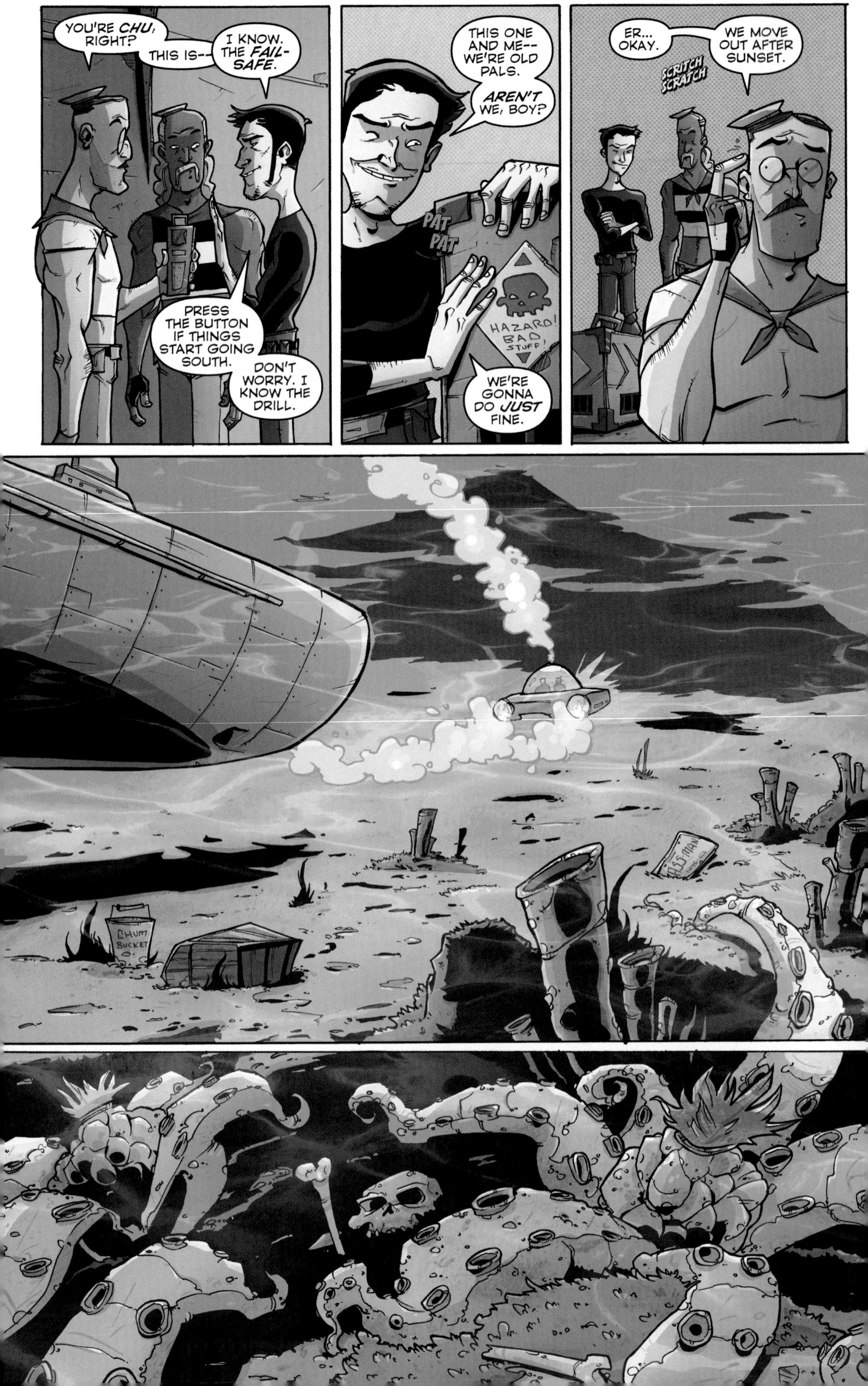
YOU'RE *CHU*, RIGHT?
THIS IS--
I KNOW. THE *FAIL-SAFE*.
PRESS THE BUTTON IF THINGS START GOING SOUTH.
DON'T WORRY. I KNOW THE DRILL.
THIS ONE AND ME-- WE'RE OLD PALS.
AREN'T WE, BOY?
PAT PAT
HAZARD! BAD STUFF!
WE'RE GONNA DO *JUST* FINE.
ER... OKAY.
WE MOVE OUT AFTER SUNSET.
SCRITCH SCRATCH
CHUM BUCKET

FORT YAMAPALU

ZZZZZ

ZZZZZ

ALRIGHT, CHALAZA.

DON'T MAKE ANY NOISE. DON'T TRY ANYTHING STUPID.

YOU'RE COMING WITH US.

THOU SHALT NOT EAT THE SACRED EGGS

KRACK

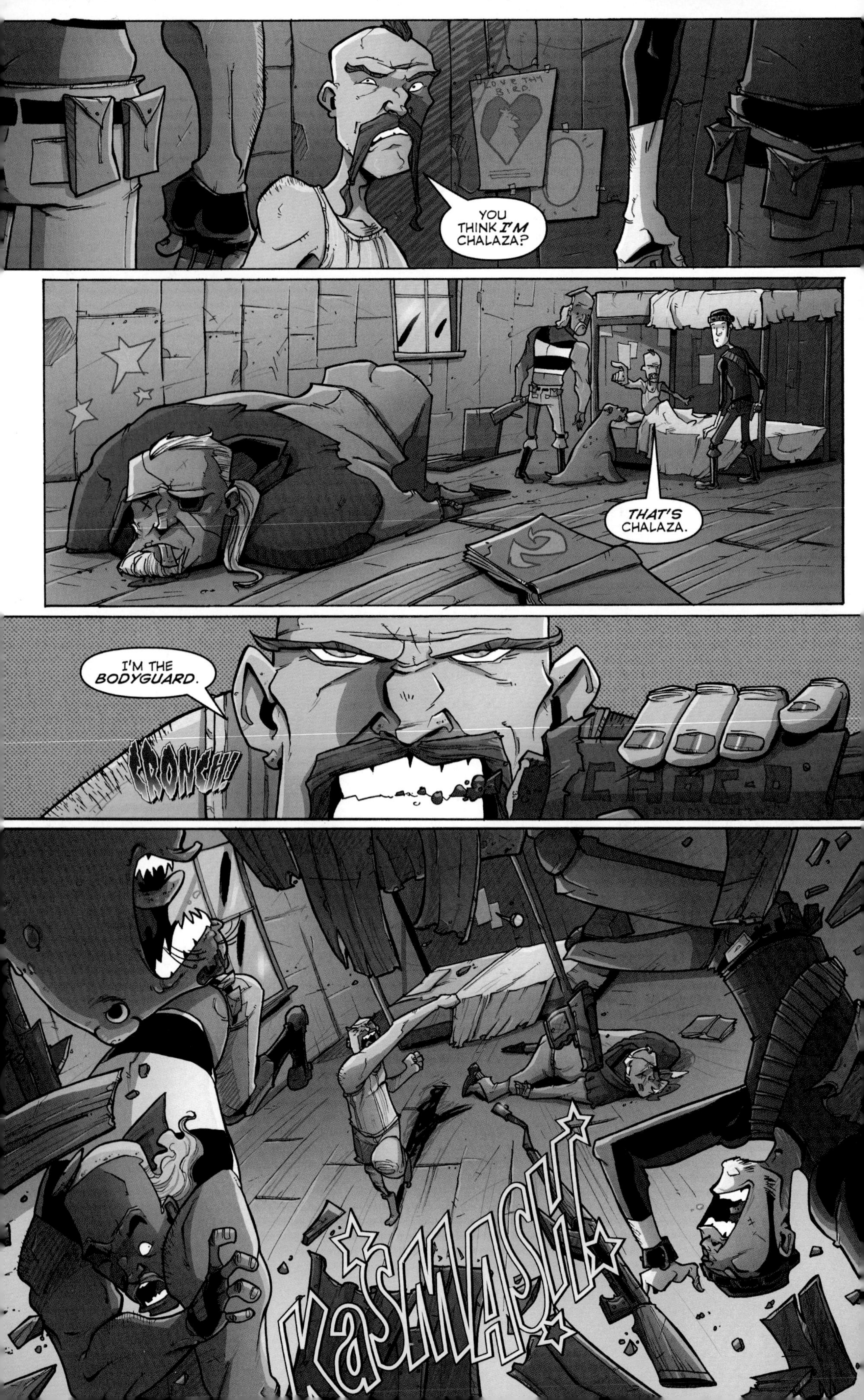
LOVE THY BIRD
YOU THINK I'M CHALAZA?
THAT'S CHALAZA.
I'M THE BODYGUARD.
CRONCH!
KASMASH!

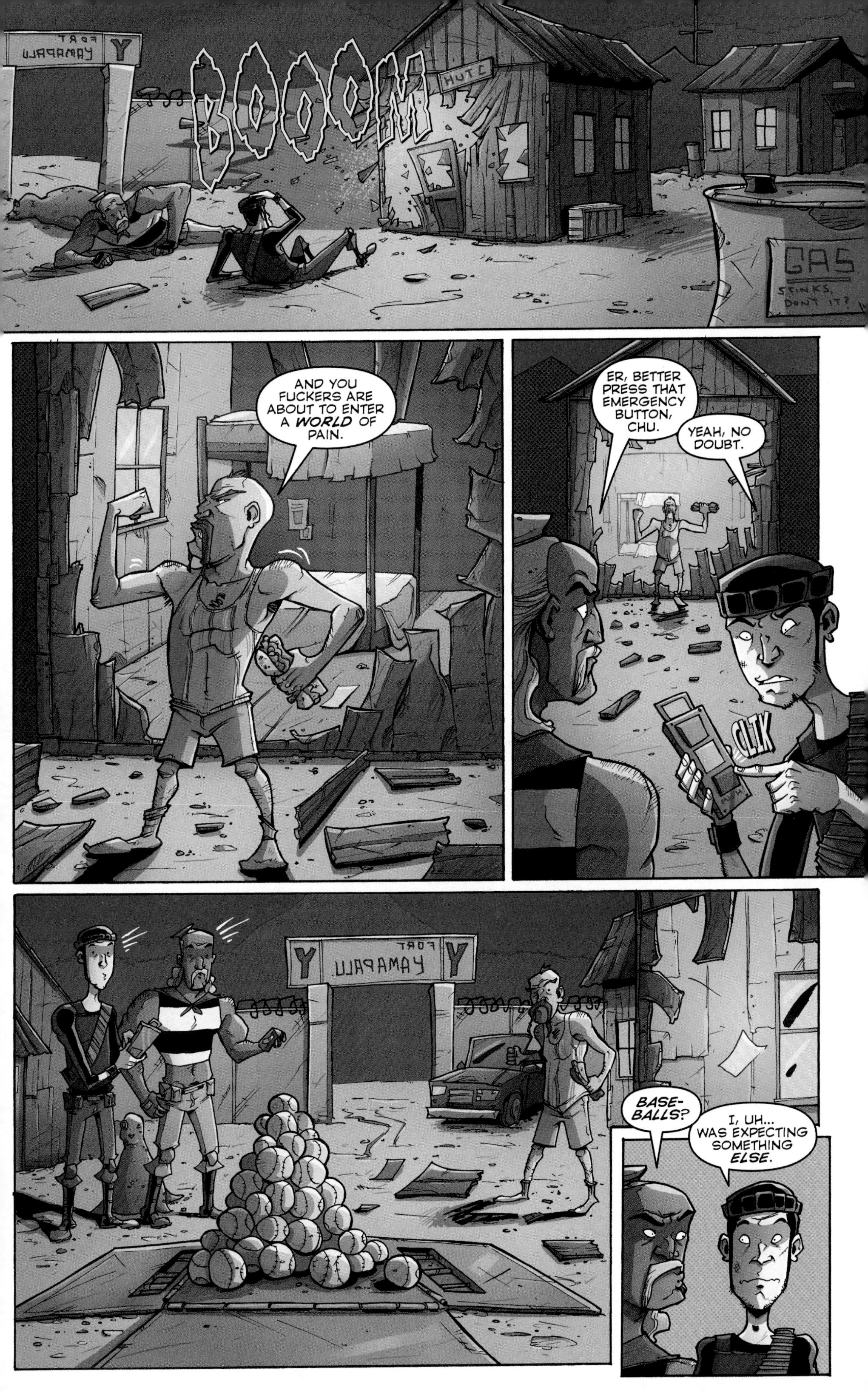
BOOOM
GAS
STINKS, DON'T IT?
AND YOU FUCKERS ARE ABOUT TO ENTER A *WORLD* OF PAIN.
ER, BETTER PRESS THAT EMERGENCY BUTTON, CHU.
YEAH, NO DOUBT.
CLIK
BASE-BALLS?
I, UH... WAS EXPECTING SOMETHING *ELSE*.

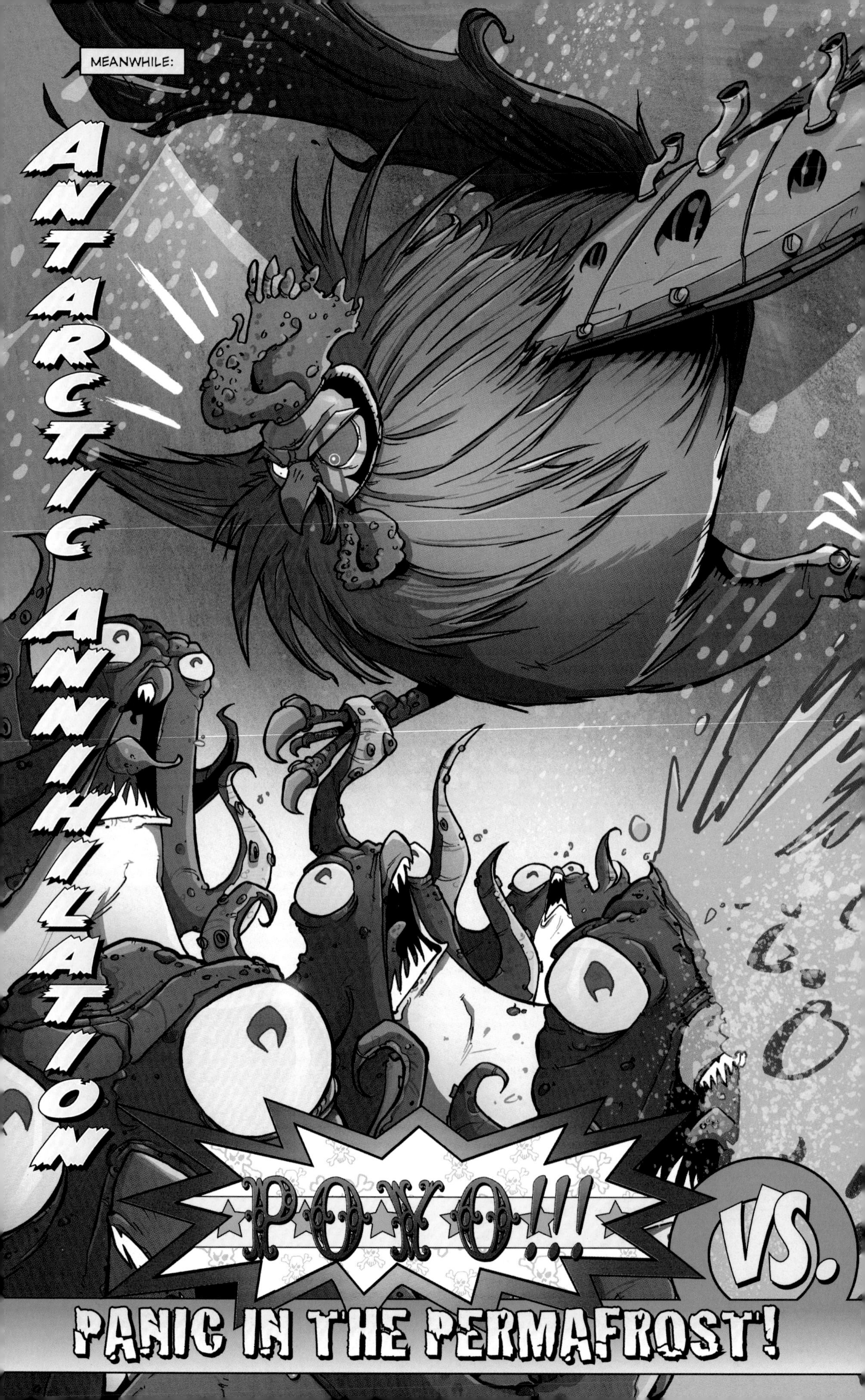
MEANWHILE:
ANTARCTIC ANNIHILATION
POXO!!!
VS.
PANIC IN THE PERMAFROST!

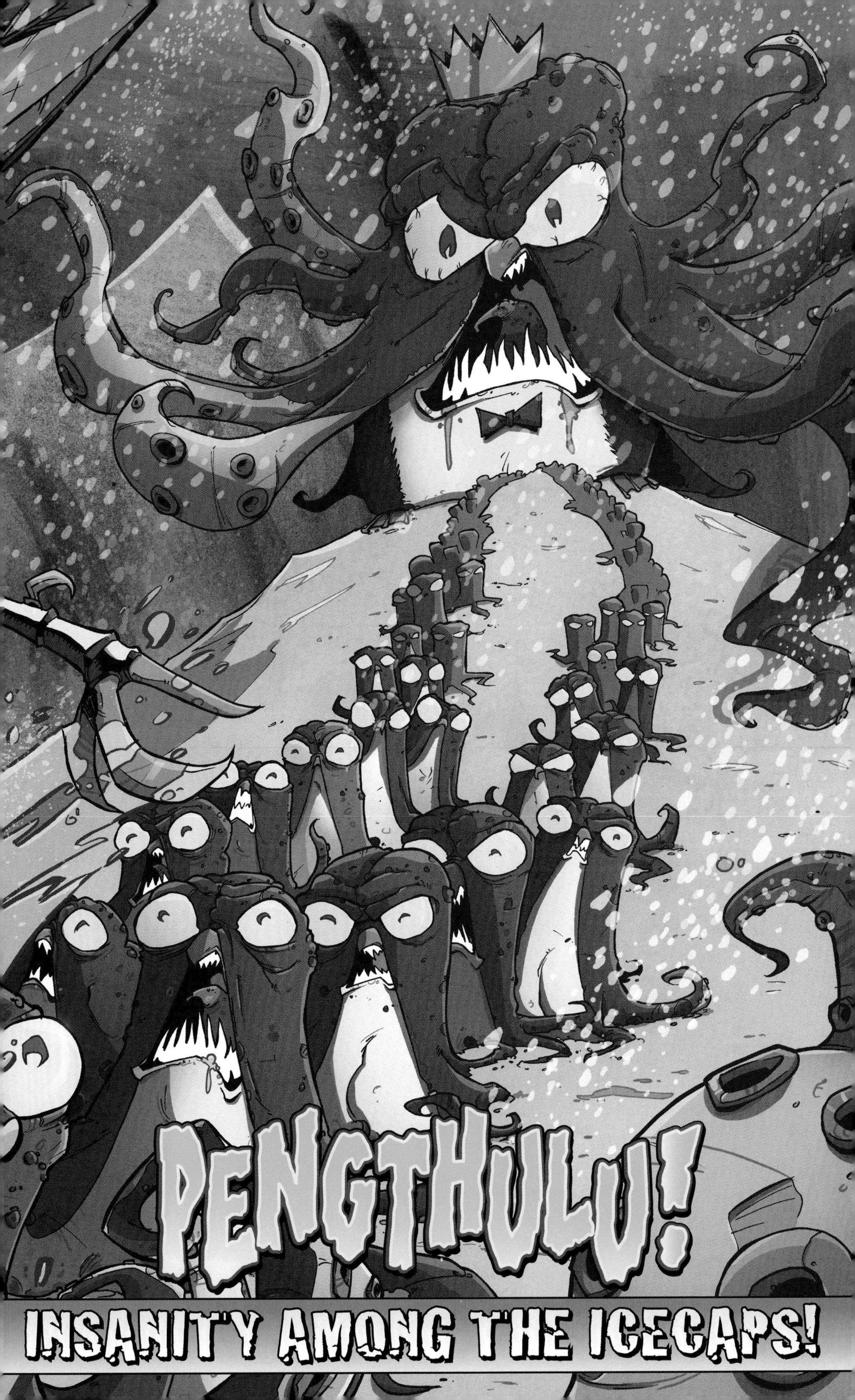
PENGTHULU!
INSANITY AMONG THE ICECAPS!

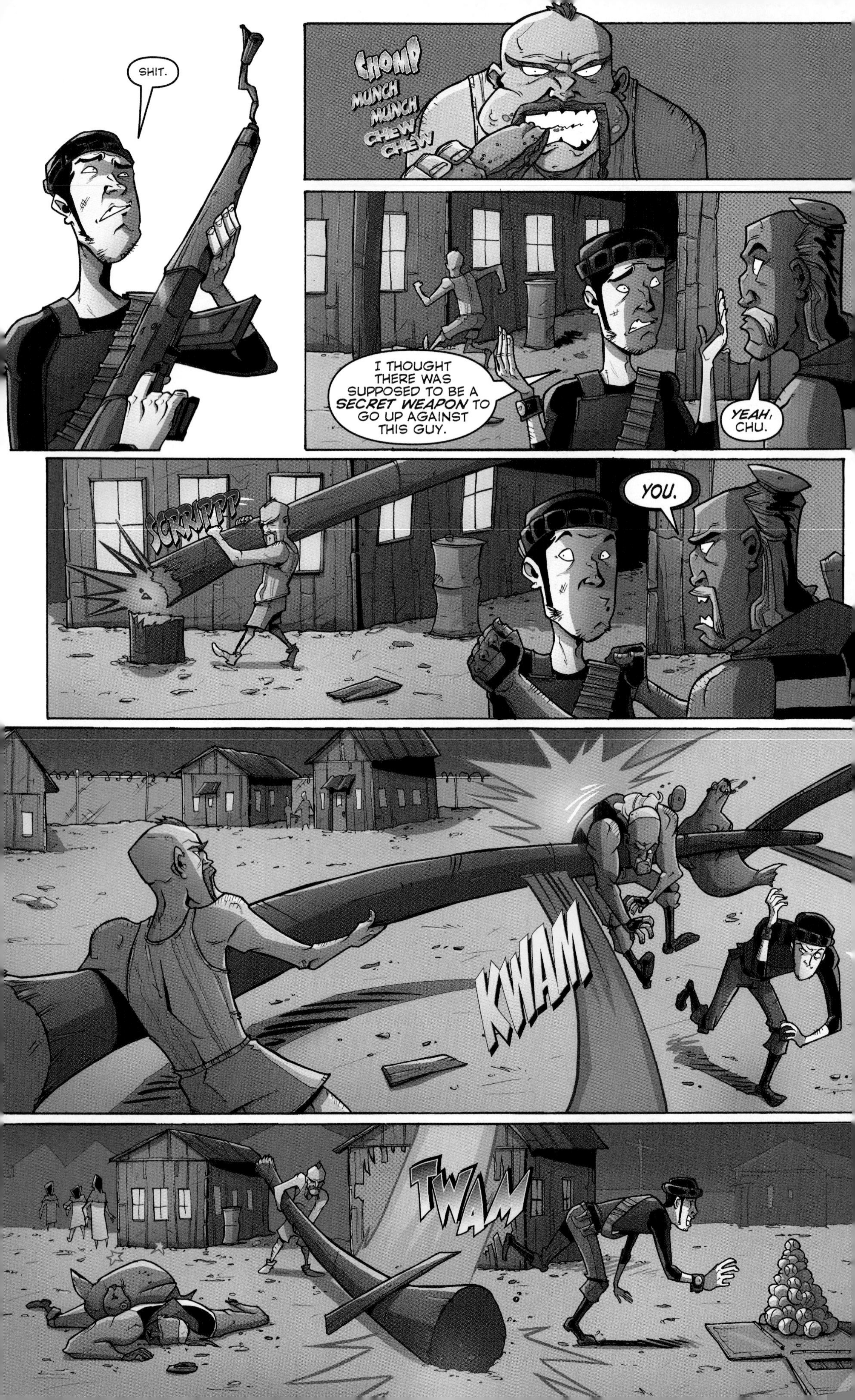
SHIT.
CHOMP
MUNCH
MUNCH
CHEW
CHEW
I THOUGHT THERE WAS SUPPOSED TO BE A SECRET WEAPON TO GO UP AGAINST THIS GUY.
YEAH, CHU.
SCRRIPPP
YOU.
KWAM
TWAM

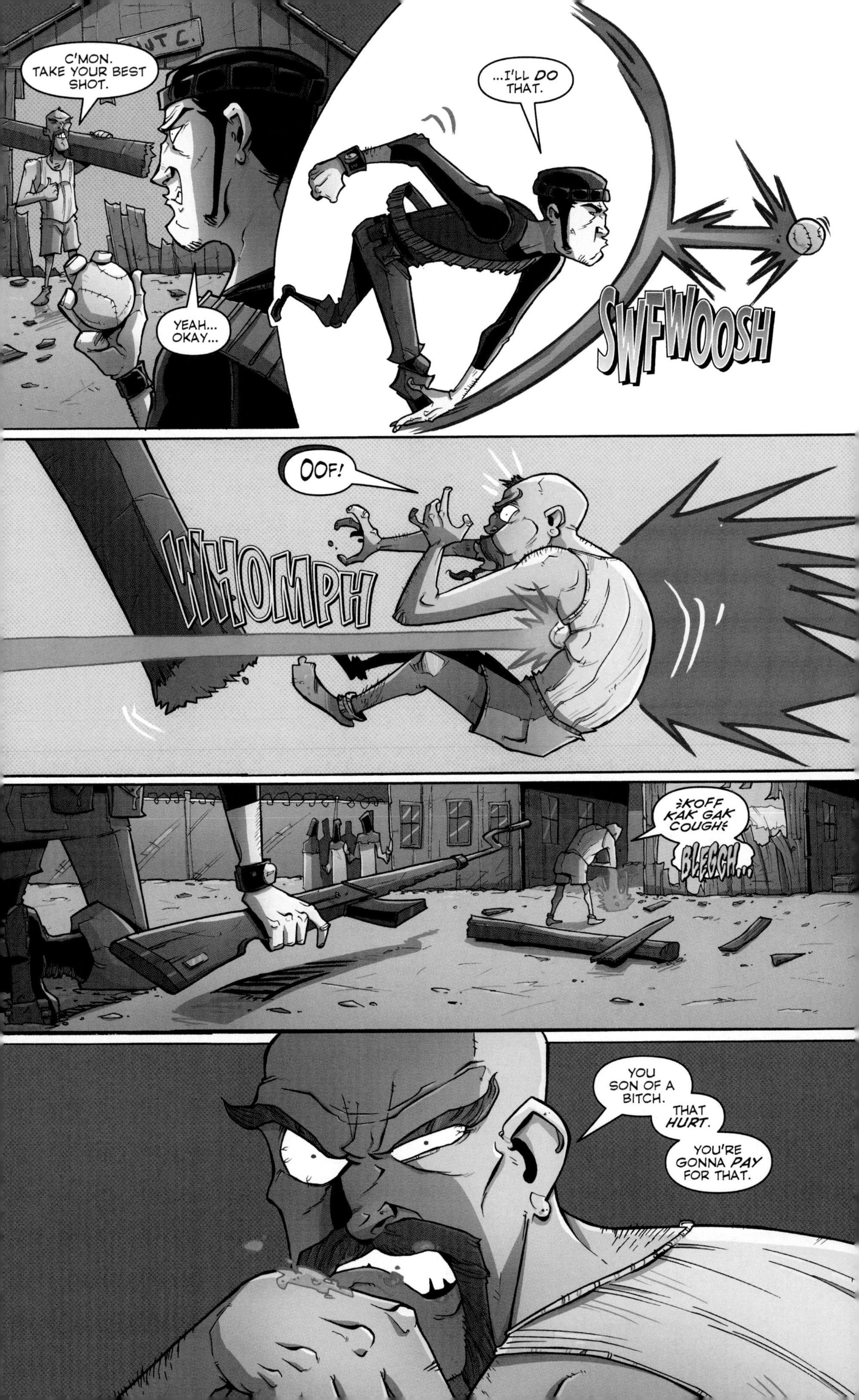
C'MON. TAKE YOUR BEST SHOT.
YEAH... OKAY...
...I'LL DO THAT.
SWFWOOSH
OOF!
WHOMPH
KOFF KAK GAK COUGH
BLEGCH...
YOU SON OF A BITCH.
THAT HURT.
YOU'RE GONNA PAY FOR THAT.

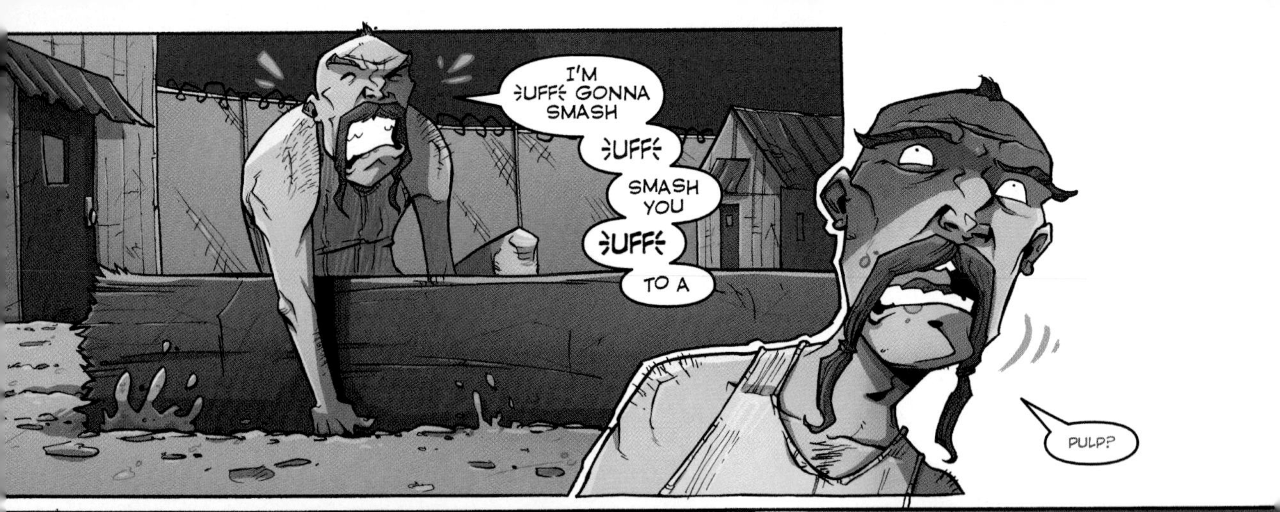
I'M
UFF GONNA
SMASH
UFF
SMASH
YOU
UFF
TO A
PULP?
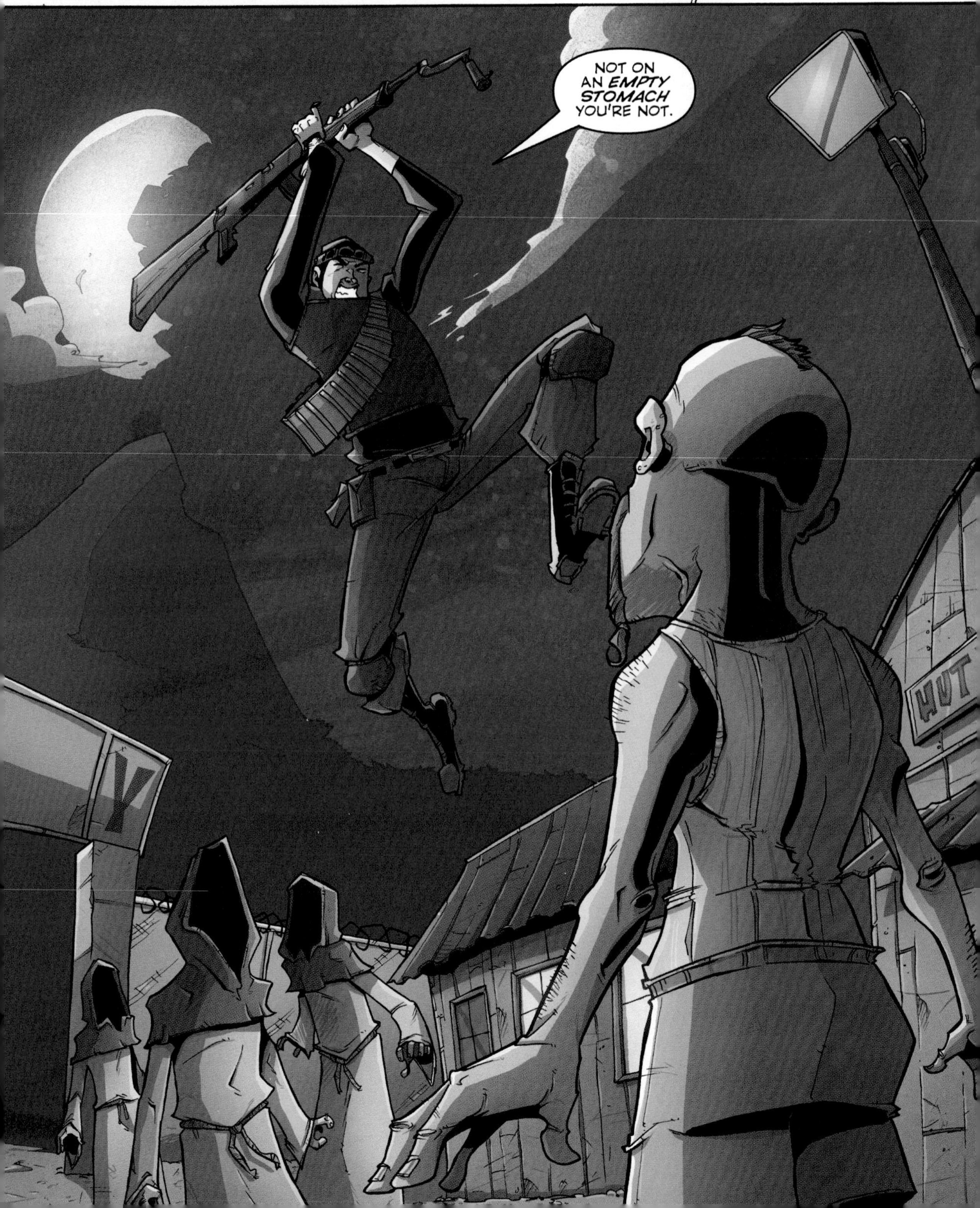
NOT ON AN EMPTY STOMACH YOU'RE NOT.
HUT

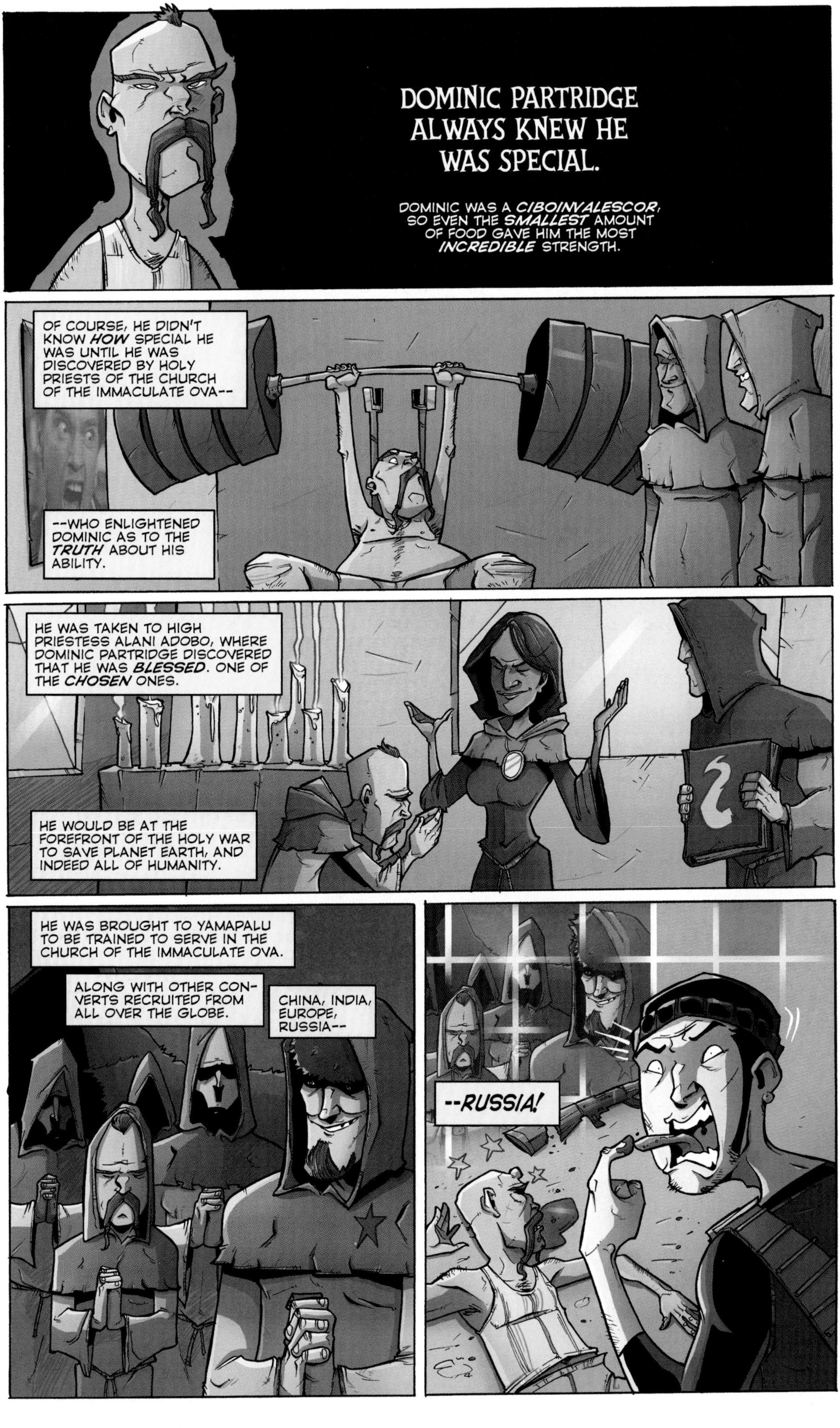
DOMINIC PARTRIDGE ALWAYS KNEW HE WAS SPECIAL.
DOMINIC WAS A CIBOINVALESCOR, SO EVEN THE SMALLEST AMOUNT OF FOOD GAVE HIM THE MOST INCREDIBLE STRENGTH.
OF COURSE, HE DIDN'T KNOW HOW SPECIAL HE WAS UNTIL HE WAS DISCOVERED BY HOLY PRIESTS OF THE CHURCH OF THE IMMACULATE OVA--
--WHO ENLIGHTENED DOMINIC AS TO THE TRUTH ABOUT HIS ABILITY.
HE WAS TAKEN TO HIGH PRIESTESS ALANI ADOBO, WHERE DOMINIC PARTRIDGE DISCOVERED THAT HE WAS BLESSED. ONE OF THE CHOSEN ONES.
HE WOULD BE AT THE FOREFRONT OF THE HOLY WAR TO SAVE PLANET EARTH, AND INDEED ALL OF HUMANITY.
HE WAS BROUGHT TO YAMAPALU TO BE TRAINED TO SERVE IN THE CHURCH OF THE IMMACULATE OVA.
ALONG WITH OTHER CON-VERTS RECRUITED FROM ALL OVER THE GLOBE.
CHINA, INDIA, EUROPE, RUSSIA--
--RUSSIA!

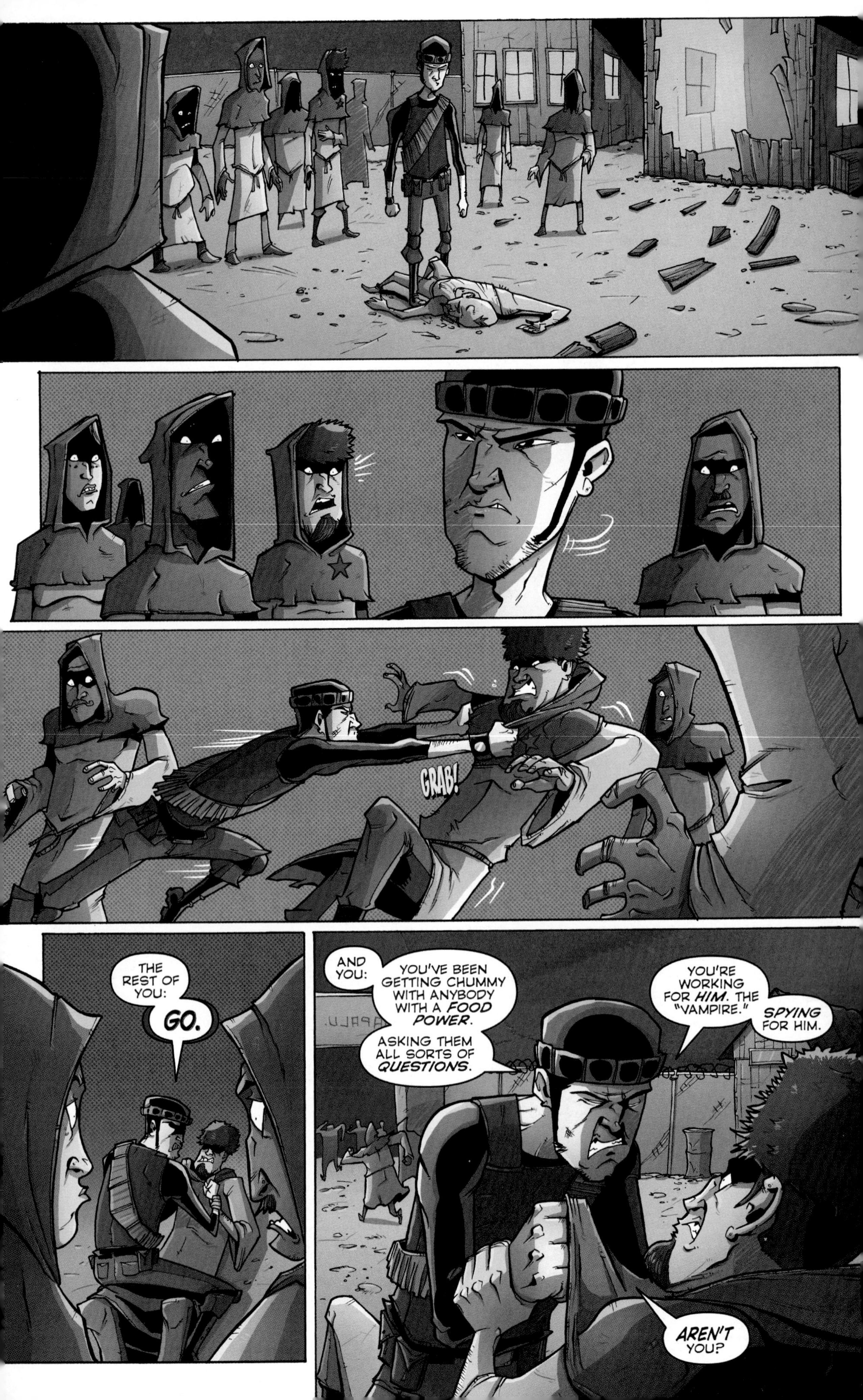

GRAB!
THE REST OF YOU: GO.
AND YOU:
YOU'VE BEEN GETTING CHUMMY WITH ANYBODY WITH A FOOD POWER.
ASKING THEM ALL SORTS OF QUESTIONS.
YOU'RE WORKING FOR HIM. THE "VAMPIRE."
SPYING FOR HIM.
AREN'T YOU?

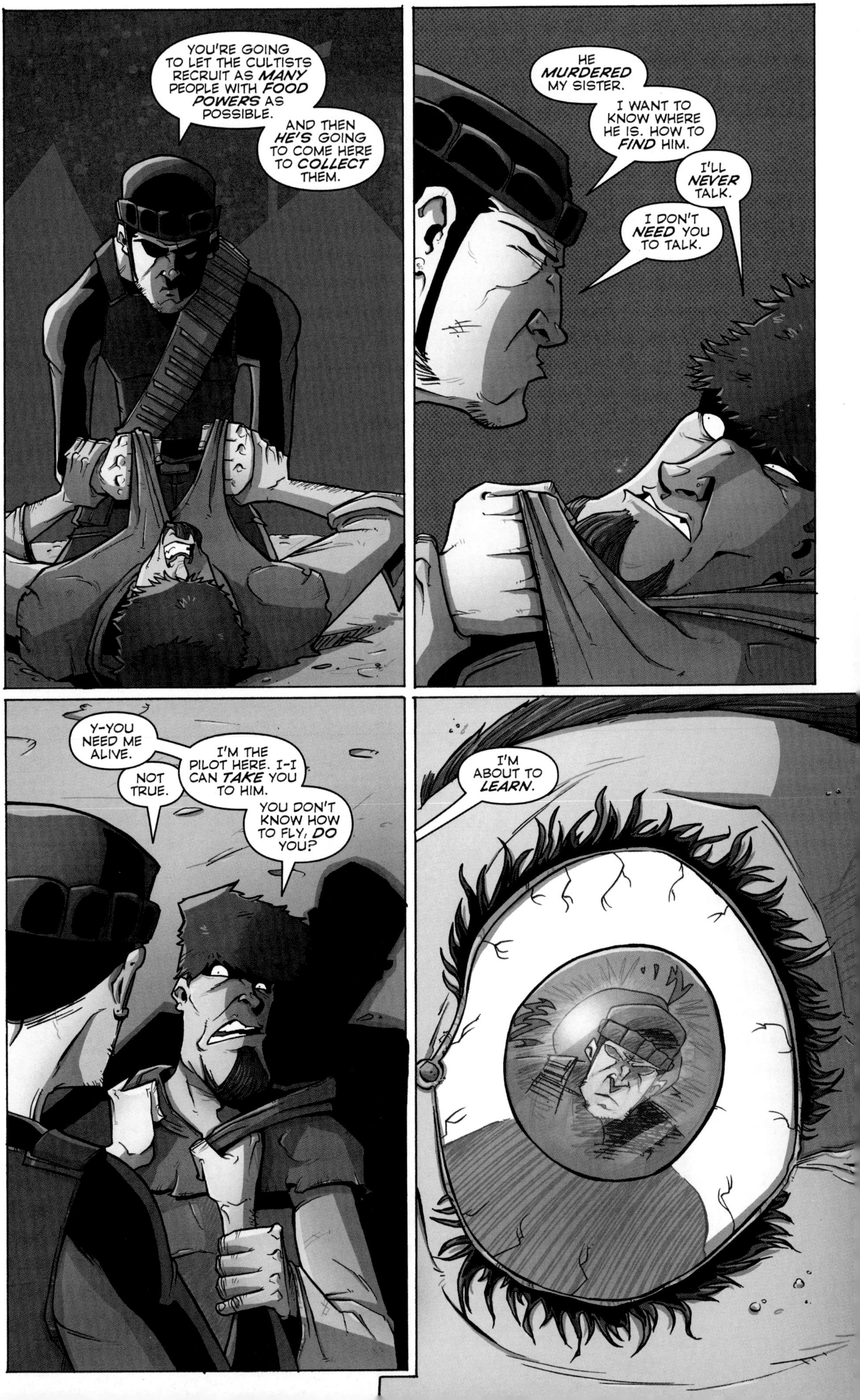
YOU'RE GOING TO LET THE CULTISTS RECRUIT AS MANY PEOPLE WITH FOOD POWERS AS POSSIBLE.
AND THEN HE'S GOING TO COME HERE TO COLLECT THEM.
HE MURDERED MY SISTER.
I WANT TO KNOW WHERE HE IS. HOW TO FIND HIM.
I'LL NEVER TALK.
I DON'T NEED YOU TO TALK.
Y-YOU NEED ME ALIVE.
NOT TRUE.
I'M THE PILOT HERE. I-I CAN TAKE YOU TO HIM.
YOU DON'T KNOW HOW TO FLY, DO YOU?
I'M ABOUT TO LEARN.

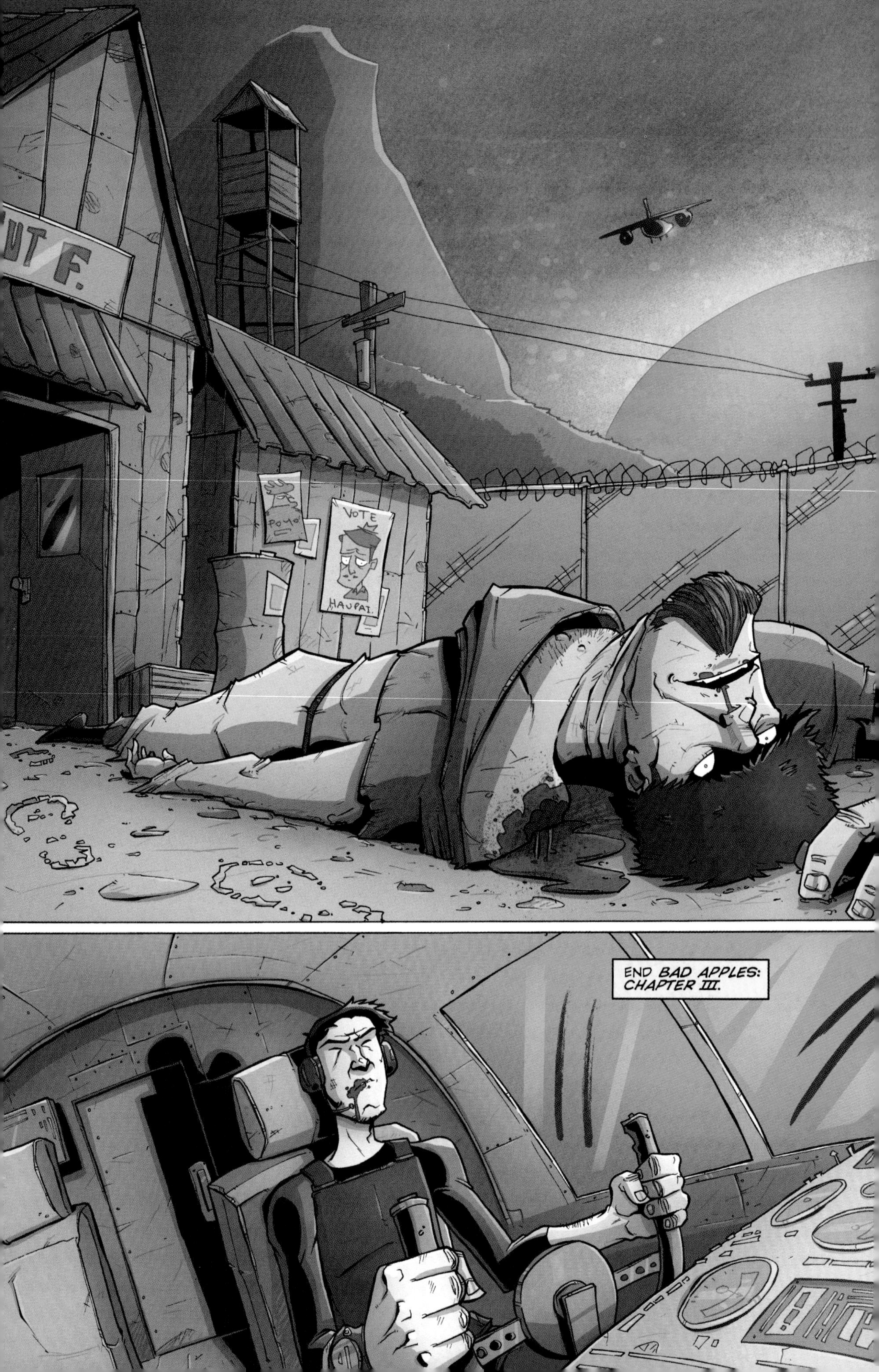
VOTE
HAUPAI.
END BAD APPLES: CHAPTER III.

Chapter Four

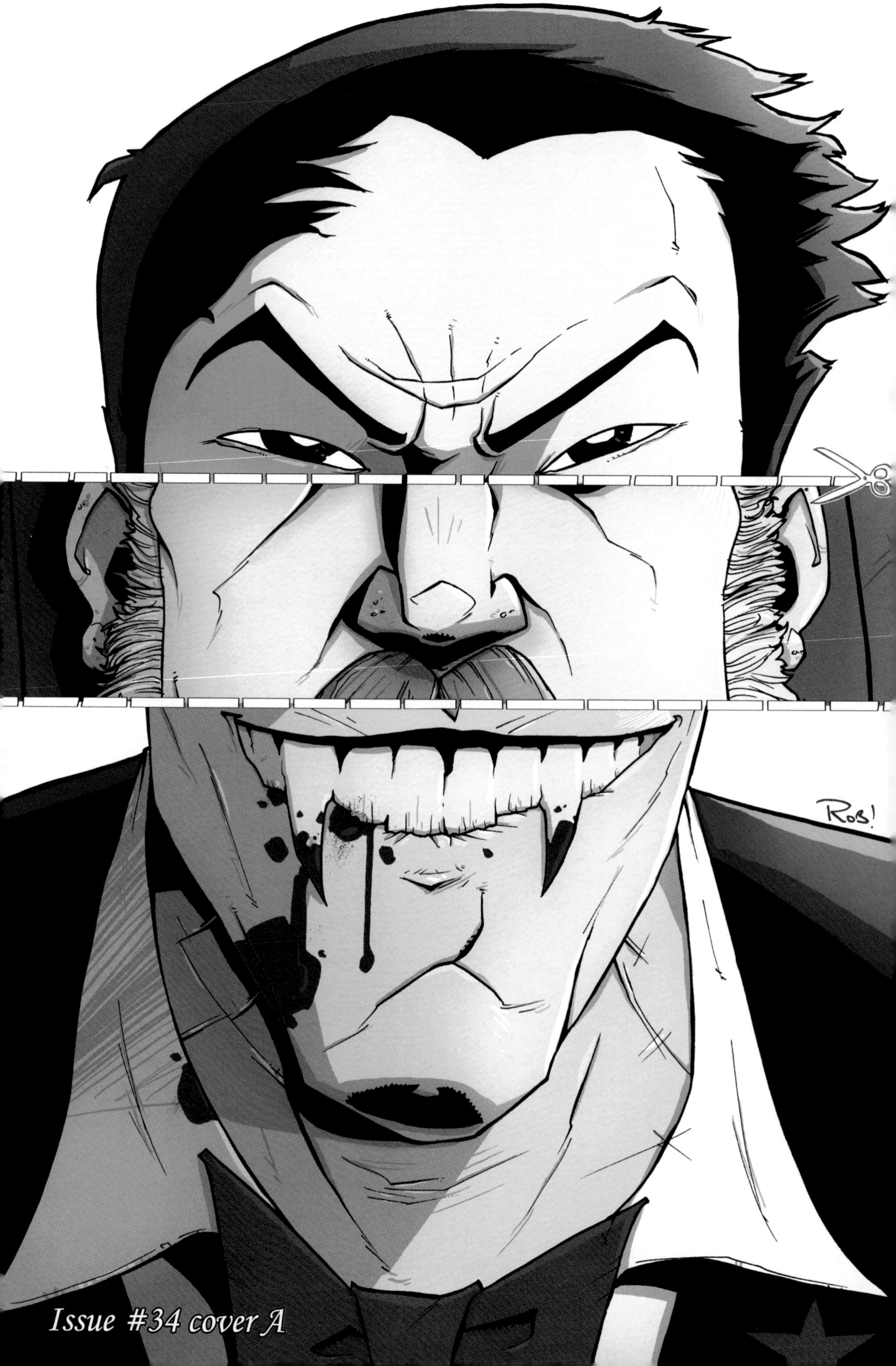
ROB!

Issue #34 cover A

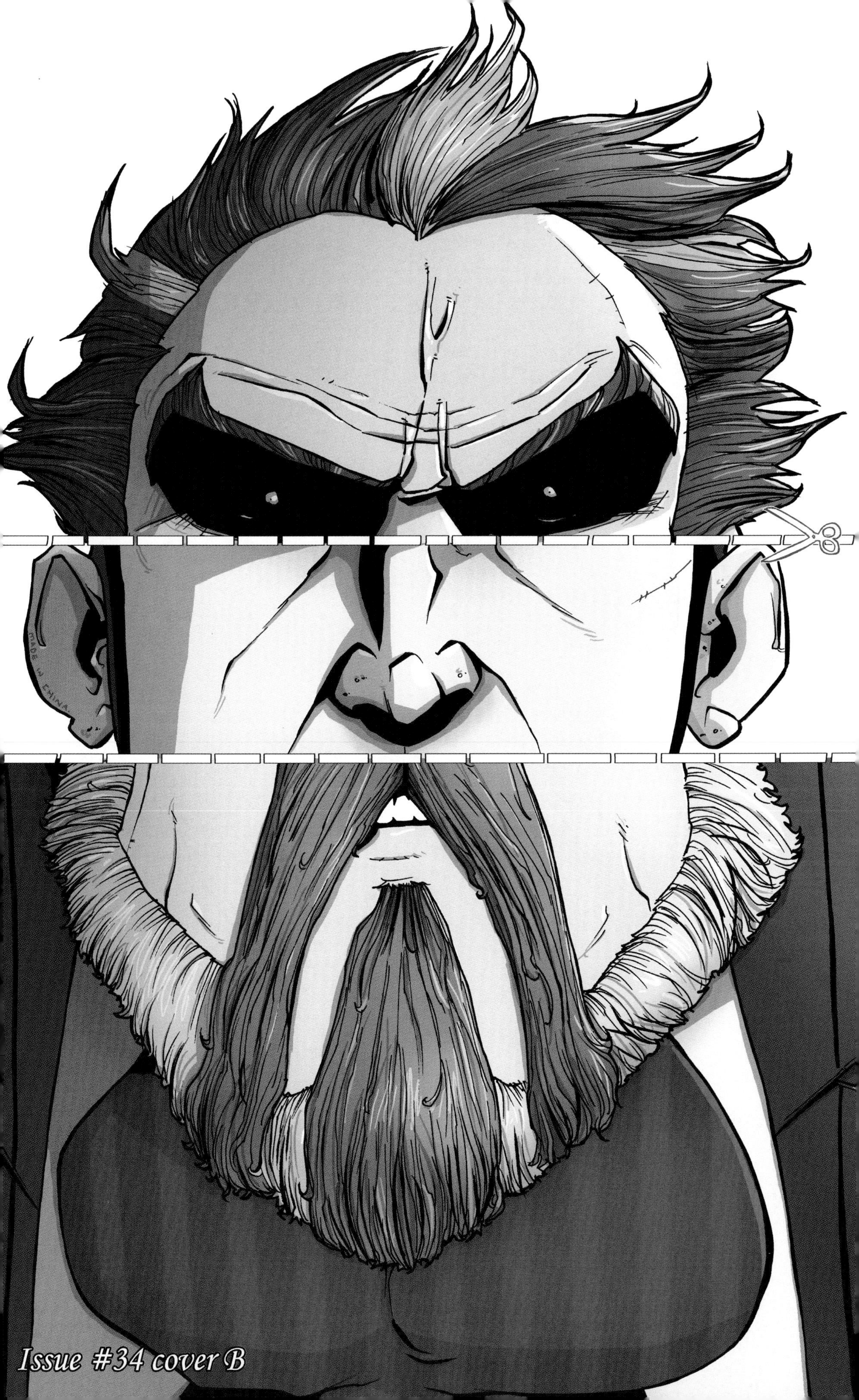
MADE IN CHINA

Issue #34 cover B

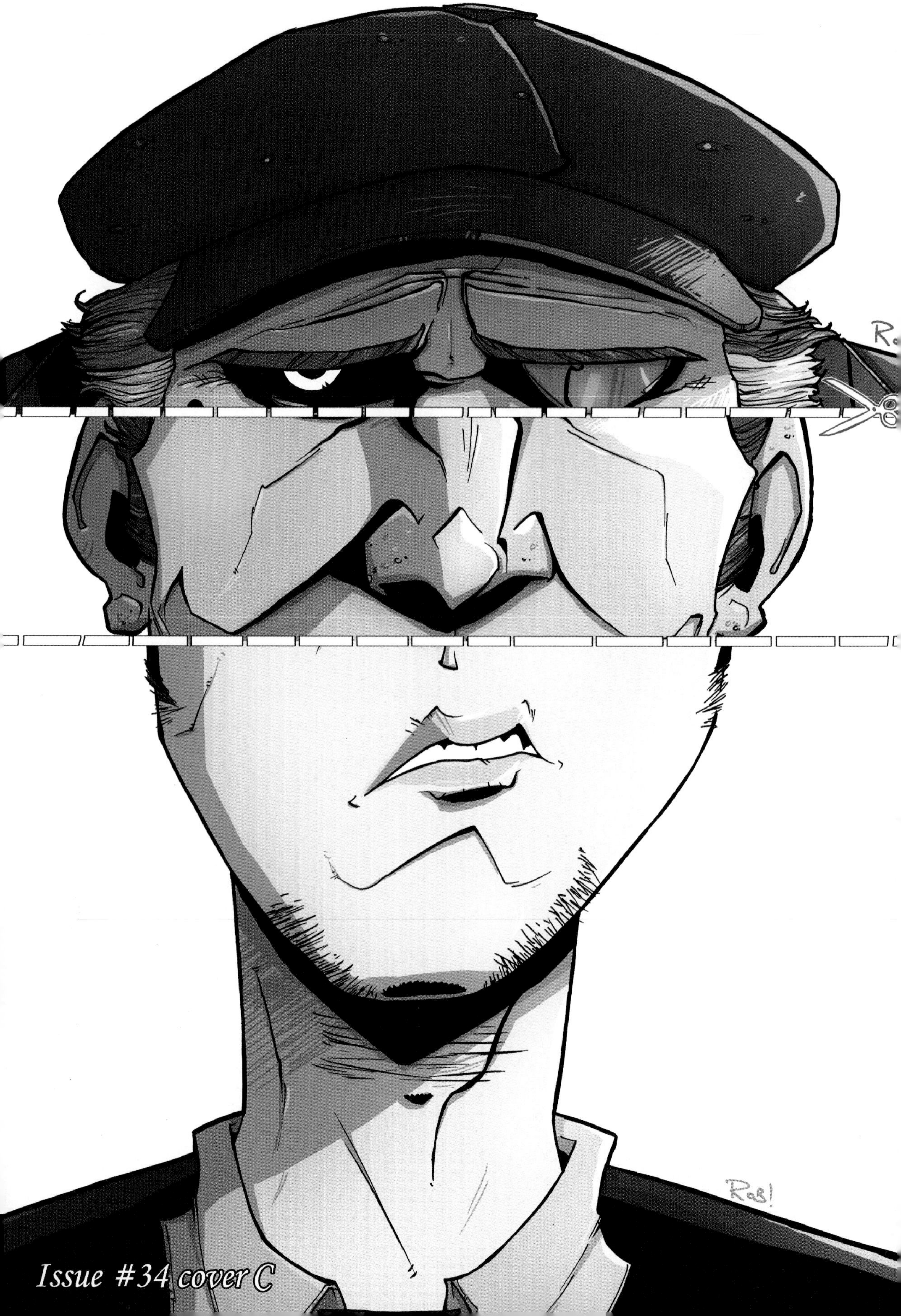

Issue #34 cover C

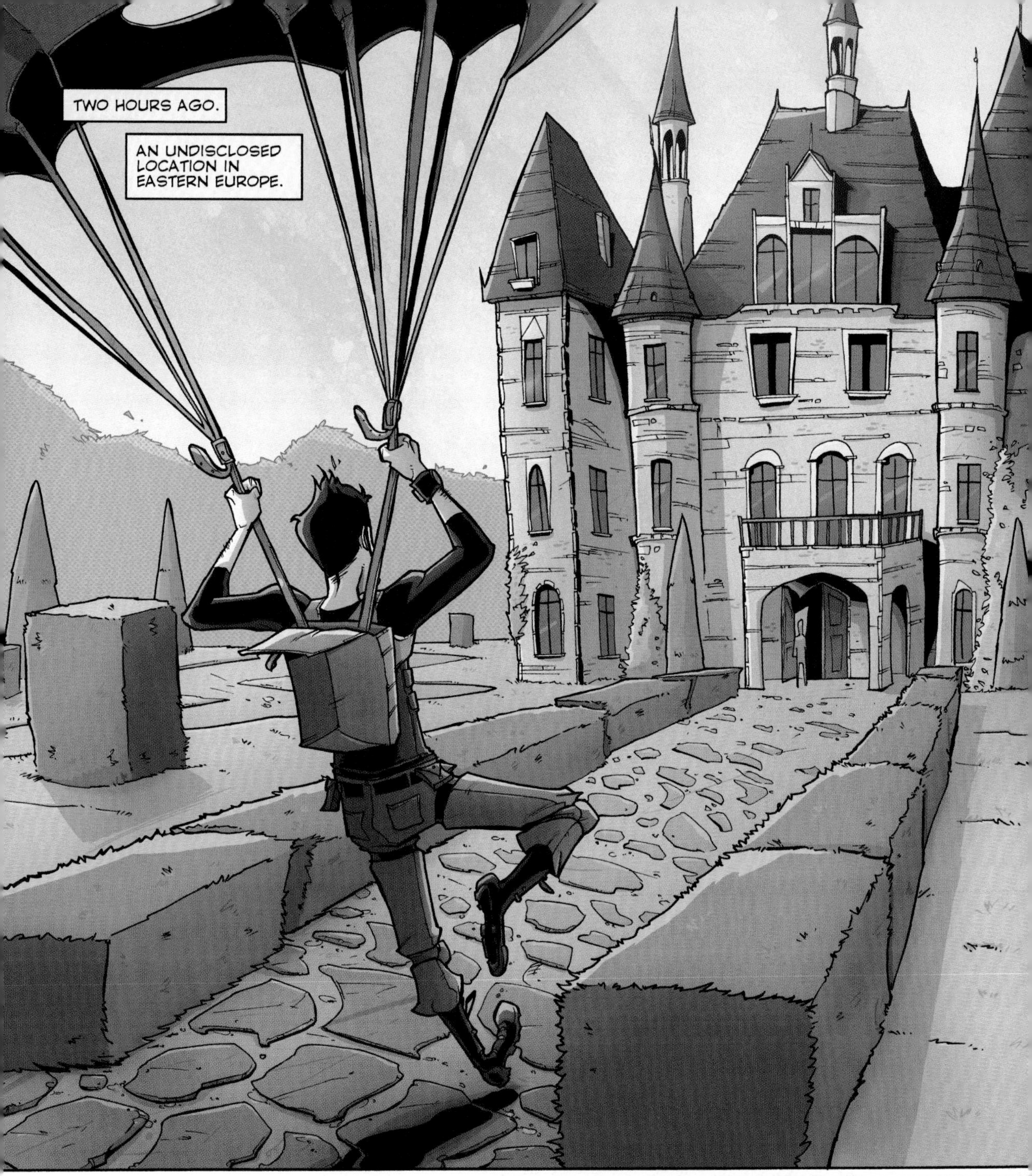
TWO HOURS AGO.
AN UNDISCLOSED LOCATION IN EASTERN EUROPE.

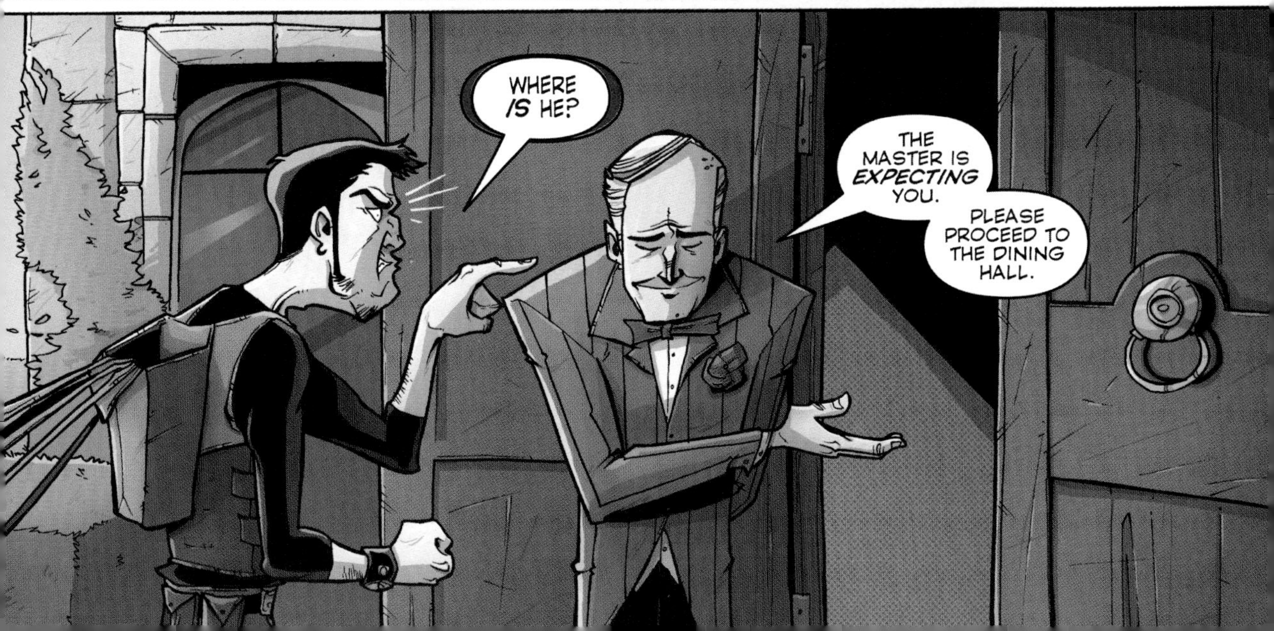
WHERE *IS* HE?
THE MASTER IS *EXPECTING* YOU.
PLEASE PROCEED TO THE DINING HALL.

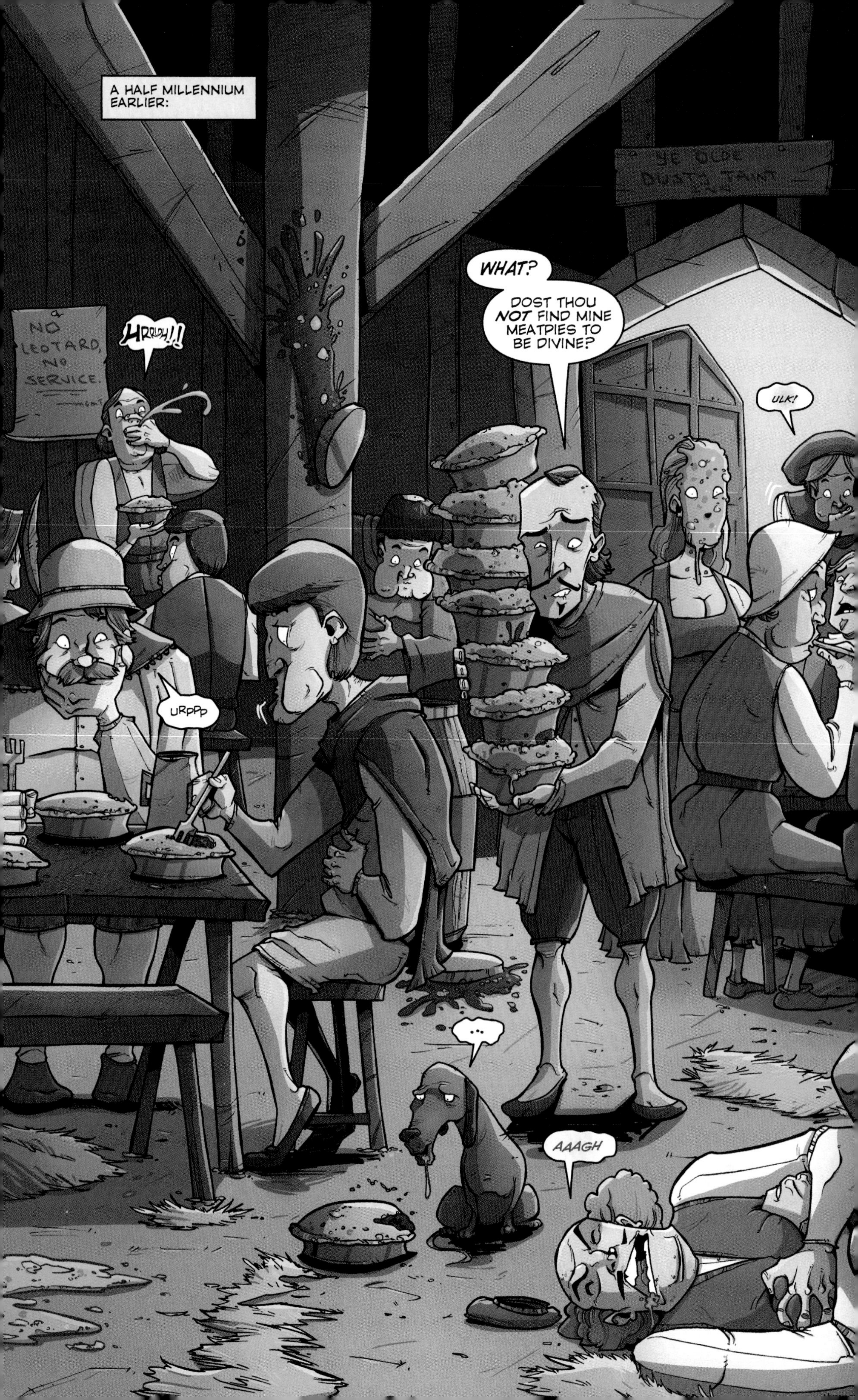
A HALF MILLENNIUM EARLIER:
YE OLDE DUSTY TAINT INN
NO LEOTARD, NO SERVICE.
HRRLDH!!
WHAT?
DOST THOU NOT FIND MINE MEATPIES TO BE DIVINE?
ULK!
URPPP
...
AAAGH

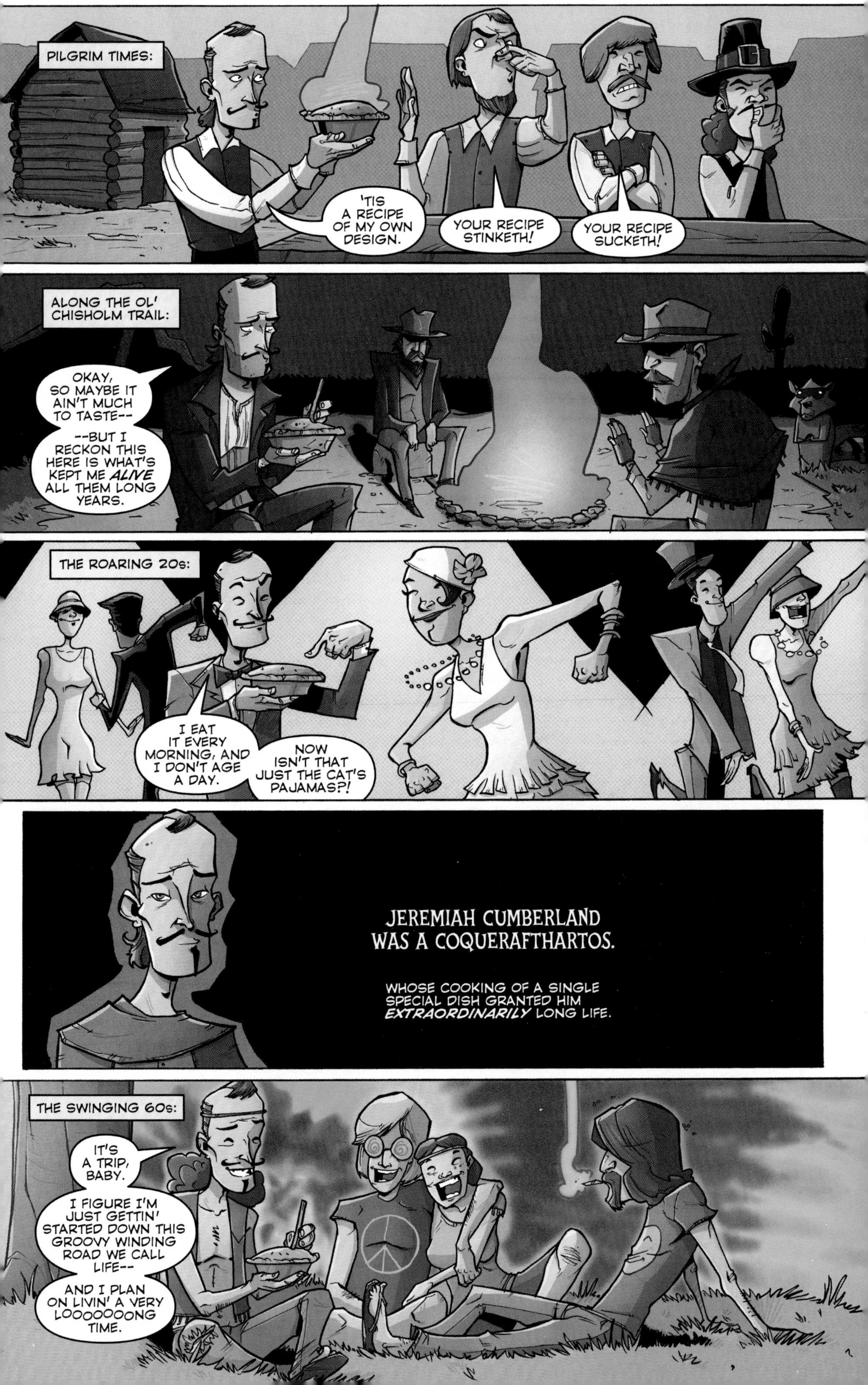
PILGRIM TIMES:
'TIS A RECIPE OF MY OWN DESIGN.
YOUR RECIPE STINKETH!
YOUR RECIPE SUCKETH!
ALONG THE OL' CHISHOLM TRAIL:
OKAY, SO MAYBE IT AIN'T MUCH TO TASTE--
--BUT I RECKON THIS HERE IS WHAT'S KEPT ME *ALIVE* ALL THEM LONG YEARS.
THE ROARING 20s:
I EAT IT EVERY MORNING, AND I DON'T AGE A DAY.
NOW ISN'T THAT JUST THE CAT'S PAJAMAS?!
JEREMIAH CUMBERLAND WAS A COQUERAFTHARTOS.
WHOSE COOKING OF A SINGLE SPECIAL DISH GRANTED HIM *EXTRAORDINARILY* LONG LIFE.
THE SWINGING 60s:
IT'S A TRIP, BABY.
I FIGURE I'M JUST GETTIN' STARTED DOWN THIS GROOVY WINDING ROAD WE CALL LIFE--
AND I PLAN ON LIVIN' A VERY LOOOOOOONG TIME.

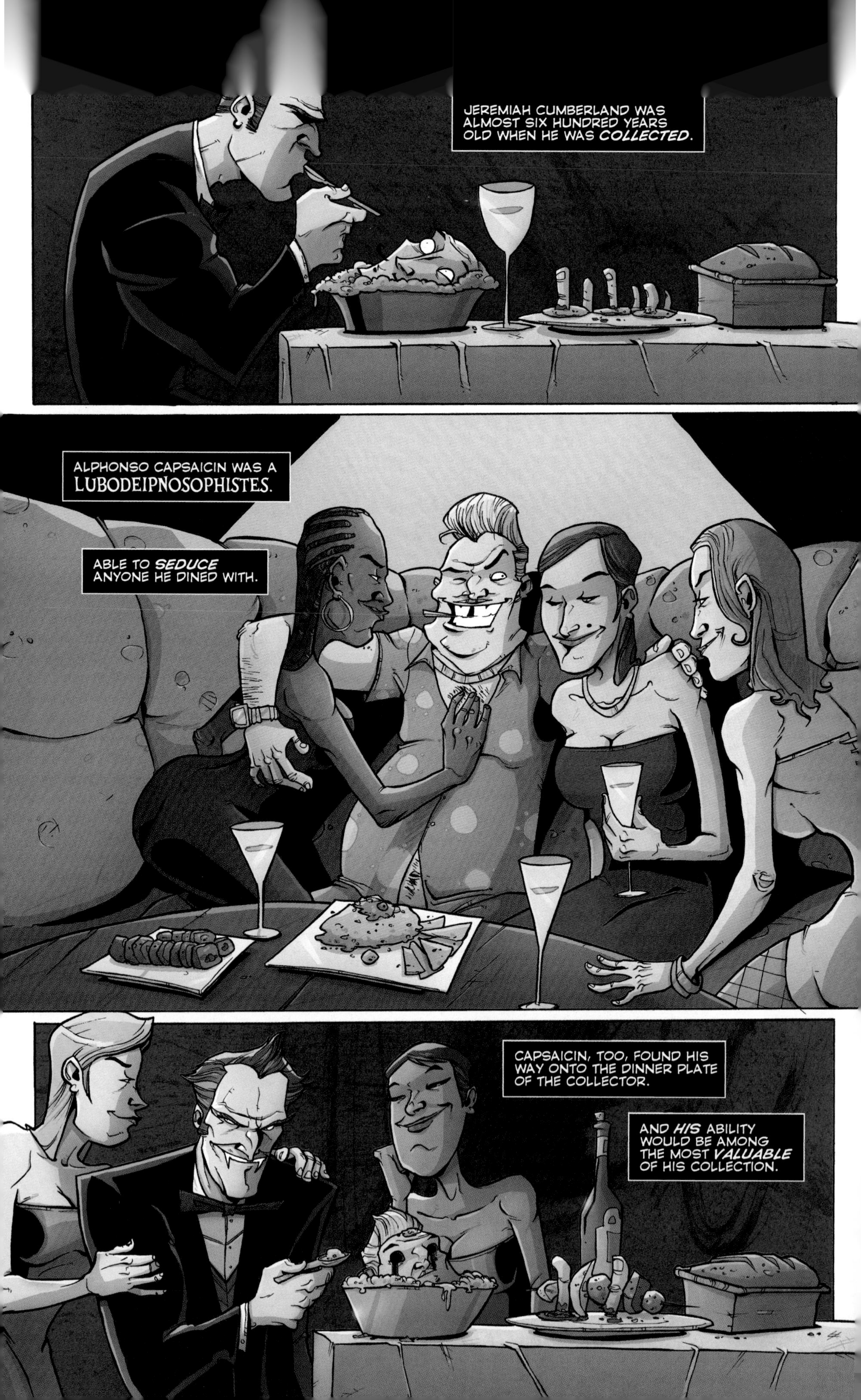

JEREMIAH CUMBERLAND WAS ALMOST SIX HUNDRED YEARS OLD WHEN HE WAS *COLLECTED*.
ALPHONSO CAPSAICIN WAS A LUBODEIPNOSOPHISTES.
ABLE TO *SEDUCE* ANYONE HE DINED WITH.
CAPSAICIN, TOO, FOUND HIS WAY ONTO THE DINNER PLATE OF THE COLLECTOR.
AND *HIS* ABILITY WOULD BE AMONG THE MOST *VALUABLE* OF HIS COLLECTION.

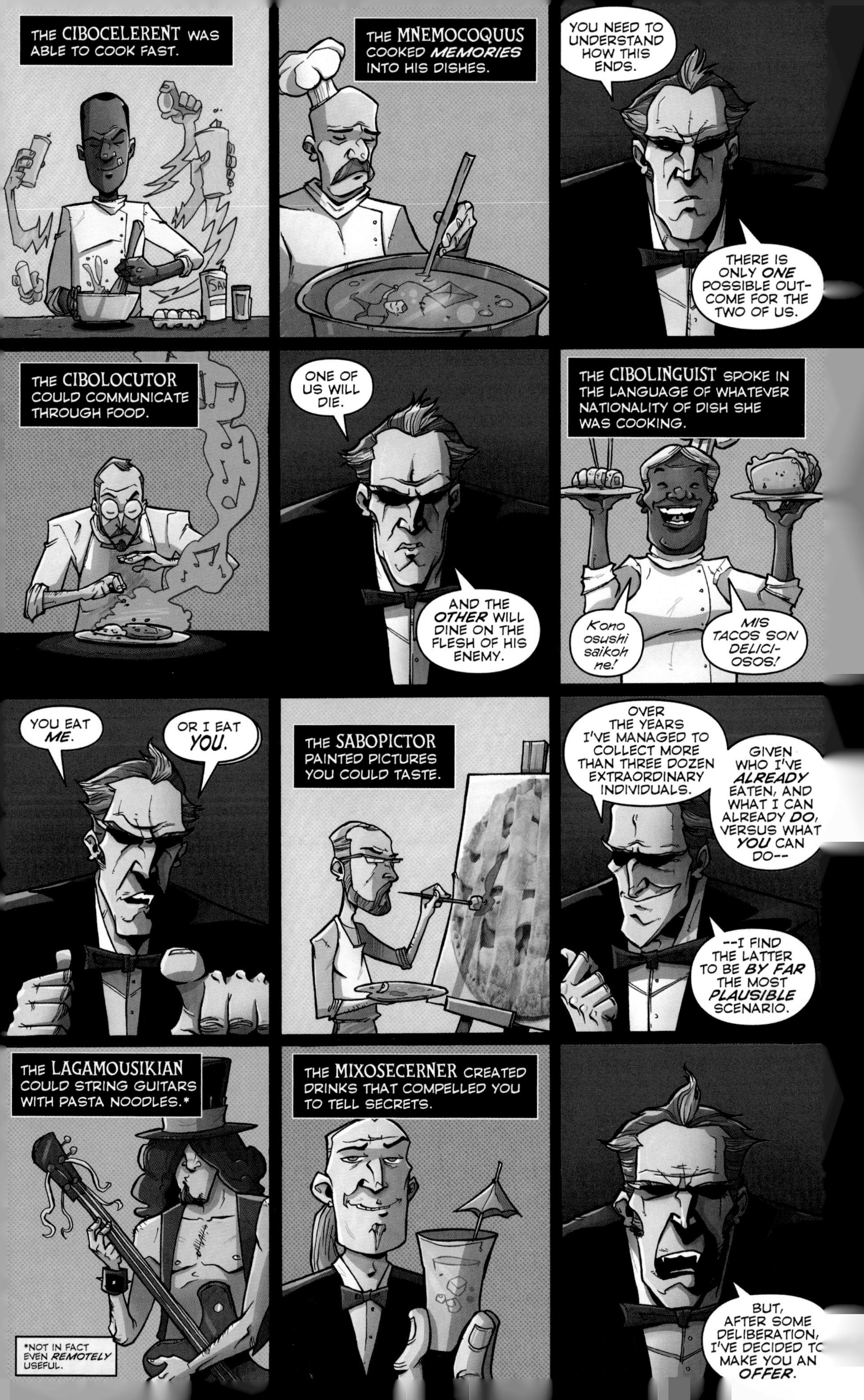
THE CIBOCELERENT WAS ABLE TO COOK FAST.
THE MNEMOCOQUUS COOKED MEMORIES INTO HIS DISHES.
YOU NEED TO UNDERSTAND HOW THIS ENDS.
THERE IS ONLY ONE POSSIBLE OUT-COME FOR THE TWO OF US.
THE CIBOLOCUTOR COULD COMMUNICATE THROUGH FOOD.
ONE OF US WILL DIE.
AND THE OTHER WILL DINE ON THE FLESH OF HIS ENEMY.
THE CIBOLINGUIST SPOKE IN THE LANGUAGE OF WHATEVER NATIONALITY OF DISH SHE WAS COOKING.
Kono osushi saikoh ne!
MIS TACOS SON DELICI-OSOS!
YOU EAT ME.
OR I EAT YOU.
THE SABOPICTOR PAINTED PICTURES YOU COULD TASTE.
OVER THE YEARS I'VE MANAGED TO COLLECT MORE THAN THREE DOZEN EXTRAORDINARY INDIVIDUALS.
GIVEN WHO I'VE ALREADY EATEN, AND WHAT I CAN ALREADY DO, VERSUS WHAT YOU CAN DO--
--I FIND THE LATTER TO BE BY FAR THE MOST PLAUSIBLE SCENARIO.
THE LAGAMOUSIKIAN COULD STRING GUITARS WITH PASTA NOODLES.*
*NOT IN FACT EVEN REMOTELY USEFUL.
THE MIXOSECERNER CREATED DRINKS THAT COMPELLED YOU TO TELL SECRETS.
BUT, AFTER SOME DELIBERATION, I'VE DECIDED TO MAKE YOU AN OFFER.

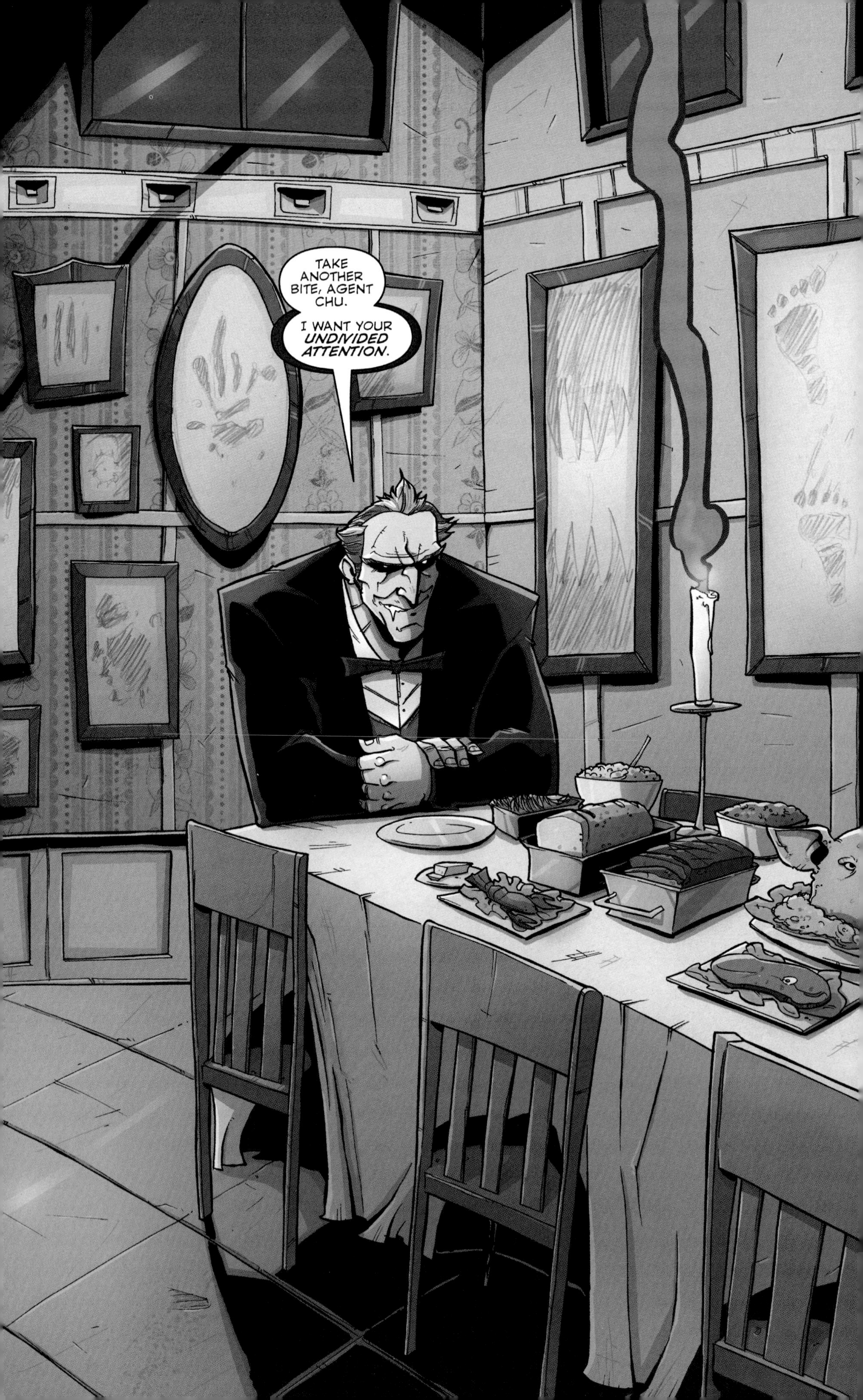
TAKE ANOTHER BITE, AGENT CHU.
I WANT YOUR *UNDIVIDED ATTENTION*.

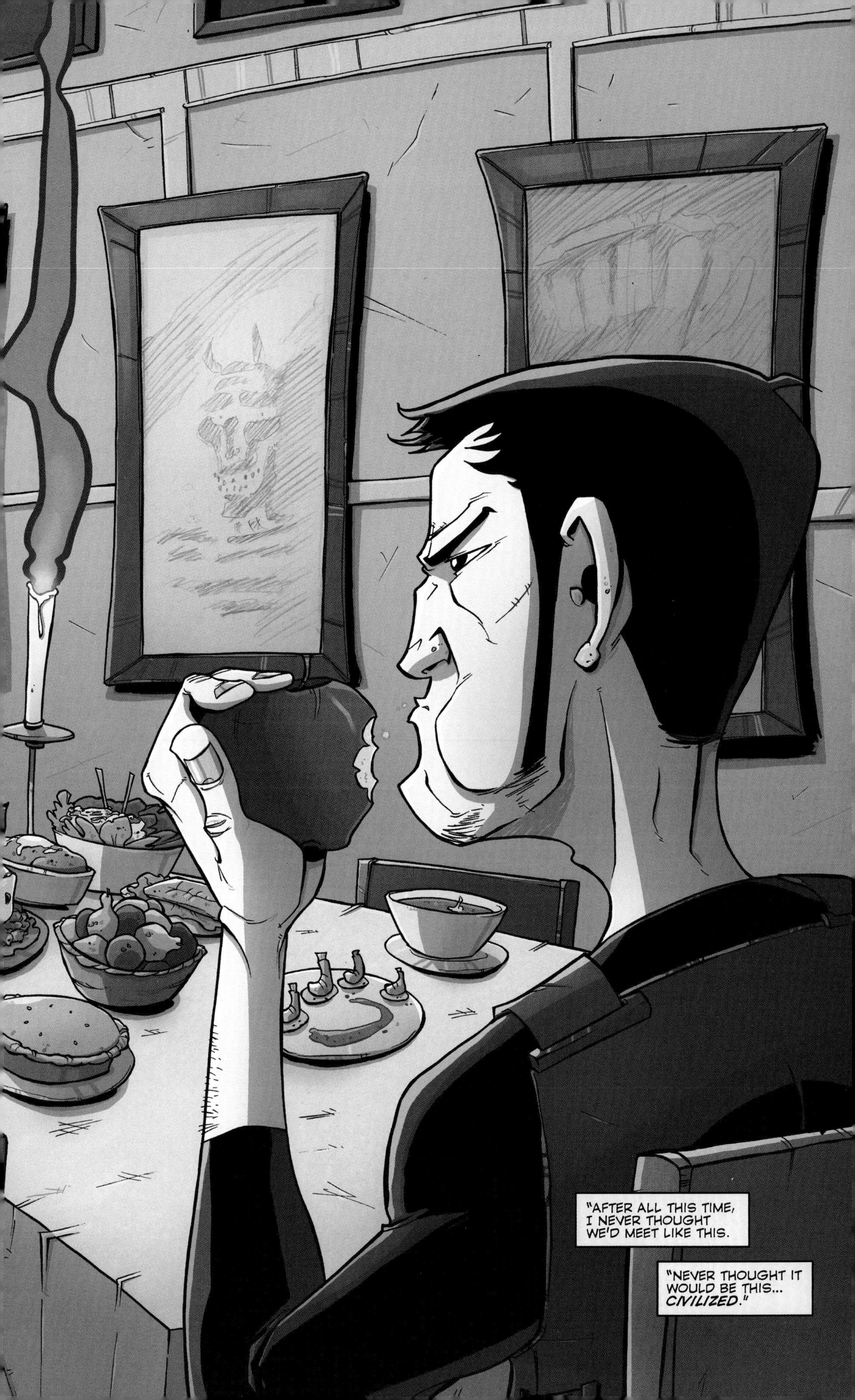
"AFTER ALL THIS TIME, I NEVER THOUGHT WE'D MEET LIKE THIS.
"NEVER THOUGHT IT WOULD BE THIS... *CIVILIZED*."

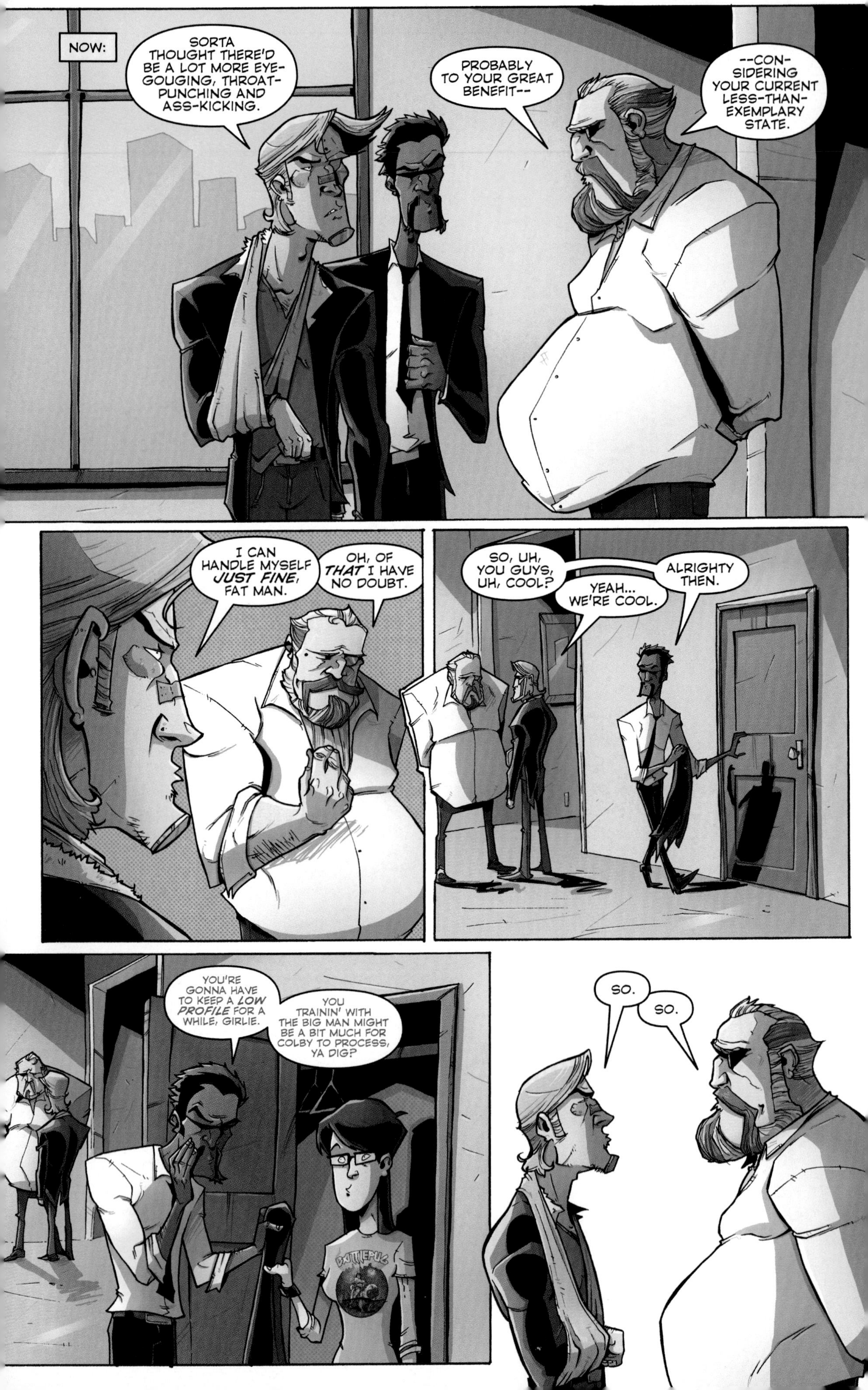
NOW:
SORTA THOUGHT THERE'D BE A LOT MORE EYE-GOUGING, THROAT-PUNCHING AND ASS-KICKING.
PROBABLY TO YOUR GREAT BENEFIT--
--CONSIDERING YOUR CURRENT LESS-THAN-EXEMPLARY STATE.
I CAN HANDLE MYSELF *JUST FINE*, FAT MAN.
OH, OF *THAT* I HAVE NO DOUBT.
SO, UH, YOU GUYS, UH, COOL?
YEAH... WE'RE COOL.
ALRIGHTY THEN.
YOU'RE GONNA HAVE TO KEEP A *LOW PROFILE* FOR A WHILE, GIRLIE.
YOU TRAININ' WITH THE BIG MAN MIGHT BE A BIT MUCH FOR COLBY TO PROCESS, YA DIG?
SO.
SO.

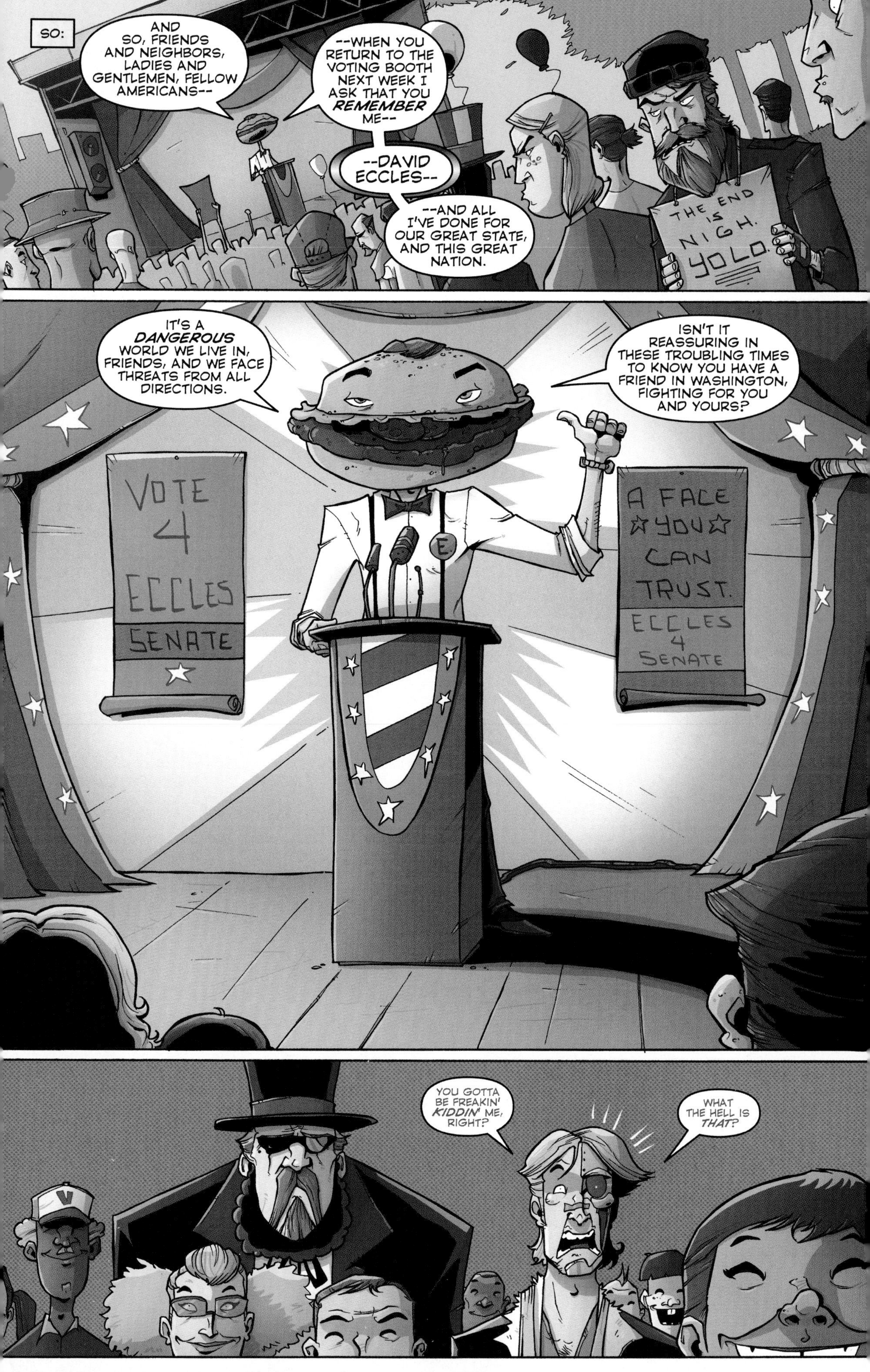
SO:
AND SO, FRIENDS AND NEIGHBORS, LADIES AND GENTLEMEN, FELLOW AMERICANS--
--WHEN YOU RETURN TO THE VOTING BOOTH NEXT WEEK I ASK THAT YOU REMEMBER ME--
--DAVID ECCLES--
--AND ALL I'VE DONE FOR OUR GREAT STATE, AND THIS GREAT NATION.
THE END IS NIGH. YOLO.
IT'S A DANGEROUS WORLD WE LIVE IN, FRIENDS, AND WE FACE THREATS FROM ALL DIRECTIONS.
ISN'T IT REASSURING IN THESE TROUBLING TIMES TO KNOW YOU HAVE A FRIEND IN WASHINGTON, FIGHTING FOR YOU AND YOURS?
VOTE 4 ECCLES SENATE
A FACE YOU CAN TRUST. ECCLES 4 SENATE
E
YOU GOTTA BE FREAKIN' KIDDIN' ME, RIGHT?
WHAT THE HELL IS THAT?

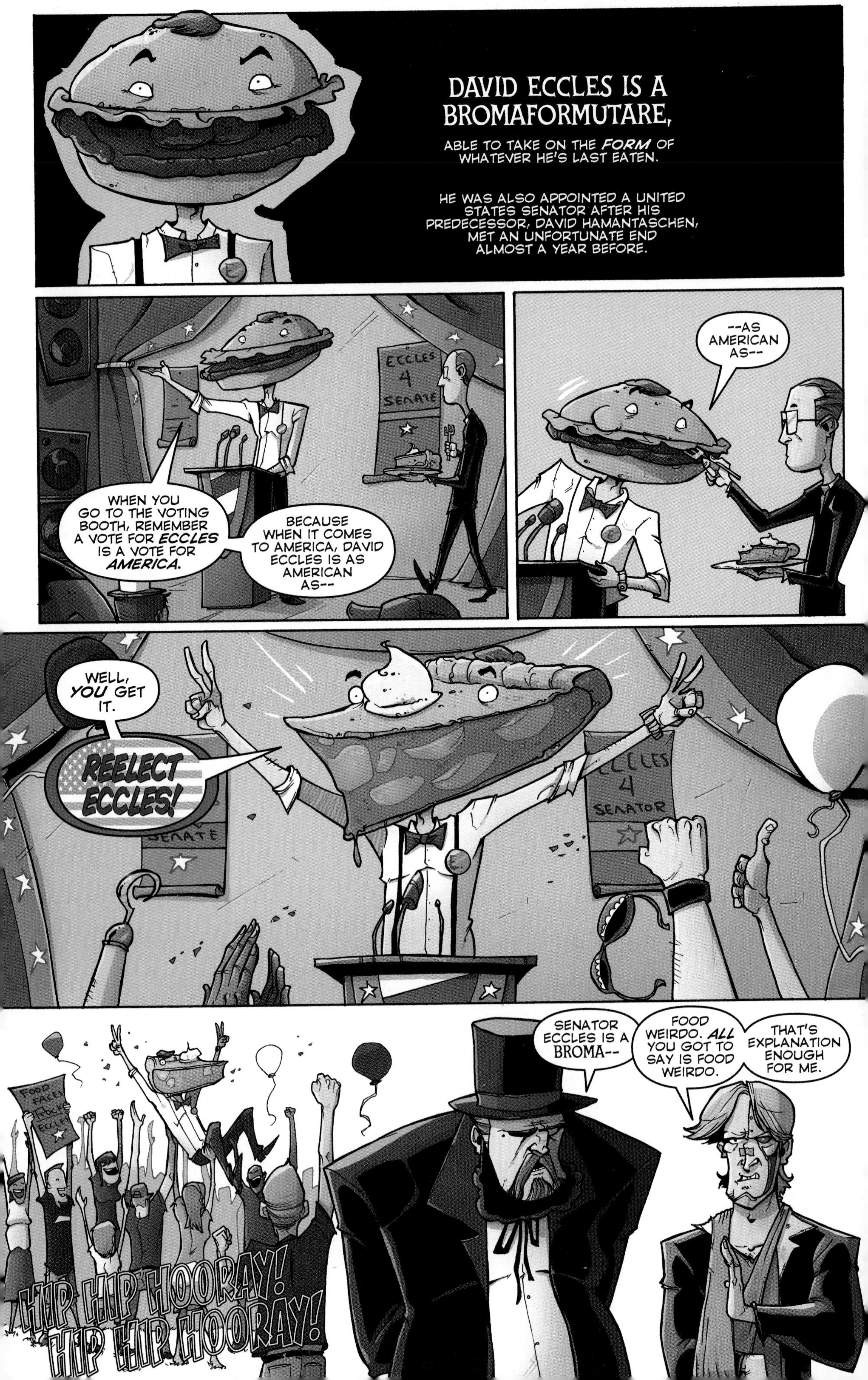
DAVID ECCLES IS A BROMAFORMUTARE,
ABLE TO TAKE ON THE FORM OF WHATEVER HE'S LAST EATEN.
HE WAS ALSO APPOINTED A UNITED STATES SENATOR AFTER HIS PREDECESSOR, DAVID HAMANTASCHEN, MET AN UNFORTUNATE END ALMOST A YEAR BEFORE.
ECCLES 4 SENATE
WHEN YOU GO TO THE VOTING BOOTH, REMEMBER A VOTE FOR ECCLES IS A VOTE FOR AMERICA.
BECAUSE WHEN IT COMES TO AMERICA, DAVID ECCLES IS AS AMERICAN AS--
--AS AMERICAN AS--
WELL, YOU GET IT.
REELECT ECCLES!
ECCLES 4 SENATOR
SENATE
FOOD FACES ROCK ECCLES
SENATOR ECCLES IS A BROMA--
FOOD WEIRDO. ALL YOU GOT TO SAY IS FOOD WEIRDO.
THAT'S EXPLANATION ENOUGH FOR ME.
HIP HIP HOORAY! HIP HIP HOORAY!

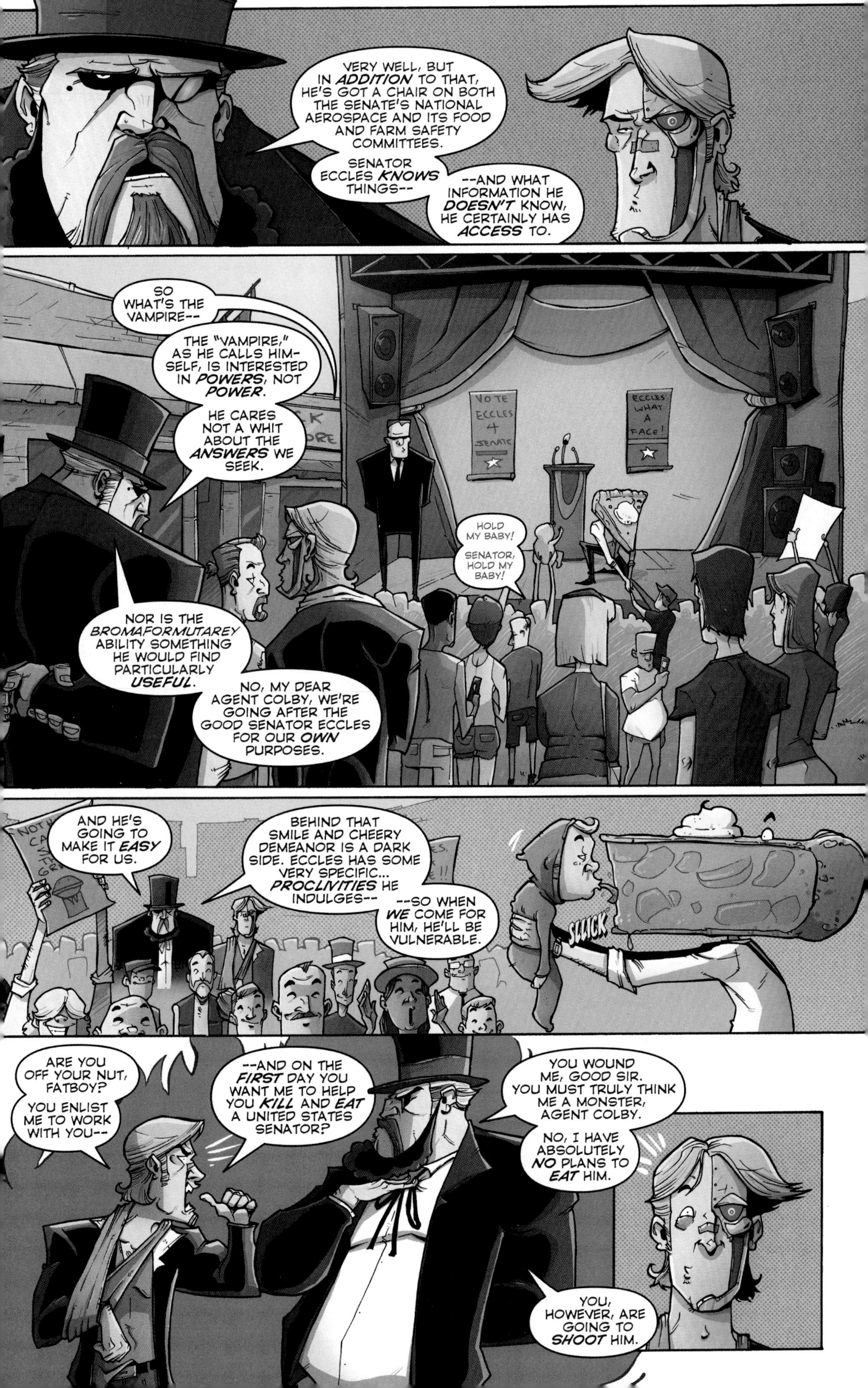
VERY WELL, BUT IN ADDITION TO THAT, HE'S GOT A CHAIR ON BOTH THE SENATE'S NATIONAL AEROSPACE AND ITS FOOD AND FARM SAFETY COMMITTEES.
SENATOR ECCLES KNOWS THINGS--
--AND WHAT INFORMATION HE DOESN'T KNOW, HE CERTAINLY HAS ACCESS TO.
SO WHAT'S THE VAMPIRE--
THE "VAMPIRE," AS HE CALLS HIMSELF, IS INTERESTED IN POWERS, NOT POWER.
HE CARES NOT A WHIT ABOUT THE ANSWERS WE SEEK.
VOTE ECCLES 4 SENATE
ECCLES' WHAT A FACE!
HOLD MY BABY!
SENATOR, HOLD MY BABY!
NOR IS THE BROMAFORMUTAREY ABILITY SOMETHING HE WOULD FIND PARTICULARLY USEFUL.
NO, MY DEAR AGENT COLBY, WE'RE GOING AFTER THE GOOD SENATOR ECCLES FOR OUR OWN PURPOSES.
AND HE'S GOING TO MAKE IT EASY FOR US.
BEHIND THAT SMILE AND CHEERY DEMEANOR IS A DARK SIDE. ECCLES HAS SOME VERY SPECIFIC... PROCLIVITIES HE INDULGES--
--SO WHEN WE COME FOR HIM, HE'LL BE VULNERABLE.
SLLICK
ARE YOU OFF YOUR NUT, FATBOY?
YOU ENLIST ME TO WORK WITH YOU--
--AND ON THE FIRST DAY YOU WANT ME TO HELP YOU KILL AND EAT A UNITED STATES SENATOR?
YOU WOUND ME, GOOD SIR. YOU MUST TRULY THINK ME A MONSTER, AGENT COLBY.
NO, I HAVE ABSOLUTELY NO PLANS TO EAT HIM.
YOU, HOWEVER, ARE GOING TO SHOOT HIM.

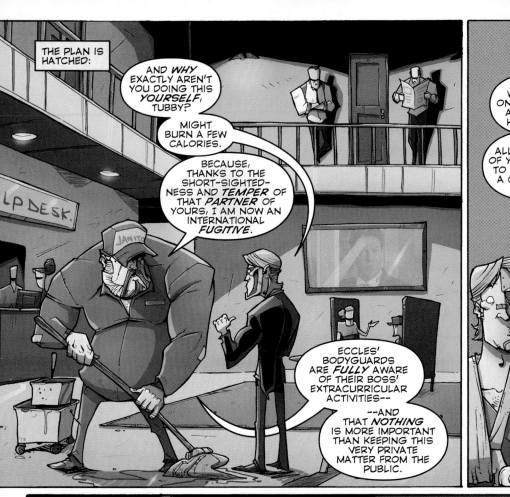

THE PLAN IS HATCHED:

AND *WHY* EXACTLY AREN'T YOU DOING THIS *YOURSELF*, TUBBY?

MIGHT BURN A FEW CALORIES.

BECAUSE, THANKS TO THE SHORT-SIGHTED-NESS AND *TEMPER* OF THAT *PARTNER* OF YOURS, I AM NOW AN INTERNATIONAL *FUGITIVE.*

ECCLES' BODYGUARDS ARE *FULLY* AWARE OF THEIR BOSS' EXTRACURRICULAR ACTIVITIES--

--AND THAT *NOTHING* IS MORE IMPORTANT THAN KEEPING THIS VERY PRIVATE MATTER FROM THE PUBLIC.

LP DESK.

JANITOR

THEY WOULD FIRE ON ME WITHOUT A MOMENT'S HESITATION.

AS IT IS, ALL THAT *BADGE* OF YOURS IS GOING TO DO IS BUY YOU A COUPLE EXTRA SECONDS.

JANITOR

"LET'S HOPE IT'S ENOUGH."

NOT ANOTHER STEP. WHAT DO YOU WANT, TIN MAN?

AGENT JOHN COLBY. FDA. HERE TA SEE YOUR *BOSS.*

SORRY, GRUESOME. THE SENATOR ISN'T ACCEPTING VISITORS AT THE MOMENT.

LEMME GET YOUR BADGE NUMBER AND HE'LL GET BACK TO YOU AT HIS CON-VENIENCE.

WHAT DO YOU WANT THE SENATOR FOR ANYWAY?

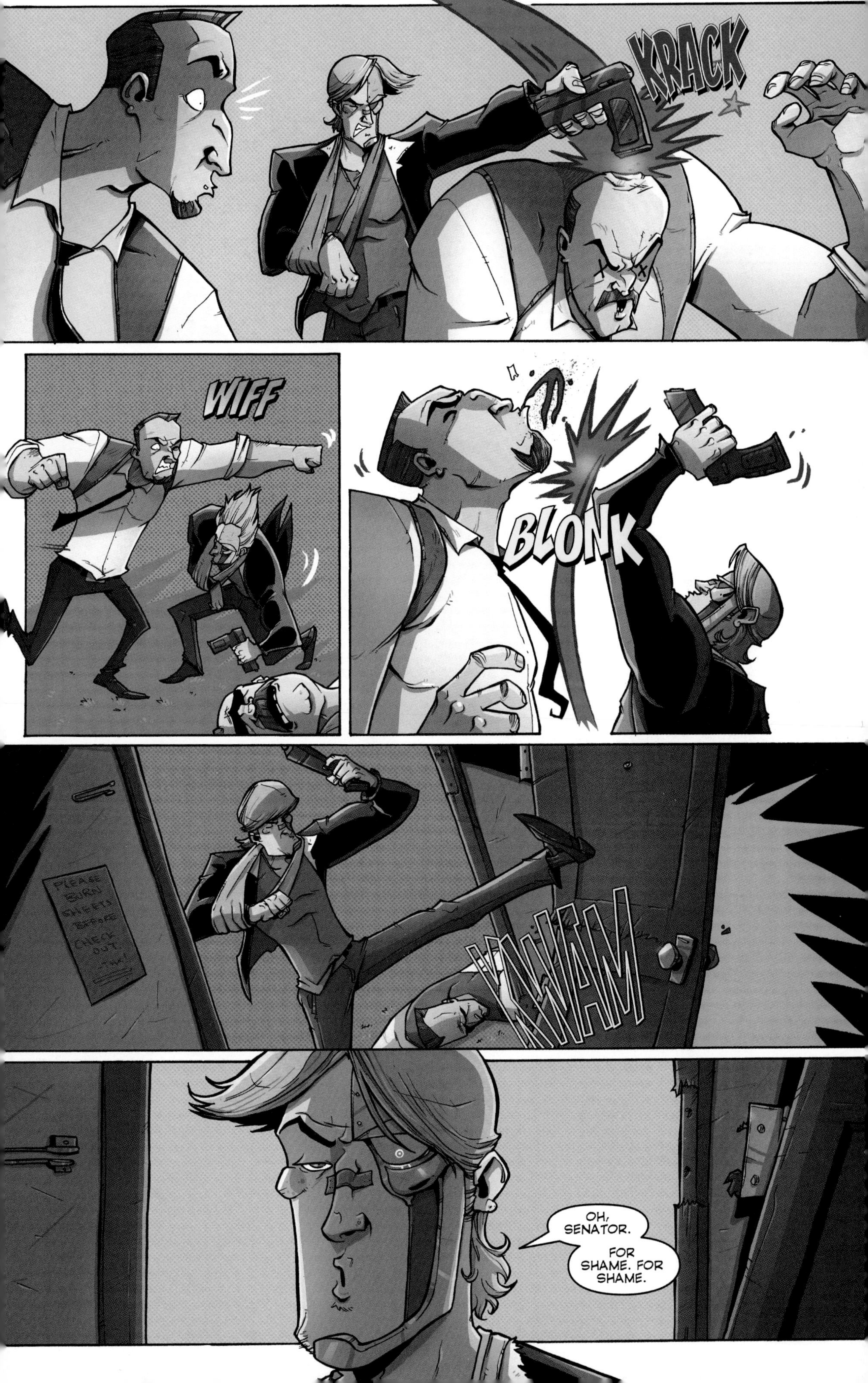
KRACK
WIFF
BLONK
PLEASE BURN SHEETS BEFORE CHECK OUT
KWAM
OH, SENATOR.
FOR SHAME. FOR SHAME.

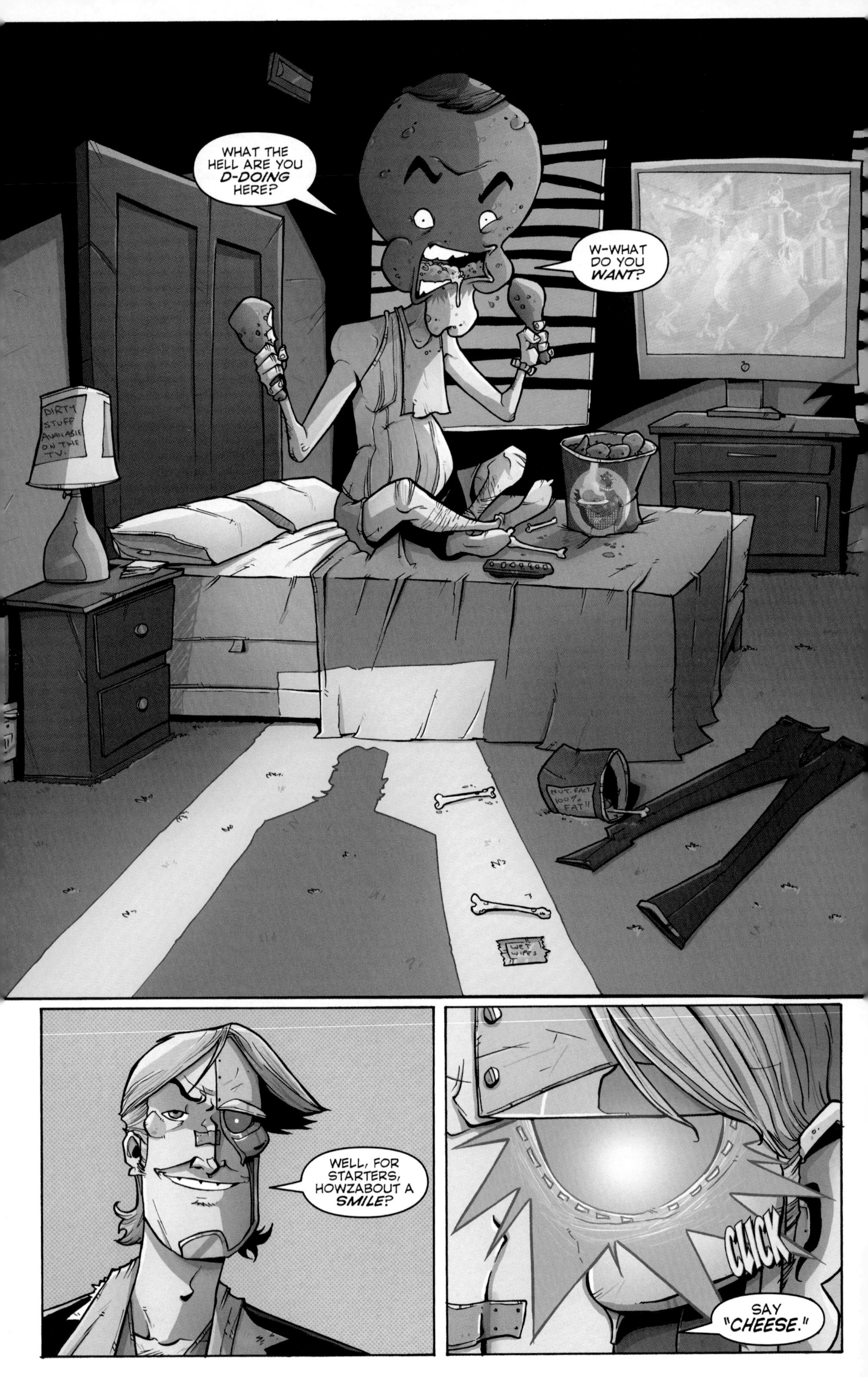

WHAT THE HELL ARE YOU *D-DOING* HERE?
W-WHAT DO YOU *WANT?*
DIRTY STUFF AVAILABLE ON THE TV.
NUT. FACT. 100% FAT!!
WET WIPES
WELL, FOR STARTERS, HOWZABOUT A *SMILE?*
CLICK
SAY "*CHEESE.*"

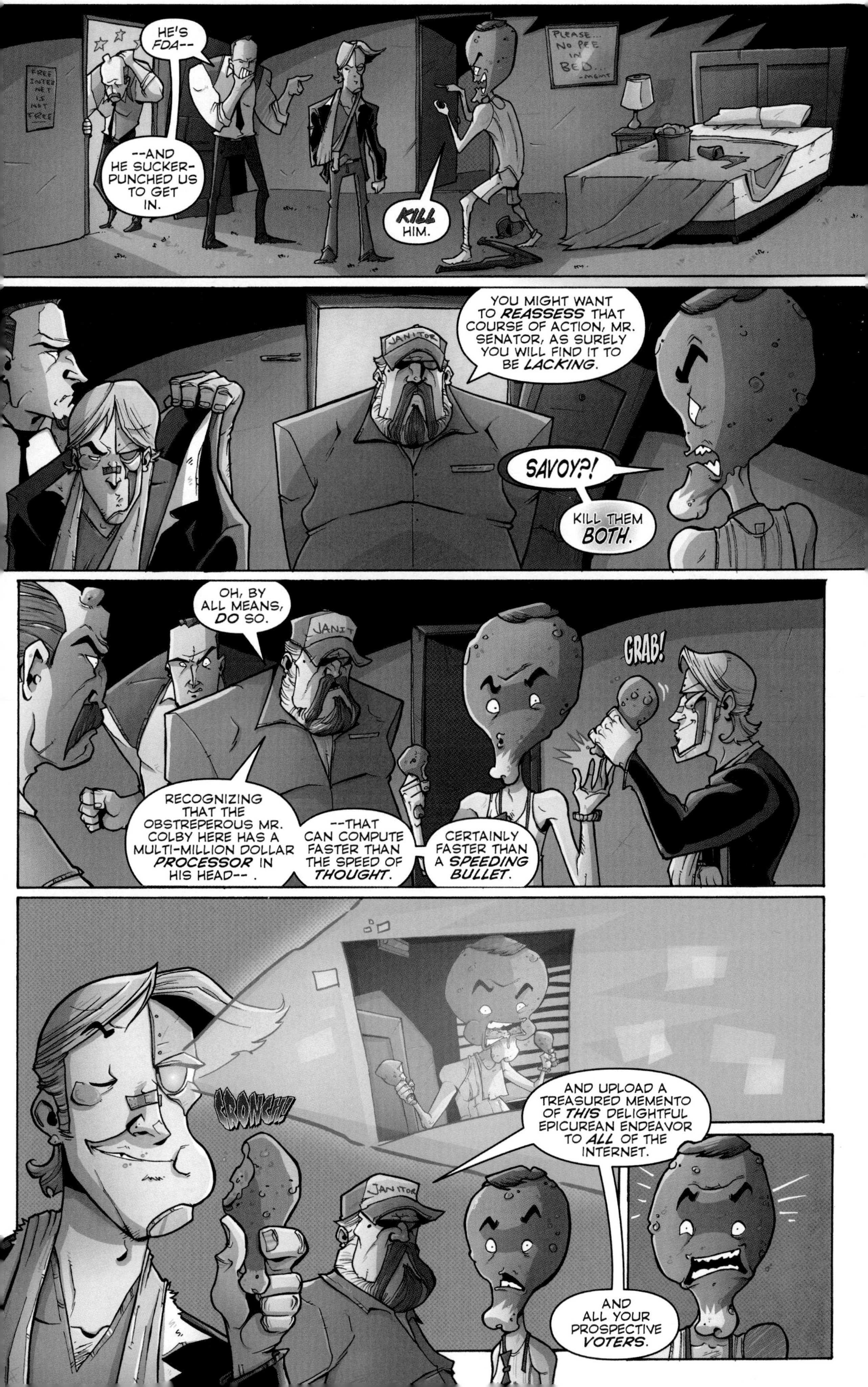
FREE INTERNET IS NOT FREE
PLEASE... NO PEE IN BED... -MGMT
HE'S *FDA*--
--AND HE SUCKER-PUNCHED US TO GET IN.
KILL HIM.
JANITOR
YOU MIGHT WANT TO ***REASSESS*** THAT COURSE OF ACTION, MR. SENATOR, AS SURELY YOU WILL FIND IT TO BE ***LACKING***.
SAVOY?!
KILL THEM ***BOTH***.
OH, BY ALL MEANS, ***DO*** SO.
GRAB!
RECOGNIZING THAT THE OBSTREPEROUS MR. COLBY HERE HAS A MULTI-MILLION DOLLAR ***PROCESSOR*** IN HIS HEAD-- .
--THAT CAN COMPUTE FASTER THAN THE SPEED OF ***THOUGHT***.
CERTAINLY FASTER THAN A ***SPEEDING BULLET***.
CRONCH!
AND UPLOAD A TREASURED MEMENTO OF ***THIS*** DELIGHTFUL EPICUREAN ENDEAVOR TO ***ALL*** OF THE INTERNET.
JANITOR
AND ALL YOUR PROSPECTIVE ***VOTERS***.

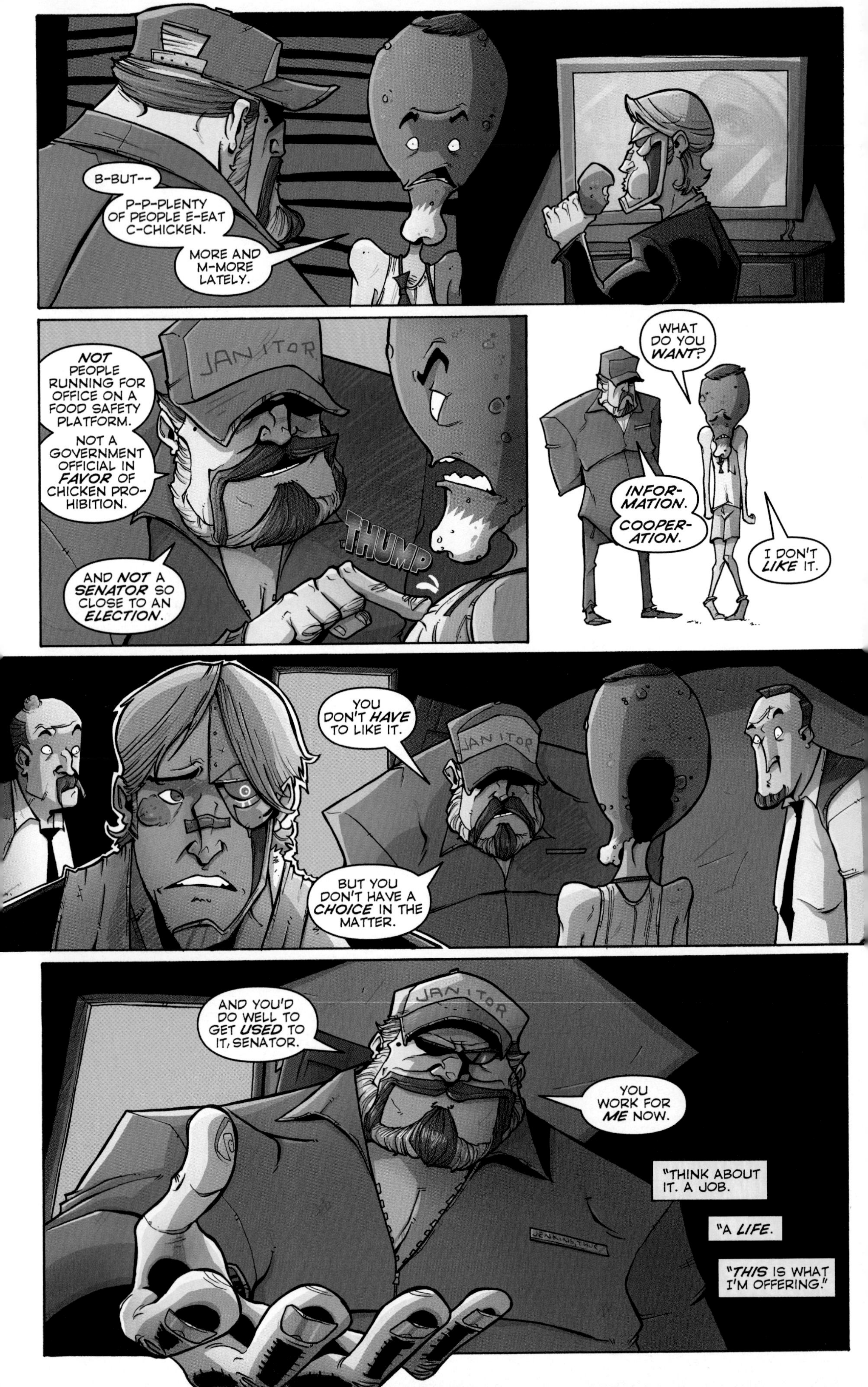
B-BUT--
P-P-PLENTY OF PEOPLE E-EAT C-CHICKEN.
MORE AND M-MORE LATELY.
JANITOR
NOT PEOPLE RUNNING FOR OFFICE ON A FOOD SAFETY PLATFORM.
NOT A GOVERNMENT OFFICIAL IN FAVOR OF CHICKEN PRO-HIBITION.
THUMP
AND NOT A SENATOR SO CLOSE TO AN ELECTION.
WHAT DO YOU WANT?
INFOR-MATION.
COOPER-ATION.
I DON'T LIKE IT.
YOU DON'T HAVE TO LIKE IT.
JANITOR
BUT YOU DON'T HAVE A CHOICE IN THE MATTER.
JANITOR
AND YOU'D DO WELL TO GET USED TO IT, SENATOR.
YOU WORK FOR ME NOW.
"THINK ABOUT IT. A JOB.
"A LIFE.
"THIS IS WHAT I'M OFFERING."

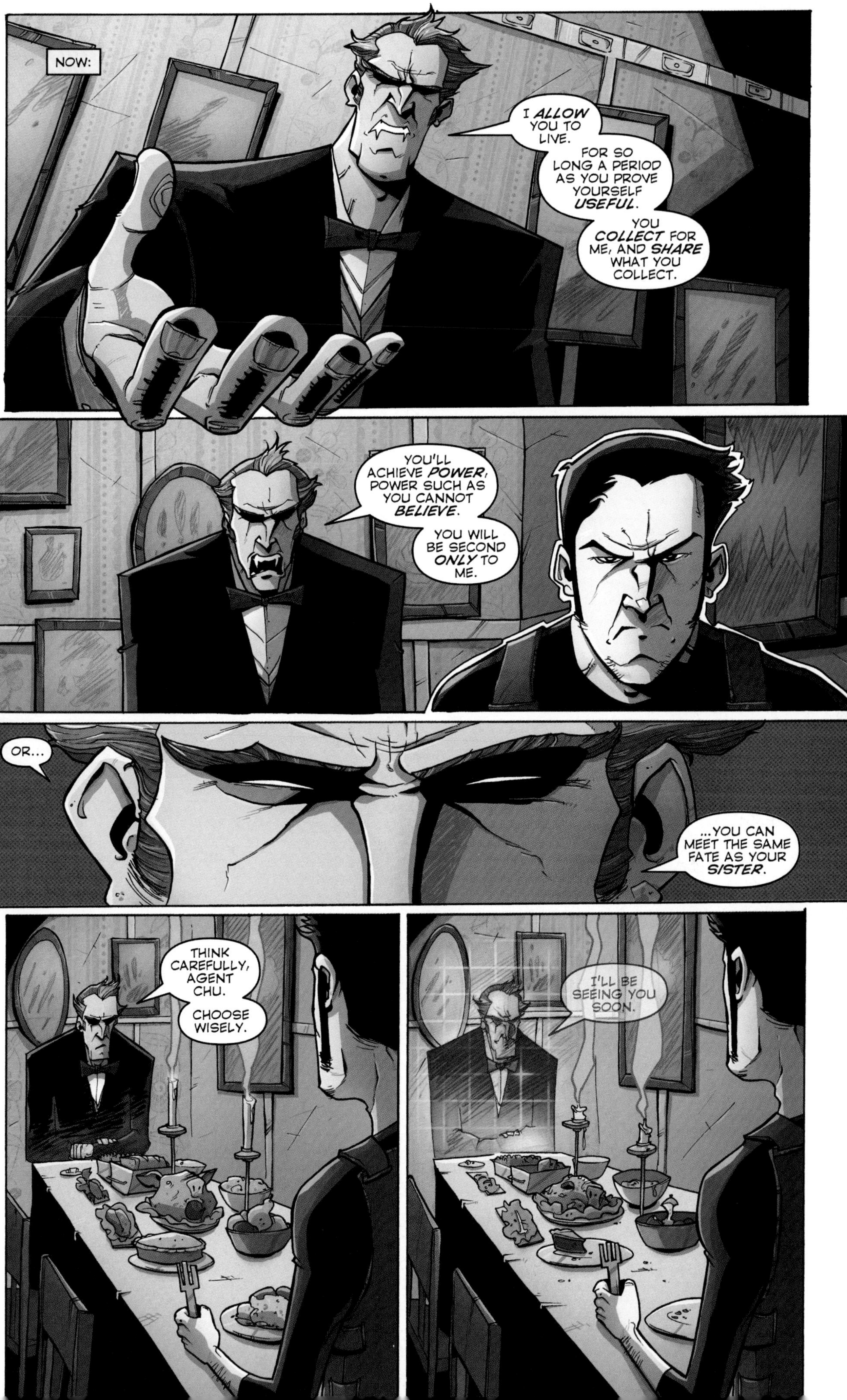
NOW:
I ALLOW YOU TO LIVE.
FOR SO LONG A PERIOD AS YOU PROVE YOURSELF USEFUL.
YOU COLLECT FOR ME, AND SHARE WHAT YOU COLLECT.
YOU'LL ACHIEVE POWER, POWER SUCH AS YOU CANNOT BELIEVE.
YOU WILL BE SECOND ONLY TO ME.
OR...
...YOU CAN MEET THE SAME FATE AS YOUR SISTER.
THINK CAREFULLY, AGENT CHU.
CHOOSE WISELY.
I'LL BE SEEING YOU SOON.

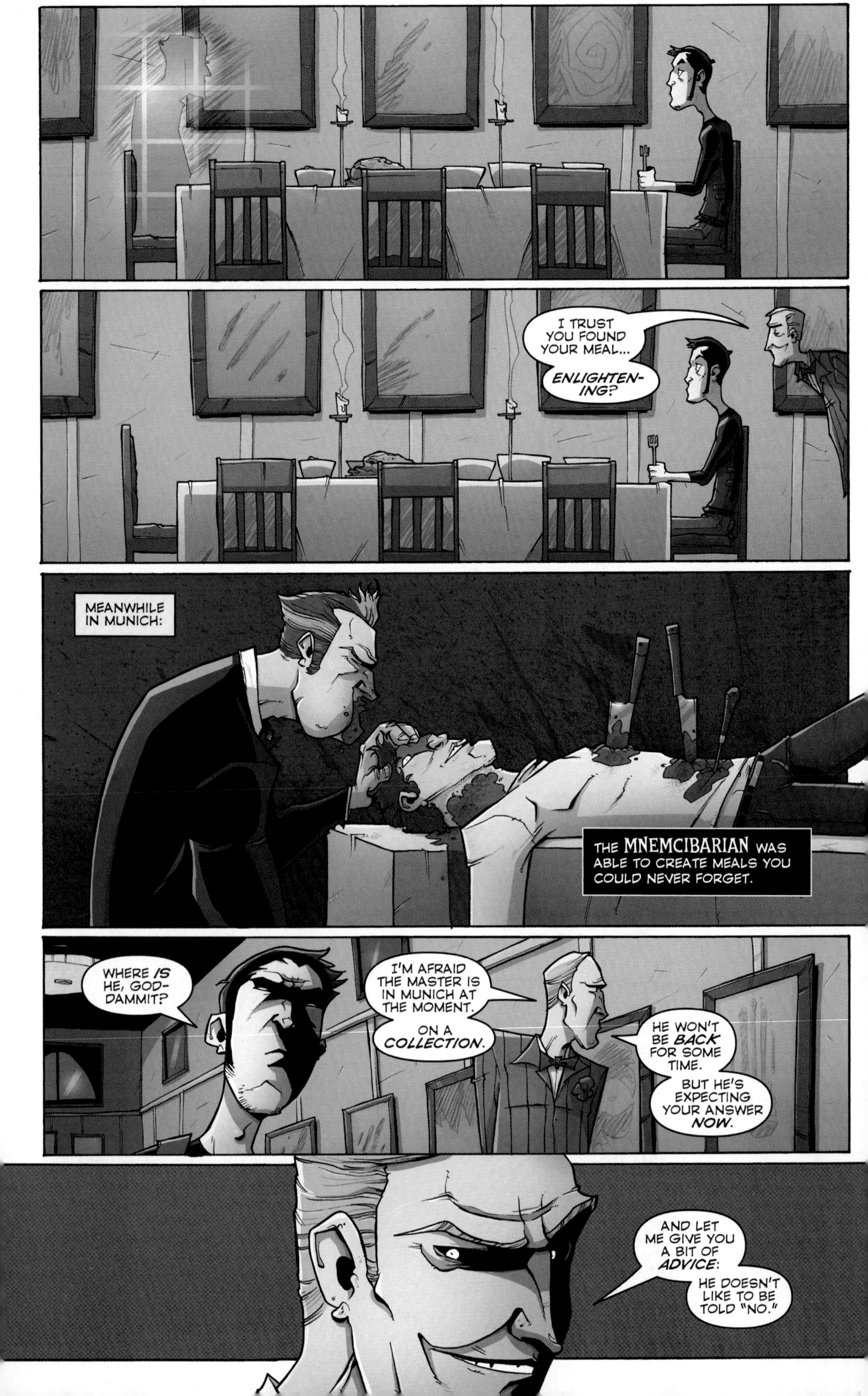
I TRUST YOU FOUND YOUR MEAL... ENLIGHTENING?
MEANWHILE IN MUNICH:
THE MNEMCIBARIAN WAS ABLE TO CREATE MEALS YOU COULD NEVER FORGET.
WHERE IS HE, GOD-DAMMIT?
I'M AFRAID THE MASTER IS IN MUNICH AT THE MOMENT.
ON A COLLECTION.
HE WON'T BE BACK FOR SOME TIME.
BUT HE'S EXPECTING YOUR ANSWER NOW.
AND LET ME GIVE YOU A BIT OF ADVICE:
HE DOESN'T LIKE TO BE TOLD "NO."

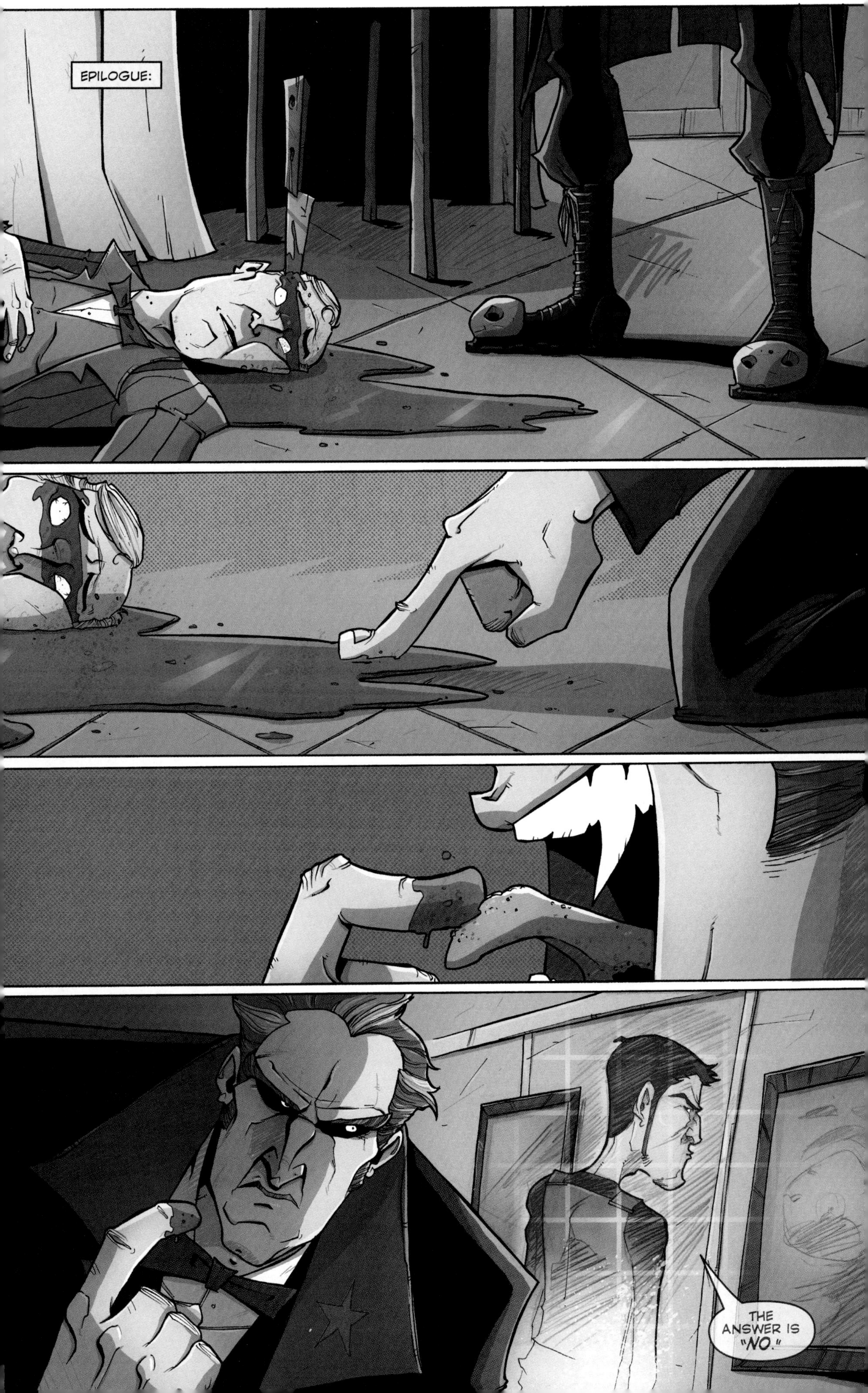
EPILOGUE:
THE ANSWER IS "NO."

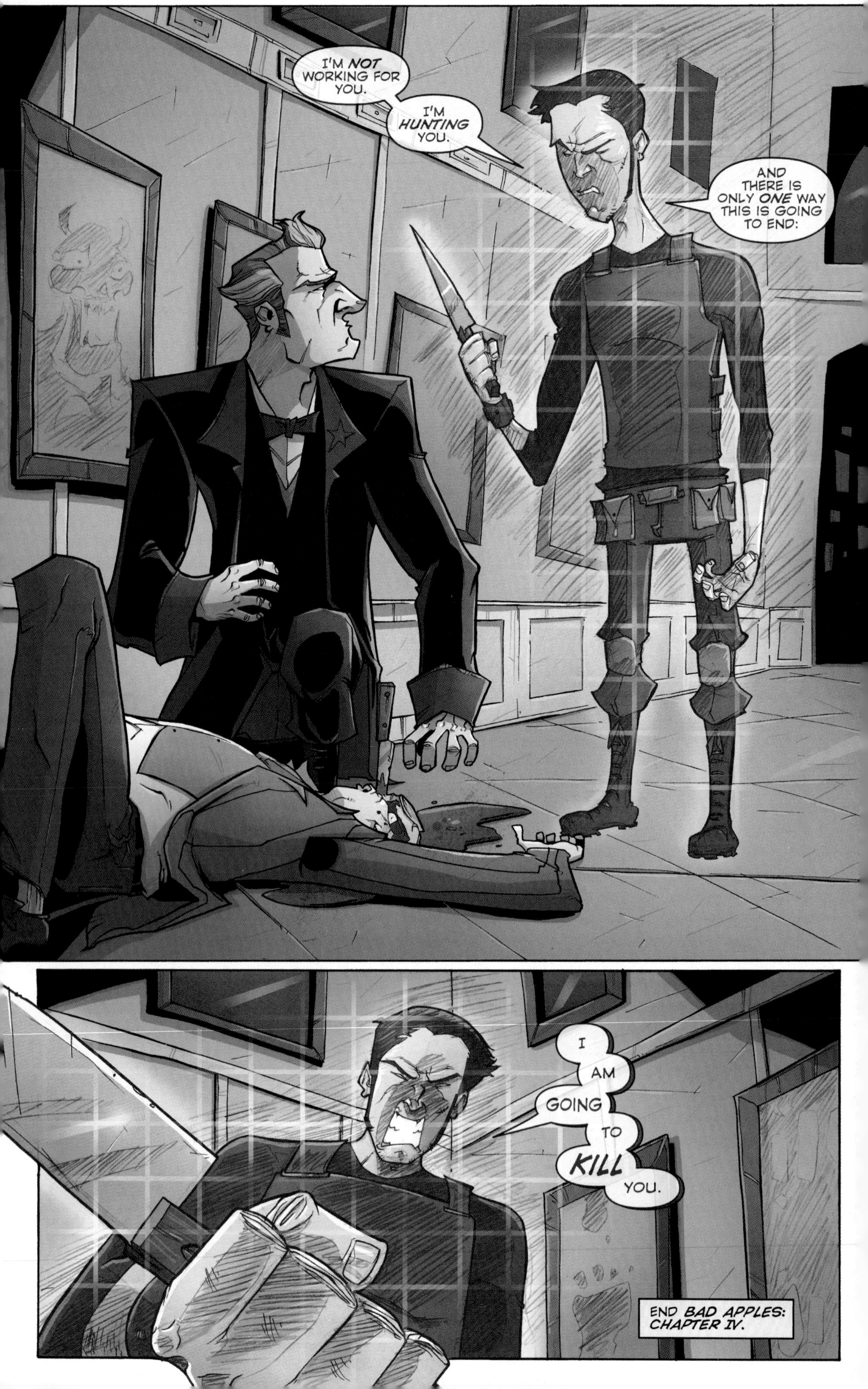
I'M NOT WORKING FOR YOU.
I'M HUNTING YOU.
AND THERE IS ONLY ONE WAY THIS IS GOING TO END:
I AM GOING TO KILL YOU.
END BAD APPLES: CHAPTER IV.

Chapter Five

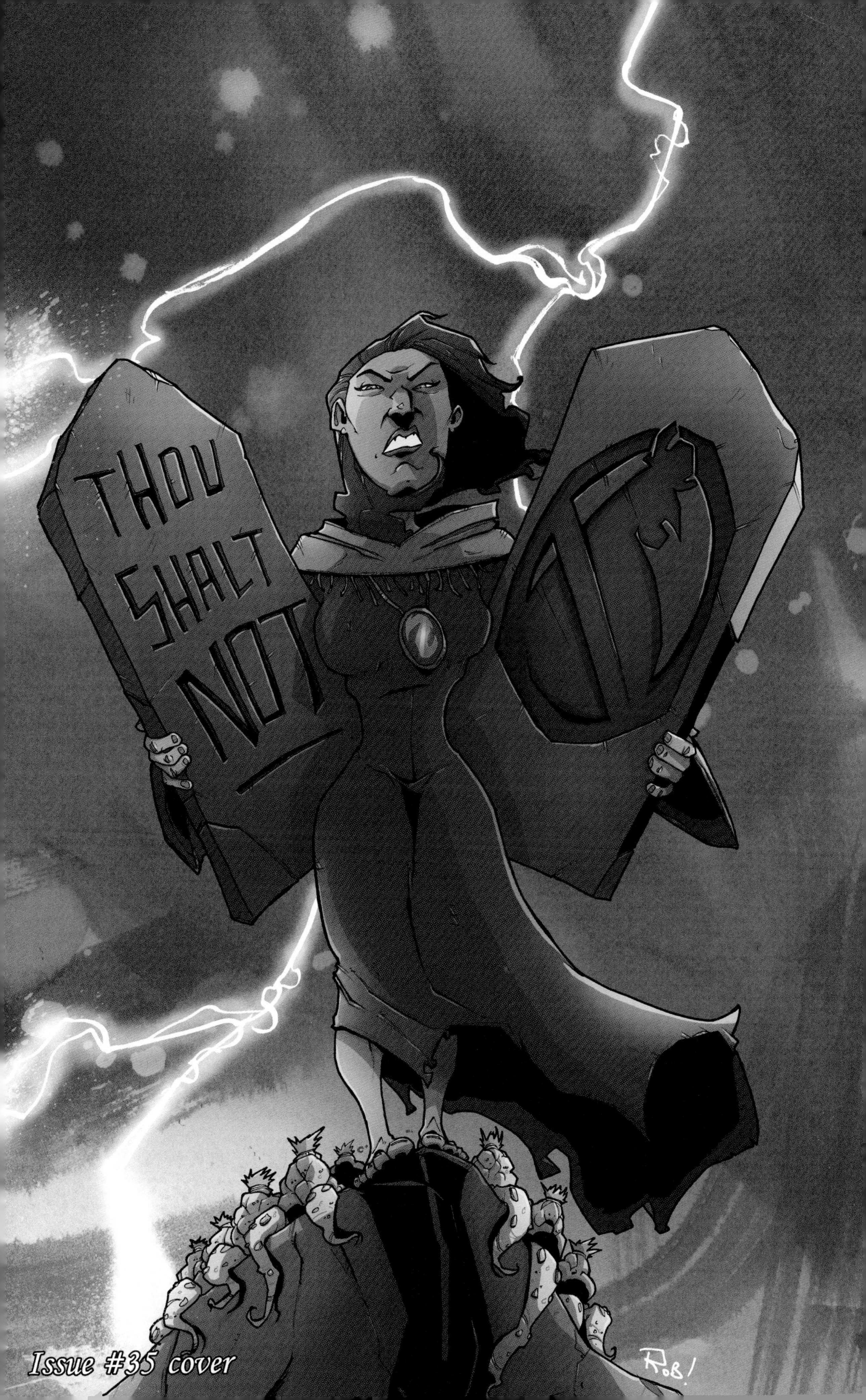
THOU SHALT NOT
ROB!
Issue #35 cover

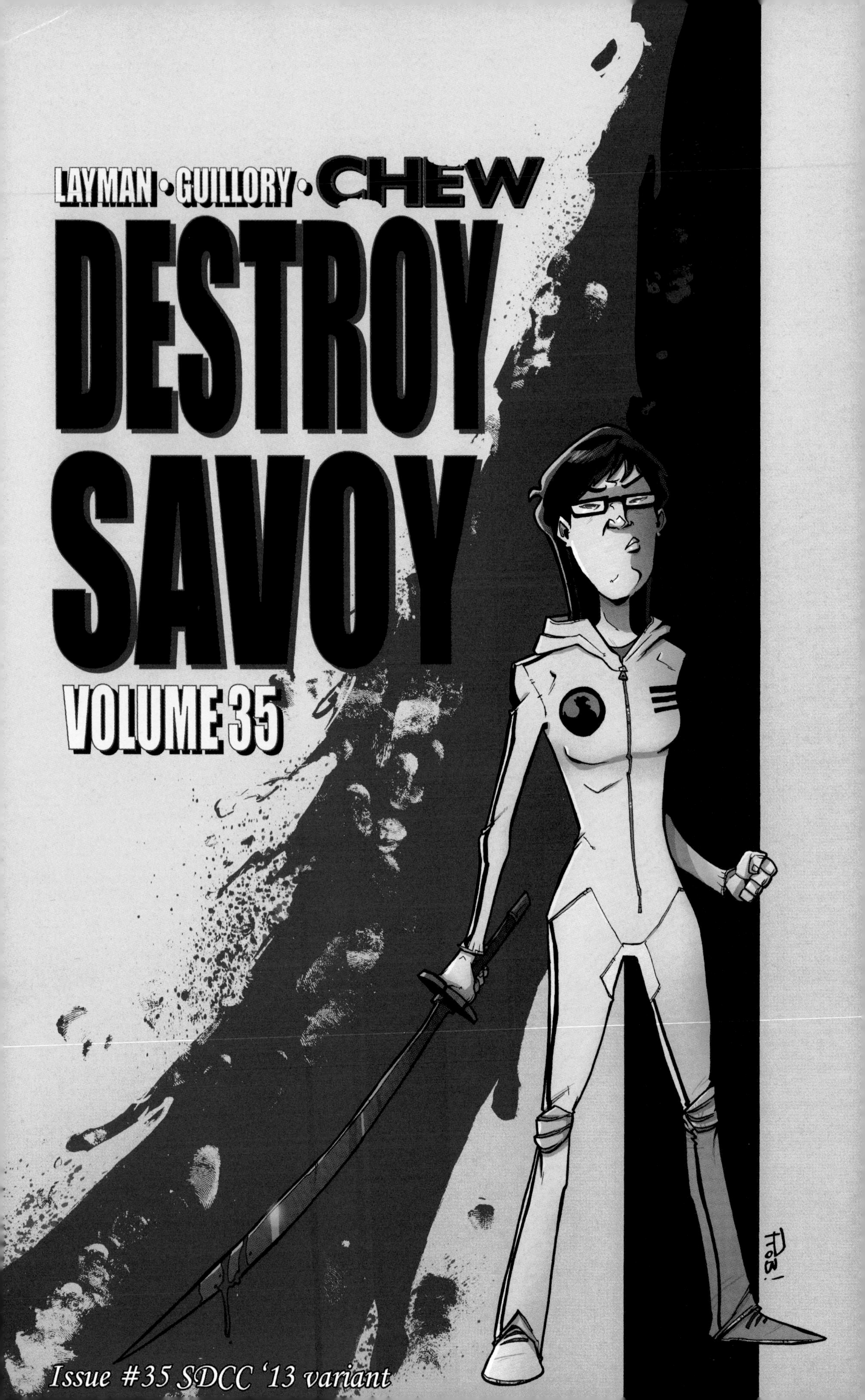
LAYMAN · GUILLORY · CHEW
DESTROY SAVOY
VOLUME 35
Issue #35 SDCC '13 variant

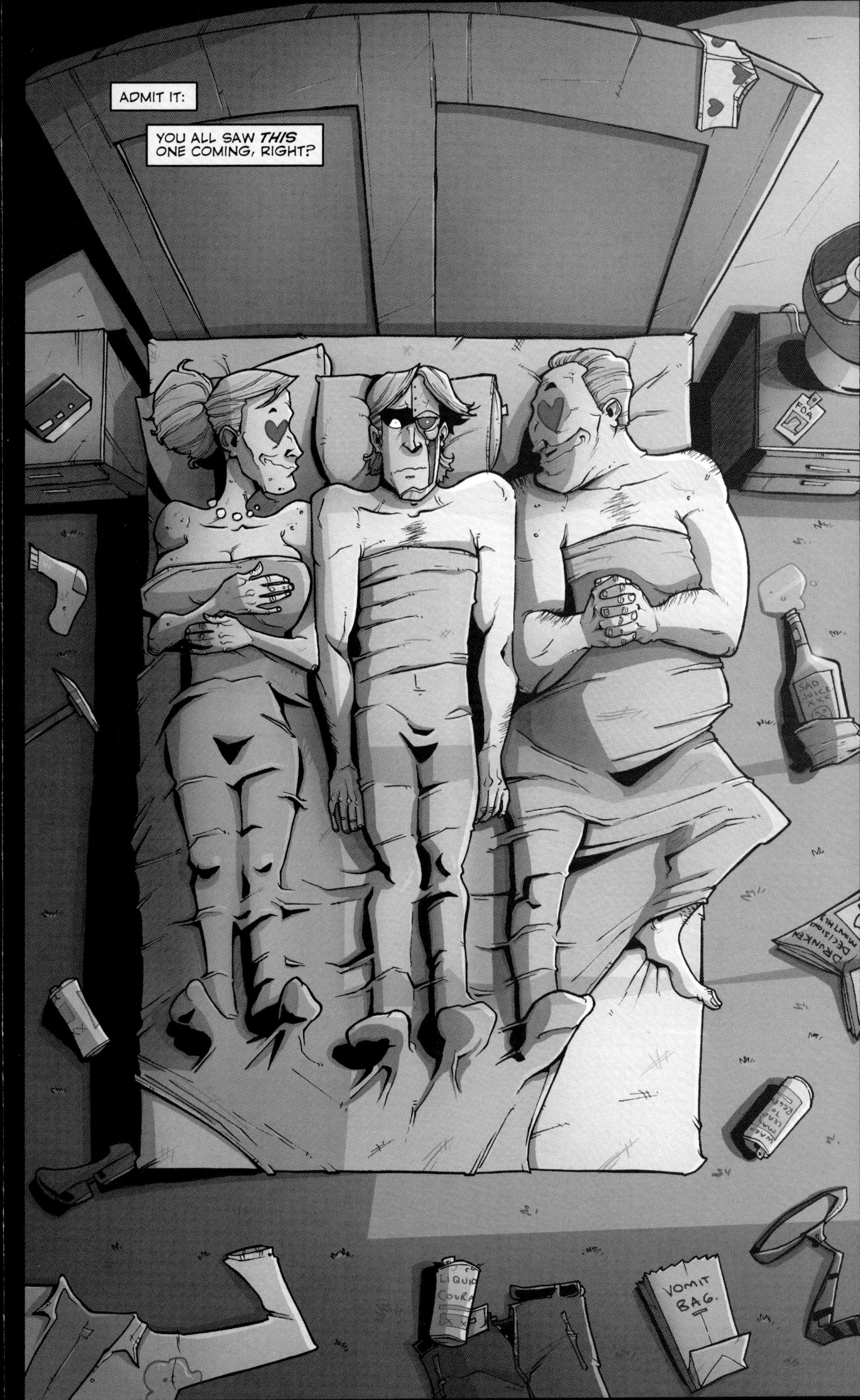
ADMIT IT:
YOU ALL SAW *THIS* ONE COMING, RIGHT?
VOMIT BAG.

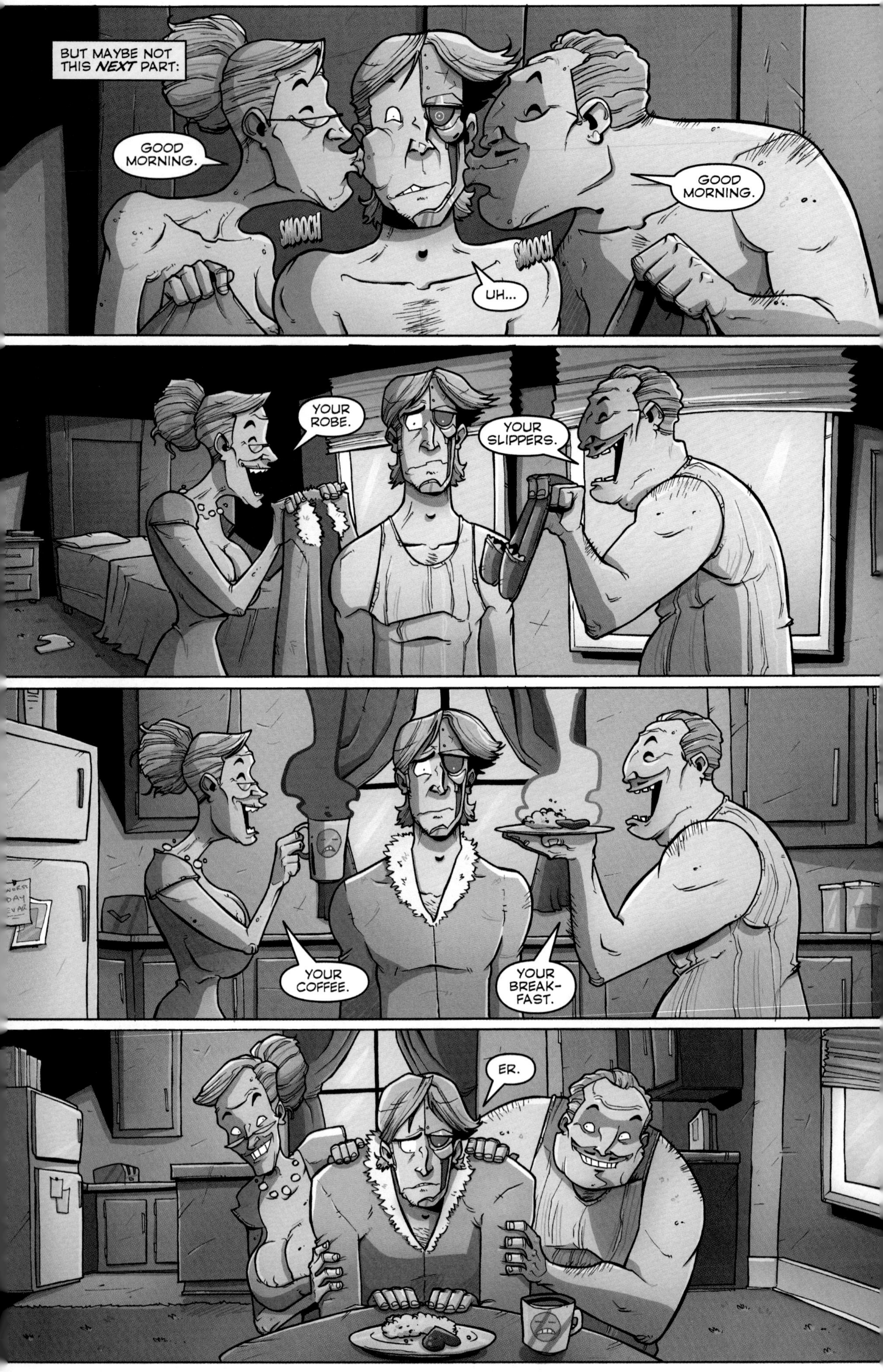
BUT MAYBE NOT THIS NEXT PART:
GOOD MORNING.
SMOOCH
GOOD MORNING.
SMOOCH
UH...
YOUR ROBE.
YOUR SLIPPERS.
YOUR COFFEE.
YOUR BREAK-FAST.
ER.

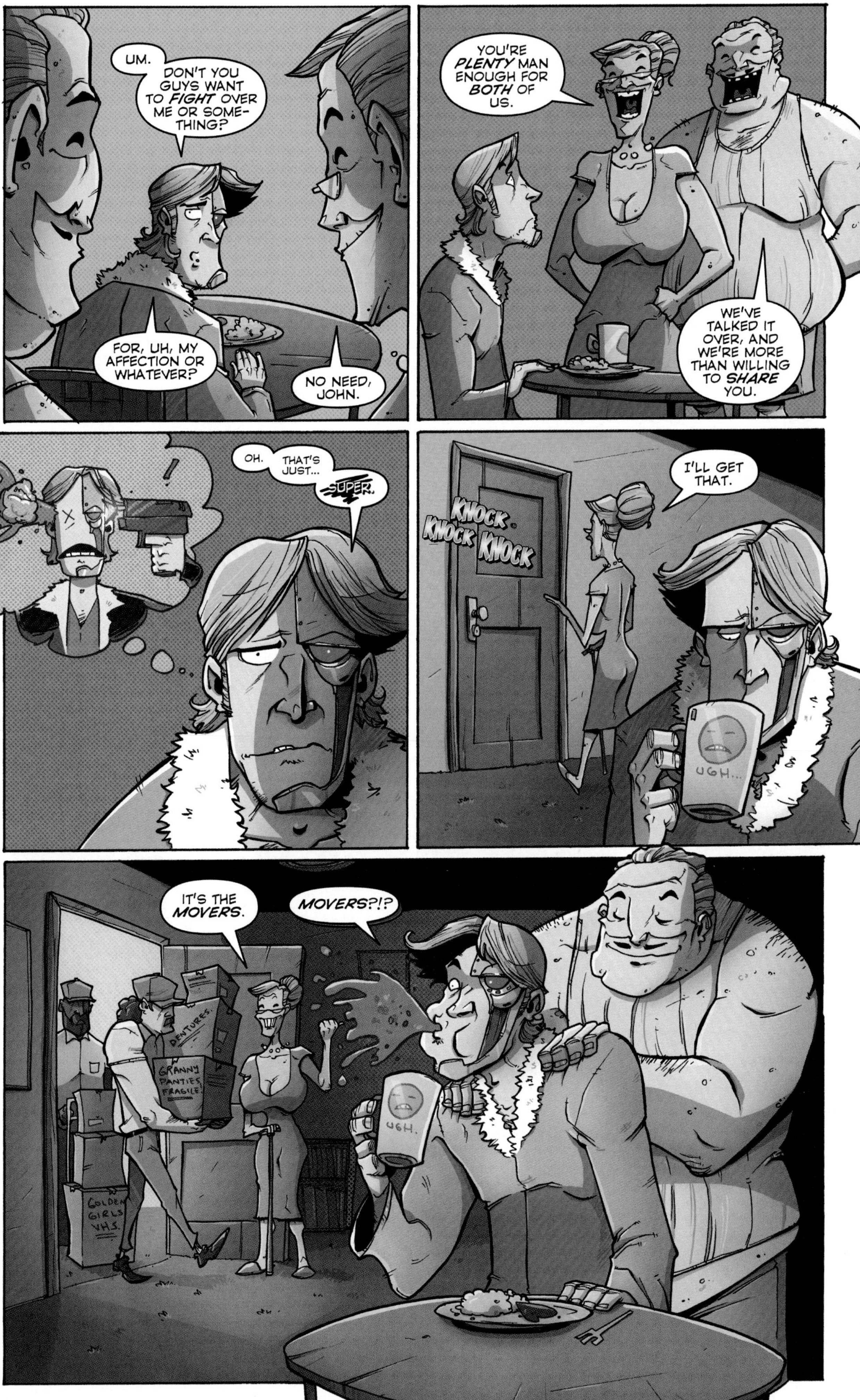
UM.
DON'T YOU GUYS WANT TO FIGHT OVER ME OR SOME-THING?
FOR, UH, MY AFFECTION OR WHATEVER?
NO NEED, JOHN.
YOU'RE PLENTY MAN ENOUGH FOR BOTH OF US.
WE'VE TALKED IT OVER, AND WE'RE MORE THAN WILLING TO SHARE YOU.
!
OH.
THAT'S JUST...
SUPER.
KNOCK KNOCK KNOCK
I'LL GET THAT.
UGH...
IT'S THE MOVERS.
MOVERS?!?
DENTURES.
GRANNY PANTIES FRAGILE
GOLDEN GIRLS V.H.S.
UGH.

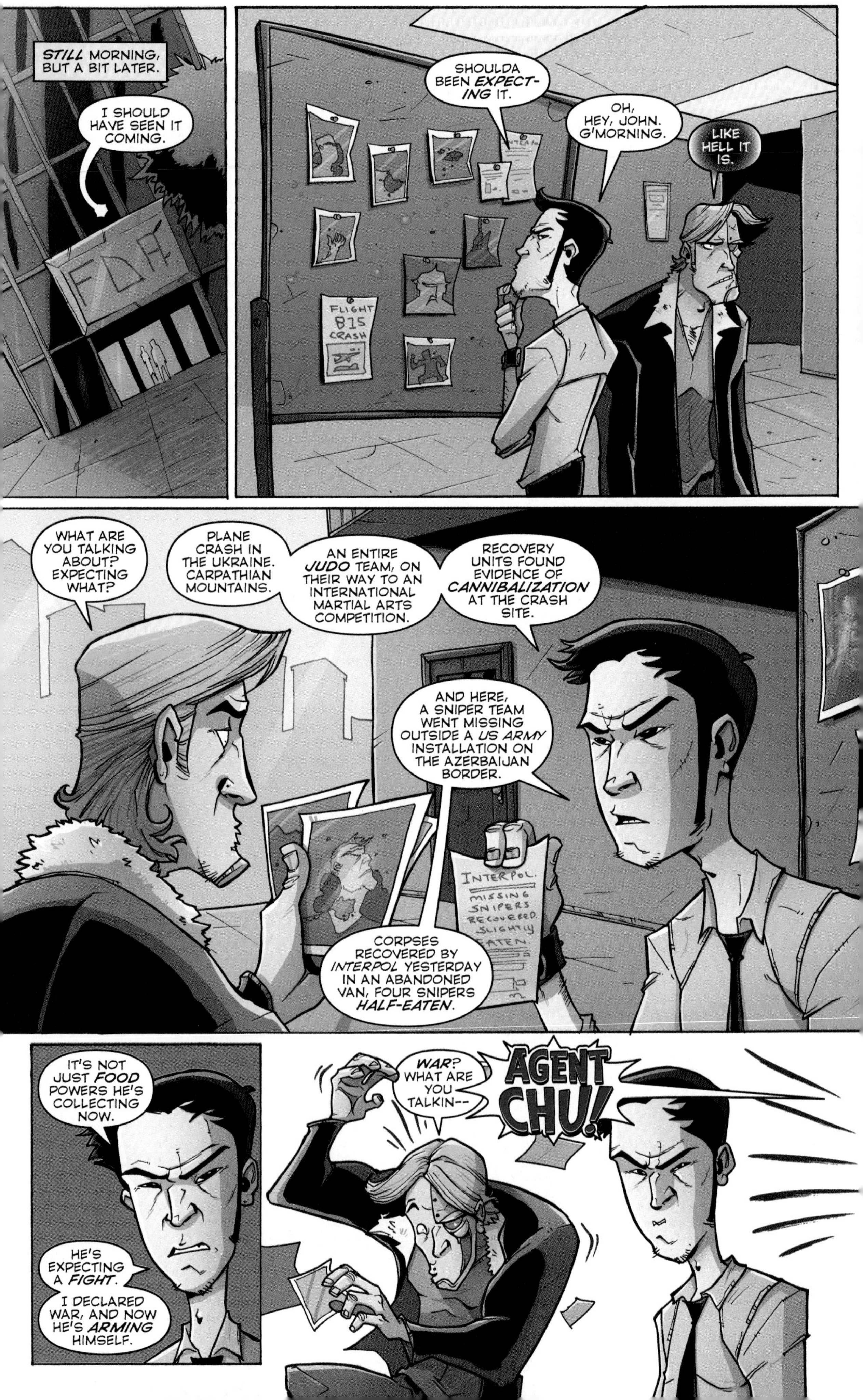

STILL MORNING, BUT A BIT LATER.
I SHOULD HAVE SEEN IT COMING.
FDA
SHOULDA BEEN EXPECTING IT.
OH, HEY, JOHN. G'MORNING.
LIKE HELL IT IS.
FLIGHT 815 CRASH
WHAT ARE YOU TALKING ABOUT? EXPECTING WHAT?
PLANE CRASH IN THE UKRAINE. CARPATHIAN MOUNTAINS.
AN ENTIRE JUDO TEAM, ON THEIR WAY TO AN INTERNATIONAL MARTIAL ARTS COMPETITION.
RECOVERY UNITS FOUND EVIDENCE OF CANNIBALIZATION AT THE CRASH SITE.
AND HERE, A SNIPER TEAM WENT MISSING OUTSIDE A US ARMY INSTALLATION ON THE AZERBAIJAN BORDER.
INTERPOL. MISSING SNIPERS RECOVERED. SLIGHTLY EATEN.
CORPSES RECOVERED BY INTERPOL YESTERDAY IN AN ABANDONED VAN, FOUR SNIPERS HALF-EATEN.
IT'S NOT JUST FOOD POWERS HE'S COLLECTING NOW.
HE'S EXPECTING A FIGHT.
I DECLARED WAR, AND NOW HE'S ARMING HIMSELF.
WAR? WHAT ARE YOU TALKIN--
AGENT CHU!

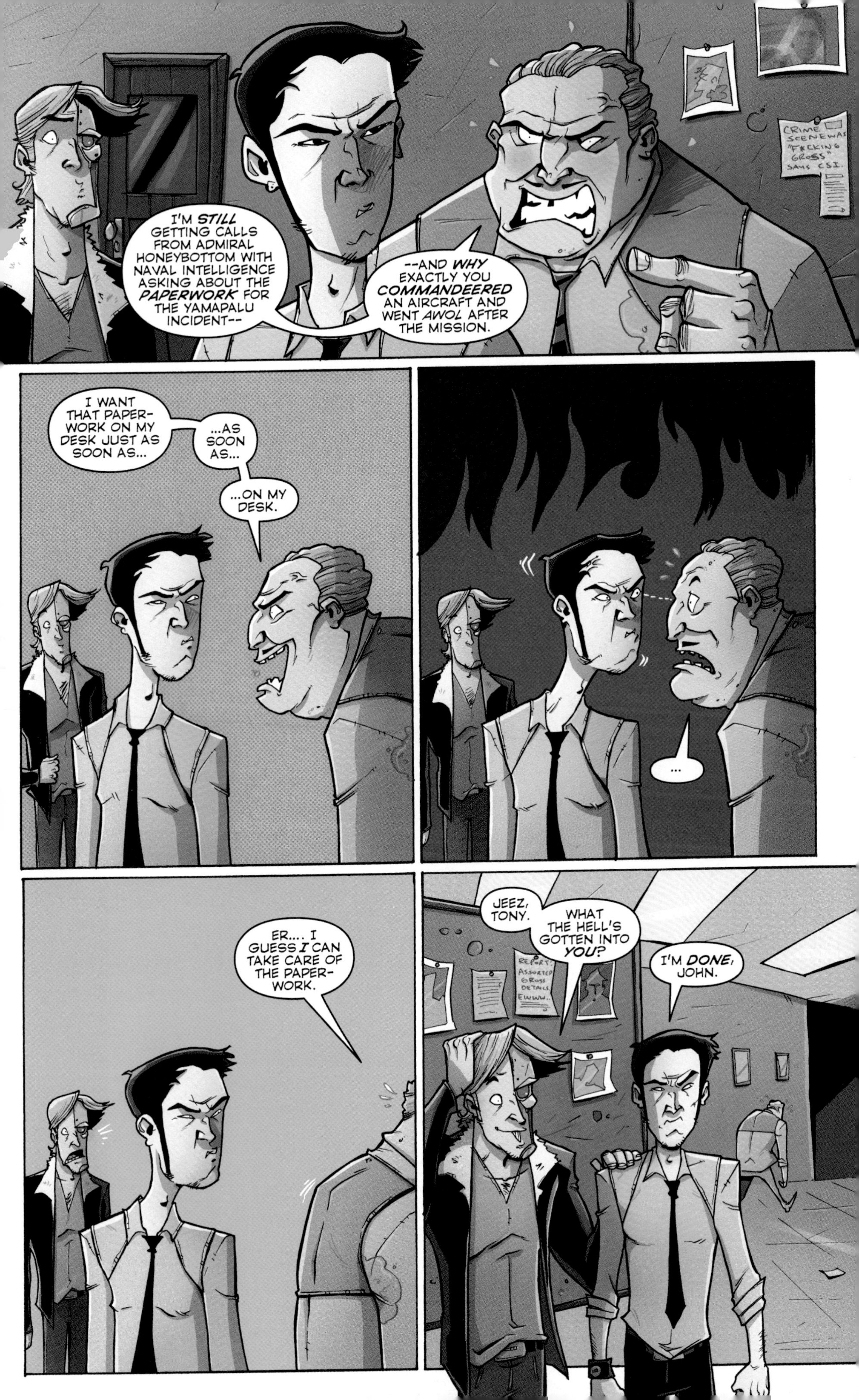
CRIME SCENE WAS "F#CKING GROSS" SAYS CSI.
I'M STILL GETTING CALLS FROM ADMIRAL HONEYBOTTOM WITH NAVAL INTELLIGENCE ASKING ABOUT THE PAPERWORK FOR THE YAMAPALU INCIDENT--
--AND WHY EXACTLY YOU COMMANDEERED AN AIRCRAFT AND WENT AWOL AFTER THE MISSION.
I WANT THAT PAPER-WORK ON MY DESK JUST AS SOON AS...
...AS SOON AS...
...ON MY DESK.
...
ER.... I GUESS I CAN TAKE CARE OF THE PAPER-WORK.
JEEZ, TONY.
WHAT THE HELL'S GOTTEN INTO YOU?
I'M DONE, JOHN.
REPORT: ASSORTED GROSS DETAILS. EWWW.

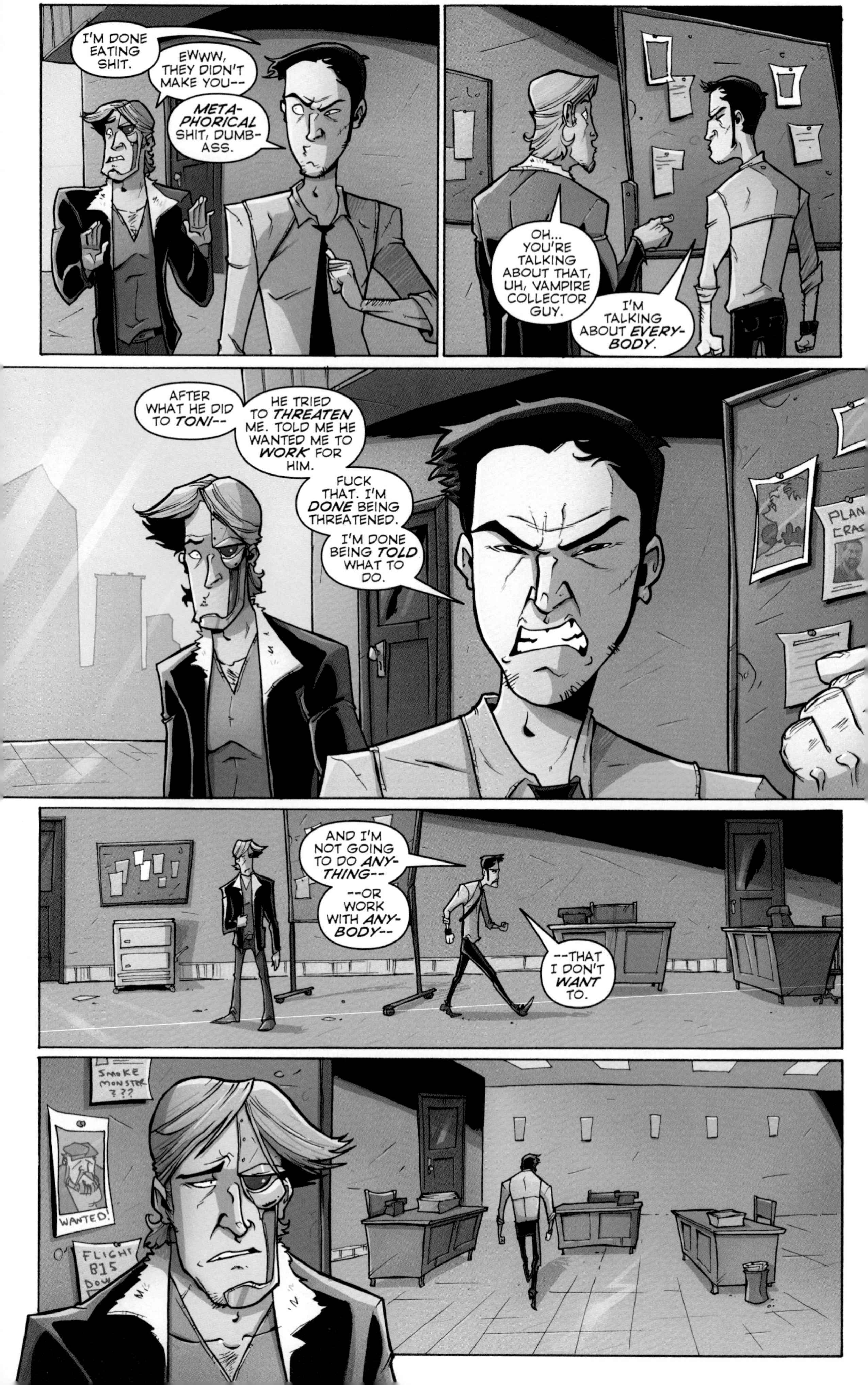
I'M DONE EATING SHIT.
EWWW, THEY DIDN'T MAKE YOU--
METAPHORICAL SHIT, DUMB-ASS.
OH... YOU'RE TALKING ABOUT THAT, UH, VAMPIRE COLLECTOR GUY.
I'M TALKING ABOUT EVERYBODY.
AFTER WHAT HE DID TO TONI--
HE TRIED TO THREATEN ME. TOLD ME HE WANTED ME TO WORK FOR HIM.
FUCK THAT. I'M DONE BEING THREATENED.
I'M DONE BEING TOLD WHAT TO DO.
PLAN CRAS
AND I'M NOT GOING TO DO ANYTHING--
--OR WORK WITH ANYBODY--
--THAT I DON'T WANT TO.
SMOKE MONSTER ???
WANTED!
FLIGHT 815 DOW

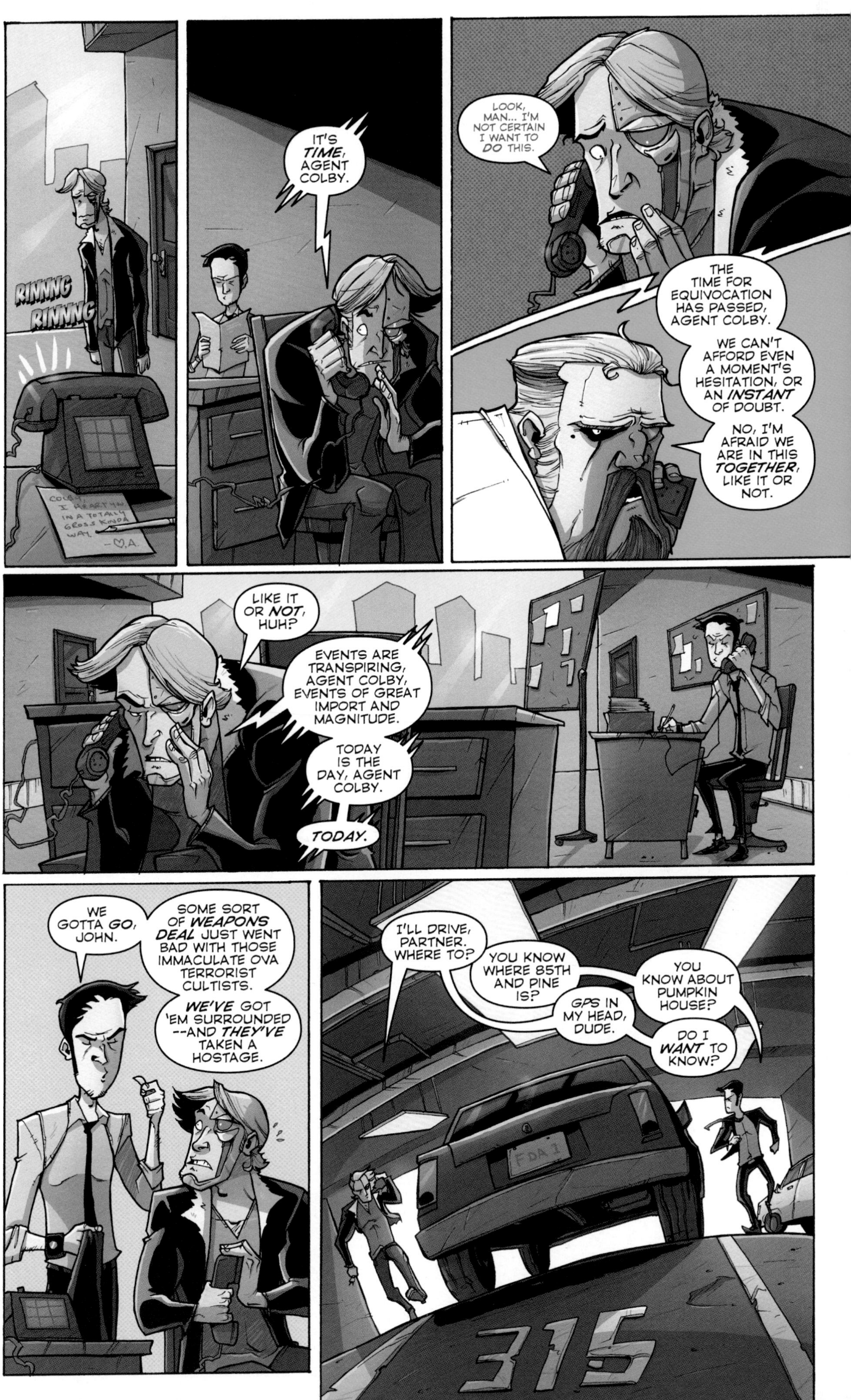
RINNNG
RINNNG
I HEART YOU
IN A TOTALLY GROSS KINDA WAY.
—♡.A.
IT'S *TIME*, AGENT COLBY.
LOOK, MAN... I'M NOT CERTAIN I WANT TO *DO* THIS.
THE TIME FOR EQUIVOCATION HAS PASSED, AGENT COLBY.
WE CAN'T AFFORD EVEN A MOMENT'S HESITATION, OR AN *INSTANT* OF DOUBT.
NO, I'M AFRAID WE ARE IN THIS *TOGETHER*, LIKE IT OR NOT.
LIKE IT OR *NOT*, HUH?
EVENTS ARE TRANSPIRING, AGENT COLBY, EVENTS OF GREAT IMPORT AND MAGNITUDE.
TODAY IS THE DAY, AGENT COLBY.
TODAY.
WE GOTTA *GO*, JOHN.
SOME SORT OF ***WEAPONS DEAL*** JUST WENT BAD WITH THOSE IMMACULATE OVA TERRORIST CULTISTS.
WE'VE GOT 'EM SURROUNDED --AND ***THEY'VE*** TAKEN A HOSTAGE.
I'LL DRIVE, PARTNER. WHERE TO?
YOU KNOW WHERE 85TH AND PINE IS?
GPS IN MY HEAD, DUDE.
YOU KNOW ABOUT PUMPKIN HOUSE?
DO I *WANT* TO KNOW?
FDA 1
315

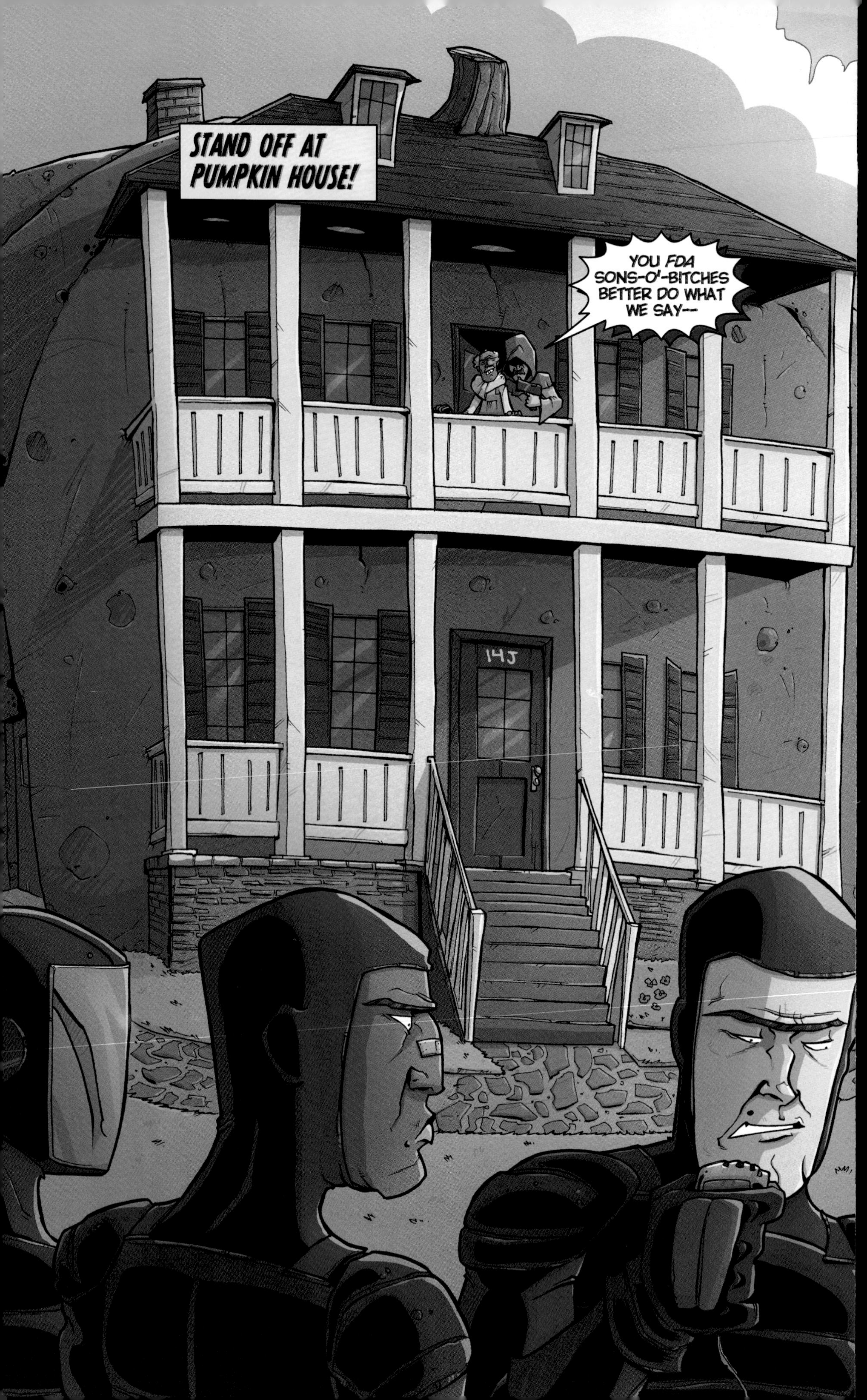
STAND OFF AT PUMPKIN HOUSE!
YOU FDA SONS-O'-BITCHES BETTER DO WHAT WE SAY--
14J

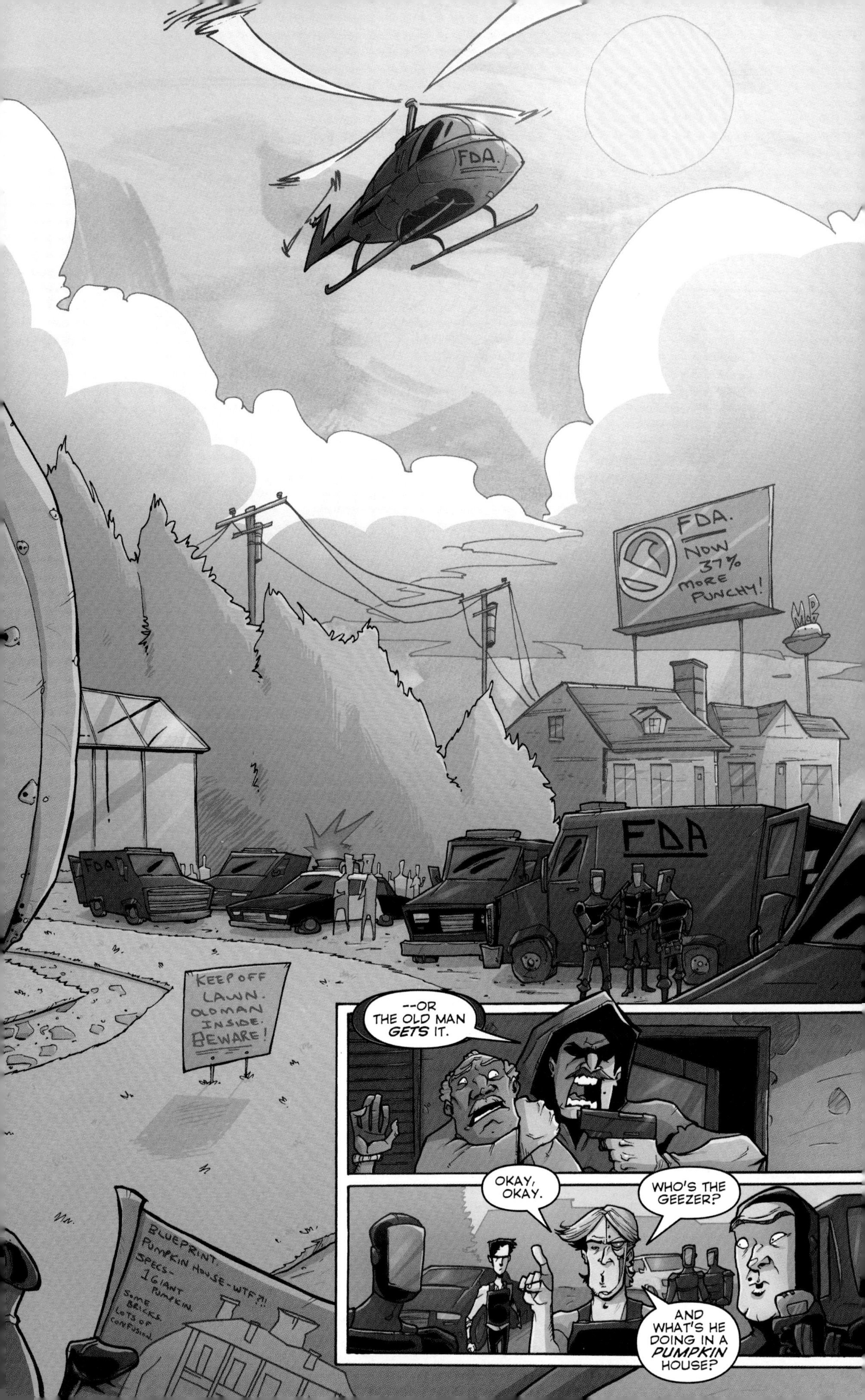
FDA.
FDA. NOW 37% MORE PUNCHY!
FDA
KEEP OFF LAWN. OLD MAN INSIDE. BEWARE!
--OR THE OLD MAN GETS IT.
OKAY, OKAY.
WHO'S THE GEEZER?
AND WHAT'S HE DOING IN A PUMPKIN HOUSE?
BLUEPRINT. PUMPKIN HOUSE-WTF?!! SPECS- 1 GIANT PUMPKIN. SOME BRICKS. LOTS OF CONFUSION.

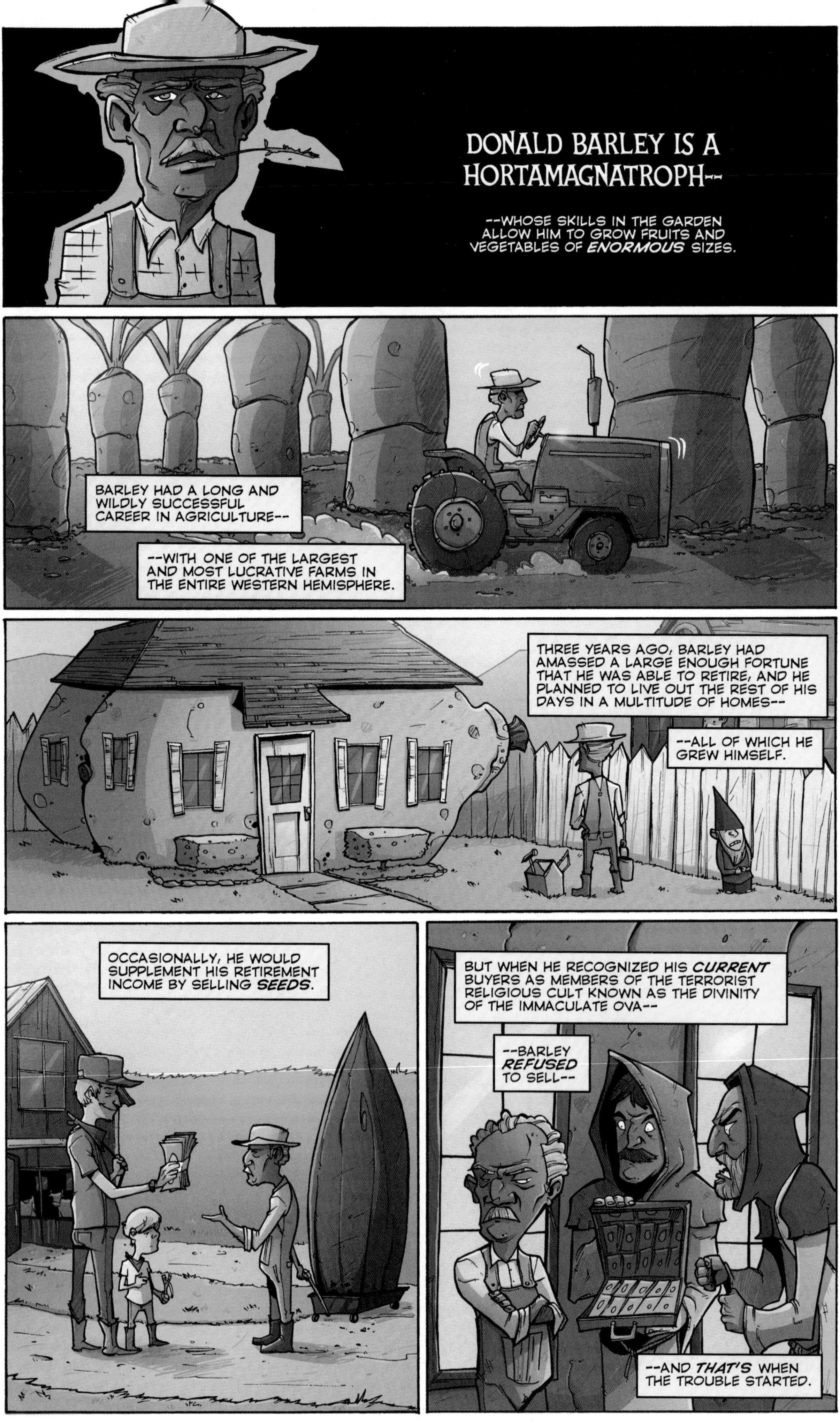
DONALD BARLEY IS A HORTAMAGNATROPH--
--WHOSE SKILLS IN THE GARDEN ALLOW HIM TO GROW FRUITS AND VEGETABLES OF *ENORMOUS* SIZES.
BARLEY HAD A LONG AND WILDLY SUCCESSFUL CAREER IN AGRICULTURE--
--WITH ONE OF THE LARGEST AND MOST LUCRATIVE FARMS IN THE ENTIRE WESTERN HEMISPHERE.
THREE YEARS AGO, BARLEY HAD AMASSED A LARGE ENOUGH FORTUNE THAT HE WAS ABLE TO RETIRE, AND HE PLANNED TO LIVE OUT THE REST OF HIS DAYS IN A MULTITUDE OF HOMES--
--ALL OF WHICH HE GREW HIMSELF.
OCCASIONALLY, HE WOULD SUPPLEMENT HIS RETIREMENT INCOME BY SELLING *SEEDS*.
BUT WHEN HE RECOGNIZED HIS *CURRENT* BUYERS AS MEMBERS OF THE TERRORIST RELIGIOUS CULT KNOWN AS THE DIVINITY OF THE IMMACULATE OVA--
--BARLEY *REFUSED* TO SELL--
--AND *THAT'S* WHEN THE TROUBLE STARTED.

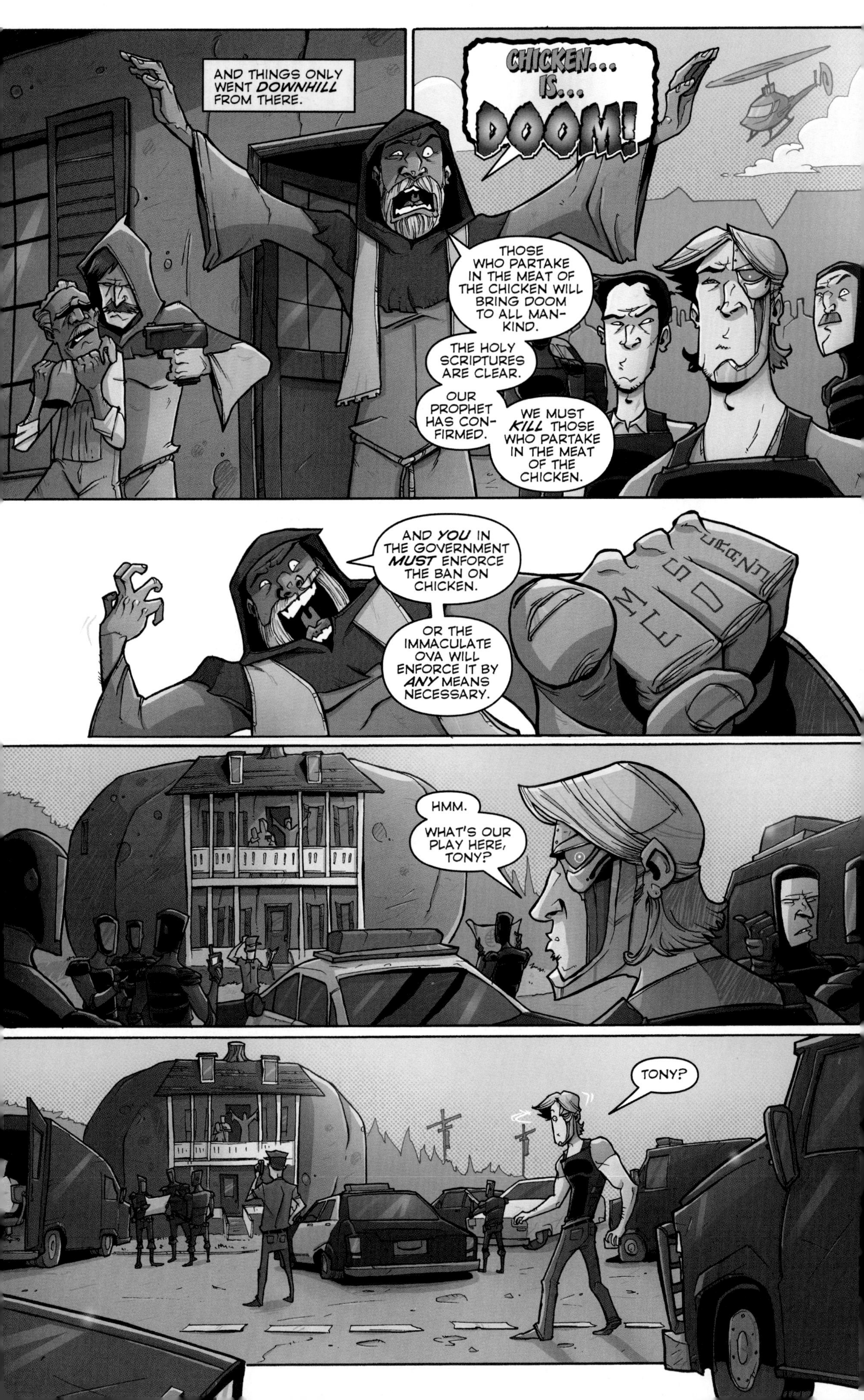
AND THINGS ONLY WENT DOWNHILL FROM THERE.
CHICKEN... IS... DOOM!
THOSE WHO PARTAKE IN THE MEAT OF THE CHICKEN WILL BRING DOOM TO ALL MAN-KIND.
THE HOLY SCRIPTURES ARE CLEAR.
OUR PROPHET HAS CON-FIRMED.
WE MUST KILL THOSE WHO PARTAKE IN THE MEAT OF THE CHICKEN.
AND YOU IN THE GOVERNMENT MUST ENFORCE THE BAN ON CHICKEN.
OR THE IMMACULATE OVA WILL ENFORCE IT BY ANY MEANS NECESSARY.
HMM.
WHAT'S OUR PLAY HERE, TONY?
TONY?

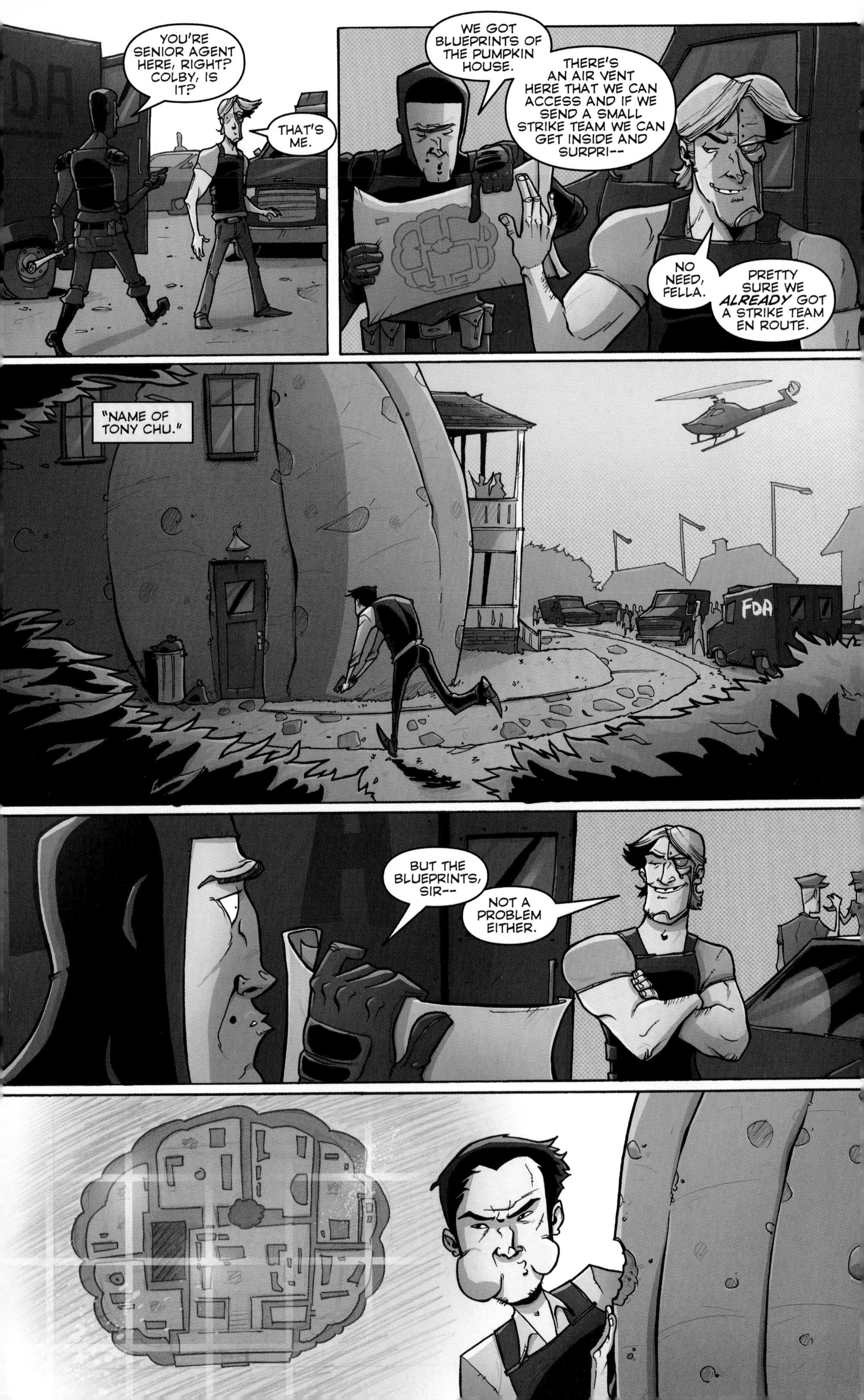
YOU'RE SENIOR AGENT HERE, RIGHT? COLBY, IS IT?
THAT'S ME.
WE GOT BLUEPRINTS OF THE PUMPKIN HOUSE.
THERE'S AN AIR VENT HERE THAT WE CAN ACCESS AND IF WE SEND A SMALL STRIKE TEAM WE CAN GET INSIDE AND SURPRI--
NO NEED, FELLA.
PRETTY SURE WE ALREADY GOT A STRIKE TEAM EN ROUTE.
"NAME OF TONY CHU."
FDA
BUT THE BLUEPRINTS, SIR--
NOT A PROBLEM EITHER.

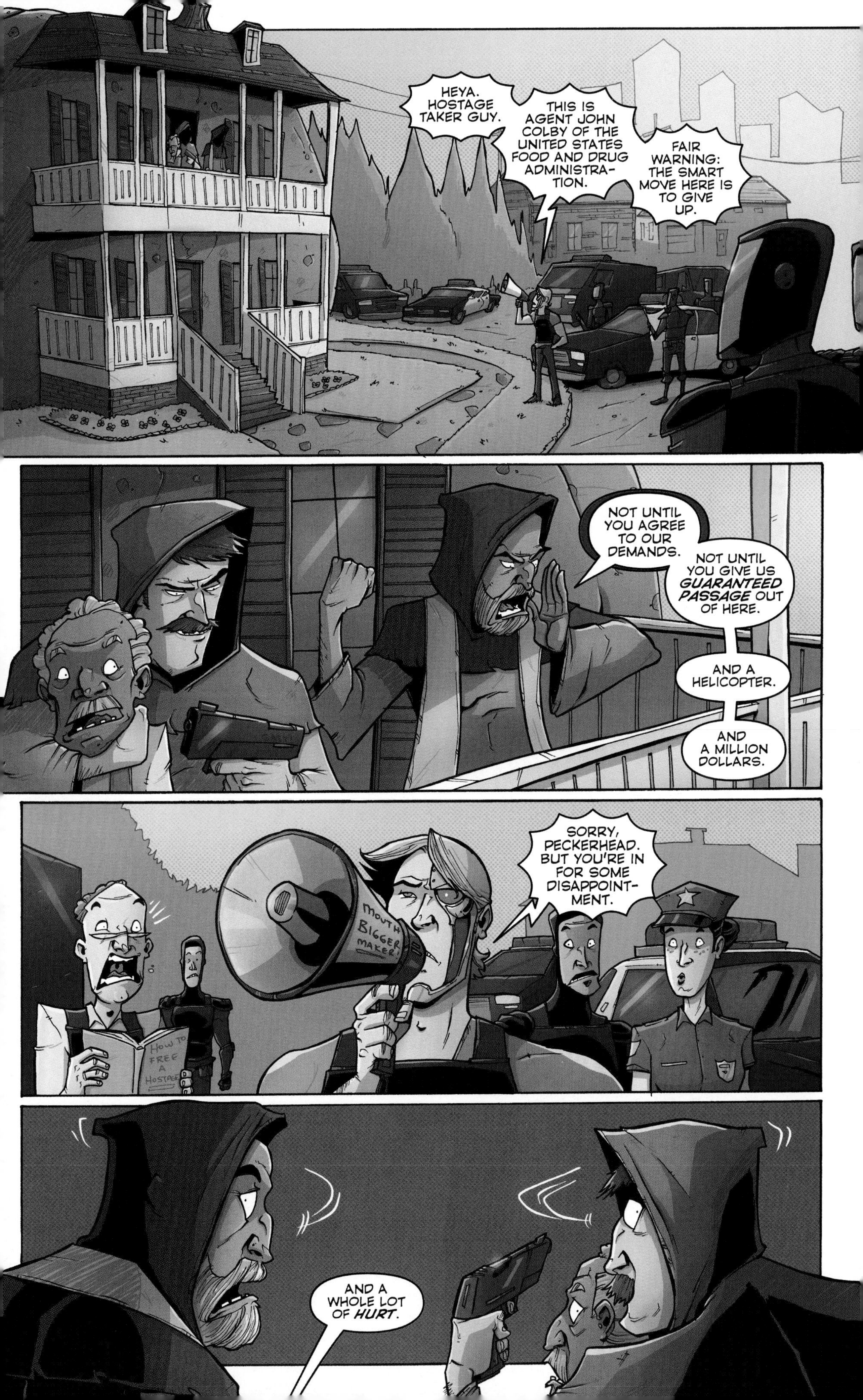
HEYA. HOSTAGE TAKER GUY.
THIS IS AGENT JOHN COLBY OF THE UNITED STATES FOOD AND DRUG ADMINISTRATION.
FAIR WARNING: THE SMART MOVE HERE IS TO GIVE UP.
NOT UNTIL YOU AGREE TO OUR DEMANDS.
NOT UNTIL YOU GIVE US ***GUARANTEED PASSAGE*** OUT OF HERE.
AND A HELICOPTER.
AND A MILLION DOLLARS.
MOUTH BIGGER MAKER!
HOW TO FREE A
SORRY, PECKERHEAD. BUT YOU'RE IN FOR SOME DISAPPOINTMENT.
AND A WHOLE LOT OF ***HURT***.

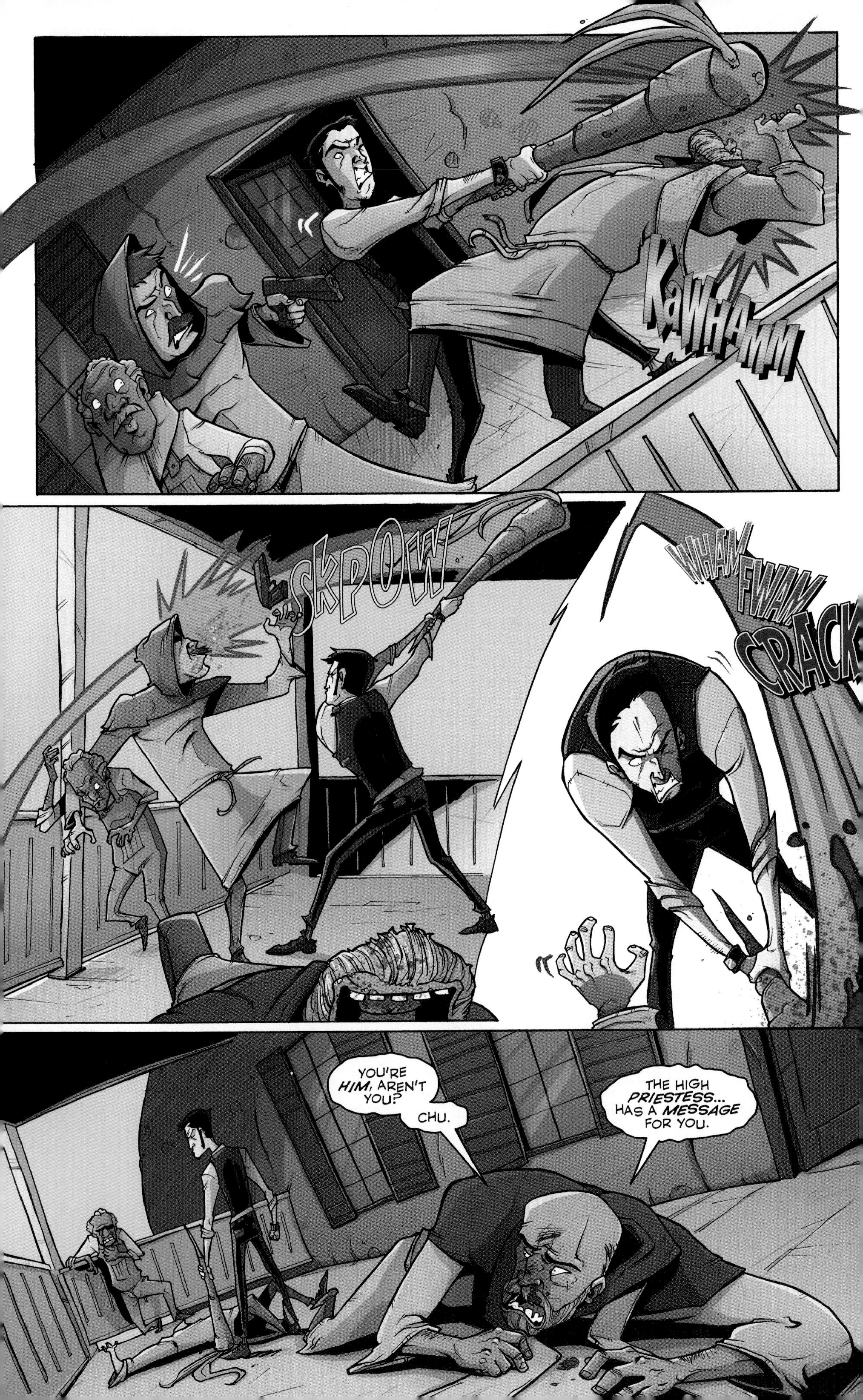
KaWHAMM
SKPOW
WHAM FWAM CRACK
YOU'RE *HIM*, AREN'T YOU?
CHU.
THE HIGH *PRIESTESS*... HAS A *MESSAGE* FOR YOU.

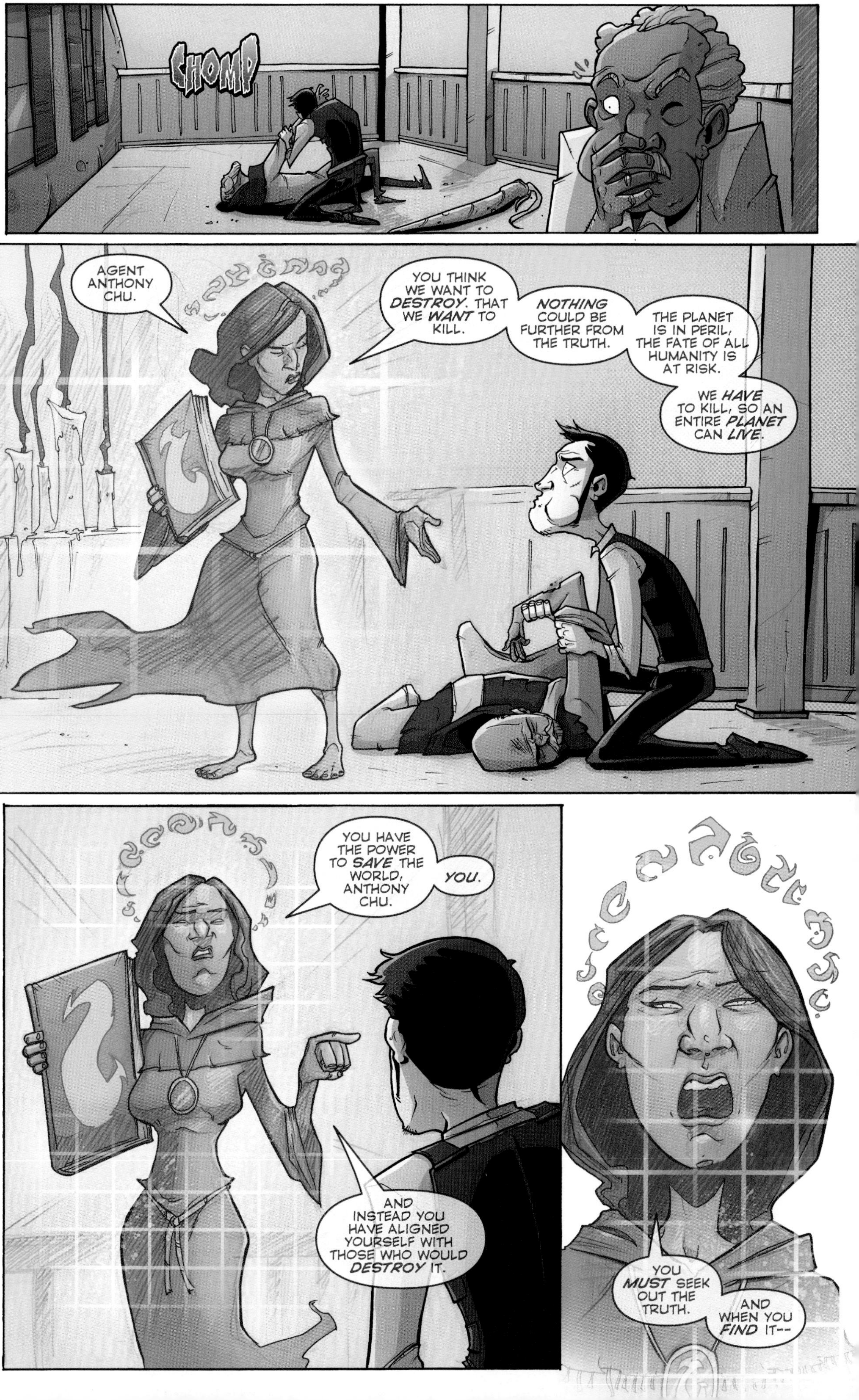
CHOMP
AGENT ANTHONY CHU.
YOU THINK WE WANT TO DESTROY. THAT WE WANT TO KILL.
NOTHING COULD BE FURTHER FROM THE TRUTH.
THE PLANET IS IN PERIL, THE FATE OF ALL HUMANITY IS AT RISK.
WE HAVE TO KILL, SO AN ENTIRE PLANET CAN LIVE.
YOU HAVE THE POWER TO SAVE THE WORLD, ANTHONY CHU.
YOU.
AND INSTEAD YOU HAVE ALIGNED YOURSELF WITH THOSE WHO WOULD DESTROY IT.
YOU MUST SEEK OUT THE TRUTH.
AND WHEN YOU FIND IT--

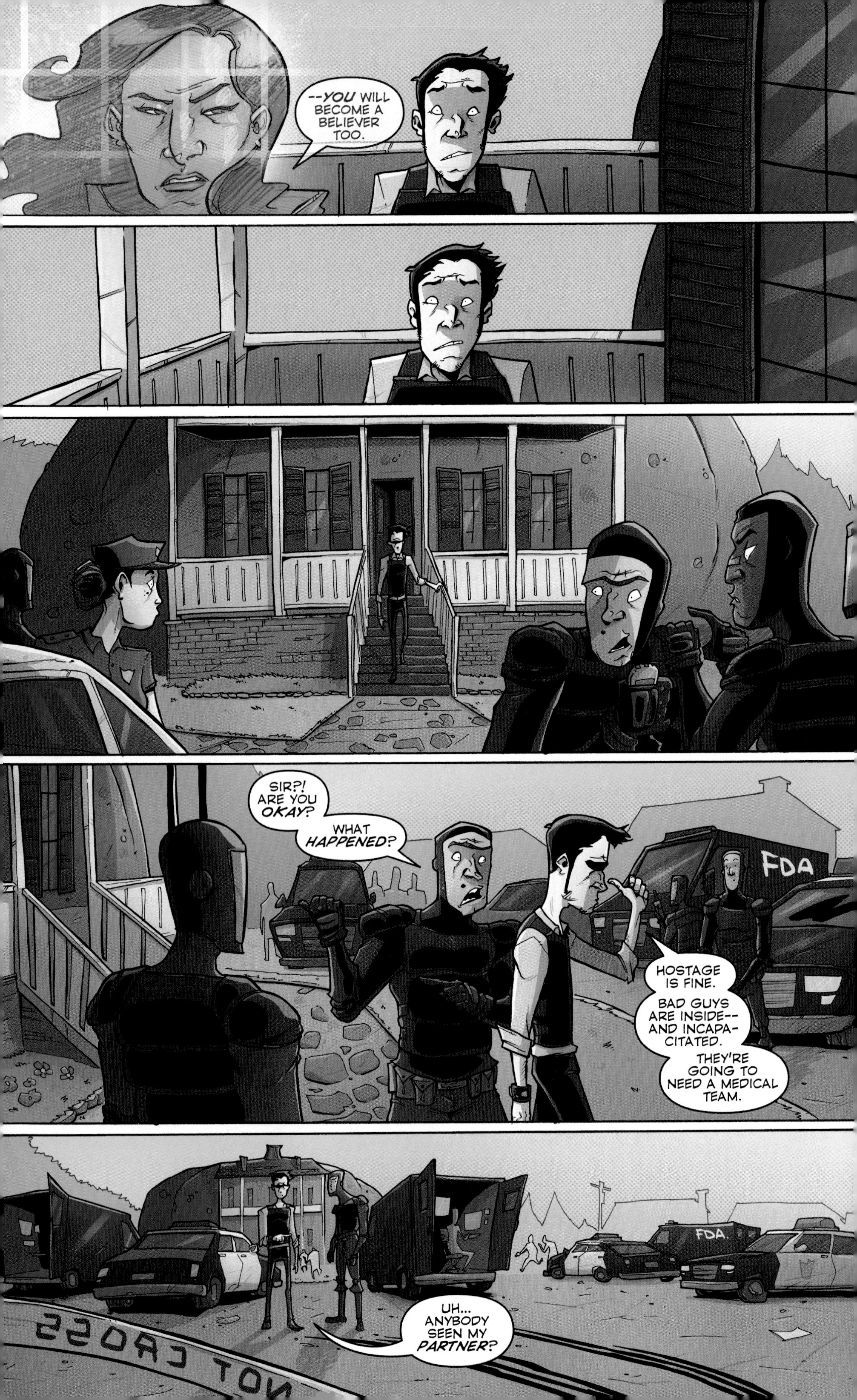
--*YOU* WILL BECOME A BELIEVER TOO.
SIR?! ARE YOU *OKAY*?
WHAT *HAPPENED*?
HOSTAGE IS FINE.
BAD GUYS ARE INSIDE-- AND INCAPACITATED.
THEY'RE GOING TO NEED A MEDICAL TEAM.
FDA
FDA.
UH... ANYBODY SEEN MY *PARTNER*?
NOT CROSS

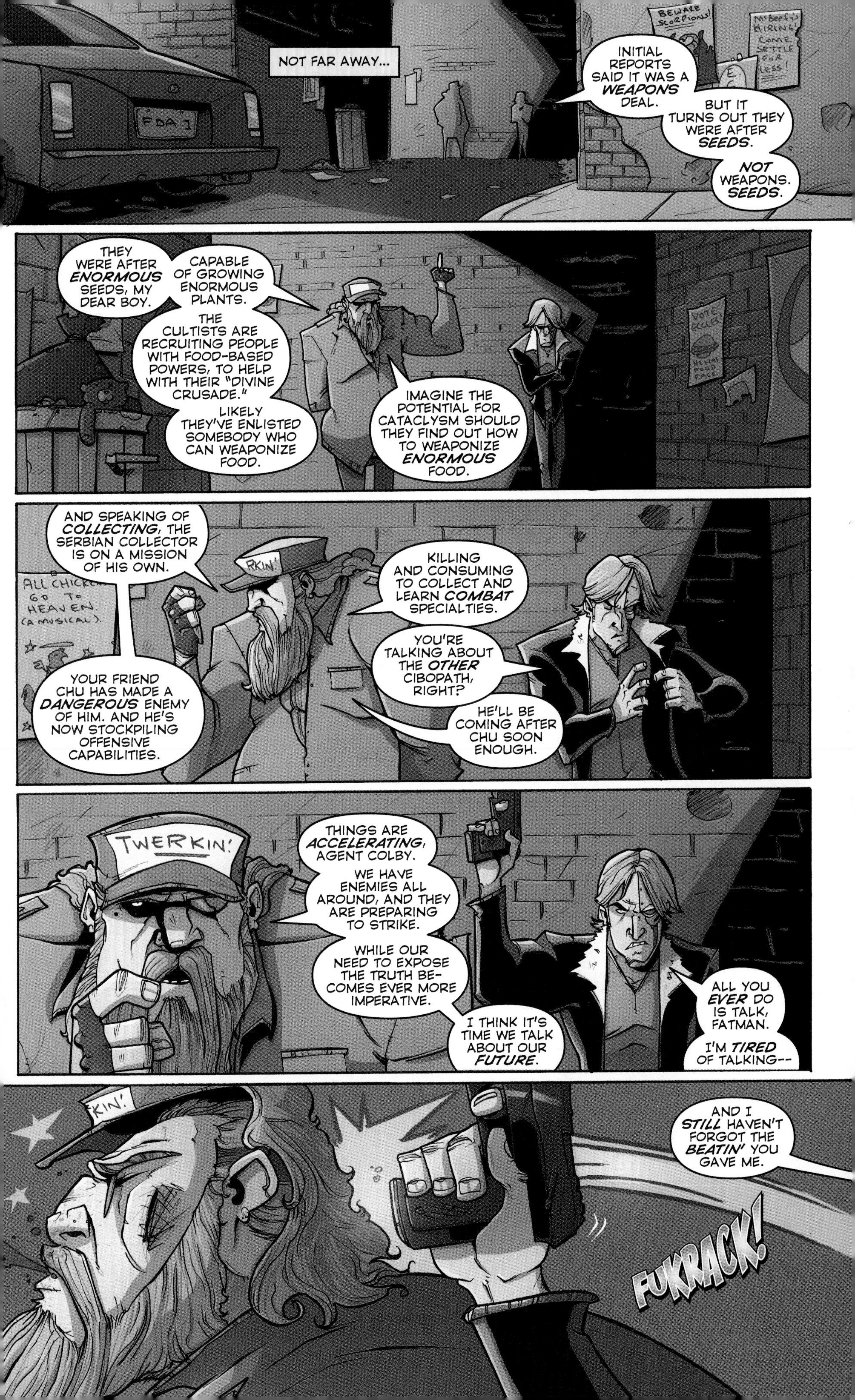
NOT FAR AWAY...
FDA 1
BEWARE SCORPIONS!
McBEEFY'S HIRING! COME SETTLE FOR LESS!
INITIAL REPORTS SAID IT WAS A WEAPONS DEAL.
BUT IT TURNS OUT THEY WERE AFTER SEEDS.
NOT WEAPONS. SEEDS.
THEY WERE AFTER ENORMOUS SEEDS, MY DEAR BOY.
CAPABLE OF GROWING ENORMOUS PLANTS.
THE CULTISTS ARE RECRUITING PEOPLE WITH FOOD-BASED POWERS, TO HELP WITH THEIR "DIVINE CRUSADE."
LIKELY THEY'VE ENLISTED SOMEBODY WHO CAN WEAPONIZE FOOD.
IMAGINE THE POTENTIAL FOR CATACLYSM SHOULD THEY FIND OUT HOW TO WEAPONIZE ENORMOUS FOOD.
VOTE ECCLES! HE HAS FOOD FACE
AND SPEAKING OF COLLECTING, THE SERBIAN COLLECTOR IS ON A MISSION OF HIS OWN.
KILLING AND CONSUMING TO COLLECT AND LEARN COMBAT SPECIALTIES.
YOUR FRIEND CHU HAS MADE A DANGEROUS ENEMY OF HIM. AND HE'S NOW STOCKPILING OFFENSIVE CAPABILITIES.
YOU'RE TALKING ABOUT THE OTHER CIBOPATH, RIGHT?
HE'LL BE COMING AFTER CHU SOON ENOUGH.
TWERKIN!
THINGS ARE ACCELERATING, AGENT COLBY.
WE HAVE ENEMIES ALL AROUND, AND THEY ARE PREPARING TO STRIKE.
WHILE OUR NEED TO EXPOSE THE TRUTH BECOMES EVER MORE IMPERATIVE.
I THINK IT'S TIME WE TALK ABOUT OUR FUTURE.
ALL YOU EVER DO IS TALK, FATMAN.
I'M TIRED OF TALKING--
AND I STILL HAVEN'T FORGOT THE BEATIN' YOU GAVE ME.
FUKRACK!

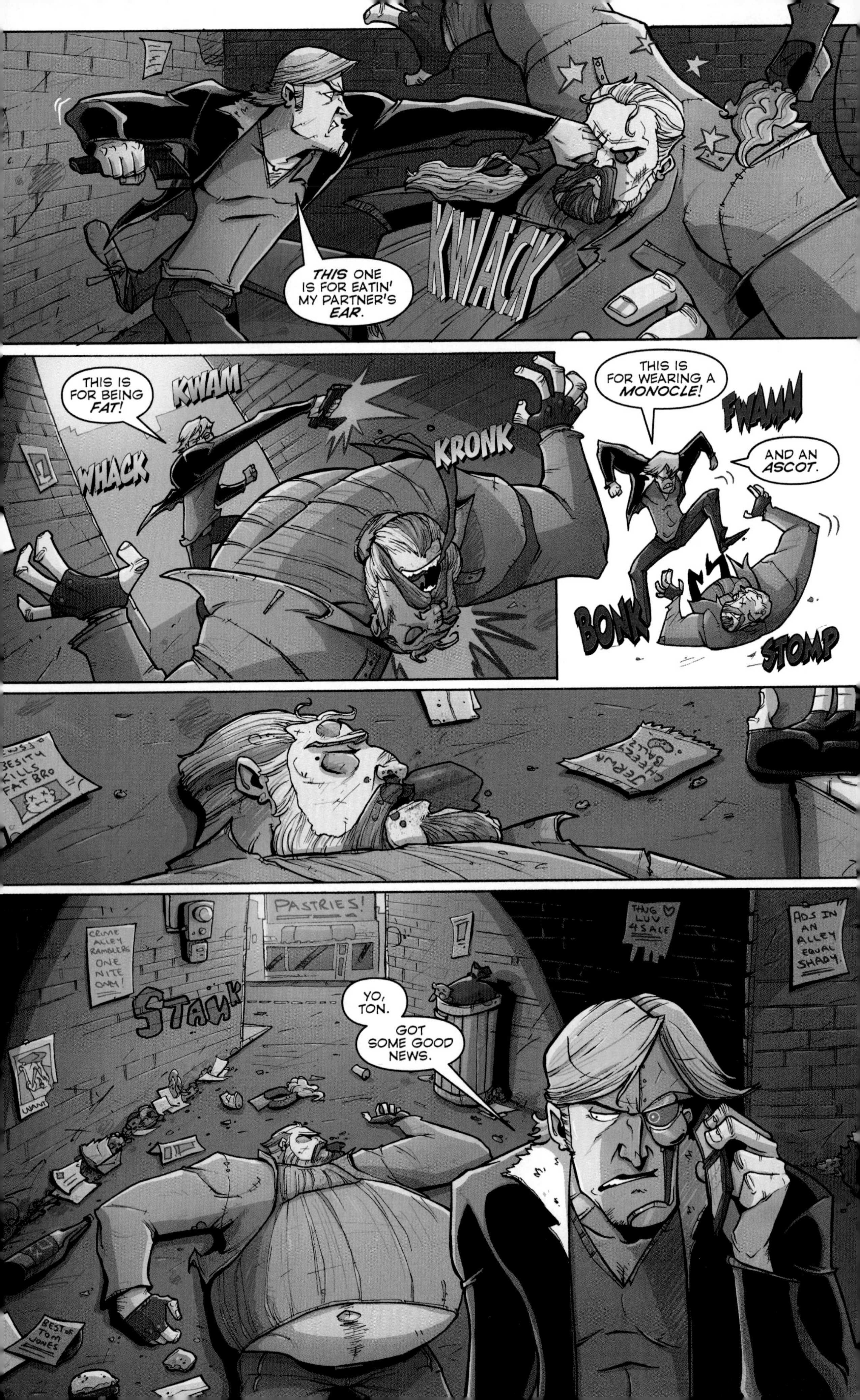
THIS ONE IS FOR EATIN' MY PARTNER'S EAR.
KWACK
THIS IS FOR BEING FAT!
KWAM
WHACK
KRONK
THIS IS FOR WEARING A MONOCLE!
FWAMM
AND AN ASCOT.
BONK
STOMP
BESITY KILLS FAT BRO
PASTRIES!
CRIME ALLEY RAMBLERS ONE NITE ONLY!
THUG LUV 4 SALE
ADS IN AN ALLEY EQUAL SHADY.
STANK
WANT
YO, TON.
GOT SOME GOOD NEWS.
BEST OF TOM JONES

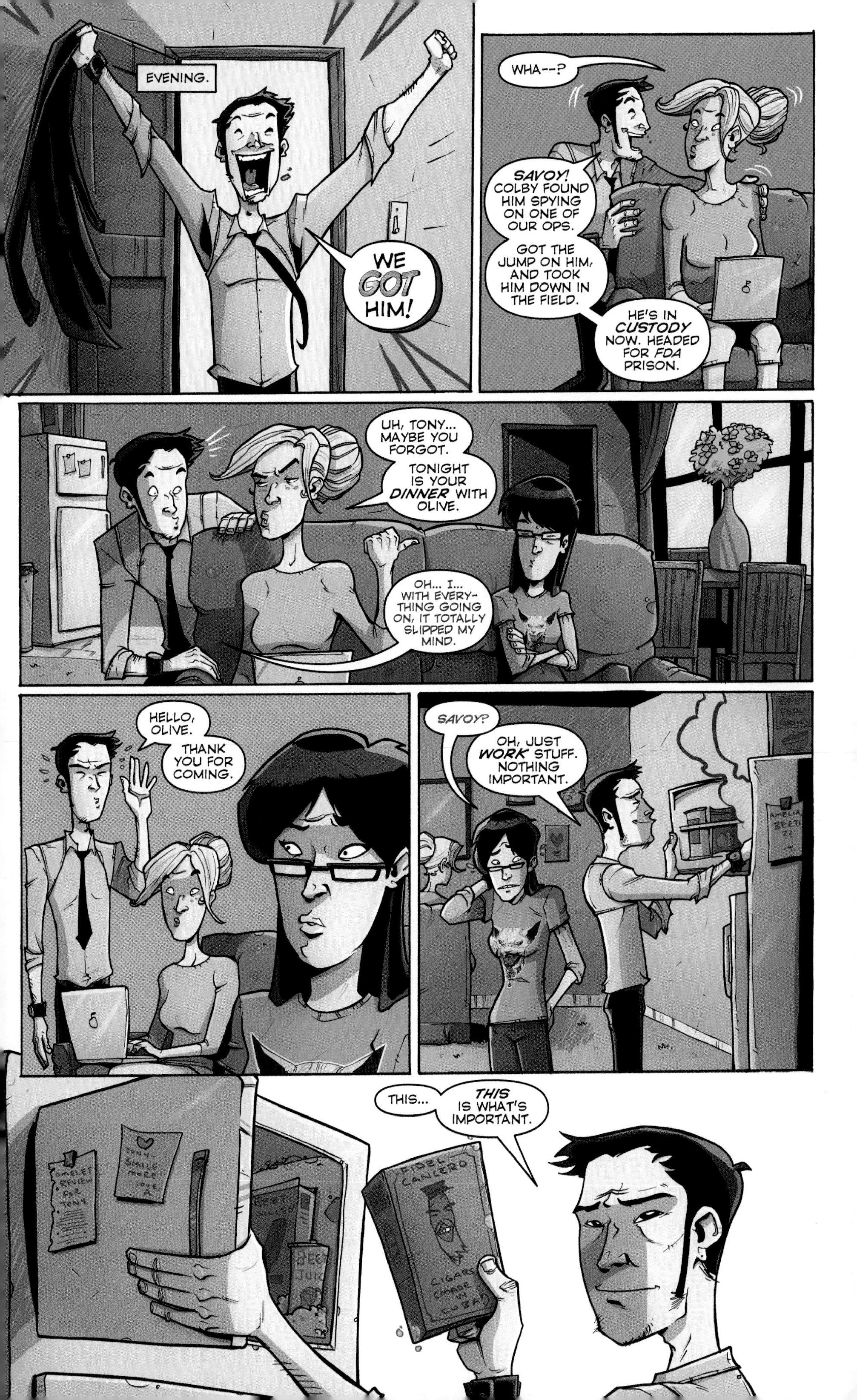
EVENING.
WE GOT HIM!
WHA--?
SAVOY! COLBY FOUND HIM SPYING ON ONE OF OUR OPS.
GOT THE JUMP ON HIM, AND TOOK HIM DOWN IN THE FIELD.
HE'S IN CUSTODY NOW. HEADED FOR FDA PRISON.
UH, TONY... MAYBE YOU FORGOT.
TONIGHT IS YOUR DINNER WITH OLIVE.
OH... I... WITH EVERY-THING GOING ON, IT TOTALLY SLIPPED MY MIND.
HELLO, OLIVE.
THANK YOU FOR COMING.
SAVOY?
OH, JUST WORK STUFF. NOTHING IMPORTANT.
THIS...
THIS IS WHAT'S IMPORTANT.
OMELET REVIEW FOR TONY.
TONY- SMILE MORE! LOVE, A.
FIDEL CANLERO
CIGARS (MADE IN CUBA)

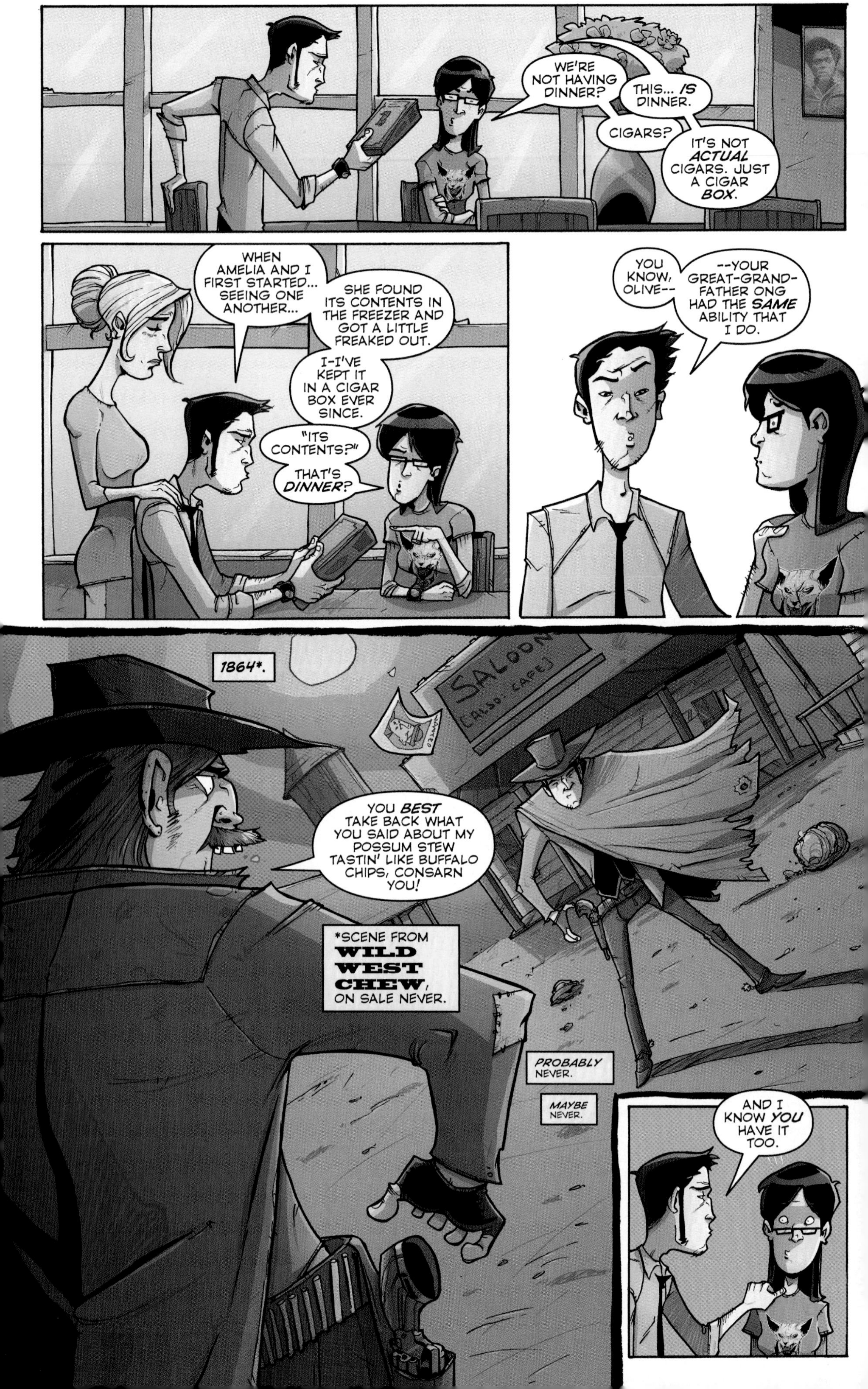
WE'RE NOT HAVING DINNER?
THIS... *IS* DINNER.
CIGARS?
IT'S NOT *ACTUAL* CIGARS. JUST A CIGAR *BOX*.
WHEN AMELIA AND I FIRST STARTED... SEEING ONE ANOTHER...
SHE FOUND ITS CONTENTS IN THE FREEZER AND GOT A LITTLE FREAKED OUT.
I-I'VE KEPT IT IN A CIGAR BOX EVER SINCE.
"ITS CONTENTS?"
THAT'S *DINNER*?
YOU KNOW, OLIVE--
--YOUR GREAT-GRAND-FATHER ONG HAD THE *SAME* ABILITY THAT I DO.
*1864**.
SALOON
[ALSO: CAFE]
WANTED
YOU *BEST* TAKE BACK WHAT YOU SAID ABOUT MY POSSUM STEW TASTIN' LIKE BUFFALO CHIPS, CONSARN YOU!
*SCENE FROM **WILD WEST CHEW**, ON SALE NEVER.
PROBABLY NEVER.
MAYBE NEVER.
AND I KNOW *YOU* HAVE IT TOO.

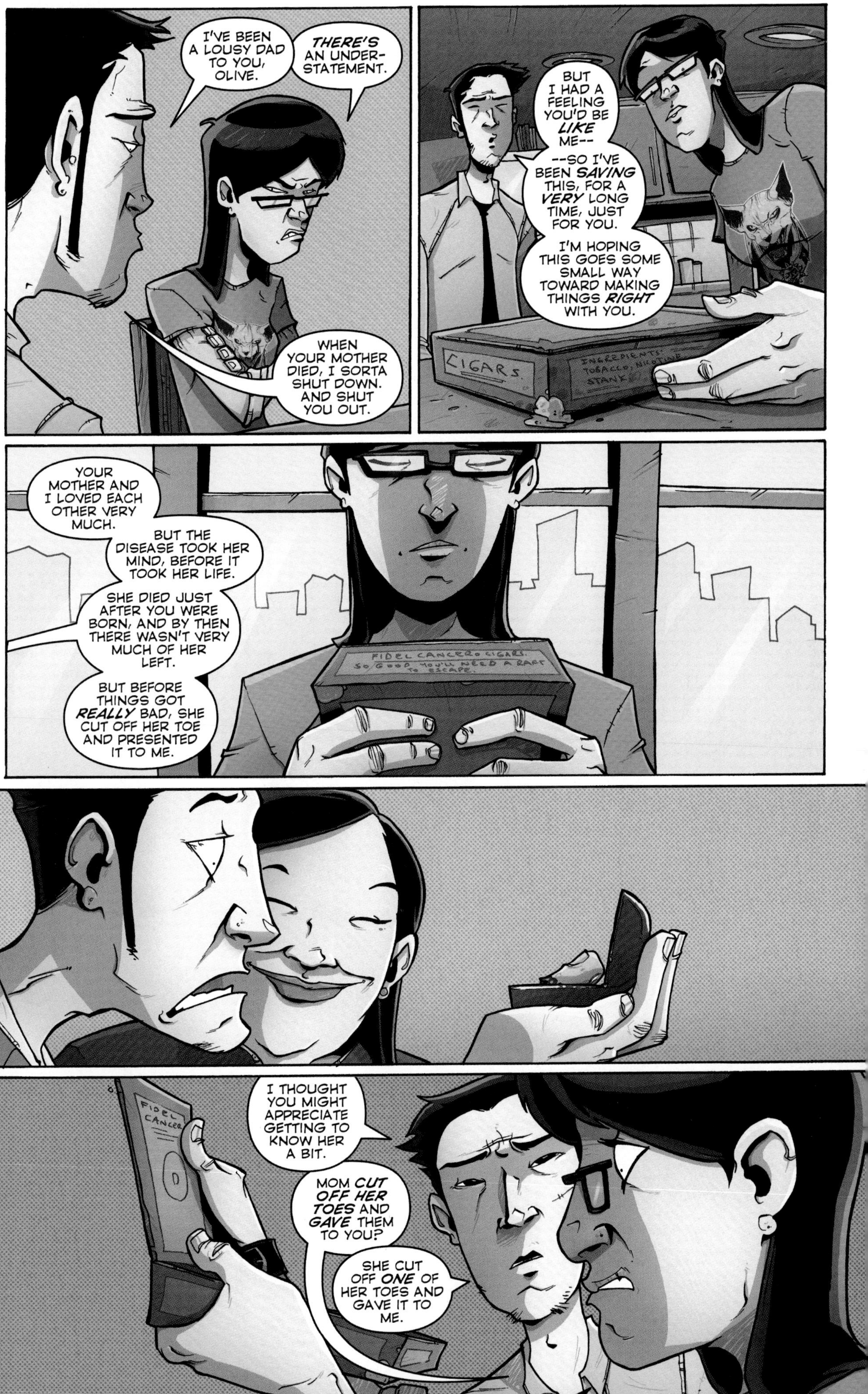
I'VE BEEN A LOUSY DAD TO YOU, OLIVE.
THERE'S AN UNDER-STATEMENT.
WHEN YOUR MOTHER DIED, I SORTA SHUT DOWN. AND SHUT YOU OUT.
BUT I HAD A FEELING YOU'D BE *LIKE* ME--
--SO I'VE BEEN *SAVING* THIS, FOR A *VERY* LONG TIME, JUST FOR YOU.
I'M HOPING THIS GOES SOME SMALL WAY TOWARD MAKING THINGS *RIGHT* WITH YOU.
CIGARS
INGREDIENTS: TOBACCO, NICOTINE, STANK
YOUR MOTHER AND I LOVED EACH OTHER VERY MUCH.
BUT THE DISEASE TOOK HER MIND, BEFORE IT TOOK HER LIFE.
SHE DIED JUST AFTER YOU WERE BORN, AND BY THEN THERE WASN'T VERY MUCH OF HER LEFT.
BUT BEFORE THINGS GOT *REALLY* BAD, SHE CUT OFF HER TOE AND PRESENTED IT TO ME.
FIDEL CANCERO CIGARS. SO GOOD YOU'LL NEED A RAFT TO ESCAPE.
I THOUGHT YOU MIGHT APPRECIATE GETTING TO KNOW HER A BIT.
MOM *CUT OFF HER TOES* AND *GAVE* THEM TO YOU?
SHE CUT OFF *ONE* OF HER TOES AND GAVE IT TO ME.

THERE'S *TWO TOES* HERE, DAD.

FIDEL CANCERO 21 EARS, MADE IN CUBA.) "WE THE STANKIEST!"

ANTONELLE!

END *CHEW BOOK VII: BAD APPLES.*

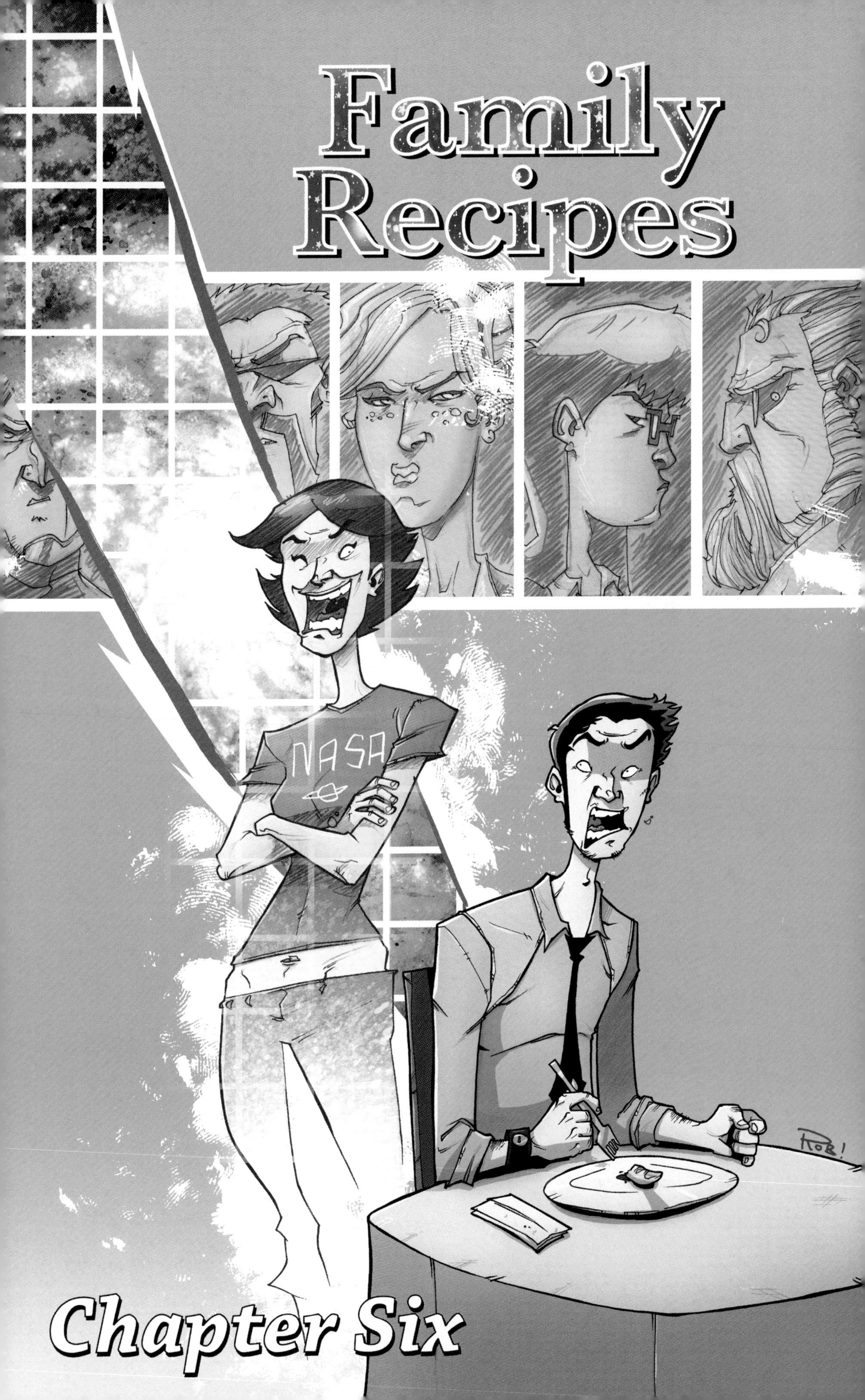
Family Recipes
NASA
ROB!
Chapter Six

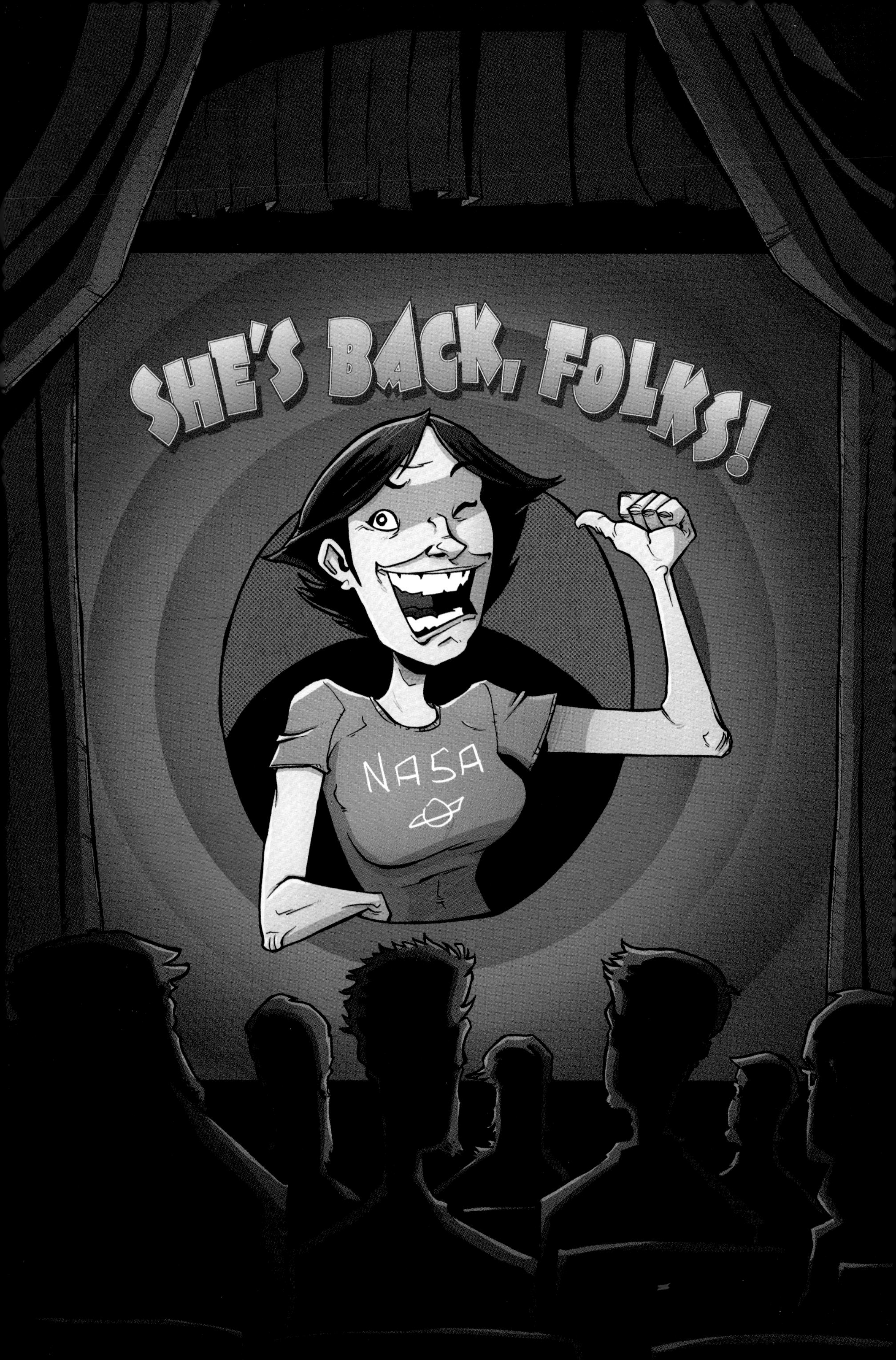
SHE'S BACK, FOLKS!
NASA

Issue #36 cover

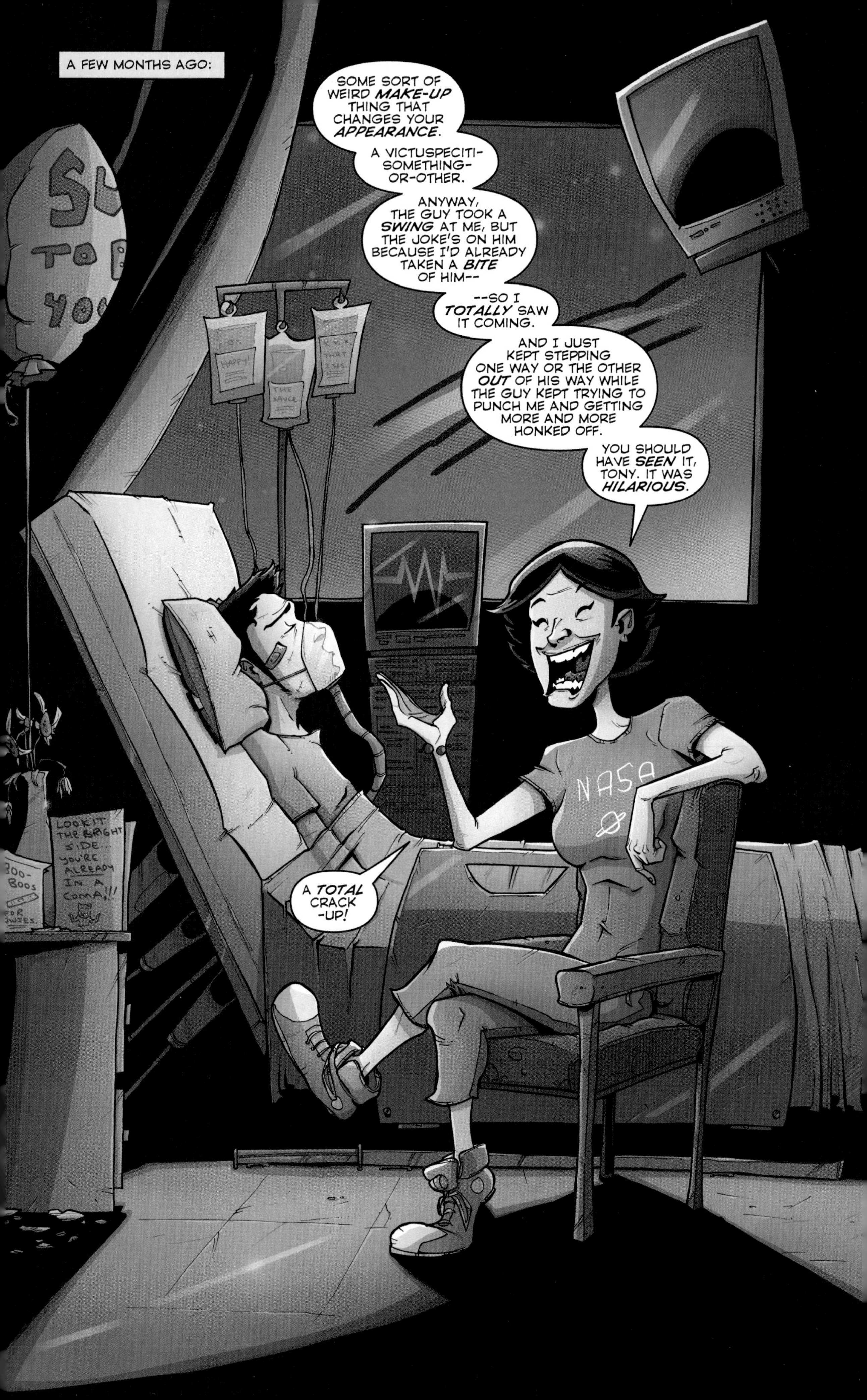
A FEW MONTHS AGO:
SOME SORT OF WEIRD MAKE-UP THING THAT CHANGES YOUR APPEARANCE.
A VICTUSPECITI-SOMETHING-OR-OTHER.
ANYWAY, THE GUY TOOK A SWING AT ME, BUT THE JOKE'S ON HIM BECAUSE I'D ALREADY TAKEN A BITE OF HIM--
--SO I TOTALLY SAW IT COMING.
AND I JUST KEPT STEPPING ONE WAY OR THE OTHER OUT OF HIS WAY WHILE THE GUY KEPT TRYING TO PUNCH ME AND GETTING MORE AND MORE HONKED OFF.
YOU SHOULD HAVE SEEN IT, TONY. IT WAS HILARIOUS.
A TOTAL CRACK-UP!
NASA
LOOKIT THE BRIGHT SIDE... YOU'RE ALREADY IN A COMA!!!

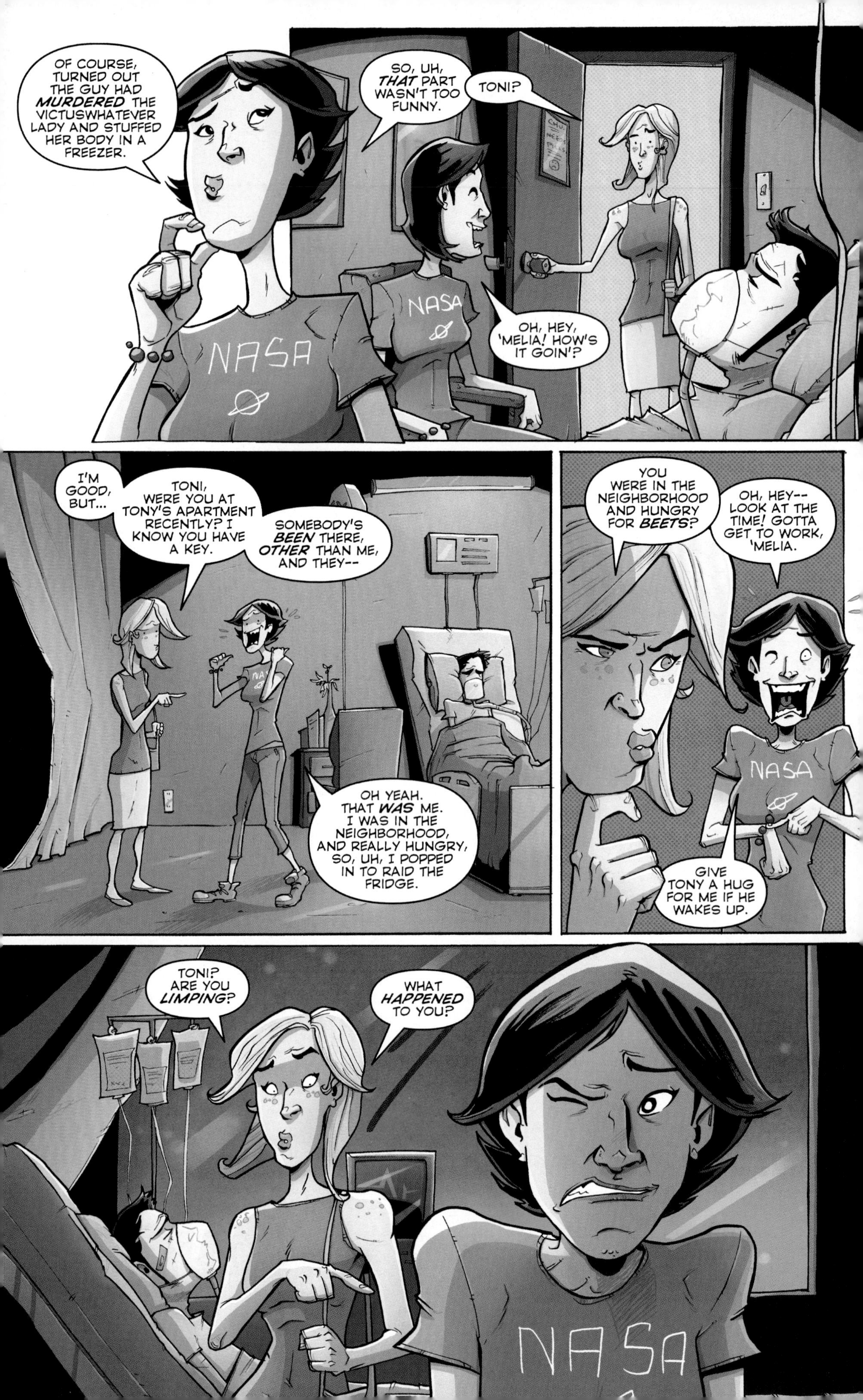
OF COURSE, TURNED OUT THE GUY HAD *MURDERED* THE VICTUSWHATEVER LADY AND STUFFED HER BODY IN A FREEZER.
SO, UH, *THAT* PART WASN'T TOO FUNNY.
TONI?
OH, HEY, 'MELIA! HOW'S IT GOIN'?
I'M GOOD, BUT...
TONI, WERE YOU AT TONY'S APARTMENT RECENTLY? I KNOW YOU HAVE A KEY.
SOMEBODY'S *BEEN* THERE, *OTHER* THAN ME, AND THEY--
OH YEAH. THAT *WAS* ME. I WAS IN THE NEIGHBORHOOD, AND REALLY HUNGRY, SO, UH, I POPPED IN TO RAID THE FRIDGE.
YOU WERE IN THE NEIGHBORHOOD AND HUNGRY FOR *BEETS*?
OH, HEY-- LOOK AT THE TIME! GOTTA GET TO WORK, 'MELIA.
GIVE TONY A HUG FOR ME IF HE WAKES UP.
TONI? ARE YOU *LIMPING*?
WHAT *HAPPENED* TO YOU?

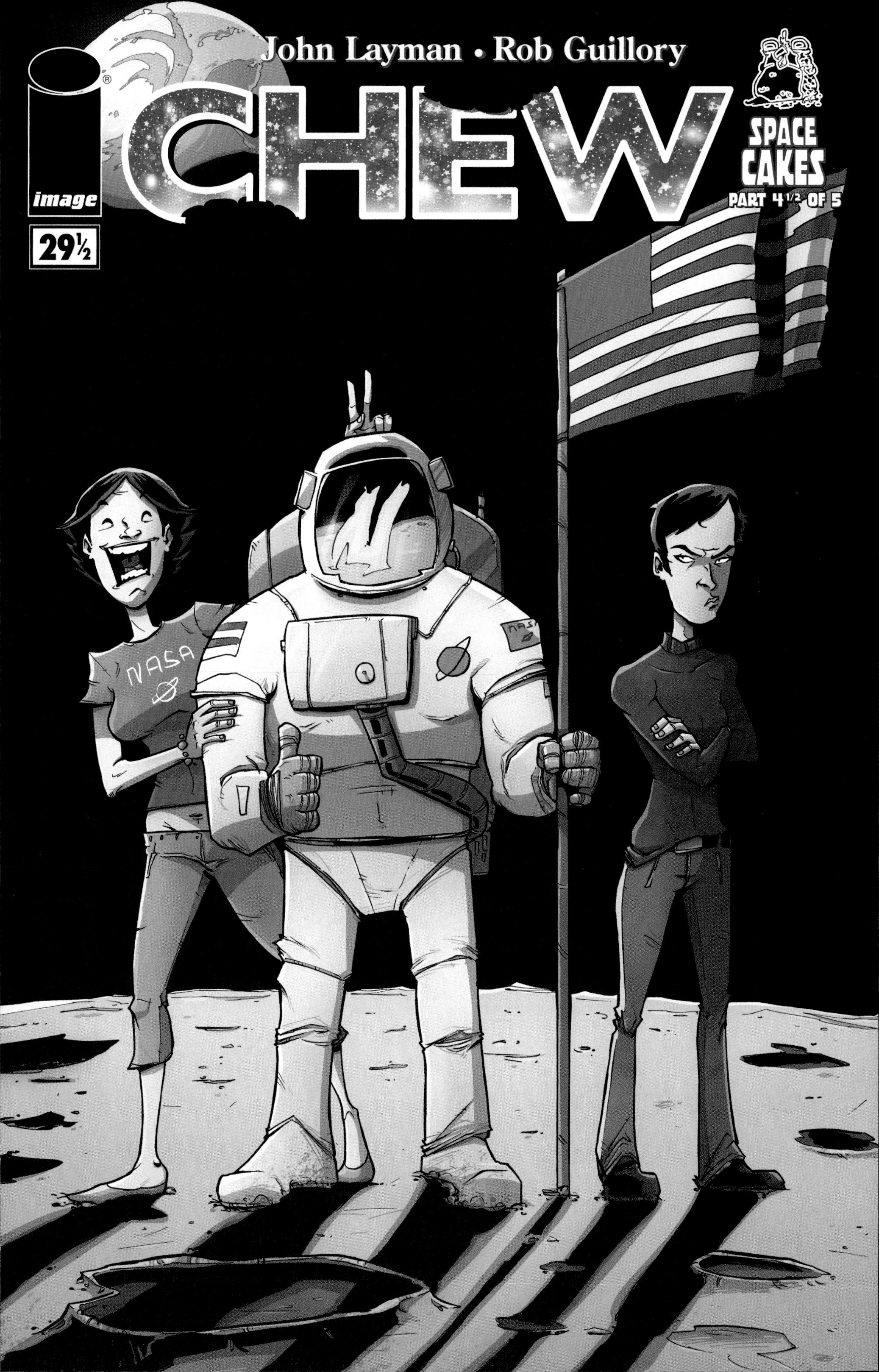
John Layman • Rob Guillory
image
CHEW
29½
SPACE CAKES
PART 4½ OF 5
NASA
NASA

image comics presents

CHEW

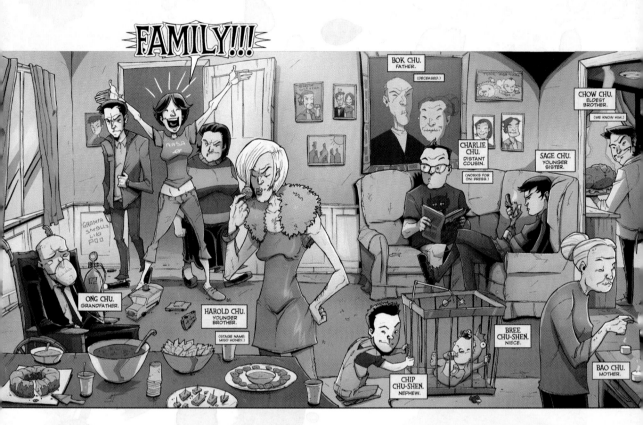

FAMILY!!!
GRAMPA SMELLZ LIK POO
ONG CHU. GRANDFATHER.
HAROLD CHU. YOUNGER BROTHER.
(STAGE NAME: MISO HONEY.)
BOK CHU. FATHER.
(DECEASED.)
CHARLIE CHU. DISTANT COUSIN.
(WORKS FOR ONI PRESS.)
CHIP CHU-SHEN. NEPHEW.
BREE CHU-SHEN. NIECE.
SAGE CHU. YOUNGER SISTER.
CHOW CHU. ELDEST BROTHER.
(WE KNOW HIM.)
BAO CHU. MOTHER.

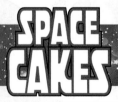

SPACE CAKES

PART 4 1/2 OF 5

written & lettered by
John Layman

drawn & coloured by
Rob Guillory

Color Assists: Taylor Wells

Fonts: Comicraft (comicbookfonts.com)
Logo: Tombgraphics (tombgraphics.com)
Book Design: Rob Guillory & John Layman

www.ChewComic.com

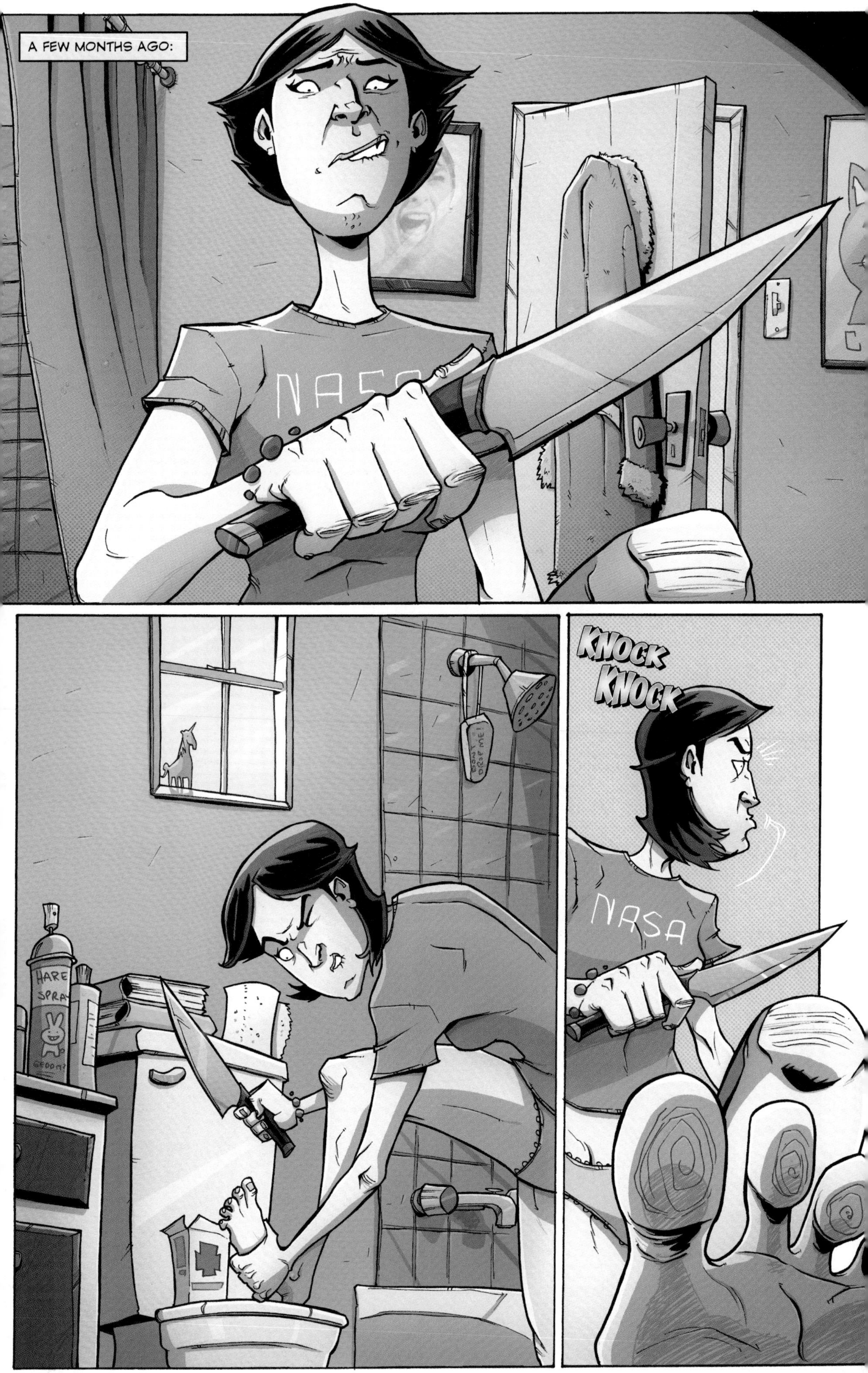
A FEW MONTHS AGO:
NASA
KNOCK
KNOCK
NASA

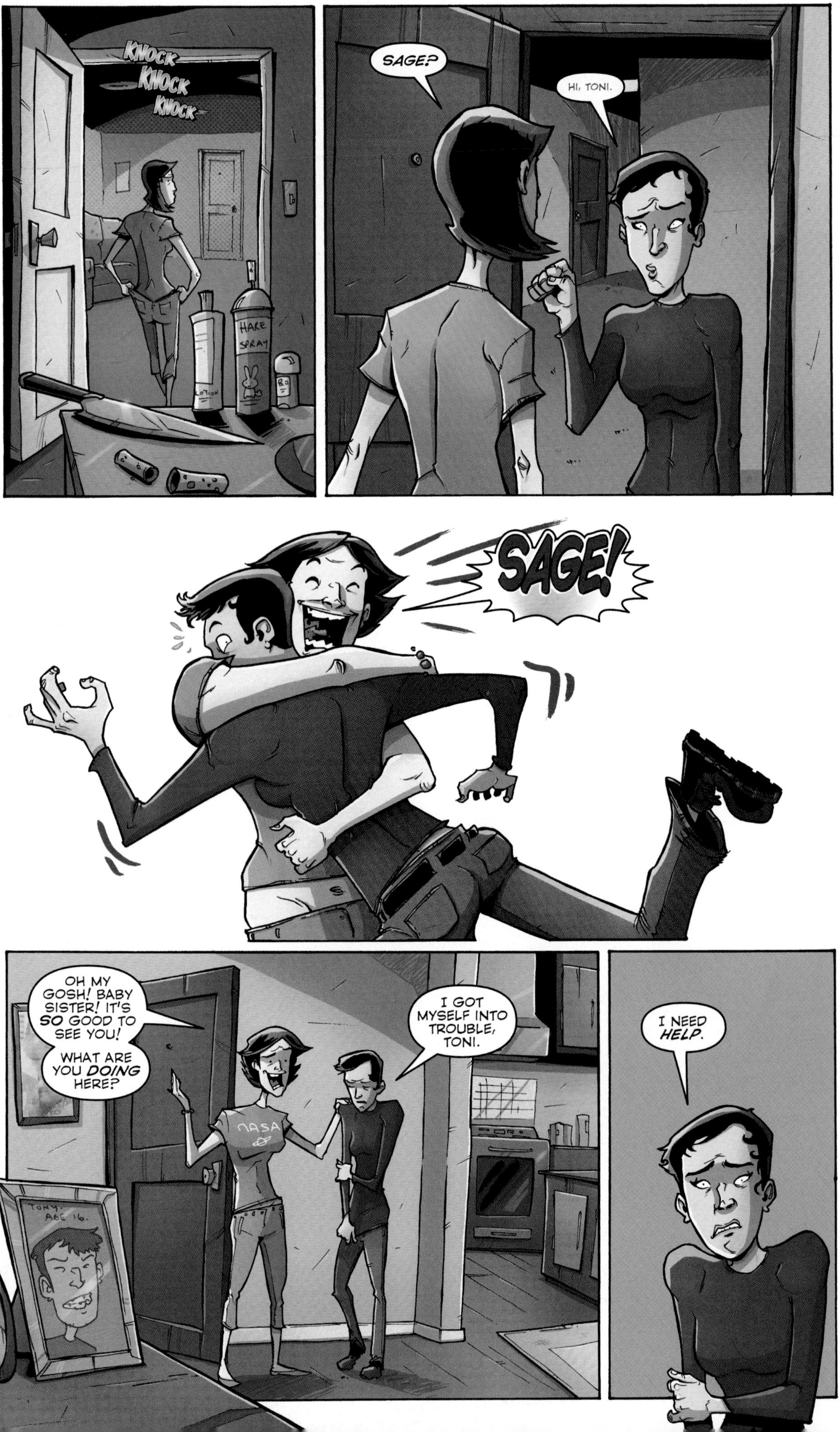
KNOCK
KNOCK
KNOCK
HARE SPRAY
LOTION
SAGE?
HI, TONI.
SAGE!
OH MY GOSH! BABY SISTER! IT'S **SO** GOOD TO SEE YOU!
WHAT ARE YOU ***DOING*** HERE?
NASA
I GOT MYSELF INTO TROUBLE, TONI.
I NEED ***HELP.***

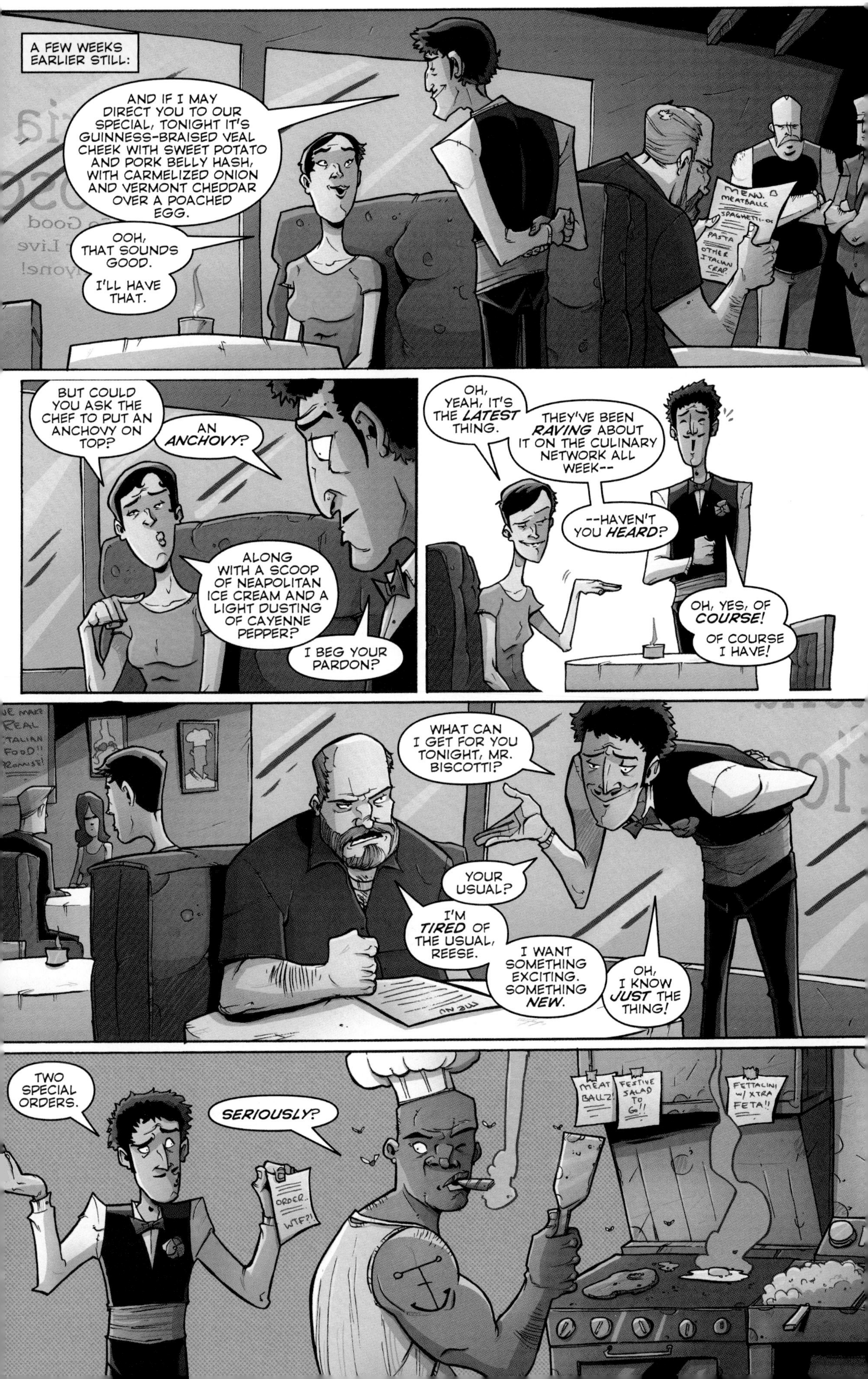
A FEW WEEKS EARLIER STILL:
AND IF I MAY DIRECT YOU TO OUR SPECIAL, TONIGHT IT'S GUINNESS-BRAISED VEAL CHEEK WITH SWEET POTATO AND PORK BELLY HASH, WITH CARMELIZED ONION AND VERMONT CHEDDAR OVER A POACHED EGG.
OOH, THAT SOUNDS GOOD.
I'LL HAVE THAT.
MENU
MEATBALLS
SPAGHETTI-OS
PASTA
OTHER ITALIAN CRAP
BUT COULD YOU ASK THE CHEF TO PUT AN ANCHOVY ON TOP?
AN *ANCHOVY*?
ALONG WITH A SCOOP OF NEAPOLITAN ICE CREAM AND A LIGHT DUSTING OF CAYENNE PEPPER?
I BEG YOUR PARDON?
OH, YEAH, IT'S THE *LATEST* THING.
THEY'VE BEEN *RAVING* ABOUT IT ON THE CULINARY NETWORK ALL WEEK--
--HAVEN'T YOU *HEARD*?
OH, YES, OF *COURSE*!
OF COURSE I HAVE!
WHAT CAN I GET FOR YOU TONIGHT, MR. BISCOTTI?
YOUR USUAL?
I'M *TIRED* OF THE USUAL, REESE.
I WANT SOMETHING EXCITING. SOMETHING *NEW*.
OH, I KNOW *JUST* THE THING!
TWO SPECIAL ORDERS.
SERIOUSLY?
ORDER.. WTF?!
MEAT BALLZ!
FESTIVE SALAD TO GO!!
FETTACINI w/ XTRA FETA!!

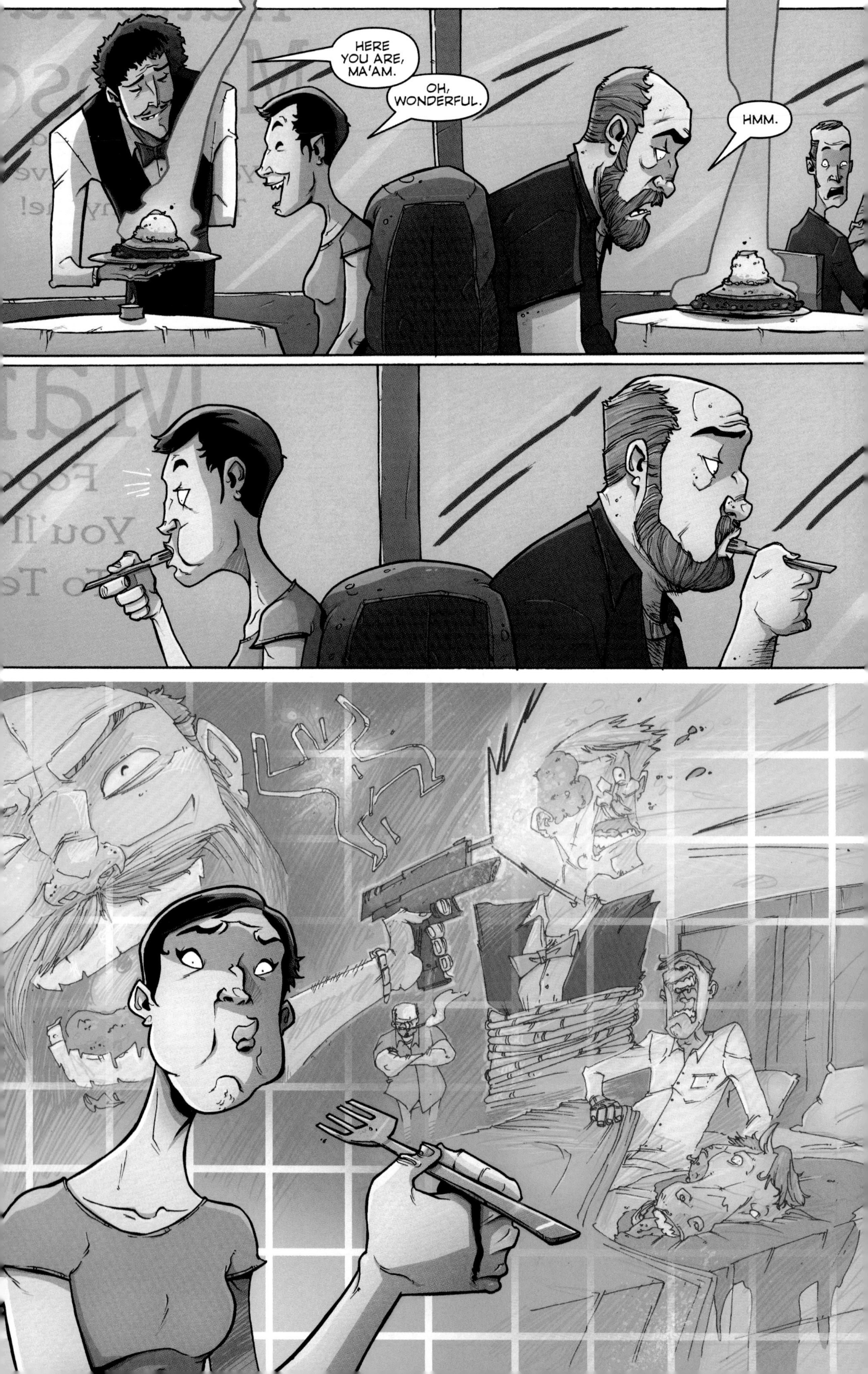
HERE YOU ARE, MA'AM.
OH, WONDERFUL.
HMM.

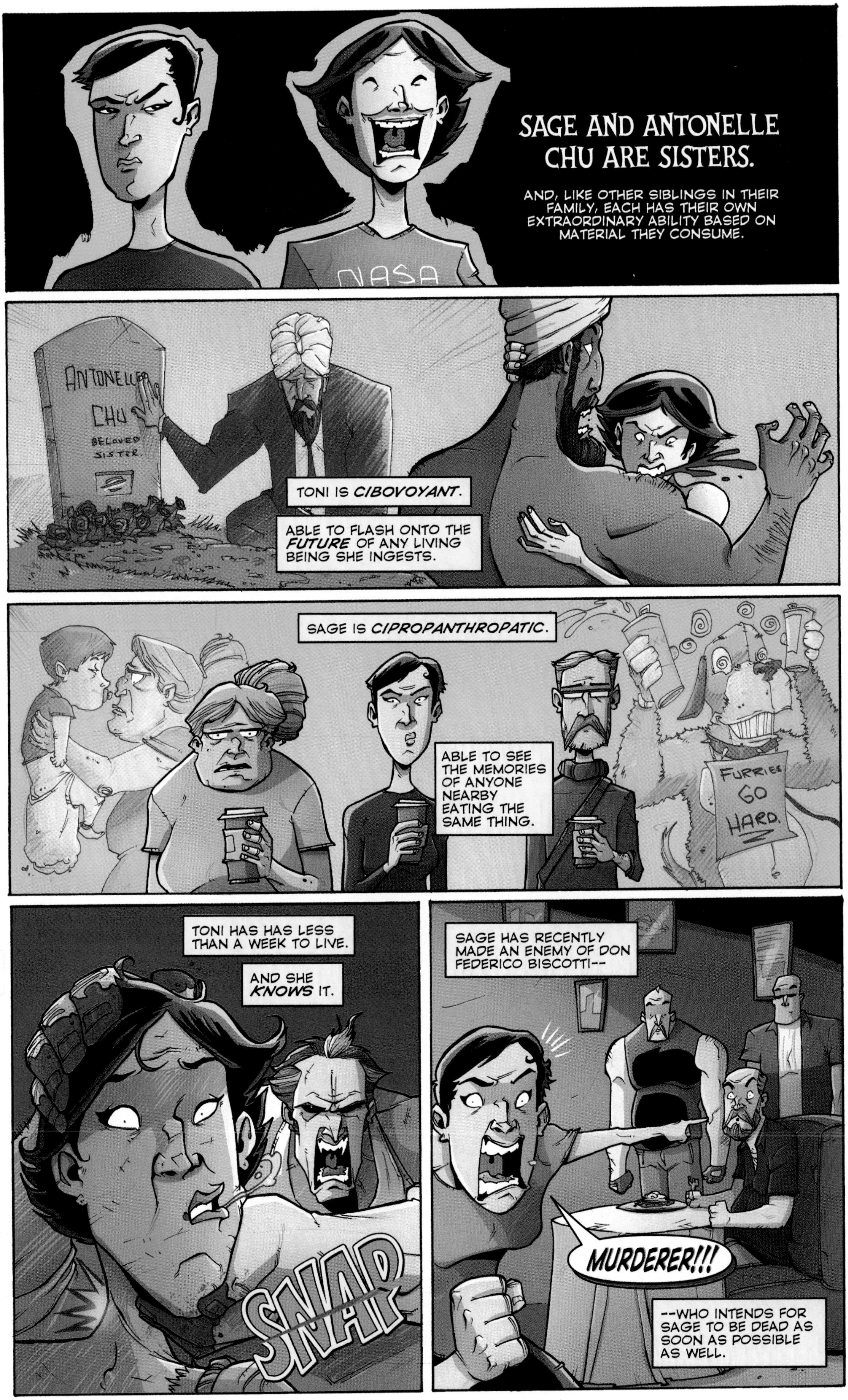
SAGE AND ANTONELLE CHU ARE SISTERS.
AND, LIKE OTHER SIBLINGS IN THEIR FAMILY, EACH HAS THEIR OWN EXTRAORDINARY ABILITY BASED ON MATERIAL THEY CONSUME.
NASA
ANTONELLE CHU BELOVED SISTER.
TONI IS CIBOVOYANT.
ABLE TO FLASH ONTO THE FUTURE OF ANY LIVING BEING SHE INGESTS.
SAGE IS CIPROPANTHROPATIC.
ABLE TO SEE THE MEMORIES OF ANYONE NEARBY EATING THE SAME THING.
FURRIES GO HARD.
TONI HAS HAS LESS THAN A WEEK TO LIVE.
AND SHE KNOWS IT.
SNAP
SAGE HAS RECENTLY MADE AN ENEMY OF DON FEDERICO BISCOTTI--
MURDERER!!!
--WHO INTENDS FOR SAGE TO BE DEAD AS SOON AS POSSIBLE AS WELL.

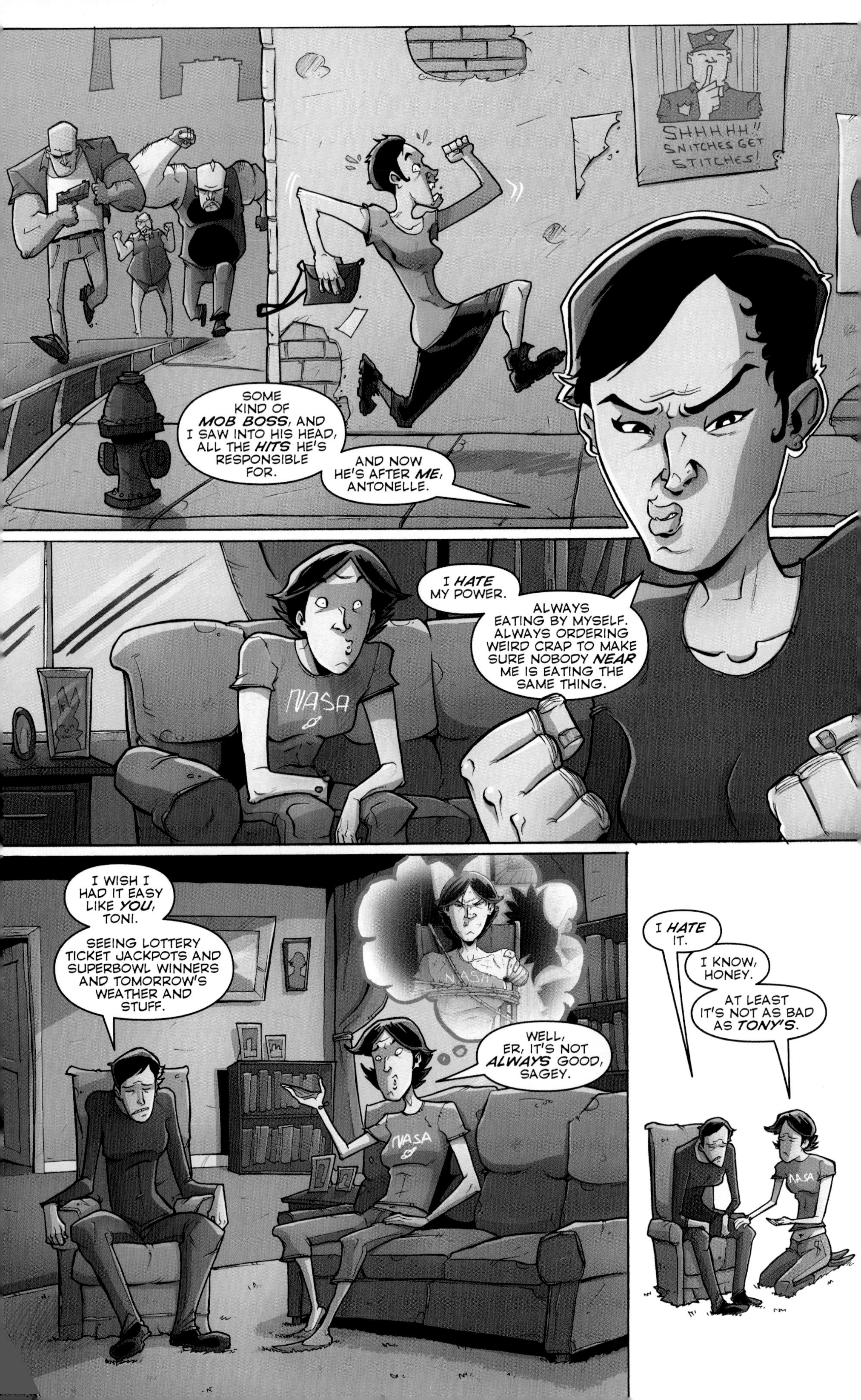
SHHHHH!! SNITCHES GET STITCHES!
SOME KIND OF MOB BOSS, AND I SAW INTO HIS HEAD, ALL THE HITS HE'S RESPONSIBLE FOR.
AND NOW HE'S AFTER ME, ANTONELLE.
I HATE MY POWER.
ALWAYS EATING BY MYSELF. ALWAYS ORDERING WEIRD CRAP TO MAKE SURE NOBODY NEAR ME IS EATING THE SAME THING.
I WISH I HAD IT EASY LIKE YOU, TONI.
SEEING LOTTERY TICKET JACKPOTS AND SUPERBOWL WINNERS AND TOMORROW'S WEATHER AND STUFF.
WELL, ER, IT'S NOT ALWAYS GOOD, SAGEY.
I HATE IT.
I KNOW, HONEY.
AT LEAST IT'S NOT AS BAD AS TONY'S.

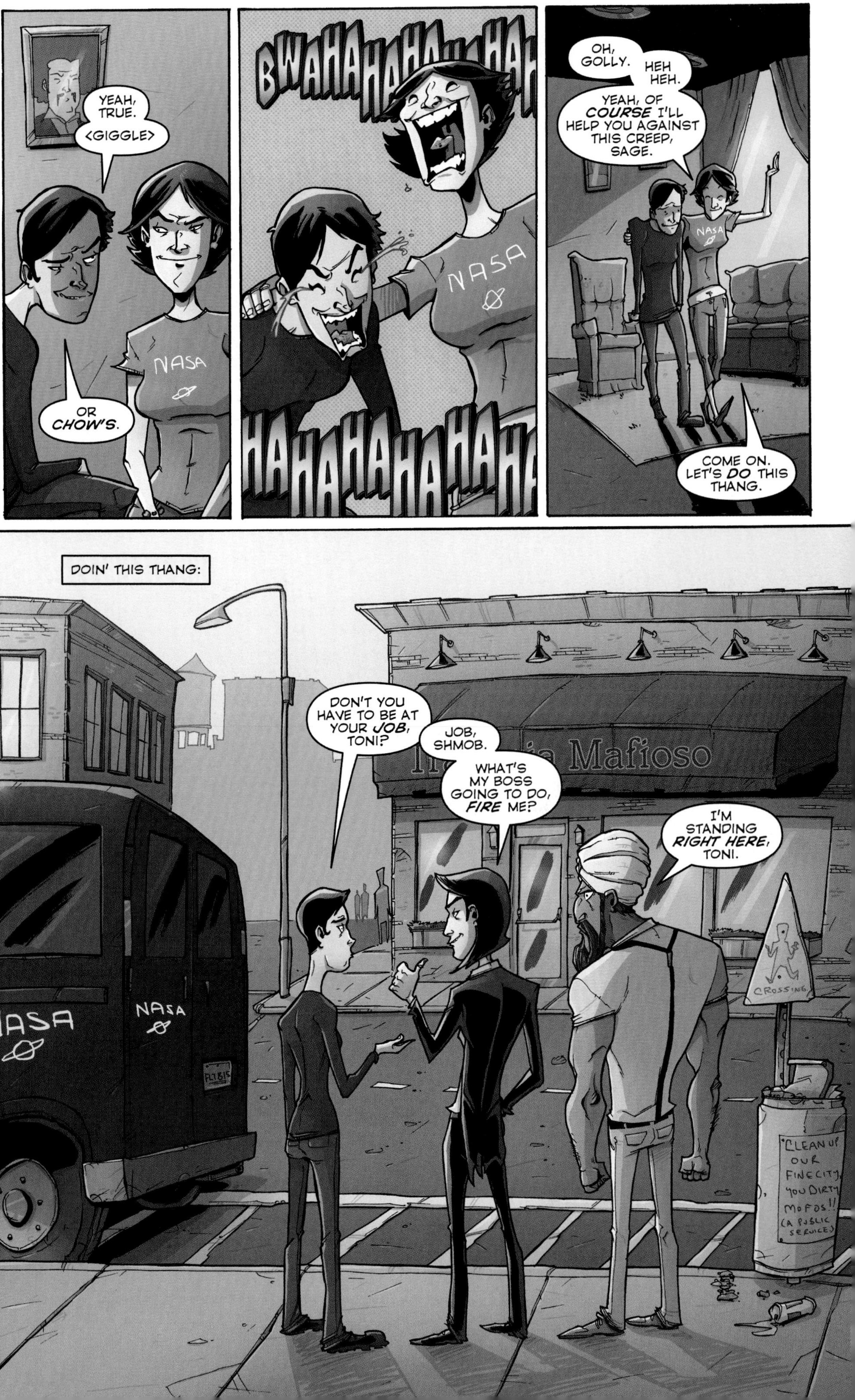
YEAH, TRUE.
<GIGGLE>
OR CHOW'S.
BWAHAHAHAHAHAHAHAHAHAHAHAHAHAHAHA
OH, GOLLY.
HEH HEH.
YEAH, OF COURSE I'LL HELP YOU AGAINST THIS CREEP, SAGE.
COME ON. LET'S DO THIS THANG.
DOIN' THIS THANG:
DON'T YOU HAVE TO BE AT YOUR JOB, TONI?
JOB, SHMOB.
WHAT'S MY BOSS GOING TO DO, FIRE ME?
I'M STANDING RIGHT HERE, TONI.
Mafioso
NASA
CROSSING
"CLEAN UP OUR FINE CITY, YOU DIRTY MOFOS!! (A PUBLIC SERVICE)

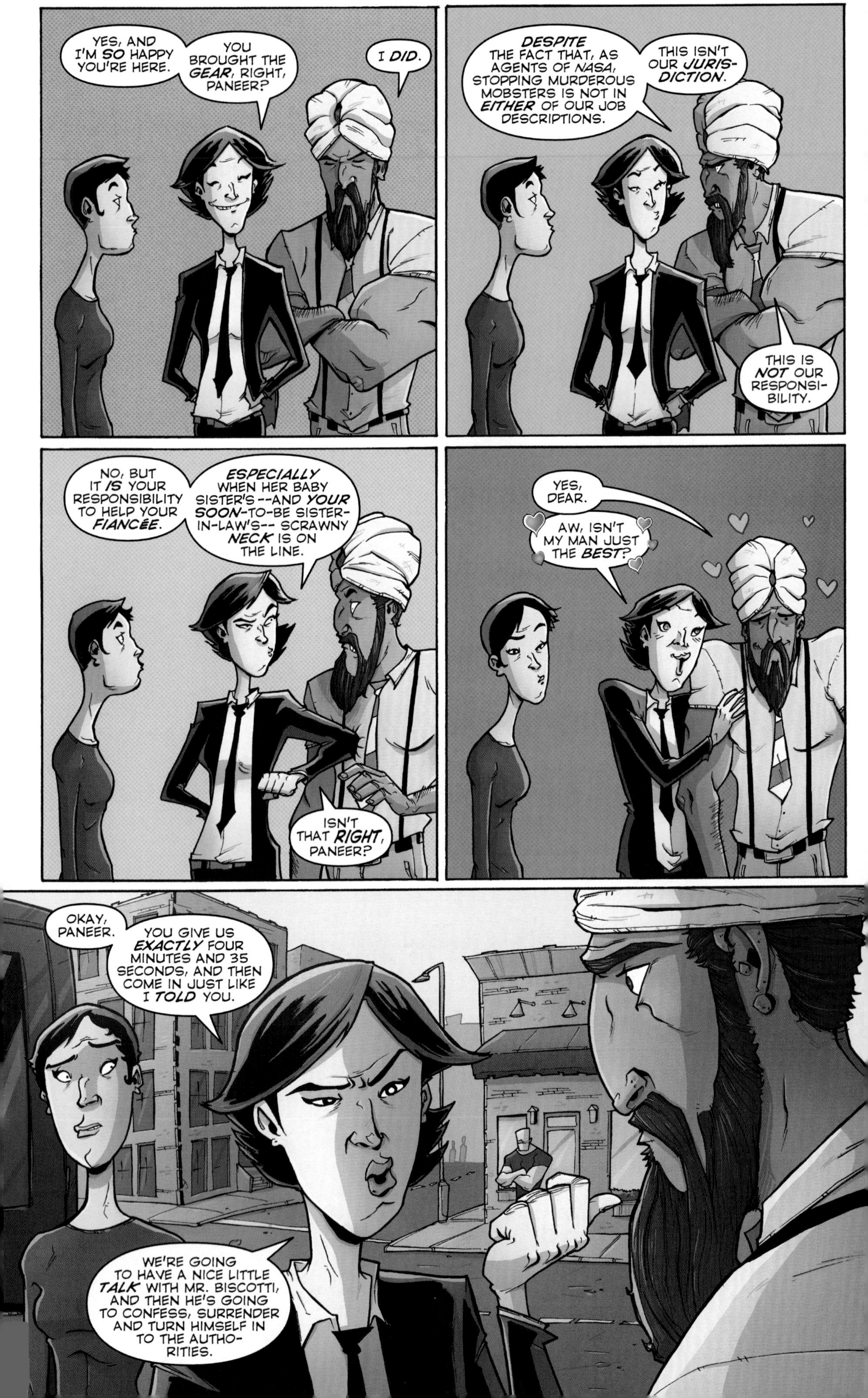

YES, AND I'M SO HAPPY YOU'RE HERE.
YOU BROUGHT THE GEAR, RIGHT, PANEER?
I DID.
DESPITE THE FACT THAT, AS AGENTS OF NASA, STOPPING MURDEROUS MOBSTERS IS NOT IN EITHER OF OUR JOB DESCRIPTIONS.
THIS ISN'T OUR JURIS-DICTION.
THIS IS NOT OUR RESPONSI-BILITY.
NO, BUT IT IS YOUR RESPONSIBILITY TO HELP YOUR FIANCÉE.
ESPECIALLY WHEN HER BABY SISTER'S--AND YOUR SOON-TO-BE SISTER-IN-LAW'S-- SCRAWNY NECK IS ON THE LINE.
ISN'T THAT RIGHT, PANEER?
YES, DEAR.
AW, ISN'T MY MAN JUST THE BEST?
OKAY, PANEER.
YOU GIVE US EXACTLY FOUR MINUTES AND 35 SECONDS, AND THEN COME IN JUST LIKE I TOLD YOU.
WE'RE GOING TO HAVE A NICE LITTLE TALK WITH MR. BISCOTTI, AND THEN HE'S GOING TO CONFESS, SURRENDER AND TURN HIMSELF IN TO THE AUTHO-RITIES.

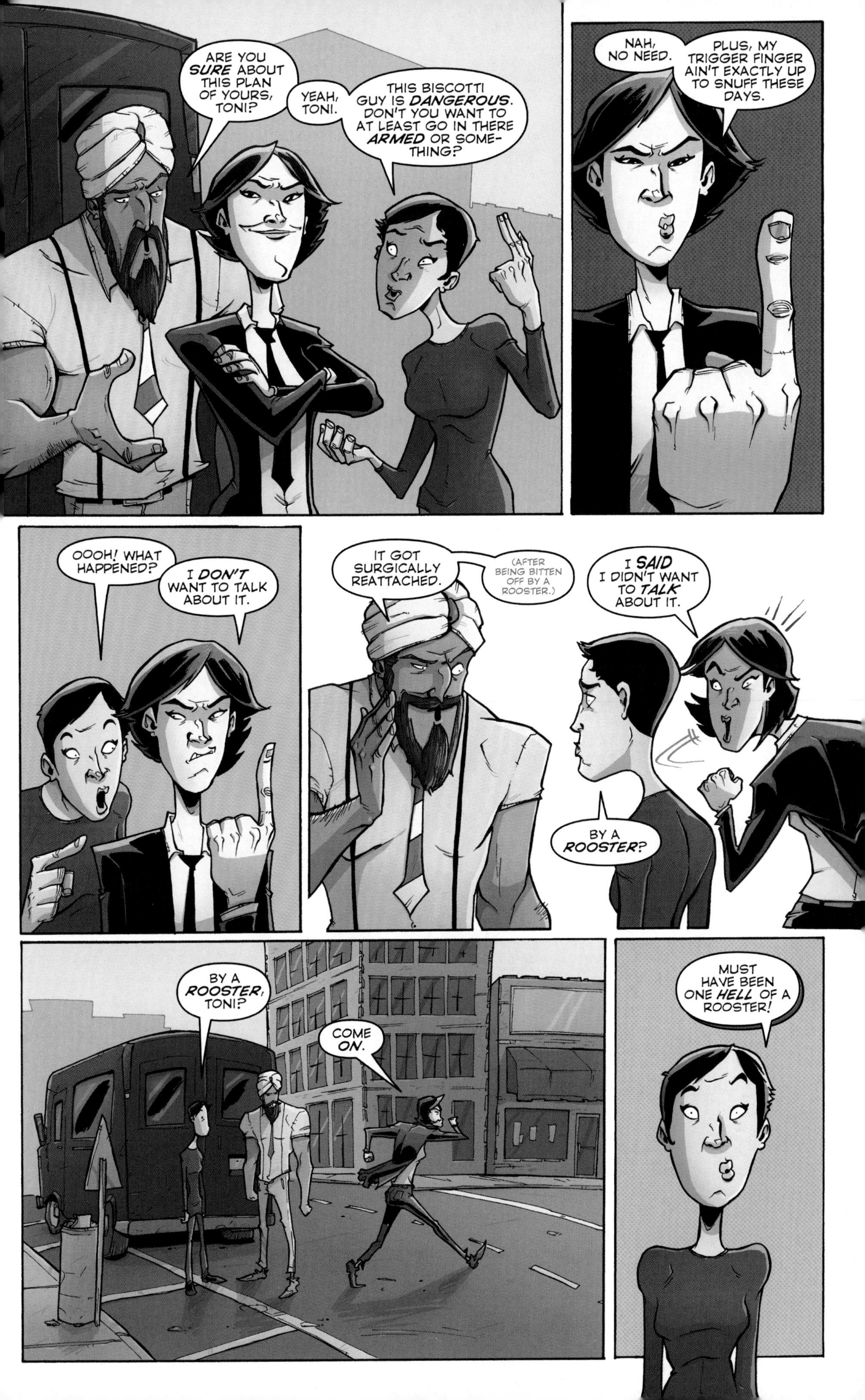

ARE YOU SURE ABOUT THIS PLAN OF YOURS, TONI?
YEAH, TONI.
THIS BISCOTTI GUY IS DANGEROUS. DON'T YOU WANT TO AT LEAST GO IN THERE ARMED OR SOMETHING?
NAH, NO NEED.
PLUS, MY TRIGGER FINGER AIN'T EXACTLY UP TO SNUFF THESE DAYS.
OOOH! WHAT HAPPENED?
I DON'T WANT TO TALK ABOUT IT.
IT GOT SURGICALLY REATTACHED.
(AFTER BEING BITTEN OFF BY A ROOSTER.)
I SAID I DIDN'T WANT TO TALK ABOUT IT.
BY A ROOSTER?
BY A ROOSTER, TONI?
COME ON.
MUST HAVE BEEN ONE HELL OF A ROOSTER!

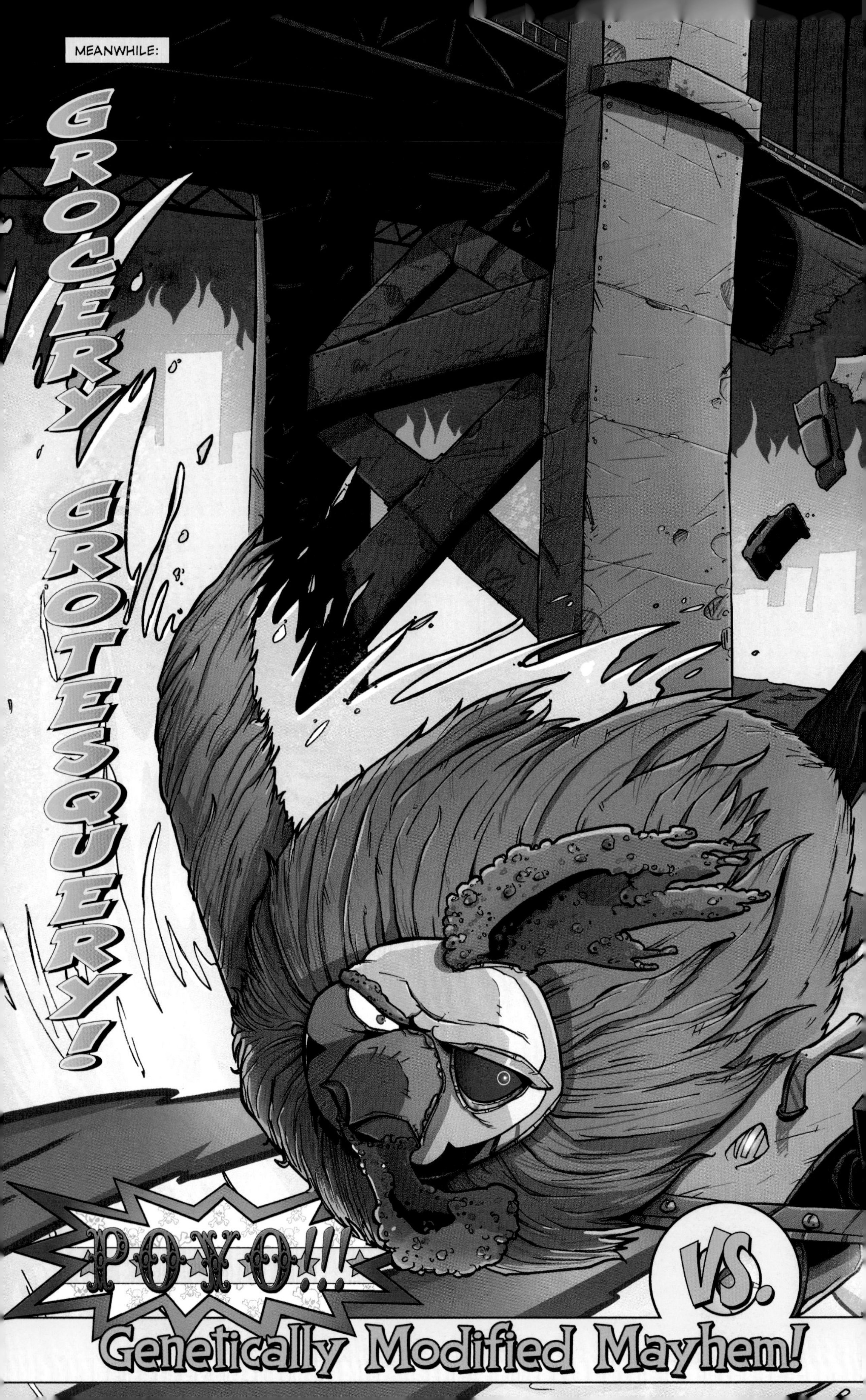
MEANWHILE:
GROCERY GROTESQUERY!
POYO!!!
VS.
Genetically Modified Mayhem!

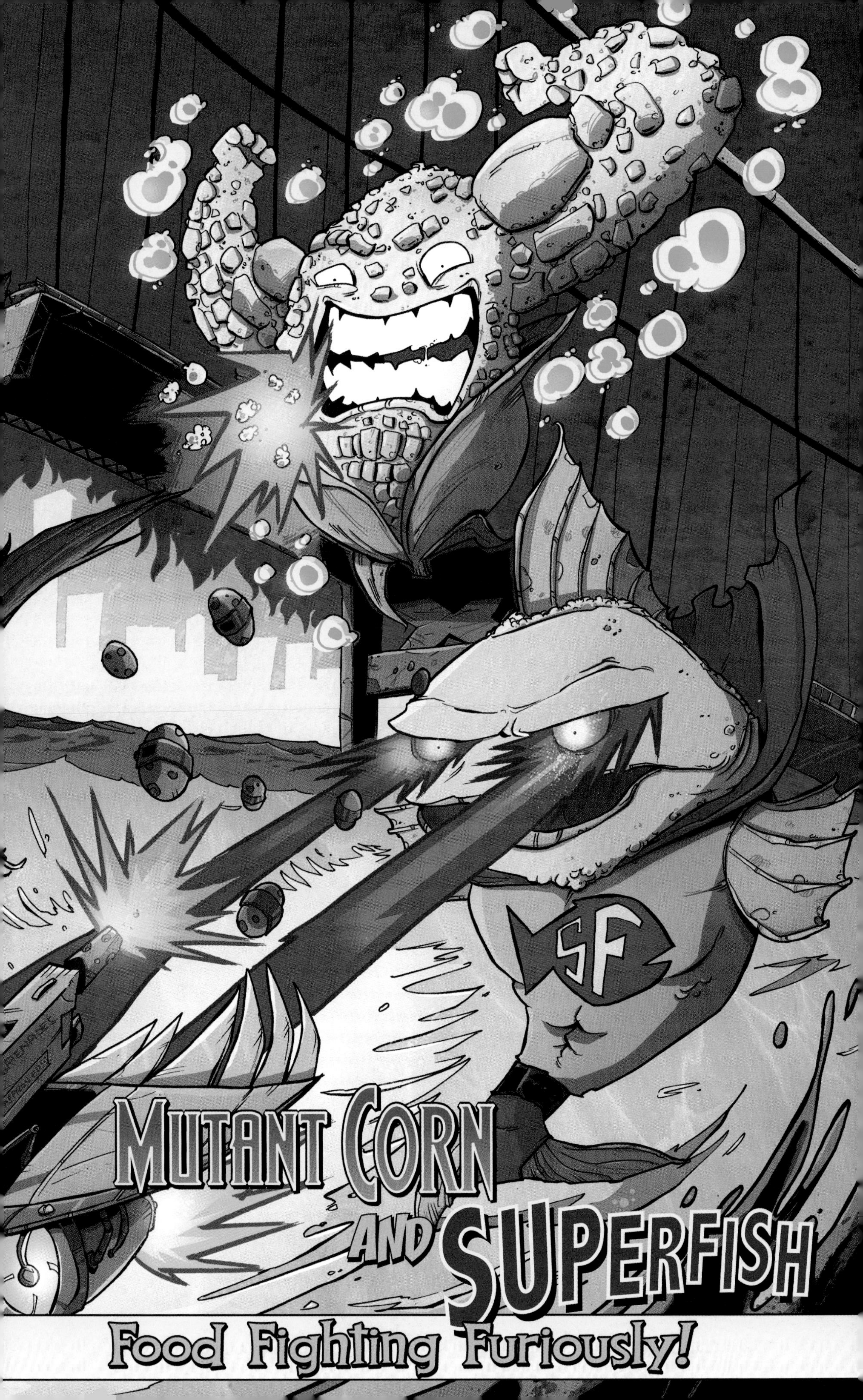
MUTANT CORN
AND SUPERFISH
SF
Food Fighting Furiously!

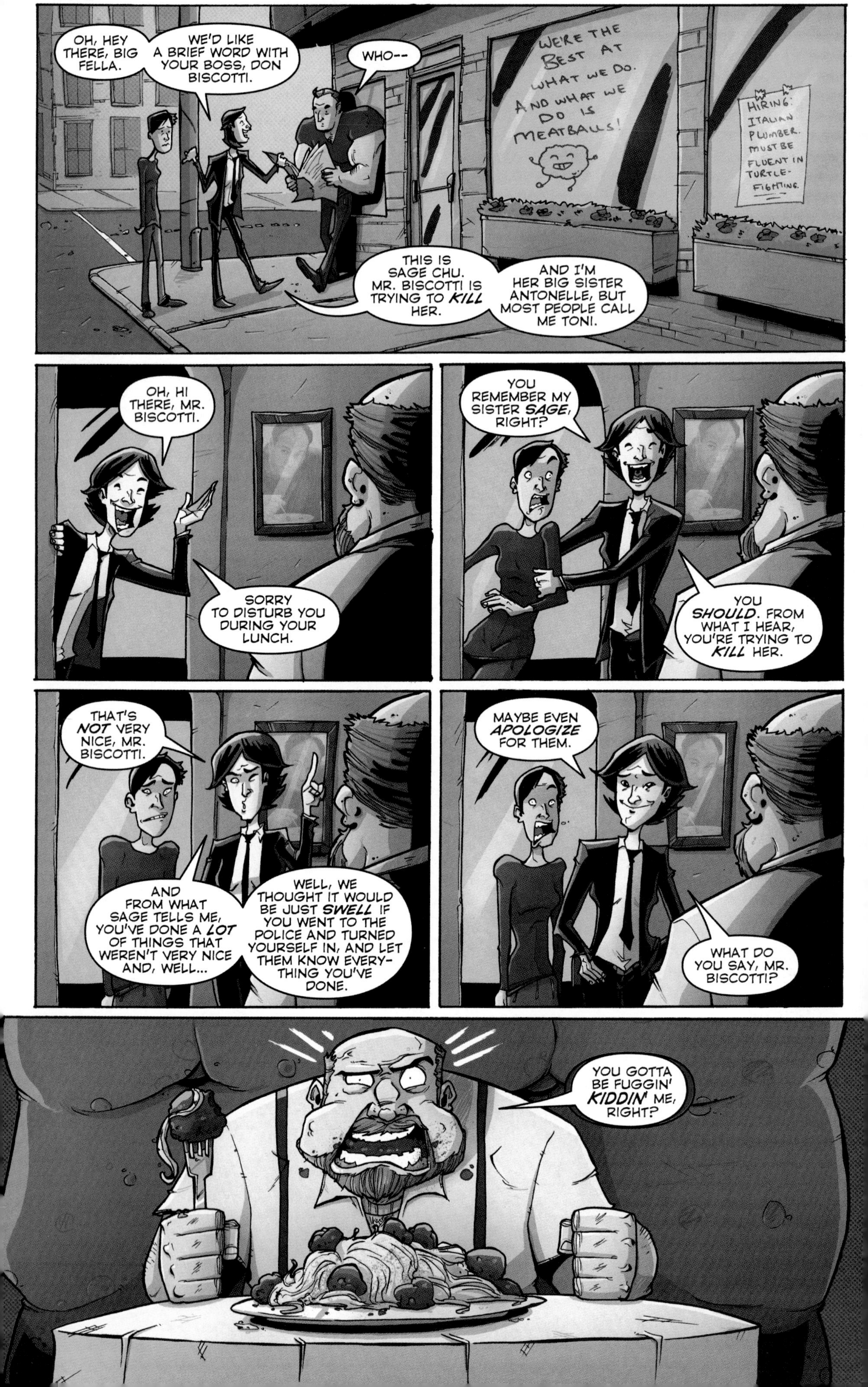
OH, HEY THERE, BIG FELLA.
WE'D LIKE A BRIEF WORD WITH YOUR BOSS, DON BISCOTTI.
WHO--
WE'RE THE BEST AT WHAT WE DO. AND WHAT WE DO IS MEATBALLS!
HIRING: ITALIAN PLUMBER. MUST BE FLUENT IN TURTLE-FIGHTING.
THIS IS SAGE CHU. MR. BISCOTTI IS TRYING TO KILL HER.
AND I'M HER BIG SISTER ANTONELLE, BUT MOST PEOPLE CALL ME TONI.
OH, HI THERE, MR. BISCOTTI.
SORRY TO DISTURB YOU DURING YOUR LUNCH.
YOU REMEMBER MY SISTER SAGE, RIGHT?
YOU SHOULD. FROM WHAT I HEAR, YOU'RE TRYING TO KILL HER.
THAT'S NOT VERY NICE, MR. BISCOTTI.
AND FROM WHAT SAGE TELLS ME, YOU'VE DONE A LOT OF THINGS THAT WEREN'T VERY NICE AND, WELL...
WELL, WE THOUGHT IT WOULD BE JUST SWELL IF YOU WENT TO THE POLICE AND TURNED YOURSELF IN, AND LET THEM KNOW EVERYTHING YOU'VE DONE.
MAYBE EVEN APOLOGIZE FOR THEM.
WHAT DO YOU SAY, MR. BISCOTTI?
YOU GOTTA BE FUGGIN' KIDDIN' ME, RIGHT?

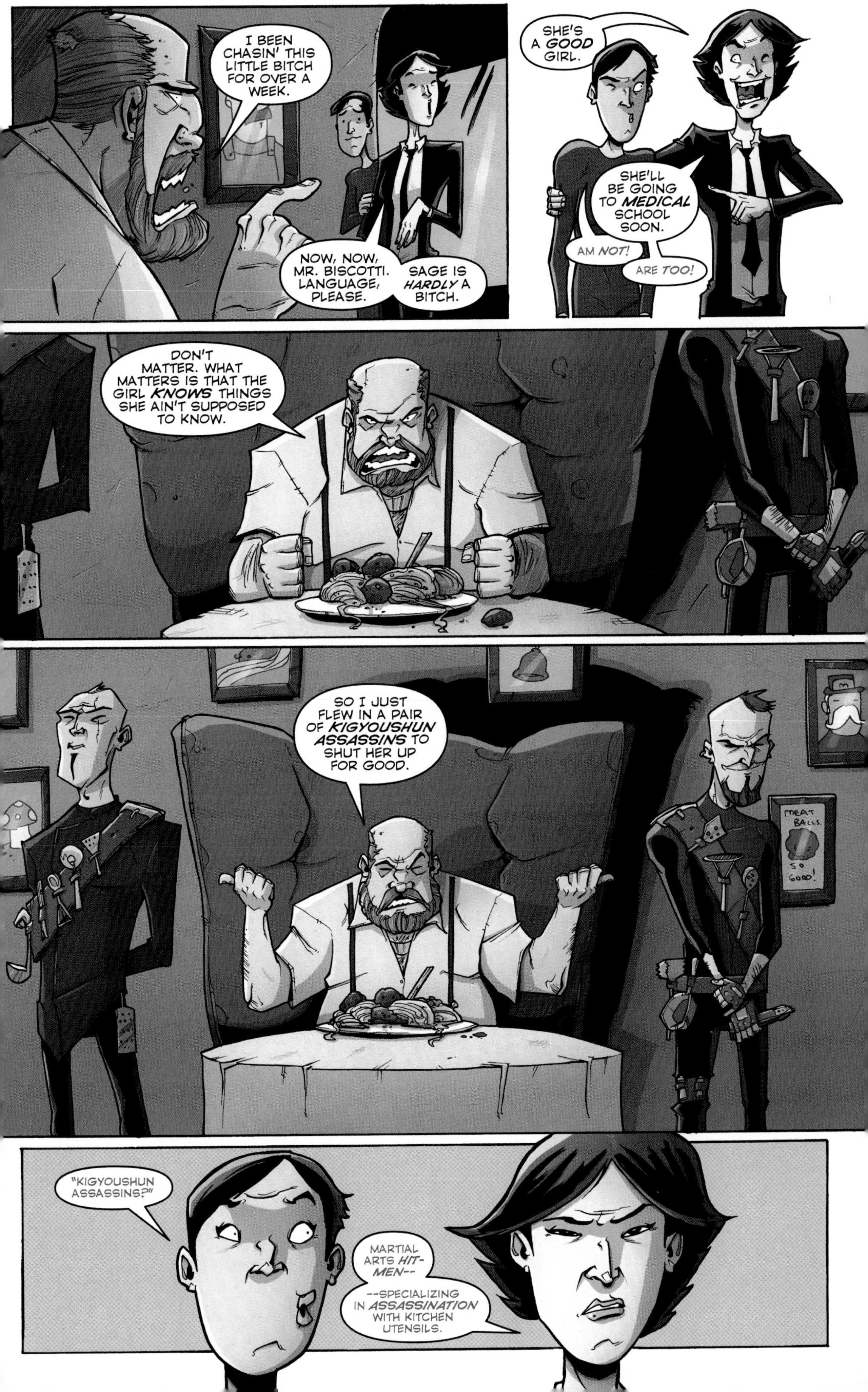
I BEEN CHASIN' THIS LITTLE BITCH FOR OVER A WEEK.
NOW, NOW, MR. BISCOTTI. LANGUAGE, PLEASE.
SAGE IS *HARDLY* A BITCH.
SHE'S A *GOOD* GIRL.
SHE'LL BE GOING TO *MEDICAL* SCHOOL SOON.
AM *NOT!*
ARE *TOO!*
DON'T MATTER. WHAT MATTERS IS THAT THE GIRL *KNOWS* THINGS SHE AIN'T SUPPOSED TO KNOW.
SO I JUST FLEW IN A PAIR OF *KIGYOUSHUN ASSASSINS* TO SHUT HER UP FOR GOOD.
MEAT BALLS. SO GOOD!
"KIGYOUSHUN ASSASSINS?"
MARTIAL ARTS *HIT-MEN--*
--SPECIALIZING IN *ASSASSINATION* WITH KITCHEN UTENSILS.

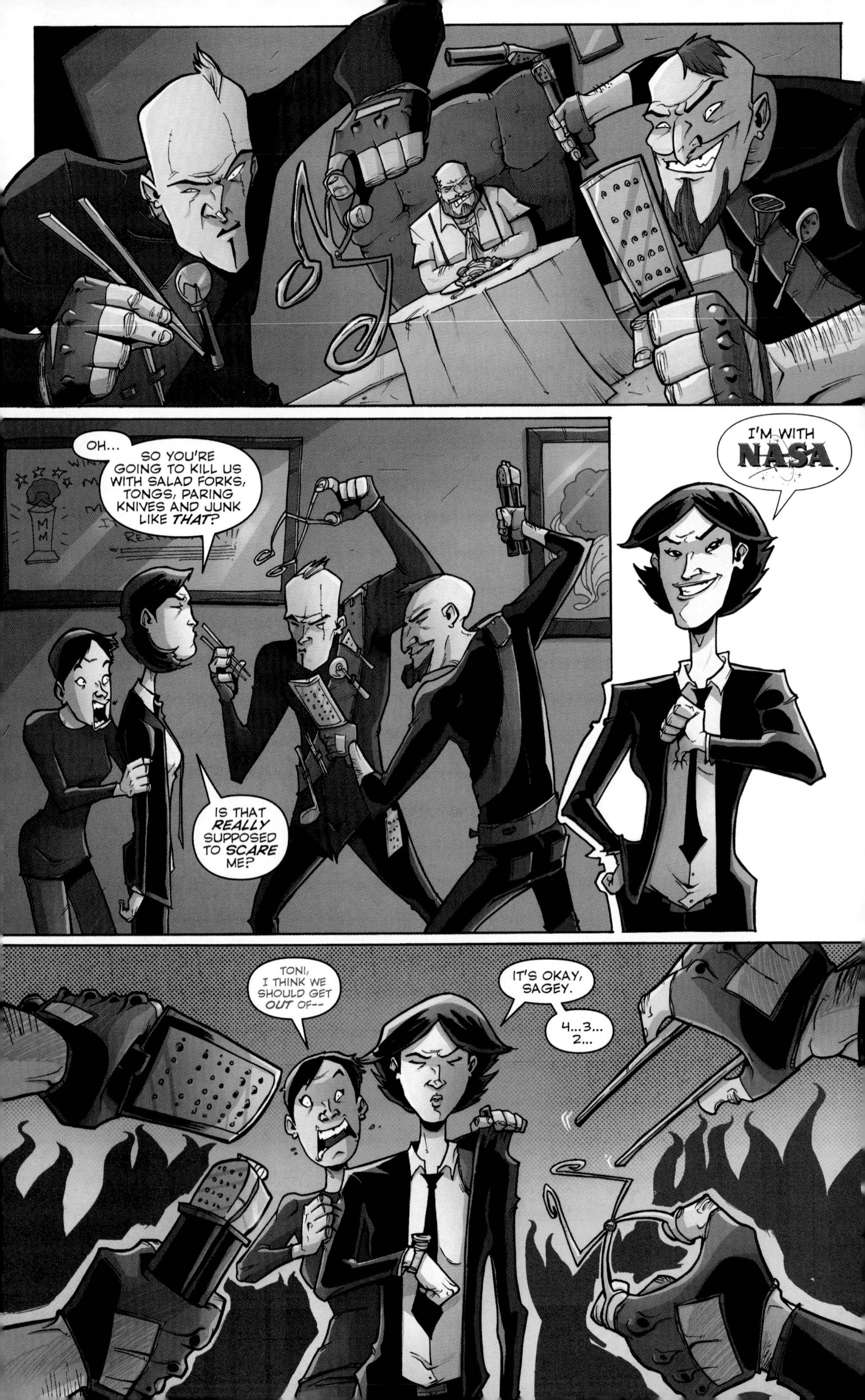
OH...
SO YOU'RE GOING TO KILL US WITH SALAD FORKS, TONGS, PARING KNIVES AND JUNK LIKE *THAT*?
IS THAT *REALLY* SUPPOSED TO *SCARE* ME?
I'M WITH NASA.
TONI, I THINK WE SHOULD GET *OUT* OF--
IT'S OKAY, SAGEY.
4...3... 2...

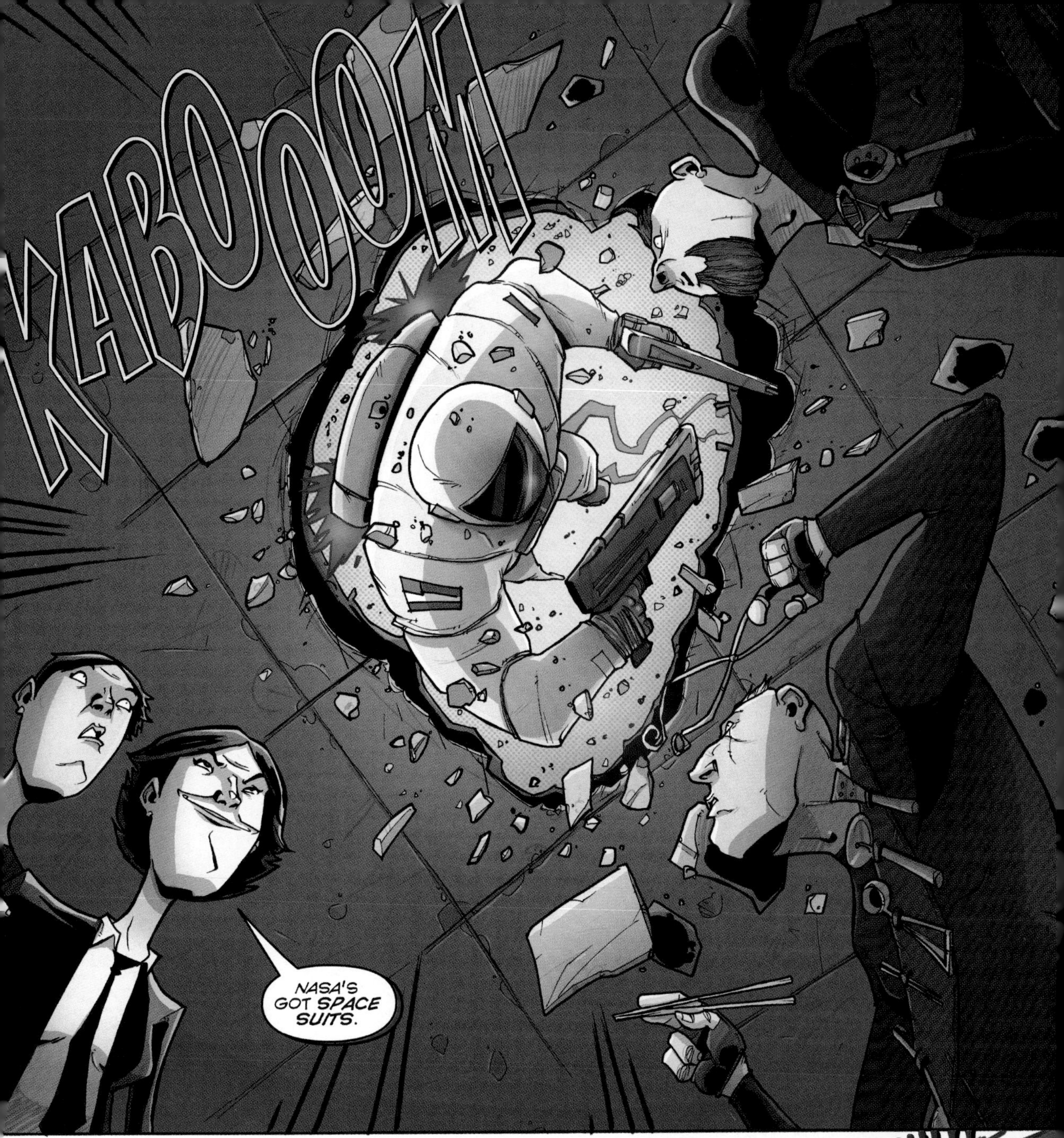
KABOOOM
NASA'S GOT SPACE SUITS.

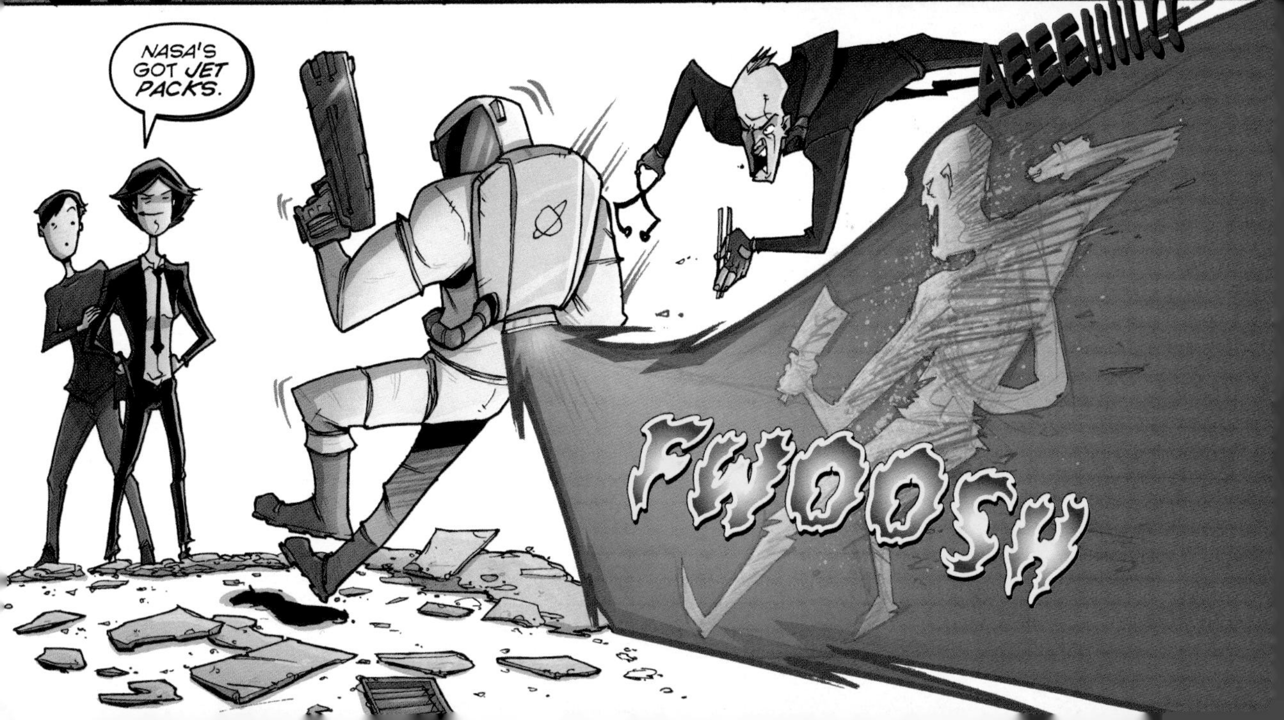
NASA'S GOT JET PACKS.
AEEEIIIII!!
FWOOSH

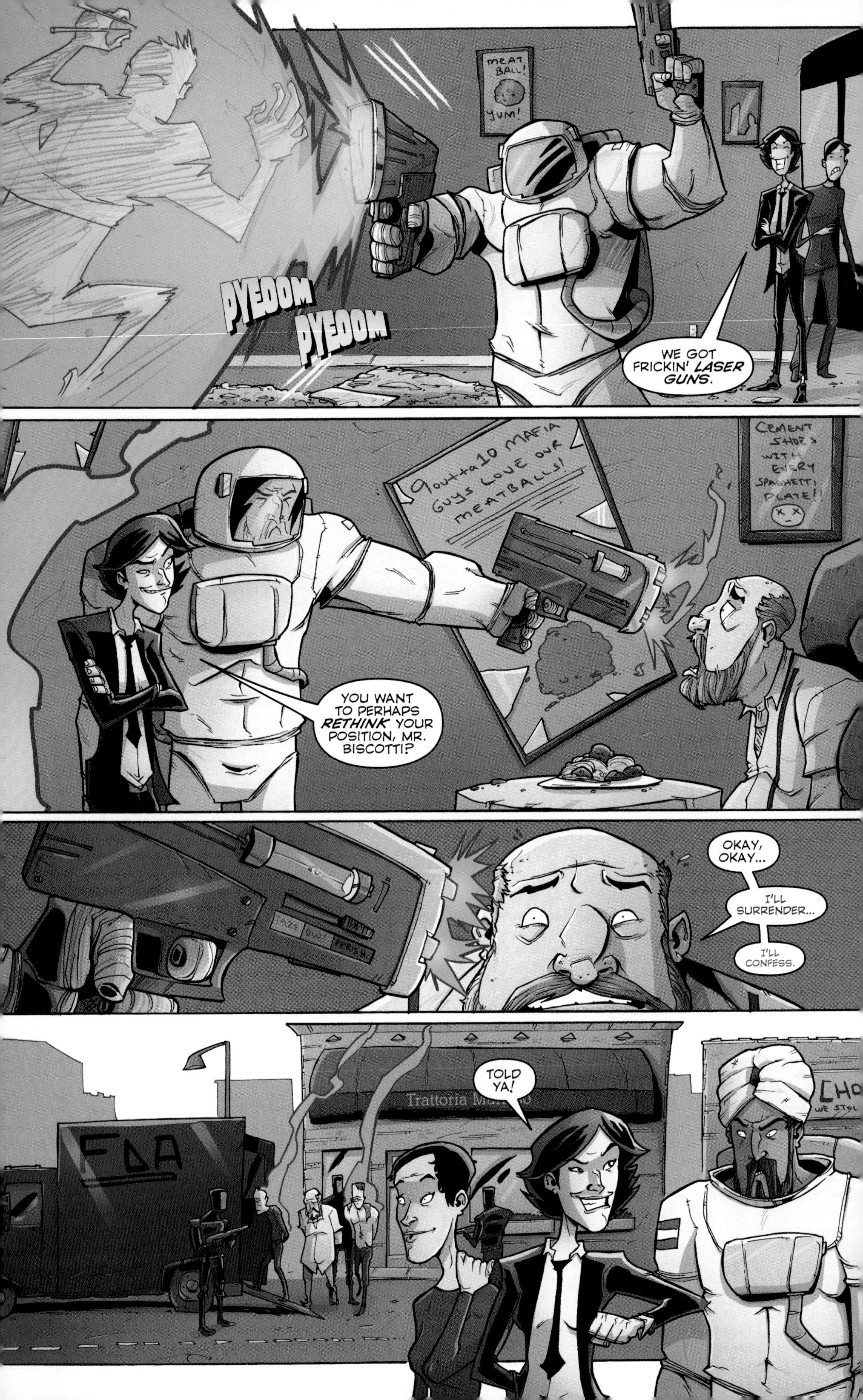
MEAT BALL! YUM!
PYEOOM
PYEOOM
WE GOT FRICKIN' LASER GUNS.
9outta10 MAFIA GUYS LOVE OUR MEATBALLS!
CEMENT SHOES WITH EVERY SPAGHETTI PLATE!!
YOU WANT TO PERHAPS RETHINK YOUR POSITION, MR. BISCOTTI?
TAZE
OW!
PERISH.
OKAY, OKAY...
I'LL SURRENDER...
I'LL CONFESS.
FDA
Trattoria
TOLD YA!

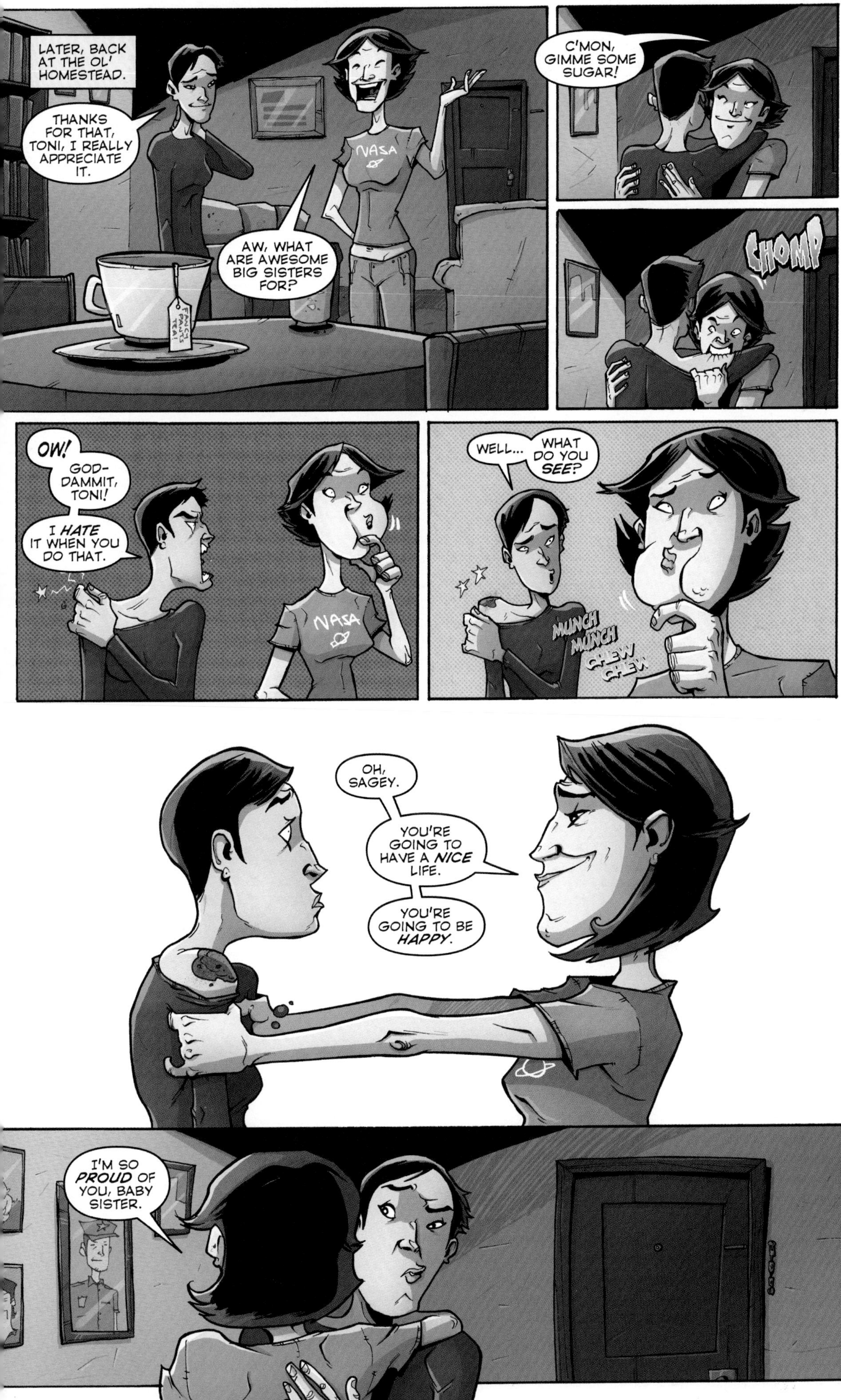
LATER, BACK AT THE OL' HOMESTEAD.
THANKS FOR THAT, TONI, I REALLY APPRECIATE IT.
AW, WHAT ARE AWESOME BIG SISTERS FOR?
C'MON, GIMME SOME SUGAR!
CHOMP
OW!
GOD-DAMMIT, TONI!
I HATE IT WHEN YOU DO THAT.
WELL...
WHAT DO YOU SEE?
MUNCH MUNCH CHEW CHEW
OH, SAGEY.
YOU'RE GOING TO HAVE A NICE LIFE.
YOU'RE GOING TO BE HAPPY.
I'M SO PROUD OF YOU, BABY SISTER.

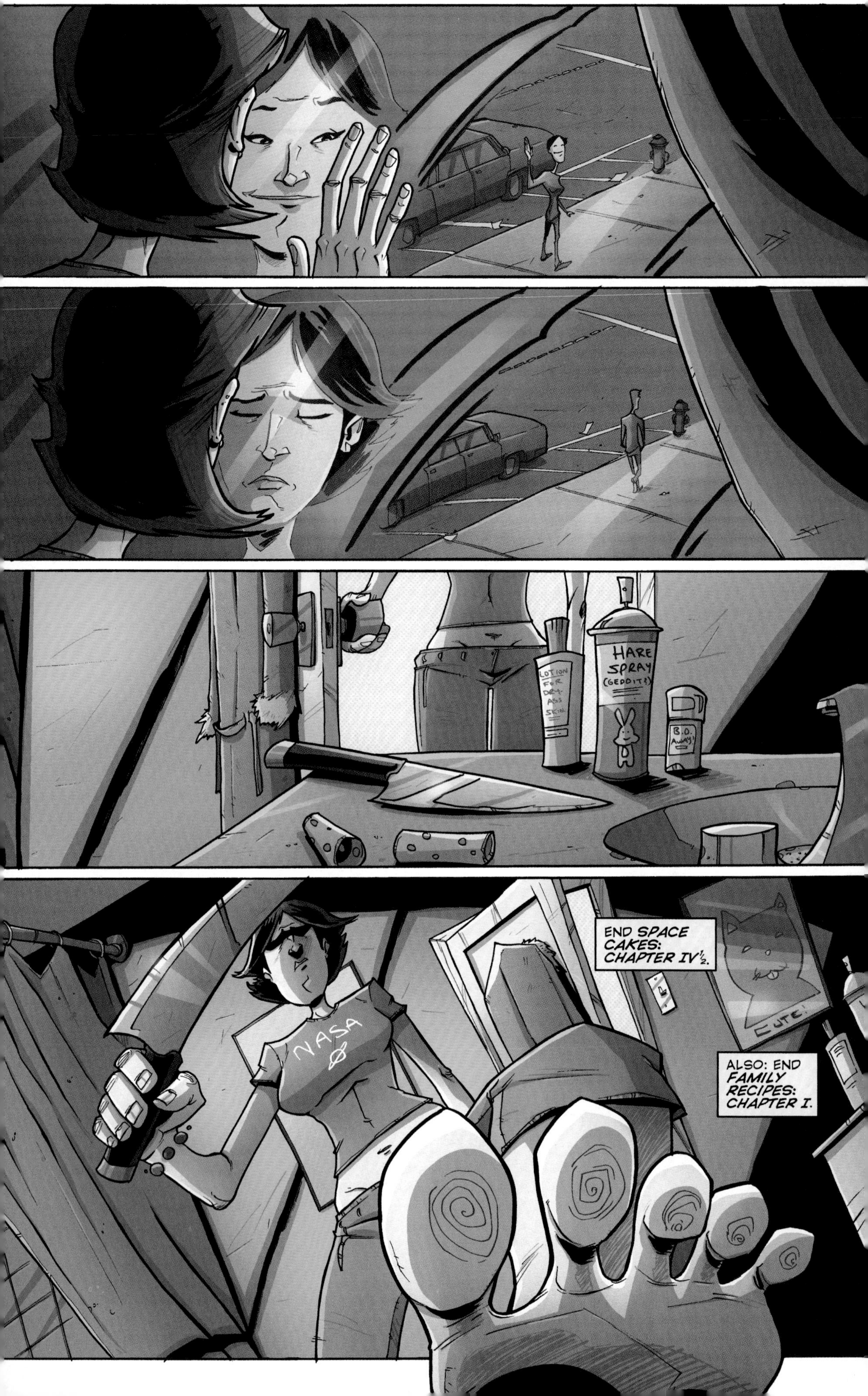
LOTION FOR DRY-ASS SKIN
HARE SPRAY (GEDDIT?)
B.O. AWAY!
NASA
CUTE.
END SPACE CAKES: CHAPTER IV½.
ALSO: END FAMILY RECIPES: CHAPTER I.

Chapter Seven

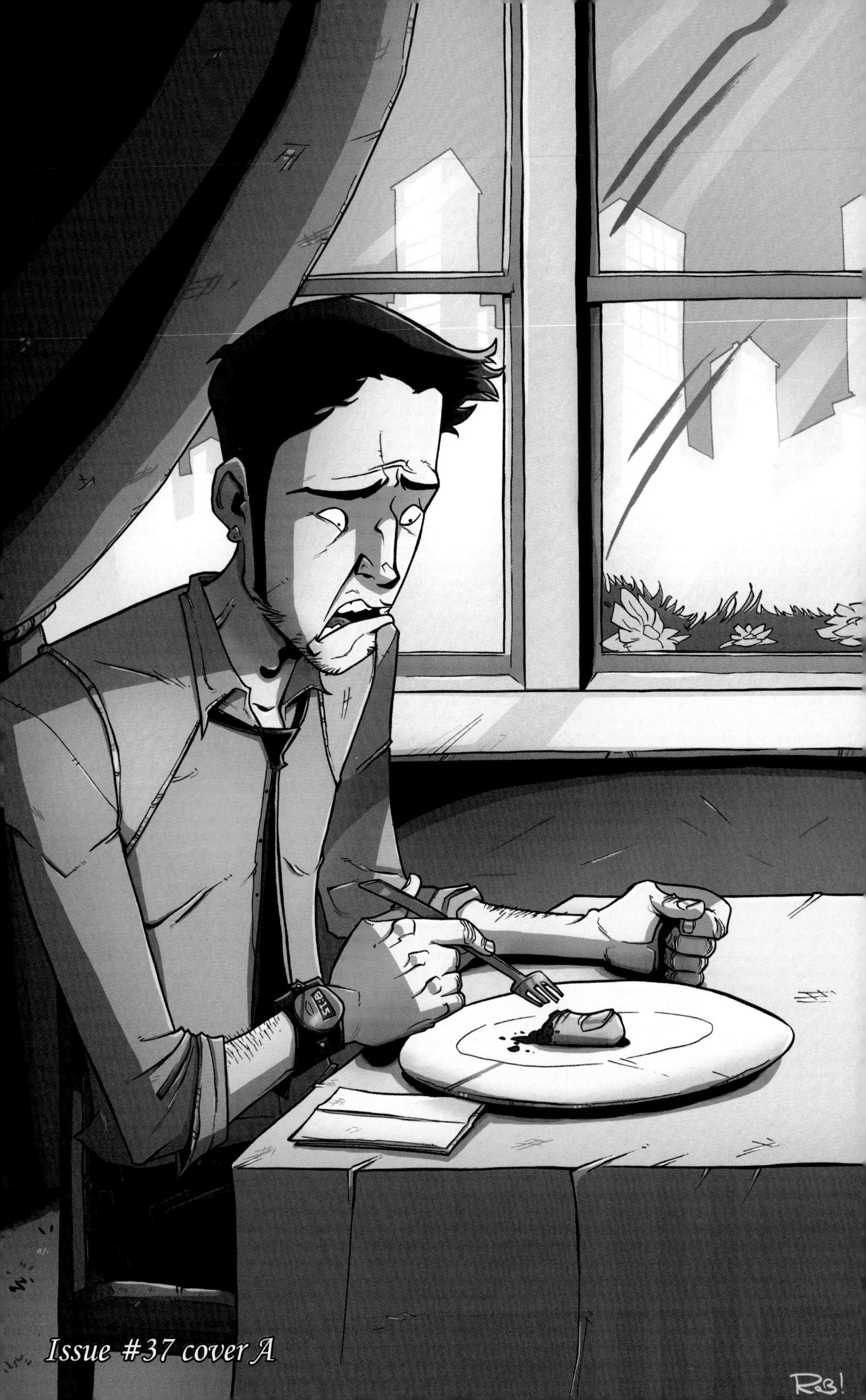

Issue #37 cover A

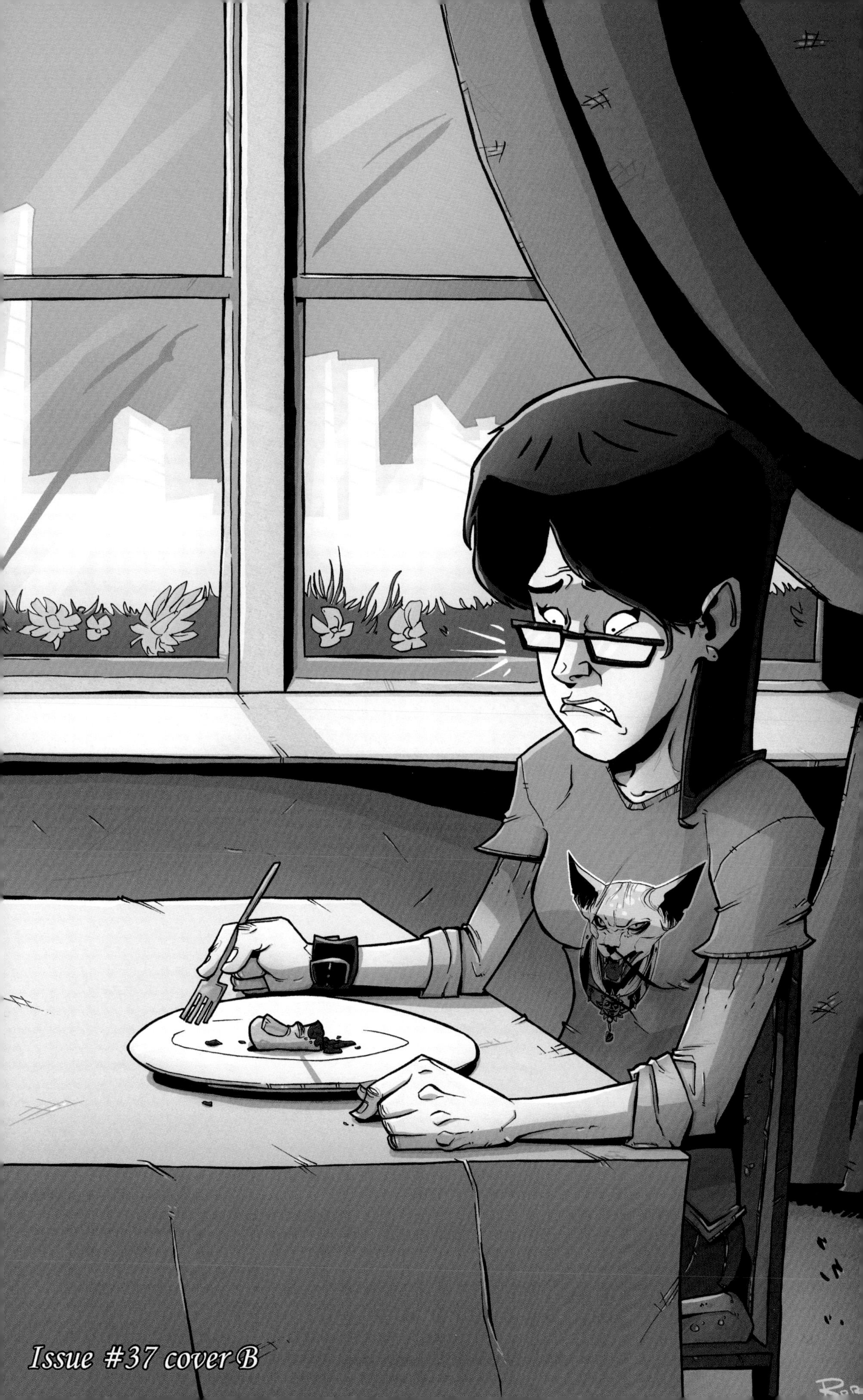

Issue #37 cover B

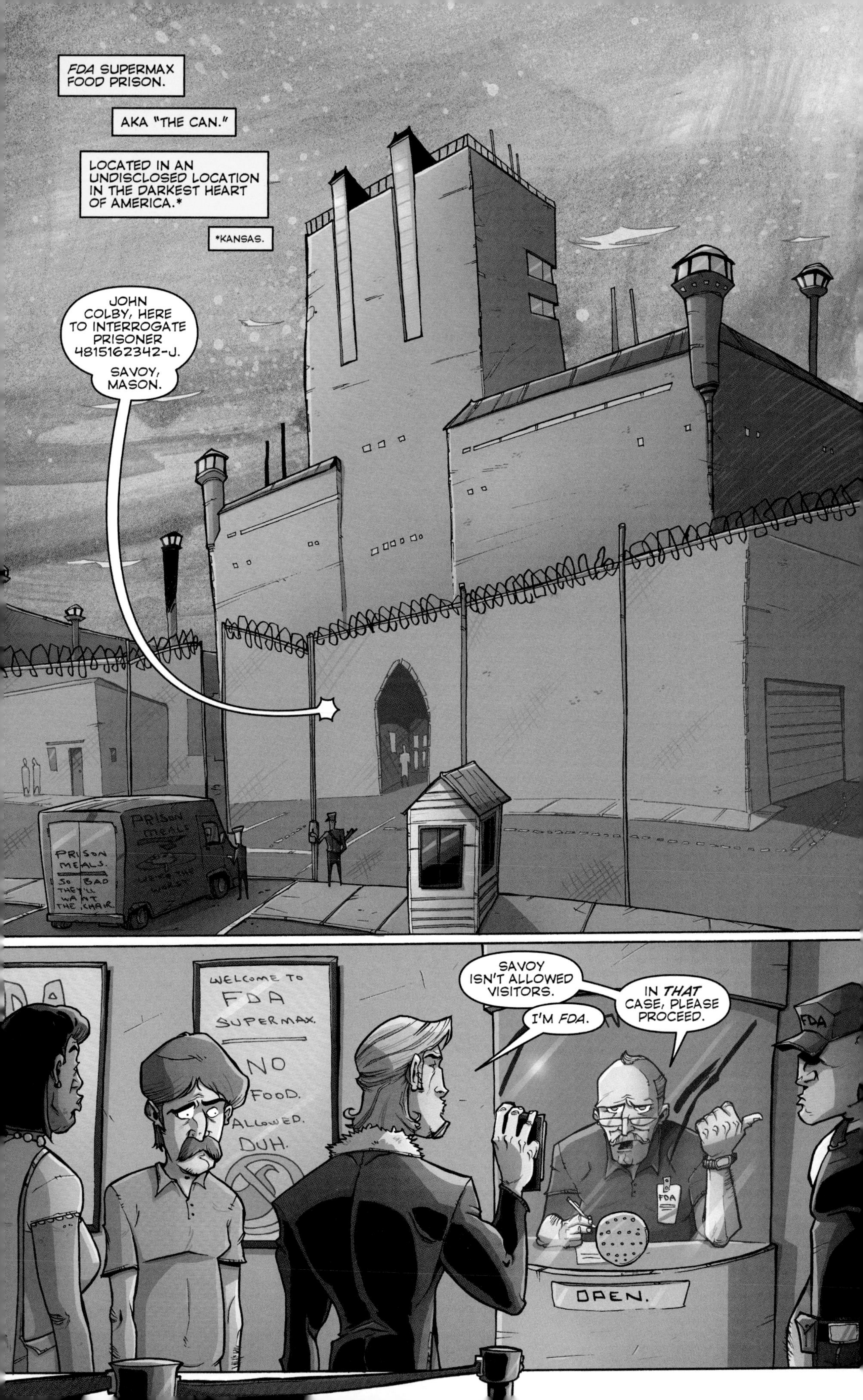

FDA SUPERMAX FOOD PRISON.
AKA "THE CAN."
LOCATED IN AN UNDISCLOSED LOCATION IN THE DARKEST HEART OF AMERICA.*
*KANSAS.
JOHN COLBY, HERE TO INTERROGATE PRISONER 4815162342-J.
SAVOY, MASON.
PRISON MEALS
PRISON MEALS. SO BAD THEY'LL WANT THE CHAIR.
WELCOME TO FDA SUPERMAX.
NO FOOD. ALLOWED. DUH.
SAVOY ISN'T ALLOWED VISITORS.
I'M FDA.
IN THAT CASE, PLEASE PROCEED.
FDA
OPEN.

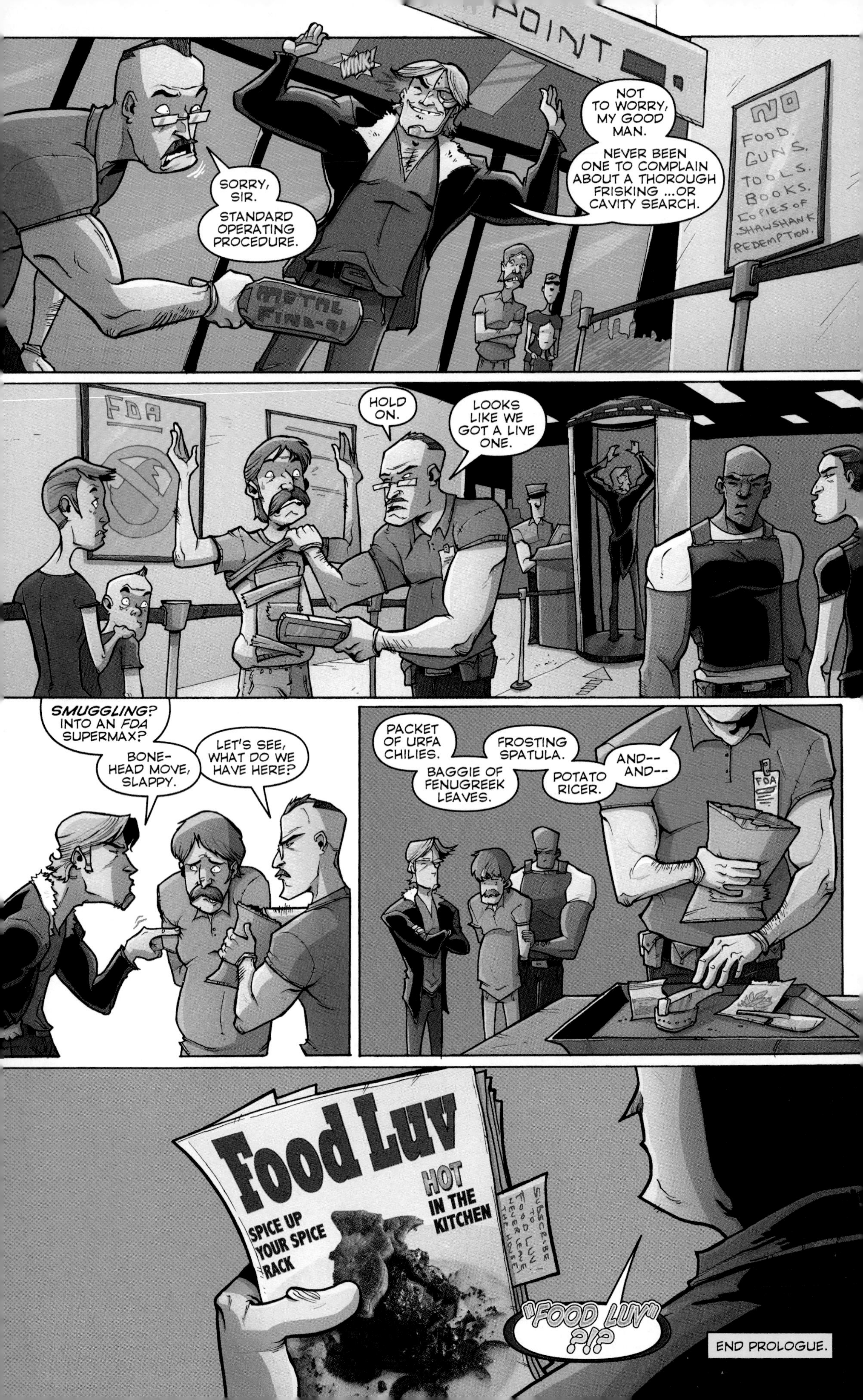
POINT
WINK!
SORRY, SIR.
STANDARD OPERATING PROCEDURE.
NOT TO WORRY, MY GOOD MAN.
NEVER BEEN ONE TO COMPLAIN ABOUT A THOROUGH FRISKING ...OR CAVITY SEARCH.
NO FOOD. GUNS. TOOLS. BOOKS. COPIES OF SHAWSHANK REDEMPTION.
METAL FIND-O!
FDA
HOLD ON.
LOOKS LIKE WE GOT A LIVE ONE.
SMUGGLING? INTO AN *FDA* SUPERMAX?
BONE-HEAD MOVE, SLAPPY.
LET'S SEE, WHAT DO WE HAVE HERE?
PACKET OF URFA CHILIES.
BAGGIE OF FENUGREEK LEAVES.
FROSTING SPATULA.
POTATO RICER.
AND-- AND--
FDA
Food Luv
HOT IN THE KITCHEN
SPICE UP YOUR SPICE RACK
SUBSCRIBE TO FOOD LUV! NEVER LEAVE THE HOUSE!
"FOOD LUV" ?!?
END PROLOGUE.

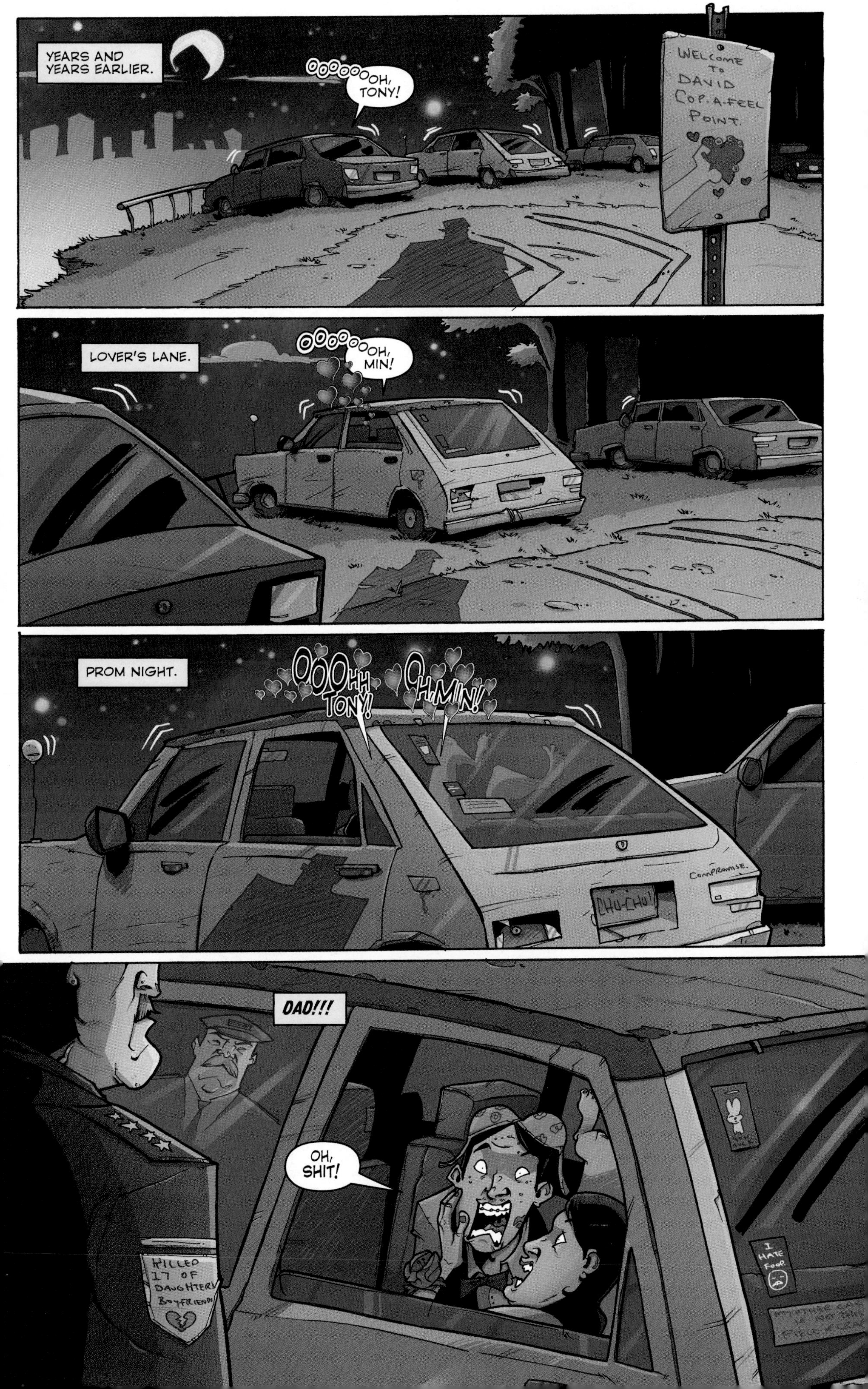
YEARS AND YEARS EARLIER.
OOOOOOOH, TONY!
WELCOME TO DAVID COP-A-FEEL POINT.
LOVER'S LANE.
OOOOOOOH, MIN!
PROM NIGHT.
OOOHH TONY!
OH, MIN!
COMPROMISE.
CHU-CHU
DAD!!!
OH, SHIT!
KILLED 17 OF DAUGHTER'S BOYFRIENDS
I HATE FOOD.

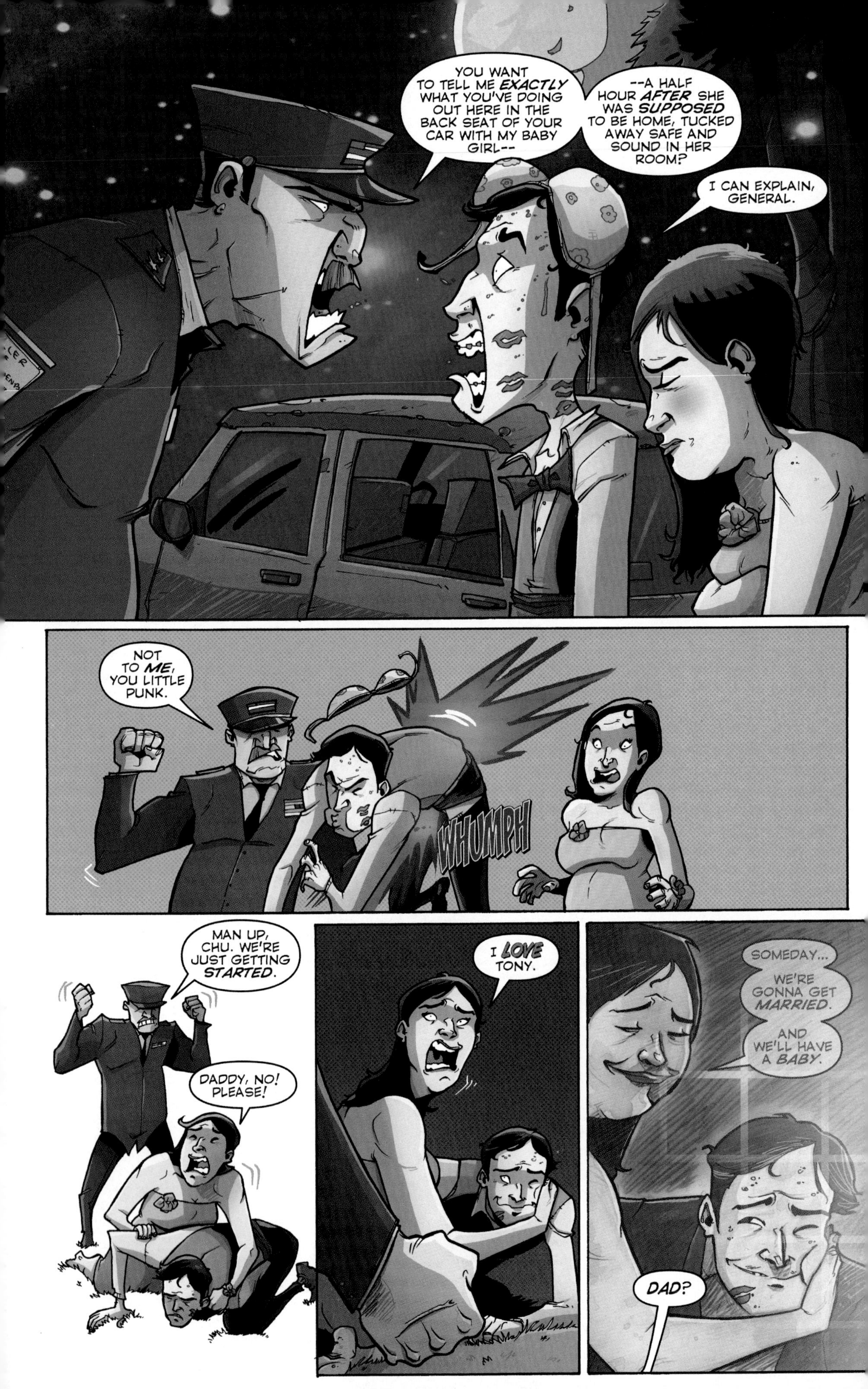
YOU WANT TO TELL ME EXACTLY WHAT YOU'VE DOING OUT HERE IN THE BACK SEAT OF YOUR CAR WITH MY BABY GIRL--
--A HALF HOUR AFTER SHE WAS SUPPOSED TO BE HOME, TUCKED AWAY SAFE AND SOUND IN HER ROOM?
I CAN EXPLAIN, GENERAL.
NOT TO ME, YOU LITTLE PUNK.
WHUMPH
MAN UP, CHU. WE'RE JUST GETTING STARTED.
DADDY, NO! PLEASE!
I LOVE TONY.
SOMEDAY...
WE'RE GONNA GET MARRIED.
AND WE'LL HAVE A BABY.
DAD?

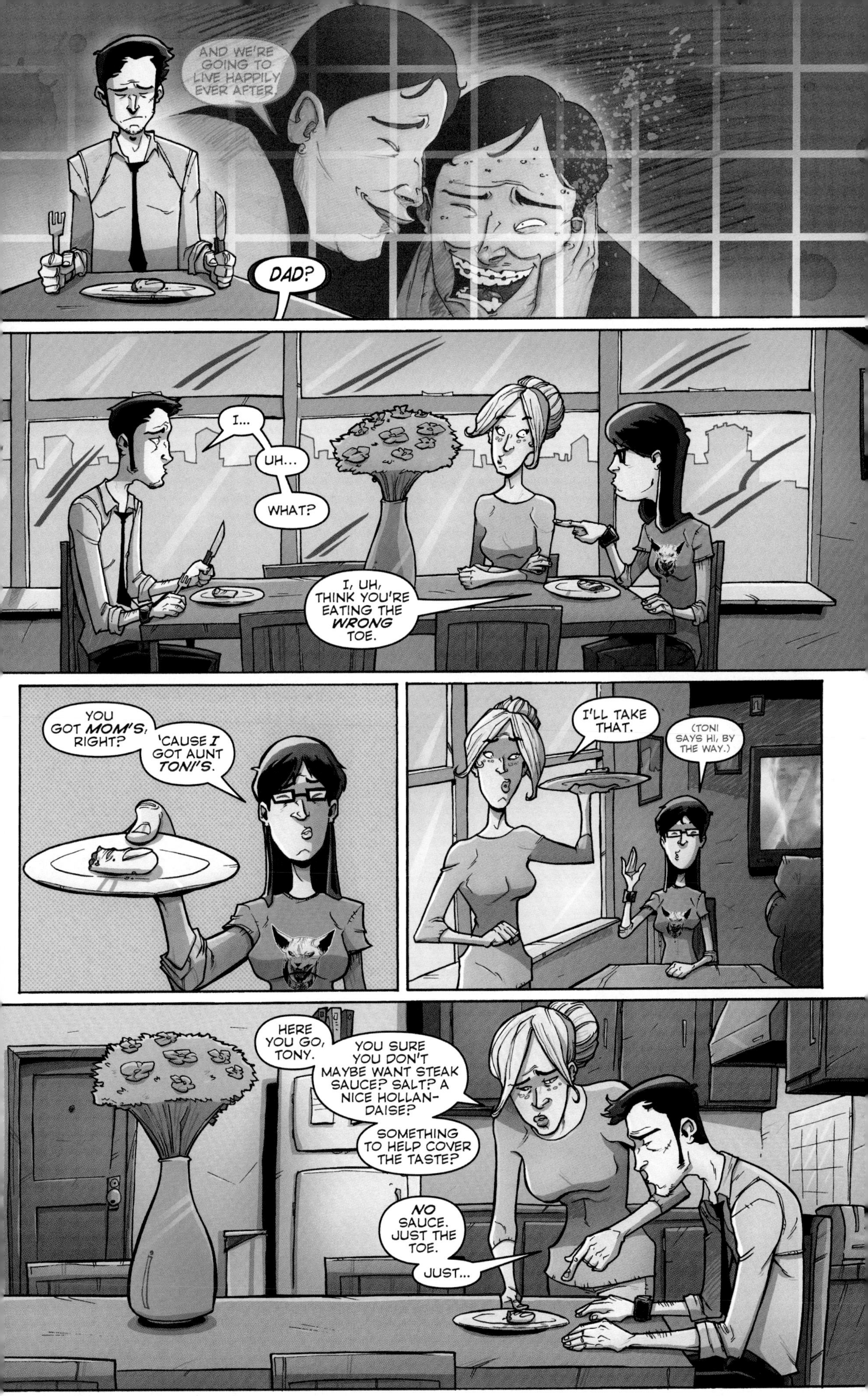
AND WE'RE GOING TO LIVE HAPPILY EVER AFTER.
DAD?
I...
UH...
WHAT?
I, UH, THINK YOU'RE EATING THE WRONG TOE.
YOU GOT MOM'S, RIGHT?
'CAUSE I GOT AUNT TONI'S.
I'LL TAKE THAT.
(TONI SAYS HI, BY THE WAY.)
HERE YOU GO, TONY.
YOU SURE YOU DON'T MAYBE WANT STEAK SAUCE? SALT? A NICE HOLLAN-DAISE?
SOMETHING TO HELP COVER THE TASTE?
NO SAUCE. JUST THE TOE.
JUST...

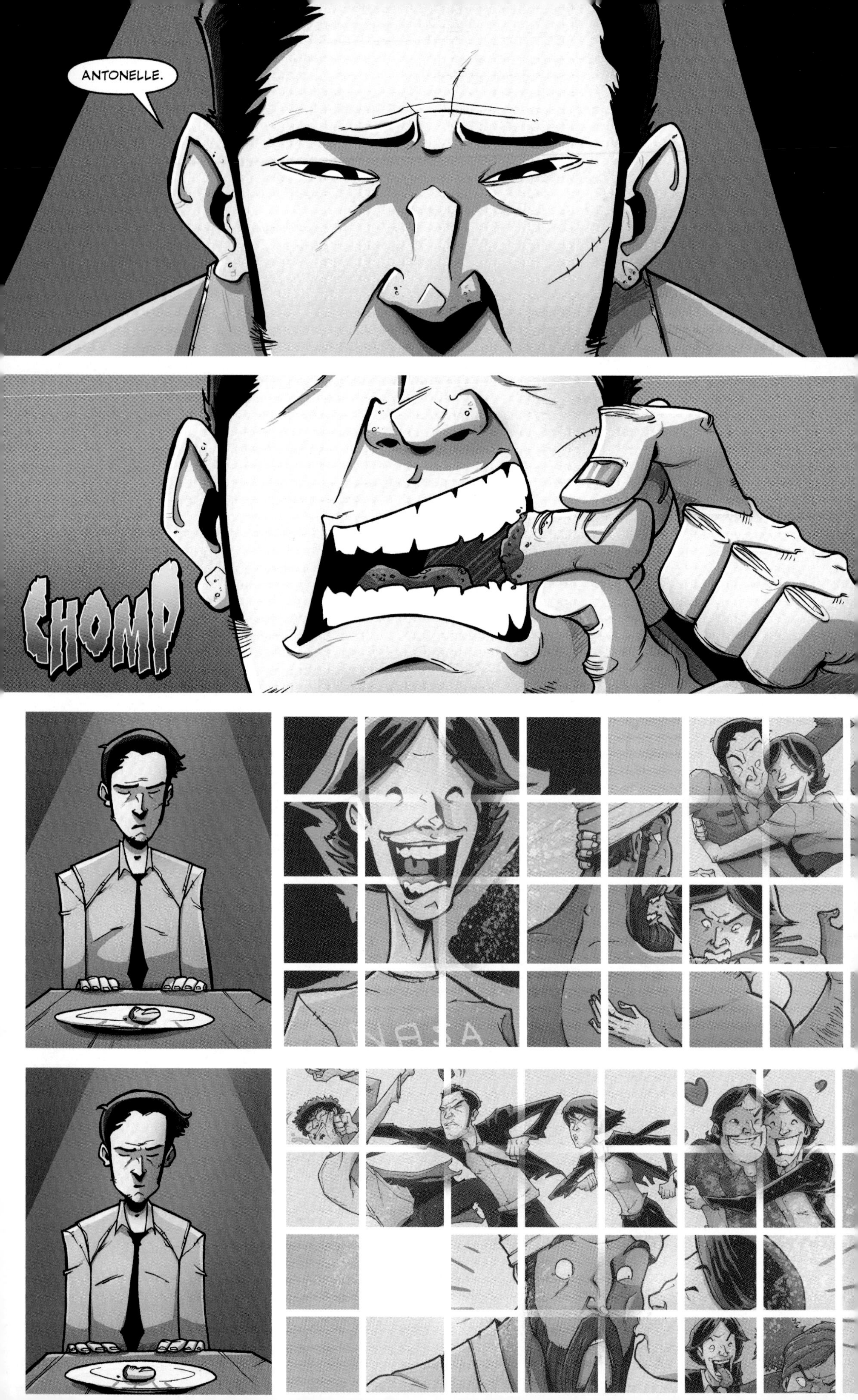
ANTONELLE.
CHOMP

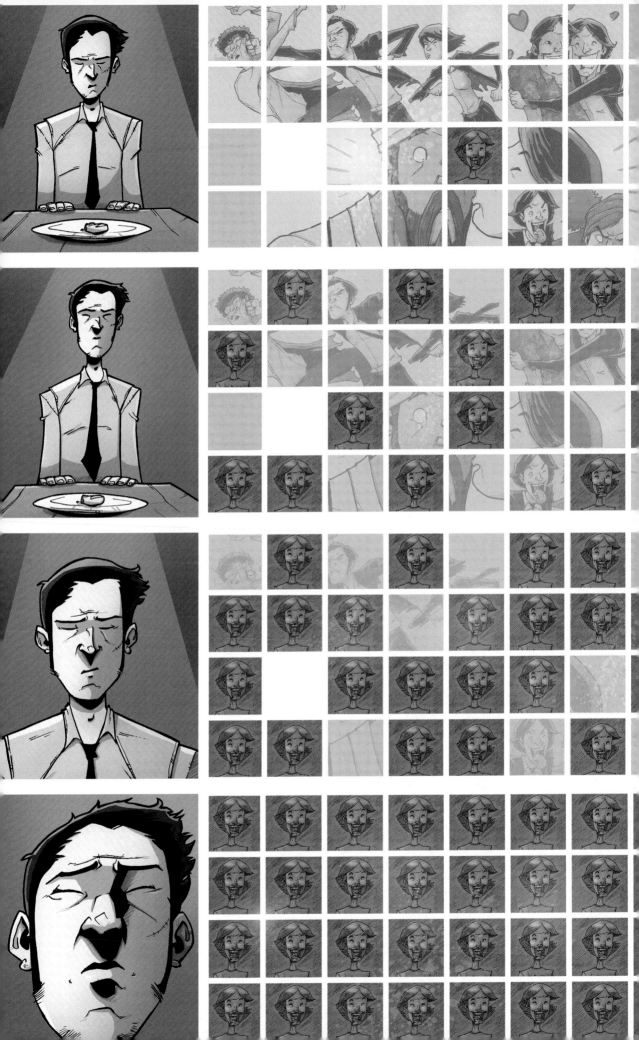

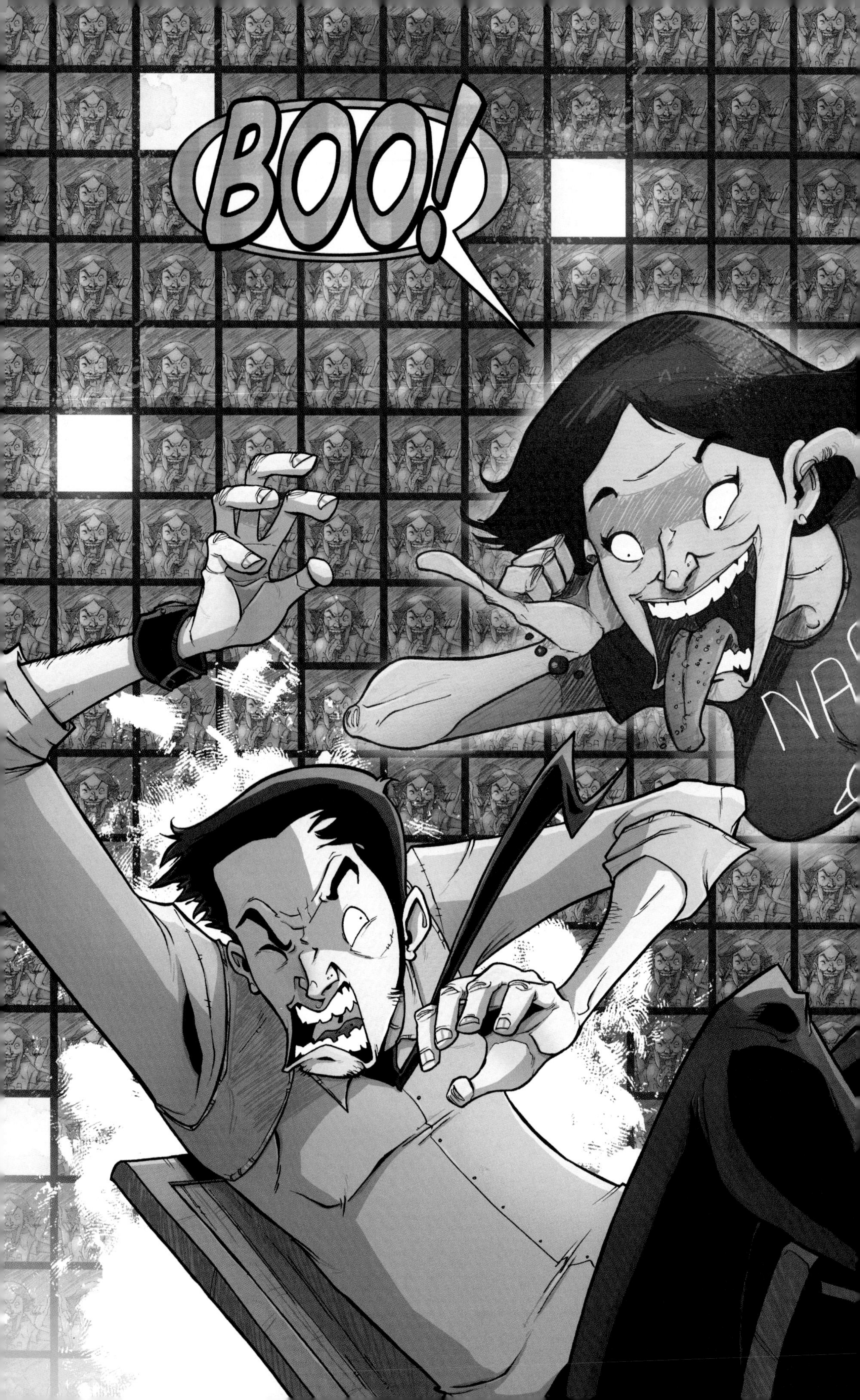
BOO!

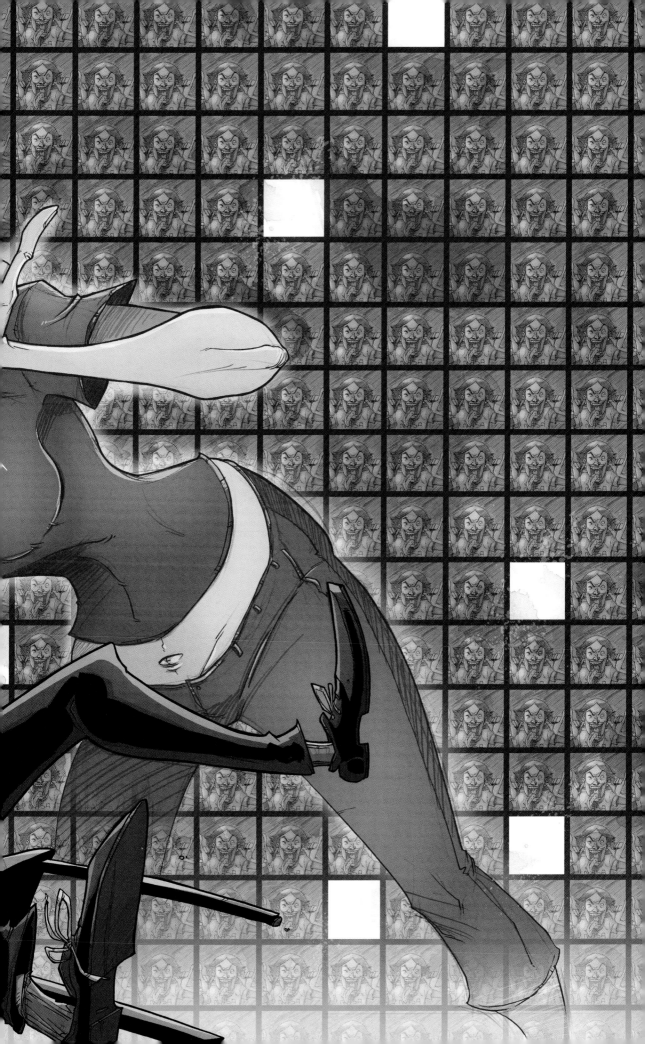

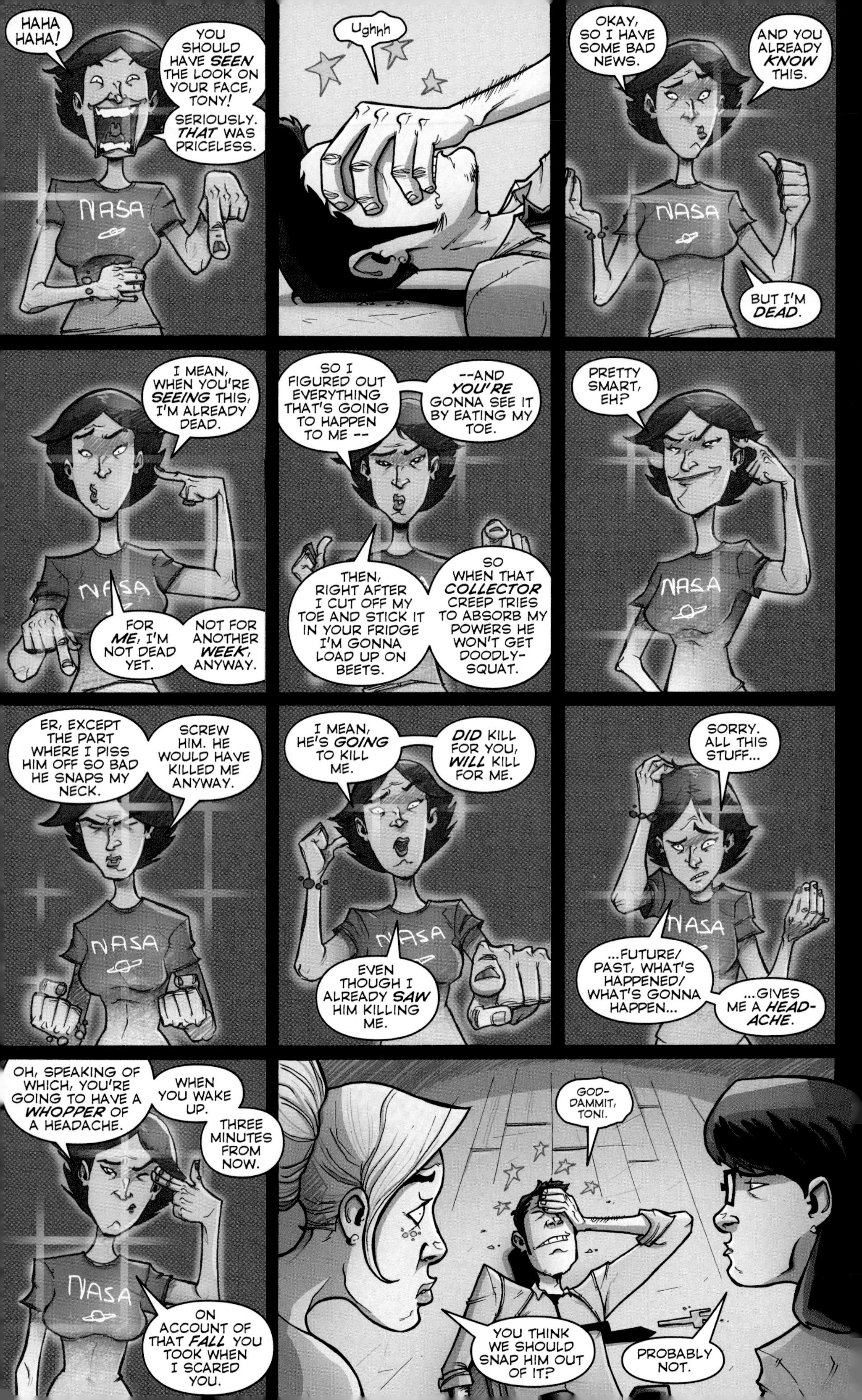
HAHA HAHA!
YOU SHOULD HAVE SEEN THE LOOK ON YOUR FACE, TONY!
SERIOUSLY. THAT WAS PRICELESS.
Ughhh
OKAY, SO I HAVE SOME BAD NEWS.
AND YOU ALREADY KNOW THIS.
BUT I'M DEAD.
I MEAN, WHEN YOU'RE SEEING THIS, I'M ALREADY DEAD.
FOR ME, I'M NOT DEAD YET.
NOT FOR ANOTHER WEEK, ANYWAY.
SO I FIGURED OUT EVERYTHING THAT'S GOING TO HAPPEN TO ME --
--AND YOU'RE GONNA SEE IT BY EATING MY TOE.
THEN, RIGHT AFTER I CUT OFF MY TOE AND STICK IT IN YOUR FRIDGE I'M GONNA LOAD UP ON BEETS.
SO WHEN THAT COLLECTOR CREEP TRIES TO ABSORB MY POWERS HE WON'T GET DOODLY-SQUAT.
PRETTY SMART, EH?
ER, EXCEPT THE PART WHERE I PISS HIM OFF SO BAD HE SNAPS MY NECK.
SCREW HIM. HE WOULD HAVE KILLED ME ANYWAY.
I MEAN, HE'S GOING TO KILL ME.
DID KILL FOR YOU, WILL KILL FOR ME.
EVEN THOUGH I ALREADY SAW HIM KILLING ME.
SORRY. ALL THIS STUFF...
...FUTURE/ PAST, WHAT'S HAPPENED/ WHAT'S GONNA HAPPEN...
...GIVES ME A HEAD-ACHE.
OH, SPEAKING OF WHICH, YOU'RE GOING TO HAVE A WHOPPER OF A HEADACHE.
WHEN YOU WAKE UP.
THREE MINUTES FROM NOW.
ON ACCOUNT OF THAT FALL YOU TOOK WHEN I SCARED YOU.
GOD-DAMMIT, TONI.
YOU THINK WE SHOULD SNAP HIM OUT OF IT?
PROBABLY NOT.

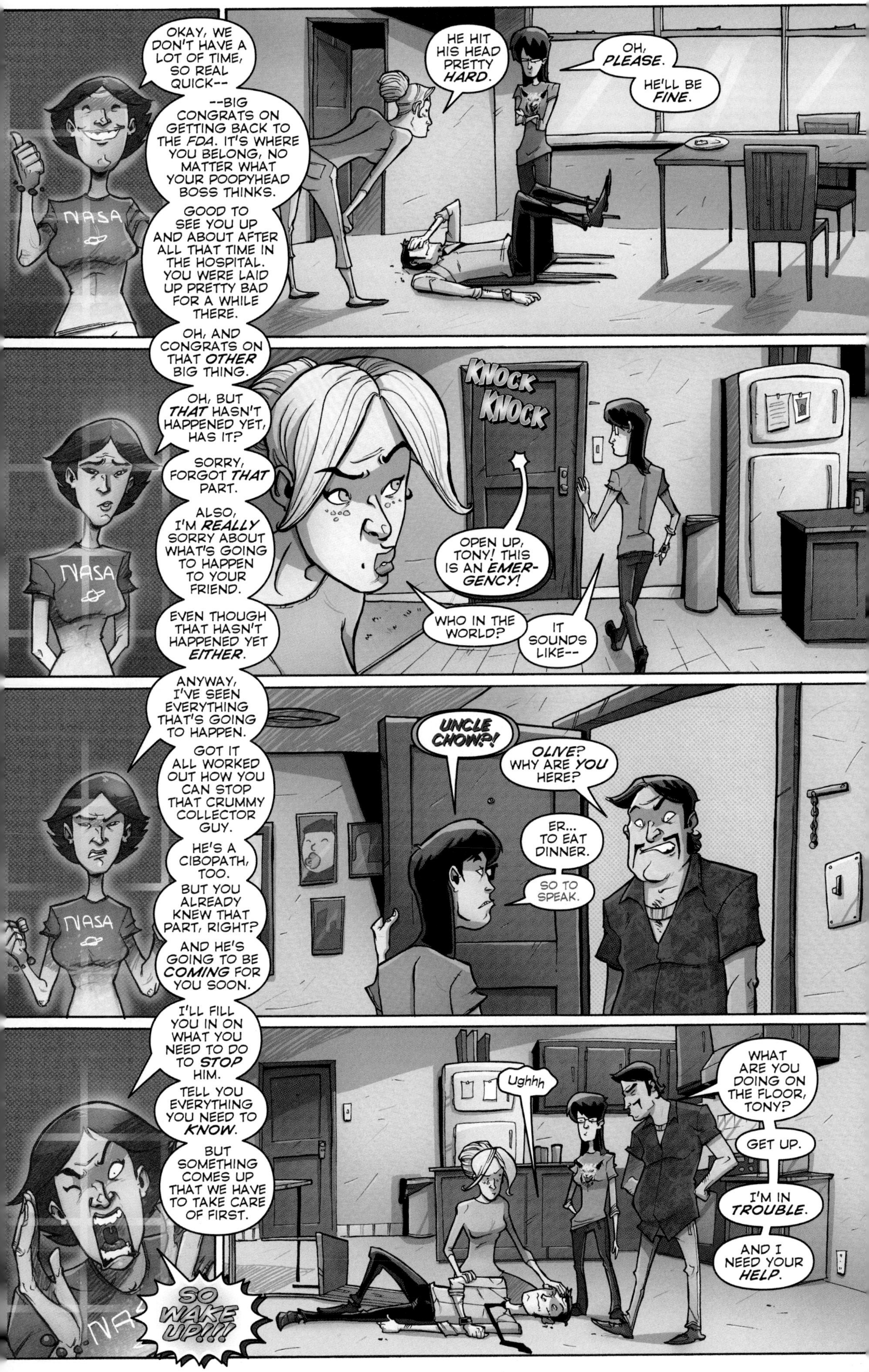
OKAY, WE DON'T HAVE A LOT OF TIME, SO REAL QUICK--
HE HIT HIS HEAD PRETTY HARD.
OH, PLEASE.
HE'LL BE FINE.
--BIG CONGRATS ON GETTING BACK TO THE FDA. IT'S WHERE YOU BELONG, NO MATTER WHAT YOUR POOPYHEAD BOSS THINKS.
GOOD TO SEE YOU UP AND ABOUT AFTER ALL THAT TIME IN THE HOSPITAL. YOU WERE LAID UP PRETTY BAD FOR A WHILE THERE.
OH, AND CONGRATS ON THAT OTHER BIG THING.
OH, BUT THAT HASN'T HAPPENED YET, HAS IT?
SORRY, FORGOT THAT PART.
ALSO, I'M REALLY SORRY ABOUT WHAT'S GOING TO HAPPEN TO YOUR FRIEND.
EVEN THOUGH THAT HASN'T HAPPENED YET EITHER.
KNOCK KNOCK
OPEN UP, TONY! THIS IS AN EMERGENCY!
WHO IN THE WORLD?
IT SOUNDS LIKE--
ANYWAY, I'VE SEEN EVERYTHING THAT'S GOING TO HAPPEN.
GOT IT ALL WORKED OUT HOW YOU CAN STOP THAT CRUMMY COLLECTOR GUY.
HE'S A CIBOPATH, TOO.
BUT YOU ALREADY KNEW THAT PART, RIGHT?
AND HE'S GOING TO BE COMING FOR YOU SOON.
UNCLE CHOW?!
OLIVE? WHY ARE YOU HERE?
ER... TO EAT DINNER.
SO TO SPEAK.
I'LL FILL YOU IN ON WHAT YOU NEED TO DO TO STOP HIM.
TELL YOU EVERYTHING YOU NEED TO KNOW.
BUT SOMETHING COMES UP THAT WE HAVE TO TAKE CARE OF FIRST.
SO WAKE UP!!!
Ughhh
WHAT ARE YOU DOING ON THE FLOOR, TONY?
GET UP.
I'M IN TROUBLE.
AND I NEED YOUR HELP.

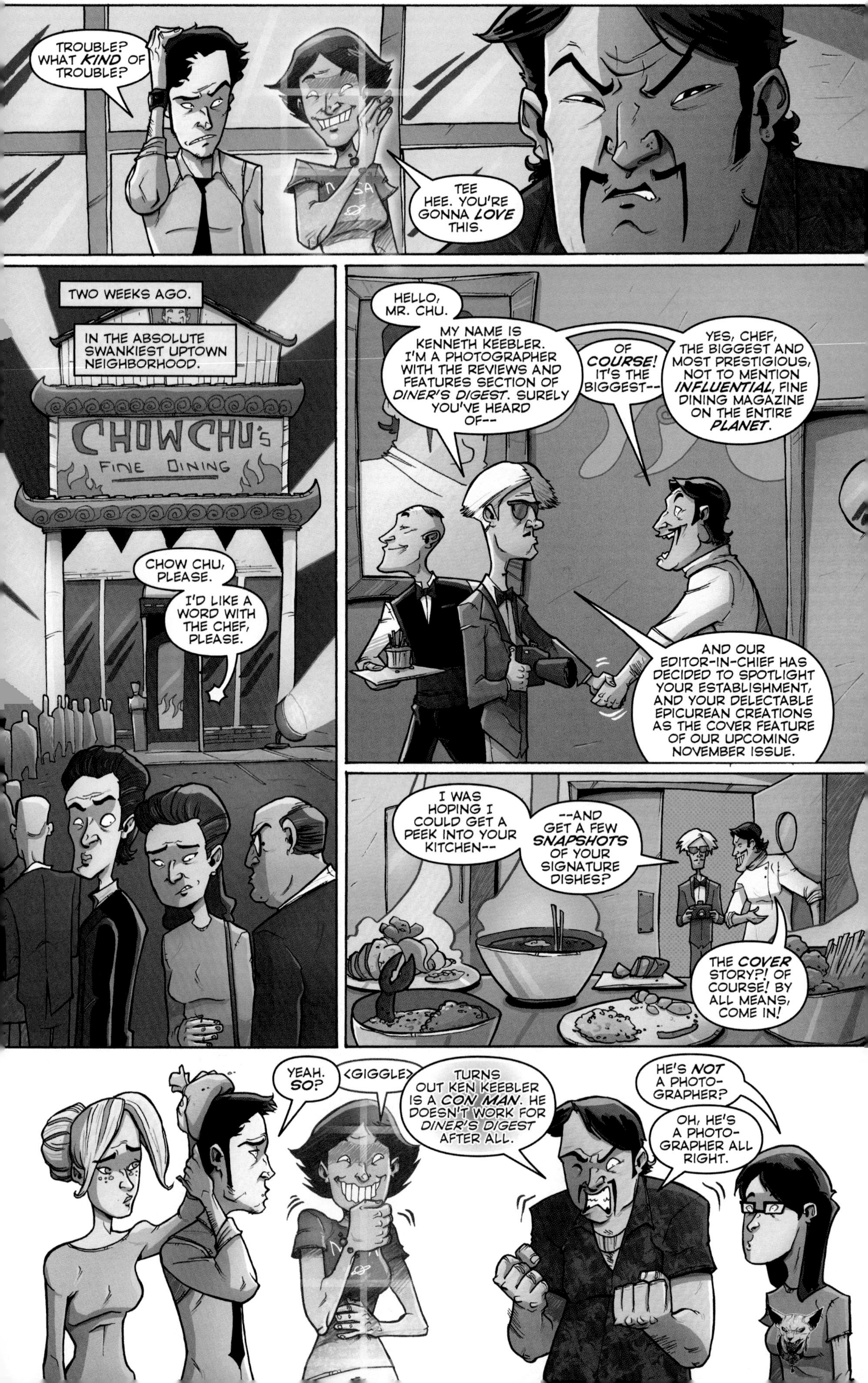
TROUBLE? WHAT KIND OF TROUBLE?
TEE HEE. YOU'RE GONNA LOVE THIS.
TWO WEEKS AGO.
IN THE ABSOLUTE SWANKIEST UPTOWN NEIGHBORHOOD.
CHOWCHU'S FINE DINING
CHOW CHU, PLEASE.
I'D LIKE A WORD WITH THE CHEF, PLEASE.
HELLO, MR. CHU.
MY NAME IS KENNETH KEEBLER. I'M A PHOTOGRAPHER WITH THE REVIEWS AND FEATURES SECTION OF DINER'S DIGEST. SURELY YOU'VE HEARD OF--
OF COURSE! IT'S THE BIGGEST--
YES, CHEF, THE BIGGEST AND MOST PRESTIGIOUS, NOT TO MENTION INFLUENTIAL, FINE DINING MAGAZINE ON THE ENTIRE PLANET.
AND OUR EDITOR-IN-CHIEF HAS DECIDED TO SPOTLIGHT YOUR ESTABLISHMENT, AND YOUR DELECTABLE EPICUREAN CREATIONS AS THE COVER FEATURE OF OUR UPCOMING NOVEMBER ISSUE.
I WAS HOPING I COULD GET A PEEK INTO YOUR KITCHEN--
--AND GET A FEW SNAPSHOTS OF YOUR SIGNATURE DISHES?
THE COVER STORY?! OF COURSE! BY ALL MEANS, COME IN!
YEAH. SO?
<GIGGLE>
TURNS OUT KEN KEEBLER IS A CON MAN. HE DOESN'T WORK FOR DINER'S DIGEST AFTER ALL.
HE'S NOT A PHOTOGRAPHER?
OH, HE'S A PHOTOGRAPHER ALL RIGHT.

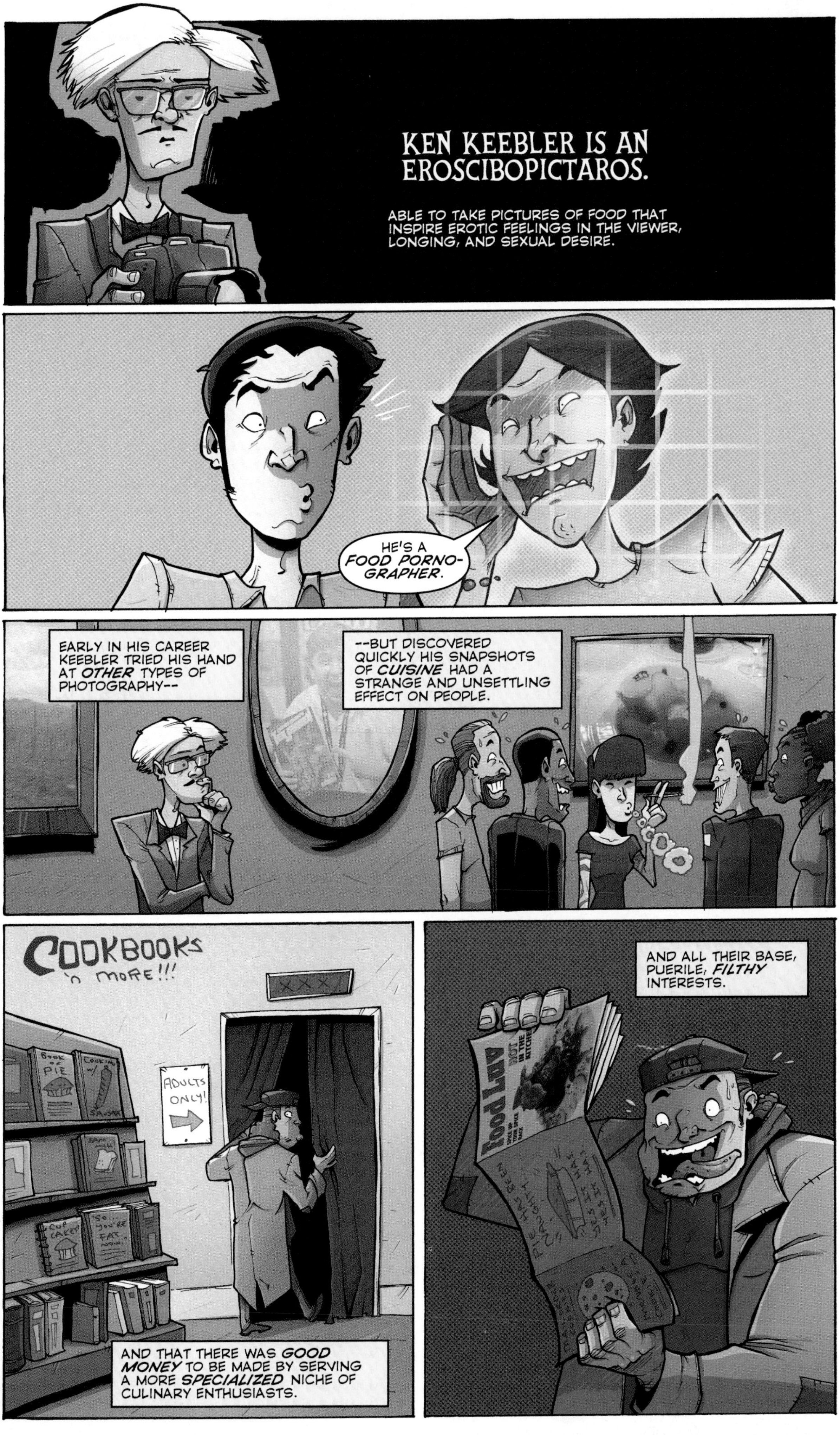
KEN KEEBLER IS AN EROSCIBOPICTAROS.
ABLE TO TAKE PICTURES OF FOOD THAT INSPIRE EROTIC FEELINGS IN THE VIEWER, LONGING, AND SEXUAL DESIRE.
HE'S A FOOD PORNOGRAPHER.
EARLY IN HIS CAREER KEEBLER TRIED HIS HAND AT OTHER TYPES OF PHOTOGRAPHY--
--BUT DISCOVERED QUICKLY HIS SNAPSHOTS OF CUISINE HAD A STRANGE AND UNSETTLING EFFECT ON PEOPLE.
COOKBOOKS 'n MORE!!!
XXX
ADULTS ONLY!
BOOK OF PIE.
COOKING w/ SAUSAGE
CUP CAKES
SO... YOU'RE FAT NOW.
AND THAT THERE WAS GOOD MONEY TO BE MADE BY SERVING A MORE SPECIALIZED NICHE OF CULINARY ENTHUSIASTS.
AND ALL THEIR BASE, PUERILE, FILTHY INTERESTS.
Food Lust

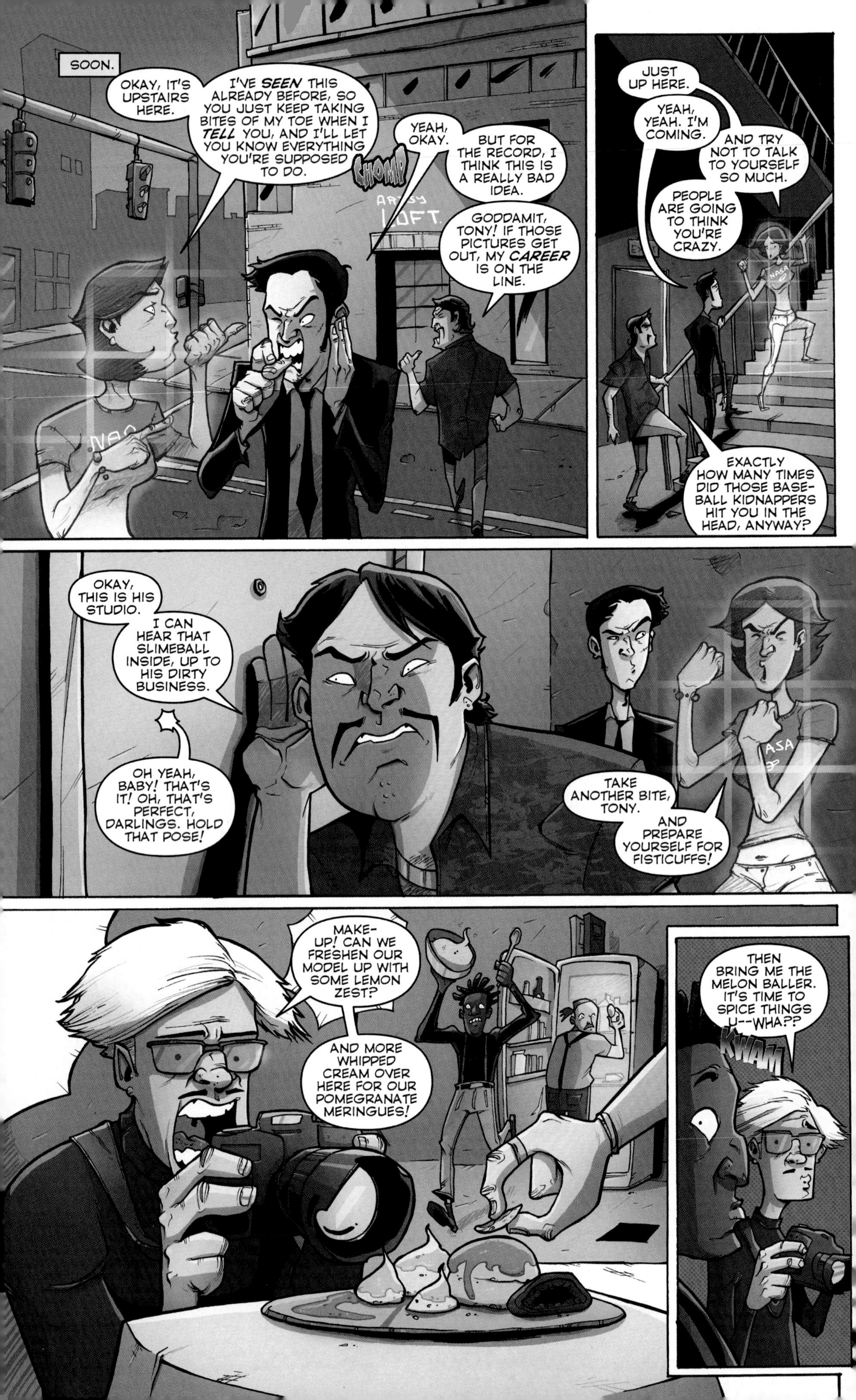
SOON.
OKAY, IT'S UPSTAIRS HERE.
I'VE SEEN THIS ALREADY BEFORE, SO YOU JUST KEEP TAKING BITES OF MY TOE WHEN I TELL YOU, AND I'LL LET YOU KNOW EVERYTHING YOU'RE SUPPOSED TO DO.
CHOMP
YEAH, OKAY.
BUT FOR THE RECORD, I THINK THIS IS A REALLY BAD IDEA.
LOFT
GODDAMIT, TONY! IF THOSE PICTURES GET OUT, MY CAREER IS ON THE LINE.
JUST UP HERE.
YEAH, YEAH. I'M COMING.
AND TRY NOT TO TALK TO YOURSELF SO MUCH.
PEOPLE ARE GOING TO THINK YOU'RE CRAZY.
NASA
EXACTLY HOW MANY TIMES DID THOSE BASE-BALL KIDNAPPERS HIT YOU IN THE HEAD, ANYWAY?
OKAY, THIS IS HIS STUDIO.
I CAN HEAR THAT SLIMEBALL INSIDE, UP TO HIS DIRTY BUSINESS.
OH YEAH, BABY! THAT'S IT! OH, THAT'S PERFECT, DARLINGS. HOLD THAT POSE!
TAKE ANOTHER BITE, TONY.
AND PREPARE YOURSELF FOR FISTICUFFS!
MAKE-UP! CAN WE FRESHEN OUR MODEL UP WITH SOME LEMON ZEST?
AND MORE WHIPPED CREAM OVER HERE FOR OUR POMEGRANATE MERINGUES!
THEN BRING ME THE MELON BALLER. IT'S TIME TO SPICE THINGS U--WHA??
KWAM

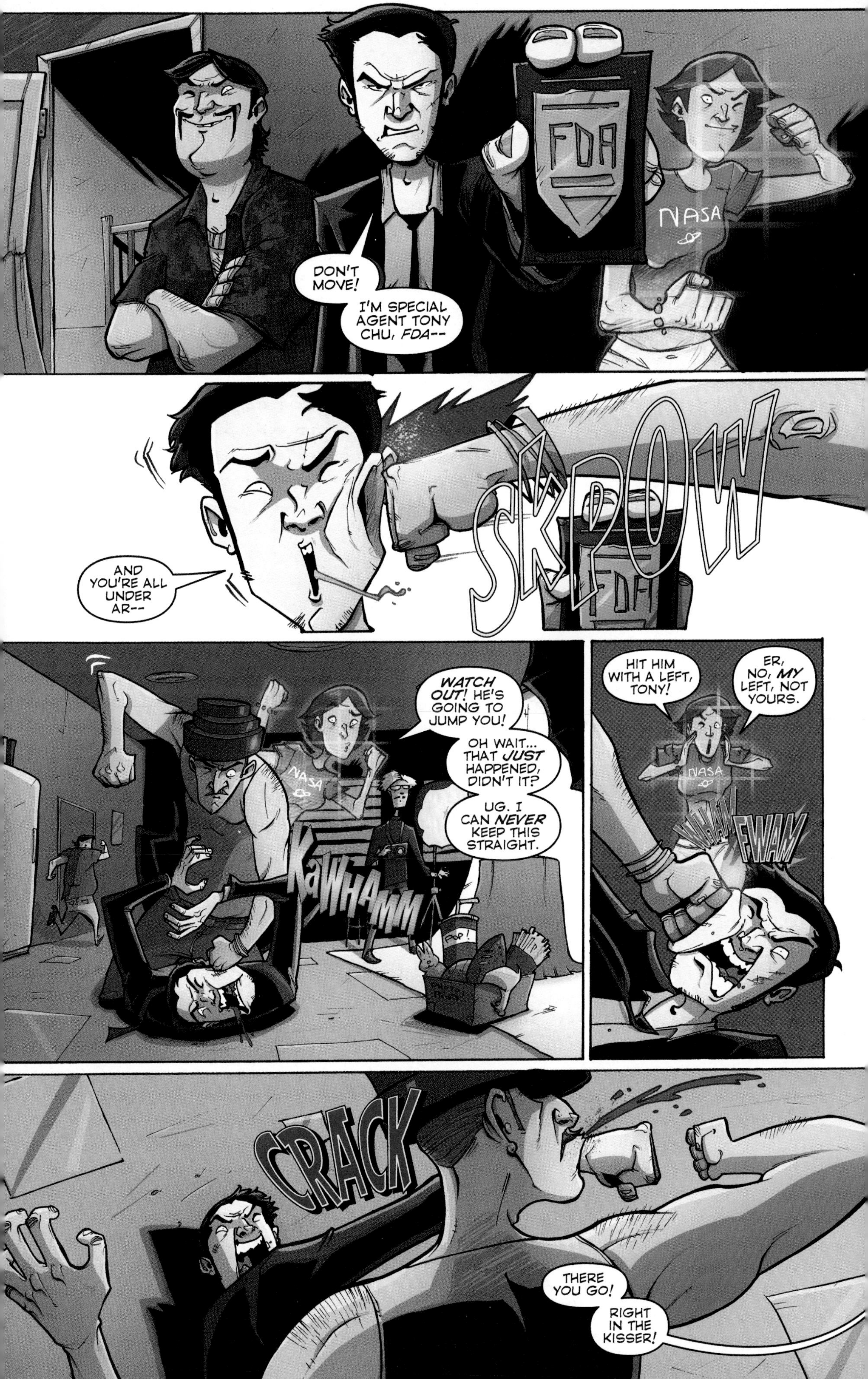
DON'T MOVE!
I'M SPECIAL AGENT TONY CHU, FDA--
NASA
FDA
AND YOU'RE ALL UNDER AR--
SKPOW
FDA
WATCH OUT! HE'S GOING TO JUMP YOU!
OH WAIT... THAT JUST HAPPENED, DIDN'T IT?
UG. I CAN NEVER KEEP THIS STRAIGHT.
NASA
KaWHAMM
POP!
HIT HIM WITH A LEFT, TONY!
ER, NO, MY LEFT, NOT YOURS.
NASA
WHAM
FWAM
CRACK
THERE YOU GO!
RIGHT IN THE KISSER!

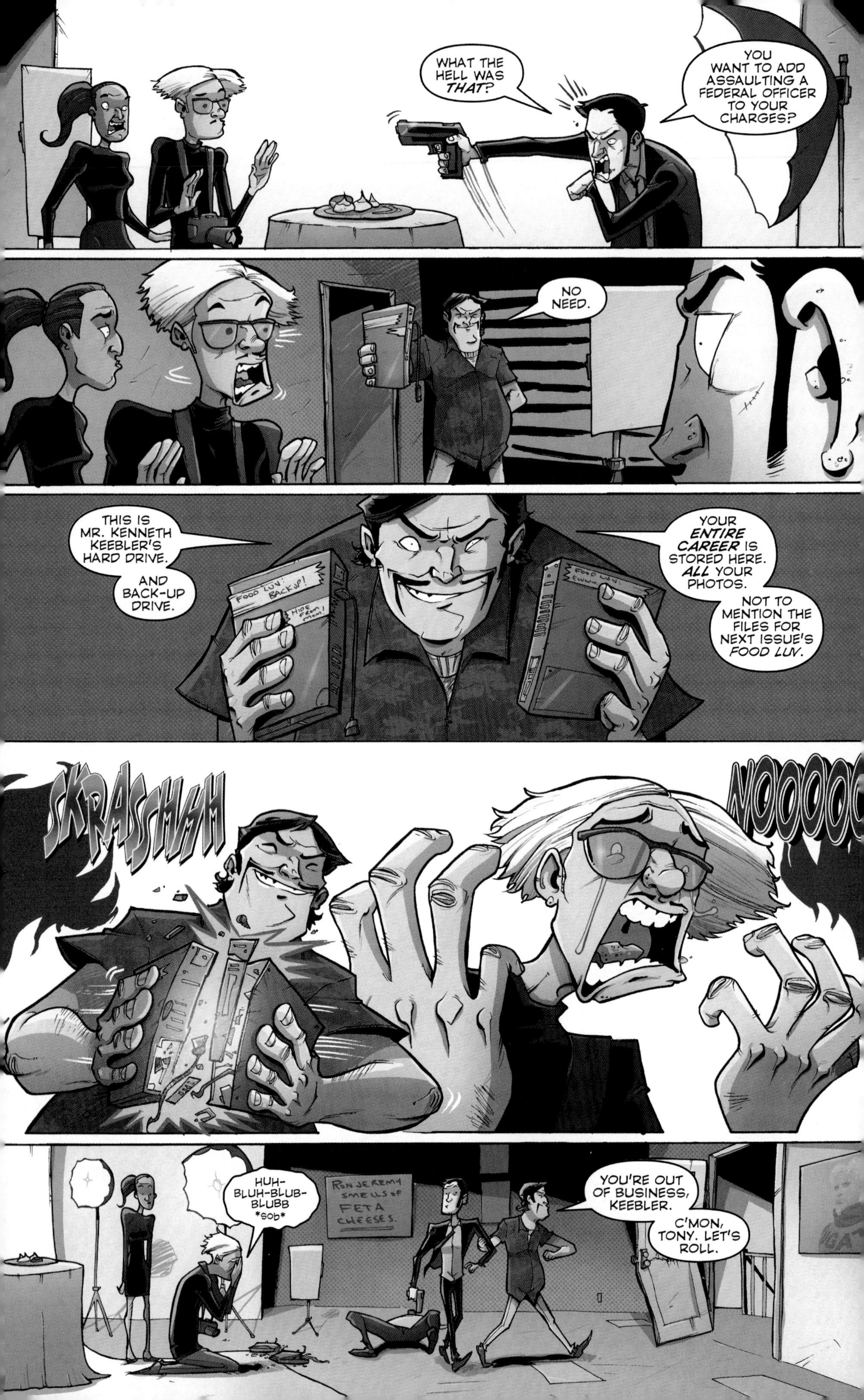
WHAT THE HELL WAS *THAT*?
YOU WANT TO ADD ASSAULTING A FEDERAL OFFICER TO YOUR CHARGES?
NO NEED.
THIS IS MR. KENNETH KEEBLER'S HARD DRIVE.
AND BACK-UP DRIVE.
FOOD LUV: BACKUP!
HIDE FROM MOM!
YOUR *ENTIRE CAREER* IS STORED HERE. *ALL* YOUR PHOTOS.
NOT TO MENTION THE FILES FOR NEXT ISSUE'S *FOOD LUV*.
SKRASSHSH
NOOOOO
HUH-BLUH-BLUB-BLUBB *sob*
RON JEREMY SMELLS OF FETA CHEESES.
YOU'RE OUT OF BUSINESS, KEEBLER.
C'MON, TONY. LET'S ROLL.

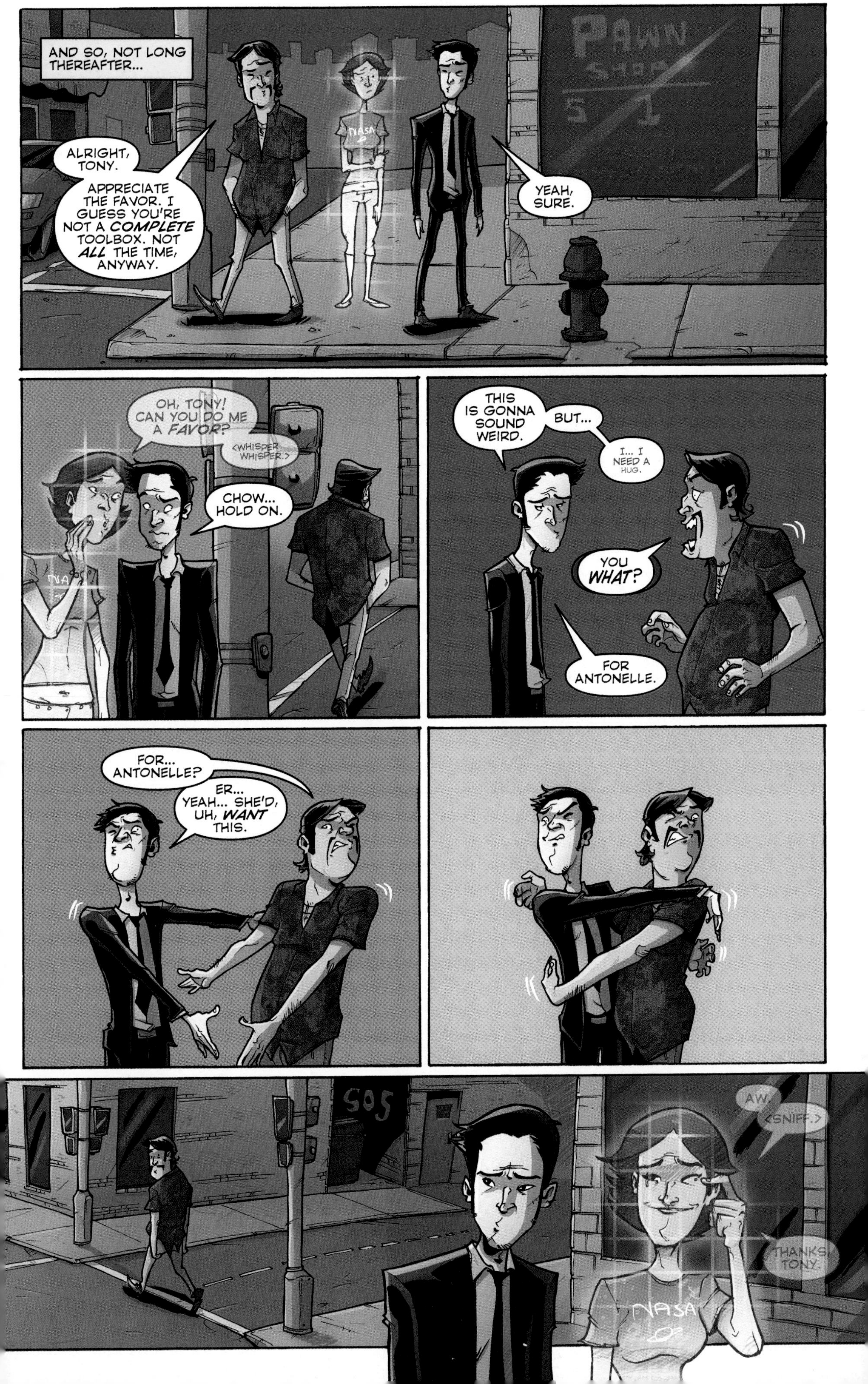
AND SO, NOT LONG THEREAFTER...
ALRIGHT, TONY.
APPRECIATE THE FAVOR. I GUESS YOU'RE NOT A COMPLETE TOOLBOX. NOT ALL THE TIME, ANYWAY.
YEAH, SURE.
PAWN SHOP
OH, TONY! CAN YOU DO ME A FAVOR?
<WHISPER WHISPER.>
CHOW... HOLD ON.
THIS IS GONNA SOUND WEIRD.
BUT...
I... I NEED A HUG.
YOU WHAT?
FOR ANTONELLE.
FOR... ANTONELLE?
ER... YEAH... SHE'D, UH, WANT THIS.
AW.
<SNIFF.>
THANKS, TONY.

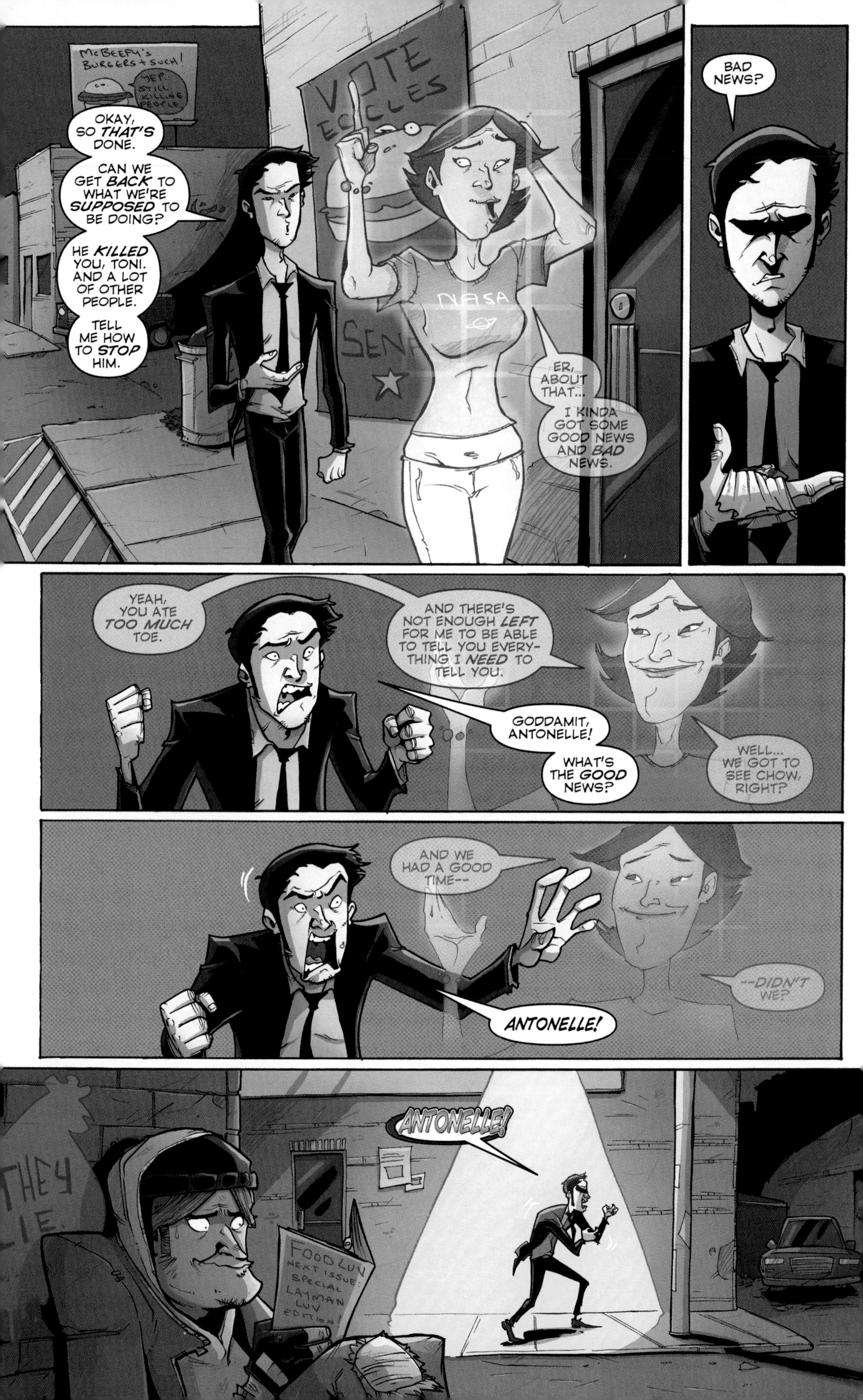
McBEEFY'S BURGERS + SUCH!
YEP. STILL KILLING PEOPLE.
VOTE ECCLES
OKAY, SO *THAT'S* DONE.
CAN WE GET *BACK* TO WHAT WE'RE *SUPPOSED* TO BE DOING?
HE *KILLED* YOU, TONI. AND A LOT OF OTHER PEOPLE.
TELL ME HOW TO *STOP* HIM.
NASA
ER, ABOUT THAT...
I KINDA GOT SOME GOOD NEWS AND *BAD* NEWS.
BAD NEWS?
YEAH, YOU ATE *TOO MUCH* TOE.
AND THERE'S NOT ENOUGH *LEFT* FOR ME TO BE ABLE TO TELL YOU EVERY-THING I *NEED* TO TELL YOU.
GODDAMIT, ANTONELLE!
WHAT'S THE *GOOD* NEWS?
WELL... WE GOT TO SEE CHOW, RIGHT?
AND WE HAD A GOOD TIME--
--*DIDN'T* WE?
ANTONELLE!
ANTONELLE!
THEY LIE.
FOOD LUV NEXT ISSUE: SPECIAL LAYMAN LUV EDITION!

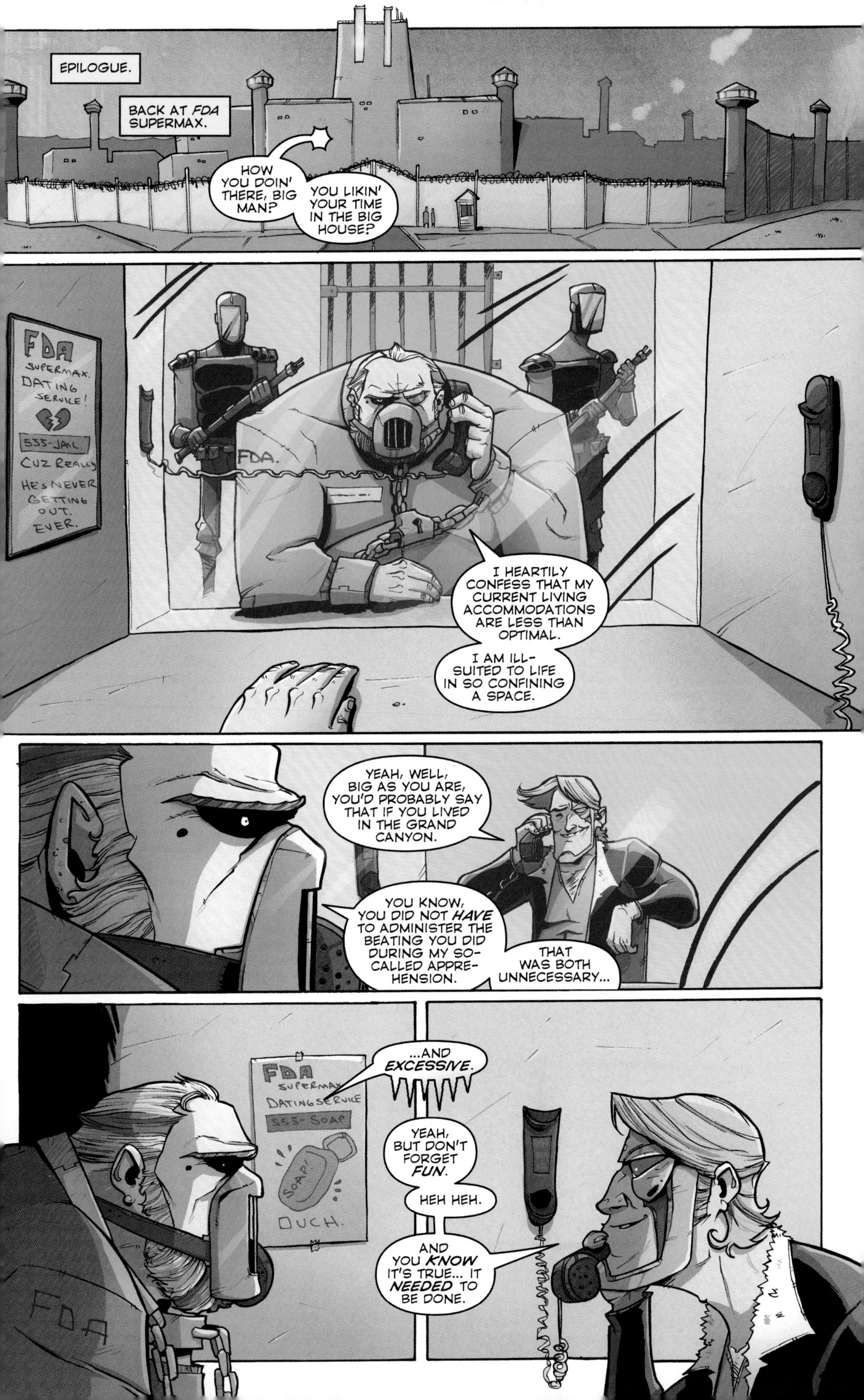
EPILOGUE.
BACK AT *FDA* SUPERMAX.
HOW YOU DOIN' THERE, BIG MAN?
YOU LIKIN' YOUR TIME IN THE BIG HOUSE?
FDA SUPERMAX. DATING SERVICE!
555-JAIL
CUZ REALLY HE'S NEVER GETTING OUT. EVER.
FDA.
I HEARTILY CONFESS THAT MY CURRENT LIVING ACCOMMODATIONS ARE LESS THAN OPTIMAL.
I AM ILL-SUITED TO LIFE IN SO CONFINING A SPACE.
YEAH, WELL, BIG AS YOU ARE, YOU'D PROBABLY SAY THAT IF YOU LIVED IN THE GRAND CANYON.
YOU KNOW, YOU DID NOT ***HAVE*** TO ADMINISTER THE BEATING YOU DID DURING MY SO-CALLED APPRE-HENSION.
THAT WAS BOTH UNNECESSARY...
...AND ***EXCESSIVE***.
FDA SUPERMAX DATING SERVICE
555-SOAP
SOAP!
OUCH.
YEAH, BUT DON'T FORGET ***FUN***.
HEH HEH.
AND YOU ***KNOW*** IT'S TRUE... IT ***NEEDED*** TO BE DONE.
FDA

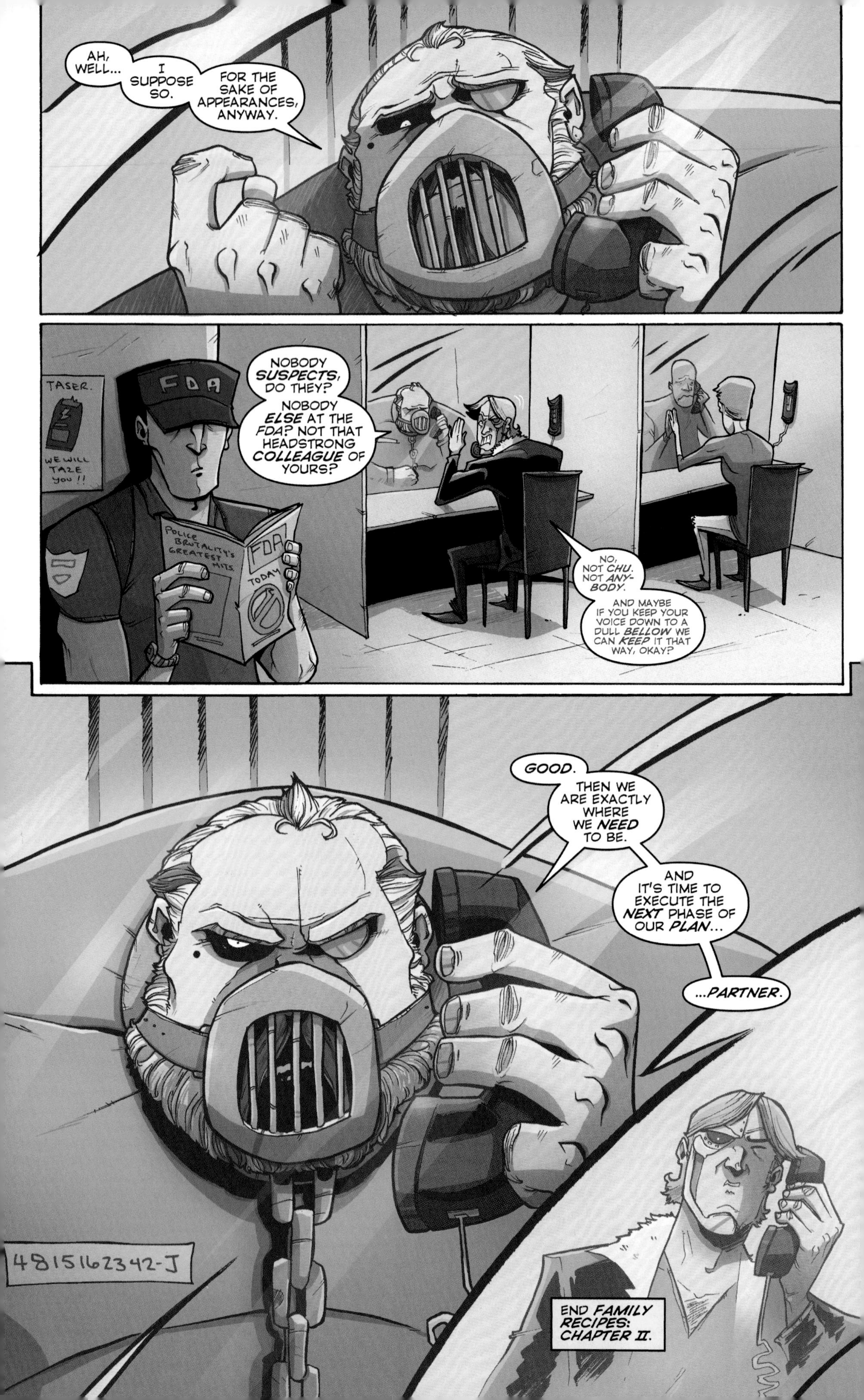
AH, WELL...
I SUPPOSE SO.
FOR THE SAKE OF APPEARANCES, ANYWAY.
TASER.
WE WILL TAZE YOU !!
FDA
NOBODY SUSPECTS, DO THEY?
NOBODY ELSE AT THE FDA? NOT THAT HEADSTRONG COLLEAGUE OF YOURS?
POLICE BRUTALITY'S GREATEST HITS.
FDA TODAY
NO, NOT CHU. NOT ANY-BODY.
AND MAYBE IF YOU KEEP YOUR VOICE DOWN TO A DULL BELLOW WE CAN KEEP IT THAT WAY, OKAY?
GOOD.
THEN WE ARE EXACTLY WHERE WE NEED TO BE.
AND IT'S TIME TO EXECUTE THE NEXT PHASE OF OUR PLAN...
...PARTNER.
4815162342-J
END FAMILY RECIPES: CHAPTER II.

Chapter Eight

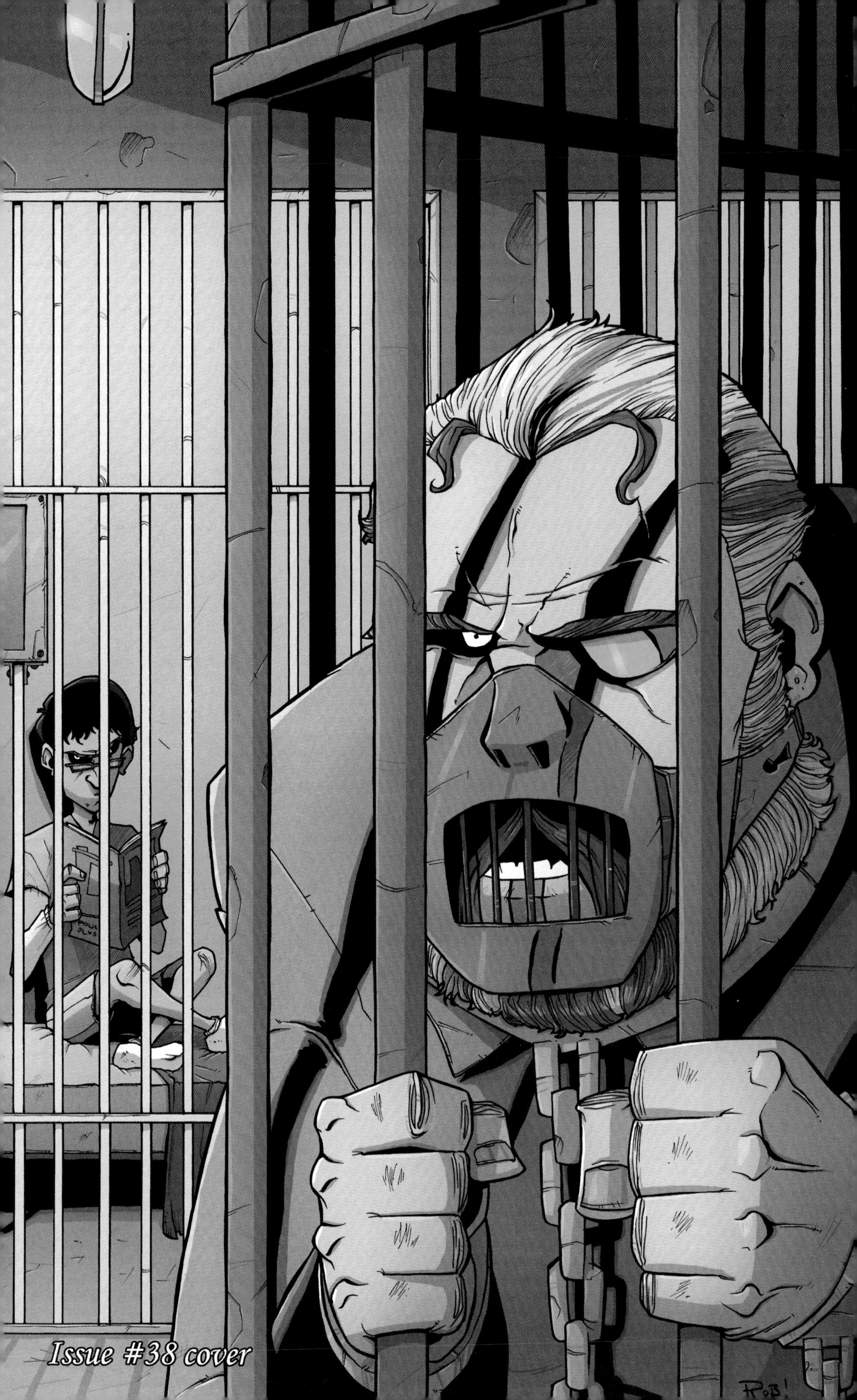
Issue #38 cover

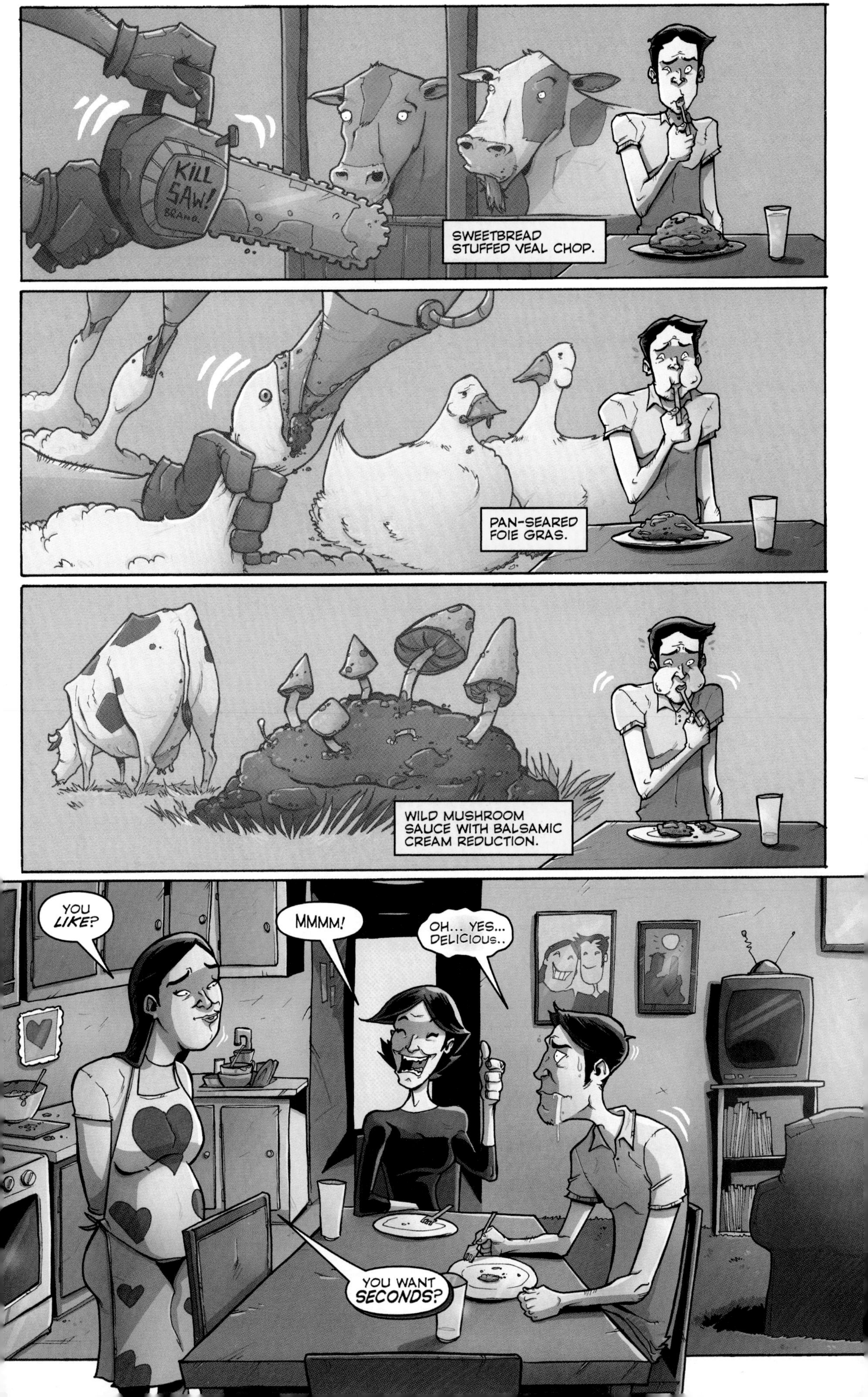
KILL SAW! BRAND.
SWEETBREAD STUFFED VEAL CHOP.
PAN-SEARED FOIE GRAS.
WILD MUSHROOM SAUCE WITH BALSAMIC CREAM REDUCTION.
YOU LIKE?
MMMM!
OH... YES... DELICIOUS..
YOU WANT SECONDS?

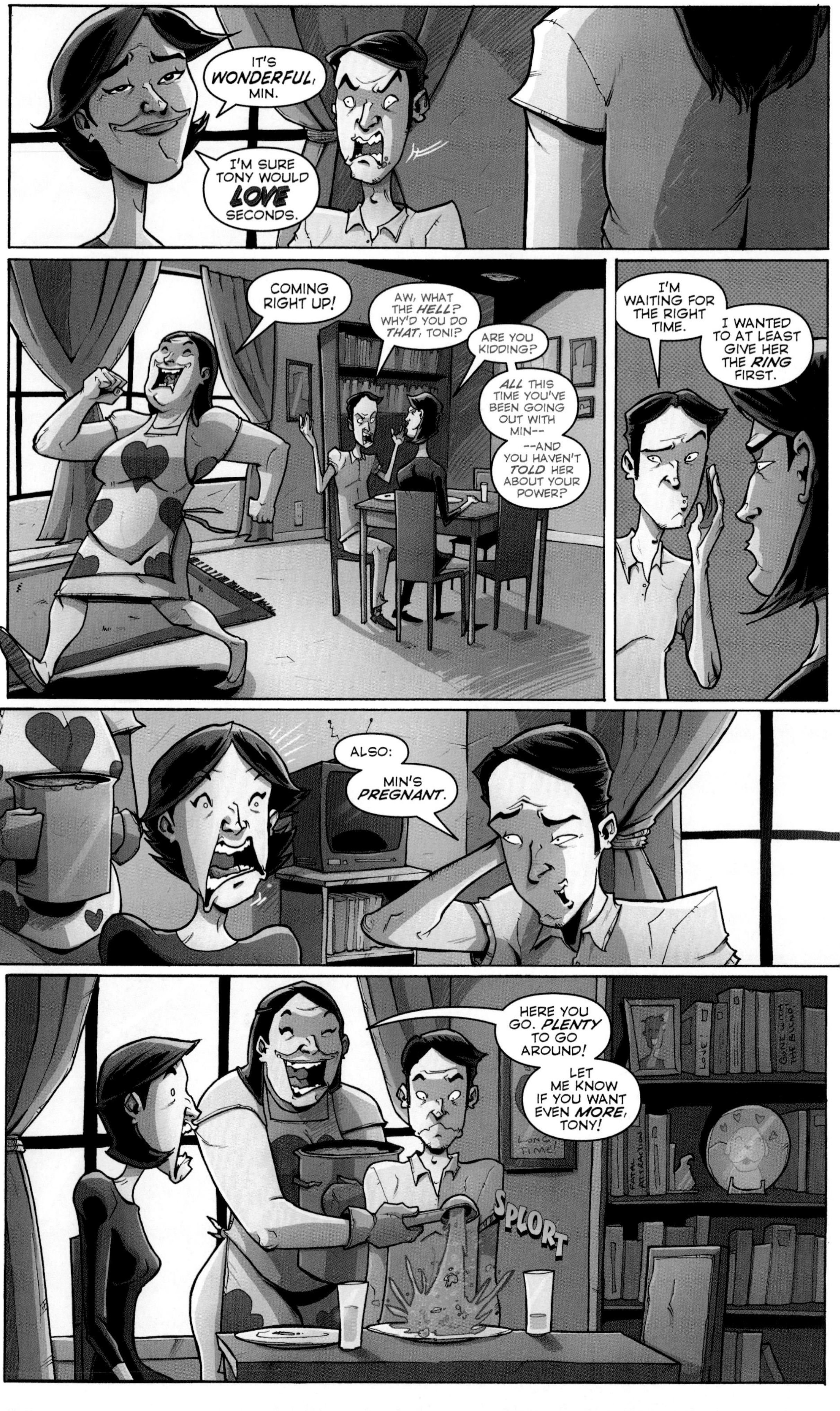
IT'S WONDERFUL, MIN.
I'M SURE TONY WOULD LOVE SECONDS.
COMING RIGHT UP!
AW, WHAT THE HELL? WHY'D YOU DO THAT, TONI?
ARE YOU KIDDING?
ALL THIS TIME YOU'VE BEEN GOING OUT WITH MIN--
--AND YOU HAVEN'T TOLD HER ABOUT YOUR POWER?
I'M WAITING FOR THE RIGHT TIME.
I WANTED TO AT LEAST GIVE HER THE RING FIRST.
ALSO:
MIN'S PREGNANT.
HERE YOU GO. PLENTY TO GO AROUND!
LET ME KNOW IF YOU WANT EVEN MORE, TONY!
SPLORT

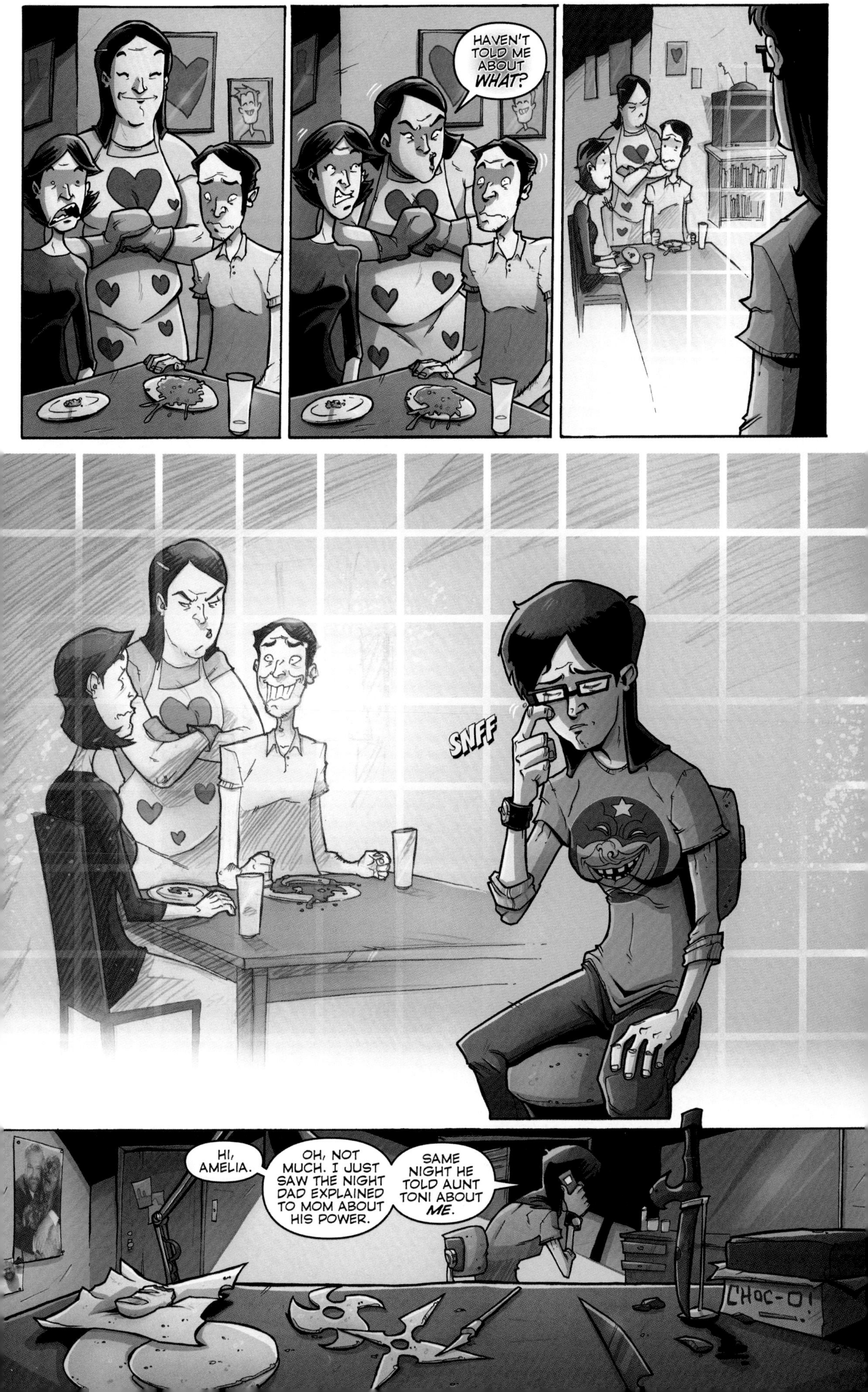
HAVEN'T TOLD ME ABOUT *WHAT?*
SNFF
HI, AMELIA.
OH, NOT MUCH. I JUST SAW THE NIGHT DAD EXPLAINED TO MOM ABOUT HIS POWER.
SAME NIGHT HE TOLD AUNT TONI ABOUT *ME*.
CHOC-O!

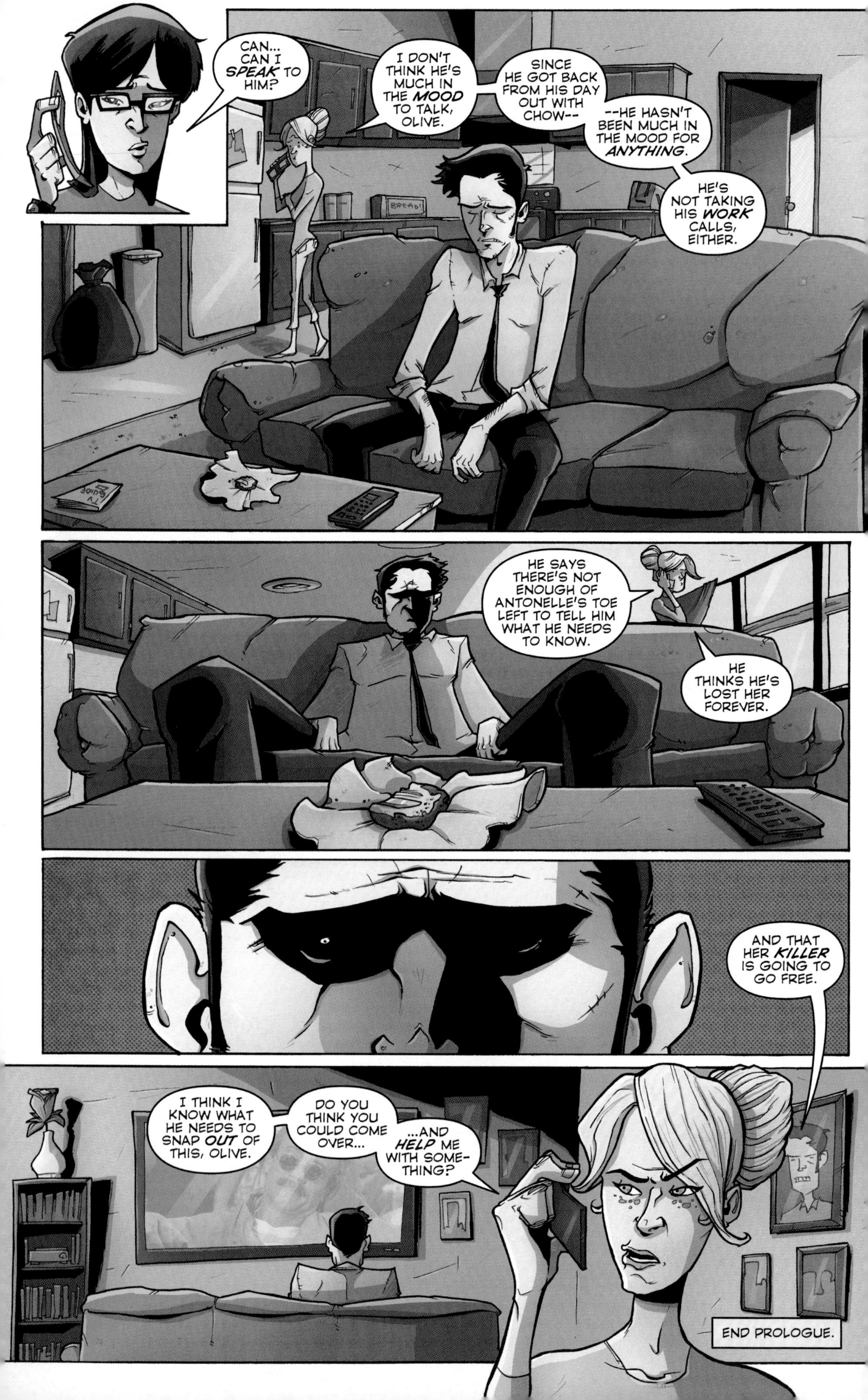
CAN... CAN I SPEAK TO HIM?
I DON'T THINK HE'S MUCH IN THE MOOD TO TALK, OLIVE.
SINCE HE GOT BACK FROM HIS DAY OUT WITH CHOW--
--HE HASN'T BEEN MUCH IN THE MOOD FOR ANYTHING.
HE'S NOT TAKING HIS WORK CALLS, EITHER.
BREAD
TV GUIDE
HE SAYS THERE'S NOT ENOUGH OF ANTONELLE'S TOE LEFT TO TELL HIM WHAT HE NEEDS TO KNOW.
HE THINKS HE'S LOST HER FOREVER.
AND THAT HER KILLER IS GOING TO GO FREE.
I THINK I KNOW WHAT HE NEEDS TO SNAP OUT OF THIS, OLIVE.
DO YOU THINK YOU COULD COME OVER...
...AND HELP ME WITH SOME-THING?
END PROLOGUE.

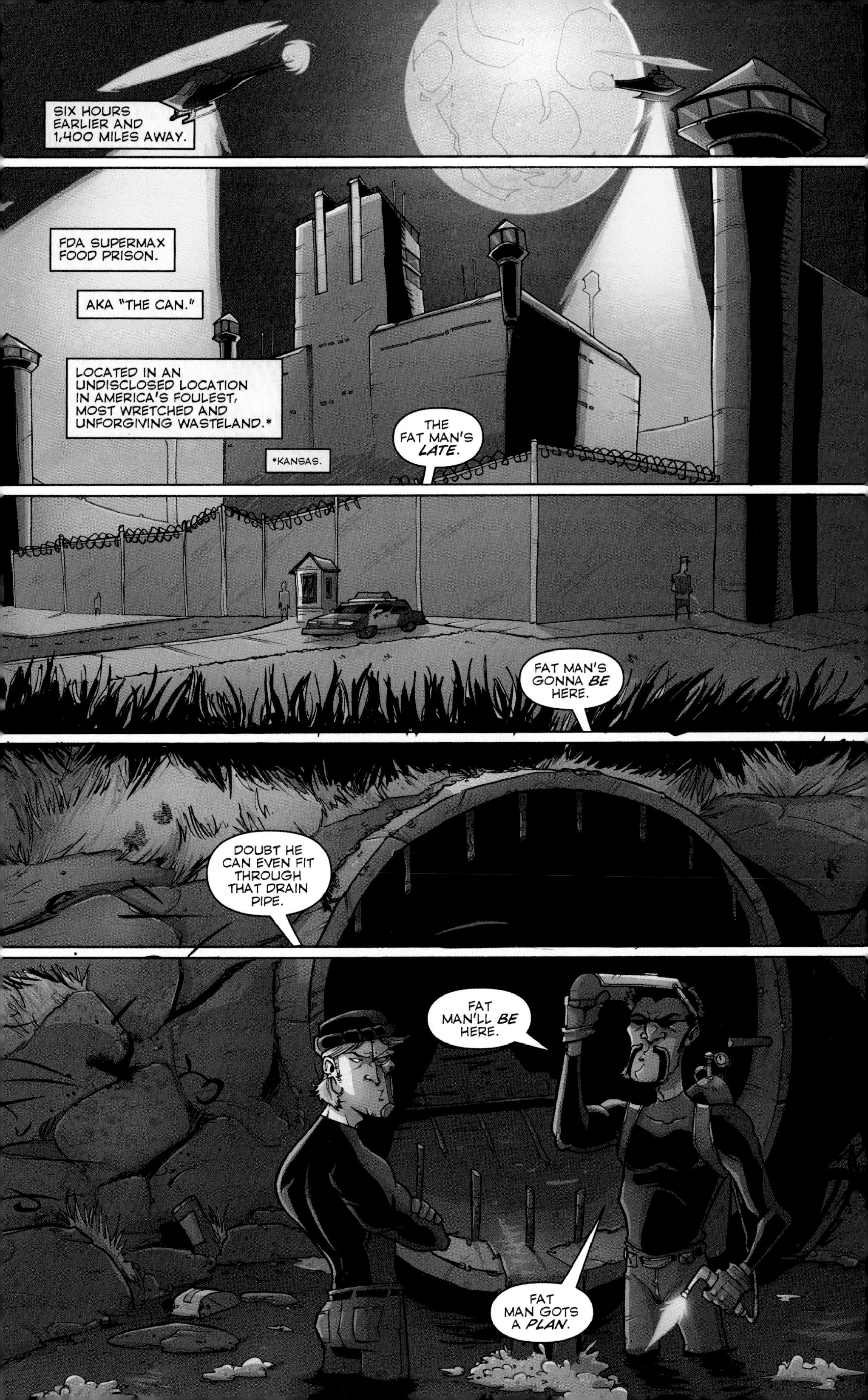

SIX HOURS EARLIER AND 1,400 MILES AWAY.
FDA SUPERMAX FOOD PRISON.
AKA "THE CAN."
LOCATED IN AN UNDISCLOSED LOCATION IN AMERICA'S FOULEST, MOST WRETCHED AND UNFORGIVING WASTELAND.*
*KANSAS.
THE FAT MAN'S LATE.
FAT MAN'S GONNA BE HERE.
DOUBT HE CAN EVEN FIT THROUGH THAT DRAIN PIPE.
FAT MAN'LL BE HERE.
FAT MAN GOTS A PLAN.

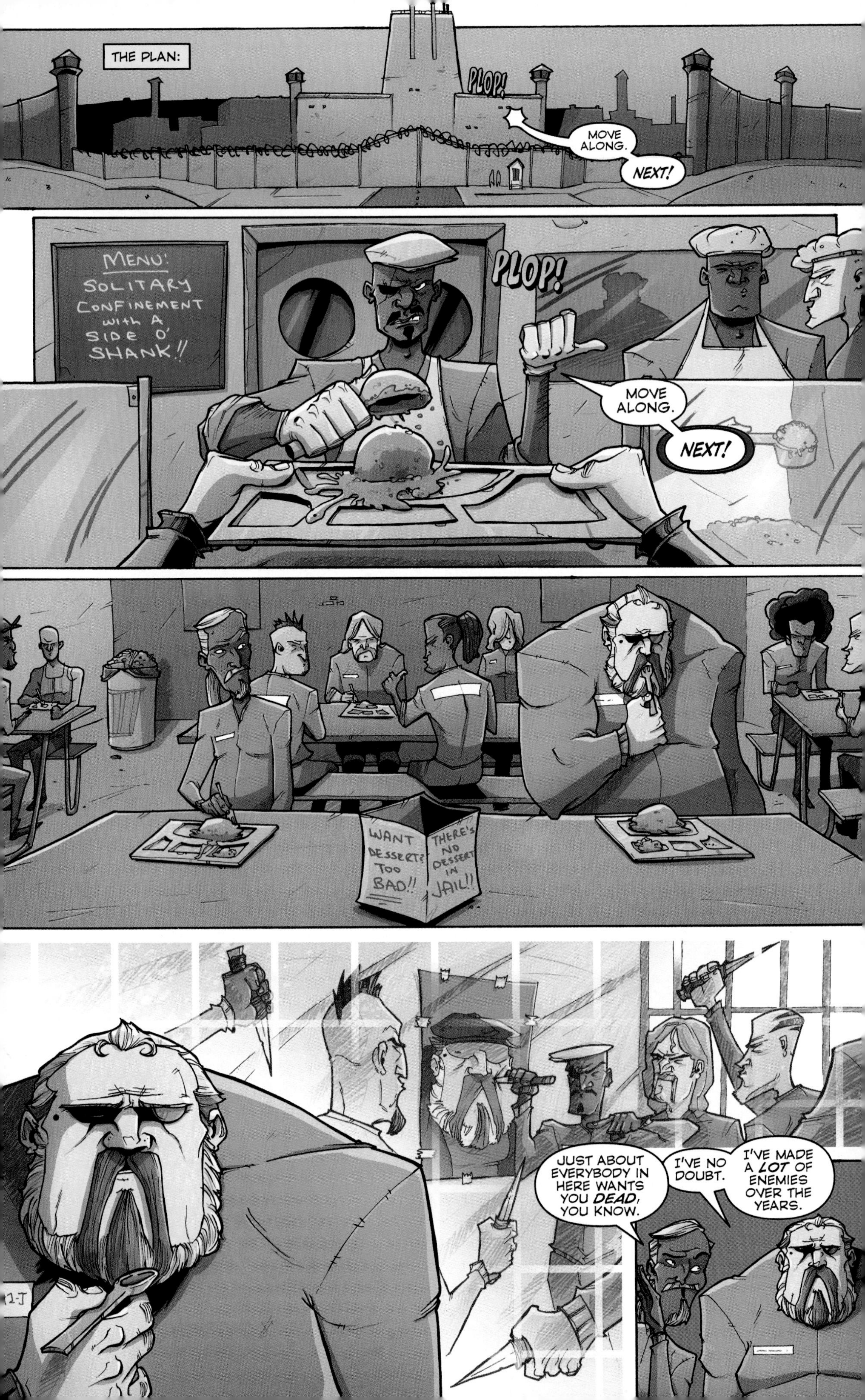
THE PLAN:
PLOP!
MOVE ALONG.
NEXT!
MENU: SOLITARY CONFINEMENT with A SIDE O' SHANK!!
PLOP!
MOVE ALONG.
NEXT!
WANT DESSERT? TOO BAD!!
THERE'S NO DESSERT IN JAIL!!
JUST ABOUT EVERYBODY IN HERE WANTS YOU DEAD, YOU KNOW.
I'VE NO DOUBT.
I'VE MADE A LOT OF ENEMIES OVER THE YEARS.

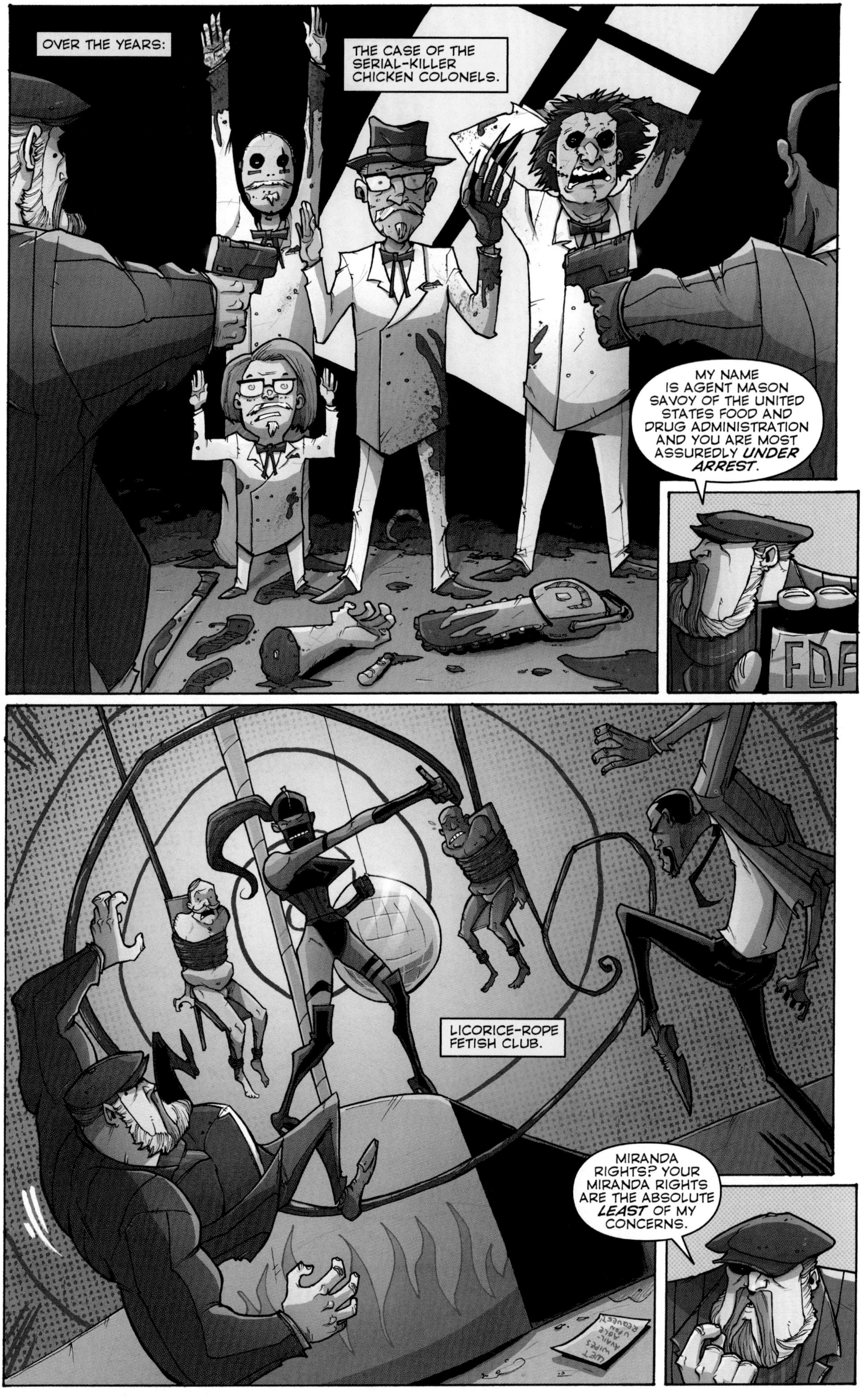
OVER THE YEARS:
THE CASE OF THE SERIAL-KILLER CHICKEN COLONELS.
MY NAME IS AGENT MASON SAVOY OF THE UNITED STATES FOOD AND DRUG ADMINISTRATION AND YOU ARE MOST ASSUREDLY UNDER ARREST.
LICORICE-ROPE FETISH CLUB.
MIRANDA RIGHTS? YOUR MIRANDA RIGHTS ARE THE ABSOLUTE LEAST OF MY CONCERNS.

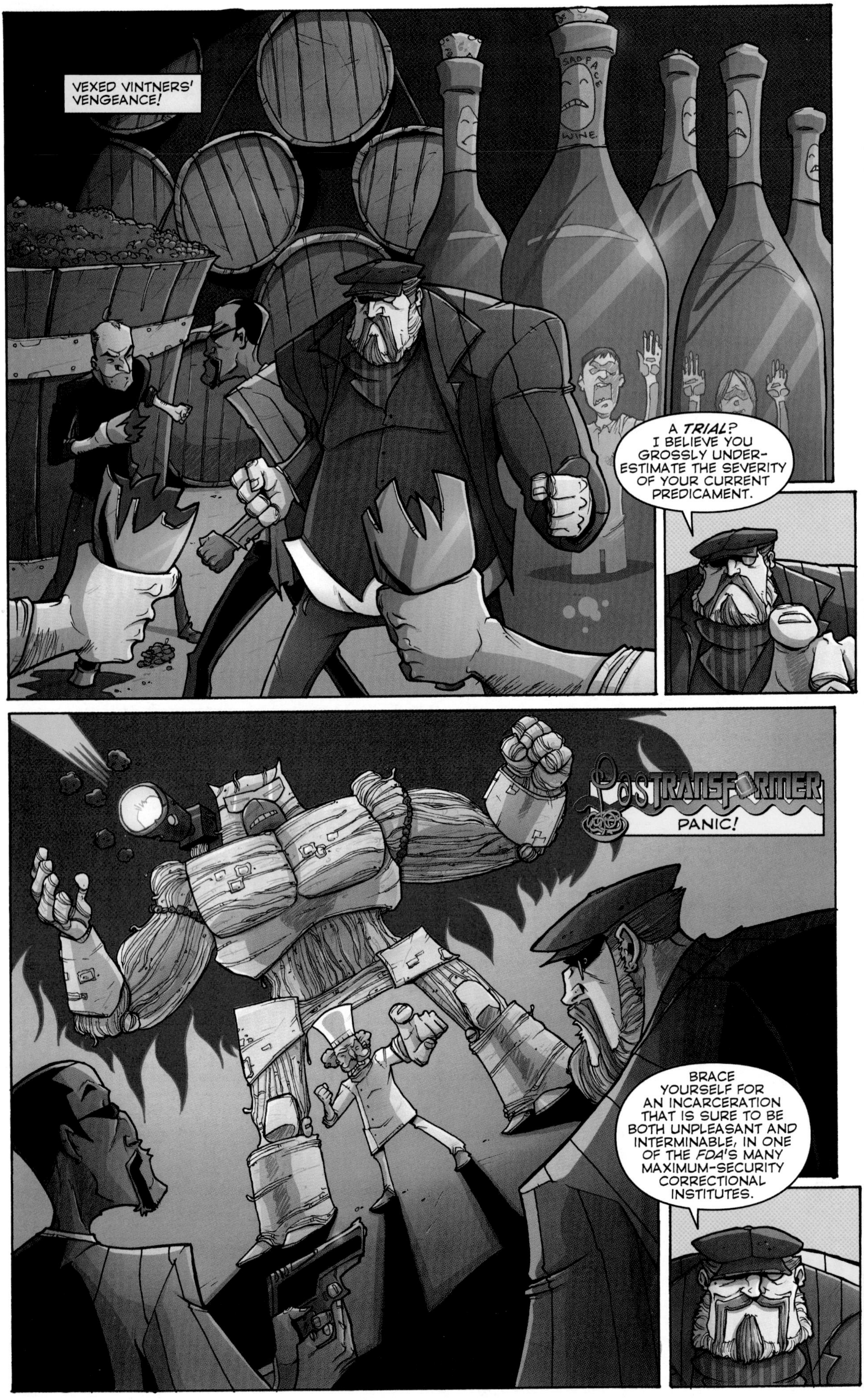
VEXED VINTNERS' VENGEANCE!
SAD FACE WINE.
A *TRIAL*? I BELIEVE YOU GROSSLY UNDER-ESTIMATE THE SEVERITY OF YOUR CURRENT PREDICAMENT.
PASTRANSFORMER PANIC!
BRACE YOURSELF FOR AN INCARCERATION THAT IS SURE TO BE BOTH UNPLEASANT AND INTERMINABLE, IN ONE OF THE *FDA*'S MANY MAXIMUM-SECURITY CORRECTIONAL INSTITUTES.

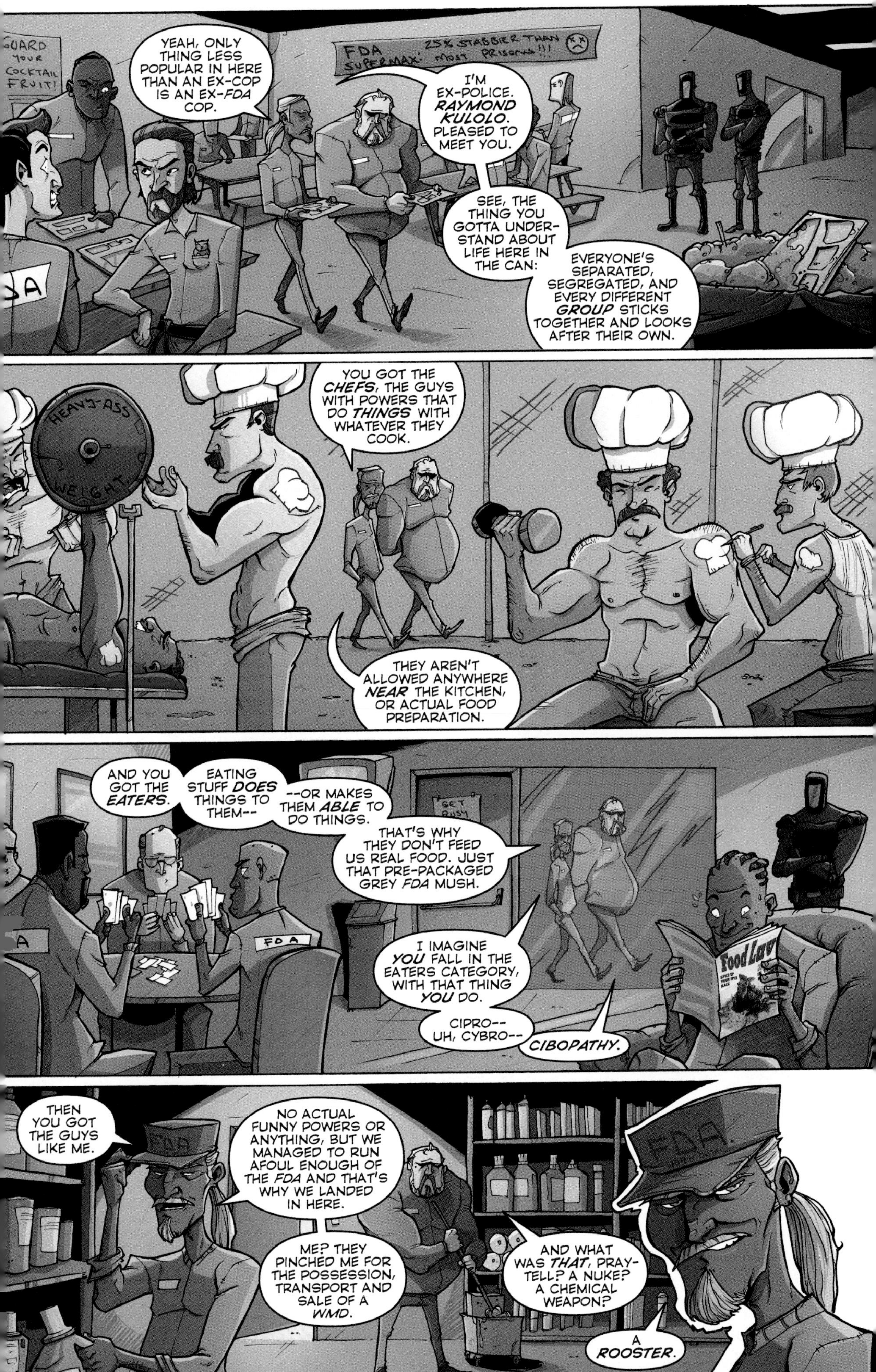
GUARD YOUR COCKTAIL FRUIT!
FDA SUPERMAX: 25% STABBIER THAN MOST PRISONS!!!
YEAH, ONLY THING LESS POPULAR IN HERE THAN AN EX-COP IS AN EX-FDA COP.
I'M EX-POLICE. RAYMOND KULOLO. PLEASED TO MEET YOU.
SEE, THE THING YOU GOTTA UNDERSTAND ABOUT LIFE HERE IN THE CAN:
EVERYONE'S SEPARATED, SEGREGATED, AND EVERY DIFFERENT GROUP STICKS TOGETHER AND LOOKS AFTER THEIR OWN.
HEAVY-ASS WEIGHT
YOU GOT THE CHEFS, THE GUYS WITH POWERS THAT DO THINGS WITH WHATEVER THEY COOK.
THEY AREN'T ALLOWED ANYWHERE NEAR THE KITCHEN, OR ACTUAL FOOD PREPARATION.
AND YOU GOT THE EATERS.
EATING STUFF DOES THINGS TO THEM--
--OR MAKES THEM ABLE TO DO THINGS.
THAT'S WHY THEY DON'T FEED US REAL FOOD. JUST THAT PRE-PACKAGED GREY FDA MUSH.
GET BUSY
FDA
Food Luv
I IMAGINE YOU FALL IN THE EATERS CATEGORY, WITH THAT THING YOU DO.
CIPRO-- UH, CYBRO--
CIBOPATHY.
THEN YOU GOT THE GUYS LIKE ME.
NO ACTUAL FUNNY POWERS OR ANYTHING, BUT WE MANAGED TO RUN AFOUL ENOUGH OF THE FDA AND THAT'S WHY WE LANDED IN HERE.
ME? THEY PINCHED ME FOR THE POSSESSION, TRANSPORT AND SALE OF A WMD.
AND WHAT WAS THAT, PRAY-TELL? A NUKE? A CHEMICAL WEAPON?
A ROOSTER.
F.D.A.
POOP BE GONE!

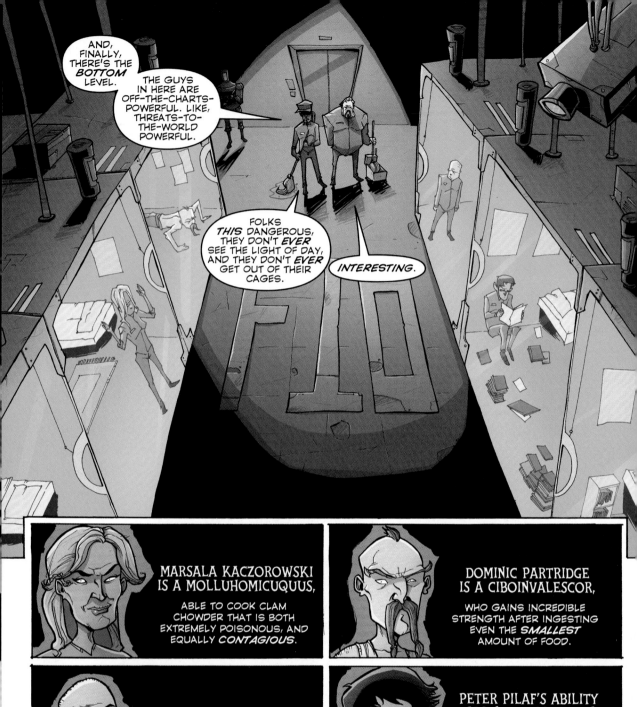

AND, FINALLY, THERE'S THE *BOTTOM* LEVEL. THE GUYS IN HERE ARE OFF-THE-CHARTS-POWERFUL. LIKE, THREATS-TO-THE-WORLD POWERFUL.

FOLKS *THIS* DANGEROUS, THEY DON'T *EVER* SEE THE LIGHT OF DAY, AND THEY DON'T *EVER* GET OUT OF THEIR CAGES.

INTERESTING.

MARSALA KACZOROWSKI IS A MOLLUHOMICUQUUS,

ABLE TO COOK CLAM CHOWDER THAT IS BOTH EXTREMELY POISONOUS, AND EQUALLY *CONTAGIOUS*.

DOMINIC PARTRIDGE IS A CIBOINVALESCOR,

WHO GAINS INCREDIBLE STRENGTH AFTER INGESTING EVEN THE *SMALLEST* AMOUNT OF FOOD.

BRANN JERWAR IS A PEDEREXPLODIER,

ABLE TO PRODUCE FLATULENCE MORE POWERFUL THAN A 14-KILOTON BOMB.

PETER PILAF'S ABILITY HAS NOT FULLY BEEN IDENTIFIED,

BUT HE IS THOUGHT TO POSSESS THE MOST POWERFUL --AND *LETHAL*-- FOOD-RELATED ABILITIES ON THE FACE OF THE PLANET.

BACKING UP JUST A BIT:

ACCORDING TO THE BLUEPRINTS, THEY'RE HOLDING HIM DOWN *THERE*.

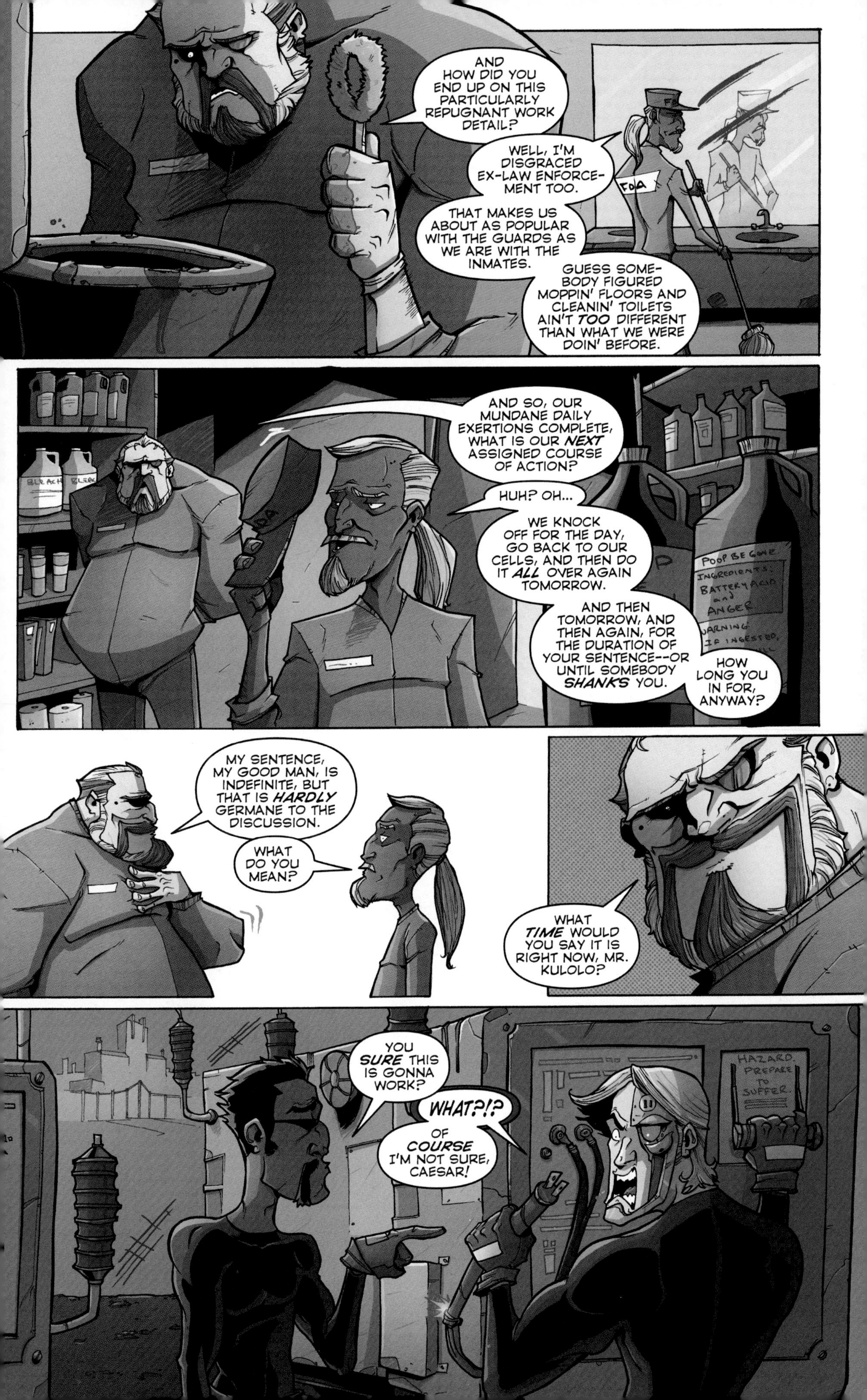
AND HOW DID YOU END UP ON THIS PARTICULARLY REPUGNANT WORK DETAIL?
WELL, I'M DISGRACED EX-LAW ENFORCEMENT TOO.
THAT MAKES US ABOUT AS POPULAR WITH THE GUARDS AS WE ARE WITH THE INMATES.
GUESS SOMEBODY FIGURED MOPPIN' FLOORS AND CLEANIN' TOILETS AIN'T TOO DIFFERENT THAN WHAT WE WERE DOIN' BEFORE.
FDA
AND SO, OUR MUNDANE DAILY EXERTIONS COMPLETE, WHAT IS OUR NEXT ASSIGNED COURSE OF ACTION?
HUH? OH...
WE KNOCK OFF FOR THE DAY, GO BACK TO OUR CELLS, AND THEN DO IT ALL OVER AGAIN TOMORROW.
AND THEN TOMORROW, AND THEN AGAIN, FOR THE DURATION OF YOUR SENTENCE--OR UNTIL SOMEBODY SHANKS YOU.
HOW LONG YOU IN FOR, ANYWAY?
BLEACH
POOP BE GONE
INGREDIENTS: BATTERY ACID and ANGER
WARNING: IF INGESTED,
MY SENTENCE, MY GOOD MAN, IS INDEFINITE, BUT THAT IS HARDLY GERMANE TO THE DISCUSSION.
WHAT DO YOU MEAN?
WHAT TIME WOULD YOU SAY IT IS RIGHT NOW, MR. KULOLO?
YOU SURE THIS IS GONNA WORK?
WHAT?!?
OF COURSE I'M NOT SURE, CAESAR!
HAZARD. PREPARE TO SUFFER.

IT WASN'T *MY* IDEA TO HACK MY ROBOTIC HALF-BRAIN INTO THE SECURITY SYSTEM OF A TOP-SECRET SUPER-MAX GOVERNMENT FOOD PRISON.

BIG MAN'S GOT A *PLAN*, COLBY.

BIG MAN'S GOT IT *ALL* WORKED OU--

FRZZZTT-

REEooo REEoooo

WHAT THE HELL WAS *THAT*?

THAT, MR. KULOLO, IS THE SOUND OF *FREEDOM*... AND *ENLIGHTENMENT*.

OF COMPUTER AND SECURITY *OVERRIDE*.

OF THUMB-PRINTS AND RETINAL SCANNERS THAT --FOR THE NEXT FOUR-AND-A-HALF MINUTES-- RECOGNIZE ME, AND *ONLY* ME.

WHILE *LOCKING OUT* ANYONE WHO IS *NOT* ME.

CARE TO COME ALONG?

CRACK

WHACK

YOU--YOU'RE BREAKING *OUT* OF HERE? ARE YOU *KIDDING*?

EVERY EXIT IS GOING TO BE *SWARMING* WITH GUARDS WITH *FULL* AUTHORITY TO SHOOT TO KILL.

I HAVE NO INTENTION OF GOING ANY-WHERE *NEAR* AN EXIT.

IN FACT, I'LL BE GOING IN THE *OPPOSITE* DIRECTION.

YOU'RE GOING TO THE *BOTTOM* LEVEL?

NO.

I'M GOING TO THE FLOOR *BELOW* THE BOTTOM LEVEL.

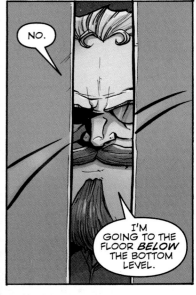

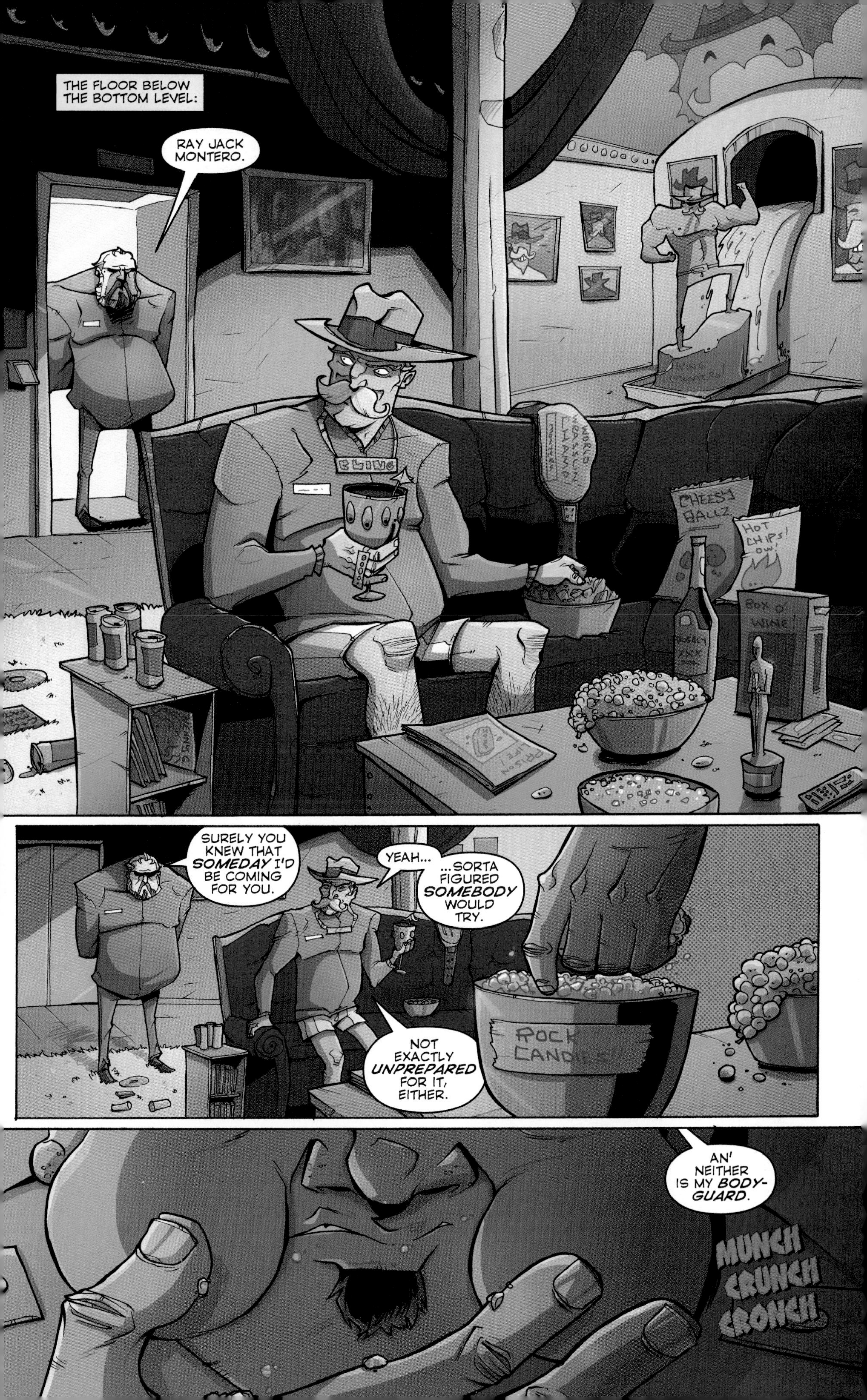
THE FLOOR BELOW THE BOTTOM LEVEL:
RAY JACK MONTERO.
BLING
WORLD WRASSLIN' CHAMP!
CHEESY BALLZ
HOT CHIPS! OW!
BOX O' WINE!
SURELY YOU KNEW THAT *SOMEDAY* I'D BE COMING FOR YOU.
YEAH...
...SORTA FIGURED *SOMEBODY* WOULD TRY.
NOT EXACTLY *UNPREPARED* FOR IT, EITHER.
ROCK CANDIES!!
AN' NEITHER IS MY *BODY-GUARD*.
MUNCH CRUNCH CRONCH

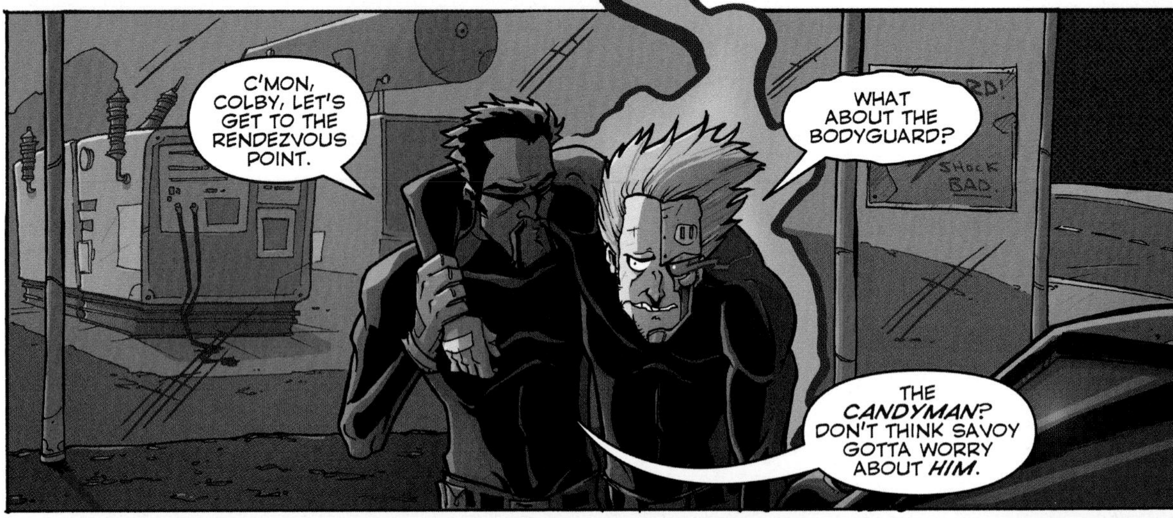
C'MON, COLBY, LET'S GET TO THE RENDEZVOUS POINT.
WHAT ABOUT THE BODYGUARD?
THE CANDYMAN? DON'T THINK SAVOY GOTTA WORRY ABOUT HIM.

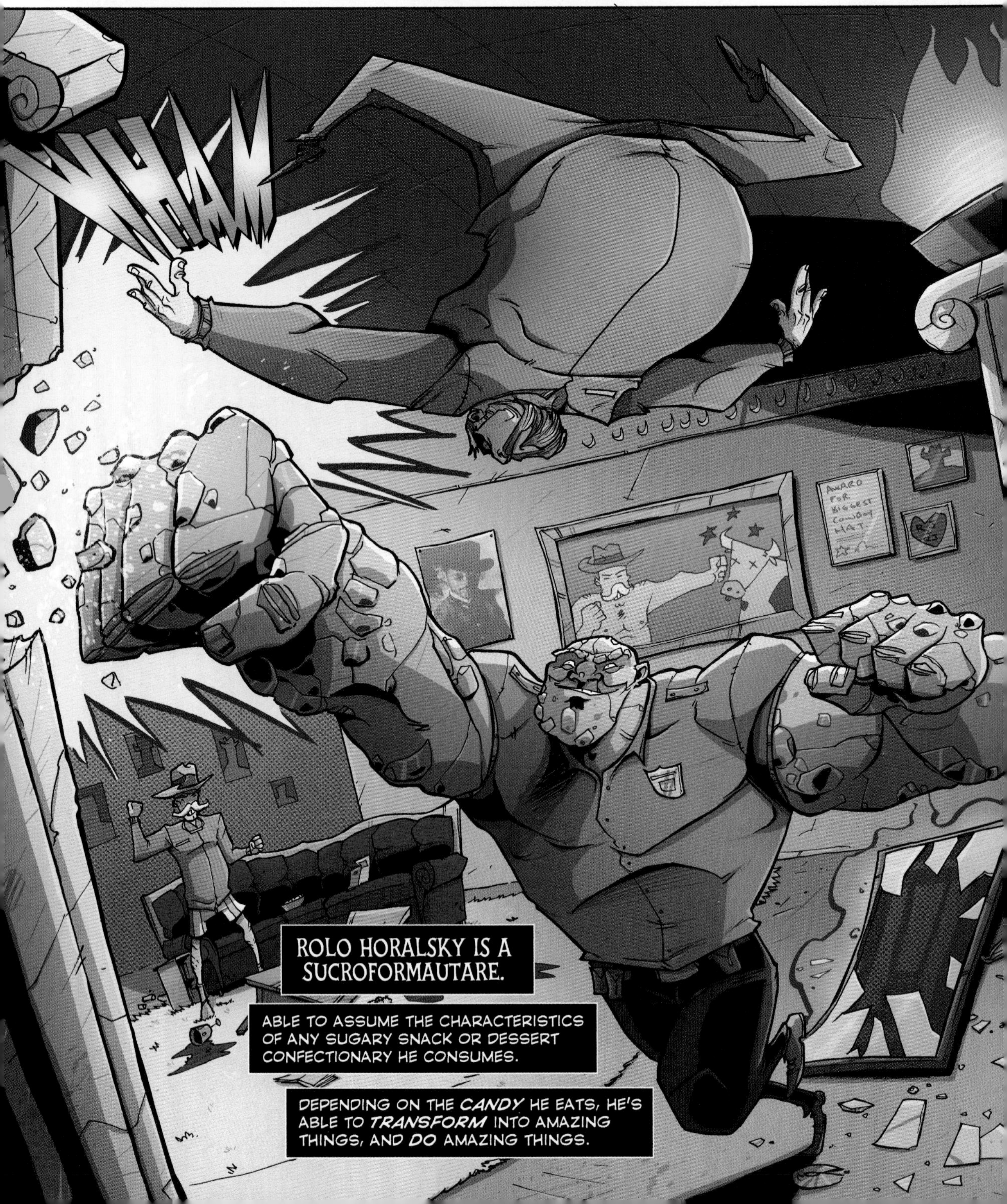
WHAM
AWARD FOR BIGGEST COWBOY HAT
ROLO HORALSKY IS A SUCROFORMAUTARE.
ABLE TO ASSUME THE CHARACTERISTICS OF ANY SUGARY SNACK OR DESSERT CONFECTIONARY HE CONSUMES.
DEPENDING ON THE CANDY HE EATS, HE'S ABLE TO TRANSFORM INTO AMAZING THINGS, AND DO AMAZING THINGS.

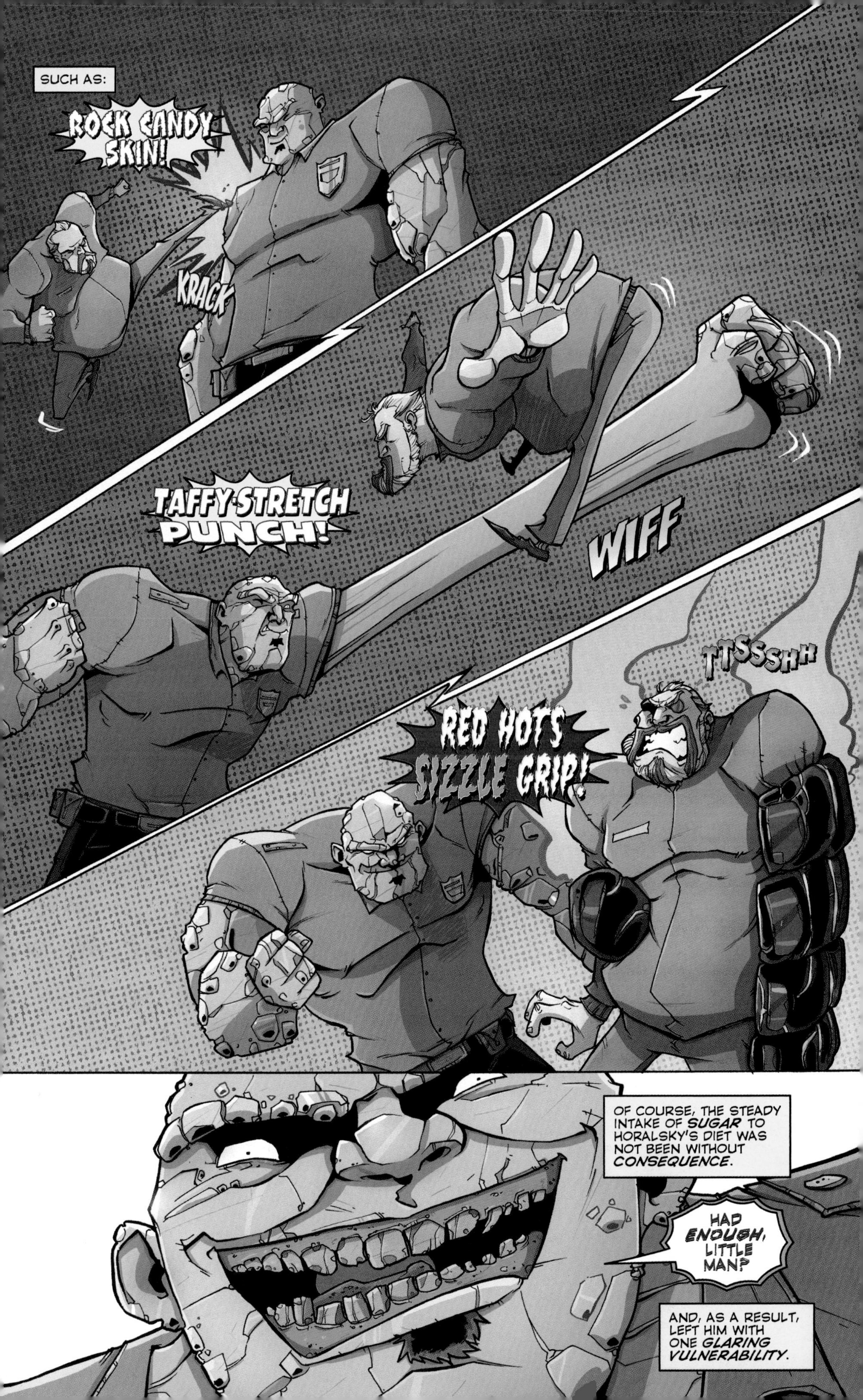
SUCH AS:
ROCK CANDY SKIN!
KRACK
TAFFY-STRETCH PUNCH!
WIFF
TTSSSHH
RED HOTS SIZZLE GRIP!
OF COURSE, THE STEADY INTAKE OF SUGAR TO HORALSKY'S DIET WAS NOT BEEN WITHOUT CONSEQUENCE.
HAD ENOUGH, LITTLE MAN?
AND, AS A RESULT, LEFT HIM WITH ONE GLARING VULNERABILITY.

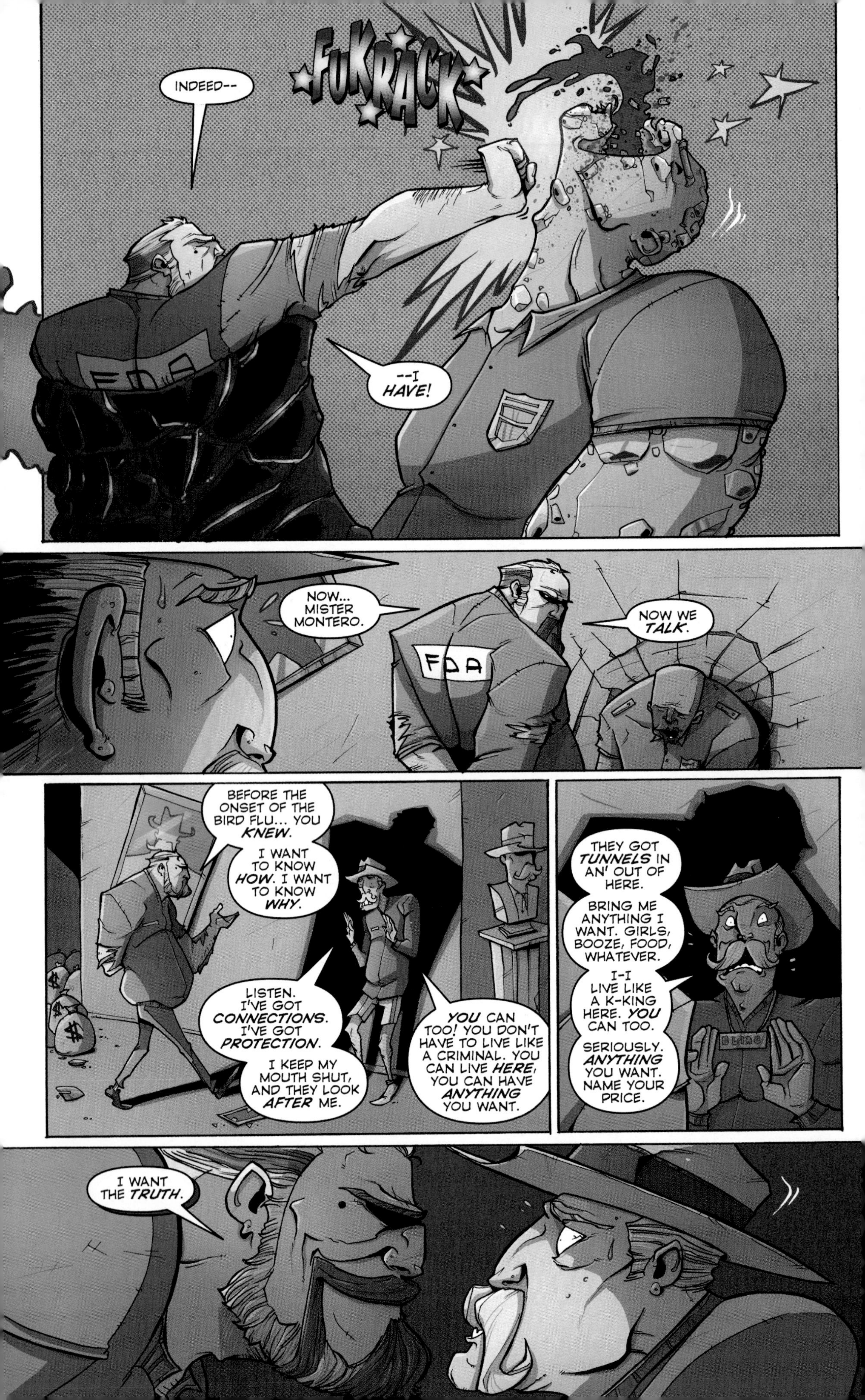
INDEED--
FUKRACK
--I *HAVE*!
NOW... MISTER MONTERO.
FDA
NOW WE *TALK*.
BEFORE THE ONSET OF THE BIRD FLU... YOU *KNEW*.
I WANT TO KNOW *HOW*. I WANT TO KNOW *WHY*.
LISTEN. I'VE GOT *CONNECTIONS*. I'VE GOT *PROTECTION*.
I KEEP MY MOUTH SHUT, AND THEY LOOK *AFTER* ME.
YOU CAN TOO! YOU DON'T HAVE TO LIVE LIKE A CRIMINAL. YOU CAN LIVE *HERE*, YOU CAN HAVE *ANYTHING* YOU WANT.
THEY GOT *TUNNELS* IN AN' OUT OF HERE.
BRING ME ANYTHING I WANT. GIRLS, BOOZE, FOOD, WHATEVER.
I-I LIVE LIKE A K-KING HERE. *YOU* CAN TOO.
SERIOUSLY. *ANYTHING* YOU WANT. NAME YOUR PRICE.
I WANT THE *TRUTH*.

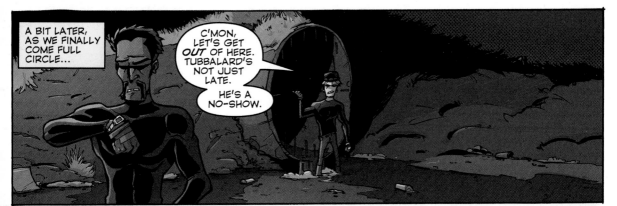

A BIT LATER, AS WE FINALLY COME FULL CIRCLE...

C'MON, LET'S GET *OUT* OF HERE. TUBBALARD'S NOT JUST LATE.

HE'S A NO-SHOW.

AHEM. I SEE THAT A LACK OF *PATIENCE* IS HIGH AMONG YOUR ALMOST *LIMITLESS* CHARACTER FAILINGS, AGENT COLBY.

YOU PULLED IT OFF, THEN? YOU *GOT* WHAT YOU WERE AFTER?

WHAT *WE* WERE AFTER, AGENT COLBY. WHAT WE *ARE* AFTER.

AND YES, I DO BELIEVE I *DID*.

THOUGH IT MIGHT TAKE SOME TIME TO... *DIGEST*... SUCH AN OVERABUNDANCE OF INFORMATION.

BACK AT THE SUPERMAX:

UHHH...

OOOOH...

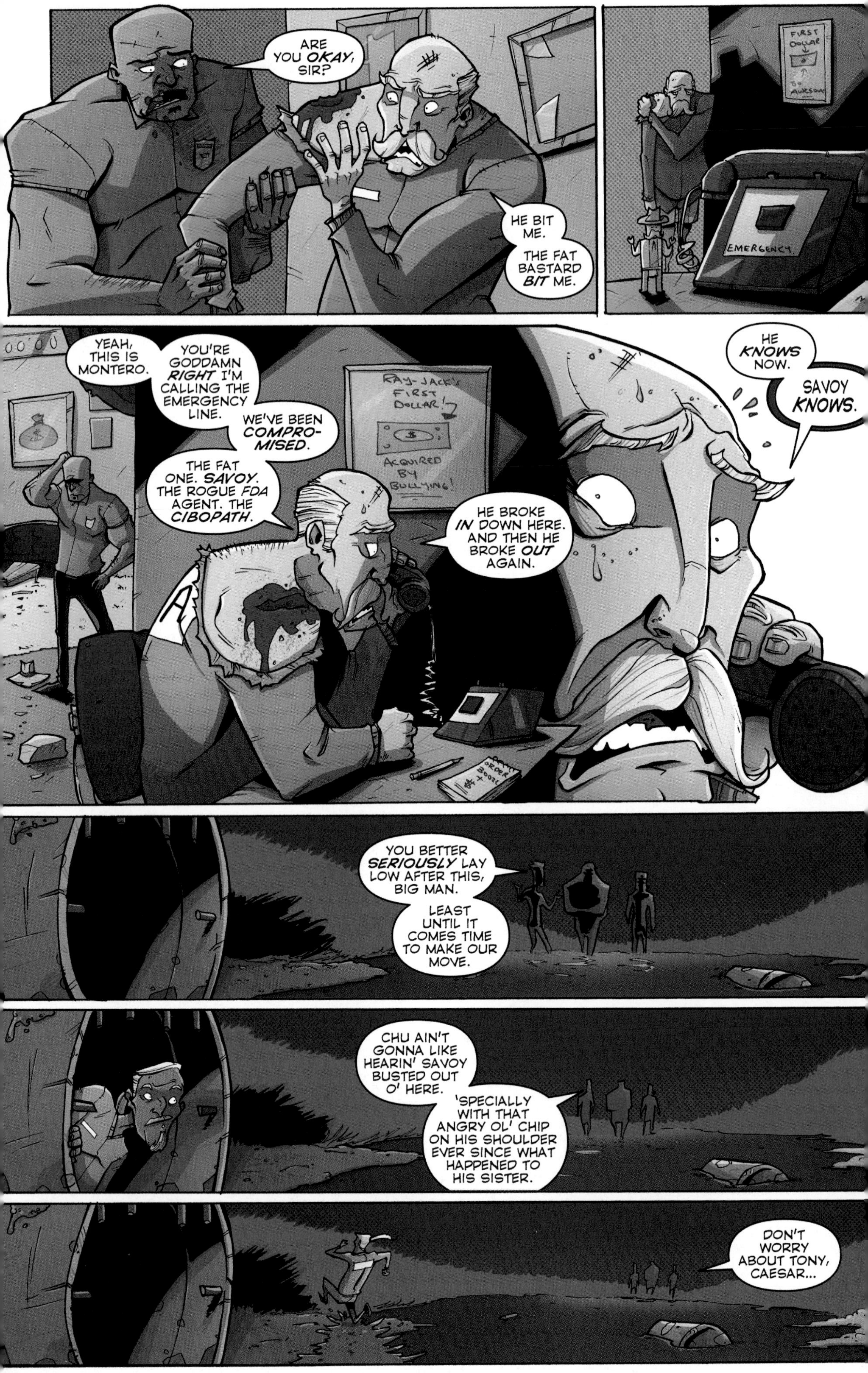

ARE YOU *OKAY*, SIR?
HE BIT ME.
THE FAT BASTARD *BIT* ME.
FIRST DOLLAR
EMERGENCY
YEAH, THIS IS MONTERO.
YOU'RE GODDAMN *RIGHT* I'M CALLING THE EMERGENCY LINE.
WE'VE BEEN *COMPROMISED*.
THE FAT ONE. *SAVOY*. THE ROGUE *FDA* AGENT. THE *CIBOPATH*.
RAY-JACK'S FIRST DOLLAR!
ACQUIRED BY BULLYING!
HE BROKE *IN* DOWN HERE. AND THEN HE BROKE *OUT* AGAIN.
HE *KNOWS* NOW.
SAVOY *KNOWS*.
YOU BETTER *SERIOUSLY* LAY LOW AFTER THIS, BIG MAN.
LEAST UNTIL IT COMES TIME TO MAKE OUR MOVE.
CHU AIN'T GONNA LIKE HEARIN' SAVOY BUSTED OUT O' HERE.
'SPECIALLY WITH THAT ANGRY OL' CHIP ON HIS SHOULDER EVER SINCE WHAT HAPPENED TO HIS SISTER.
DON'T WORRY ABOUT TONY, CAESAR...

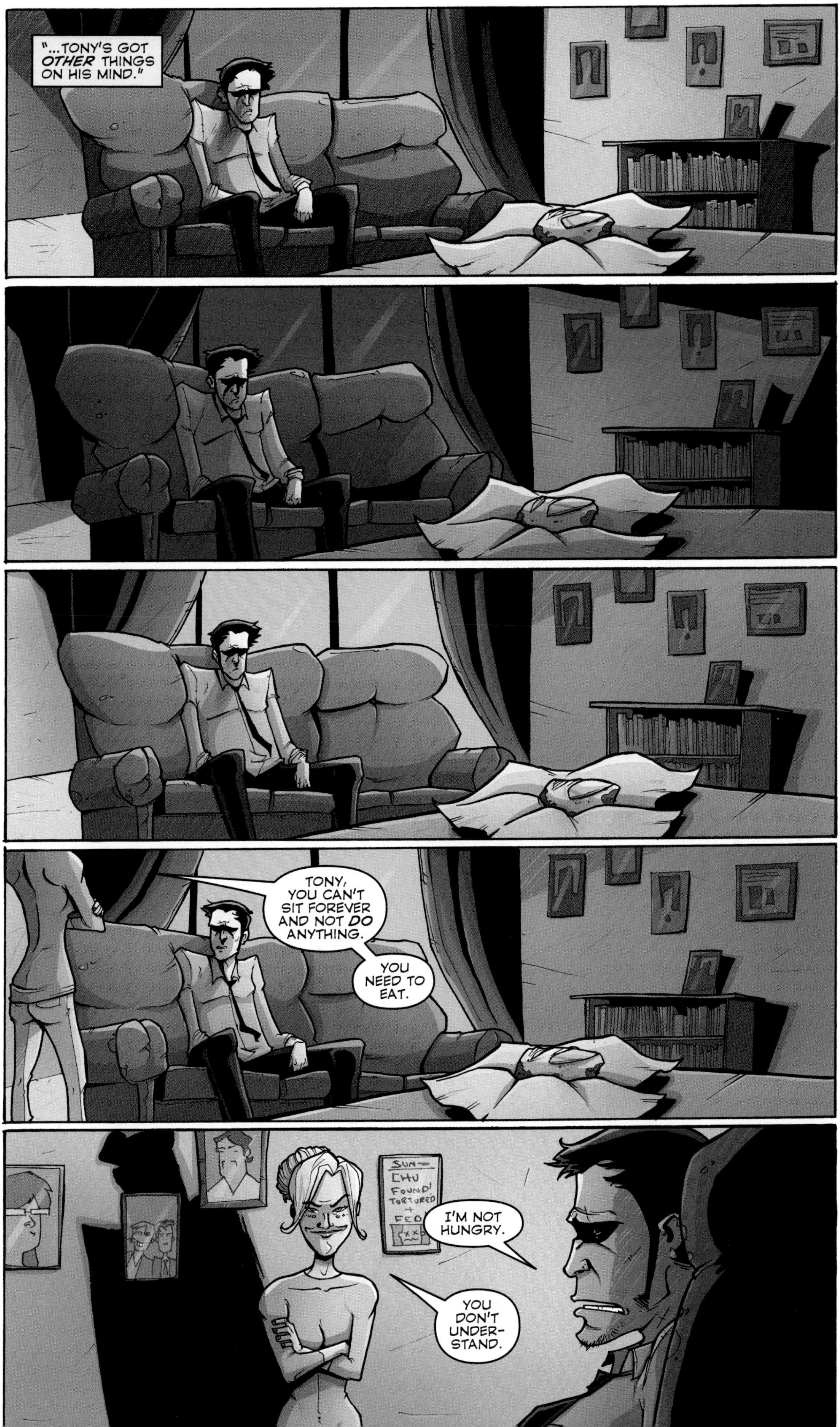
"...TONY'S GOT *OTHER* THINGS ON HIS MIND."
TONY, YOU CAN'T SIT FOREVER AND NOT *DO* ANYTHING.
YOU NEED TO EAT.
I'M NOT HUNGRY.
YOU DON'T UNDER-STAND.

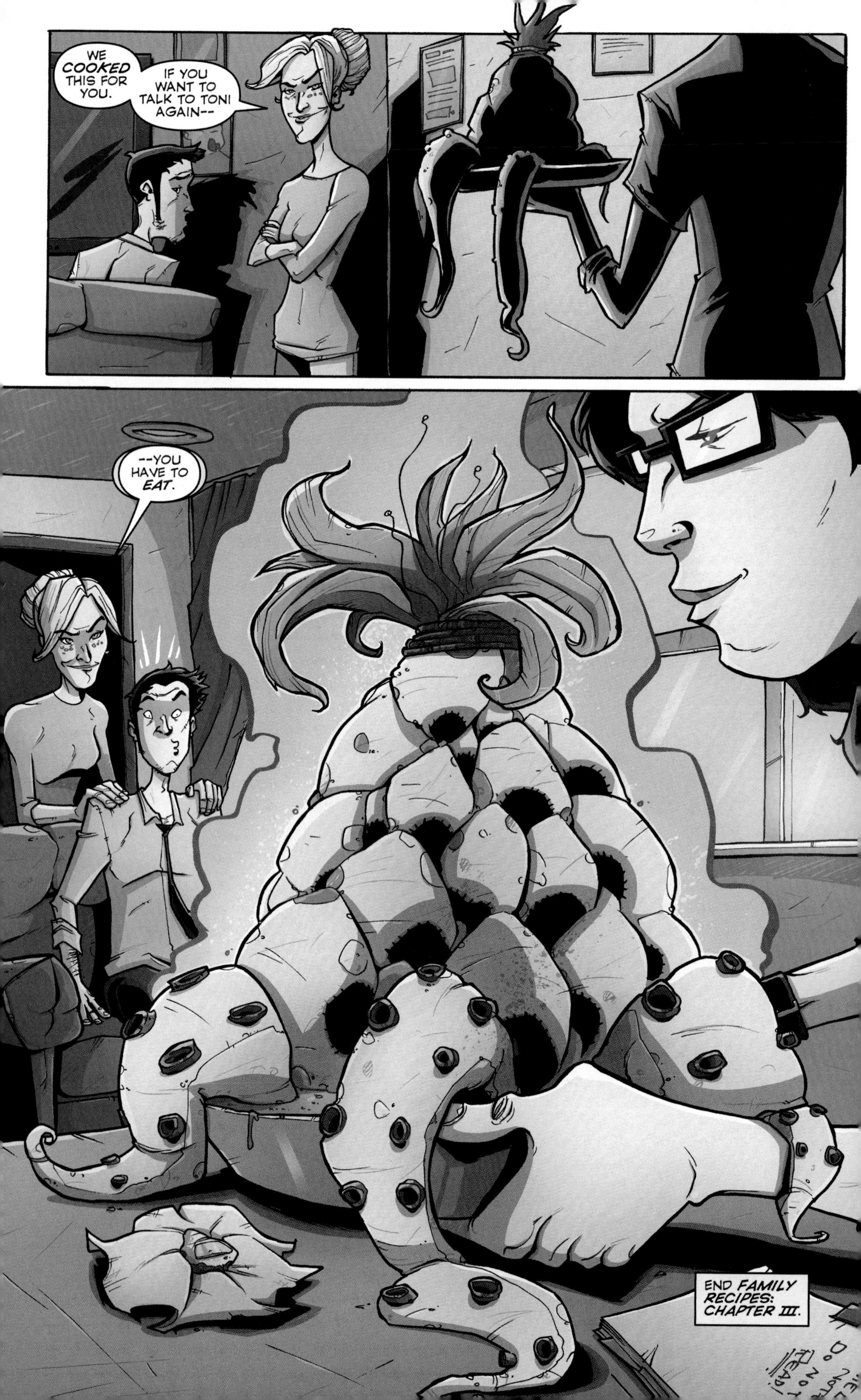
WE COOKED THIS FOR YOU.
IF YOU WANT TO TALK TO TONI AGAIN--
--YOU HAVE TO EAT.
END FAMILY RECIPES: CHAPTER III.

Chapter Nine

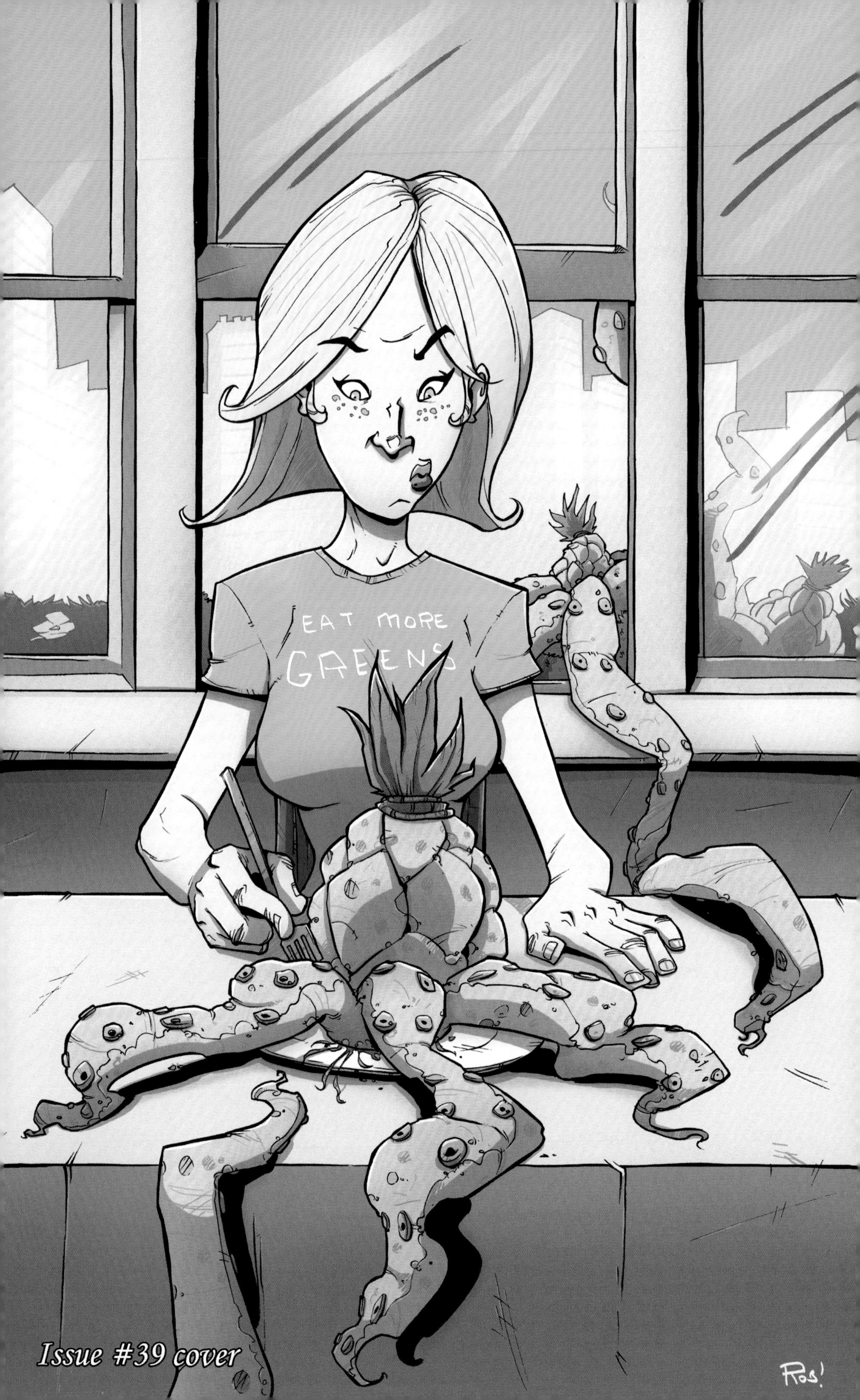
EAT MORE GREENS
Ros!

Issue #39 cover

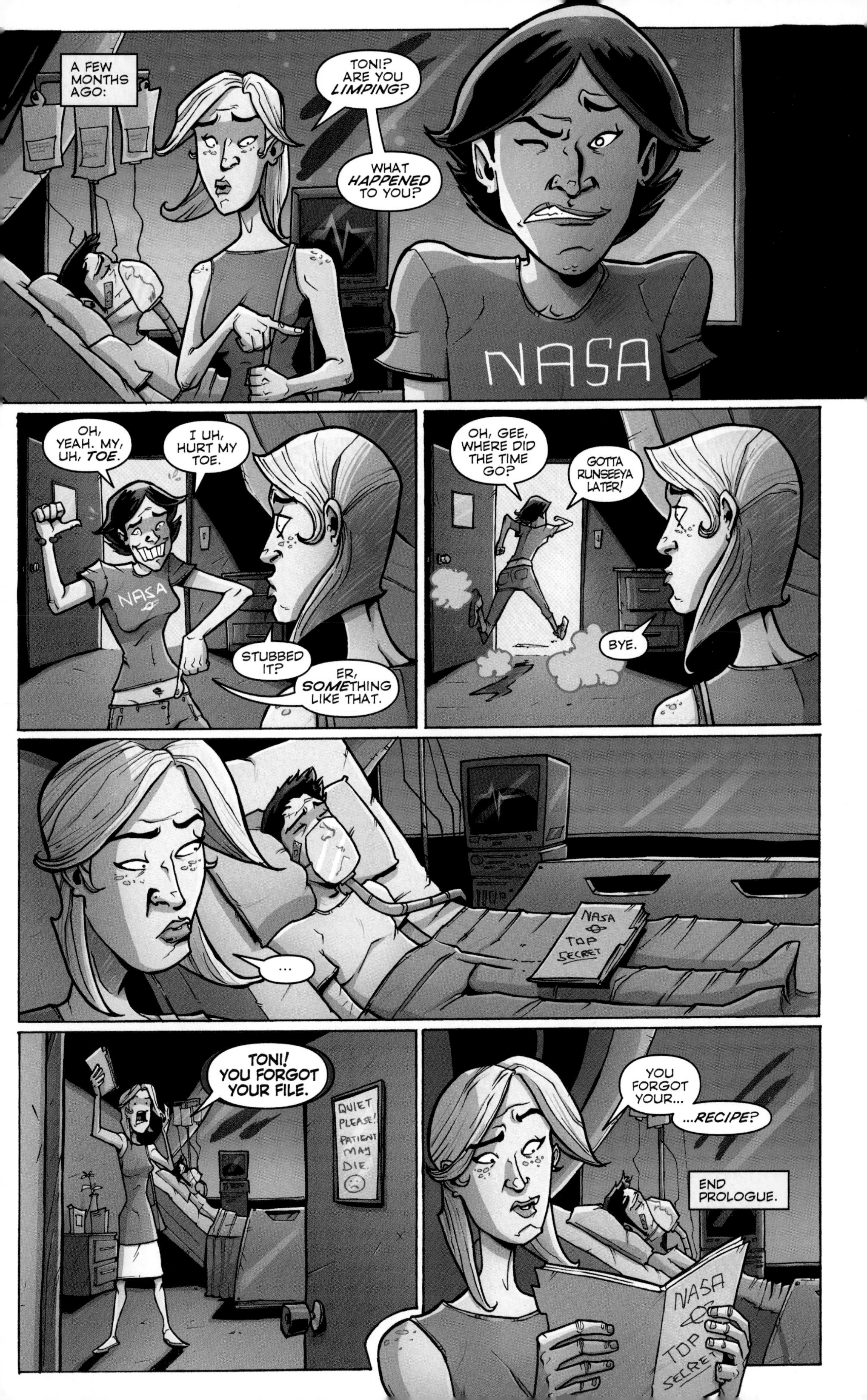
A FEW MONTHS AGO:
TONI? ARE YOU LIMPING?
WHAT HAPPENED TO YOU?
NASA
OH, YEAH. MY, UH, TOE.
I UH, HURT MY TOE.
NASA
STUBBED IT?
ER, SOMETHING LIKE THAT.
OH, GEE, WHERE DID THE TIME GO?
GOTTA RUNSEEYA LATER!
BYE.
NASA
TOP SECRET
...
TONI! YOU FORGOT YOUR FILE.
QUIET PLEASE! PATIENT MAY DIE.
YOU FORGOT YOUR...
...RECIPE?
END PROLOGUE.
NASA
TOP SECRET

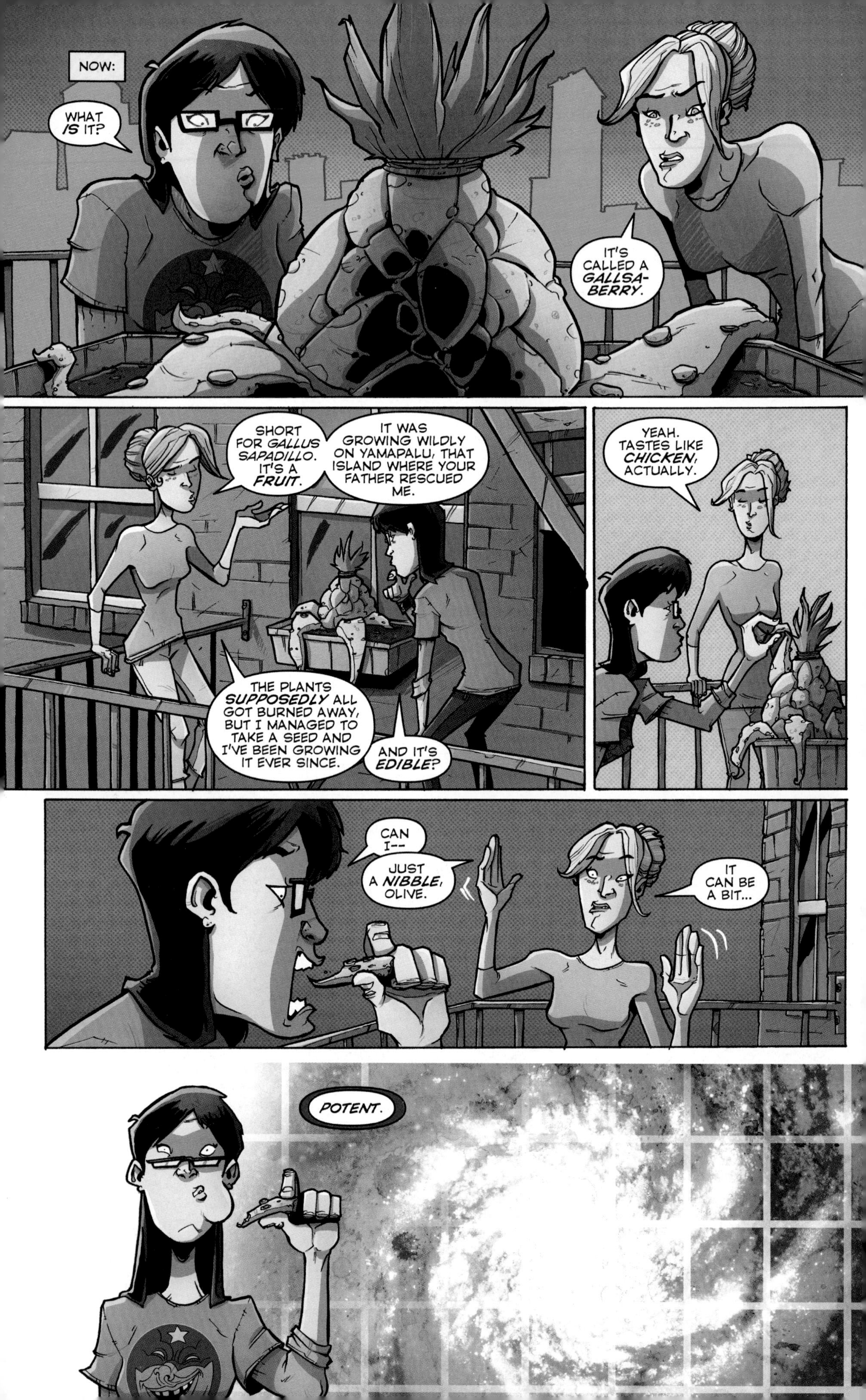
NOW:
WHAT IS IT?
IT'S CALLED A GALLSA-BERRY.
SHORT FOR GALLUS SAPADILLO. IT'S A FRUIT.
IT WAS GROWING WILDLY ON YAMAPALU, THAT ISLAND WHERE YOUR FATHER RESCUED ME.
THE PLANTS SUPPOSEDLY ALL GOT BURNED AWAY, BUT I MANAGED TO TAKE A SEED AND I'VE BEEN GROWING IT EVER SINCE.
AND IT'S EDIBLE?
YEAH. TASTES LIKE CHICKEN, ACTUALLY.
CAN I--
JUST A NIBBLE, OLIVE.
IT CAN BE A BIT...
POTENT.

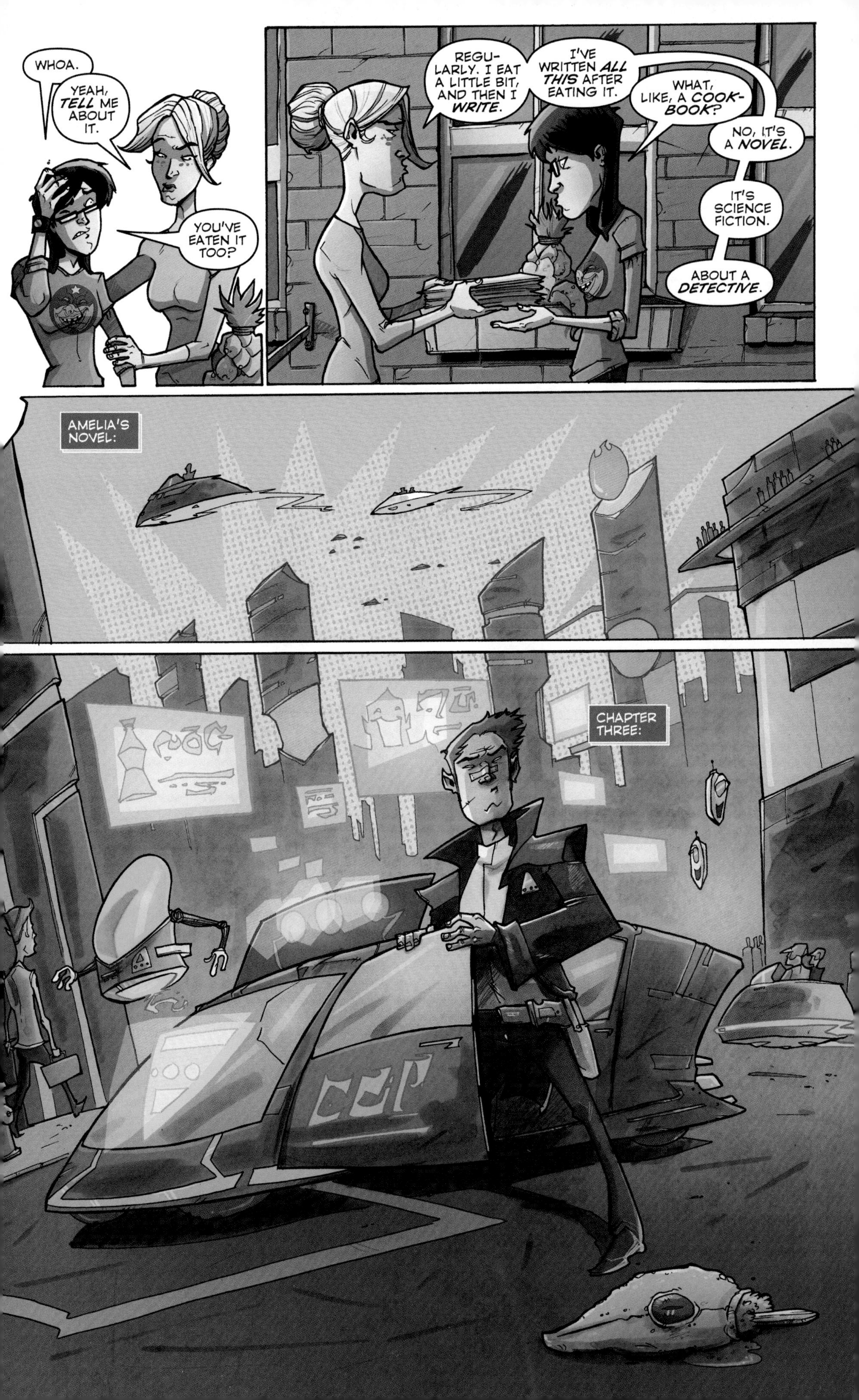
WHOA.
YEAH, TELL ME ABOUT IT.
YOU'VE EATEN IT TOO?
REGU-LARLY. I EAT A LITTLE BIT, AND THEN I WRITE.
I'VE WRITTEN ALL THIS AFTER EATING IT.
WHAT, LIKE, A COOK-BOOK?
NO, IT'S A NOVEL.
IT'S SCIENCE FICTION.
ABOUT A DETECTIVE.
AMELIA'S NOVEL:
CHAPTER THREE:

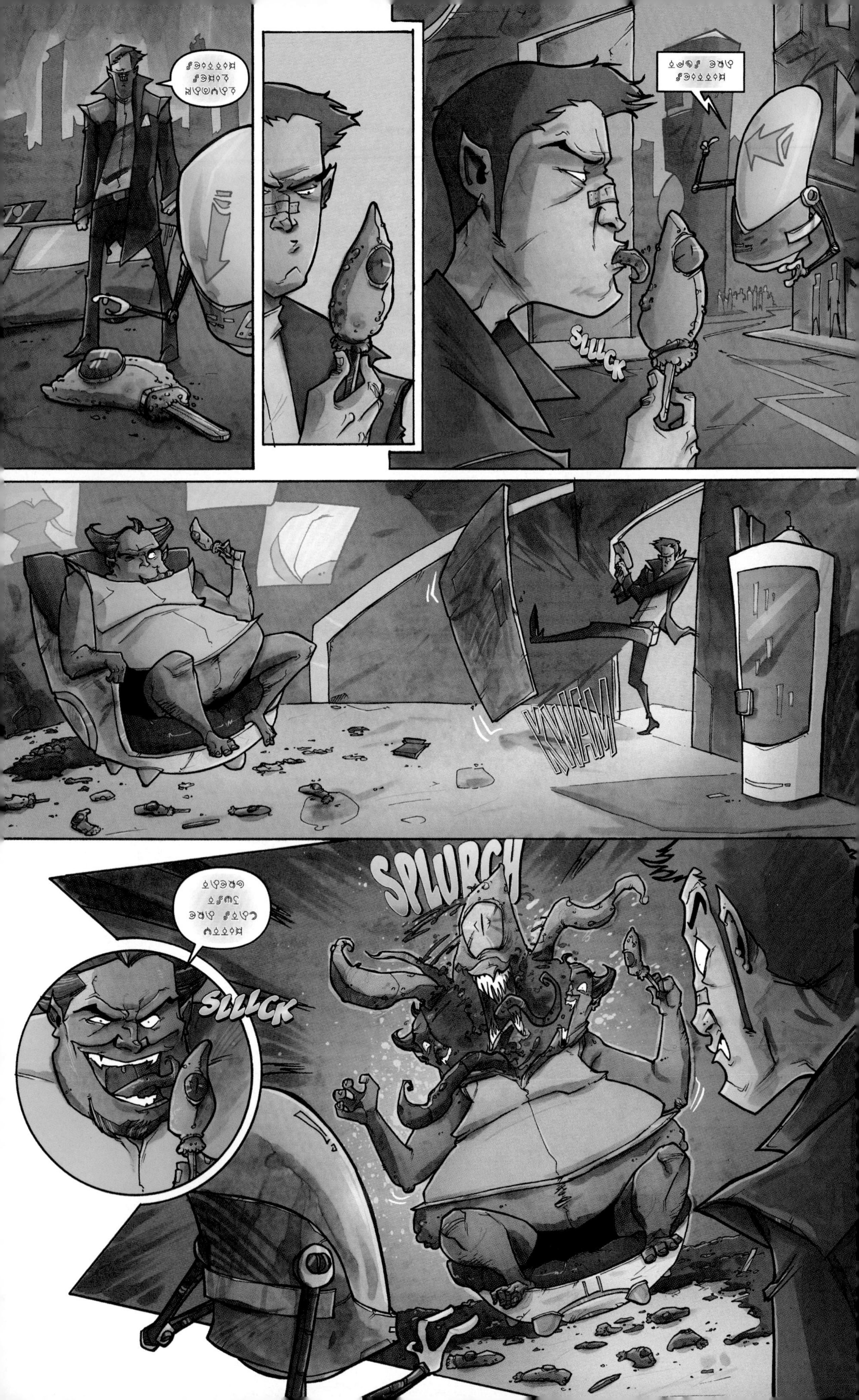
SLLLCK
SPLURCH
SLLLCK

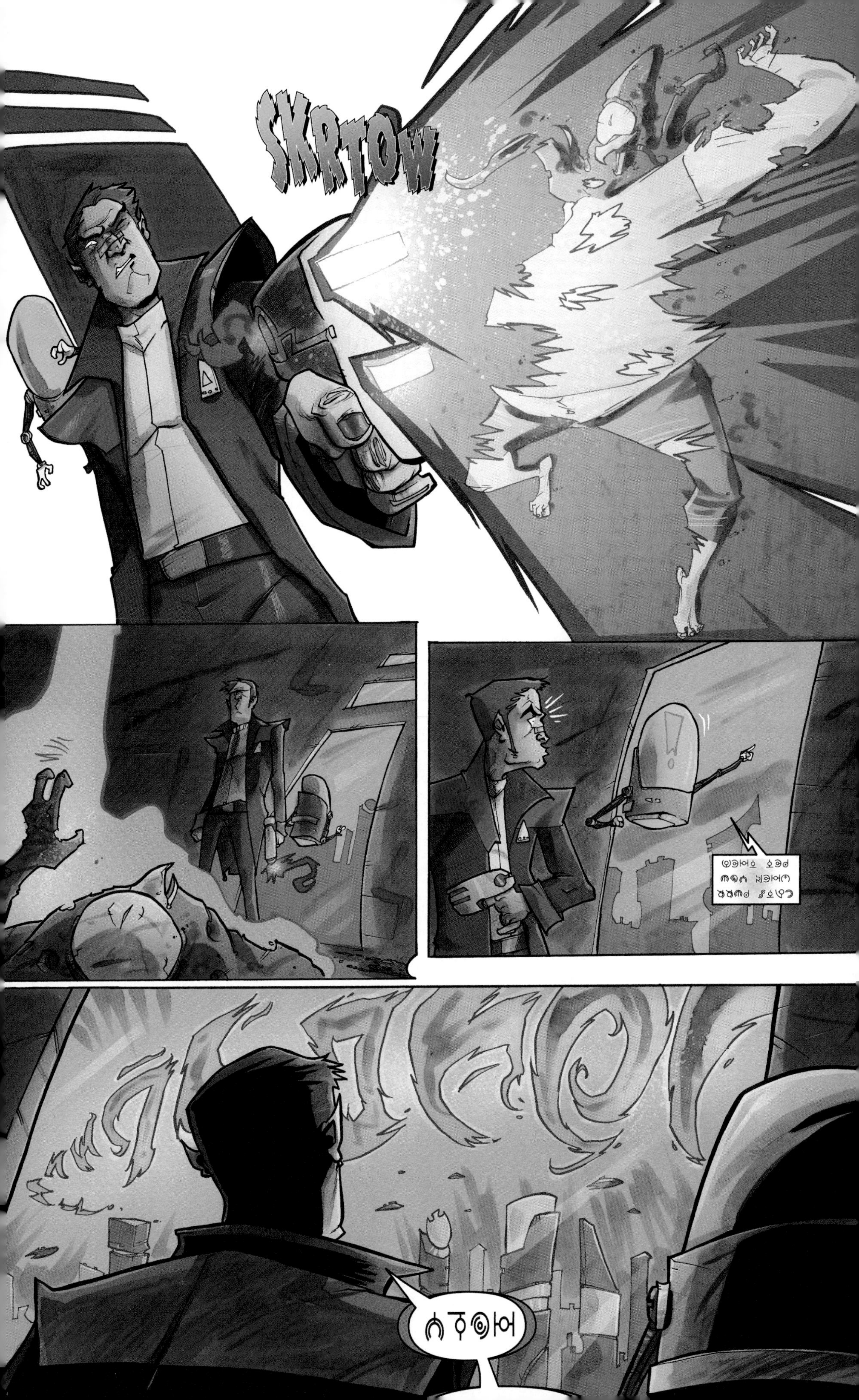
SKRTOW

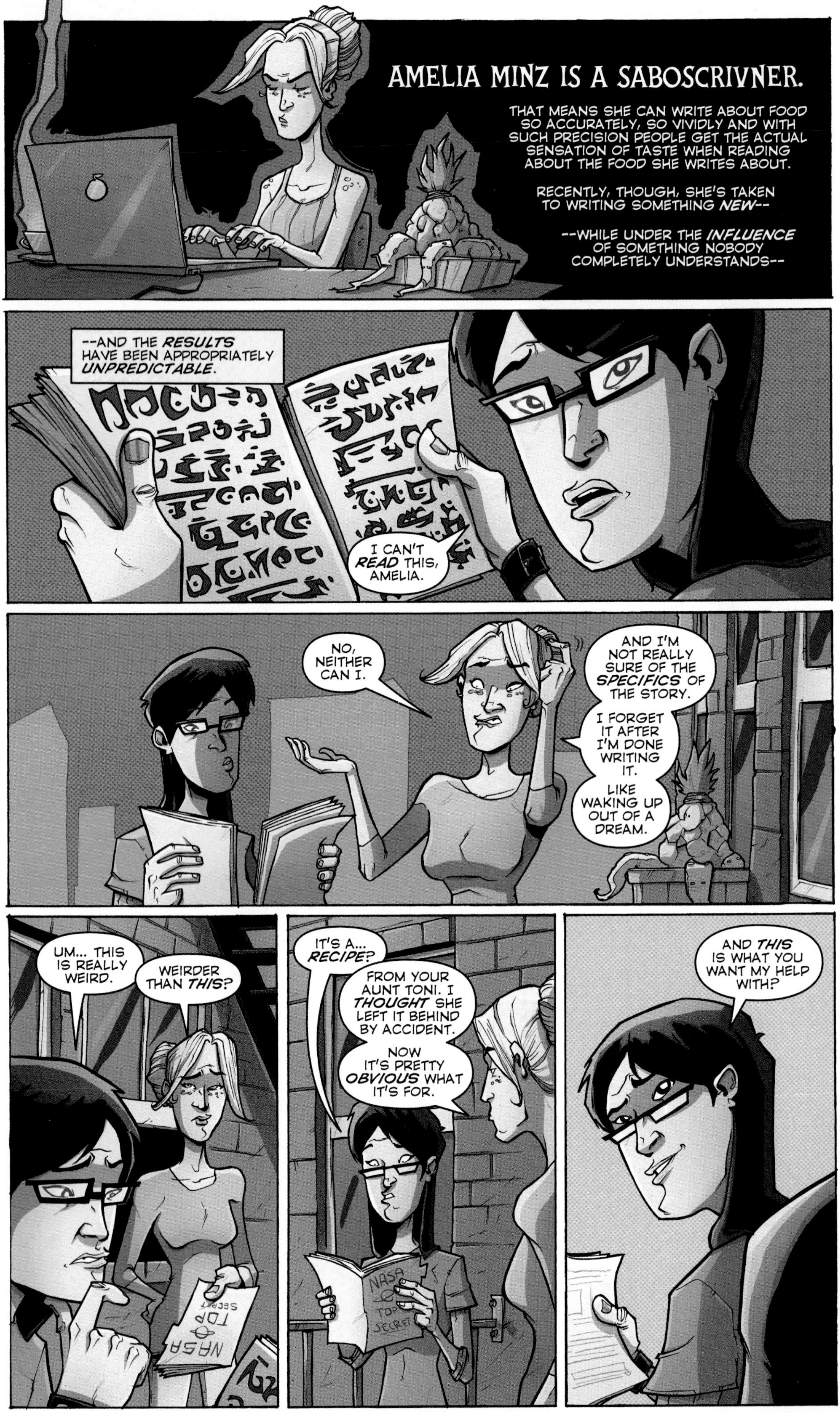
AMELIA MINZ IS A SABOSCRIVNER.
THAT MEANS SHE CAN WRITE ABOUT FOOD SO ACCURATELY, SO VIVIDLY AND WITH SUCH PRECISION PEOPLE GET THE ACTUAL SENSATION OF TASTE WHEN READING ABOUT THE FOOD SHE WRITES ABOUT.
RECENTLY, THOUGH, SHE'S TAKEN TO WRITING SOMETHING NEW--
--WHILE UNDER THE INFLUENCE OF SOMETHING NOBODY COMPLETELY UNDERSTANDS--
--AND THE RESULTS HAVE BEEN APPROPRIATELY UNPREDICTABLE.
I CAN'T READ THIS, AMELIA.
NO, NEITHER CAN I.
AND I'M NOT REALLY SURE OF THE SPECIFICS OF THE STORY.
I FORGET IT AFTER I'M DONE WRITING IT.
LIKE WAKING UP OUT OF A DREAM.
UM... THIS IS REALLY WEIRD.
WEIRDER THAN THIS?
NASA TOP SECRET
IT'S A... RECIPE?
FROM YOUR AUNT TONI. I THOUGHT SHE LEFT IT BEHIND BY ACCIDENT.
NOW IT'S PRETTY OBVIOUS WHAT IT'S FOR.
NASA TOP SECRET
AND THIS IS WHAT YOU WANT MY HELP WITH?

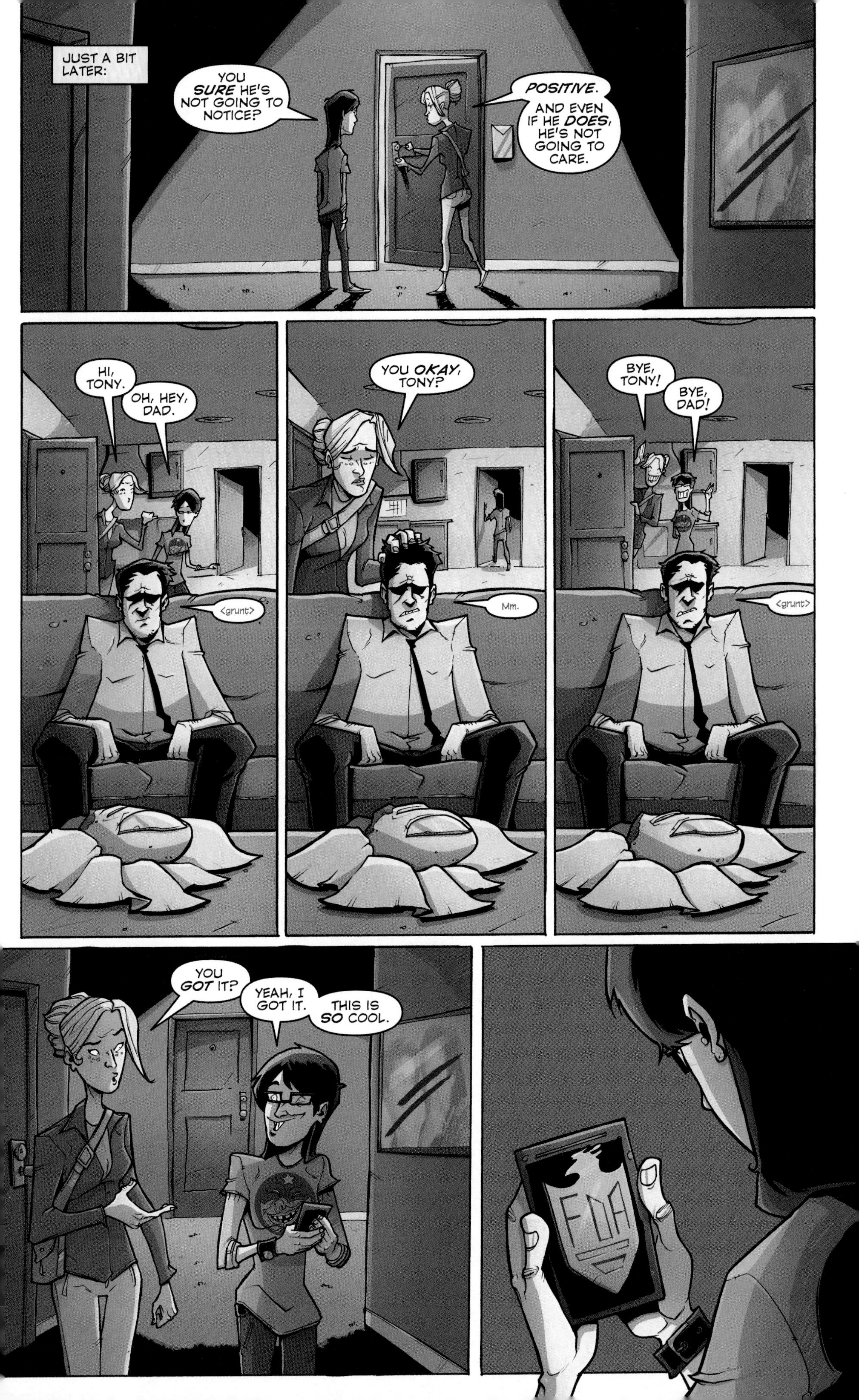
JUST A BIT LATER:
YOU SURE HE'S NOT GOING TO NOTICE?
POSITIVE.
AND EVEN IF HE DOES, HE'S NOT GOING TO CARE.
HI, TONY.
OH, HEY, DAD.
<grunt>
YOU OKAY, TONY?
Mm.
BYE, TONY!
BYE, DAD!
<grunt>
YOU GOT IT?
YEAH, I GOT IT.
THIS IS SO COOL.

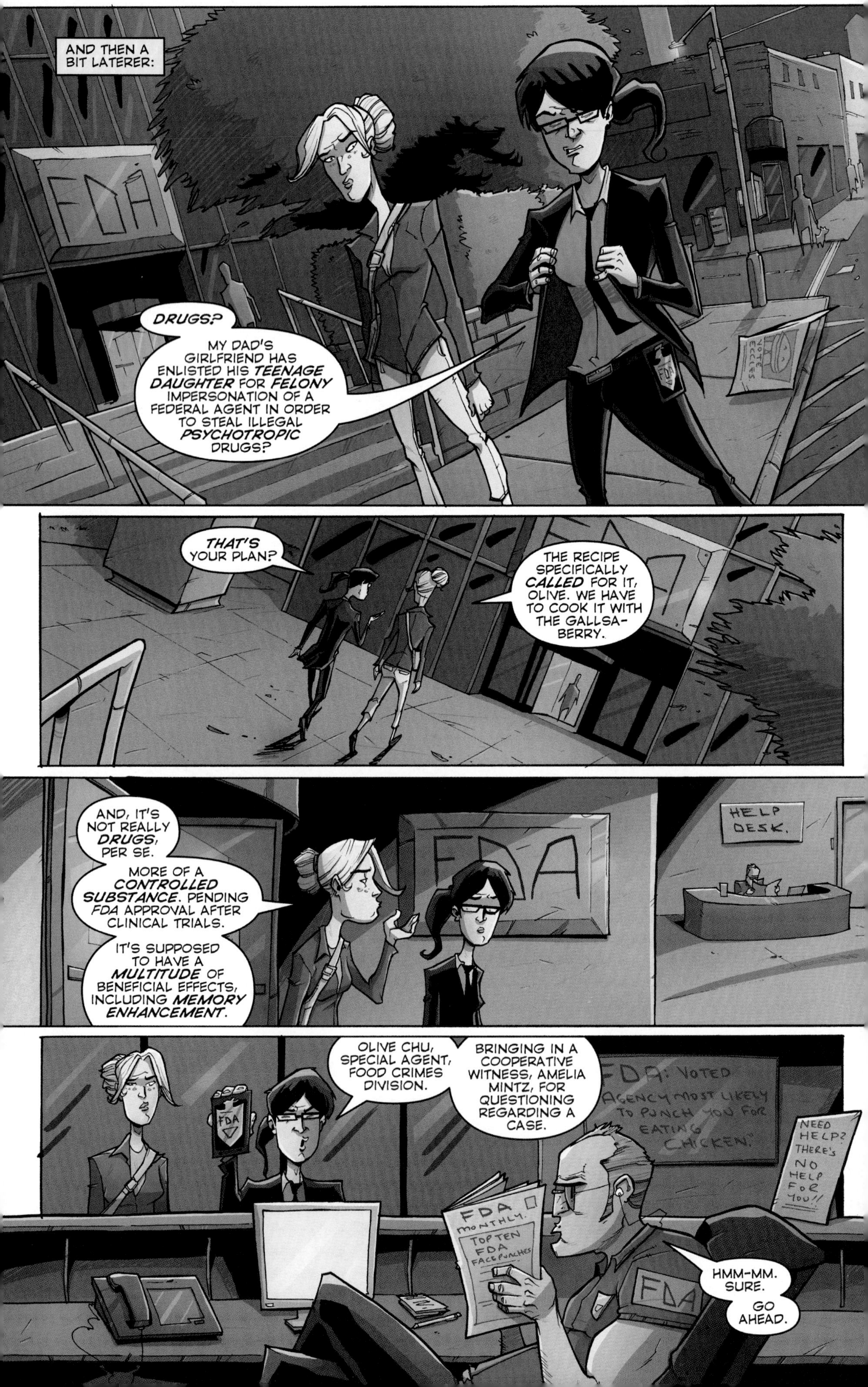
AND THEN A BIT LATERER:
FDA
DRUGS?
MY DAD'S GIRLFRIEND HAS ENLISTED HIS TEENAGE DAUGHTER FOR FELONY IMPERSONATION OF A FEDERAL AGENT IN ORDER TO STEAL ILLEGAL PSYCHOTROPIC DRUGS?
VOTE ECCLES
THAT'S YOUR PLAN?
THE RECIPE SPECIFICALLY CALLED FOR IT, OLIVE. WE HAVE TO COOK IT WITH THE GALLSA-BERRY.
AND, IT'S NOT REALLY DRUGS, PER SE.
MORE OF A CONTROLLED SUBSTANCE. PENDING FDA APPROVAL AFTER CLINICAL TRIALS.
IT'S SUPPOSED TO HAVE A MULTITUDE OF BENEFICIAL EFFECTS, INCLUDING MEMORY ENHANCEMENT.
FDA
HELP DESK.
OLIVE CHU, SPECIAL AGENT, FOOD CRIMES DIVISION.
BRINGING IN A COOPERATIVE WITNESS, AMELIA MINTZ, FOR QUESTIONING REGARDING A CASE.
FDA: VOTED AGENCY MOST LIKELY TO PUNCH YOU FOR EATING CHICKEN.
NEED HELP? THERE'S NO HELP FOR YOU!!
FDA MONTHLY. TOP TEN FDA FACE PUNCHES
HMM-MM. SURE.
GO AHEAD.

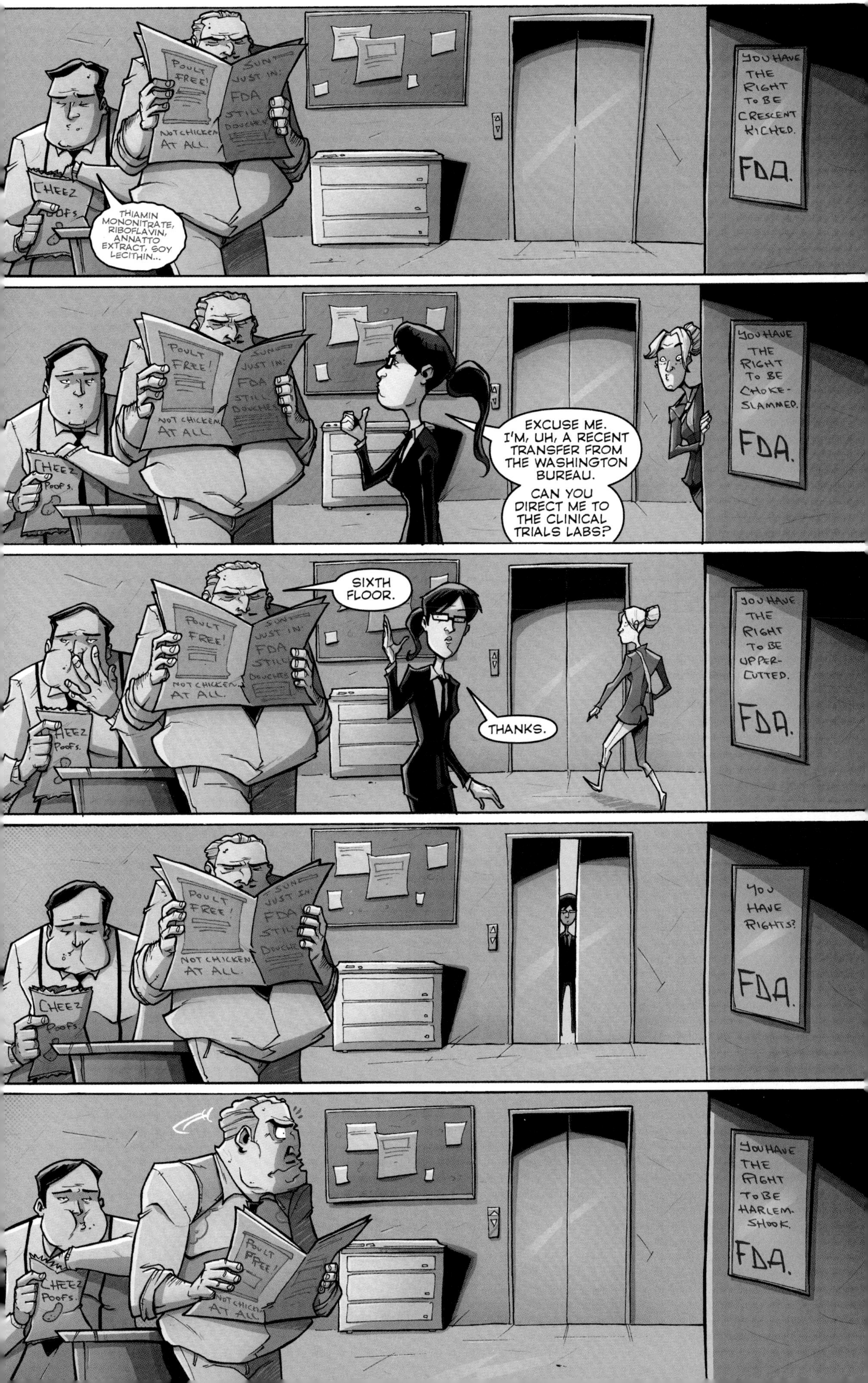

POULT FREE!
SUN JUST IN: FDA STILL
NOT CHICKEN AT ALL
CHEEZ POOFS
THIAMIN MONONITRATE, RIBOFLAVIN, ANNATTO EXTRACT, SOY LECITHIN...
YOU HAVE THE RIGHT TO BE CRESCENT KICKED. FDA.
EXCUSE ME. I'M, UH, A RECENT TRANSFER FROM THE WASHINGTON BUREAU.
CAN YOU DIRECT ME TO THE CLINICAL TRIALS LABS?
YOU HAVE THE RIGHT TO BE CHOKE-SLAMMED. FDA.
SIXTH FLOOR.
THANKS.
YOU HAVE THE RIGHT TO BE UPPER-CUTTED. FDA.
YOU HAVE RIGHTS? FDA.
YOU HAVE THE RIGHT TO BE HARLEM-SHOOK. FDA.

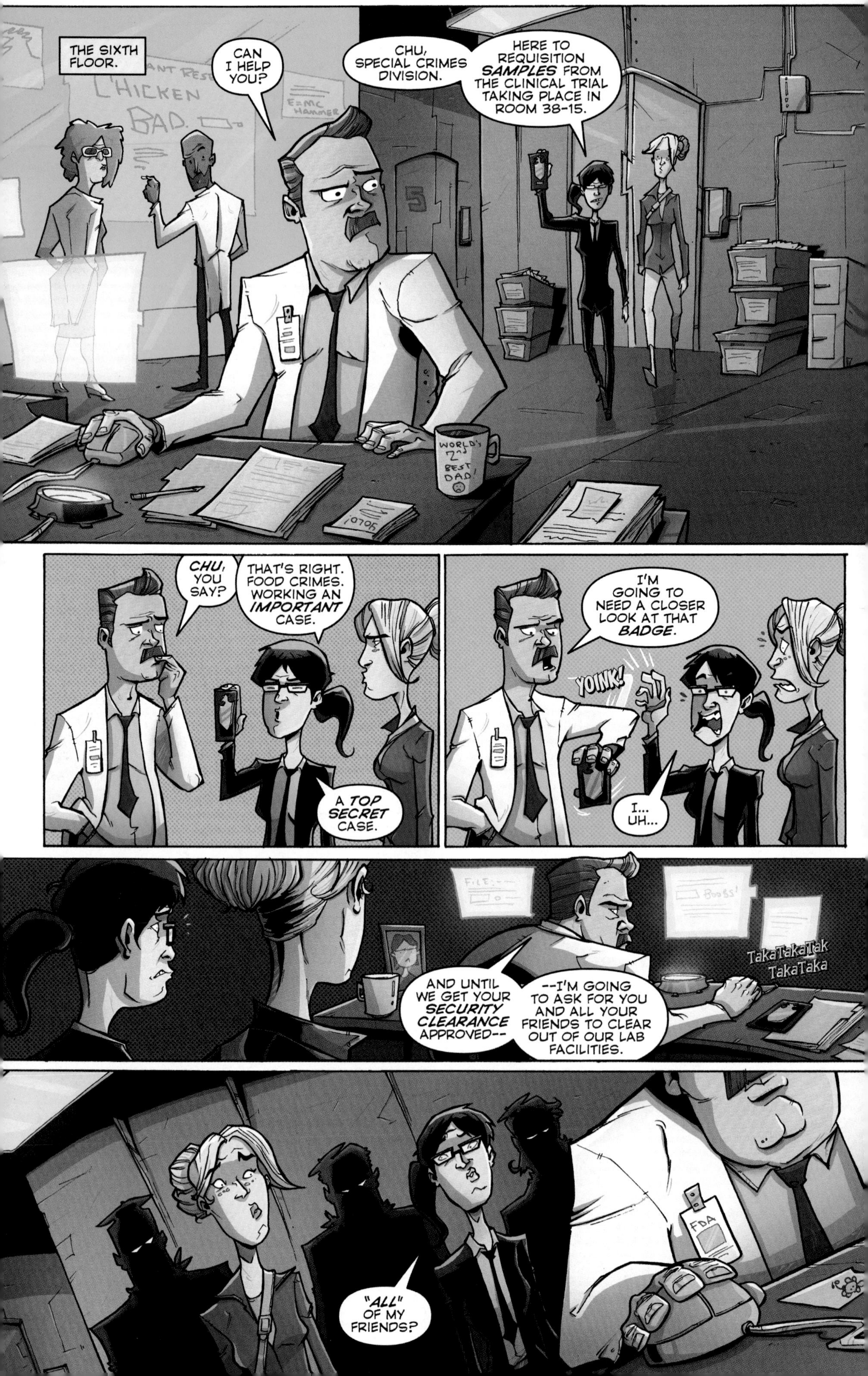
THE SIXTH FLOOR.
CAN I HELP YOU?
CHU, SPECIAL CRIMES DIVISION.
HERE TO REQUISITION *SAMPLES* FROM THE CLINICAL TRIAL TAKING PLACE IN ROOM 38-15.
CHICKEN BAD.
E=MC HAMMER
WORLD'S 2ND BEST DAD!
CHU, YOU SAY?
THAT'S RIGHT. FOOD CRIMES. WORKING AN *IMPORTANT* CASE.
A *TOP SECRET* CASE.
I'M GOING TO NEED A CLOSER LOOK AT THAT *BADGE*.
YOINK!
I... UH...
TakaTakaTak TakaTaka
AND UNTIL WE GET YOUR *SECURITY CLEARANCE* APPROVED--
--I'M GOING TO ASK FOR YOU AND ALL YOUR FRIENDS TO CLEAR OUT OF OUR LAB FACILITIES.
"*ALL*" OF MY FRIENDS?
FDA

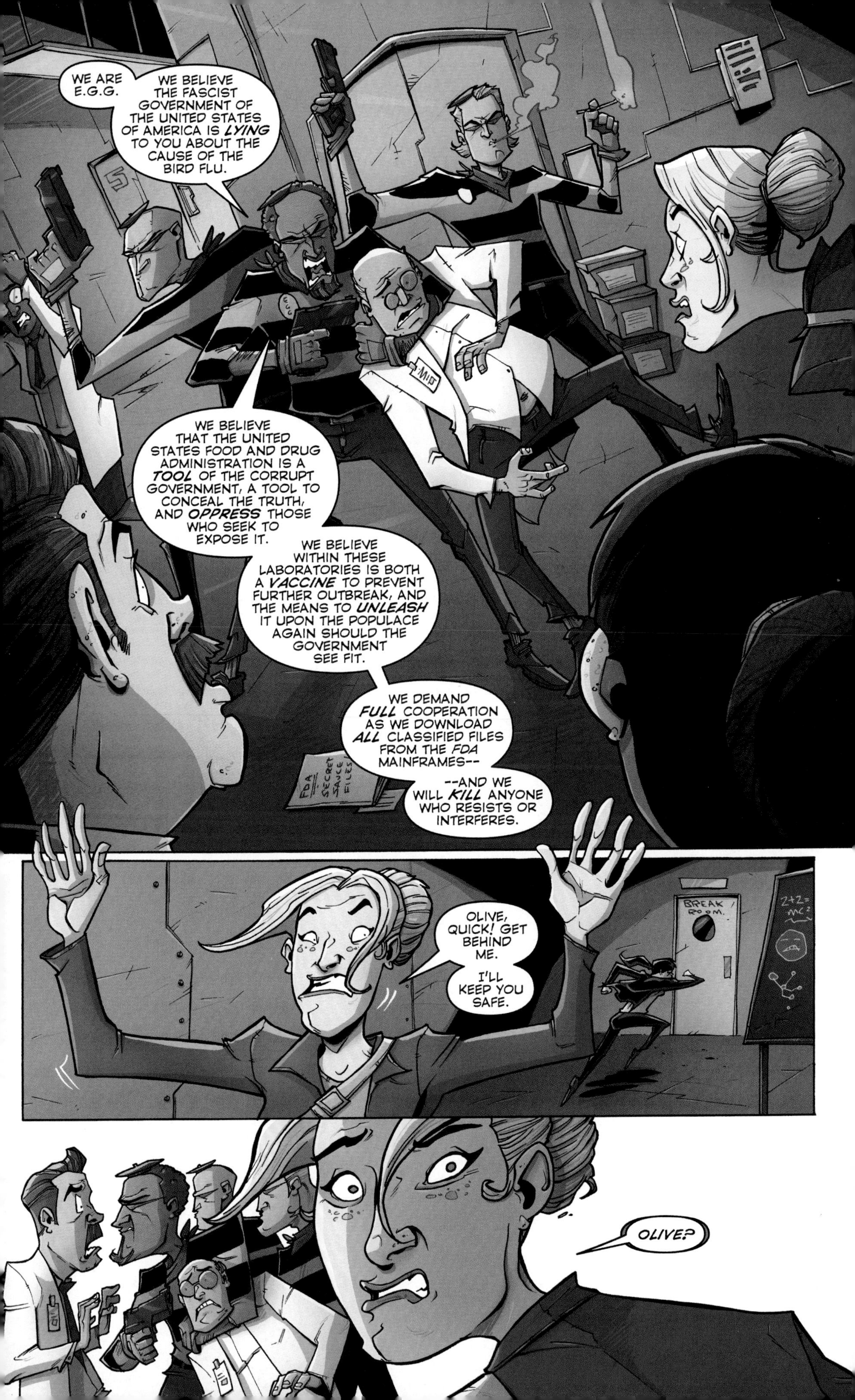

WE ARE E.G.G.
WE BELIEVE THE FASCIST GOVERNMENT OF THE UNITED STATES OF AMERICA IS *LYING* TO YOU ABOUT THE CAUSE OF THE BIRD FLU.
WE BELIEVE THAT THE UNITED STATES FOOD AND DRUG ADMINISTRATION IS A *TOOL* OF THE CORRUPT GOVERNMENT, A TOOL TO CONCEAL THE TRUTH, AND *OPPRESS* THOSE WHO SEEK TO EXPOSE IT.
WE BELIEVE WITHIN THESE LABORATORIES IS BOTH A *VACCINE* TO PREVENT FURTHER OUTBREAK, AND THE MEANS TO *UNLEASH* IT UPON THE POPULACE AGAIN SHOULD THE GOVERNMENT SEE FIT.
WE DEMAND *FULL* COOPERATION AS WE DOWNLOAD *ALL* CLASSIFIED FILES FROM THE *FDA* MAINFRAMES--
--AND WE WILL *KILL* ANYONE WHO RESISTS OR INTERFERES.
FDA
SECRET SAUCE FILES
BREAK ROOM.
OLIVE, QUICK! GET BEHIND ME.
I'LL KEEP YOU SAFE.
OLIVE?

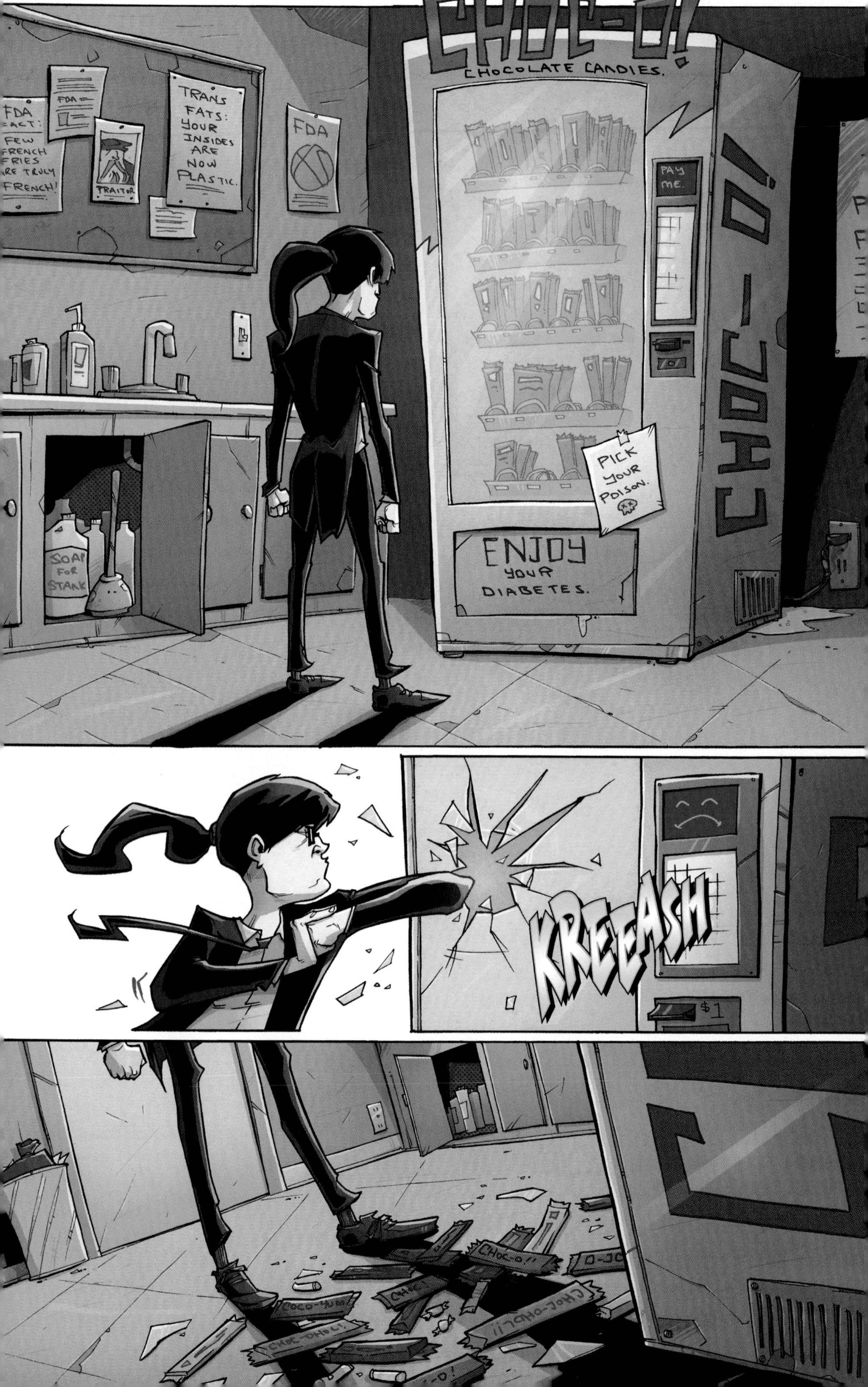
CHOC-O!
CHOCOLATE CANDIES.
FDA
FEW FRENCH FRIES
FRENCH!
FDA
TRAITOR
TRANS FATS: YOUR INSIDES ARE NOW PLASTIC.
FDA
PAY ME.
CHOC-O!
PICK YOUR POISON.
ENJOY YOUR DIABETES.
SOAP FOR STARK
KREEASH
$1
CHOC-O!!
COCO-YUM
CHOC-OHOL!

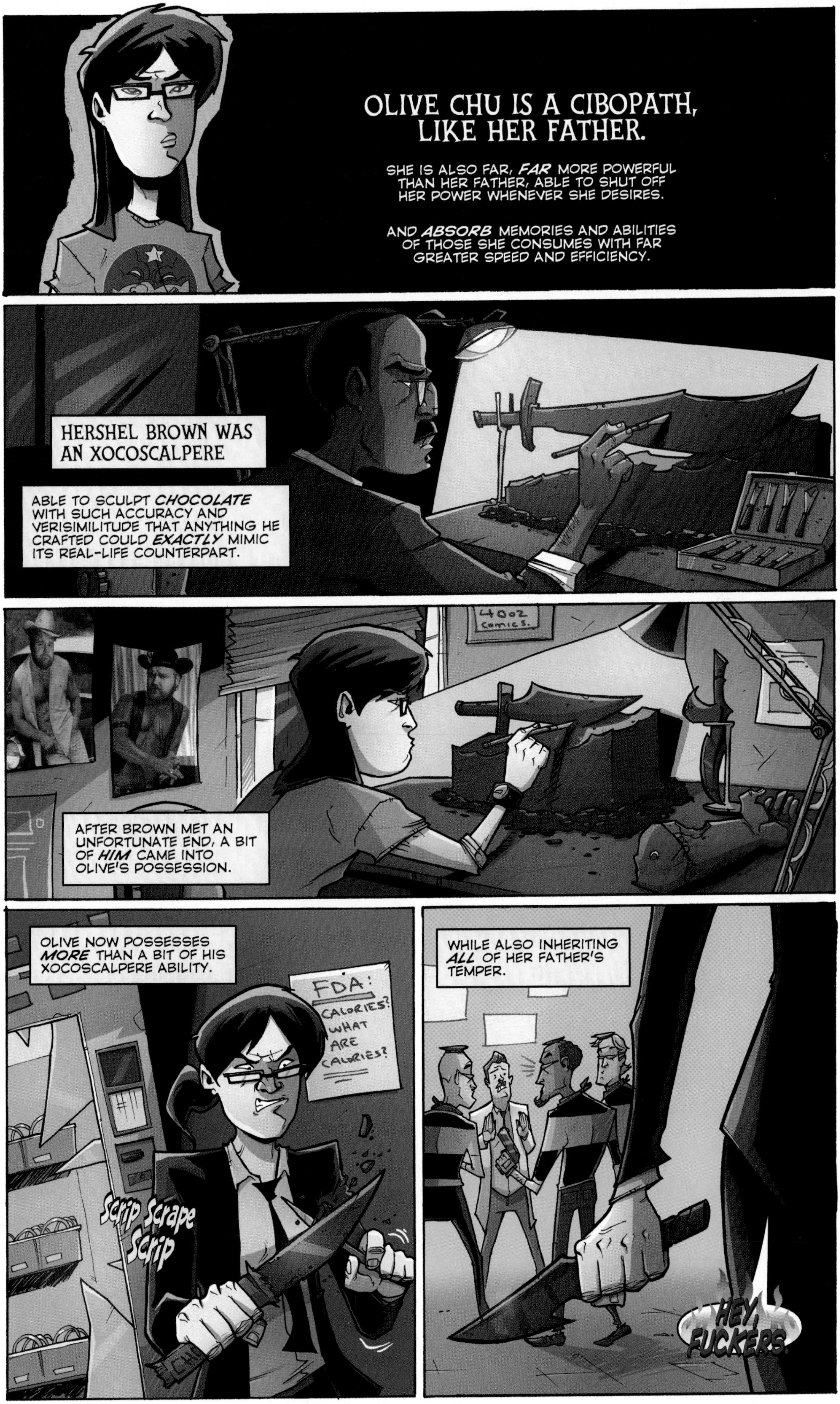
OLIVE CHU IS A CIBOPATH, LIKE HER FATHER.
SHE IS ALSO FAR, FAR MORE POWERFUL THAN HER FATHER, ABLE TO SHUT OFF HER POWER WHENEVER SHE DESIRES.
AND ABSORB MEMORIES AND ABILITIES OF THOSE SHE CONSUMES WITH FAR GREATER SPEED AND EFFICIENCY.
HERSHEL BROWN WAS AN XOCOSCALPERE
ABLE TO SCULPT CHOCOLATE WITH SUCH ACCURACY AND VERISIMILITUDE THAT ANYTHING HE CRAFTED COULD EXACTLY MIMIC ITS REAL-LIFE COUNTERPART.
AFTER BROWN MET AN UNFORTUNATE END, A BIT OF HIM CAME INTO OLIVE'S POSSESSION.
OLIVE NOW POSSESSES MORE THAN A BIT OF HIS XOCOSCALPERE ABILITY.
FDA: CALORIES? WHAT ARE CALORIES?
Scrip Scrape Scrip
WHILE ALSO INHERITING ALL OF HER FATHER'S TEMPER.
HEY, FUCKERS.

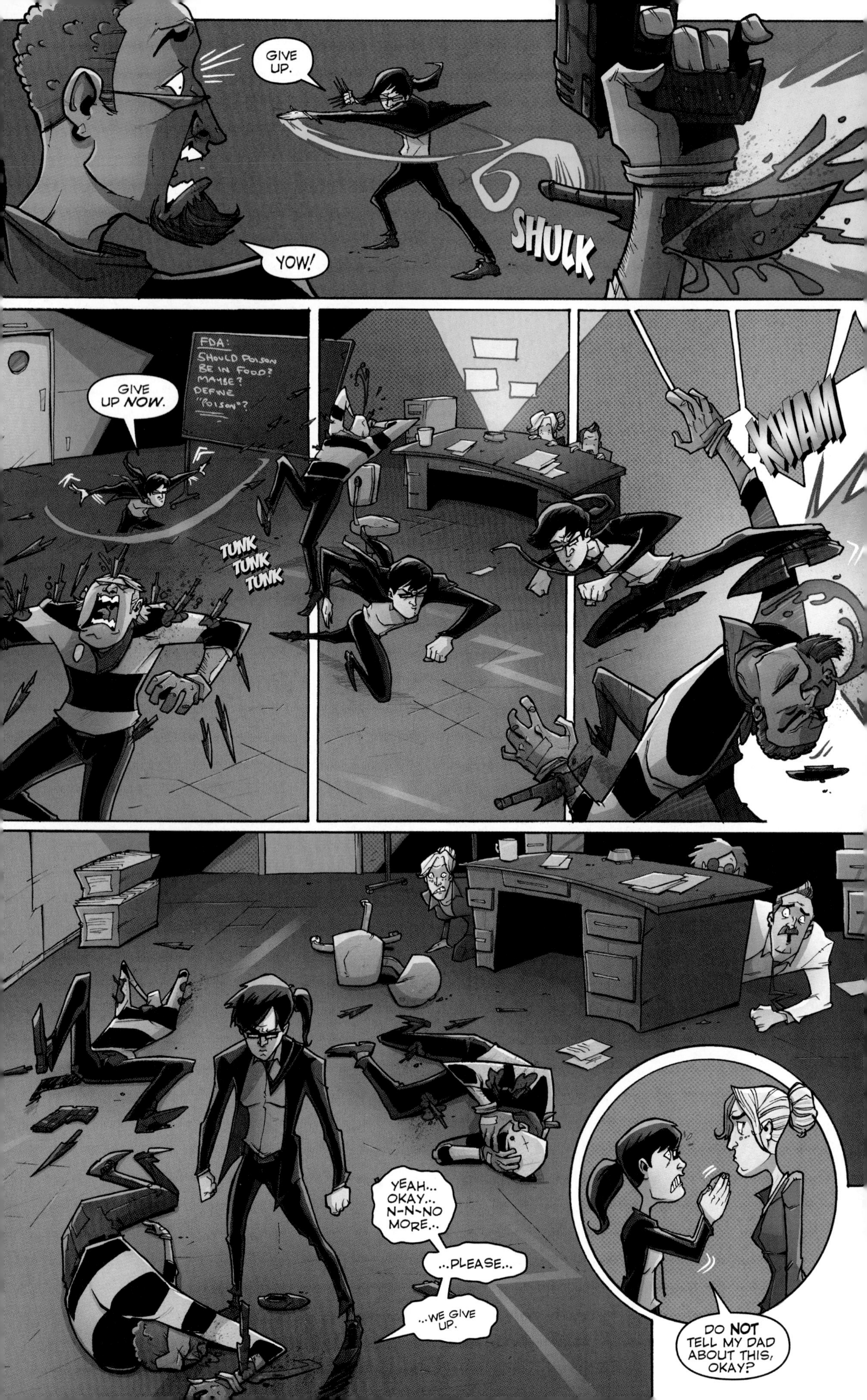
GIVE UP.
YOW!
SHULK
GIVE UP NOW.
FDA:
SHOULD POISON BE IN FOOD?
MAYBE?
DEFINE "POISON"?
TUNK TUNK TUNK
KWAM
YEAH... OKAY... N-N-NO MORE...
...PLEASE...
...WE GIVE UP.
DO NOT TELL MY DAD ABOUT THIS, OKAY?

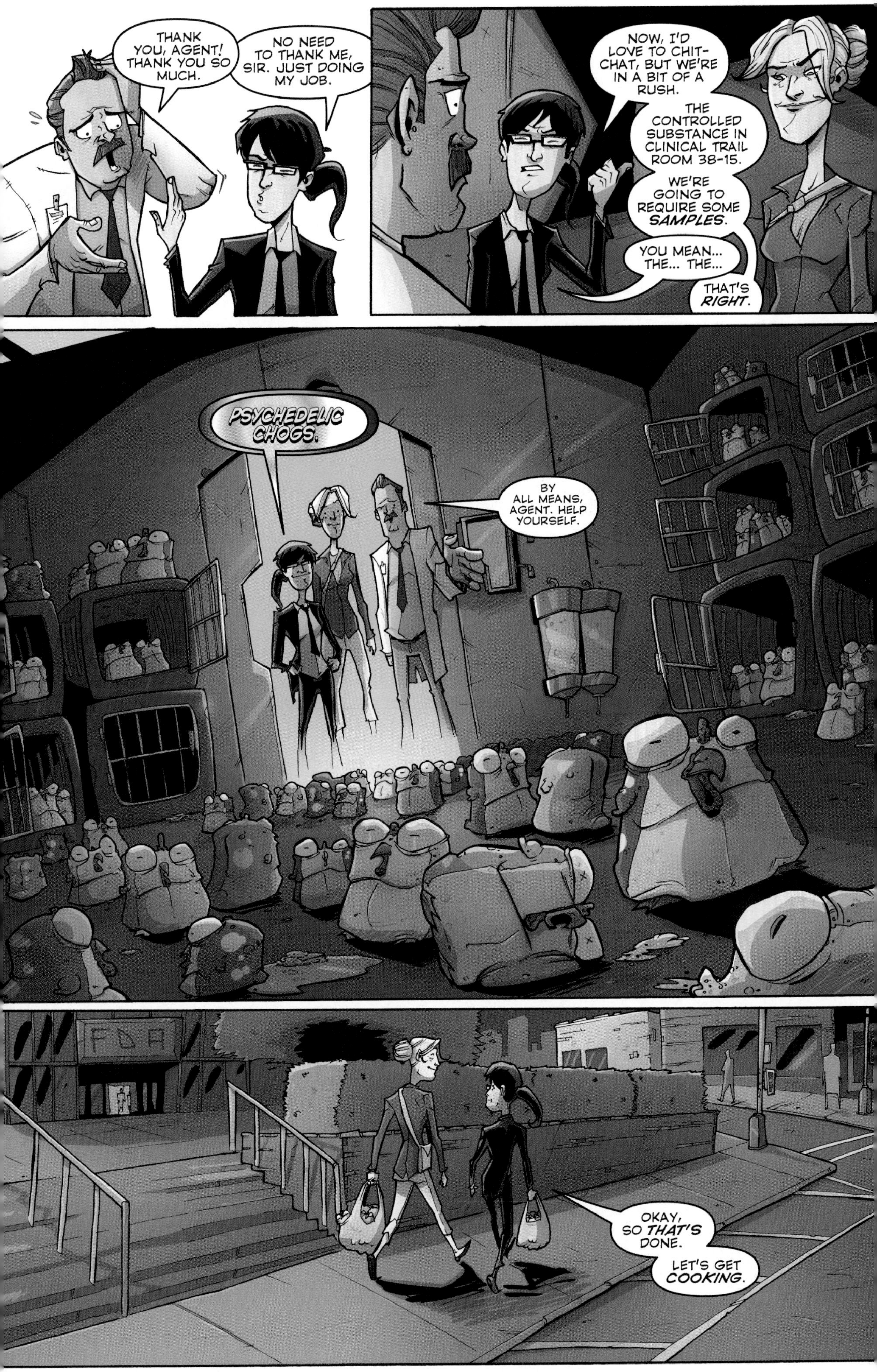

THANK YOU, AGENT! THANK YOU SO MUCH.
NO NEED TO THANK ME, SIR. JUST DOING MY JOB.
NOW, I'D LOVE TO CHIT-CHAT, BUT WE'RE IN A BIT OF A RUSH.
THE CONTROLLED SUBSTANCE IN CLINICAL TRAIL ROOM 38-15.
WE'RE GOING TO REQUIRE SOME *SAMPLES*.
YOU MEAN... THE... THE...
THAT'S *RIGHT*.
PSYCHEDELIC CHOGS.
BY ALL MEANS, AGENT. HELP YOURSELF.
FDA
OKAY, SO *THAT'S* DONE.
LET'S GET *COOKING*.

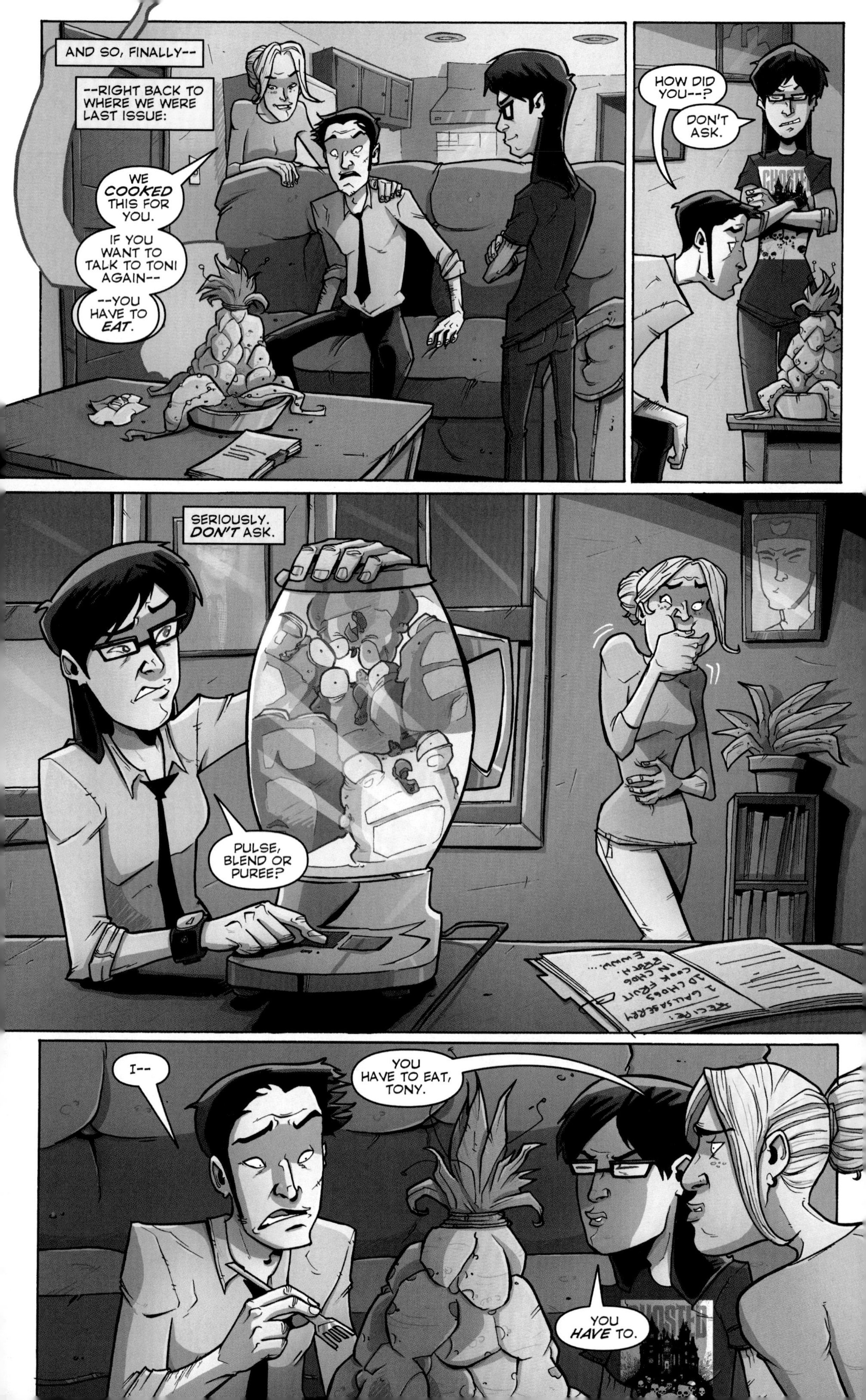

AND SO, FINALLY--
--RIGHT BACK TO WHERE WE WERE LAST ISSUE:
WE *COOKED* THIS FOR YOU.
IF YOU WANT TO TALK TO TONI AGAIN--
--YOU HAVE TO *EAT*.
HOW DID YOU--?
DON'T ASK.
SERIOUSLY. *DON'T* ASK.
PULSE, BLEND OR PUREE?
RECIPE:
1 GALLSABERRY
1D CHOGS
COOK FRUIT
IN CHOG
BROTH.
EWWW...
I--
YOU HAVE TO EAT, TONY.
YOU *HAVE* TO.

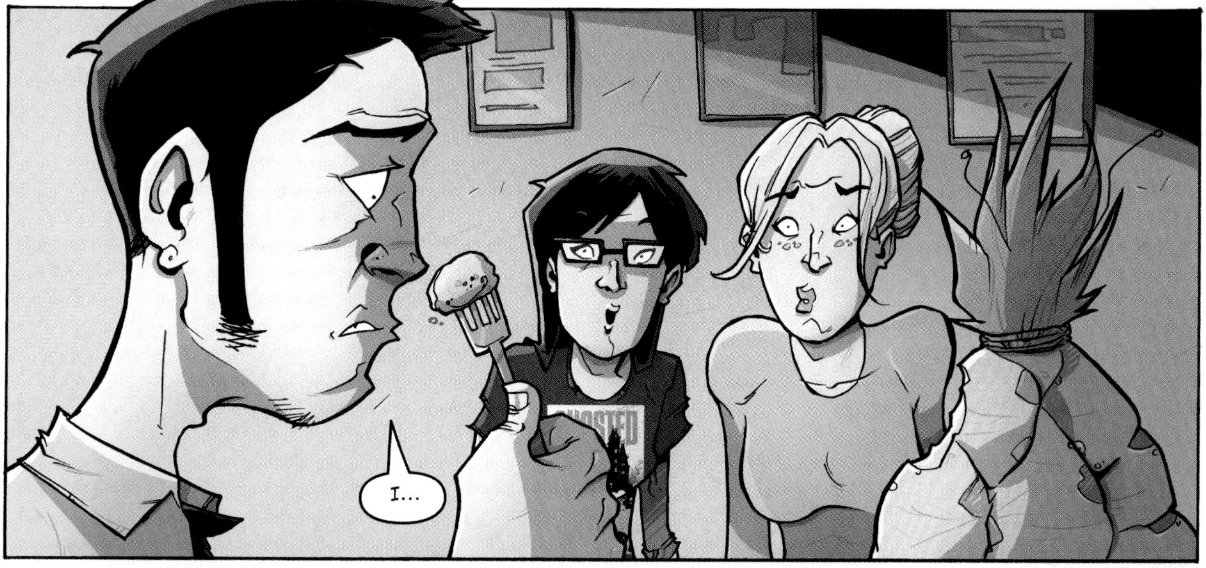
I...

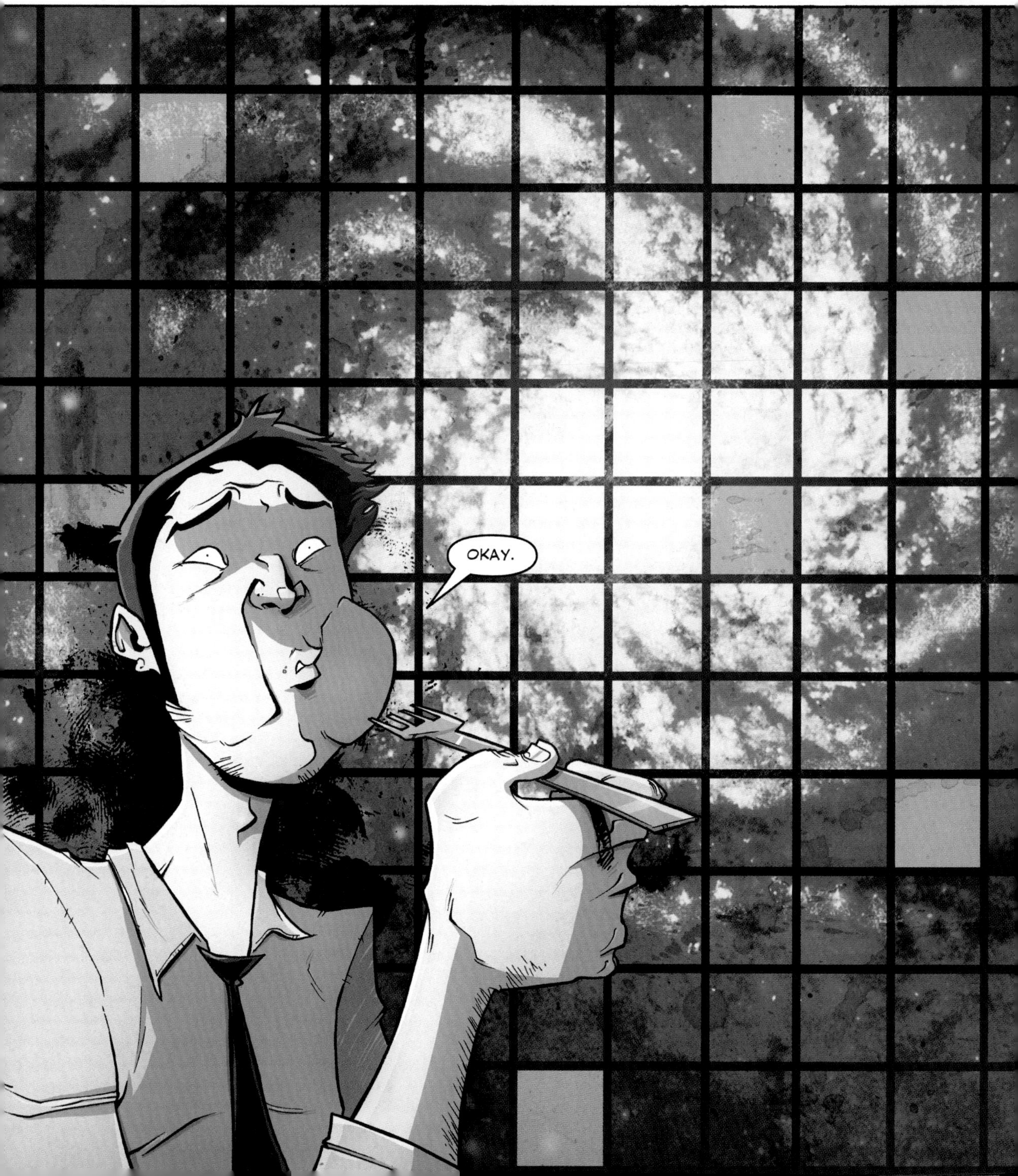
OKAY.

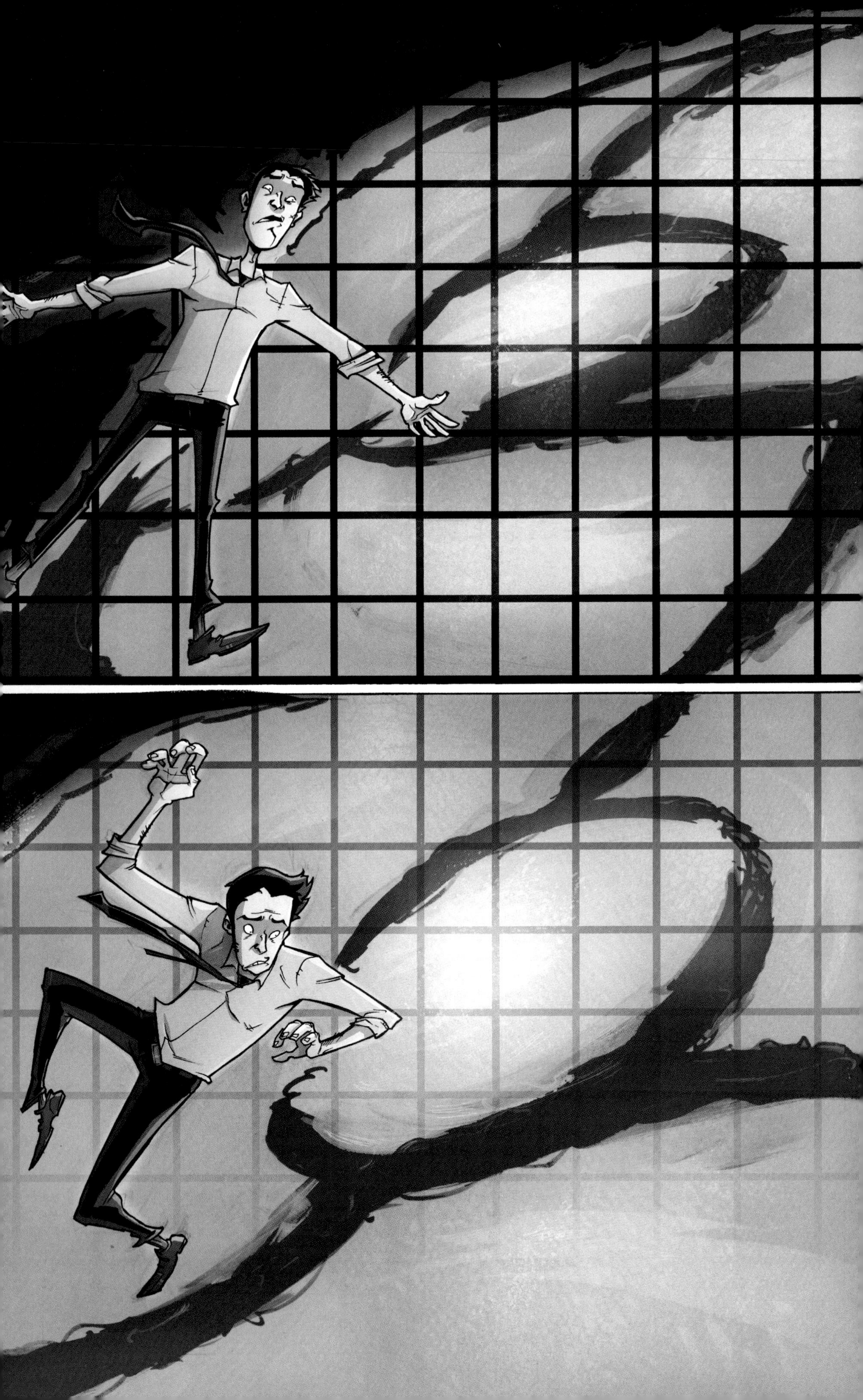

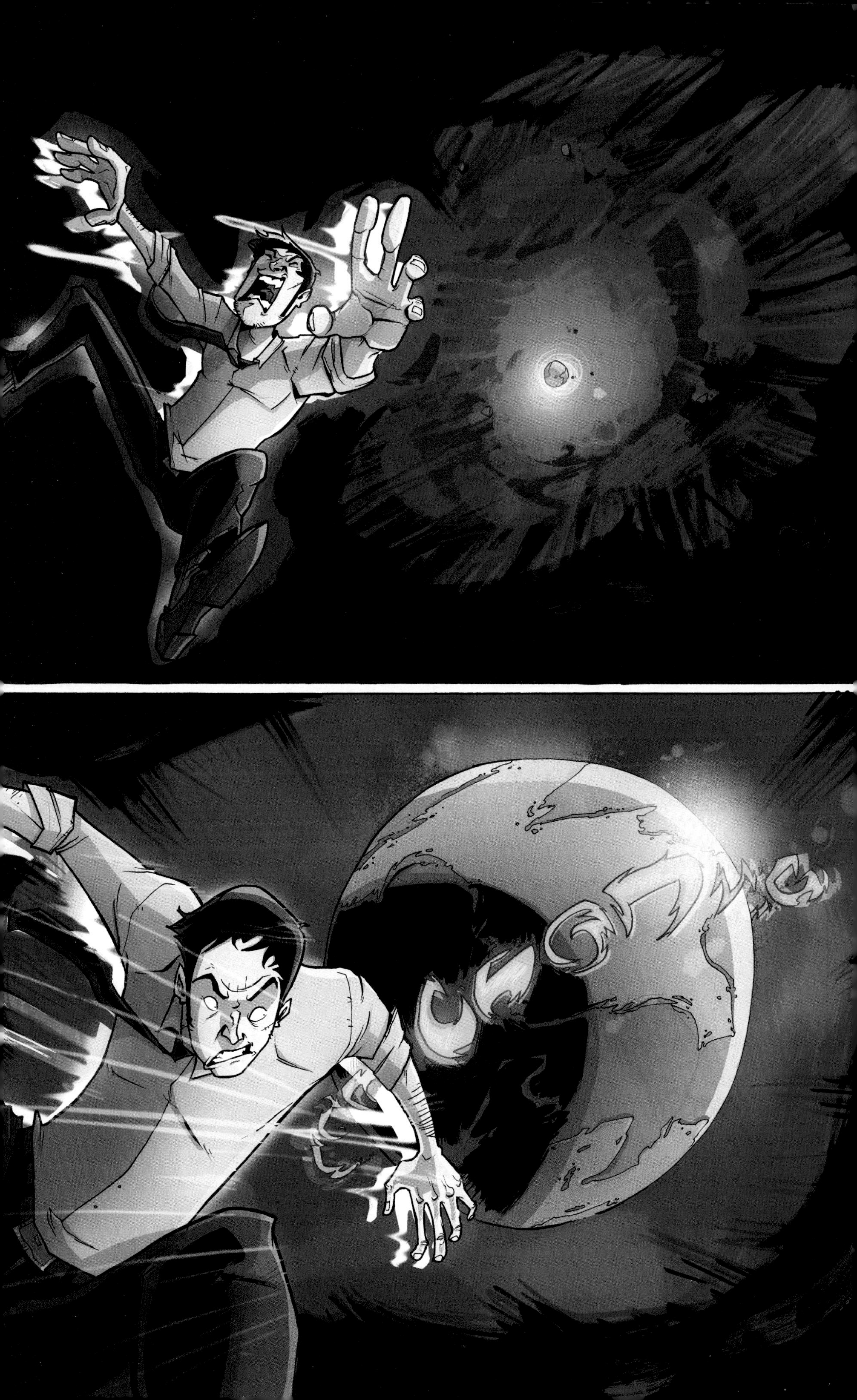

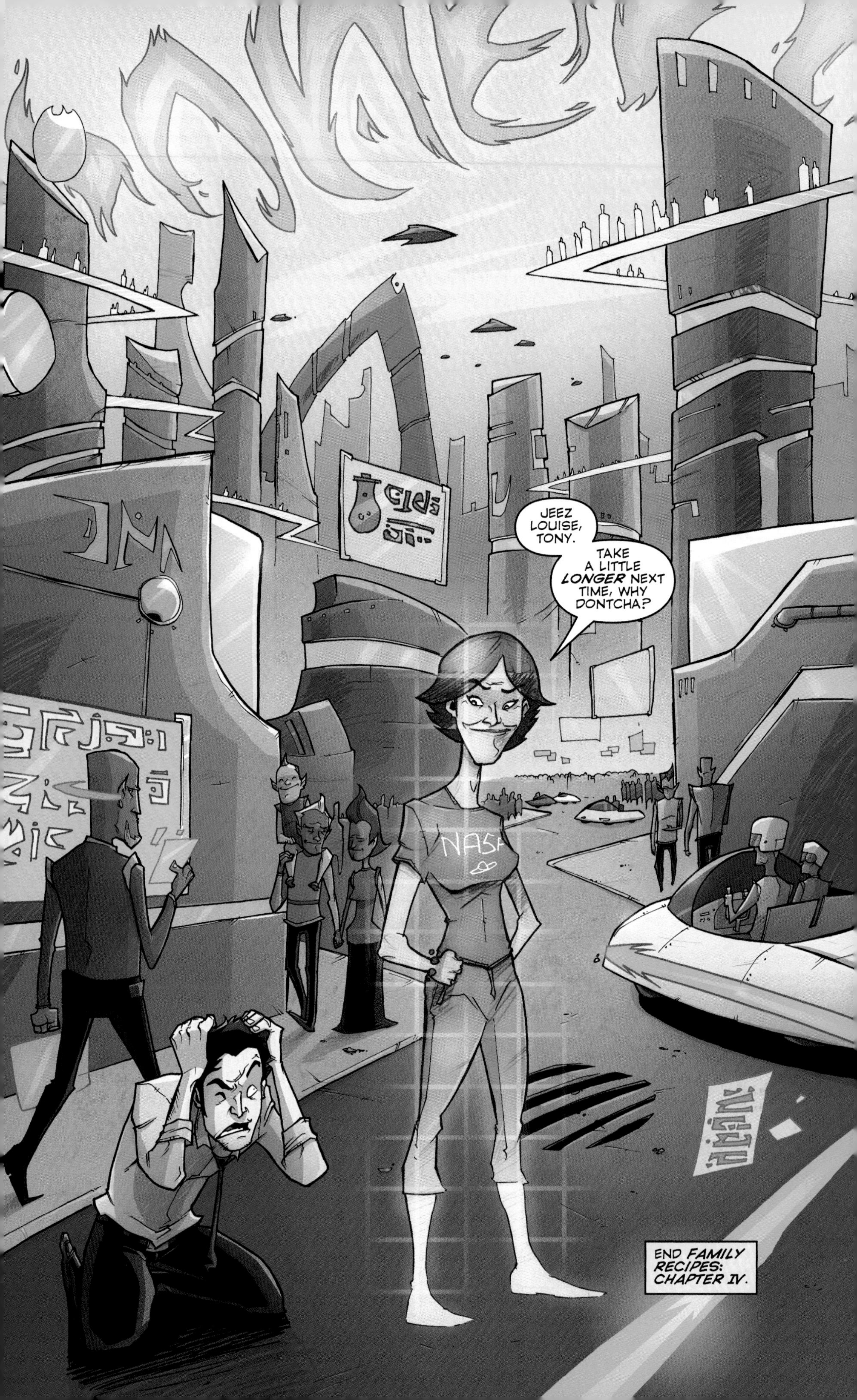
JEEZ LOUISE, TONY.
TAKE A LITTLE LONGER NEXT TIME, WHY DONTCHA?
END FAMILY RECIPES: CHAPTER IV.

Chapter Ten

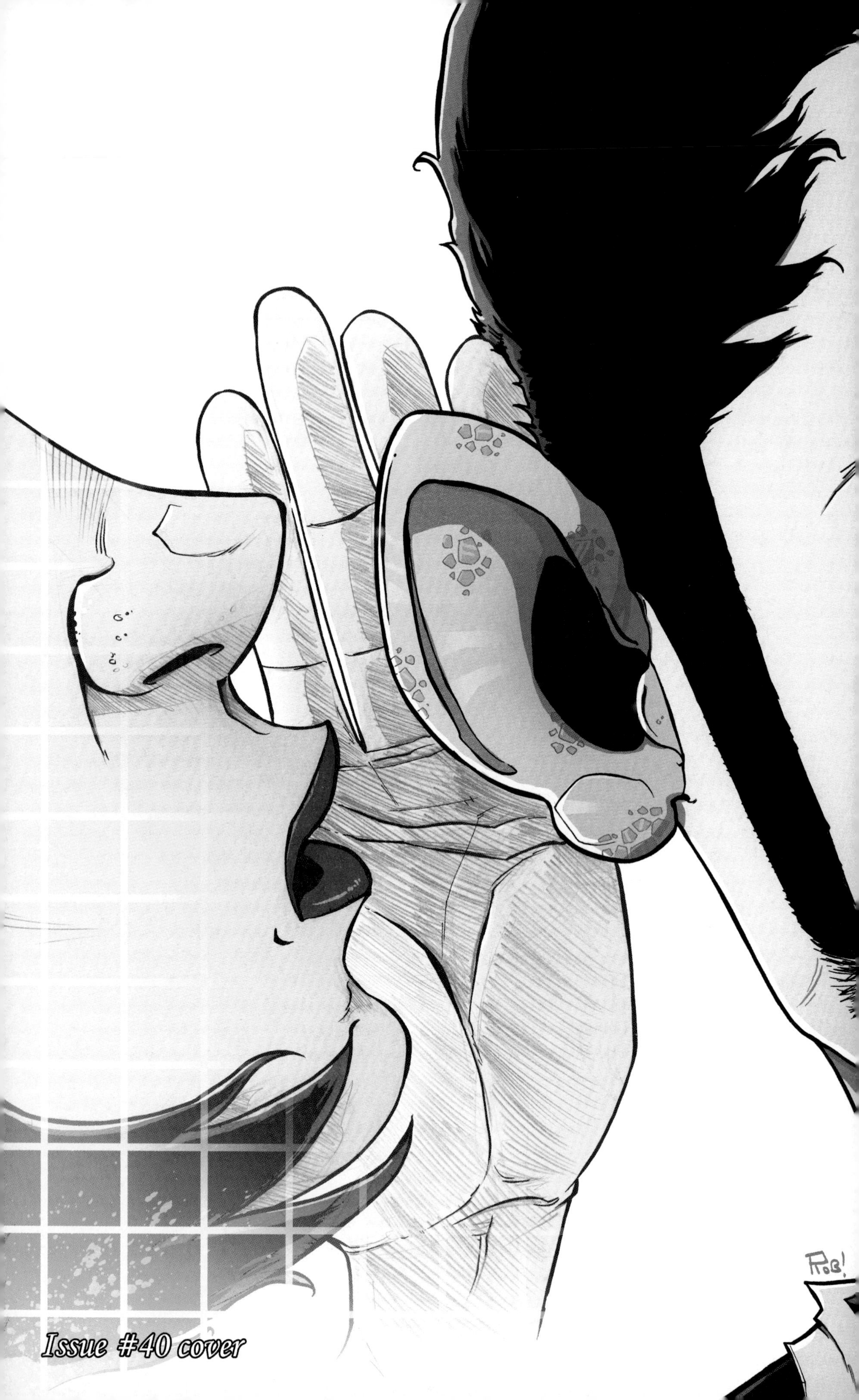
ROB!

Issue #40 cover

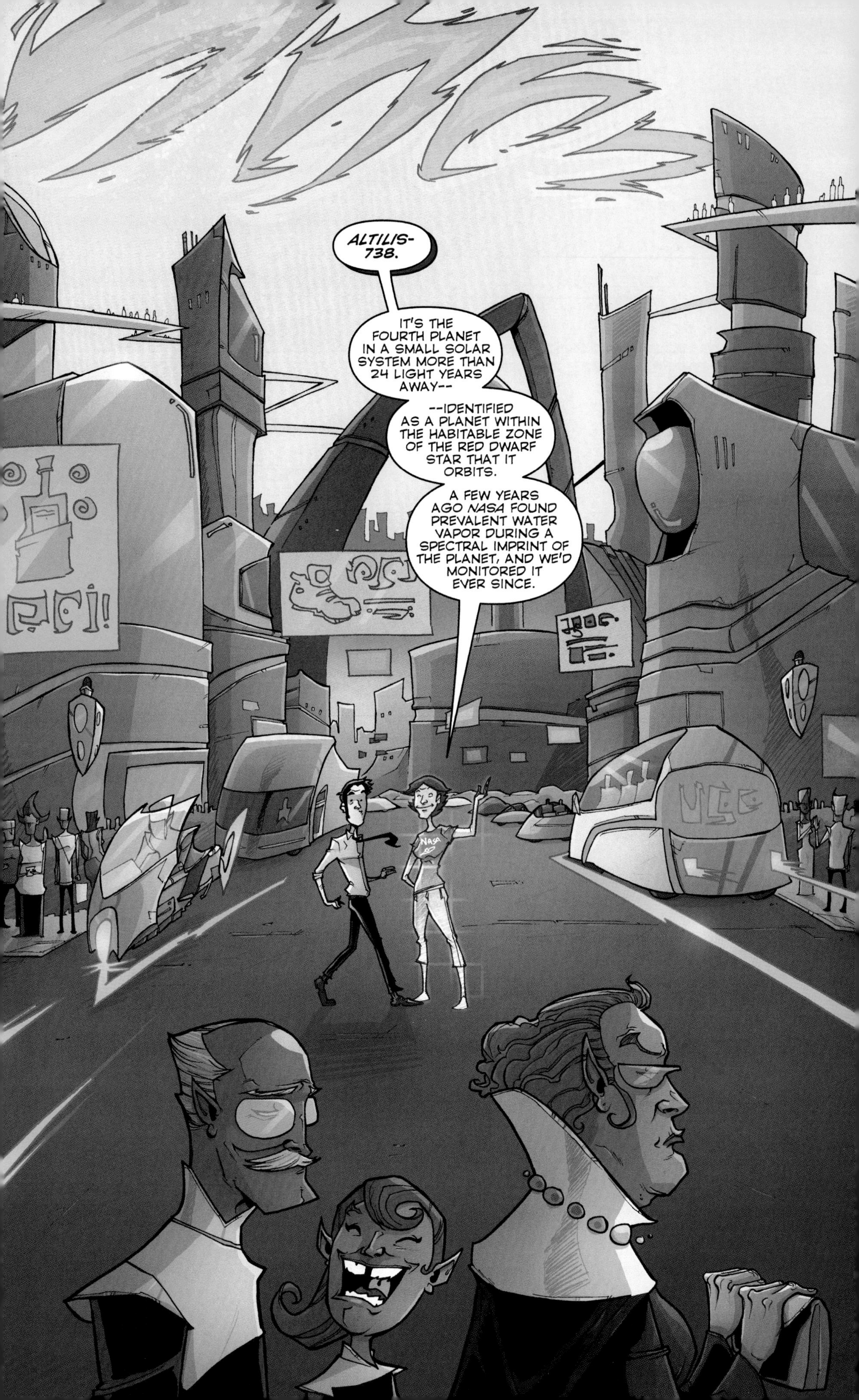
ALTILIS-738.
IT'S THE FOURTH PLANET IN A SMALL SOLAR SYSTEM MORE THAN 24 LIGHT YEARS AWAY--
--IDENTIFIED AS A PLANET WITHIN THE HABITABLE ZONE OF THE RED DWARF STAR THAT IT ORBITS.
A FEW YEARS AGO NASA FOUND PREVALENT WATER VAPOR DURING A SPECTRAL IMPRINT OF THE PLANET, AND WE'D MONITORED IT EVER SINCE.
NASA

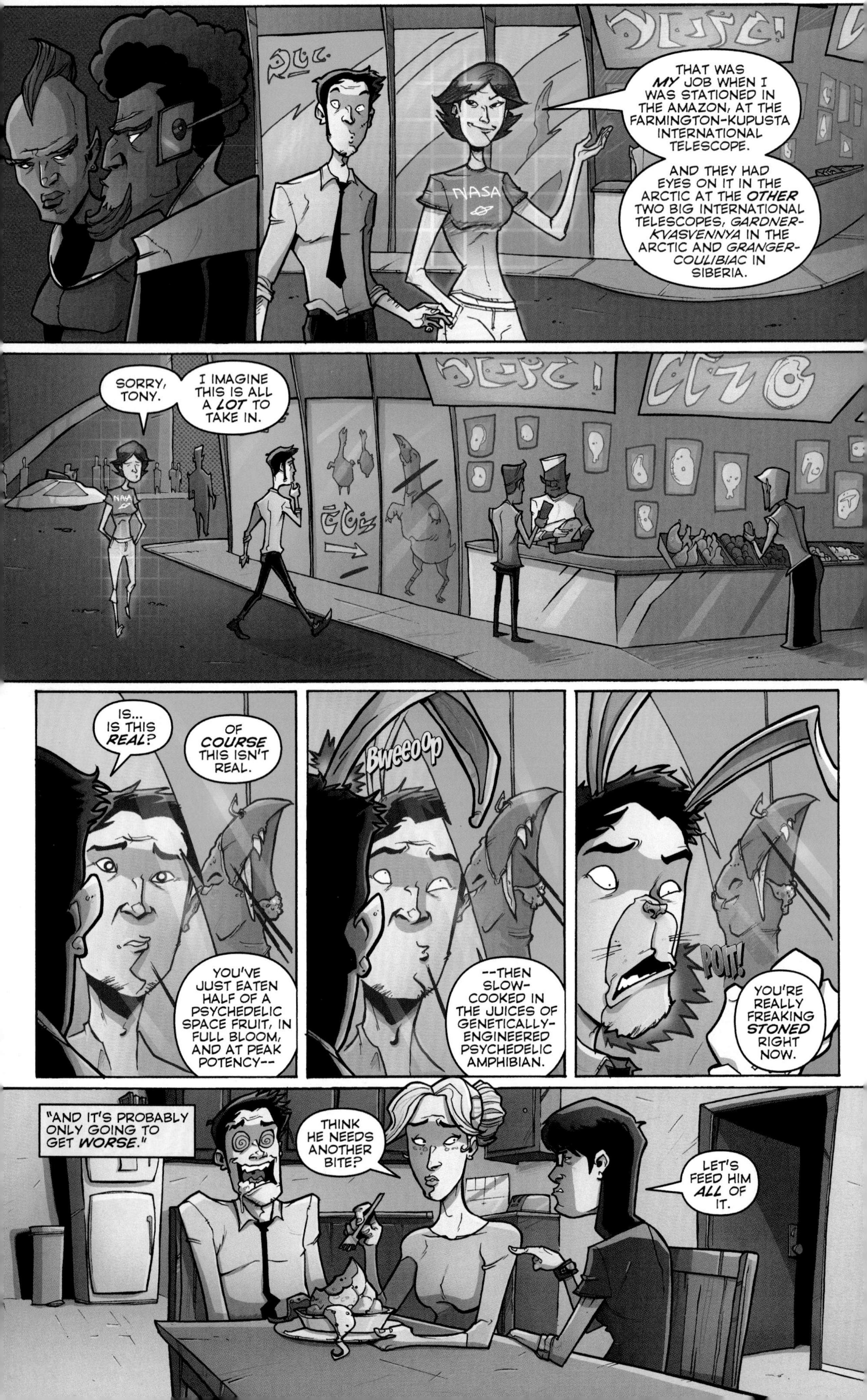
THAT WAS MY JOB WHEN I WAS STATIONED IN THE AMAZON, AT THE FARMINGTON-KUPUSTA INTERNATIONAL TELESCOPE.
AND THEY HAD EYES ON IT IN THE ARCTIC AT THE OTHER TWO BIG INTERNATIONAL TELESCOPES, GARDNER-KVASVENNYA IN THE ARCTIC AND GRANGER-COULIBIAC IN SIBERIA.
NASA
SORRY, TONY.
I IMAGINE THIS IS ALL A LOT TO TAKE IN.
IS... IS THIS REAL?
OF COURSE THIS ISN'T REAL.
YOU'VE JUST EATEN HALF OF A PSYCHEDELIC SPACE FRUIT, IN FULL BLOOM, AND AT PEAK POTENCY--
Bweeoop
--THEN SLOW-COOKED IN THE JUICES OF GENETICALLY-ENGINEERED PSYCHEDELIC AMPHIBIAN.
POIT!
YOU'RE REALLY FREAKING STONED RIGHT NOW.
"AND IT'S PROBABLY ONLY GOING TO GET WORSE."
THINK HE NEEDS ANOTHER BITE?
LET'S FEED HIM ALL OF IT.

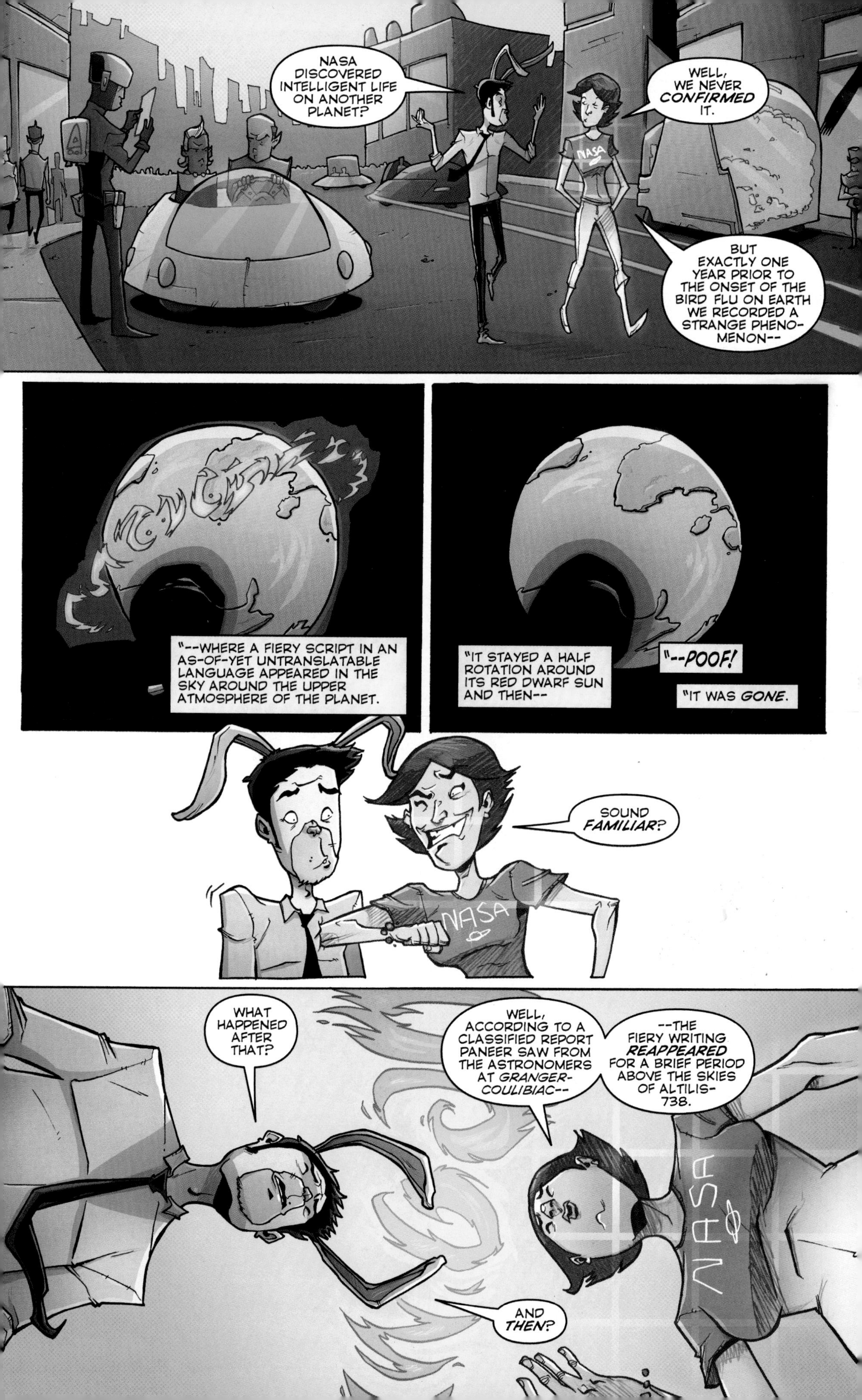
NASA DISCOVERED INTELLIGENT LIFE ON ANOTHER PLANET?
WELL, WE NEVER CONFIRMED IT.
BUT EXACTLY ONE YEAR PRIOR TO THE ONSET OF THE BIRD FLU ON EARTH WE RECORDED A STRANGE PHENO-MENON--
"--WHERE A FIERY SCRIPT IN AN AS-OF-YET UNTRANSLATABLE LANGUAGE APPEARED IN THE SKY AROUND THE UPPER ATMOSPHERE OF THE PLANET.
"IT STAYED A HALF ROTATION AROUND ITS RED DWARF SUN AND THEN--
"--POOF!
"IT WAS GONE.
SOUND FAMILIAR?
WHAT HAPPENED AFTER THAT?
WELL, ACCORDING TO A CLASSIFIED REPORT PANEER SAW FROM THE ASTRONOMERS AT GRANGER-COULIBIAC--
--THE FIERY WRITING REAPPEARED FOR A BRIEF PERIOD ABOVE THE SKIES OF ALTILIS-738.
AND THEN?

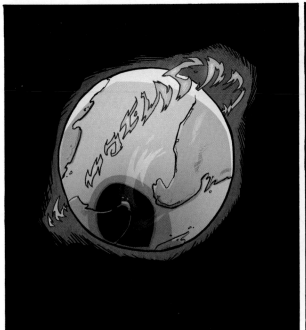

AND THEN **BOOM.**

NO MORE ALTILIS-738.

KNOCK KNOCK

KNOCK KNOCK KNOCK

YOU'RE GONNA WANT TO *GET* THAT.

WHERE THE HELL HAVE YOU *BEEN,* TONY?

WHY HAVEN'T YOU BEEN ANSWERING YOUR PHONE?

WE'VE GOT *WORK* TO DO.

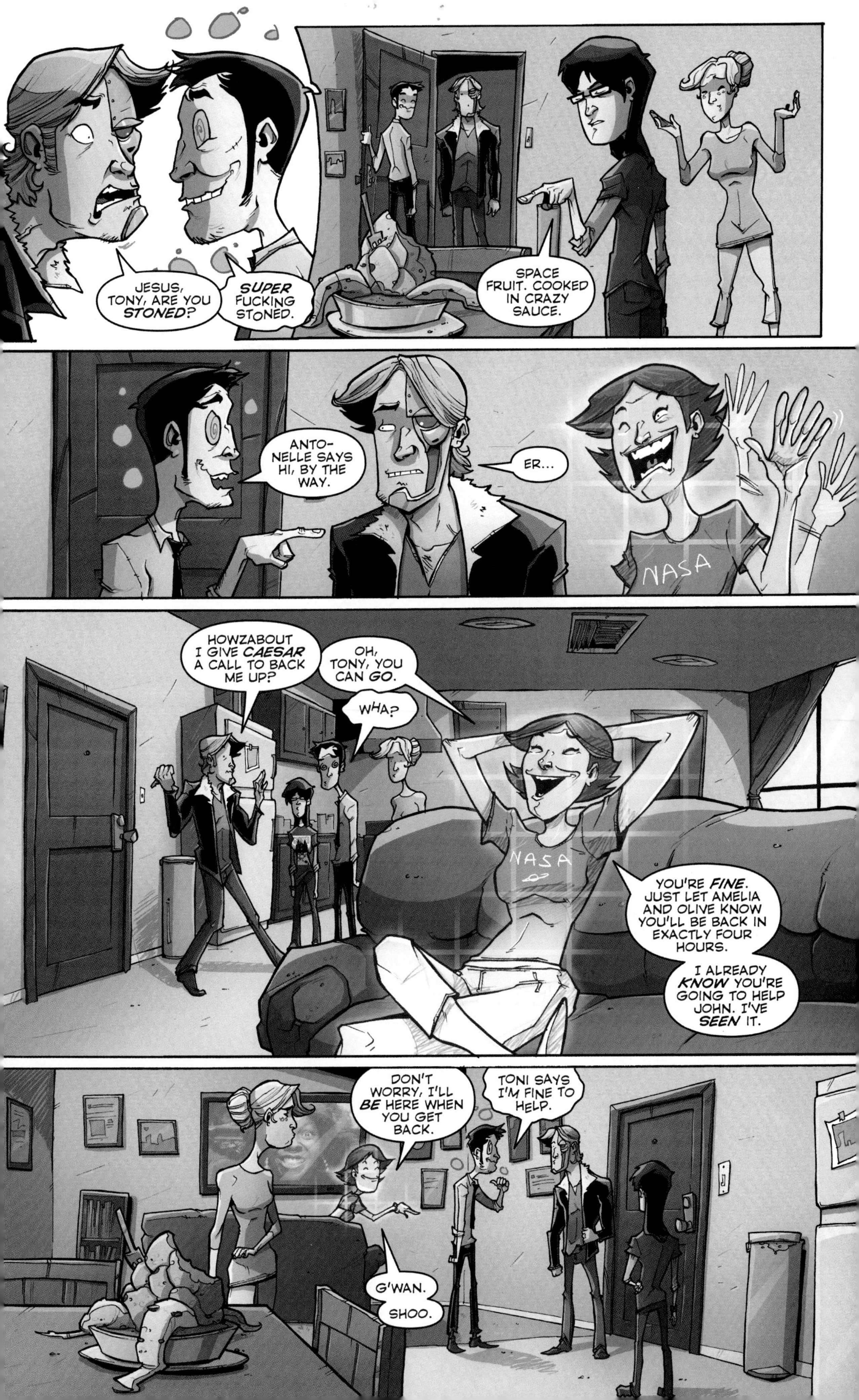
JESUS, TONY, ARE YOU STONED?
SUPER FUCKING STONED.
SPACE FRUIT. COOKED IN CRAZY SAUCE.
ANTO-NELLE SAYS HI, BY THE WAY.
ER...
NASA
HOWZABOUT I GIVE CAESAR A CALL TO BACK ME UP?
OH, TONY, YOU CAN GO.
WHA?
NASA
YOU'RE FINE. JUST LET AMELIA AND OLIVE KNOW YOU'LL BE BACK IN EXACTLY FOUR HOURS.
I ALREADY KNOW YOU'RE GOING TO HELP JOHN. I'VE SEEN IT.
DON'T WORRY, I'LL BE HERE WHEN YOU GET BACK.
TONI SAYS I'M FINE TO HELP.
G'WAN.
SHOO.

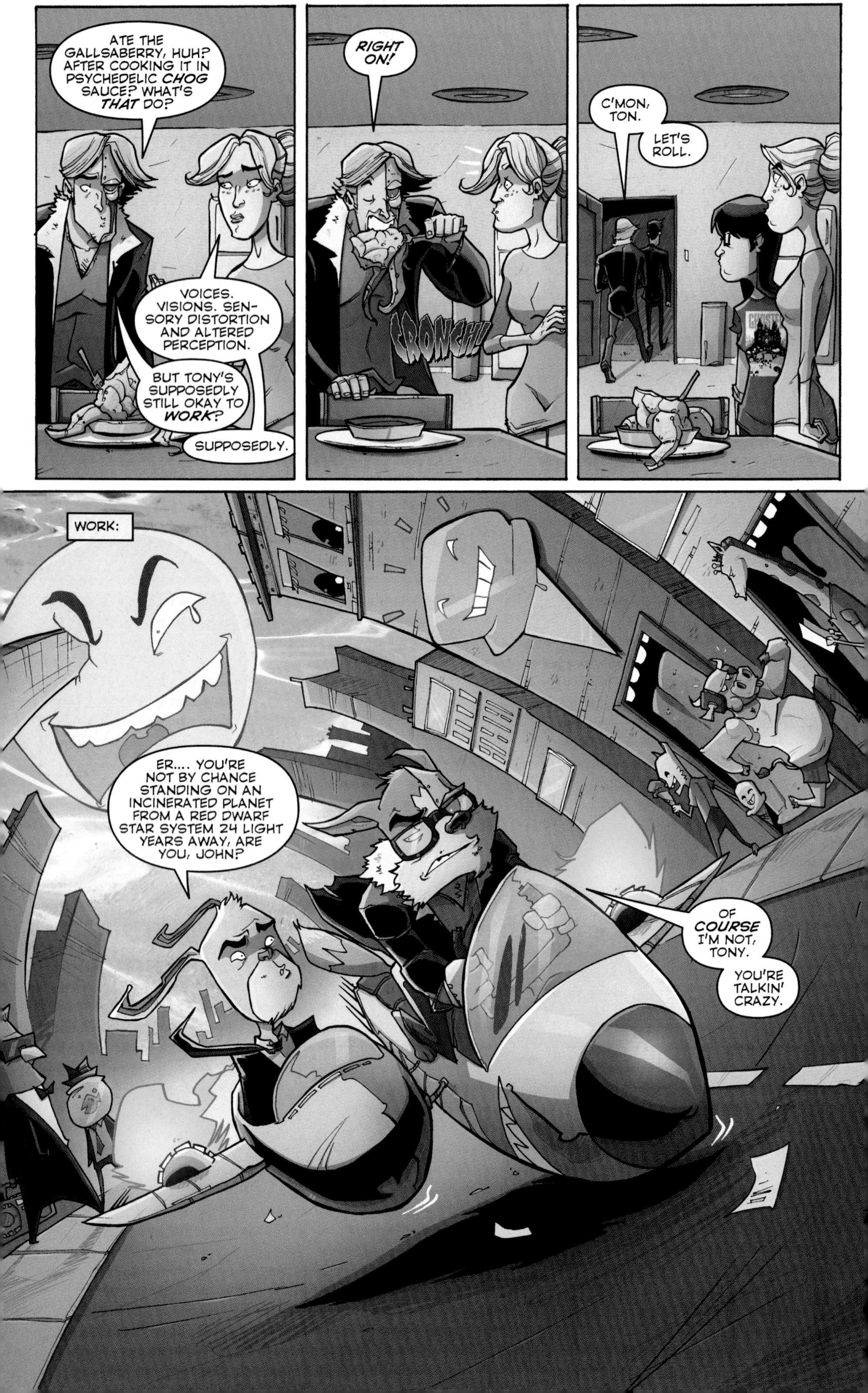

ATE THE GALLSABERRY, HUH? AFTER COOKING IT IN PSYCHEDELIC CHOG SAUCE? WHAT'S THAT DO?
VOICES. VISIONS. SENSORY DISTORTION AND ALTERED PERCEPTION.
BUT TONY'S SUPPOSEDLY STILL OKAY TO WORK?
SUPPOSEDLY.
RIGHT ON!
CRONCH!!
C'MON, TON.
LET'S ROLL.
WORK:
ER.... YOU'RE NOT BY CHANCE STANDING ON AN INCINERATED PLANET FROM A RED DWARF STAR SYSTEM 24 LIGHT YEARS AWAY, ARE YOU, JOHN?
OF COURSE I'M NOT, TONY.
YOU'RE TALKIN' CRAZY.

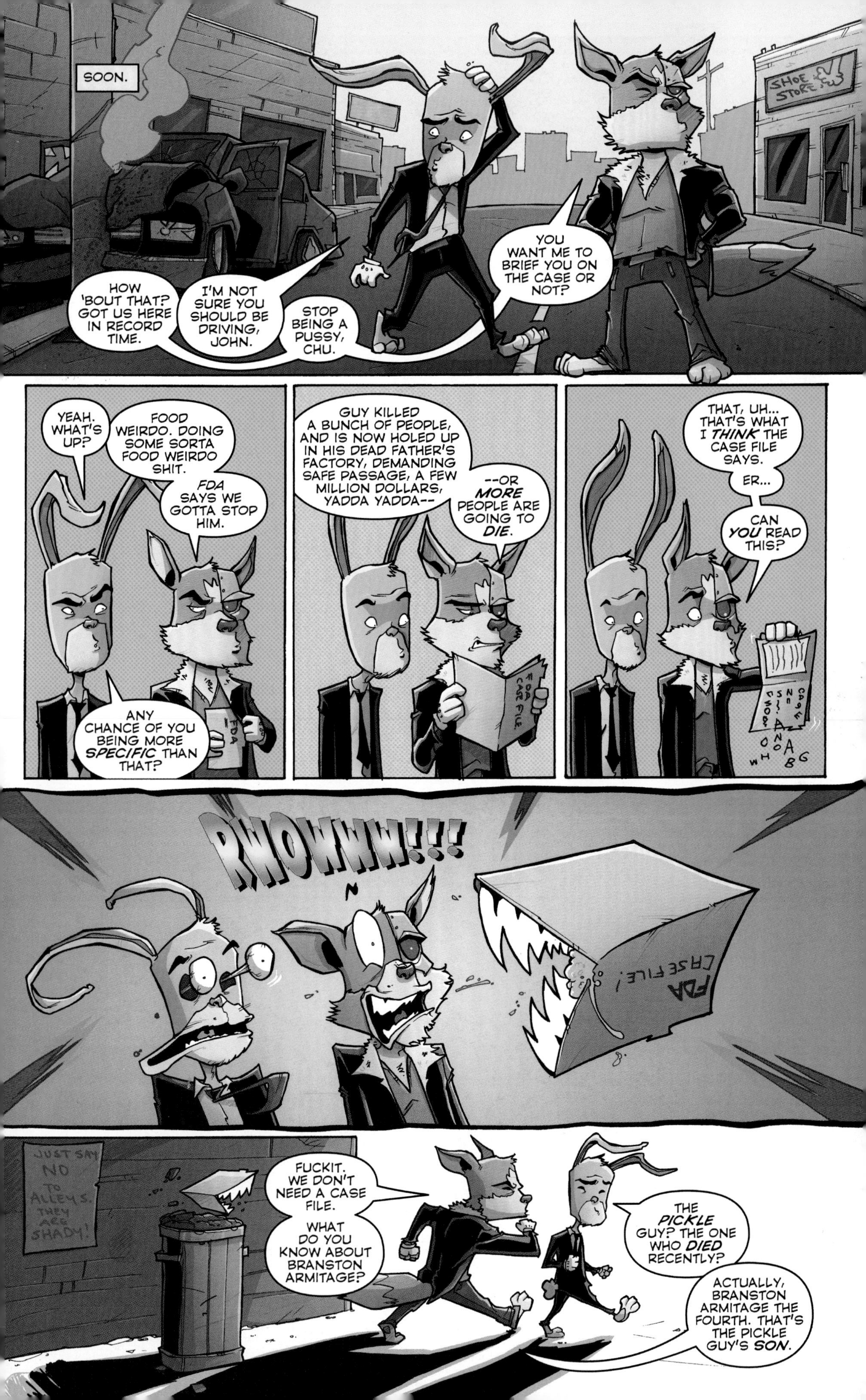
SOON.
HOW 'BOUT THAT? GOT US HERE IN RECORD TIME.
I'M NOT SURE YOU SHOULD BE DRIVING, JOHN.
STOP BEING A PUSSY, CHU.
YOU WANT ME TO BRIEF YOU ON THE CASE OR NOT?
SHOE STORE
YEAH. WHAT'S UP?
FOOD WEIRDO. DOING SOME SORTA FOOD WEIRDO SHIT.
FDA SAYS WE GOTTA STOP HIM.
ANY CHANCE OF YOU BEING MORE SPECIFIC THAN THAT?
FDA
GUY KILLED A BUNCH OF PEOPLE, AND IS NOW HOLED UP IN HIS DEAD FATHER'S FACTORY, DEMANDING SAFE PASSAGE, A FEW MILLION DOLLARS, YADDA YADDA--
--OR MORE PEOPLE ARE GOING TO DIE.
FDA CASE FILE
THAT, UH... THAT'S WHAT I THINK THE CASE FILE SAYS.
ER...
CAN YOU READ THIS?
RWOWWW!!!
FDA CASE FILE!
JUST SAY NO TO ALLEYS. THEY ARE SHADY!
FUCKIT. WE DON'T NEED A CASE FILE.
WHAT DO YOU KNOW ABOUT BRANSTON ARMITAGE?
THE PICKLE GUY? THE ONE WHO DIED RECENTLY?
ACTUALLY, BRANSTON ARMITAGE THE FOURTH. THAT'S THE PICKLE GUY'S SON.

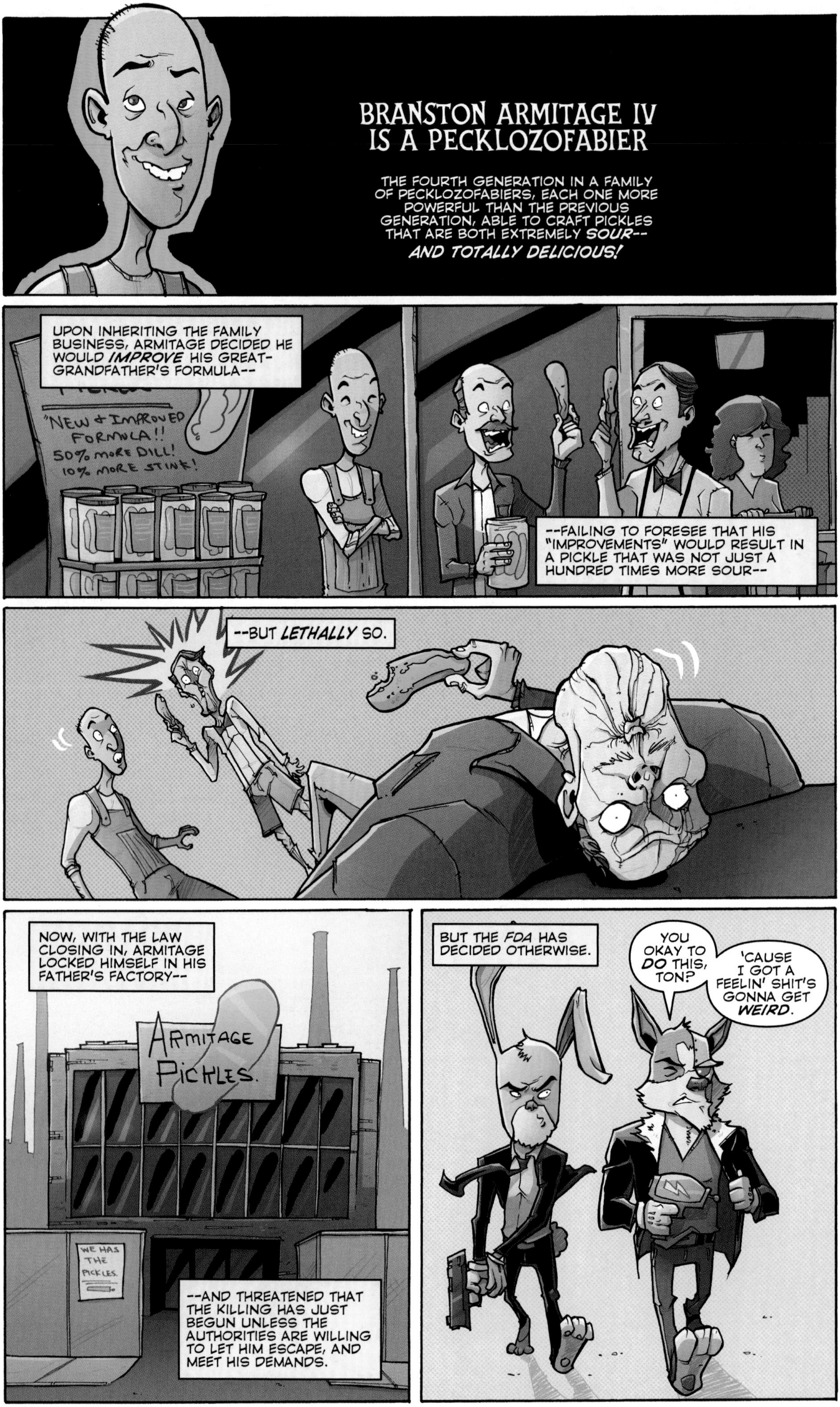
BRANSTON ARMITAGE IV
IS A PECKLOZOFABIER
THE FOURTH GENERATION IN A FAMILY OF PECKLOZOFABIERS, EACH ONE MORE POWERFUL THAN THE PREVIOUS GENERATION, ABLE TO CRAFT PICKLES THAT ARE BOTH EXTREMELY SOUR--
AND TOTALLY DELICIOUS!
UPON INHERITING THE FAMILY BUSINESS, ARMITAGE DECIDED HE WOULD IMPROVE HIS GREAT-GRANDFATHER'S FORMULA--
"NEW & IMPROVED FORMULA!! 50% MORE DILL! 10% MORE STINK!
--FAILING TO FORESEE THAT HIS "IMPROVEMENTS" WOULD RESULT IN A PICKLE THAT WAS NOT JUST A HUNDRED TIMES MORE SOUR--
--BUT LETHALLY SO.
NOW, WITH THE LAW CLOSING IN, ARMITAGE LOCKED HIMSELF IN HIS FATHER'S FACTORY--
ARMITAGE PICKLES.
WE HAS THE PICKLES.
--AND THREATENED THAT THE KILLING HAS JUST BEGUN UNLESS THE AUTHORITIES ARE WILLING TO LET HIM ESCAPE, AND MEET HIS DEMANDS.
BUT THE FDA HAS DECIDED OTHERWISE.
YOU OKAY TO DO THIS, TON?
'CAUSE I GOT A FEELIN' SHIT'S GONNA GET WEIRD.

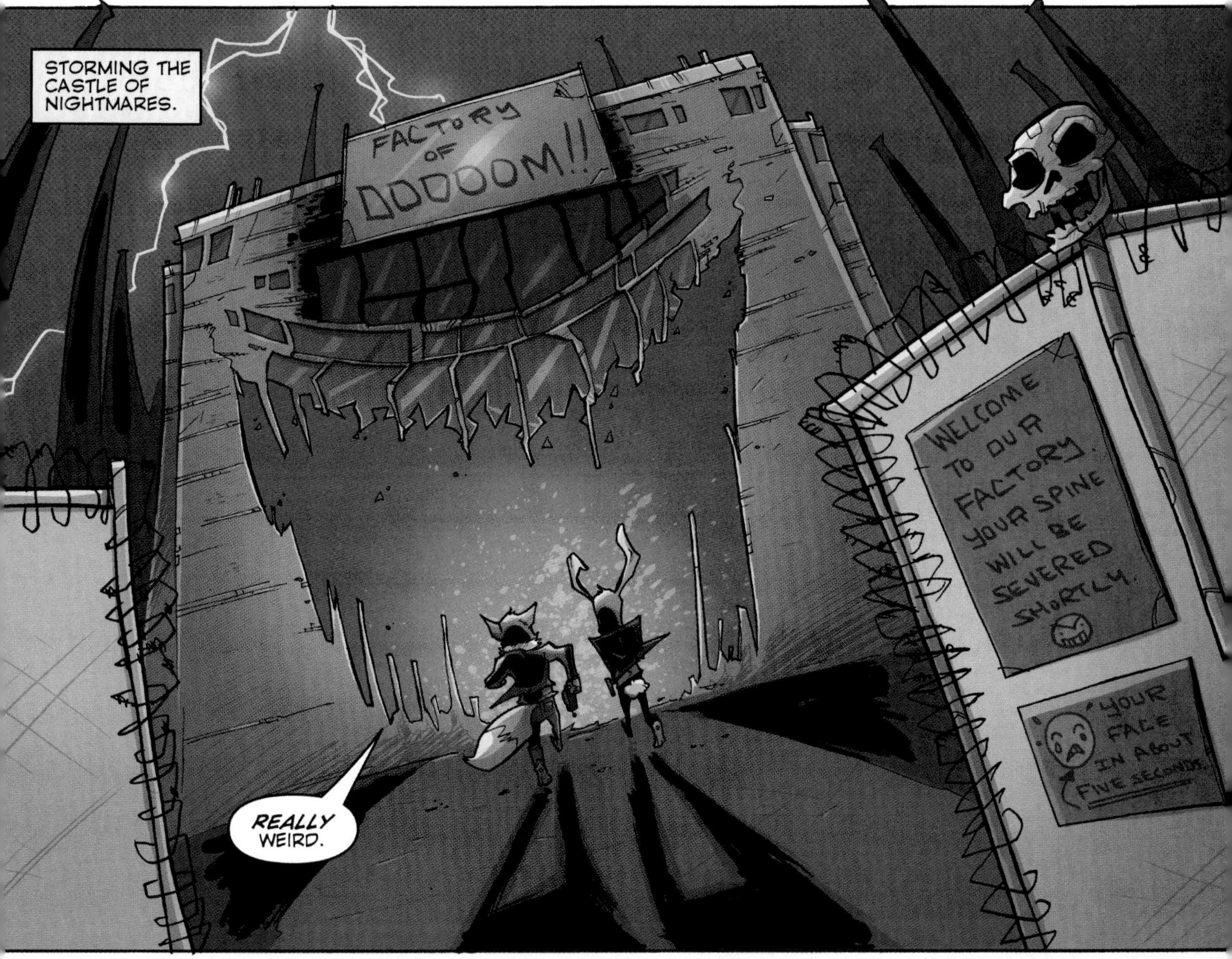
STORMING THE CASTLE OF NIGHTMARES.
FACTORY OF DOOOOM!!
WELCOME TO OUR FACTORY. YOUR SPINE WILL BE SEVERED SHORTLY.
YOUR FACE IN ABOUT FIVE SECONDS.
REALLY WEIRD.

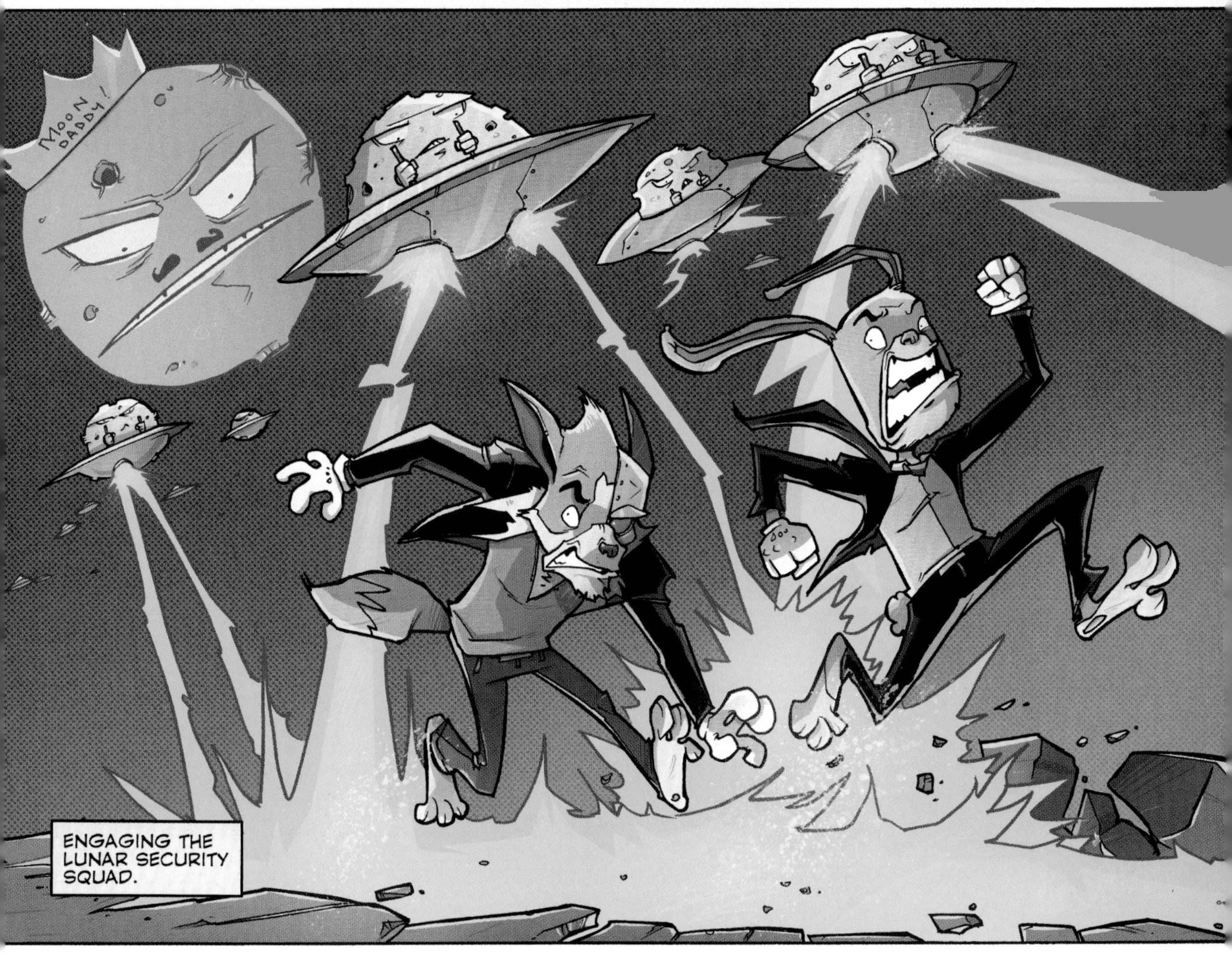
MOON DADDY!
ENGAGING THE LUNAR SECURITY SQUAD.

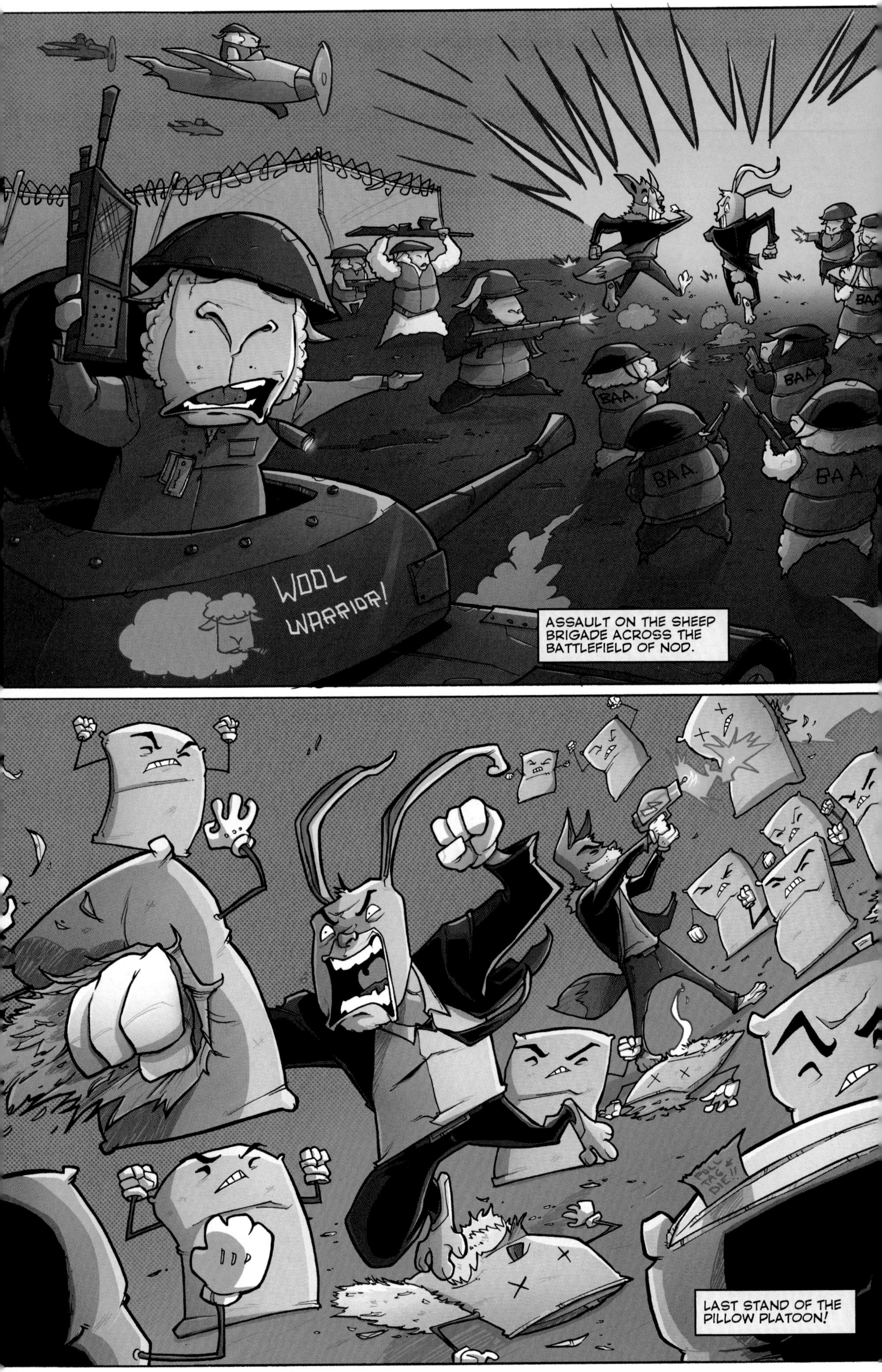
BAA.
BAA.
BAA.
BAA.
BAA.
WOOL WARRIOR!
ASSAULT ON THE SHEEP BRIGADE ACROSS THE BATTLEFIELD OF NOD.
PULL TAG DIE!!
LAST STAND OF THE PILLOW PLATOON!

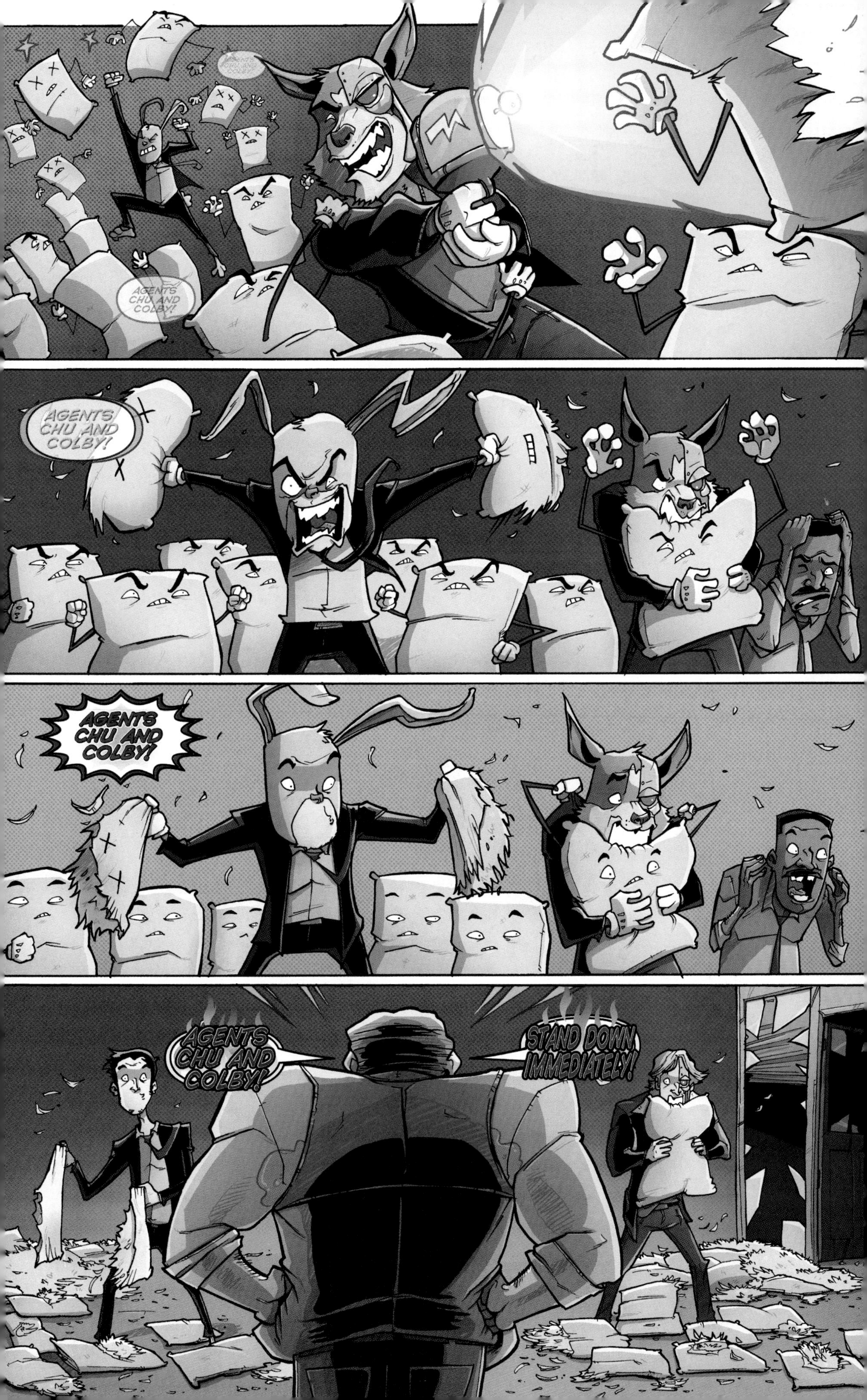

AGENTS CHU AND COLBY!
AGENTS CHU AND COLBY!
AGENTS CHU AND COLBY!
AGENTS CHU AND COLBY!
STAND DOWN IMMEDIATELY!

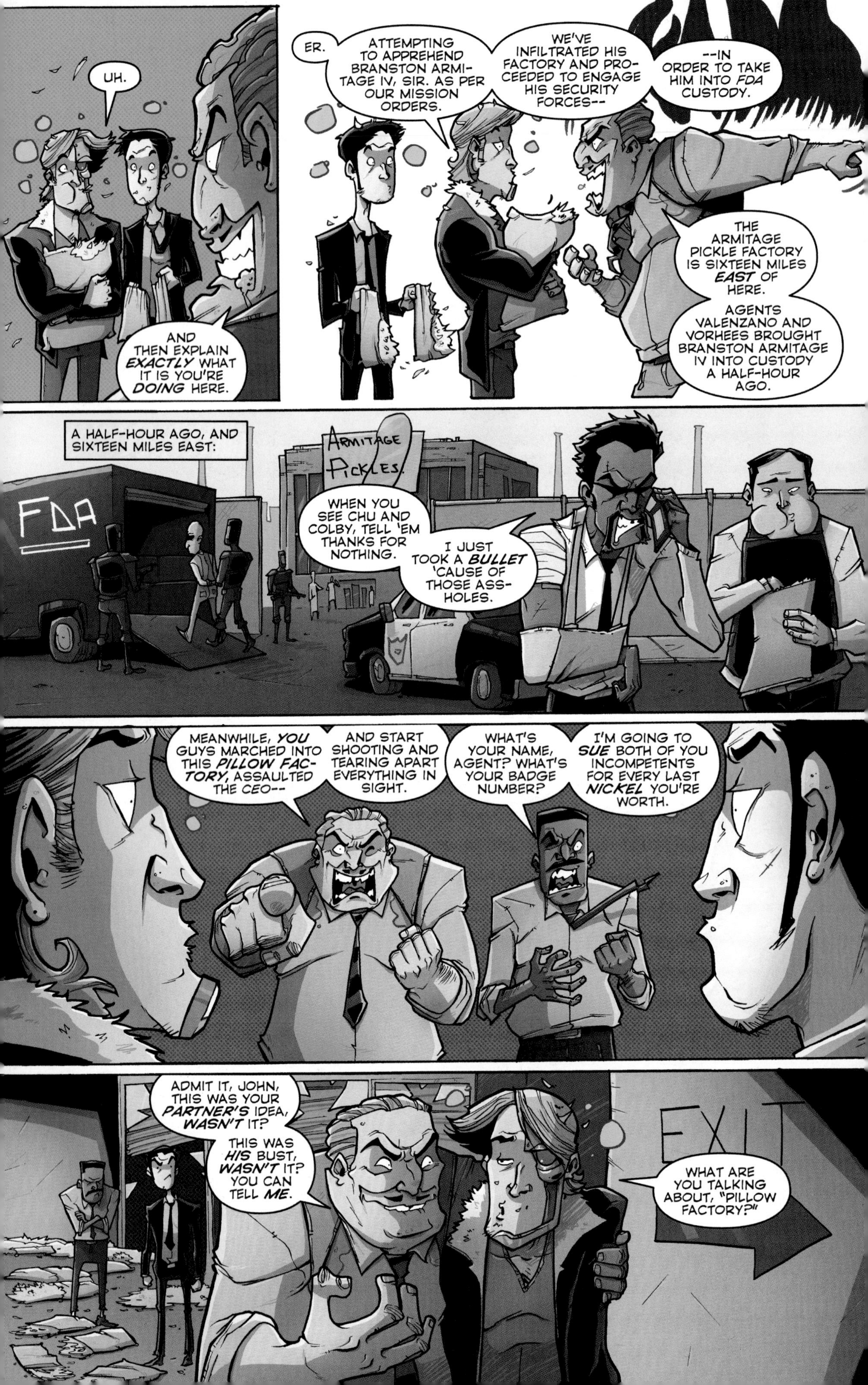

UH.
AND THEN EXPLAIN EXACTLY WHAT IT IS YOU'RE DOING HERE.
ER.
ATTEMPTING TO APPREHEND BRANSTON ARMITAGE IV, SIR. AS PER OUR MISSION ORDERS.
WE'VE INFILTRATED HIS FACTORY AND PROCEEDED TO ENGAGE HIS SECURITY FORCES--
--IN ORDER TO TAKE HIM INTO FDA CUSTODY.
THE ARMITAGE PICKLE FACTORY IS SIXTEEN MILES EAST OF HERE.
AGENTS VALENZANO AND VORHEES BROUGHT BRANSTON ARMITAGE IV INTO CUSTODY A HALF-HOUR AGO.
A HALF-HOUR AGO, AND SIXTEEN MILES EAST:
ARMITAGE PICKLES
FDA
WHEN YOU SEE CHU AND COLBY, TELL 'EM THANKS FOR NOTHING.
I JUST TOOK A BULLET 'CAUSE OF THOSE ASSHOLES.
MEANWHILE, YOU GUYS MARCHED INTO THIS PILLOW FACTORY, ASSAULTED THE CEO--
AND START SHOOTING AND TEARING APART EVERYTHING IN SIGHT.
WHAT'S YOUR NAME, AGENT? WHAT'S YOUR BADGE NUMBER?
I'M GOING TO SUE BOTH OF YOU INCOMPETENTS FOR EVERY LAST NICKEL YOU'RE WORTH.
ADMIT IT, JOHN, THIS WAS YOUR PARTNER'S IDEA, WASN'T IT?
THIS WAS HIS BUST, WASN'T IT? YOU CAN TELL ME.
EXIT
WHAT ARE YOU TALKING ABOUT, "PILLOW FACTORY?"

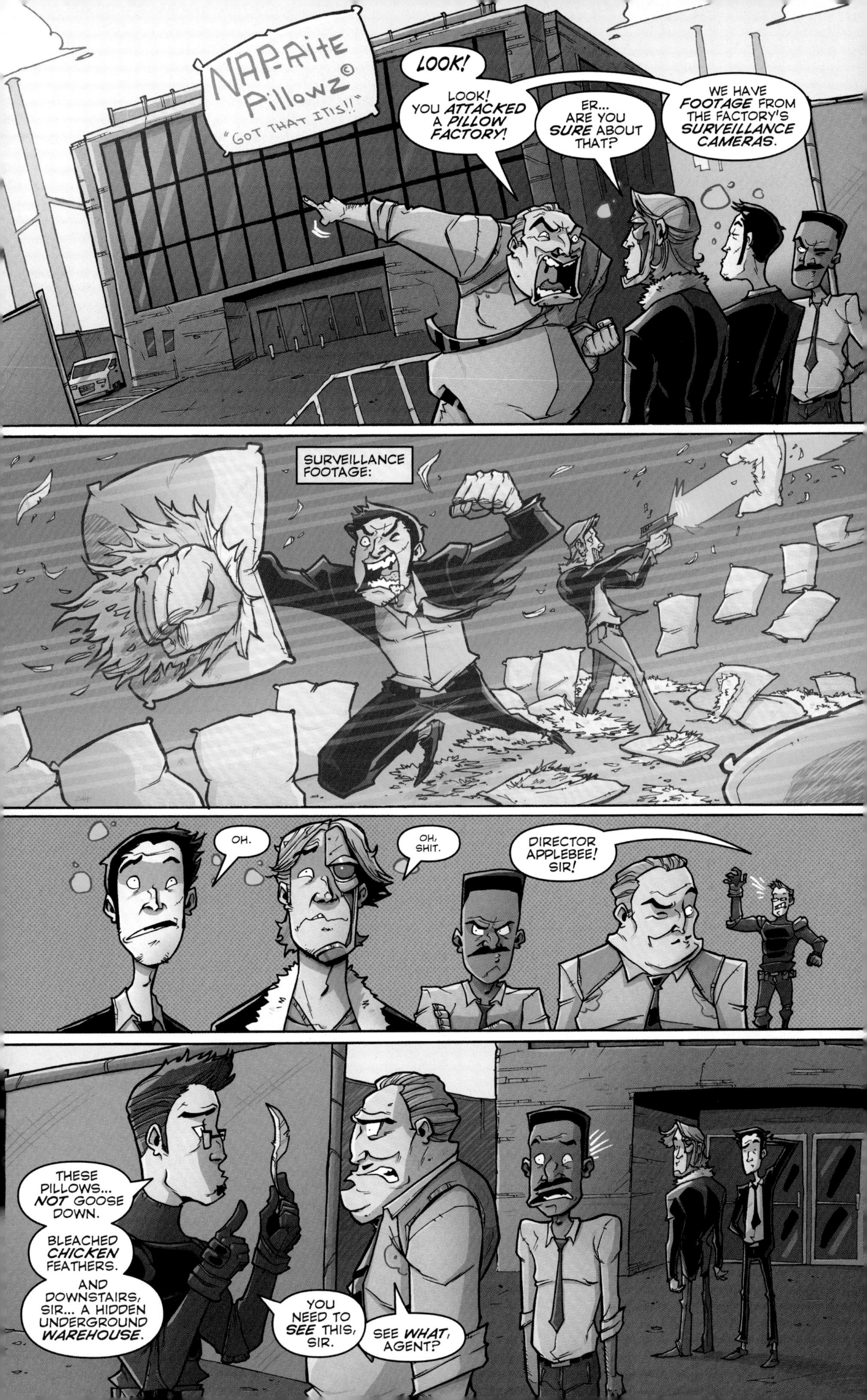
NAP-Rite Pillowz©
"GOT THAT ITIS!!"
LOOK!
LOOK! YOU ATTACKED A PILLOW FACTORY!
ER... ARE YOU SURE ABOUT THAT?
WE HAVE FOOTAGE FROM THE FACTORY'S SURVEILLANCE CAMERAS.
SURVEILLANCE FOOTAGE:
OH.
OH, SHIT.
DIRECTOR APPLEBEE! SIR!
THESE PILLOWS... NOT GOOSE DOWN.
BLEACHED CHICKEN FEATHERS.
AND DOWNSTAIRS, SIR... A HIDDEN UNDERGROUND WAREHOUSE.
YOU NEED TO SEE THIS, SIR.
SEE WHAT, AGENT?

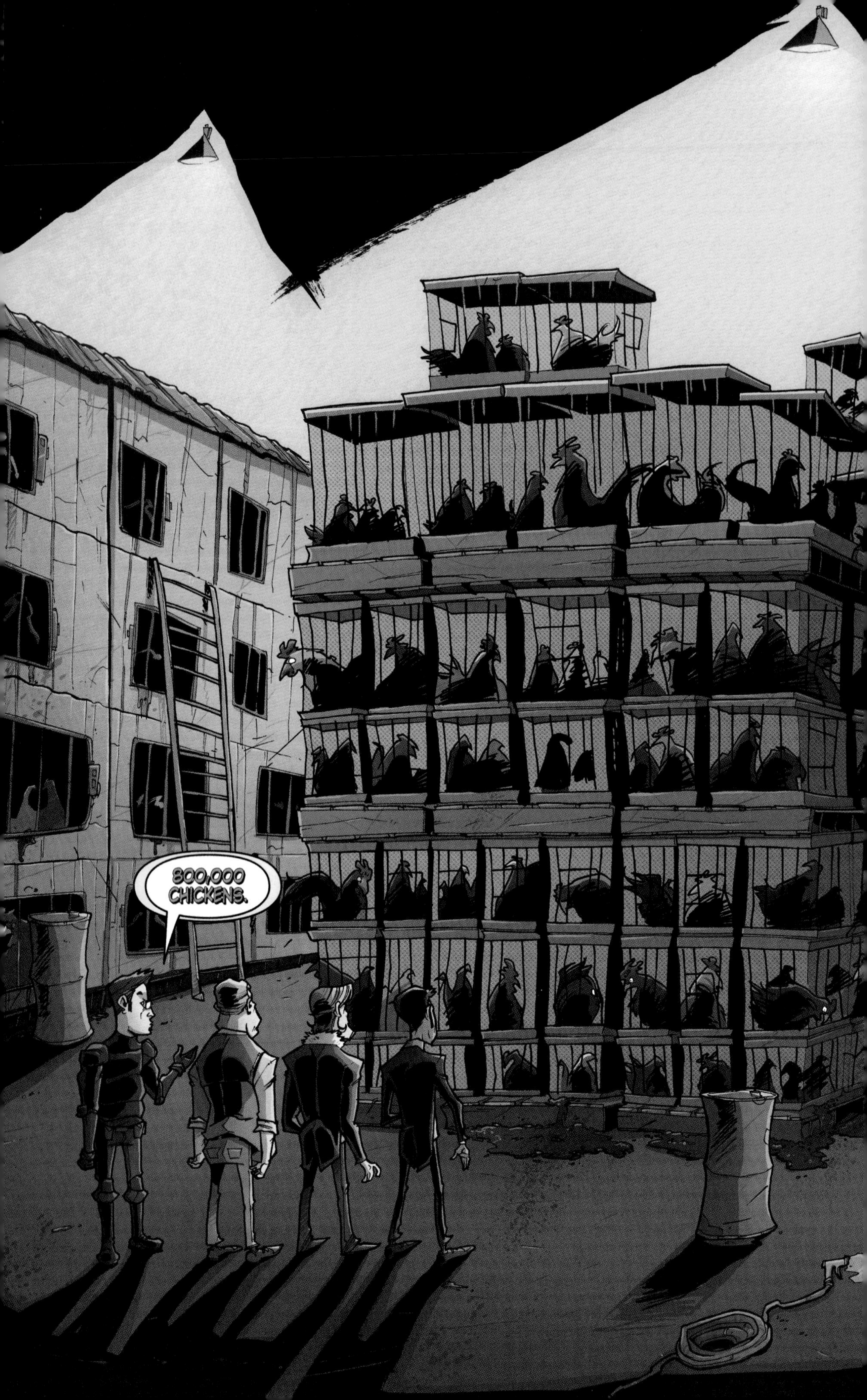
800,000 CHICKENS.

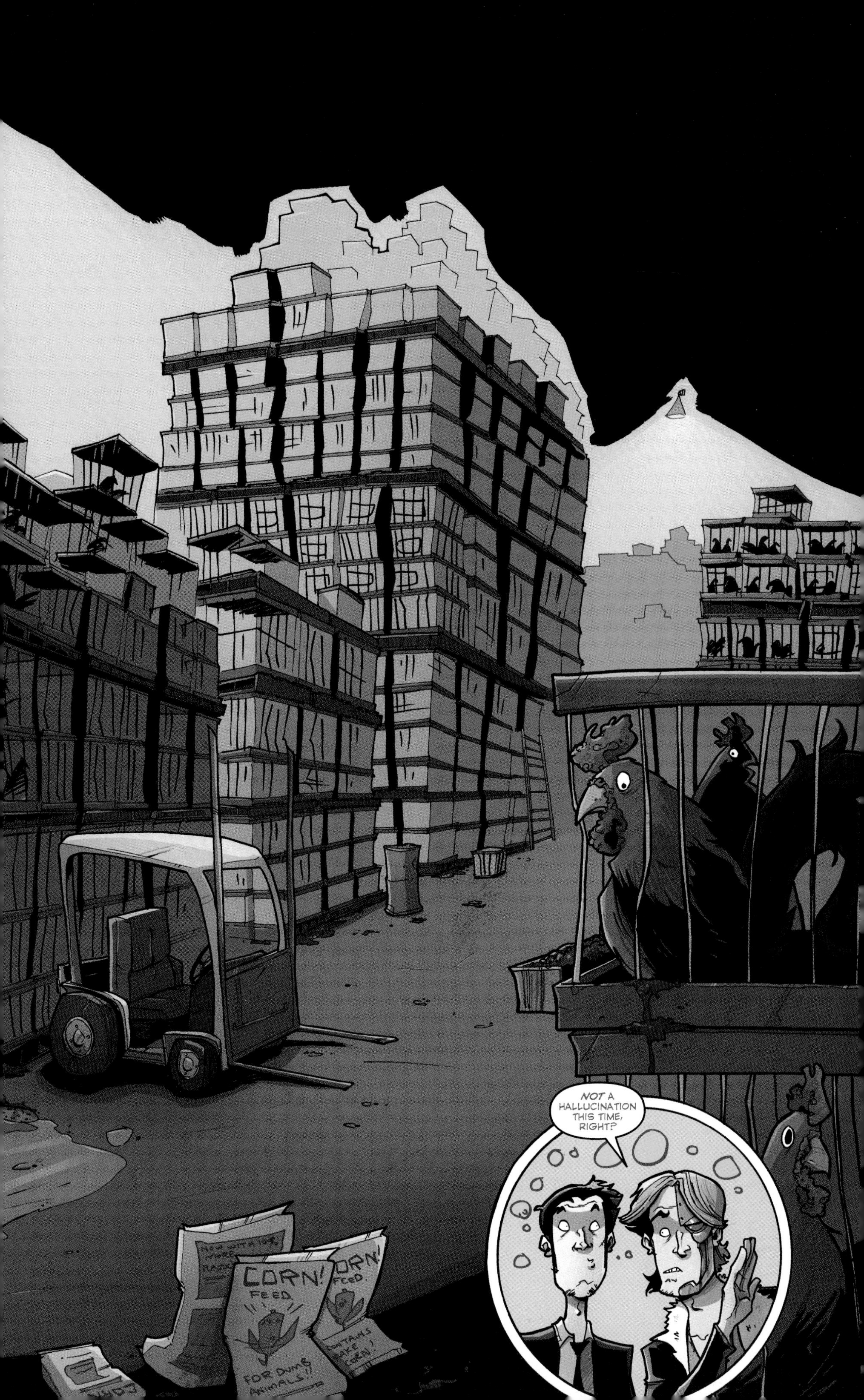
NOT A HALLUCINATION THIS TIME, RIGHT?
CORN! FEED. FOR DUMB ANIMALS!!

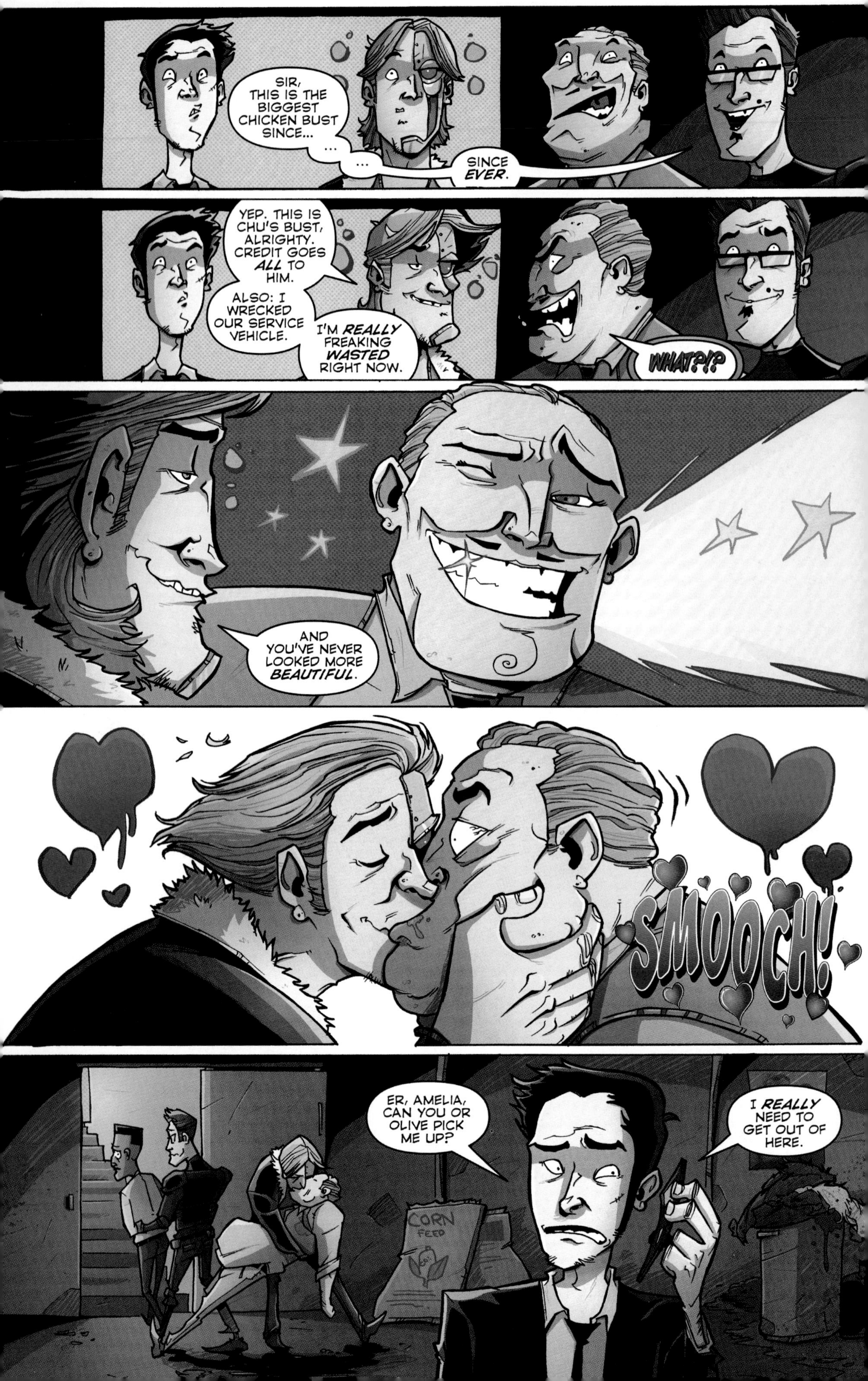

SIR, THIS IS THE BIGGEST CHICKEN BUST SINCE...
...
...
SINCE EVER.
YEP. THIS IS CHU'S BUST, ALRIGHTY. CREDIT GOES ALL TO HIM.
ALSO: I WRECKED OUR SERVICE VEHICLE.
I'M REALLY FREAKING WASTED RIGHT NOW.
WHAT?!?
AND YOU'VE NEVER LOOKED MORE BEAUTIFUL.
SMOOCH!
CORN FEED
ER, AMELIA, CAN YOU OR OLIVE PICK ME UP?
I REALLY NEED TO GET OUT OF HERE.

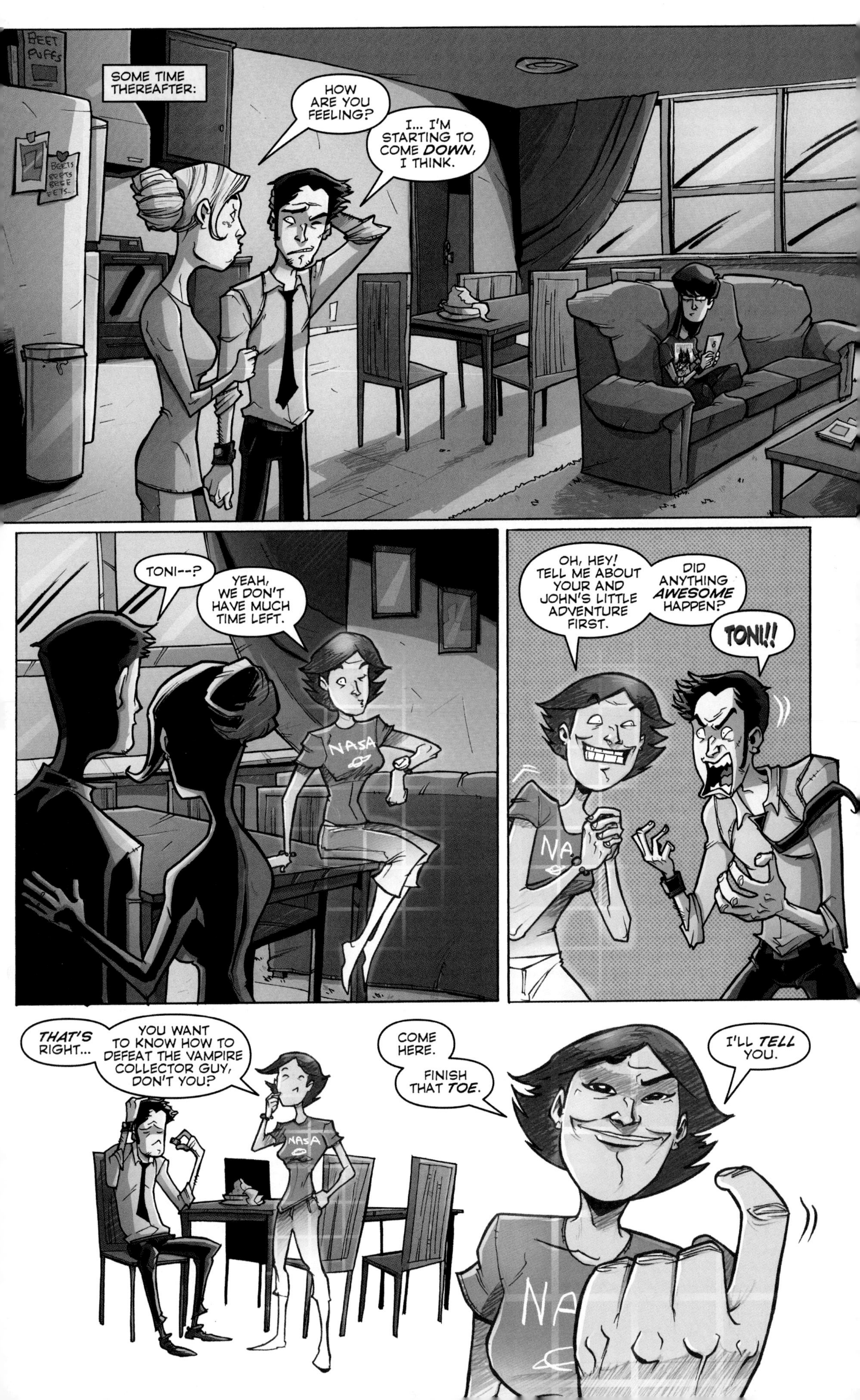
BEET PUFFS
SOME TIME THEREAFTER:
HOW ARE YOU FEELING?
I... I'M STARTING TO COME *DOWN*, I THINK.
TONI--?
YEAH, WE DON'T HAVE MUCH TIME LEFT.
OH, HEY! TELL ME ABOUT YOUR AND JOHN'S LITTLE ADVENTURE FIRST.
DID ANYTHING *AWESOME* HAPPEN?
TONI!!
THAT'S RIGHT...
YOU WANT TO KNOW HOW TO DEFEAT THE VAMPIRE COLLECTOR GUY, DON'T YOU?
COME HERE.
FINISH THAT *TOE*.
I'LL *TELL* YOU.

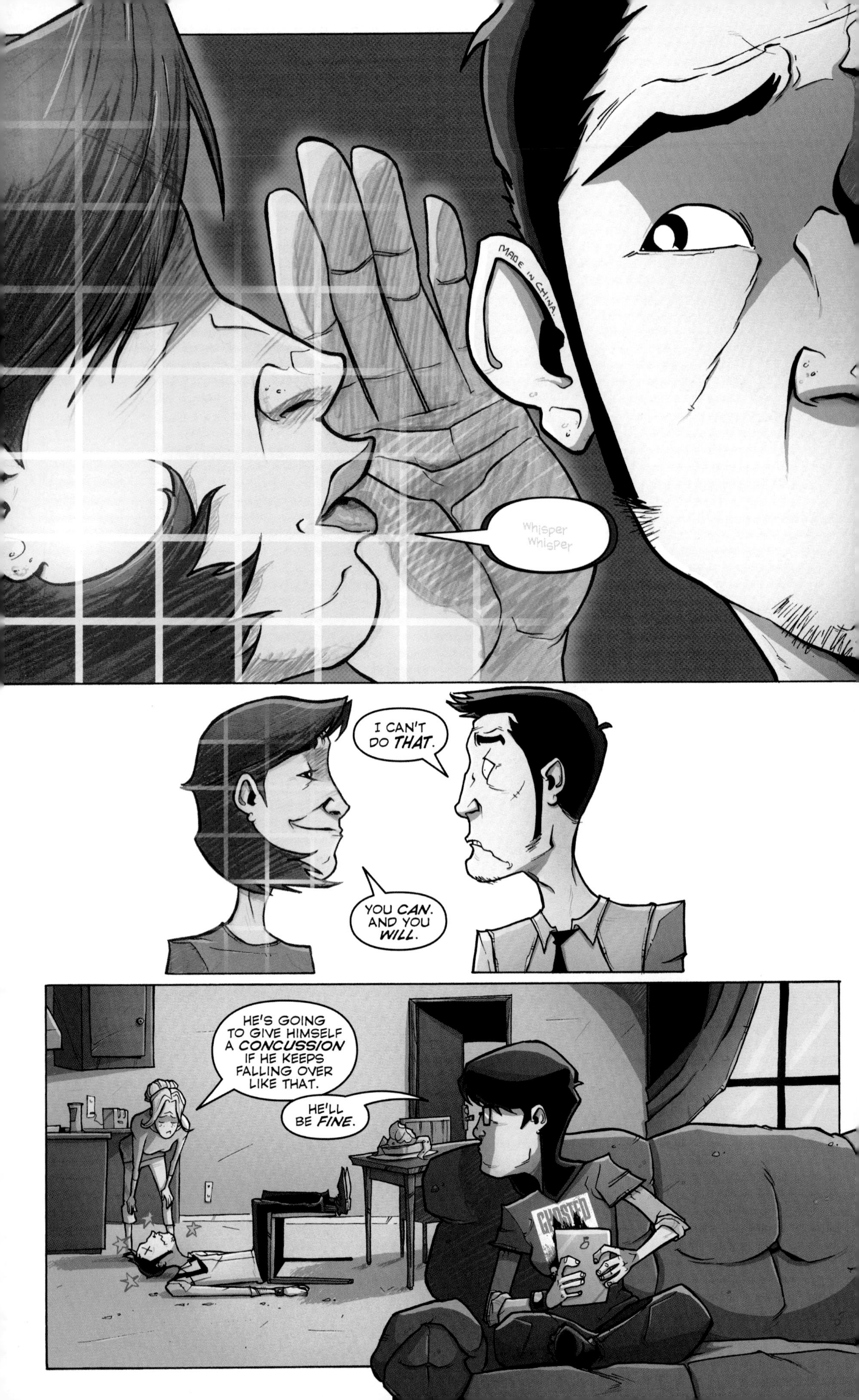
MADE IN CHINA.
whisper whisper
I CAN'T DO THAT.
YOU CAN. AND YOU WILL.
HE'S GOING TO GIVE HIMSELF A CONCUSSION IF HE KEEPS FALLING OVER LIKE THAT.
HE'LL BE FINE.
GHOSTED

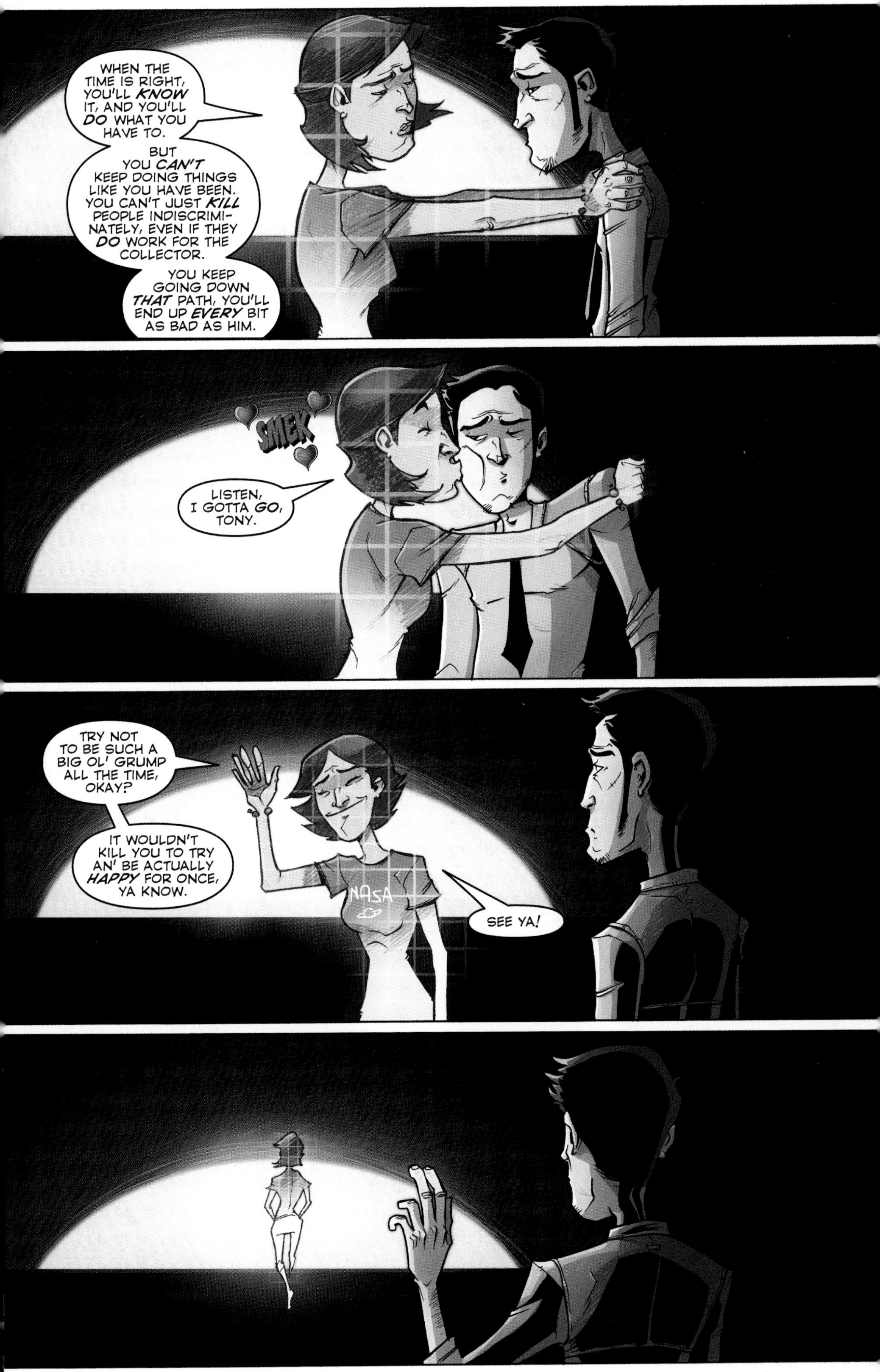
WHEN THE TIME IS RIGHT, YOU'LL KNOW IT, AND YOU'LL DO WHAT YOU HAVE TO.
BUT YOU CAN'T KEEP DOING THINGS LIKE YOU HAVE BEEN. YOU CAN'T JUST KILL PEOPLE INDISCRIMI-NATELY, EVEN IF THEY DO WORK FOR THE COLLECTOR.
YOU KEEP GOING DOWN THAT PATH, YOU'LL END UP EVERY BIT AS BAD AS HIM.
SMEK
LISTEN, I GOTTA GO, TONY.
TRY NOT TO BE SUCH A BIG OL' GRUMP ALL THE TIME, OKAY?
IT WOULDN'T KILL YOU TO TRY AN' BE ACTUALLY HAPPY FOR ONCE, YA KNOW.
NASA
SEE YA!

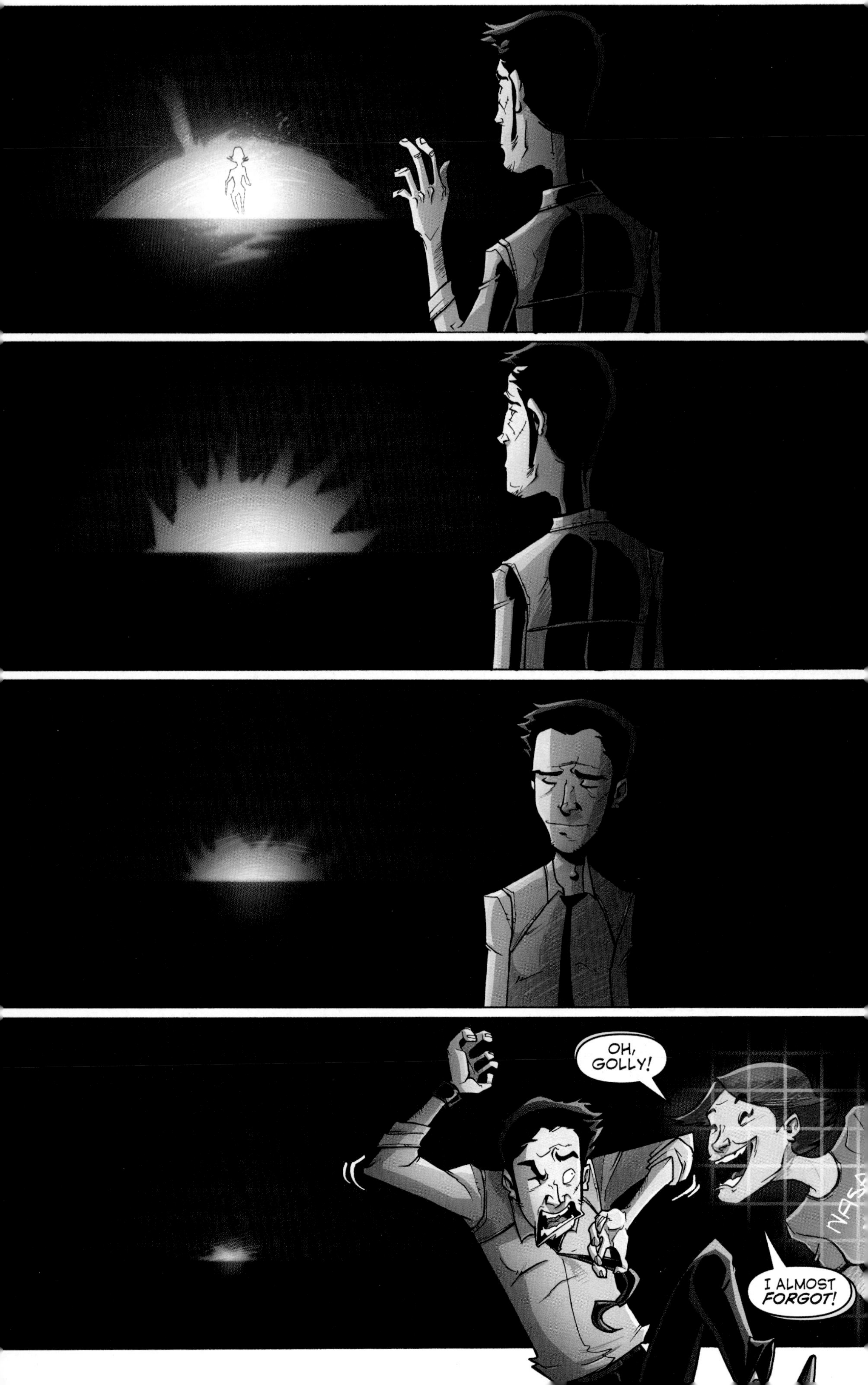
OH, GOLLY!
I ALMOST FORGOT!

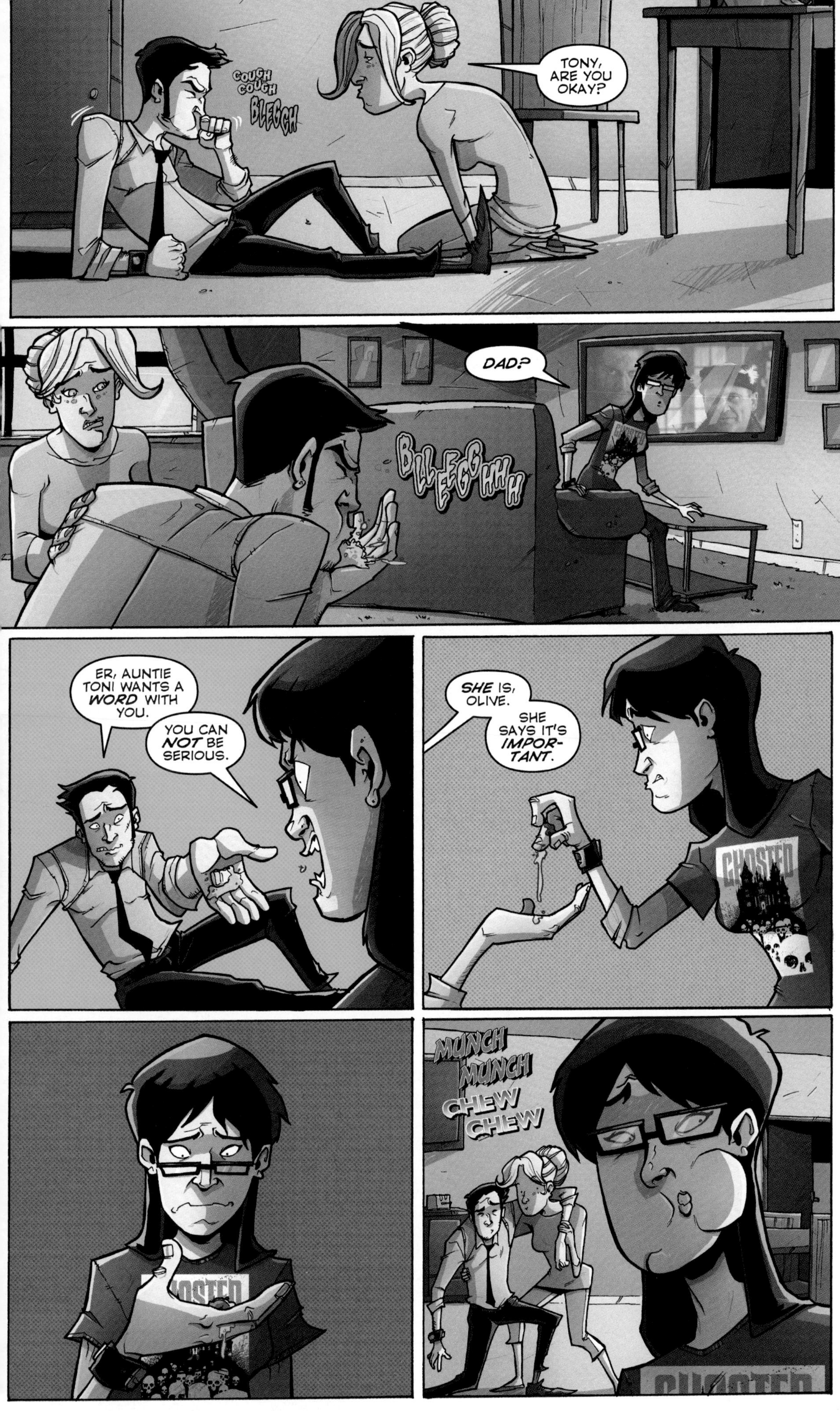
COUGH COUGH
BLEGCH
TONY, ARE YOU OKAY?
DAD?
BLLEEGGHHH
ER, AUNTIE TONI WANTS A WORD WITH YOU.
YOU CAN NOT BE SERIOUS.
SHE IS, OLIVE.
SHE SAYS IT'S IMPORTANT.
MUNCH MUNCH
CHEW CHEW

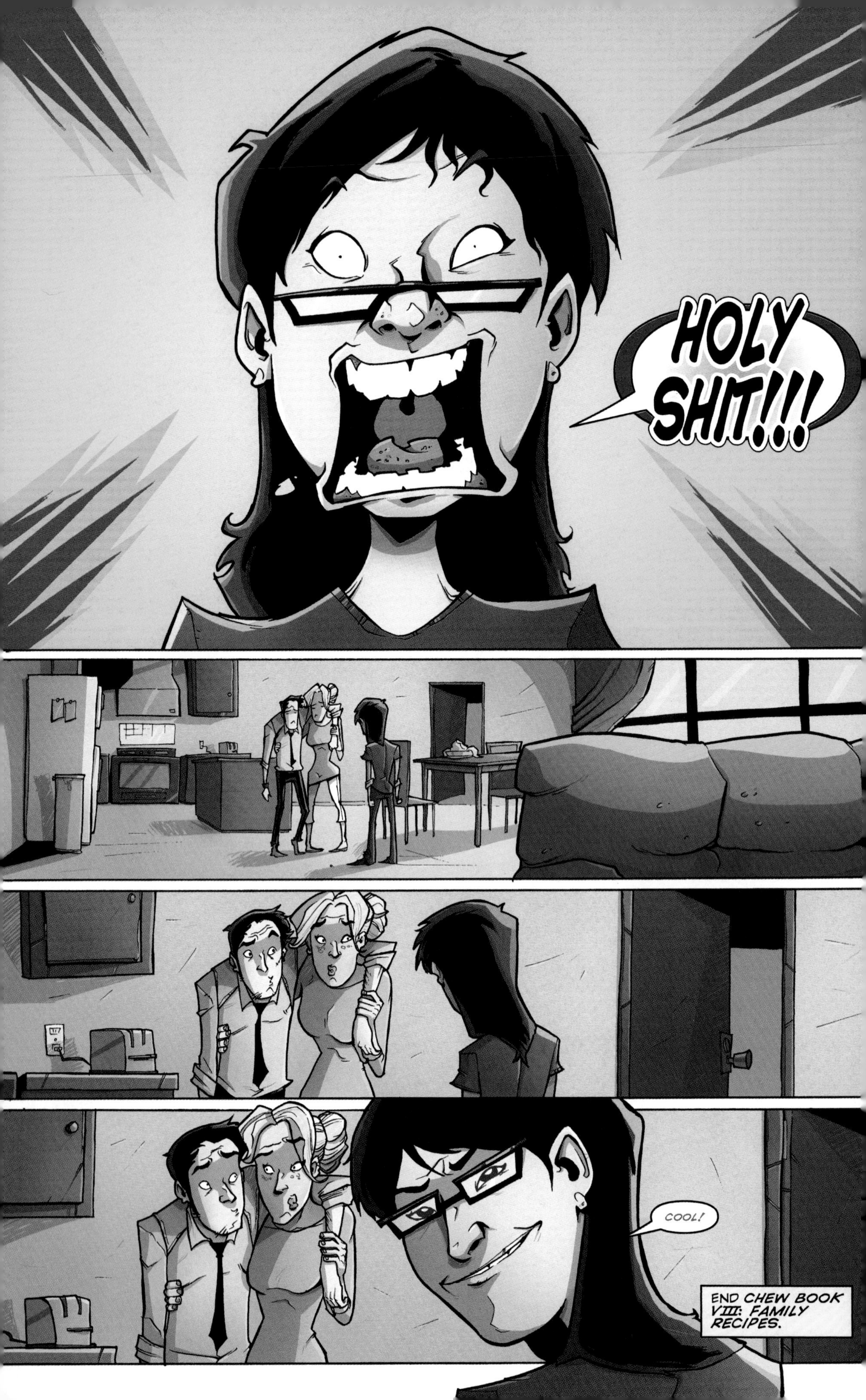
HOLY SHIT!!!
COOL!
END CHEW BOOK VIII: FAMILY RECIPES.

Extras

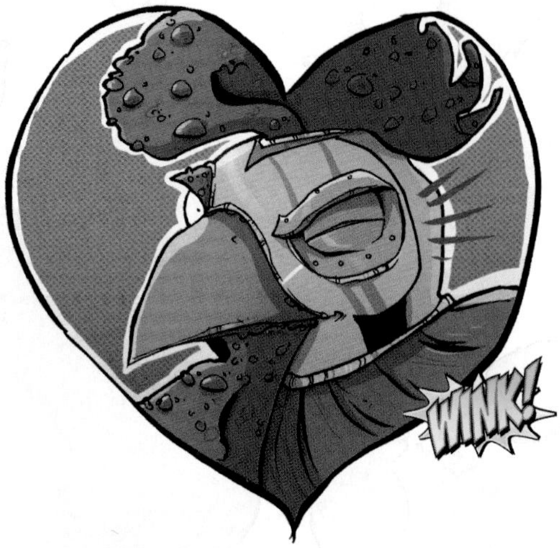
WINK!

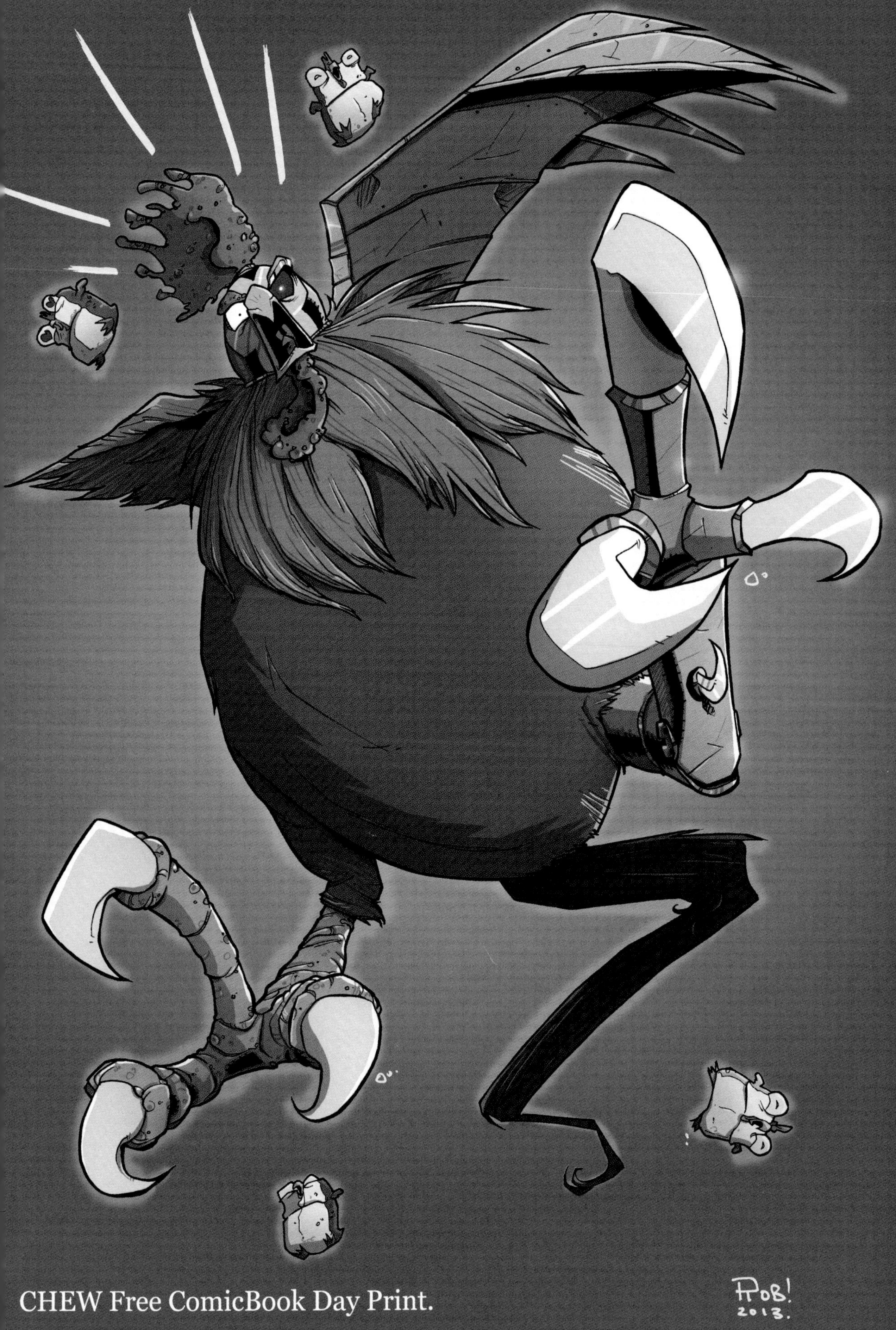
ROB!
2013.

CHEW Free ComicBook Day Print.

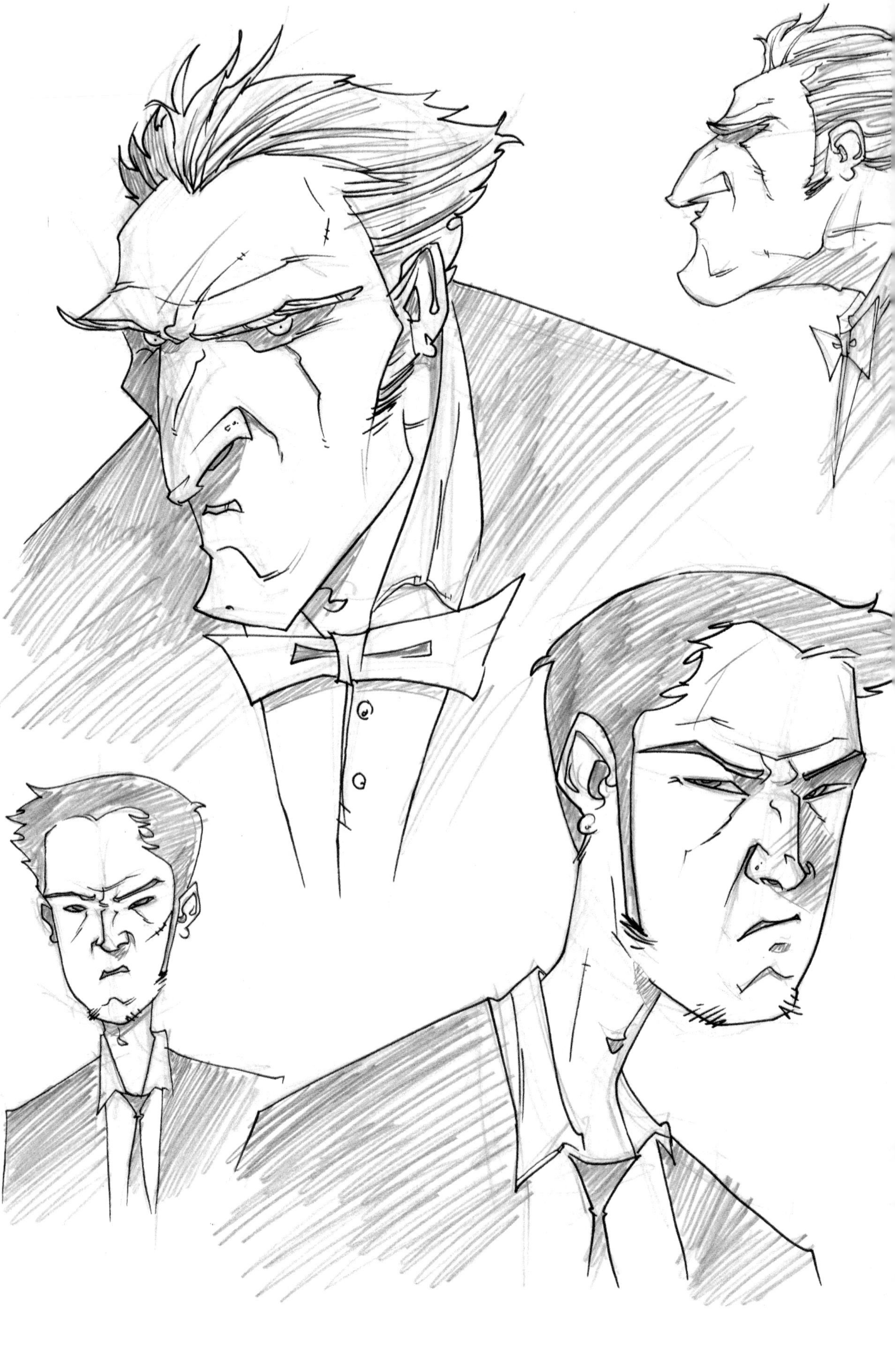

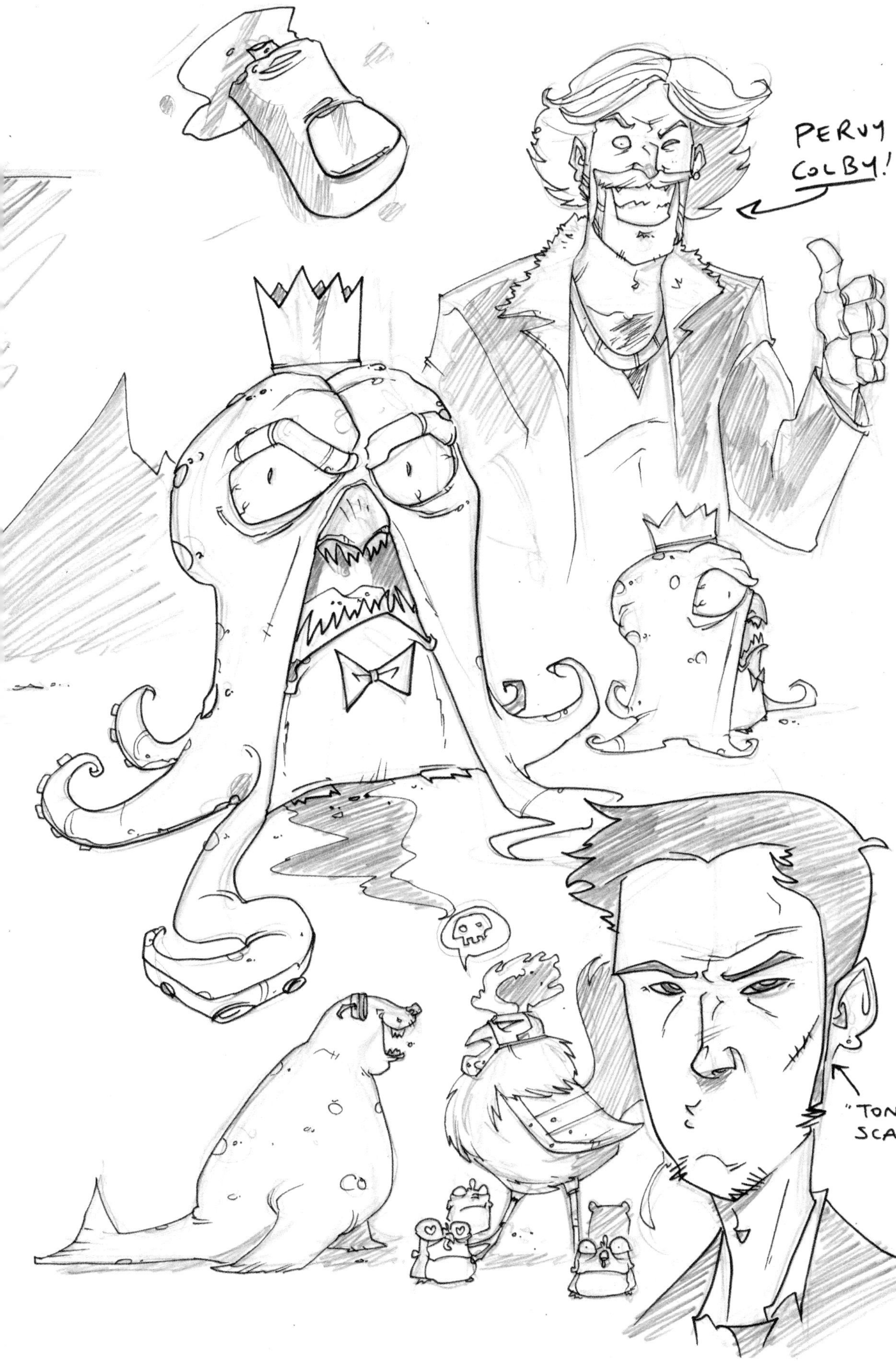
PERVY
COLBY!
"TONI
SCAR."

Random Sketchbook page.

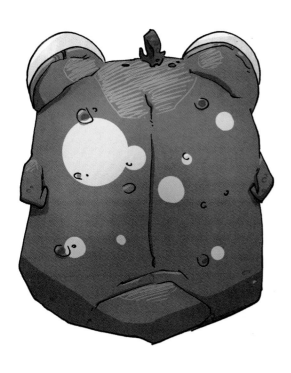

Concept drawings for a CHOG Vinyl figure.
Final Vinyl Product by Skelton Crew Studio.
(*www.skeltoncrewstudio.com*)

#34 “unmixed” Tony cover

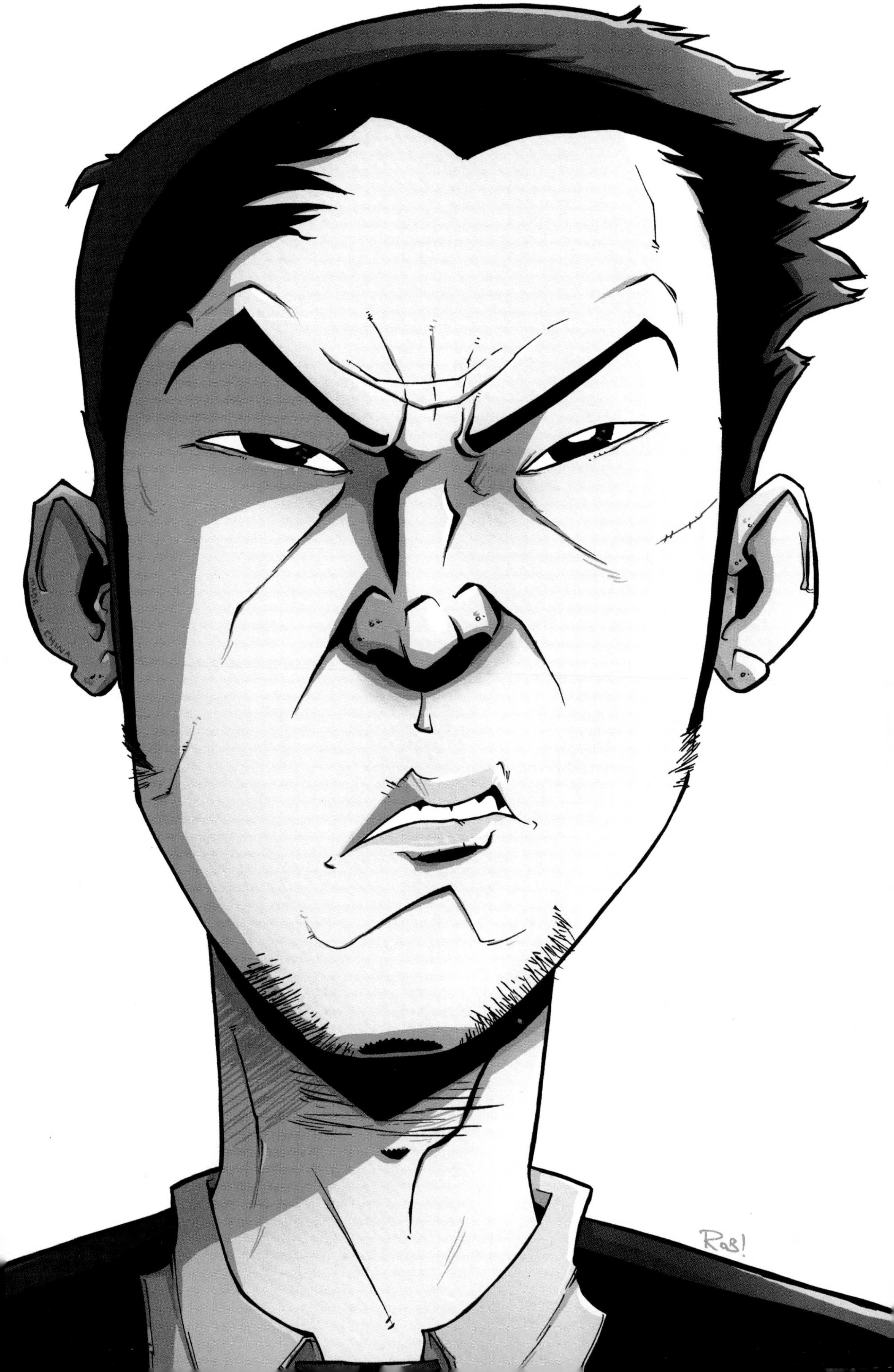

#34 “unmixed” Savoy cover

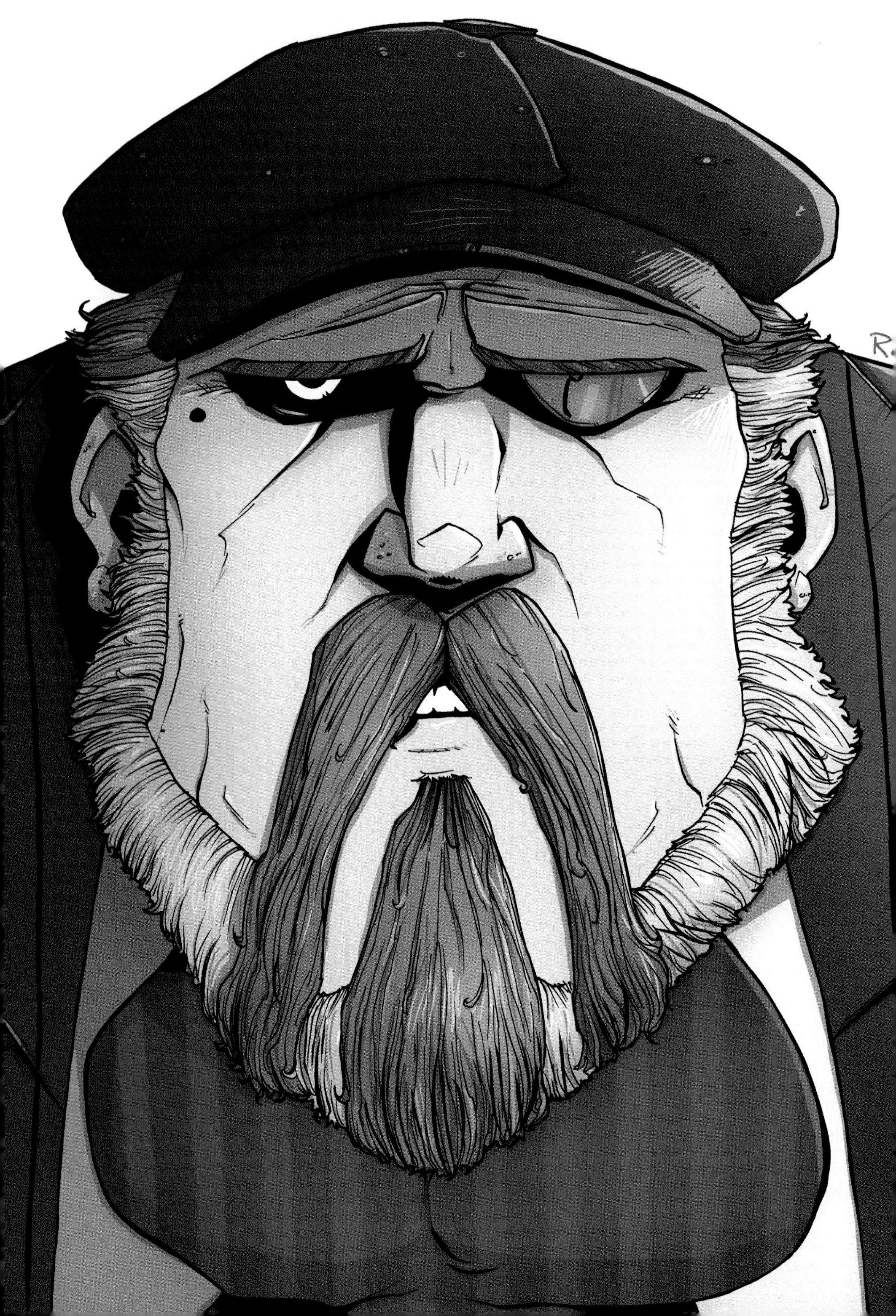

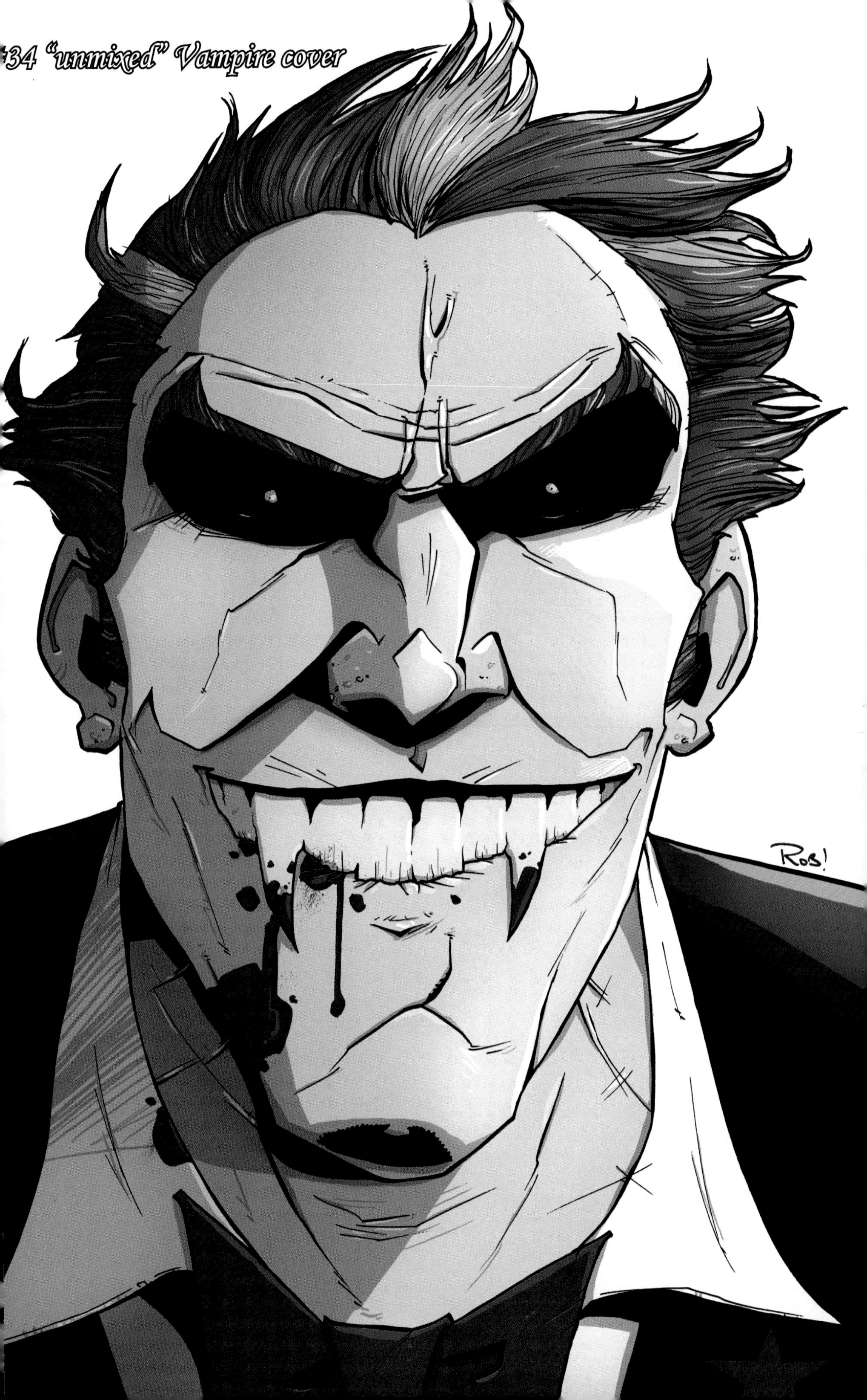
ROB!

#34 “unmixed” Vampire cover

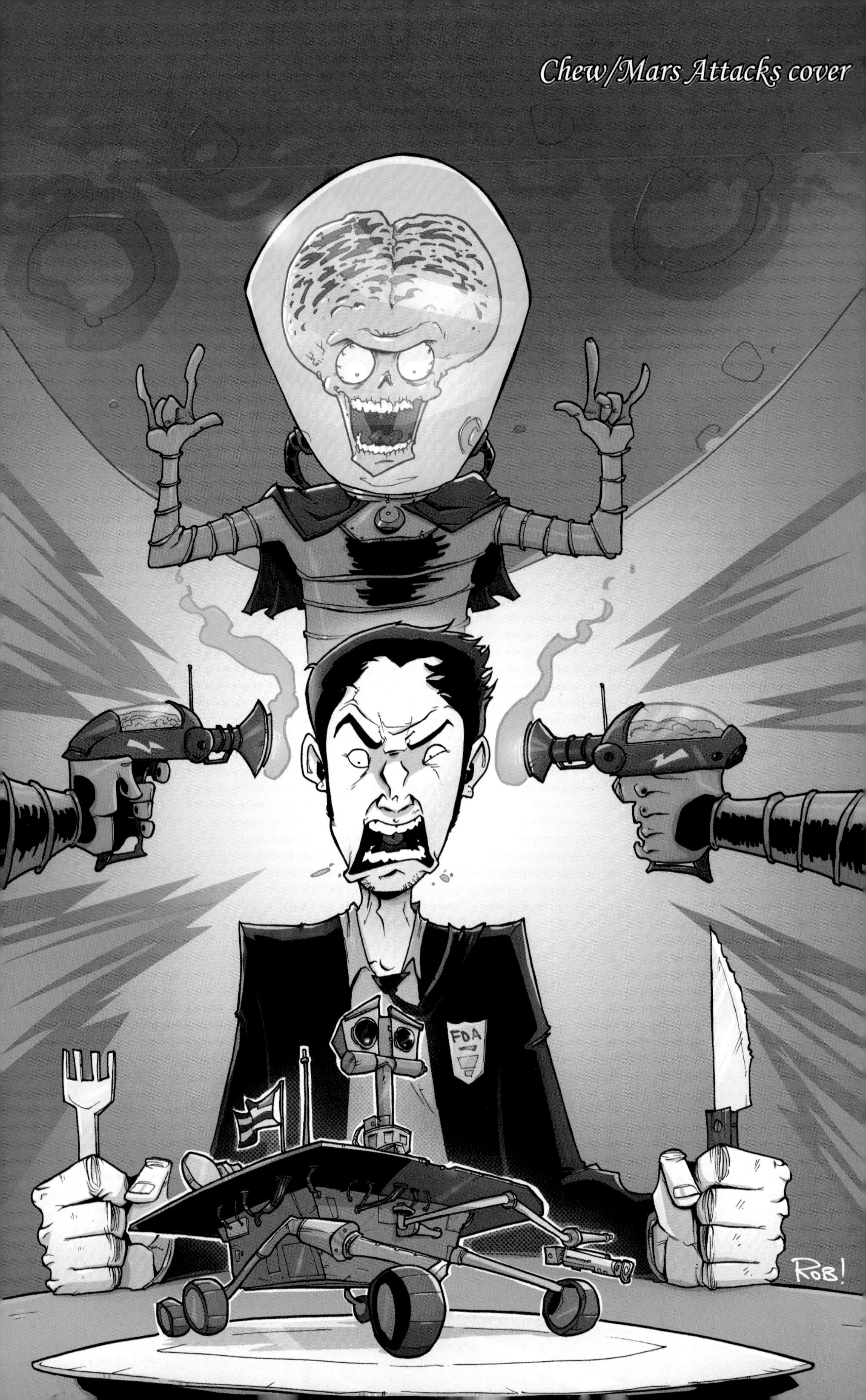
FDA
ROB!

Chew/Mars Attacks cover

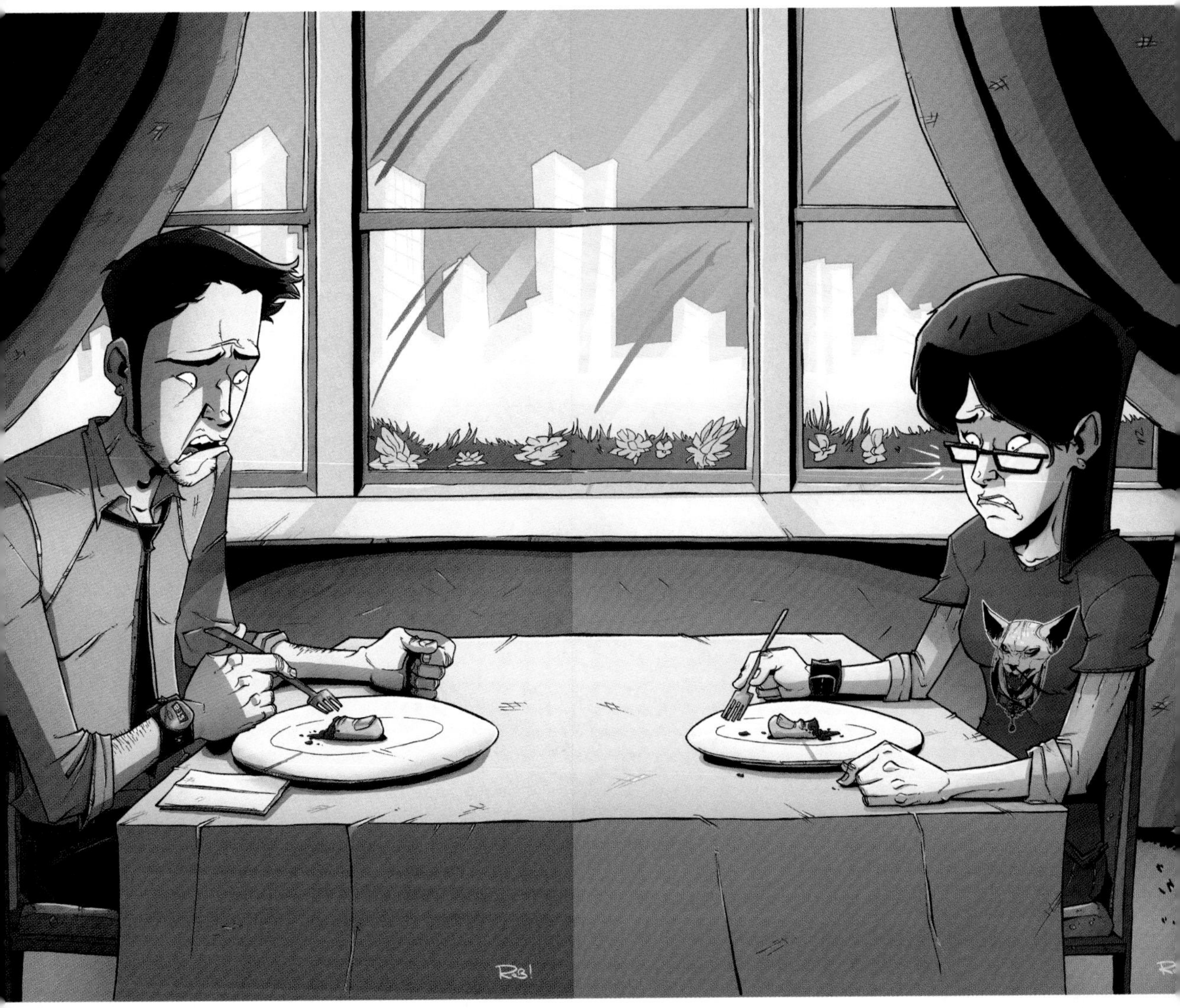

CHEW #37 Covers A +B.

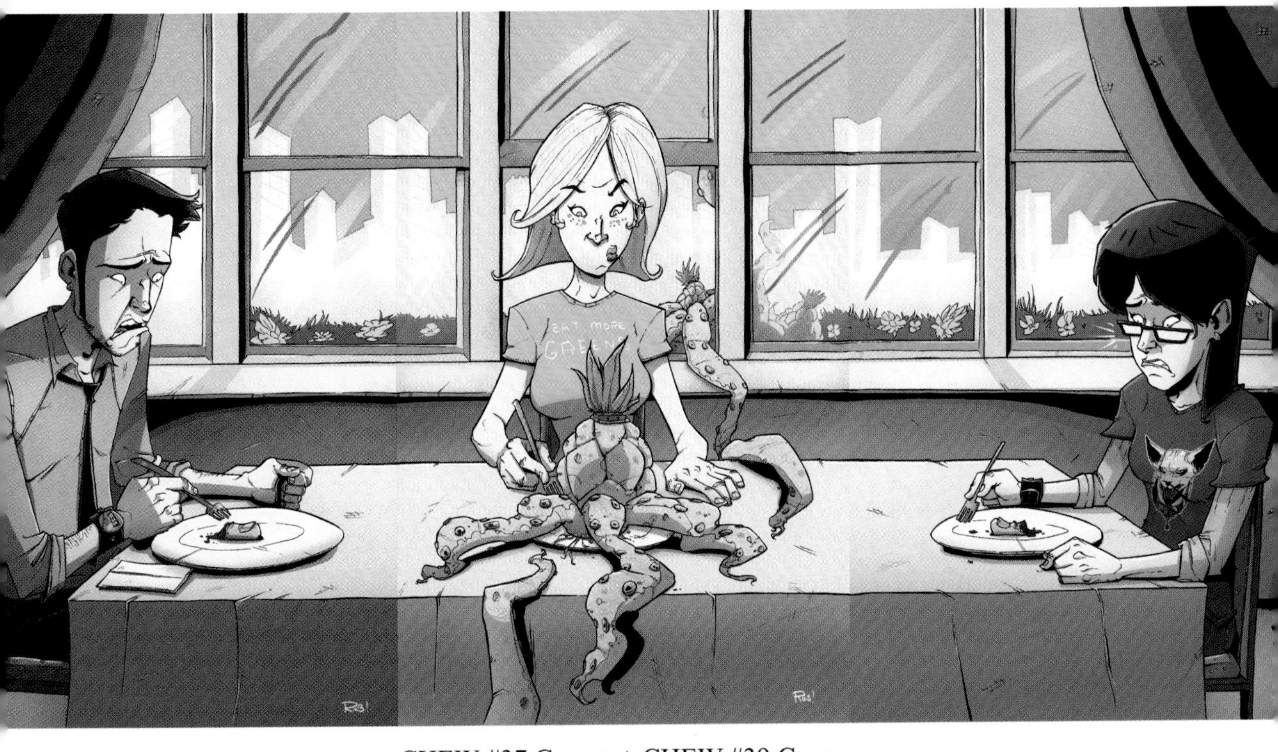
EAT MORE

CHEW #37 Covers + CHEW #39 Cover.

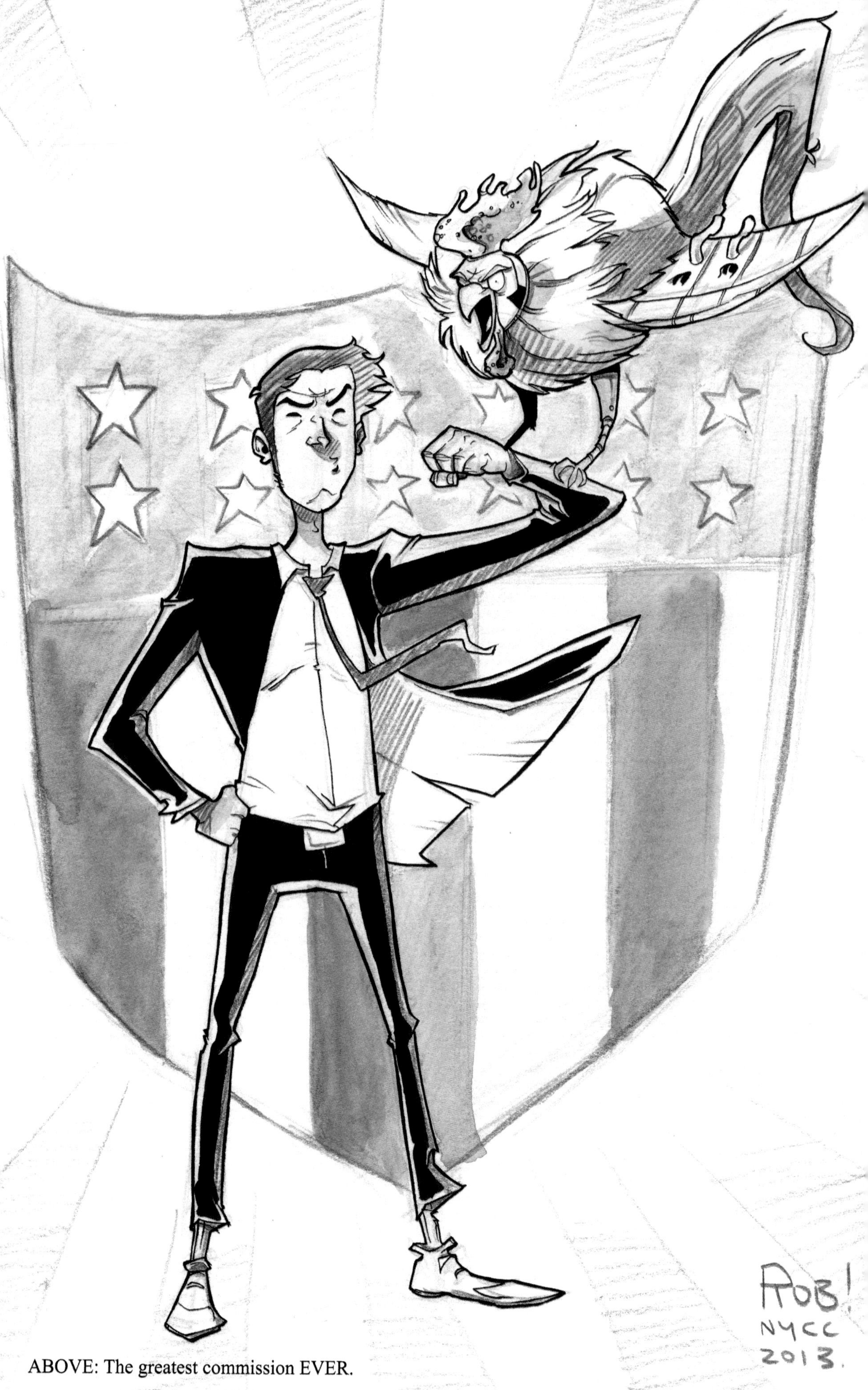
ROB!
NYCC
2013.

ABOVE: The greatest commission EVER.

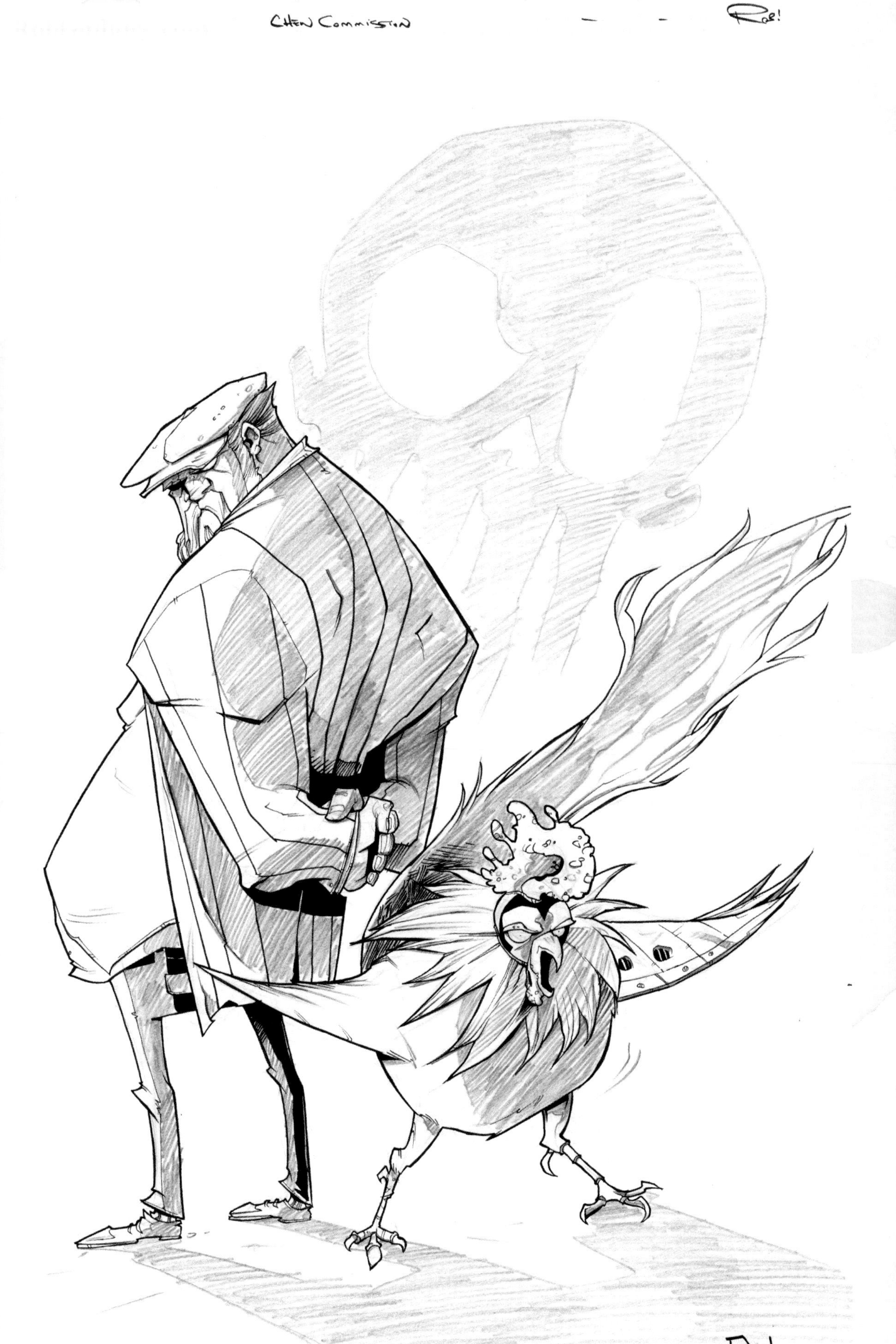
Chen Commission
Rob!
Rob!
2014.

Commission. I get a LOT of Poyo commissions.

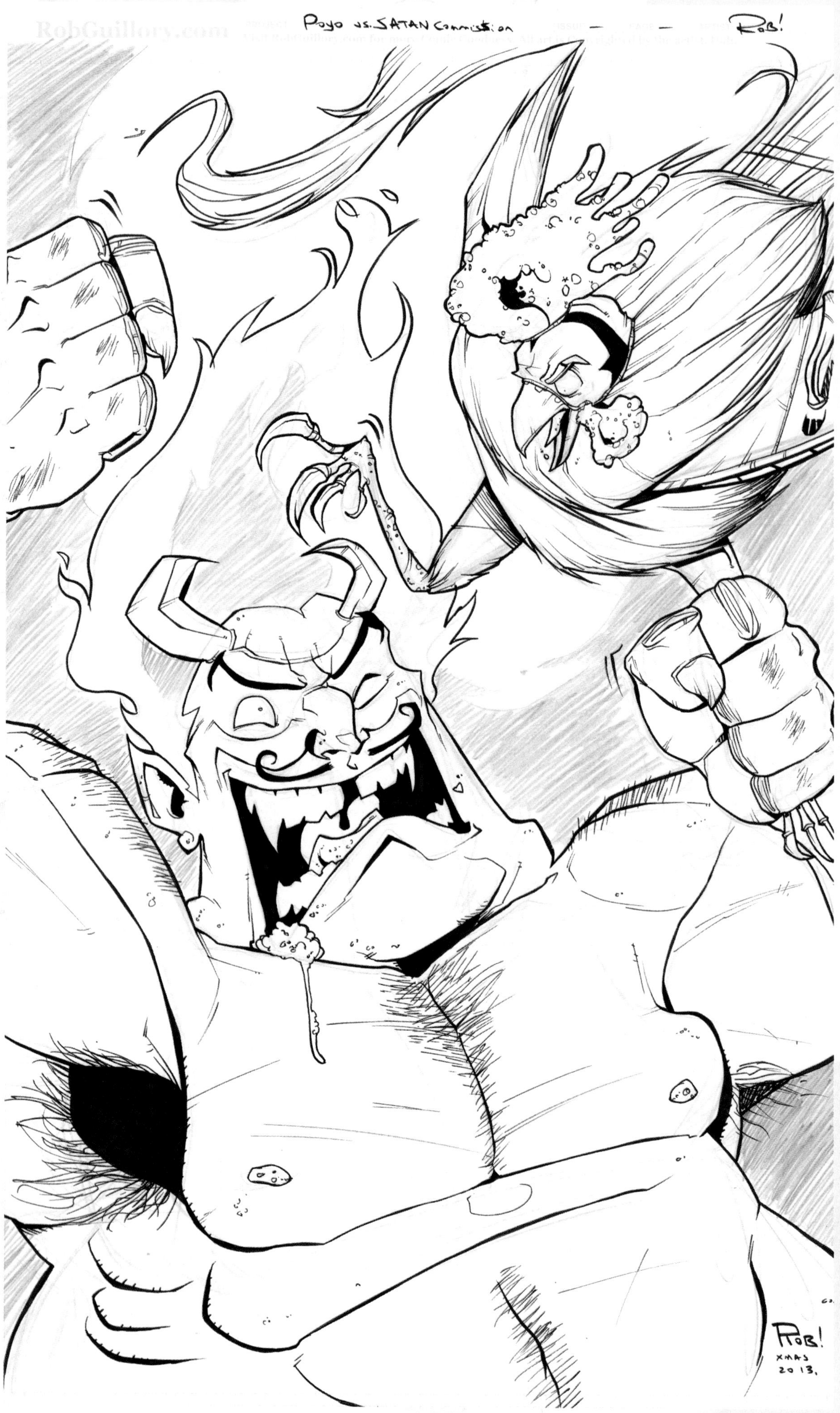
RobGuillory.com
Poyo vs. SATAN Commission
ROB!
ROB!
XMAS
2013.

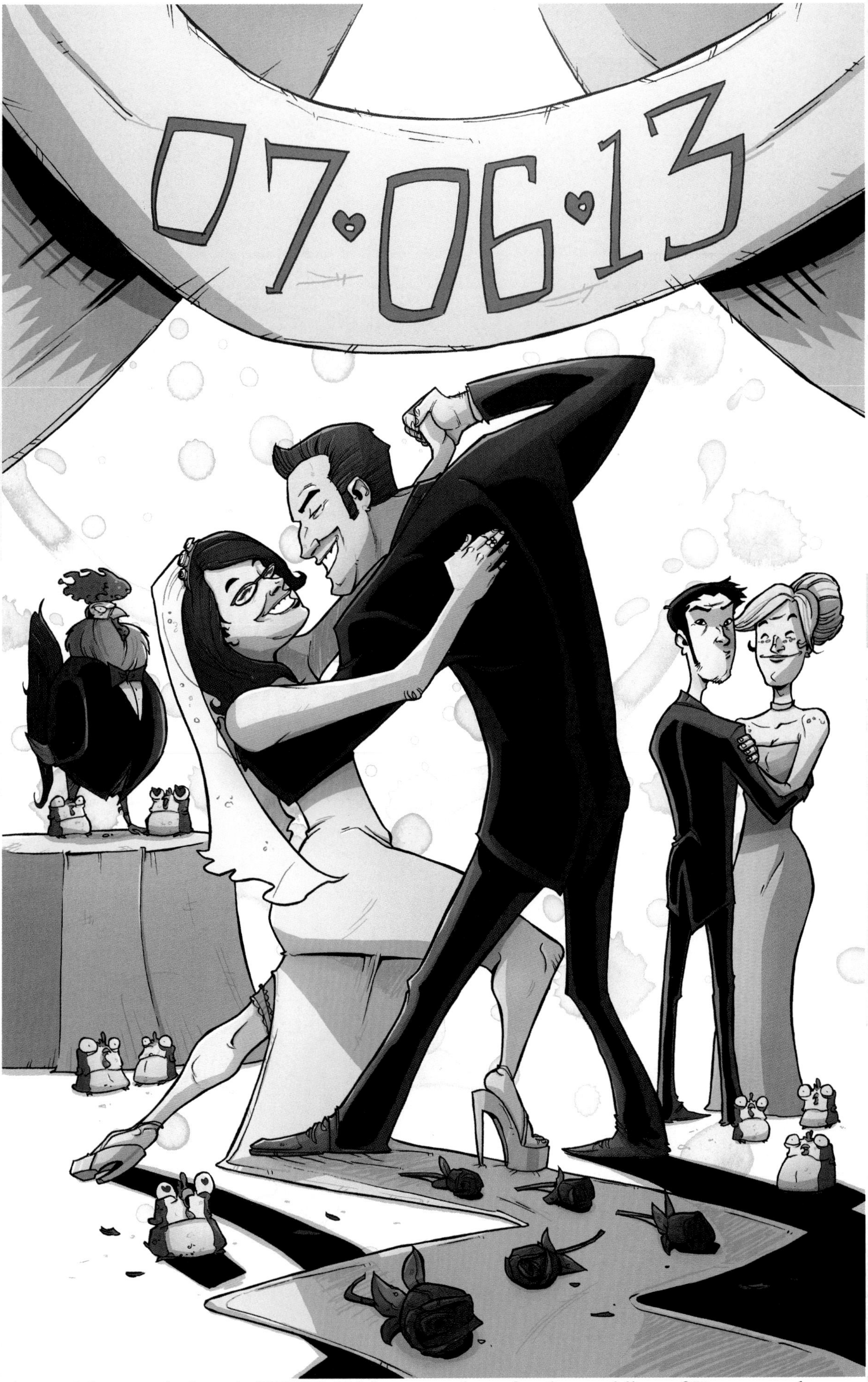
07·06·13

A special commission. A CHEW #30 homage done for the wedding of Damon and Vincie Wanamaker. To the infinite confusion of their families, no doubt!

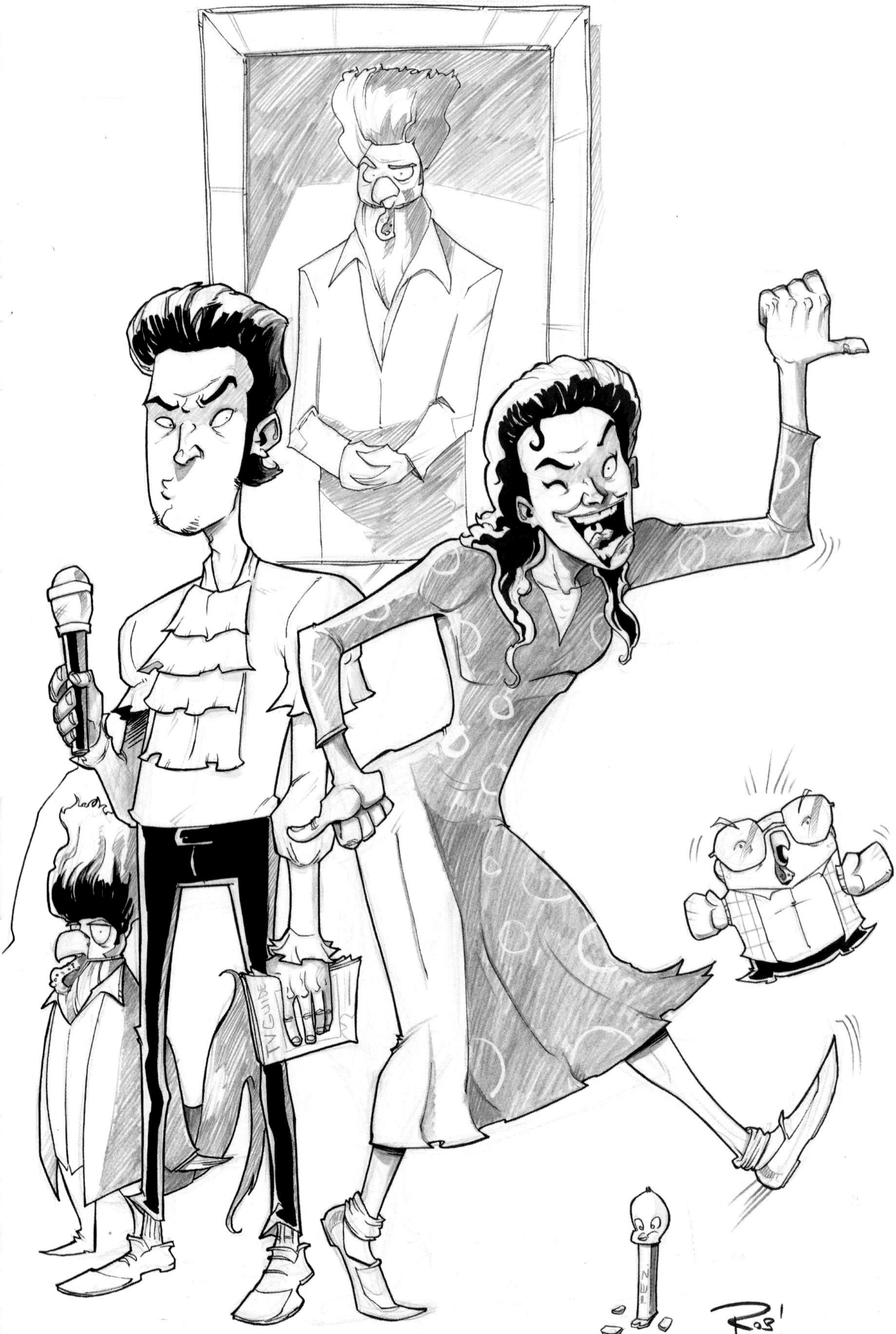
TV GUIDE
Rob!
NYCC
2013.

Commission. Toni has the little kicks.

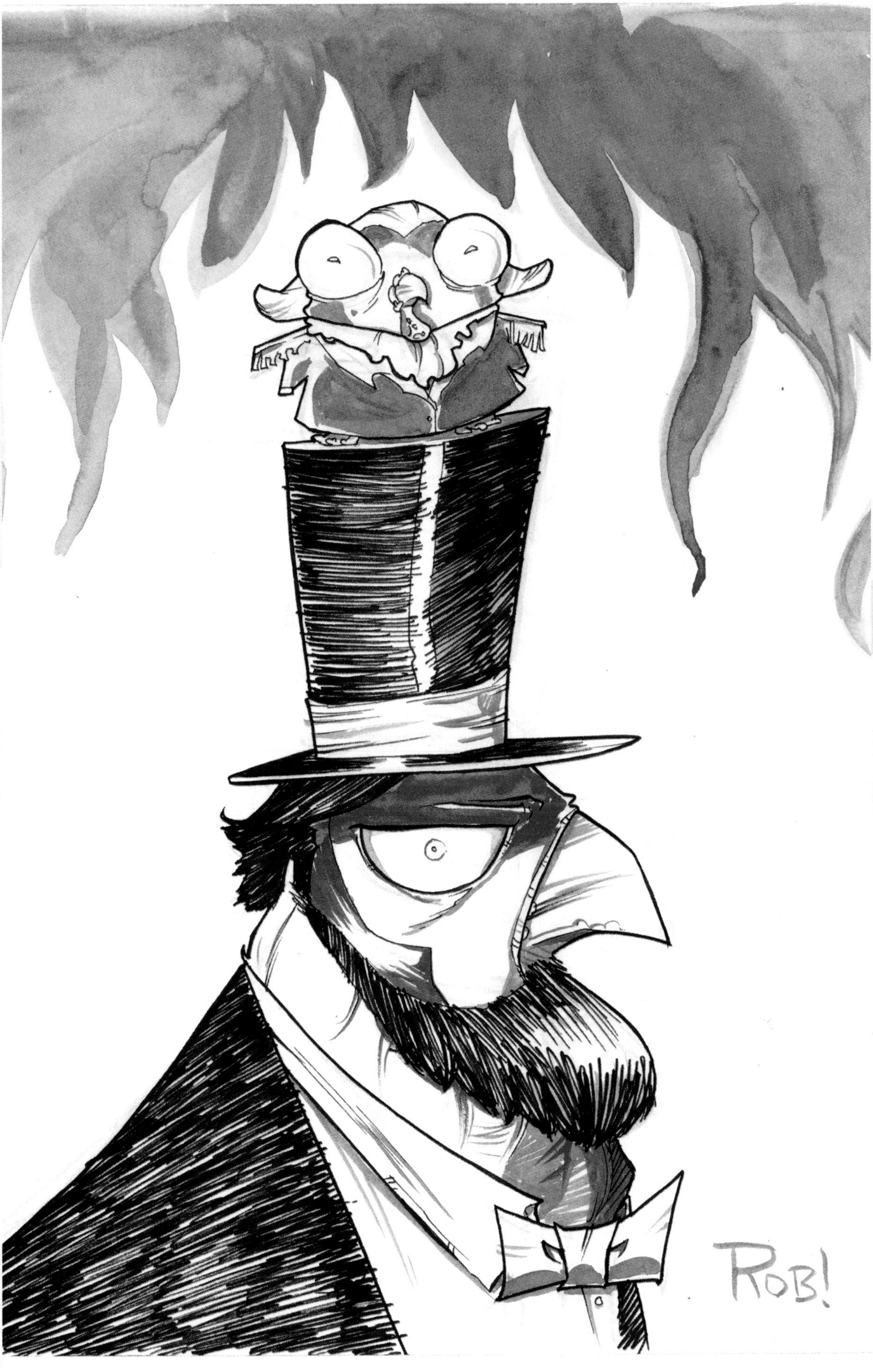
ROB!

Cover of a special CHEW sketchbook, in which Poyo and Chogs were dressed in cosplay as various obscure pop culture characters. BEST sketchbook EVER.

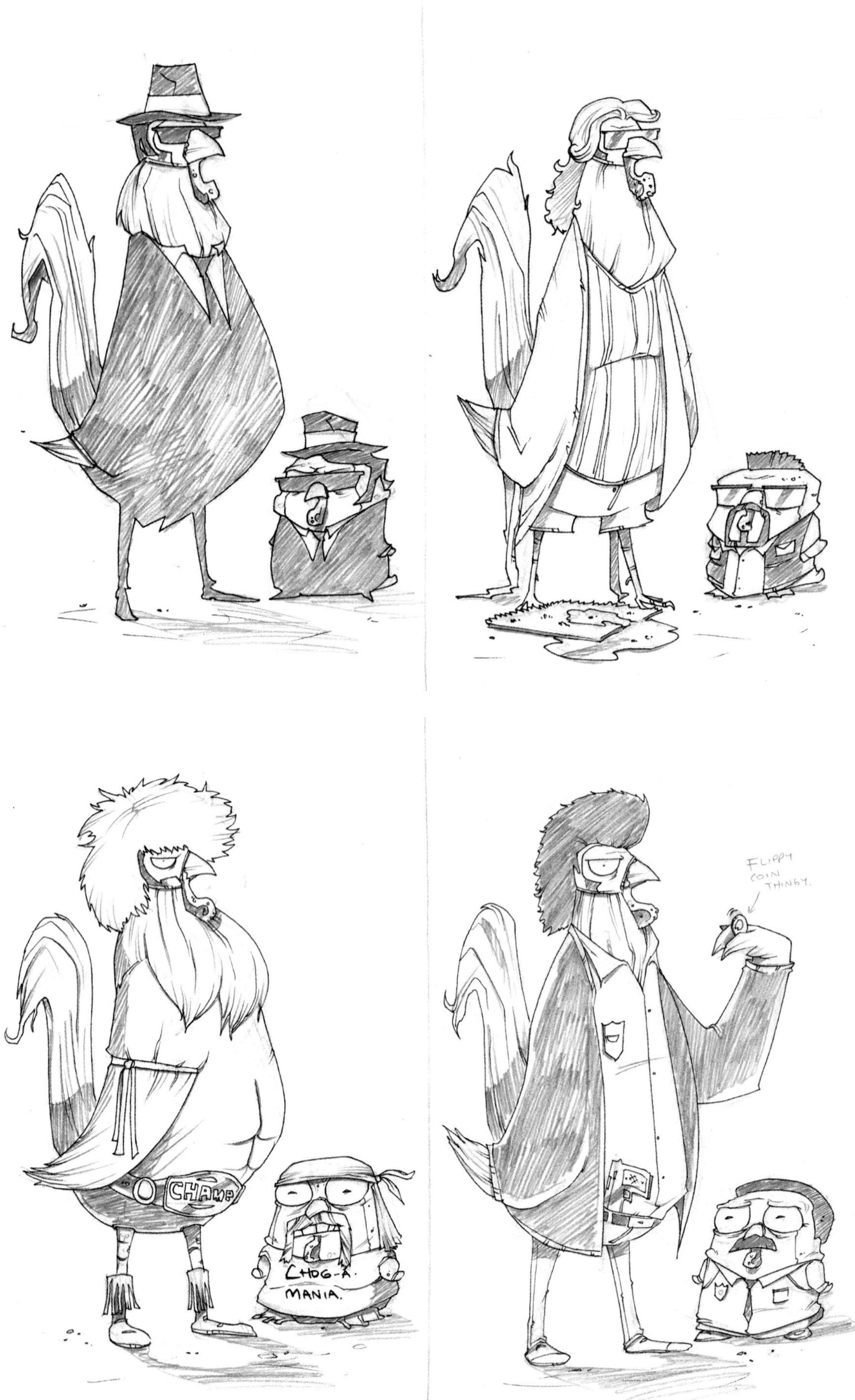
FLIPPY COIN THINGY.
CHAMP
CHOG-A-MANIA.

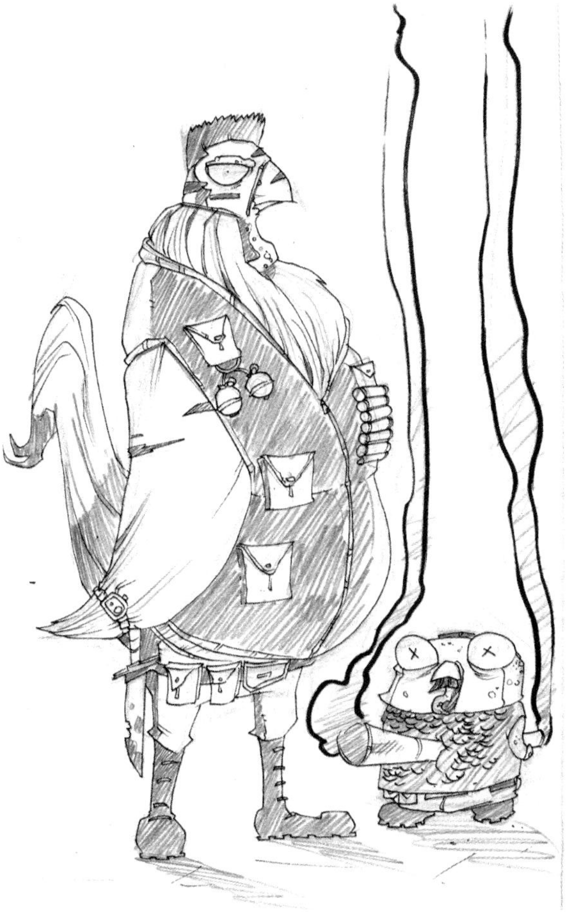

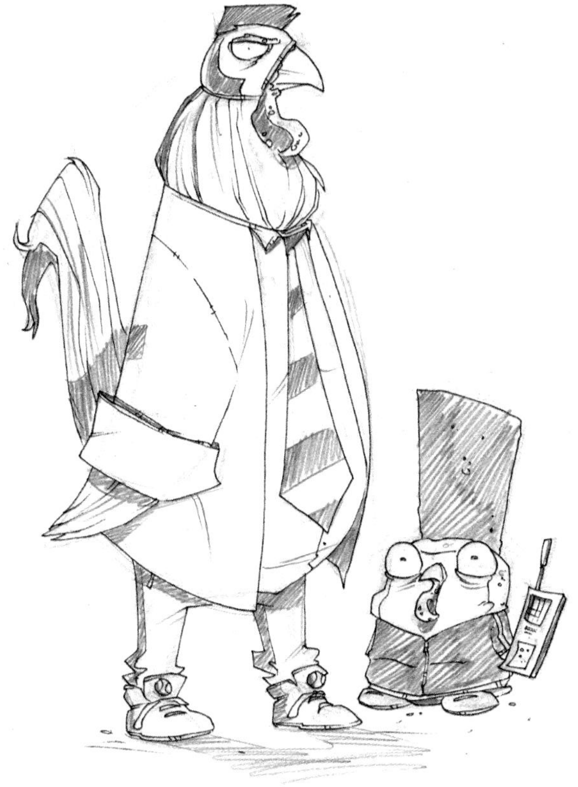

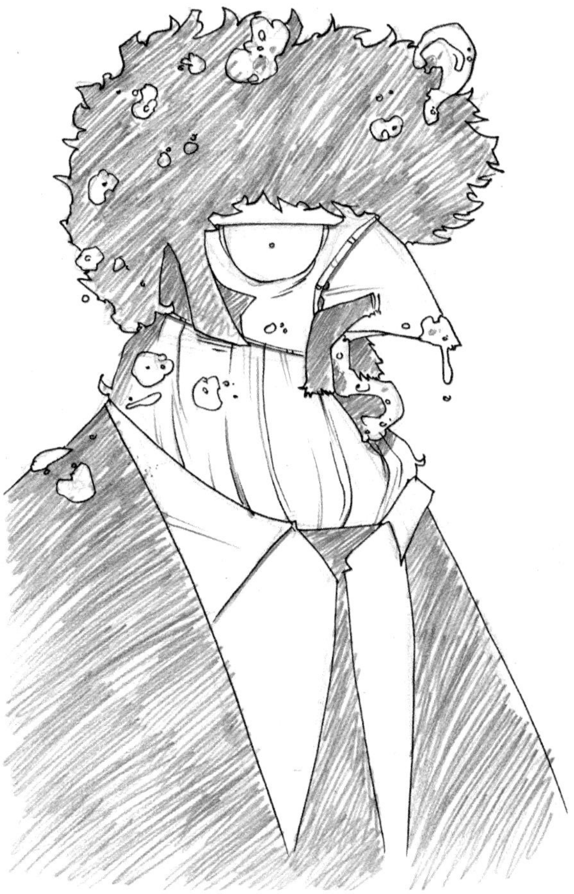

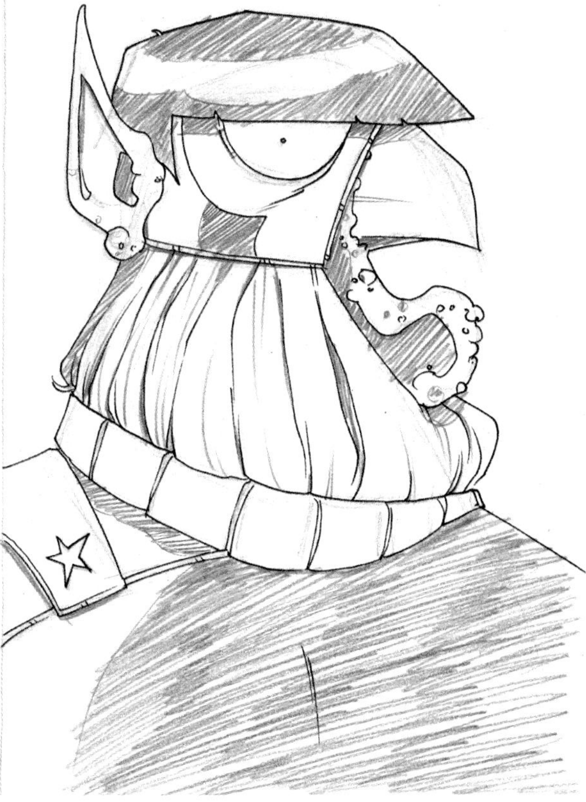

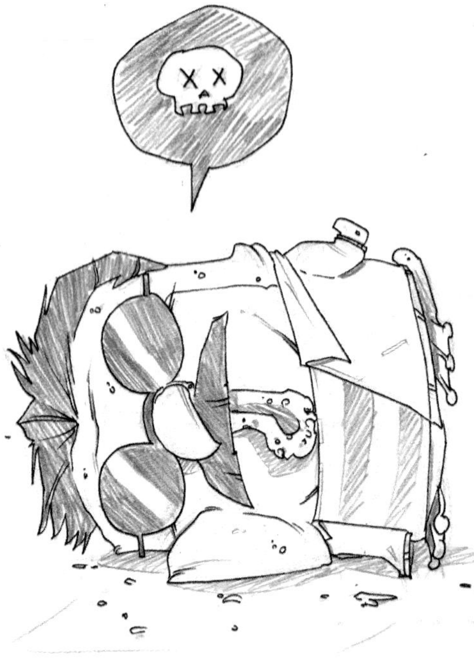

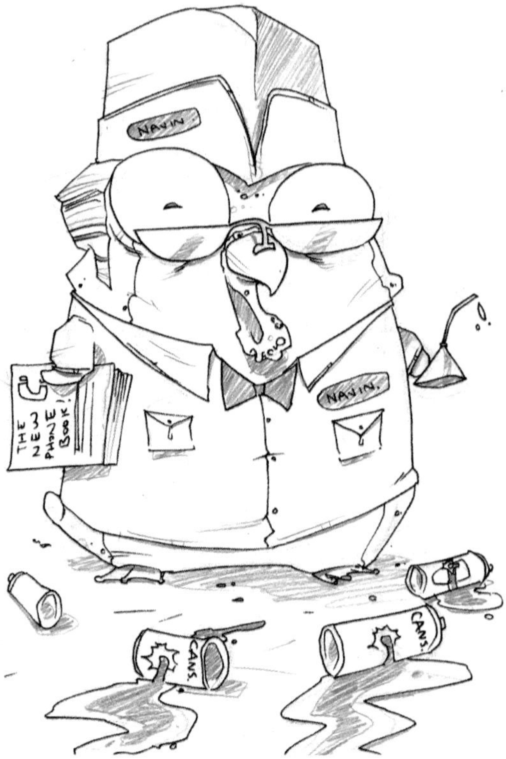
NAVIN
THE NEW PHONE BOOK!
NAVIN.
CANS.
CANS.

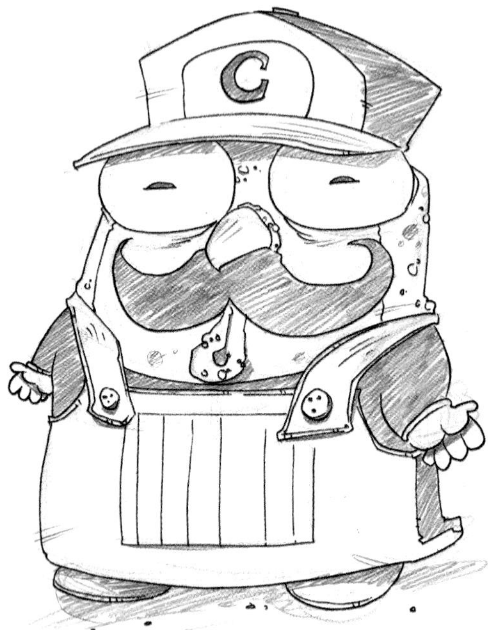
C

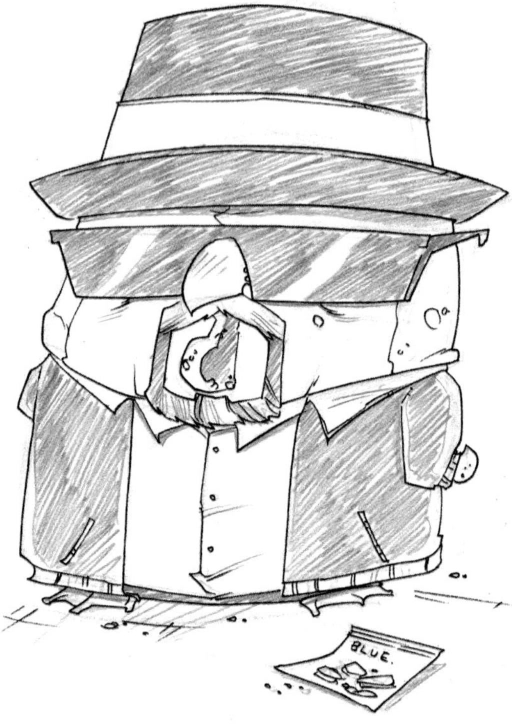
BLUE.

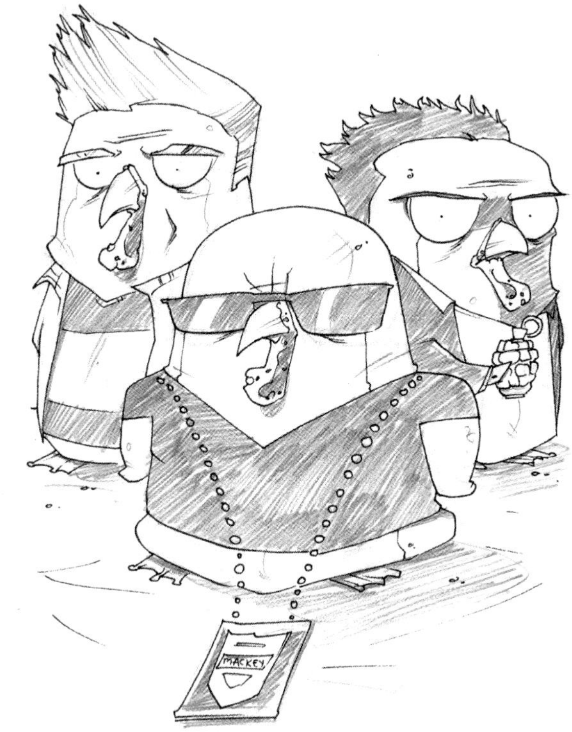
MACKEY

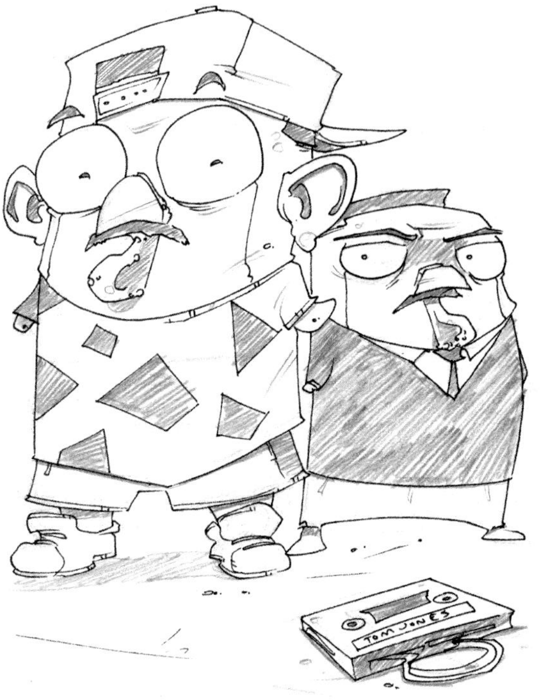
TOM JONES

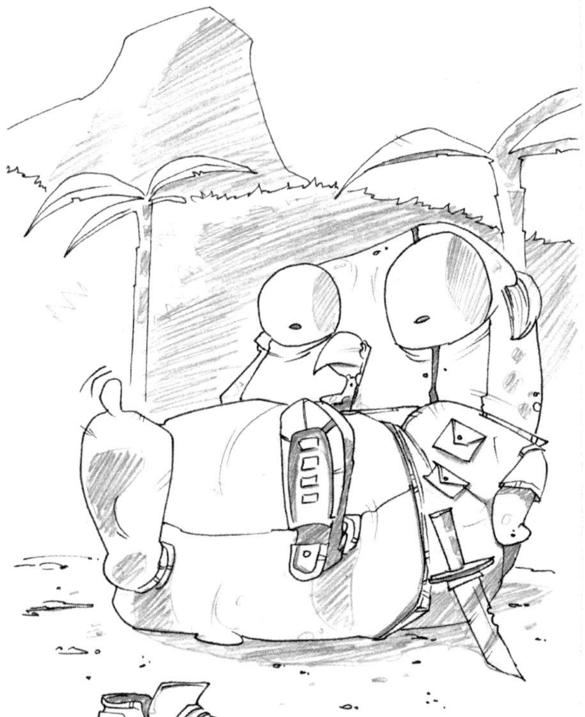

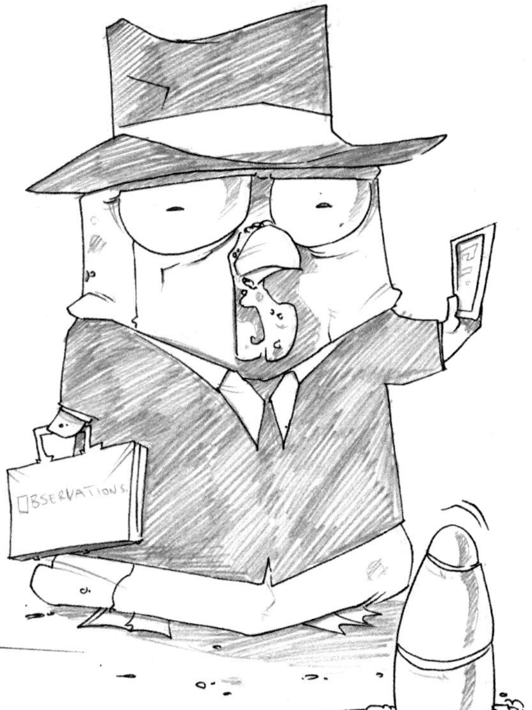
OBSERVATIONS.

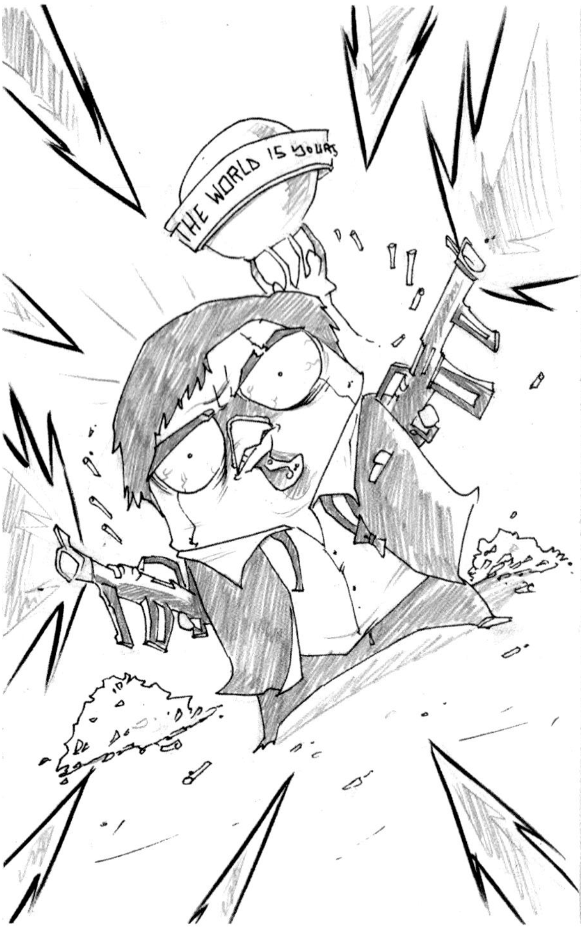
THE WORLD IS YOURS

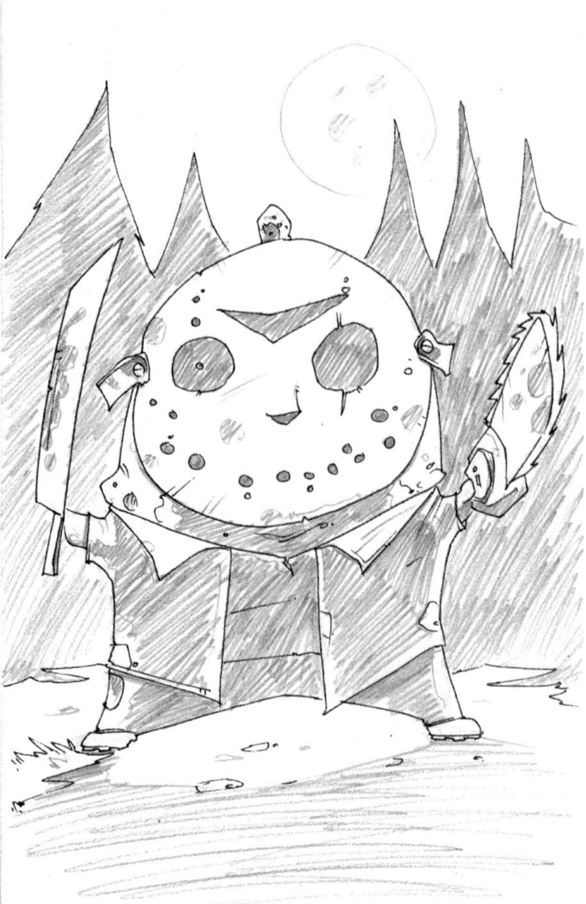

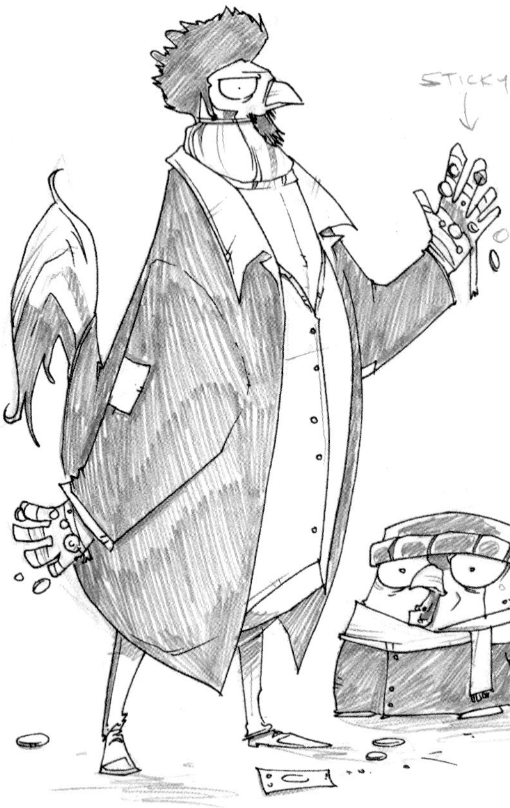
STICKY!

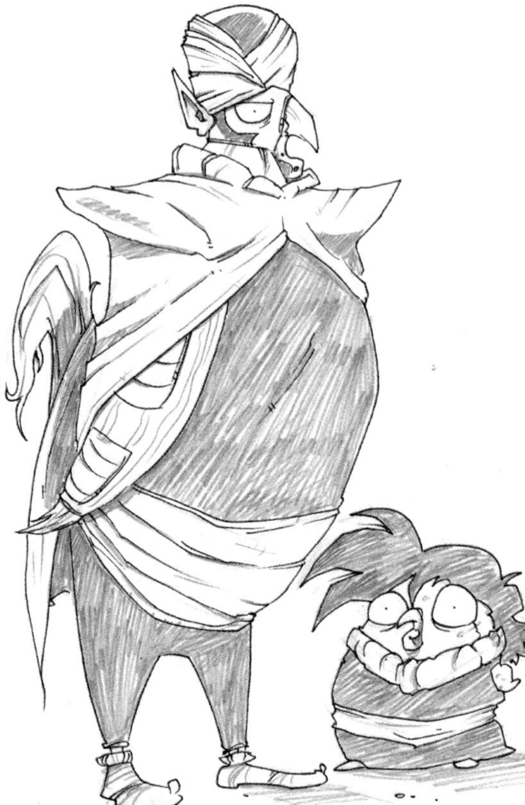

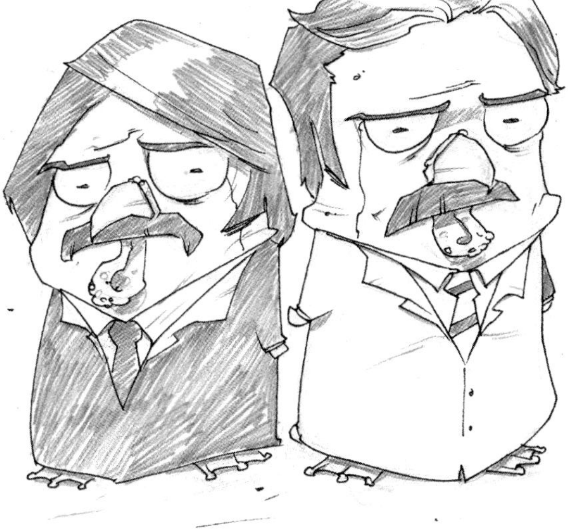

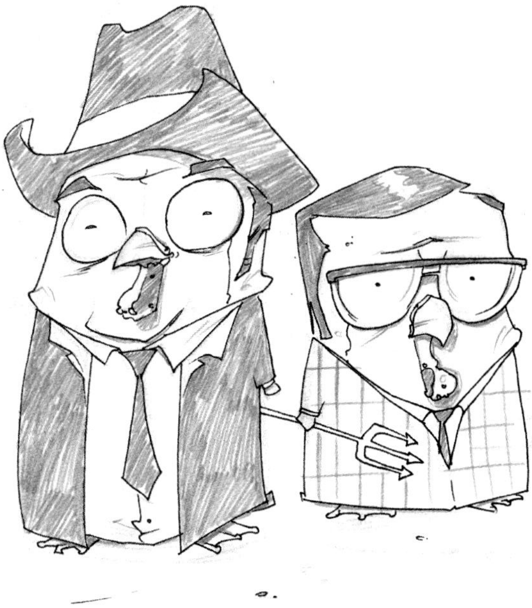

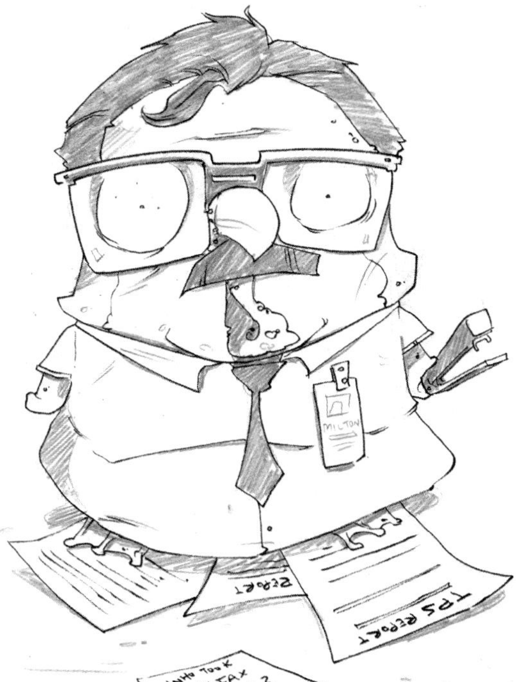
MILTON
REPORT
TPS REPORT
WHO TOOK THE FAX MACHINE?

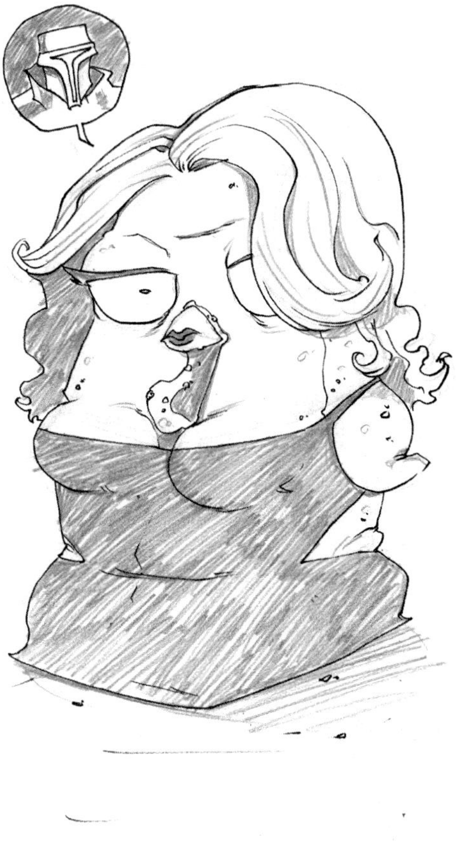

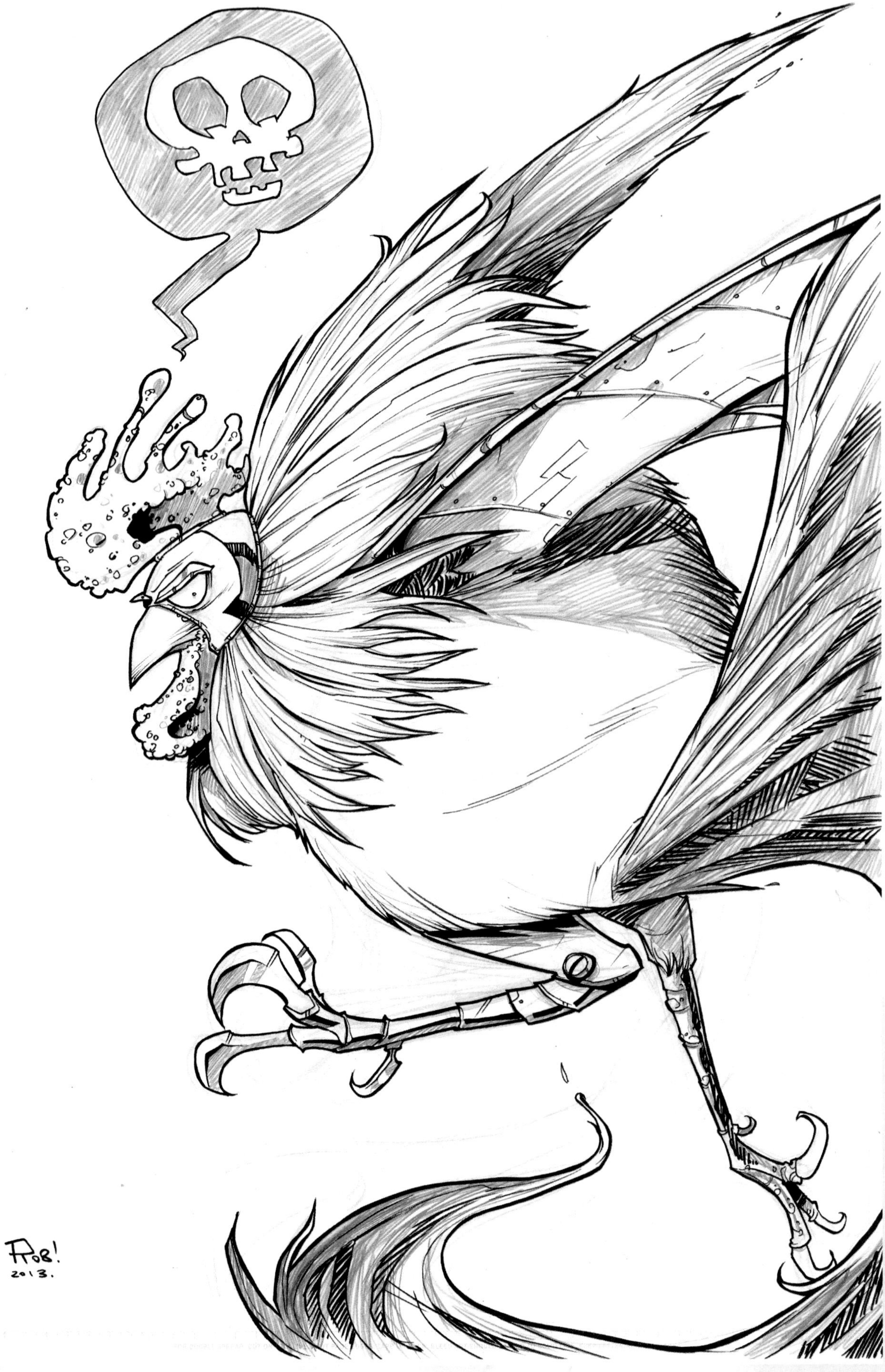
ROB!
2013.

POYO loves you. From the bottom of his murderous chicken heart.

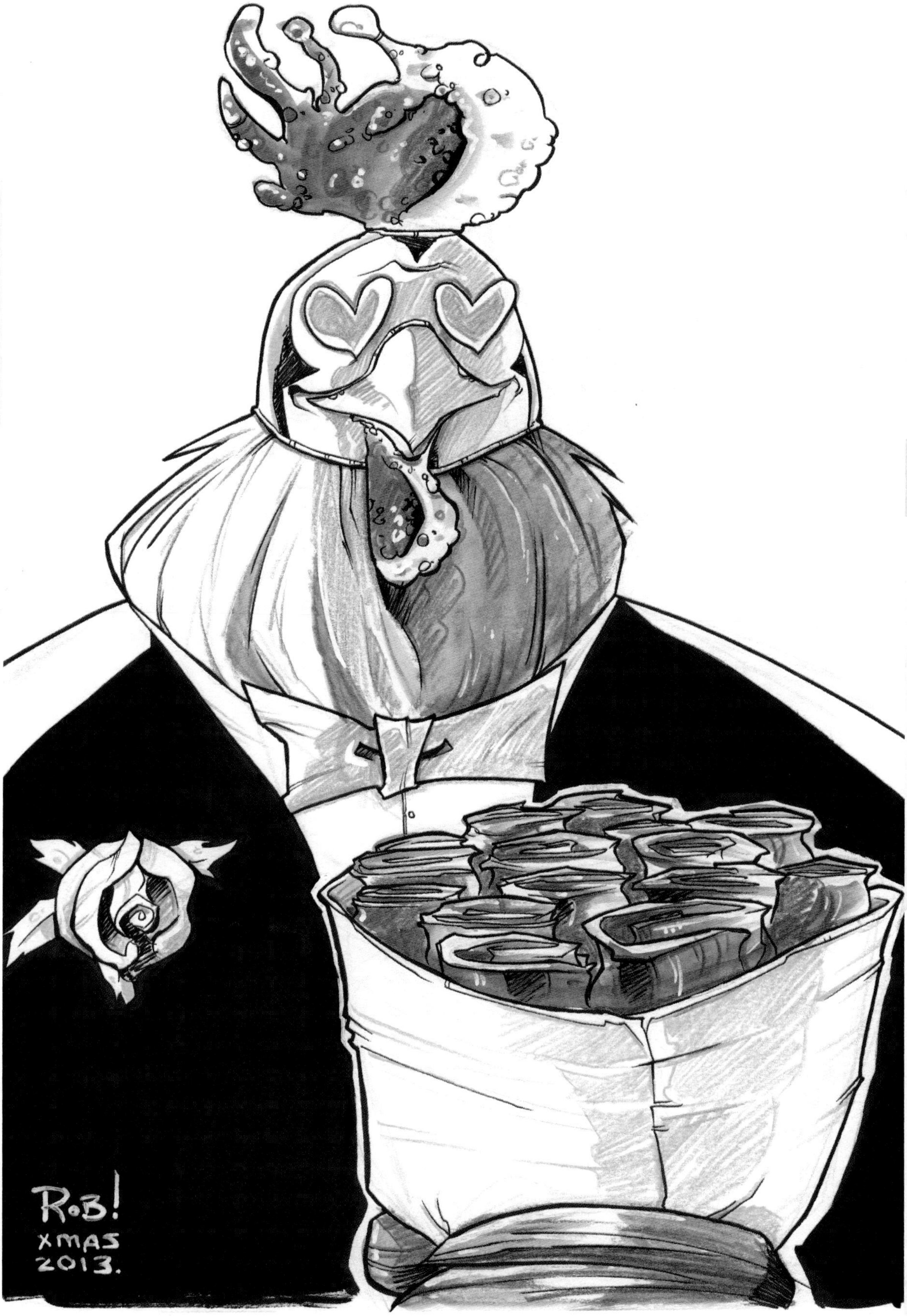
ROB!
XMAS
2013.

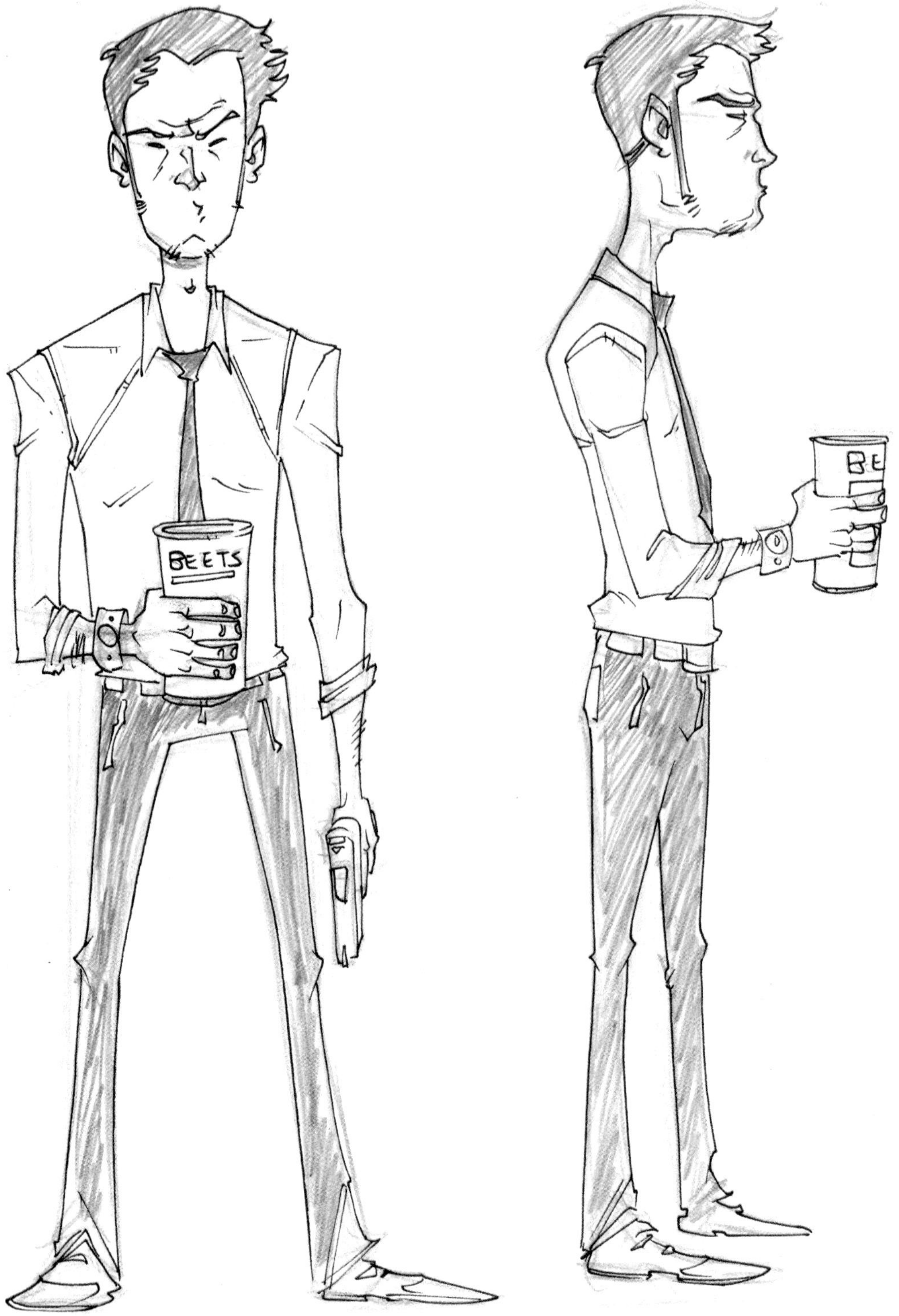
BEETS
BE

Character turnarounds, for yet-unannounced things.

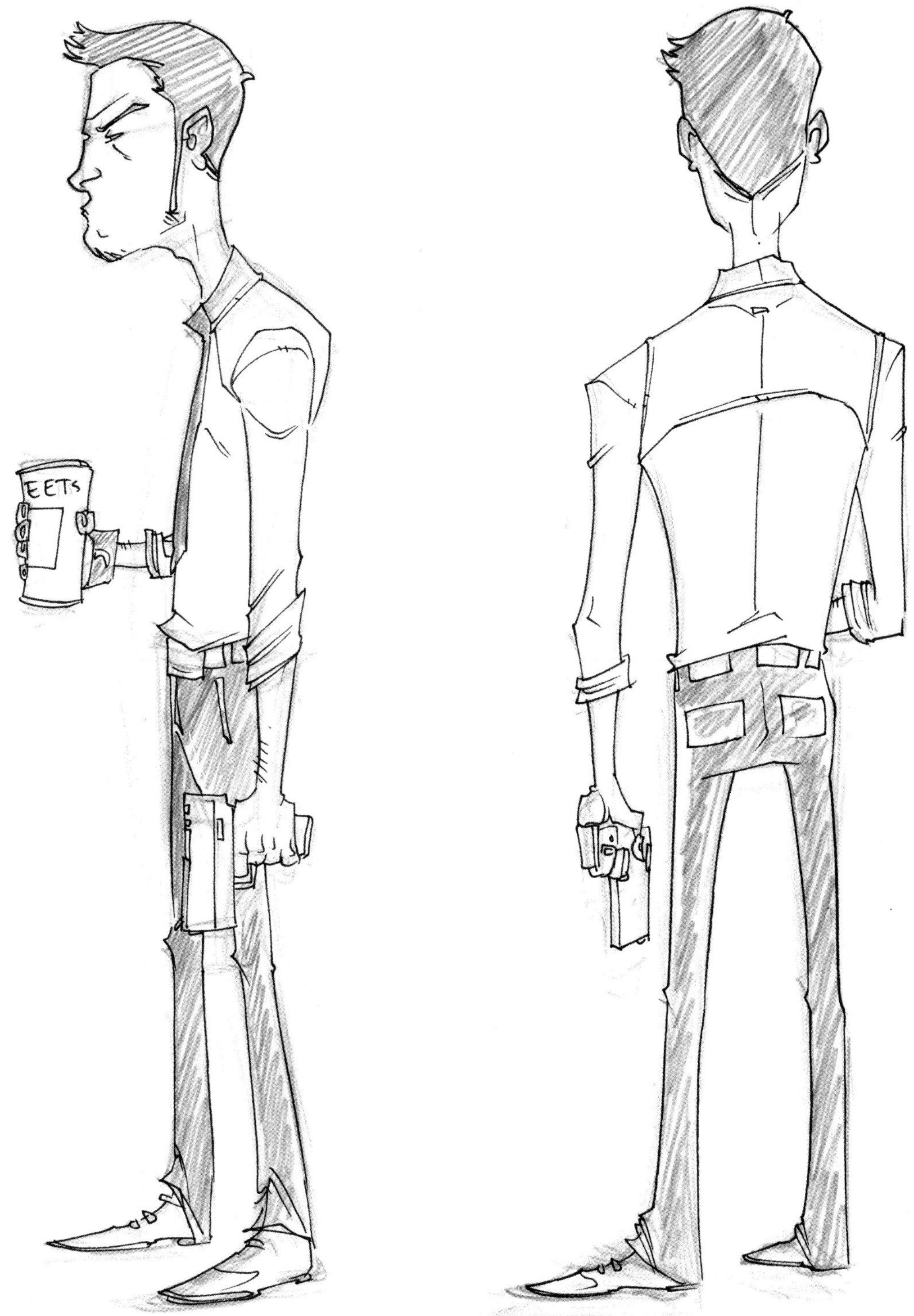
EETs

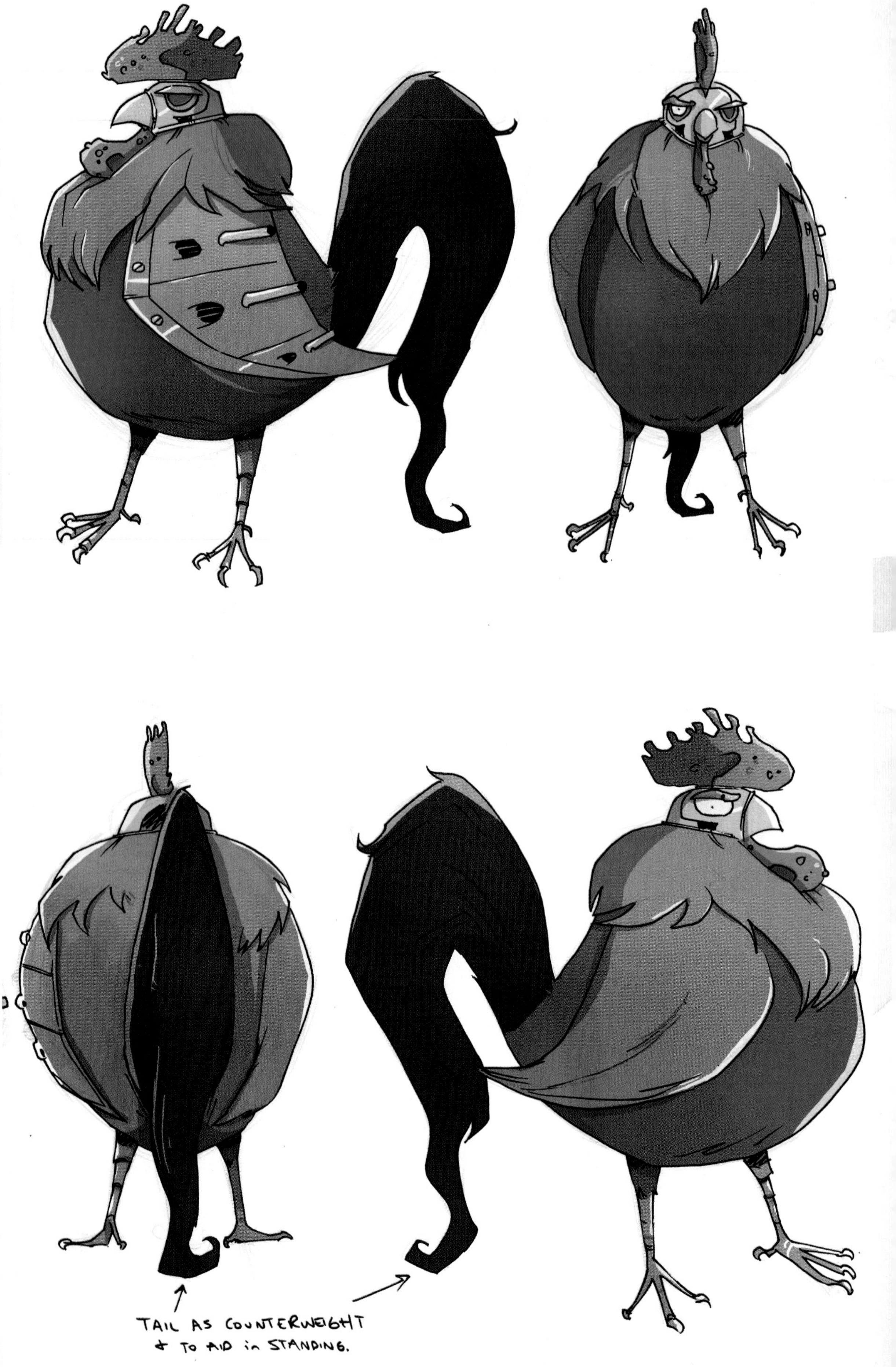
TAIL AS COUNTERWEIGHT
& TO AID in STANDING.

More turnarounds.

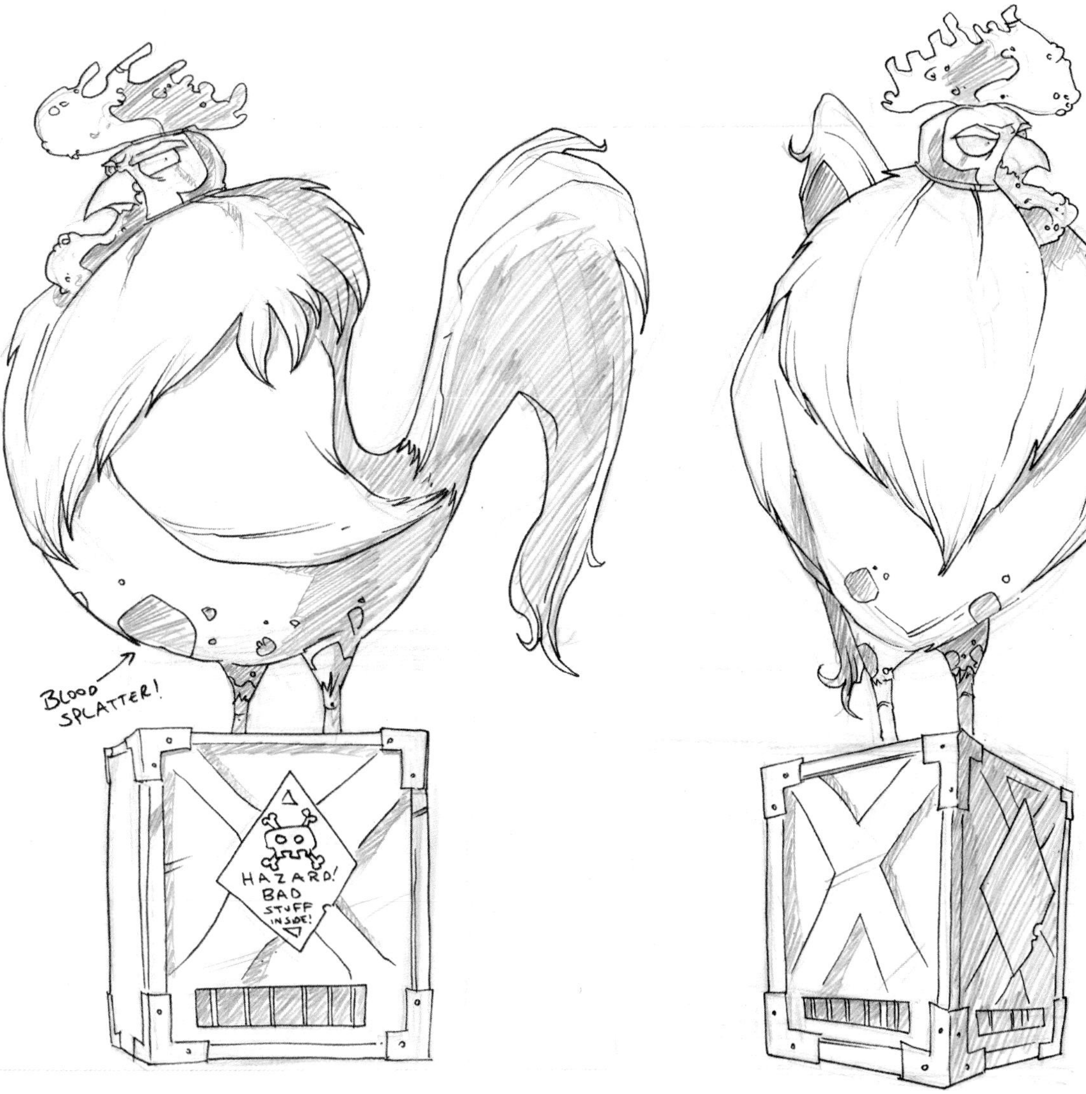
BLOOD SPLATTER!
HAZARD! BAD STUFF INSIDE!

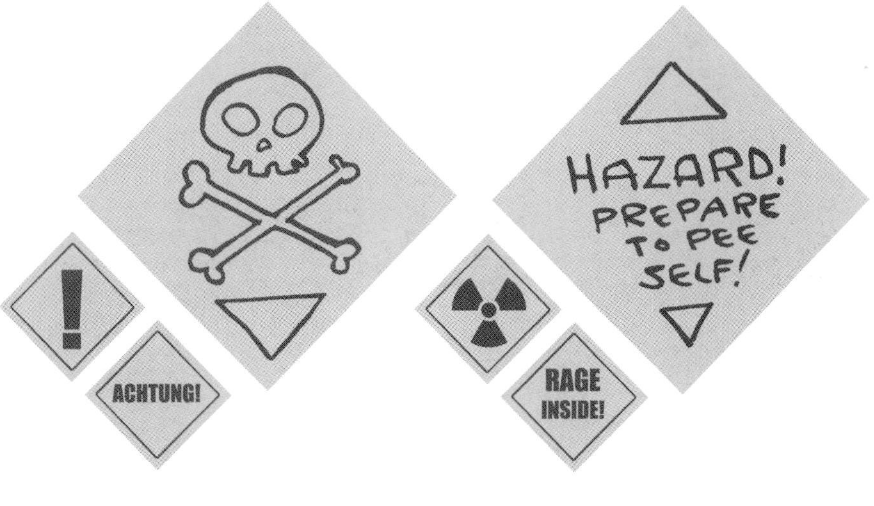
HAZARD! PREPARE TO PEE SELF!
ACHTUNG!
RAGE INSIDE!

Turnarounds for a Poyo vinyl statue.
I designed the “Warning” decals myself, just to keep with the silly humor of the book.

Layman and Rob, in Tours, France.
Feb., 2013.

JOHN LAYMAN · ROB GUILLORY
TONY CHU
DÉTECTIVE CANNIBALE
5. Première ligue
DEDICACE
LUNDI 11 FEVRIER
A PARTIR DE 14H

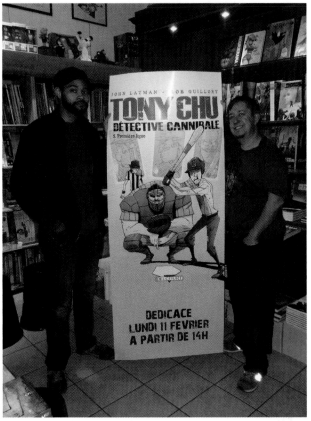

We have no idea who took this photo!

JOHN LAYMAN

John Layman recently traded in his addiction to World of Warcraft for Plants Vs. Zombies: Garden Warfare. He's got three cats, a dog, a son, a roommate, and lots of comics and Legos. He'd write more, but those plants and zombies aren't gonna kill themselves, ya know.

ROB GUILLORY

Rob Guillory is a comic artist from the Year 3000 version of Lafayette, Louisiana. There, he spends his time using his talents to encourage diplomacy between the future Cajuns and their insidious robot alligator rivals. Likes include: Pies, his wife April (who has been pregnant with their second child for the last 1000 years), his son Aiden and nonsensical bio pages.

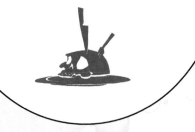

ChewComic.com

For original art: robguillorystore.com

Badass Chew stuff: http://www.skeltoncrewstudio.bigcartel.com

Layman on Twitter: @themightylayman *Rob on Twitter: @Rob_guillory*